THE DARK RESTARTER

SEAN MCMAHON

©2019 Sean McMahon.

All rights reserved.

No part of this book may be used or reproduced by any means whatsoever without prior permission from the author, except in the case of brief quotations embodied in critical articles or reviews.

This is a work of fiction. Names, characters, businesses, organisations, places, events and incidents are either the product of the author's imagination, or are used in a fictitious manner, with express permission being granted for the use of specific locations.

Any resemblance to actual events or persons, living, dead, or in Restarter form, is purely coincidental, or referenced satirically.

Author's note: utilising the abilities of a Restarter to alter the timeline to amend author-ownership is strictly prohibited.

For more information, visit:

www.restarterlodge.com

ISBN: 9781793133397

Cover by Sam Moore © 2019

Dedicated to *you*.

Because without your support you wouldn't be reading this right now, and the Restarters would cease to exist.

Thank you.

.

CHAPTER ONE
Erasing the Past

R.I Timestamp Error: Recalculating…

The Restarter slammed against the wall with a soundless thud, the absence of sound betraying the severity of the impact. He began to raise his hand up to the back of his head, certain that it would be covered in a sickly red on its return journey, but fought against the impulse knowing it would do him no favours.

A burst of nostalgia flooded through his mind as he recollected the days when he couldn't feel pain, as the razor-sharp tip of the large knife pierced through his leather jacket, t-shirt, and an unnerving number of layers of his flesh. The Restarter pushed back against the pressure, attempting to prevent the blade from travelling the extra inch into his out-of-phase heart.

Whilst the dwindling ripples of blue – and ferociously vibrant red – energy erupted from the contact between his hands, which were clenched around his attacker's wrist, he was infuriated that he seemed unable to draw upon the contact to infuse his own body with some much-needed charge. Remembering his assailant was beholden to an entirely different set of rules, he grimaced at the inconvenience, as his own remaining energy was effortlessly siphoned off into the man before him.

His adversary barked a laugh, bringing up his free hand in a swift motion to apply more pressure to the hilt, and the Restarter was forced to unclench his teeth as he gasped in agony, the blade edging a further quarter-inch into his chest.

'Just focus,' he muttered angrily at himself.

His attacker laughed again, looming over him, revelling in his victim's woe. 'What was that? I can't hear you over your whimpering.'

The Restarter looked over his soon-to-be murderer's shoulder, his friend lined up against the wall like a metaphoric lamb being prepped for a very literal slaughter. His failure in this moment would lead to everything he cared about coming undone. Dying in this form was not an option; they had seen what came after. The eternal nothingness that awaited them.

A dense white fog, one paradoxically static yet mobile, rolled across the floor, eager to cloud his mind and strip away his crucial sense of self and memories now that his charge was almost thoroughly depleted.

'Not *now* dammit!' spat the time traveller, before clenching his teeth once again, in the hope it would help him in the way of lucidity.

The gravity of the situation finally dawned on him; in his misguided attempt to cheat time and defeat the man before him, he and his team had inadvertently ended up providing a highly intelligent and equally motivated sociopath the keys to a time machine.

As if reading his mind, his assailant spoke.

'Did you honestly think I wouldn't find a way to exploit it? Exploit *you*? Did you think a force of nature like me could be contained?'

The irony wasn't lost on the Restarter.

After all, he had spent the best part of a year in the second of four alternate timelines trying to avoid hurting *anyone*, and yet he'd still managed to kill no less than three innocent people. But what if his agenda had been to actively cause harm? Unbound by remorse? Devoid of a conscience…

He looked up at his eternally invincible adversary, staring defiantly into his opponent's near-genius analytical mind and realised this was what he could have become if he had been left with nothing to focus on but revenge…

A *Dark* Restarter.

The monster pulled back the blade, noticing his

prey was losing the will to fight.

The fog seemed to sense it too, eager to correct the danger his very existence posed to reality, rolling over the Restarter.

His arms dropped to his side, leaving him utterly defenceless, with no regard to the severity of his situation, or awareness of his surroundings.

His opponent grinned, his shark-like teeth lacking glisten thanks to the ineffectual moonlight, realising he was finally about to succeed where his previous incarnations had failed.

'No more *restarts*. This world is *mine* now. And everything you love will *burn*. Not that you will be around to witness the *new world order*,' said Malcolm gleefully.

The Restarter was vaguely self-aware enough to sense the bitterness of defeat, and began to daydream about an alternate world; one where he had succeeded, one where he had saved his chosen family…

'Any last words?' said Malcolm.

'I can't think of anything,' the time traveller muttered, more in literal frustration over not being able to organise his own thoughts, rather than as a direct response to the question that had been fired at him.

As he teetered along the brink of failure, he realised that this had been Malcolm's plan all along.

Too late, he knew the dark truth that had been kept from him; he had been tricked into placing his trust in a man he should never have believed in. Every single piece of information he had been given had been by design. It had all been a lie. He had been manipulated.

As he took his last breath, a tear rolled down his cheek as he was forced to accept that after everything he'd been through, his time on this earth was over. And, worse, the woman bleeding out against the wall behind his killer would be next.

Failing *her* felt like the worst part of all.

And, in a moment that would change everything, Malcolm brought up the blade one final time, thrusting it towards the heart of the man before him with an insatiable eagerness, intoxicated by the deliciousness that only years of planning finally coming to fruition could provide, as he proceeded to overwrite not only his own future, but the potential past, present and future of millions.

CHAPTER TWO
New Beginnings

1st Cerebral Reversion – Friday, August 24th,

12:01pm

After what felt like an eternity of timelessness, the relentless sound of rushing air ceased abruptly, and there he stood, with nothing but the darkness for company.

Malcolm fell to his knees, entirely off balance, and wanting to expel the contents of his stomach, his body refusing him the indulgence. He heard footsteps above him, and quickly pulled himself together, not having felt this exposed and unprepared in a long, long time.

As his razor-sharp mind processed the best course of action, he heard the alarming sound of a key being turned in a lock, and the mundanely familiar click of a light being switched on behind him. A faint surge of light filled the room with a pathetic amber glow, the intensity inexplicably scorching his retinas and forcing him to cover his eyes.

Peering between his fingers, a tattered sofa came into focus to his right, and he dragged himself across the floor using his elbows for leverage, like a rat scurrying out of sight in the hope it would increase its mortality for just a little longer.

The unwanted guest at the top of what he could now tell were stairs began to descend, making their way towards him, each step loaded with weight, purpose, and a complete lack of urgency.

It had been a long time since Malcolm had felt this uncharacteristically afraid. A feeling that felt incredibly alien to him.

Over the past 24 years Malcolm had trained not only his body, but his most valuable asset; his mind, to be the strongest they both could be. He had studied various forms of combat, increased his understanding of his already incredible grasp of forensic science thanks to his former connections to the Metropolitan Police, and had become more than proficient in various forms of psychology.

A crucial skill that allowed him to form the necessary rapport with his works of art, prior to ending their miserable and pathetic lives.

But despite all that, he felt afraid.

Weak.

And utterly lost.

He hadn't felt this way since Oph–

'This will have to do,' said the man, now mere metres away from Malcolm, who realised all too late that one of his feet was sticking out beyond the edge of his makeshift hiding place.

There was no way in hell the man had not seen him, hiding behind the sofa like a child. Now it was just a matter of how long the person looming above him wanted to toy with him, as Malcolm desperately tried to become the man he knew himself to be, so he could take back control of this confusing mess he now found himself embroiled in.

The visitor sighed, more than a hint of disappointment in his tone as he spoke again.

'Should've spent longer looking for more suitable concealment.'

Malcolm realised the jig was up and, refusing to pander to the fear and confusion, stood up, dusted himself down, and stared at the man facing away from him with an intense glare.

'Who are you?' said Malcolm.

The man chuckled, a hoarse reverberation leaving his mouth more akin to gravel churning in a blender than possessing any real humour, and made his way to a table at the edge of the basement, offloading his bag and removing some A3 sized folders.

'Answer me,' growled Malcolm. He had no tolerance for rudeness, and despised arrogance, the irony of that totally lost on his self-absorbed mind.

Only then did it dawn on him. He *recognised* this place. 'Wait…how?' he added, more for his own benefit, not really knowing what it was that he was asking his brain to decipher.

Instead of responding, the man continued onwards with his routine, placing items around the table in an almost ceremonious manner.

Malcolm had to respect that. He too was a man of precision. But the evident lack of respect being sent his way wouldn't do. It wouldn't do at all. Malcolm took several large strides towards the man who still refused to face him and placed his hand on his shoulder, which passed right through the person's body.

Malcolm's eardrums popped, filled with the sound reminiscent of an old camera he used to own from the 80's. He recalled with unexpected fondness how the camera would always make a plinking noise when the bulb had expired, advising the user that a new one was required.

Malcolm's incredulity was replaced with a look of awe, as he pulled back his hand as if he had been burnt. He stared once more at his appendage, turning it slowly in front of his eyes, flexing his fingers one by one and forming a fist, then repeating the process, ensuring his hand had not been compromised.

He looked up too late, as the ghostly visitor span around on the spot and glided through him, his entire body phasing through Malcolm's, causing him to stagger backwards.

'Impossible,' muttered Malcolm, as his taste buds flared and his mouth filled impossibly with the taste of the colour red.

In fairness, murderous monster though he may have been, even *he* was allowed a free pass on feeling disconcerted by seeing a duplicated version of himself phasing through his own body.

It was then, in a matter of seconds, that Malcolm realised he was dead.

CHAPTER THREE
String Theory

47th Cerebral Reversion – Saturday, August 25th, 1.37pm

It didn't take Malcolm long to establish a baseline for his current predicament.

It was now his forty-seventh jump backwards in time, and he was halfway through the current cycle, making this the forty-eighth Saturday, August 25th he had relived thus far. As he stood outside what he realised to be both the cause and potential solution to all his problems, he reminisced over what led him here, and how he had so cleverly worked his way backwards to the locational equivalent of an epiphany.

Early on, it had been a simple matter for him to

employ the principle of Occam's razor; he had been presented with competing hypothetical answers to a multitude of questions that culminated in one singular truth, and he had decided early on to simply select the one that made the fewest assumptions on his part;

He was in the past.

He couldn't affect his surroundings, was surely in some form of purgatory, and in order to get out, he would have to retrace his steps to ascertain the critical moment that had led him to this proverbial dead end.

Once he had accepted these truths, he found that he had literally nothing other than an abundance of time to do just that. The "cerebral reversions" as he was calling them, seemed to confine him to a thirty-three-hour time period.

Whilst he was free to roam the surrounding area of the Pentney Lakes, he could not step foot beyond the boundary line without it accelerating the process and triggering the next Cerebral Reversion, which sent him back to precisely 12:01pm on Friday the 24th of August.

A mild inconvenience, which he would only resort to when strictly necessary in order to begin his plans anew in the event his carefully orchestrated observations proved fruitless. Case in point;

Cerebral Reversion Number 17.

During his seventeenth jump, he had decided to revisit his last memory before being delivered into his own past. It was utterly beyond the realm of possibility that the cause of his plight had been during those final moments.

Or so he had thought.

In his arrogant belief that he was untouchable, and despite having seen his own dead body lying on the floor of Kevin Barker's basement, it had taken him until his sixteenth Cerebral Reversion for him to revisit that moment.

His assumptions were embarrassingly debunked, as he had watched his past-self being held in place by an unseen force, blue arcs of lightening erupting from the eye sockets of his physical form, culminating in his last moments in the world of the living as he watched himself collapse into a humiliating heap on the floor.

He watched on, as an invisible presence ascended the staircase behind him in the form of ghostly footsteps. Malcolm dutifully followed those breadcrumbs, watching as the basement door opened of its own accord. Using this opportunity to slide through the gap, he noted how the hairs on his out-of-phase arms crackled with a blackish-red energy, and took in the sight before him; the woman in orange, and the rat-catcher bringing Kevin's creature back into the lodge.

He coughed in a pointless attempt to get their attention, then remembered he was invisible to those residing in this timeline, or rather, what *they* perceived as their present.

Malcolm cursed at the vexation of that.

As the young man and woman departed, he once

again heard footsteps, this time turning back on themselves and descending the staircase. He followed them, then quickly realised he was witnessing his final moments from a new perspective, before unceremoniously being thrust back into the past.

Upon re-entry, he quickly made his way to the boundary line of the lakes, eager to place as much distance from his ruthlessly repeating fate as possible.

But as he reached the exit sign and crossed an unseen threshold, he experienced a sensation that could only be described as being vaporised. Cut to ribbons at the molecular level, his body – or at least what constituted for it these days – eventually reformed, along with his consciousness.

His eighteenth Cerebral Reversion therefore became notable for the revelation of the curse that came with it;

There was no escape.

He couldn't leave, and he couldn't interact with anything. He was at an impasse.

In a deadlock of recurring dilated time that refused to release him, with no way of knowing the true cause behind what had thwarted his past-self and sent him to this elaborately self-contained underworld.

He had to get creative.

Which is why he was here.

The path that all roads led to.

A torso-level fence with a humble black sign attached to it, emblazoned with two golden, simple words that would change more than even he could imagine.

"Fir Lodge."

As Malcolm strode soundlessly across the shingle driveway of the lodge before him, he experienced a wave of temporal dissonance, noticing the hairs on his forearm rising once again, as another faint crackle of red energy arced between each hair.

He flattened the hairs with his large hand, rubbing his arm gently in an attempt to shrug off the odd sensation that someone had walked over his grave.

The killer winced, then smiled darkly at the loaded terminology.

Weaving around the numerous cars on the driveway, Malcolm casually entered Fir Lodge through the open front door. His ears perked up as he heard laughing coming from the end of a hallway, and a flash of garish colours danced across his field of view from the end of the lodge.

As he walked down the corridor and out through the door into the rear garden, Malcolm closed his eyes, inhaling deeply as he absorbed the mental clarity afforded to him by the music emanating from a nearby speaker, the rhythmic idle hum of the large hot tub to his left resulting in him almost forgetting, albeit for a mere second or two, that he wasn't really here at all.

He noticed the rat-catcher and orange secretary immediately, laughing and joking at opposite ends of the large expanse of grass. Suddenly, Malcolm was able to make sense of their attire; it was a party, and the outfits were costumes.

Over the past decade he hadn't had much time for either television or movies on account of his art, but he wasn't so out of touch that he couldn't place a few; Marilyn Monroe, Santa Clause, and now that he could see the rat-catcher in his full costume in the ultra-bright harsh light of day, he realised he was dressed as a Ghostbuster.

He had watched that particular film with *her* once. A long time ago. In another life. A life before she was taken—

His musings were halted, as he was brought crashing down back into the present, and he watched with malice as the insolent partygoers paraded around like idiotic children, fussing over the creature whom he immediately recognised, and would later learn was called Jerry. But that wasn't what pulled him back from his ruminations. It was the arrival of Kevin that saw to that.

A man in a black and blue plaid shirt, whom he of course knew by name before the introductions were even made.

For a moment, Malcolm wondered how Kevin had escaped from the confines of the room in the basement beneath his own lodge, and a wave of panic swept over him as he feared the man would tell these strangers all about how he had captured him.

Shaking away the ridiculous notion, the killer reminded himself that those events had not yet happened. At least from the perspective of all those in front of him, who were operating on a very different clock than him.

Malcolm smiled darkly over the fact that the man in the plaid shirt had yet to make his acquaintance, then made his way past the hot tub, striding through someone dressed in 70's disco attire.

Jasmine shuddered, as Malcolm's out-of-phase molecules effortlessly passed through her, and he positioned himself to the right-hand side of the building next to a moderately sized terracotta plant pot.

Despite his high intelligence, Malcolm was struggling to readjust his mind into thinking fourth-dimensionally. The concept wasn't complicated, but his mind was battling him constantly, refusing to grant him permission to accept the new status quo. The hairs on his neck once again reverberated, and he experienced another faint sensation of static shock.

The dog inhaled a piece of sausage and looked up at him from across the garden, cocked his head as if he could see him, and ran towards him.

Malcolm took several steps back, as Jerry sauntered towards him then stared oddly at the side of the lodge.

Malcolm followed Jerry's gaze, resting on the wooden structure, then back at the animal, before gingerly reaching out into the space between the creature and the lodge. He could almost see a ripple in the air, and as his fingers connected with it, he saw a brief spark of blue energy, which curled violently and surged into his hand like an electrified eel, causing him to pull his hand back as quickly as his reflexes allowed.

Jerry eventually lost interest, turned on the spot, and gave Malcolm a wide berth, shooting the murderer a barely perceivable sniff of indifference. Malcolm watched as the dog sped off towards the edge of the property, before stopping to sniff into empty space once again.

Jerry rolled onto his back, kicking his legs into the air, and Malcolm stared as the same ripple in reality presented itself a second time.

As the quantumly-displaced killer strode towards the animal to get a closer look, the dog jumped up onto its feet and departed, leaving even more questions for Malcolm in his wake.

An idea was forming in Malcolm's mind, but it lacked substance. He was too analytical to make halfbaked assumptions, and instead turned back to the party taking place behind him, eager to learn more. The key to his escape resided somewhere amongst these idiots, he was certain of it.

The answers were merely dormant somewhere within Fir Lodge. It was just a matter of time before he turned over the right stone to find them.

He could feel it.

*

Malcolm followed the participants of the past like a disembodied shadow lurking in the corners of their history. A poisonous serpent intent on unravelling everything that made them who they were, with the sole purpose of discarding them to the ravenous rapids of time as soon as the opportunity presented itself, so that he could find his way back to the present and continue his quest for artistic perfection.

Events took an unexpected turn when Malcolm, purely by luck, had followed the golfer named Peter into a side room.

Sensing what was slowly becoming a regular occurrence, a strange resonance of displaced energy brushed against his hand. Malcolm flexed his fingers, staring at them with interest, then continued onwards into the bedroom.

What happened next changed everything.

In an instant, the golfer was seemingly pushed against the rear wall of the room. Malcolm watched, as a faint blue sizzle of luminescence began to radiate throughout the golfer's eye sockets, before increasing in intensity to such an extent that Peter's black cheeks looked almost pale amidst the anomaly.

Malcolm moved closer, eager to see the energy up close, having only previously witnessed it fleetingly, but was forced into diverting his attention for a nanosecond, as he heard the door close gently behind him, seemingly of its own volition.

'Fascinating,' said Malcolm, drinking in the spectacle before him, eager to learn the secrets the past had to offer.

Something was clearly holding the young man in

place, preventing him from moving, and that something appeared to be connected to a mysterious blue energy that seemed to flow throughout this nefarious netherworld in which Malcolm had been imprisoned within.

For reasons he couldn't explain, he wanted to reach out and touch the ethereal power of the electricity that was twisting and turning before him. With fingertips mere millimetres away from Peter's face, he could feel the power, as it thrummed wildly. The answer to everything. The key to the doors of time could be his, if he could just grab hold of—

'Still…s-sorry,' said Peter, causing Malcolm to recoil.

He wasn't expecting the young man to be conscious, let alone lucid, and felt unexpectedly exposed. Before he could regain the courage to try again, the energy dissipated, Peter's eyelids fluttering eerily, until eventually his eyes rolled back into a healthier and altogether less erratic state.

Malcolm cursed at the missed opportunity, as Peter walked straight through him, shuddering slightly as he left Malcolm behind in the room.

*

There was little time to mull over his findings, as he noticed that the Ghostbuster he now knew to be called Hal (which he reasoned was short for Harold) and the orange secretary named Kara had set off to where Malcolm's past-iteration was currently residing.

Whilst he knew how this part played out, he

rushed ahead of them and back to Kevin's lodge. The front door was ajar, but not enough for him to pass through it, and Malcolm found himself both relieved and elated as the door moved under his touch and creaked inwards to allow him passage over and across the Welcome mat. A loophole which he would later discover was due to his proximity to his considerably more alive past-self occupying the basement below him.

He stepped across the threshold, surveying the area around him.

Everything looked ordinary. Identical to how he remembered it.

The time traveller moved out of the way as a past incarnation of himself ascended the stairs from the basement and into the living room. He watched as his duplicate navigated the room, his mannerisms and deliberate movements solidifying the notion that this was indeed a perfect recreation of himself.

Malcolm's equilibrium underwent an unexpected nosedive, as if he was being pulled by an unseen force in three directions; in the past, during his present, and from his now unwritten future.

As he attempted to dismiss the feeling, a plate resting on a worktop behind him fell to the floor of its own accord, delaying his past-self from returning to the basement as planned.

And then it dawned on him.

'Oh…' he said to himself, the truth finally revealing itself to him. 'Ohhhh! Of course,' he added, his thoughts finally taking shape and forming less a theory, and more a form of understanding that more than echoed a full-blown revelation. 'I'm not the only one here, am I?' he said, challenging the universe. Daring it to offer a counter-argument.

The realisation that he wasn't the only out-of-phase entity occupying the current timeline was about to change everything. There were clearly others in this place, plucking at invisible strings and operating in accordance with their own agenda, as evidenced by the intermittent sensation of static charges he had felt during many of his previous Cerebral Reversions.

The ripples in the surrounding environment.

Not to mention his past-self held in place by the same form of blue energy that had attacked the golfer at Fir Lodge…

Someone had changed his past. Of this he was certain. There was no other way of explaining how his plans with the man in the storage room below had come so unstuck.

But who?

Allowing the remainder of his last moments on earth to play out, a psychotic grin appeared on his face, his shark-like teeth piercing through the surrounding gloom, as two familiar faces ushered Jerry into the lodge.

He knew what he needed to do now.

It would take time to figure out precisely how he would accomplish his new mission. But luckily, that was one commodity that was not only at his disposal, it was something he had an infinite supply of.

Through all the commotion, and a multitude of moving pieces, he quickly honed in on the one constant. The one reoccurring factor that was too obvious to ignore.

Or rather, the two reoccurring factors;

Harold, and Kara.

CHAPTER FOUR
Doorway to the Grave

1,060th Cerebral Reversion – Saturday, August 25th, 8:31pm

It had taken him longer than he ever expected, but after hundreds of Cerebral Reversions, Malcolm was not just getting *through* to his past-self, he was entirely and without exception fully in control.

What started off as whispers on the wind had eventually solidified into his words granting him far more power than he ever could have hoped for.

It started small, with Malcolm's past-self mumbling the words his duplicated counterpart was muttering in frustration.

Eventually, however, Malcolm had become an

insidious conduit, channelling all of his ideas and plans into the mind of his past-self until, on one beautiful morning, he had managed to manipulate himself into killing Kevin outright, rather than simply storing him in the basement for later. It was a huge win, and one that had ultimately led him to what he was certain would be the crown jewel in an already impressive catalogue of achievements whilst he had been alive.

But today, Malcolm was playing a much more intricate, and dare he say it, reserved game. Waiting until nightfall, he skulked along the outskirts of Fir Lodge, before whispering his final instruction of the evening to his flesh-and-blood self, whose mind was so addled by his time-travelling counterpart he could barely form his own thoughts at all anymore.

'Now, remember,' said the time-traveller, once again whispering into his own ear. 'Once in position, you must stay there until I instruct you otherwise. Understood?'

Malcolm's past-self mumbled unintelligibly, and he glared disapprovingly. A party was in full swing, and he could sense the reluctance brewing in the posture of his chronologically cloned brother. 'Say it,' he hissed.

'Understood.'

'Good. Now off you go,' he said, placing his hand on his own back, causing his alive-self to shiver. It seemed to have the desired effect, as the puppet shook off the self-doubt and made his way closer to the lodge.

As per his own instruction, Malcolm watched as his double stepped quietly onto the gravel driveway of Fir Lodge, hoisted himself onto the balcony, then finally onto the roof, where he laid himself down flat in a prone position on the slates above where the dining room was situated. His positioning was crucial; his physical self would be mere meters away, albeit vertically, from Robert's room.

The restarting version of Malcolm glided happily towards the building, and slipped in through the side entrance.

Having spent the lion's share of the past thirty-two hours, seventeen minutes and thirty seconds maintaining constant contact with his past-self, he knew the power contained within his hollow body would be enough for what came next. He could feel the energy coursing through his quantumly-disentangled veins. Malcolm also knew that *they* were here. Harold and Kara. Of this he was certain.

He couldn't see them, nor could they see him. But it mattered little. He was about to pull the rug out from underneath them all the same.

It had taken Malcolm a long time to deduce that he wasn't just reliving *his* last hours on this earth, but that he was actually reliving the hours leading up to his murderer's end game; that he was *trapped* within the culmination of what was possibly hundreds of their own self-contained Cerebral Reversions. Reversions in time that had led, ultimately, to them freeing themselves. And they had achieved this, rather impressively, by altering the surrounding environment in incredibly subtle ways.

Any doubts he had of this hypothesis were immediately eliminated during the early hours of one Saturday morning in particular…

It had been a defining moment for him, and the final part of the puzzle for formulating his plan. His thoughts drifted backwards in time, as he replayed the events over in his mind…he recalled having all but given up, during a particularly intense brooding session where he had taken to staring at the moon through the kitchen window on the upper level of Fir Lodge, when two glasses on the kitchen counter moved of their own accord, gliding across the table top. The sound of glass against wood was barely audible, like gas moving through a distant pipe.

That in itself would have been enough to confirm his suspicions. But the real moment that changed everything, when he *truly* began to realise he was on to something, came when the bottle of tequila rose up impossibly into the air, fifty or so centimetres above the counter, the contents pouring into the glasses.

The shot-glasses themselves then began to levitate smoothly, the liquid within them falling out of the glass onto the floor, followed by the bottle of tequila moving slowly back into the corner of the worktop.

As the two shot-glasses lowered themselves and collided with the worktop in tandem with a revelatory clack, he realised both Harold and Kara were still, technically speaking, here with him. Carrying out their own operation to change their destiny and free themselves from the same prison he was trapped in.

He reasoned that they were echoes of a changed past. More specifically, *his* changed past. And were reliving their final moments over and over. But what did that mean for him? He couldn't see them. Merely their *actions* in the *physical* world.

But that had been their mistake. And now every single Cerebral Reversion he experienced was, in actuality, him reliving the last thirty-three hours they spent here. To beat them, he would need to foil the changes they had made. And to do that, he would need something they could never have predicted he would have access to…

"Help," he had thought. He was going to need help…

Malcolm was pulled back to what constituted the present, the arrival of a familiar face causing him to retreat from the balcony of Fir Lodge on which he was standing and return to ground level in order to greet him.

Kevin stepped onto the gravel driveway and once again found himself struggling to wrap his head around the lack of crunch the action generated.

His eyes skimmed the top of Fir Lodge, then down to the balcony, just in time to see the back of Malcolm, who he realised must have seen him arrive and would surely be making his way down to meet with him.

Kevin looked down at his own plaid shirt, and turned his back on the lodge to face his best friend, who sat there panting enthusiastically.

'What would you do?' said Kevin, addressing Jerry directly.

Jerry looked up at him, hearing his words despite being alive and entirely out of phase with his dad, before sniffing the space where his boots would have been were he alive.

He heard his name being called out behind him, and Kevin grimaced at having incorrectly assumed how much time he had left to be alone with his thoughts. Hearing Malcom's voice always made him feel like he was going to vomit, yet he somehow always managed to keep it down. Something about this place had that affect.

'Kevin!'

'Malcolm,' he said, the word dripping with disdain.

'Wonderful. I see you've reconsidered my offer?'

'Not much of an offer. Kill some kids or spend a lifetime with you.'

'And yet, here you are.'

Malcolm had him there. The truth was, Malcolm always had him over a barrel.

After sixty-eight time loops of the same thirty-three hours, forty of which Kevin and Malcolm had spent together, Kevin had tried desperately to make sense of it all. But despite finally wrapping his head around the fact he was some kind of ghostly echo reliving the past, the truth was he had no way to interact with history like Malcolm could.

He was powerless.

Though he had seen how Malcolm controlled the past version of himself, the one who existed in the physical realm, Kevin just couldn't seem to connect with himself in that way.

Sure, there had been glimmers that he was getting through to himself, but with Malcolm instructing his own respective alive-self to kill Kevin every morning it quickly became pointless. According to Malcolm, forming a bond between the past and present version of one's self required a rather inconvenient base level requirement of said self being alive.

Malcolm knew that of course.

And every time Kevin got close to reaching his alive-self after begging him to leave the Pentney Lakes, Malcolm would issue the kill order on Kevin, or just tie him up to keep him out of the way.

But today was the one exception.

Malcolm had allowed him to spend the entirety of the loop with his physical self, instructing him to maintain physical contact with "Alive-Kevin" as a reminder for what he could go back to if Kevin would just cease his infernal resisting and work *with* him.

And it certainly looked as if the only way out for him was to do just that.

Work with Malcolm. Those were the terms.

Terms which led him to break away over the past few time-loops from the psychopath and strike out on his own. But the fog grew denser, his memories were beginning to fade, a side-effect he had no way of knowing was being caused by his inability to interact with another person matching his current condition.

With that, resentfully, he was here. The exact point in space and time that Malcolm had told him to meet him should he ever grow weary of bouncing backwards through time with only the lakes for company.

"The lakes and *Jerry*," thought Kevin.

'I trust you sent your past-self back home as instructed?' asked Malcolm, referring to the other prerequisite for Kevin being granted time alone with his alive-self.

Kevin nodded.

'Don't look so sour faced!' said Malcolm, with menace-filled levity. 'Once you have assisted me with this final deed, I'll be free of this place. We *both* will. I will spare both you and your animal.'

'His name…is *Jerry*,' he replied icily.

'Yes, yes,' said Malcolm dismissively. 'Whatever. Now, do we have a deal?' and he held out his hand to Kevin, then nodded advising him to proceed.

Kevin stared up at the lodge thinking of the lives within, realising he was essentially aiding and abetting a murderer. He then looked down at Jerry, standing next to his master, his vacant expression implying his father already knew what needed to be done.

Kevin mimicked Malcolm's gesture, outstretching his hand, then pulled it away at the last moment.

'No,' said Kevin.

'No? No?!' the killer broke out into a hideous laugh.

'I'm not going to help you kill a bunch of kids. As far as I can tell, you being stuck here keeps the outside world safe. You're powerless here. And we're fading. I can feel it.'

Malcolm knew what he meant. If he strayed too far for too long from his alive-self, his thoughts became blurry. Clouded. And a literal black fog would creep its way over everything, rolling across the grass as if reclaiming the world. The same fog that reclaimed him moments before the end of each Cerebral Reversion.

'I don't know what you're talking about,' lied Malcolm.

'I think you do,' said Kevin, a bold smile stretching out across his own face and, for the first time since he got here, feeling like he knew something Malcolm didn't want him to know. 'We may not feel pain here. Or hunger. Or even thirst. But there is one thing we can feel that not even you can escape, isn't there?'

'And what would that be,' replied Malcolm, feigning boredom but willing to let Kevin have his moment just so he could rob him of it afterwards.

'Fear.'

Malcolm took a step towards the man and his dog, dropping the pretence of civility.

'I fear *nothing*. I do not fear *you*, these *children*, or—'

Kevin cut him off. 'Or eternal damnation once the fog claims you permanently? It's getting thicker, Malcolm. It's just a matter of…' he chortled, 'time.'

'Oh Kevin, you've been here for less than seventy loops. No energy to draw from, no physical-self to interact with, except today of course. A gift I gave you as a peace offering, no less. You've spent so long in the woods you haven't even figured out that music can refuel your focus.'

Kevin was dumbfounded.

He was about to ask if music really could keep the fog at bay when Malcolm quickly grabbed his hand, causing a reasonable bounty of blue sparks to fly from Kevin and into Malcolm's body, draining a confused Kevin of every last drop of his retained temporal energy.

The killer looked back at him with a smirk, his eyes a savage red, as he released his firm grip on Kevin's hand.

Kevin pulled away from the loaded handshake, resentment in his eyes, knowing something awful had just happened.

'No one will know, Kevin. Of that, you have my word.'

'I don't even know what just happened! What did you do? And your word is worth shit,' he added boldly.

Malcolm chuckled.

'I've killed some for less than that. But I'm feeling…positively reinvigorated. Now run along.'

'What was that? That blue energy?'

''Let's just say, the time you spent with your past-self today was not what you thought it was.'

'What are you going to do to them?' asked Kevin, feeling utterly drained, his thoughts fuzzy.

'I said *leave*.'

The killer's smile waned to reveal a subliminal reminder that he rarely asked twice, let alone thrice. And on that note, Malcolm turned his back on Kevin and made his way back inside Fir Lodge.

Kevin stood there, he and Jerry alone on the gravel, feeling cheated as the prospect of the consequences that would surely result from a handshake with the devil dawned on him.

He had been tricked. Whatever that energy was, Malcolm had stolen it from him. And the way it had left his body caused him to think that trying to steal it back would just empower the monster even more. All he could do now was hope whatever Malcolm was planning wouldn't work. He'd be more careful tomorrow when the nightmare started over. Would learn what the blue energy was about. Learn to wield it to fight Malcolm.

He continued to lie to himself, not wanting to admit that he knew there would not be a tomorrow at all. At least, not for him.

As he looked down at Jerry, an idea began to swirl in his mind. Maybe it wasn't too late. If he could just keep Jerry from accidentally luring the occupants to his home, maybe he could save them.

Maybe…

Jerry was important. He just wished he knew why. And then he wished he knew who Jerry was. Perhaps the dog in front of him knew the answer. But as the white fog swirled around him, it stripped him of the question. Then his mind. Then his body entirely.

*

Malcolm had been watching closely; the balloons, the falling wine bottle, the dog chasing phantoms that weren't really phantoms at all…

He was shaken from his ruminations as the golfer approached the door that led to the one called Robert's bedroom he was currently waiting patiently inside of. As the footsteps grew louder, he took a deep breath, and placed his hands against the door, positioning his legs to take the brunt of the incoming onslaught.

The door handle rattled, as it always did, and Malcolm envisioned the energy he had siphoned from Kevin building from his core and into his hands. The door began to move inwards, the killer gritting his teeth and channelling his hatred into something he could use; a manifestation of power that would act as a key to finally freeing him from this place. The door slammed shut under his force, and he heard the young man from the other side – both figuratively and literally – mumbling a quizzically-toned hum of perplexed confusion.

He was done in this place. He felt *saturated* by it, as if the moronic exchanges of those residing in Fir

Lodge were somehow *infecting* him with their banality. The door handle quivered again, and Malcolm growled, as the door began to give way under his ever-depleting charge of residual energy.

The door crept ever further open, and Malcolm heard the golfer speak.

'Rob, you in there, mate? I need to borrow your charger.'

Images flashed through Malcolm's mind, fuelling his anger, haunting his sense of self; one image in particular, of a young rat-catcher and his orange secretary.

He snarled at the thought of them, his eyes igniting with a reinvigorated red electricity that would've filled the dark room, had light been able to reflect from between Malcolm's present and the pocket of the past he was locked in.

Malcolm yelled in defiance, until the door gave way under his sheer refusal to accept that he would be beaten, and slammed shut.

And then Malcolm waited.

And waited.

Eventually, he allowed his lips to form a malicious smile. His shark-like teeth glowing under the otherworldly red hue being cast from his own eye sockets.

As the black fog arrived, much earlier than usual, he knew he had done it, the energy leaving him, rendering him powerless once more.

Coils of darkness wrapped around his body like starved snakes, ready to transport him, to spit him out on the other side of eternity for a job well done.

Malcolm fought against it, and looked up to the ceiling, knowing his alive-self was still on the roof. He transmitted one final instruction and heard the reassuring creak of his weight walking across the tiles above him.

'Not yet,' Malcolm whispered gently to the universe. There was still one more loose end to take care of.

But the clutches of time itself refused to listen and claimed him as its own. Malcolm's last thought being that of a singular hope that his physical self could handle the last will and testament of his own superior intellect.

*

'Jeez,' said Peter from the other side of the door. 'Whatever,' he grumbled, heading back down the corridor to continue what was starting to feel like a never-ending side-quest, shivering slightly as if someone had stepped over his grave, entirely unaware that the reality was much more like someone had actually just dug a fresh one for him. 'Oh,' said Peter, stopping by the double entrance doors of the lodge.

The mischievously-adorable springer spaniel sat there patiently in the moonlight, as Peter looked up the communal staircase and called out to Fearne, who was utterly preoccupied with assisting Daisy in clearing up a spillage of some kind.

'Guys?' said Peter, turning around to face Jon and Will who were playing a rather rambunctious game of pool. 'That dog's back.'

'Jerry? He's out late?' said Jon looking over at Peter briefly before lining up his next shot

Peter shrugged and opened the front door, allowing Jerry to strut into the lodge and towards the pool table, then making his way up the staircase.

'Grab the dog Peter, there's glass everywhere up here!' Daisy shouted down, uncharacteristically stressed.

Sighing at the realisation that his quest for a phone charger had run its course and silently blaming Fearne for not packing such an essential item, he squatted down to get Jerry's attention, turning the silver disc attached to the dog's collar in his open palm.

'Number 51…' he said out loud. 'Guys, what number are we?'

Jon and Will made some contradicting noises of cheers and groans as Jon sunk another yellow into the corner pocket.

Growing irritable, Peter shouted out to anyone who would listen.

'Going to take the dog back guys!'

He gestured towards the now-open door before them both. 'I'm so under-appreciated,' he mumbled. 'After you, good sir!'

Jerry wagged his tail and followed Peter's instructions.

As he stepped outside, the sound of an old-fashioned song from what must have been one of

Jon's Royal Air Force playlists faded in volume, and the cool air seemed to flood against his body, causing another involuntary shiver. He reached back for the door handle and pushed it away from him, his ears greeted by a satisfying "click", indicating it was fully closed.

An action that wasn't in and of itself *too* concerning. Unless you were a Restarter on your 165th restart, watching helplessly as their entire plan had just gone well and truly to shit, her hands pressed against the glass of the door, unable to open it with her slowly dwindling charge. A door which wasn't *really* a door at all, but had suddenly transmogrified into the vertical lid to Peter's coffin.

A Restarter, for example, who was now screaming through the glass trying to get the attention of her friend, knowing that in less that twenty-two minutes his act of apparent kindness was going to erase her from existence, sending her back to the present day, where she wouldn't be able to remember *needing* to help him, let alone be in a position to–

Peter stopped for a second, cocking his head just a little, as if he had heard something on the wind, then turned back to face the glass. Seemingly staring into not only Kara's eyes, but Hal's as well – who had returned from tripping the hot tub and was as equally imprisoned behind the door – he raised an immaculately crafted eyebrow.

'I'll be right back,' said Peter, to no one in particular.

Hal mouthed words that seemed to run along the lines of "he did *not* just say that?" as he and Kara frantically bolted through the corridor that led to the rear garden, darted to the right, and backtracked along the driveway. Their feet stopping soundlessly atop the shingle as they looked at each other and nodded, knowing Peter's only hope depended on them reaching the boundary line of Pentney Lakes in time.

But time, as always, was not on their side.

And with one simple change, a man operating in a slightly different phase to the two of them had achieved the impossible. After 1,060 Cerebral Reversions (or Restarts, depending on who you asked) everything that Hal and Kara had fought so hard to set in motion unravelled at the seams.

Their past restarted, their future changed, into an alternate reality entirely of Malcolm's design.

CHAPTER FIVE
Brave New World

R.I Timestamp Error: Recalculating…

Jess ran down the eerily quiet alley, vaulted over a fence, and moved deeper into the now abandoned amusement park, crouching down behind an overflowing litter bin to take an ill-advised but much needed moment to catch her breath.

Her stamina all but depleted, she slipped her backpack from her shoulders to take stock. As she unzipped the bag, she winced, knowing that whilst the sound may not have drawn unwanted attention, she was still hideously exposed.

She listened for a moment, satisfied that the only groans she could hear were the ones ingrained in her imagination, then ran a quick inventory; her trusty

Glock, a measly two magazines, a single grenade that in her hands was more a liability than of any real use, and a hundred or so tickets that she'd stolen from an abandoned theme park store room that were good for little more than kindling. She hadn't eaten in hours, and her bottle of water barely contained the remnants of perspiration, let alone any viable means of hydration, and she cursed herself for travelling too far for too long without replenishing the crucial supplies she needed to stay alive.

"Stupid."

Jess took a deep breath and exhaled slowly, acknowledging that she was being too hard on herself. Pressing her earpiece, she called out to her fellow survivors.

'Is anyone close to the east wing, I'm low and need back up.'

She was greeted by unhelpful static.

'Great,' she mumbled. 'Guess I'll have to do this myself. As *always*.'

Her earpiece startled her as it crackled to life and a familiar voice responded.

'I'm here,' said the voice. 'Little busy at the moment. How long can you hold out?'

It was Hal.

Not really who she was hoping for, given that her fiancé had a tendency to make terrible decisions when it came to thinking on his feet. Since the outbreak started, he often took a lone wolf approach when it came to supply-runs, and was incredibly wasteful with his ammunition.

'I have a few minutes,' she said snippily.

The earpiece crackled again, a playful tone in his voice.

'Don't get snippy, I'll be there.'

It was then that she heard the shuffling, followed by a sickening groan.

'Shit,' Jess whispered, quickly shoving her arms back through the straps of her pack and loading a magazine into her gun, making sure to keep a spare on standby.

And there it was; a decaying reanimated corpse, shuffling towards her, its eyes a fluorescent blue, equal in vibrancy to the neon signs surrounding her which were being powered by unseen generators, fortunately operating separately from the national grid.

"The Restarted," as Hal called them.

She pulled herself up from the ground and strode towards what, judging by the name-badge affixed to the now-filthy clothes it was wearing, used to be an employee of the park. Jess stuck out her tongue to concentrate, raised her gun, looked down the sights, and fired off a single bullet.

The projectile pinged off of a vending machine, a metre or so to the right of her intended target.

'Damn it,' she said, glad that Hal hadn't been around to see that. She hated smaller firearms, feeling much more confident with weapons that offered a wider spread.

Slumping her shoulders, she sulkily plodded closer to the afflicted reanimated cadaver, wondering for the billionth time if a cure would ever be found. It had been so long now. She had killed so many that they didn't even register as human to her. All she saw at this point in her zombie-killing career was a violent, rabid animal that needed to be put down so that it could finally find peace. It was a matter of survival, and death was a secondary concern to becoming infected. Coming back...becoming one of those *things*. They had all, at one point, seen it happen to the ones they loved.

Now a mere metre away, she re-raised her weapon, applying slight pressure to the trigger, then hesitated. There was only one. Noise would draw more, and she was low on ammo. Pulling her knife from its holster, she flipped it in her right hand so the blade was facing outwards, swiping savagely, placing the blade firmly into the creature's right temple.

Jess pulled the blade out quickly, fearing the weight of the zombie might pull her down with it. Absent-mindedly, she envisioned the act of wiping the blood from the blade on her jeans, trying to decide if she had time to nip into the nearby arcade whilst it was quiet, in the hope of finding a melee weapon with a bit more range.

Having calculated the risk, she jogged briskly and made her way into the claustrophobic room, the wonder of the rows of retro gaming cabinets lining the walls completely lost on her, realising immediately she had made a terrible mistake. A quick headcount indicated there were at least twenty of The Restarted shuffling around, trying to gain access to a barricaded room on the far side. She instinctively took a step backwards, ending up in the clamouring arms of another monster that was hiding in the shadows behind her. Jess yelped in what was both a combination of surprise and pain, as her attacker wrapped his arms around her and dug their nails into her forearms.

And just like that, Jess knew she was infected.

*

Hal heard the scream ring out across the open courtyard of the park, and realised he'd make a fatal mistake. At the very least, Jess would never forgive him for this. At worst…he shook the negativity from his mind as he unloaded the final rounds from his shotgun into the head of a nearby member of The Restarted, pressing his earpiece before focusing squarely on frantically attempting to reload.

He was never that great at multi-tasking.

'We need backup, east wing. Jess is in trouble,' Hal said into the receiver.

He too was greeted by static, and immediately understood how Jess must have felt, as another representative of the undead lashed out at him. He smashed the hilt of his shotgun into the jaw of his attacker, causing the beast to recoil, then gripped the loading mechanism in his right hand, using the weight of the weapon to reload itself, fully aware of how slick that must have looked.

Aiming true, he pulled the trigger, the recoil causing minimum discomfort ever since Jon had shown him how to modify it. Brains shot outwards, lining the floor with what he assumed was a foul-smelling viscous goop, not that he had ever actually been in a position to verify that theory.

Hal made haste towards the east wing, bolted down the alleyway to his right, before finally arriving at the arcade, rummaging in his bag in an attempt to gain purchase on his secret weapon…

As he reached Jess, he unloaded three rounds in quick succession, taking out the three assailants that were eager to feast on, unbeknownst to Hal, Jess's now-infected flesh.

'About damn time!' said Jess, pulling the blade from another of The Restarted.

'Blah blah, you're fine,' said Hal unapologetically. 'You wanna nag some more, or get out of here?'

Jess hesitated for a fraction longer than was necessary, seemingly unsure on if she was done fighting, but ultimately deciding she could still argue whilst on the move.

She ran past Hal, who continued to offload some rounds into the heads of what was slowly becoming a hoard, until there were too many of them for him to decide on which to aim at.

Remaining was suicide, so he shot off after Jess.

As they made their way back down the main alley, they noted that the route ahead was blocked off. Hal pulled out an old MP3 player equipped with external speakers, quickly scrolling through the playlist until he found a track that resonated with him.

'Nope, nope, ahhhh, perfect,' said Hal, as he pressed play and threw the device like a grenade into the modest gaggle in front of him.

The device landed with a flimsy clack, and for a moment Hal worried it might have glitched out on him, but his fears were eradicated as AC/DC's "Thunderstruck" filled the courtyard.

Hal looked over at Jess, eyes filled with glee.

She ignored him entirely, as she switched out her humble handgun for an MP4 semi-automatic rifle from Hal's garishly bright-pink pack.

The creatures, meanwhile, distracted by the noise coming from the music player, turned their attention away from them, allowing Hal to run past and hit the starter controls on a theme park attraction; a simple machine that rotated one-seater spaceships at varying speeds. The spaceships began to bob up and down, hilariously in time with the music filling the arena of death. Several of the creatures walked into it, beheading themselves in the process.

'Nice,' said Jess.

'Thanks,' said Hal, somewhat caught off guard by the rare display of praise.

As they made their way into the central plaza, Brian Johnson's throaty voice filled their eardrums, doing little to counteract how exposed they now were. Hoards had been drawn to the music from every nook and cranny of the park, leaving them surrounded.

Now, back to back, they knew this would be their last stand.

'You ready to do this thing?' said Hal, like a poor man's action hero.

'I always knew this was how we were going to go out.'

'Armed to the teeth in a blaze of glory?'

'I was thinking more along the lines of dying before you put that shelf up that you promised seven months ago,' she retorted.

Hal barked a laugh. 'Seems kind of a moot point right now sweetie.'

'A cow's opinion…'

'Hey, you said it,' joked Hal, intentionally ignoring the "Friends" reference.

'Douche. Where the hell is your brother, anyway?'

'Love you baby. And you know Alex, he'll be here…'

They clinked their lead-dispensing conduits of death, and reloaded.

*

Jess whirled around like a Dervish, spraying hot lead in a 360-degree arc, taking the legs out from underneath the front line of their attackers, as Hal threw a grenade into the hoard that had congregated to his right, sending body parts flying.

'Dammit Hal, we don't want crawlers, tone it down!'

Jess was right; whilst the frag grenade has taken a large amount of The Restarted out of the equation, some had inevitably survived, their legless torsos digging their nails into the ground to drag themselves forward, eager to take a bite out of their ankles. Hal finished them off with headshots, refusing to allow the commentary of his fiancée to distract him from the task at hand.

Within minutes, the entirety of the undead that were occupying the park had been drawn to them by the gunfire. The wall behind Hal and Jess acted as both a shield to being attacked from behind, as well as a lid to what would soon become their coffin. They couldn't run forwards, and they couldn't retreat. They had nowhere to run to.

As the masses of zombies brought hell itself down upon them, Hal heard the dreaded clack of a dead man's click; he was out of ammo.

Jess's weapon decided to betray her shortly after, jamming entirely. This was it. After months of planning, surviving, and mastering firearms, they were about to join the ranks of the undead.

Jess pulled out her pistol, checked her clip, and noted the three bullets remaining.

'One each…' she said, shooting one last zombie to her left for luck.

'We had a good run.'

As the hoard closed the gap, Hal and Jess didn't see the point in fighting with knives anymore. There were simply too many to make it out of this alive.

Their earpieces crackled to life.

'Sorry I'm late, was just grabbing a coffee,' said a disembodied voice. 'Where are you?'

'Central hub, central hub!' shouted Jess and Hal in unison.

'Oh man, I love this track!' said Alex, as the song started its second cycle of its endless loop.

The chorus was temporarily muted by the sound of a rocket-propelled grenade, which landed several metres in front of them, utterly obliterating a large mass of the undead that were obstructing their escape.

Alex flew in, sliding on his knees, attaching a slab of remotely detonated C4 to the leg of an unsuspecting ghoul. He jumped to his feet, said "Sup"' to his fellow zombie-slayers, and held up the detonator, it blinked green, and the horde exploded behind him. 'And for the man who has everything,' he added, restocking their ammunition and running off back into the fray, equipping a deadly-looking axe and decapitating anything that moved.

'How do you do that again?' Hal asked into his headset.

'L3 then hold Circle,' Alex replied happily, his voice partially distorted.

'Right, always forg–'

A wave of nausea suddenly attacked Hal's senses, his vision obstructed by an inexplicable sea of fog. He shook his head, and the shunt to his equilibrium evolved into an agonising migraine, causing him to drop his controller.

A ringing sound broke up the insanity as the pain gradually lessened, before dissipating entirely, and Hal realised it was his phone.

'Dammit Hal,' said Jess, 'what's wrong with you?'

Hal mumbled apologetically, grabbing his controller from the carpeted floor to resume his responsibilities. He pulled off his headset before getting back into the game as he accepted the call and propped the device between his shoulder and free ear.

'Jurassic Park, how can I direct your call?' he said into the receiver.

'Hal, we need to talk...'

'Oh, hey Kar'! What's up?

'Have you heard?'

Hal could sense an unusual amount of panic in her voice, and a notable level of distress. Horror even.

'Hang on,' said Hal. 'Guys, sorry, we need to call it.'

Both Alex and Jess groaned in disapproval, as Hal put down his controller and walked into the kitchen, his onscreen character dying within seconds.

'Bad time?' asked Kara.

'Nah,' lied Hal, 'just playing COD Zombies, can't pause an online game.'

'Uh huh, whatever. Listen. Something's wrong and...I don't know why I'm calling you really, but–'

Jess came into the kitchen and Hal mouthed the words "it's Kara" and she nodded, having already heard as much.

'Don't be too long,' said Jess quietly. 'We need to start getting ready for the funeral anyway.'

'Uh huh,' said Hal. 'I won't be long–wait. What?' he added, turning to face her.

Kara whispered hysterically down the phone to Hal.

'That's what I'm trying to tell you Hal, it's–'

What Jess said next made no sense to him at all.

'Peter's funeral, Hal…' said Jess, a puzzled look on her face laced with concern that he had seemingly forgotten the funeral of one of their closest friends.

Hal experienced a violently intense sensation of temporal dysplasia.

A voice erupted from his phone again, and he was brought back down to whatever Earth he was now stuck on.

'That's what I'm trying to tell you Hal!' repeated Kara, utterly exasperated.

'I have to go,' mumbled Hal, hanging up the phone and throwing it onto the kitchen counter.

'You're fucking with me, right?' said Hal, not finding the joke funny at all.

'No, I'm not fucking with you. We really *do* need to get ready…' said Jess, misunderstanding the question.

And with that she left him alone and trotted up the stairs, as Shelby plodded into the kitchen, staring up at Hal expectantly for a treat.

After all, he *was* in the place where treats lived.

Hal smiled distractedly and grabbed her a biscuit,

flicking it towards her head. Shelby caught it in her mouth flawlessly, then skipped away, her tiny claws clacking against the floor tiles before landing on the carpet of the hallway and allowing her to stealthily leave his sight.

'Yeah,' said Hal to himself. 'Of course. The funeral.'

How could he have forgotten?

On that sour note, he headed upstairs to prepare for an afternoon of mourning the death of a friend he had no idea had died in the first place.

CHAPTER SIX
Funeral for a Friend

Friday, October 5th, 2018, 1:04pm

It had been six weeks since Hal's stay at Fir Lodge, and during that time not one person had mentioned to him, not even in passing, that his friend Peter had died.

He slumped down in the passenger seat of Jess's car, looking down at his legs. The sun bounced intensely off of his royal blue trousers, and he noticed the left lace on his pristine black shoes had, much like his mind, come undone. Hal sub-consciously acknowledged the clock on the dashboard, electric-blue numbers that were igniting a feeling of anxiety deep within him.

Attempting to lean down and retie his rogue lace,

he was instantly pulled back by the seat belt, and groaned in irritation. Gently loosening the tautness of the belt, he finally had enough leeway to reach down and rectify the problem. As he did so, a beam of sunlight glistened off his silver cufflink, dancing across the blue sleeve of his suit jacket.

He had panicked when Jess had instructed him to get ready, having felt guilty for apparently blocking out the tragedy that had befallen one of his closest friends, feeling utterly ashamed that he hadn't so much as purchased a new suit for the occasion. But as he made his way to his wardrobe, a bright blue suit, crisp white shirt, and matching blue tie were waiting for him, all of which still had the price tag affixed to them.

'We're here,' said Jess, pulling him back into the present.

It was bad enough that he was wearing a suit he couldn't remember buying, but even worse that his past-self had chosen such a garish colour. Wearing electric blue just didn't feel right for a funeral. He decided to cut himself some slack, taking solace in the fact that he had at least somehow been functional enough to buy a suit at all.

Hal had taken up Jess's offer for her to drive, due to him not knowing which church he was meant to be driving to and feeling that asking the question would raise eyebrows. Thus far, judging by the route she was taking, all he knew was that they were heading in the general direction of Bocking town.

As they pulled into the car park, Hal read the sign for St Mary's Church.

'You okay?' said Jess, noticing his almost delirious expression.

'Yeah. Umm…it's just so much to take in, you know?' said Hal feebly, neglecting to bolster his proclamation of the obvious with what was really bothering him.

'I know, somehow it feels more real now we're actually here,' noted Jess.

The pair made their way across the courtyard, meeting up with the rest of their friends, who were engaging in the customary small-talk befitting of a situation such as this. Hal caught a few conversations on the wind, things such as "how was your drive", "traffic was murder", "traffic wasn't that bad actually" and his particular favourite; "what a lovely church", until finally, Jon approached him.

'Hey mate,' said Jon. 'Erm…nice suit?' he added, more of a question than a statement.

'Hey, Jon. Yeah…thanks,' said Hal, finding himself unable to formulate a more explanatory sentence and desperate for the exchange between them to end.

Saving him from any further embarrassment, at least for the time being, a woman stepped outside from behind the large, heavy-set entrance doors of the church, and gestured for everyone to take a seat inside.

*

As Hal took up a pew, he noticed a leaflet perched inside the cloth pouch that lined the back of the seats of the people sitting in front of him. Forcing his fingers between a haggard-looking bible and the unseen netting within the pouch itself, he plucked the expensive-feeling paper that had been created in memoriam of his friend Peter, and scanned his eyes across the information it contained, trying to restart his failing memory.

'Peter Allen, Born August 19th, 1991, died August 25th, 2018.'

He stuffed it into the pocket of his trousers, figuring he may need it later. Loosening his tie and resting his arms on his knees, Hal promptly began to lose his shit, simultaneously attempting to regulate his breathing by formulating a mental list of the things that were disturbing him. He decided to start big; how was it possible that he had no recollection of his friend kicking the bucket that was holding his soul quite adequately until two hours ago? Why couldn't he remember buying this ridiculously inappropriate, yet admittedly perfectly fitting, suit? And why did every funeral start with menacingly oppressive organ music?

The same woman who invited them into the church took up residence centre stage, and began hosting the sermon.

'We are gathered here today in memory of–' and she was off, rather unhelpfully leaving out all of the crucial details Hal was looking for. The *how*, the *why*, the *what's*…instead filling her opening speech with all of the generalised platitudes that only someone who *didn't* know Peter like he did would say, as if she were reading them from his Facebook bio. For a fleeting moment he wondered if this Reverend was in on a celestial joke somehow – almost as if she were the mastermind behind it all…

Hal felt a burning sensation in the back of his head and turned around in an attempt to identify the cause. He was greeted by the sight of Kara, staring at him, seemingly trying to utilise some form of telepathy to get him to look at her. Her eyes were wide with an emotion Hal recognised as the onset signs of what was surely insanity.

He shot her a lame nod, then turned back to face the onslaught of social media reruns being thrown up by the well-meaning host of today's madness. Suddenly, he turned back to face Kara, or rather, focused his attention on what she wearing; a well-fitting, lightning-blue dress, with a matching fascinator.

Noting the way in which he was surveying her ensemble, she shifted uneasily in her seat, her face flooding with a high level of embarrassment that caused her cheeks to flush. She shrugged apologetically, then raised an indignant eyebrow, as if to say "you can talk."

Hal felt a nudge in his ribs, and turned to his left, disarmed by Jess who nodded towards the Archbishop of Banality before them, indicating that he should be paying attention. He winced apologetically, allowing his eyes to glaze over, safe in the knowledge that he could hide in plain sight for the next presumably billion hours of whatever the hell this thing was.

But as Fearne took the stage, a sigh escaped his soul as he realised his invisibility was about to be short lived. In fact, things began to escalate so quickly that, by comparison to his current reality, it made even the weirdness levels of Highlander 2 seem like they may have actually contained an internal logic after all.

CHAPTER SEVEN
The Poet, The Widow, and The Wardrobe
Friday, October 5th, 2018, 1:27pm

There was nothing inherently peculiar about the way Fearne took to the podium. Excluding the fact that she was about to bust out a eulogy for a man that Hal wasn't entirely convinced was actually dead, given that he had spoken to him on the phone less than a week ago.

But nonetheless, something about her demeanour was putting Hal on edge. He looked back at Kara, and could tell she was experiencing the same degree of emotional disconnect.

Fearne breathed heavily into the microphone, then pulled herself together, her words starting innocently enough, but ultimately achieving little in the way of easing his understandable concerns.

'Thank you all for…coming here today,' said Fearne. 'Or should I say for coming here *then*,' she added, more than a little manically, giggling creepily to herself in the sort of way that someone did right before a Xenomorph burst forth from their chest. 'Peter is…*was*, everything to me. We were partners in everything. Which is precisely why I need you all to listen very, *very* closely to what I'm about to say.'

Hal's spider-sense flared violently as Fearne continued, causing a sickness in his stomach to rise up which was so intense he not-so-casually started to take stock of his surroundings, just in case he needed to make a sharp exit to the nearest bathroom.

'Peter *isn't* dead,' said Fearne, the words landing like three independently cast Hadouken blasts into the faces of every person lining the pews before her. All except one of course. And, unbeknownst to Hal, one other person sitting a few rows behind him. 'He's alive, I just…I just need to *fix* it and I need all of you to help me with this because I can't do this on my own! I need you all to help me get back to–'

The Reverend hosting the sermon intervened, ever so gently placing a hand on Fearne's shoulder, but enough so that she could work towards reclaiming ownership of the microphone.

'I think what Fearne is trying to reiterate is that Peter lives on in all of you. His kindness and compassion for others has left a mark on–'

Fearne grabbed the microphone back, tears rolling from her eyes and streaming down her face, her running mascara giving her a look of wildness and unpredictability, as she frantically gripped her long brunette hair in a fit of both frustration and unadulterated exasperation.

'No, I mean Peter is alive! I need you all to *hear* me! Why is no one *hearing* what I'm say–'

The Reverend whirled a finger in the direction of Rhiannon, the wholly under-appreciated organist, as if to indicate it was time to play Fearne out.

Noting that now was truly her time to shine, the musician – who ran a very under-exposed website and was available for other events such as weddings and b'nai mitzvah, whilst being equally open to private messages being sent to her via the Holy Trinity of social media platforms – dutifully obliged.

Fearne clenched her fist, mumbling to herself, and ran down the centre aisle, colliding with the double doors to the church with such ferocity that Hal wondered if the church's building insurance was up to date.

The room was filled with hushed tones, as the echoes of the chamber doors slammed behind her, with Rhiannon doing her best to maintain the flow of music, despite the irregular distractions. Not for the first time in her life, the organist contemplated why she hadn't just sacked this one off to go home and watch the latest episode of The Bake Off.

Ever the professional, their host cleared her

throat and attempted to exorcise the swamp of awkwardness that Fearne had left in her wake.

'I know you will all understand and respect this is an extremely difficult time. A loss like this is always heart-breaking, especially the loss of someone so young, their whole life taken from them so unfairly, in such tragic circumstances.'

Hal seized his opportunity, taking a cue from the organist and piping up.

'And…what *were* those circumstances exactly?' he said, recoiling at how loud his voice travelled across the acoustically-traitorous room, even over the music that was playing throughout.

Everyone turned in their seats to face him, a deafening slide of arses all working in unison, causing Hal's face to flood with a colour not that far off from beetroot purple.

'Ya know…' said Hal, his voice now a high-pitched squeal that he attempted to rectify with an equally ill-timed throat clearing that sounded like his dog Shelby when she was regurgitating a hair ball. 'You know,' he tried again. "Better", he thought. 'I just thought hearing the manner in which Peter…erm…*died*, would help…with…the *grieving*?' he added, as if vindicating the ridiculousness of his words.

"Nailed it," thought Hal.

"Fucked it," thought Kara.

The Reverend patted down her gown, utterly at a loss for the manner in which the young man was determined to derail her flow. She had practised her presentation countless times, seriously regretting her decision to take on this particular funeral just so that her fellow Reverend, Roger, could attend a beer festival in Chelmsford.

'Perhaps now,' she said in a tone that was clearly gearing towards a non-negotiable rhetoric suggestion, 'would be a good time for our next speaker to take the podium. Hal Callaghan, if you'd be so kind?'

A tidal wave of shifting bodies in seats once again echoed throughout the room, as Hal stared blankly back at her, a lopsided smile complementing his thousand-yard stare which was aimed directly back at her. The Reverend appeared to suppress her irritation upon realising the next guest speaker was the very person she was attempting to keep from derailing things further.

'Hal has kindly written a poem lamenting his friendship with Peter,' she added, gesturing towards Hal, then back towards the podium.

'I have?' asked Hal, as terror gripped him.

'What the hell is wrong with you?' whispered Jess frantically.

'I don't…I haven't written anything?!' he snapped, attempting to whisper, but ultimately loud enough for everyone to hear.

Jess nudged him in the stomach, forcing him to stand up, and he frowned at her as if he found the gesture to be nothing less than a mutiny, before making his way to the microphone.

Taking a deep breath, he looked back out into the eyes of his expectant friends. Kara in particular was leaning in, resting her elbows on her knees and her chin in her palms. Hal felt she looked a little bit too enthused with curiosity to see how this was going to pan out for him.

Adjusting his suit jacket, he reached into the interior pockets of his blazer, his sub-conscious hoping to graze against an old friend; that of the filter box he used to store his cigarettes prior to quitting six weeks ago, echoes of his addiction resulting in its presence being sorely missed.

Instead, he felt a thin sheet of paper, which he pulled out quickly, scanning the text that was typed upon it. Hal exhaled in relief, realising the poem he couldn't remember even writing was etched across it in handwriting that looked far too neat to be his own. Shrugging, he figured it best at this point to just roll with the chaos.

*

'Great poem Hal,' said Rachel as they made their way through the corridor of the glamourous, chic barn which had been hired to house the wake. 'Honestly, who knew you could write?!'

'Not me, that's for sure,' said Hal, his words far more literal that his friend could ever know. As beads of sweat trickled down his forehead, his eyes darted around the room as if he had just entered bat country and was auditioning for a part in the sequel to Fear and Loathing in Las Vegas.

'You want a drink?' asked Rachel. 'I'll get the first round in, the bar's about to open.'

'Yeah, great, whatever, JD and coke please,' said Hal absently. 'Actually, better make it neat,' he added.

'Wow, start as you mean to go on!' said Rachel, utterly perplexed by Hal's uncharacteristic dismissiveness and choice of alcohol. 'Are you okay? I mean…I know none of us are *okay* exactly, but you seem a little…'

"Like I've *slipped* into an alternate *universe*?!" he thought to himself. 'I'm fine, Rach, honest. A drink would be lovely,' he added as an extra convincer.

Hal took a deep breath, but midway through exhaling he felt a hand reach out from nowhere, pulling him entirely off balance, as he was dragged into darkness.

He tried to yell out, but a hand clasped around his mouth, turning his shout into a lamely-muted mumble. Hal struggled as he was pushed towards the rear wall of wherever the hell he now was, as the sound of a door clicked shut behind him. He spun around to face his attacker, hands ready to dish out some Judo chops.

'Oh. Hey, Kar',' said Hal.

'We. Need. To. Talk.'

'What about? Who wore it better?' said Hal, as the sliver of sunlight from the window behind him ricocheted off of her blue dress, which almost looked metallic in this light, not to mention being almost identical in tone to his own blue attire.

'Tell me I'm not losing my mind here,' said Kara, attempting to pace up and down but instead spinning on the spot due to the lack of room. 'And *me*, obviously,' she added, referring to her outfit.

Hal hummed a high-pitched tone, seemingly in disagreement. 'Hmmm debaaaateable.'

Kara dispensed her trademark scowl.

'Why did you pick blue anyway?' asked Kara.

'No idea. You?'

'I don't remember picking it at all. Can't be a coincidence, surely?' said Kara contemplatively.

'How do you have wine? The bar isn't even *open* yet?' said Hal, noticing as she picked a large glass of vino from the poorly erected shelf, feeling slightly concerned, but primarily just jealous.

Kara replied by taking a swig as if it were little more than thirst-quenching water as Hal, in an action not that time-consuming given the dimensions of the small cubby hole they were occupying, drank in their surroundings in lieu of a beverage he could call his own.

'Where even *are* we?' said Hal, trying to get his bearings. 'You couldn't find anywhere a little roomier? What is this, a wardrobe?'

'Oh, I'm sorry,' said Kara sarcastically. 'You're right, my bad–'

'Kara.'

'Maybe we should just head to the bar? In front of all our friends? Then we can–'

'*Kara*,' Hal tried again.

'–discuss how Peter, who Greg and I had *dinner* with literally *two* weeks ago, apparently *died* six weeks ago? Yeah we should definitely–'

'KARA,' shouted Hal. 'Will you calm the frack down, you're giving me heart palpitations!'

She took a breath, realising her own blood pressure was so high it was giving her a mild ice-pick migraine.

They looked at each other, the dank broom closest filling their nostrils with the aromatic scent of stale beer and cheap bleach.

'So,' said Hal, 'how have you beeeen?' he hummed, unable to come up with a more creative opener.

'What?' said Kara. 'Fine. Busy. I'm fine. You?'

'Good,' said Hal. 'So, elephant in the room time. You feel it *too,* right?'

She knew exactly what he meant. The sensation of lost time, the blackouts, the newsfeed on her own social media accounts that showed photos of places she couldn't remember going, status updates she couldn't remember writing, clothes such as the very dress she was currently wearing that she couldn't remember buying. And lastly, but most importantly of all, the death of a friend she couldn't even remember losing.

'Yeah,' said Kara. 'I feel it too. It started earlier today. A wave of nausea hit me. Some weird fog. Next thing I know, Greg's dragging me to a funeral for Peter! For *Peter*, Hal! He tells me he died at the lodge six weeks ago. They think he was murdered!'

'Murdered?' said Hal. 'Seriously? By who?'

Kara took a deep breath, and scrunched up her eyes, pinching the bridge of her nose in an attempt to collect her thoughts.

'Thank God, I thought it was just me,' said Kara. 'Greg thought I was insane, I thought it was a wind-up at first.'

There was a knock on the door and Kara turned to face the unexpected intrusion, as Rachel popped her head through to check on them.

'Oh, hey,' said Rachel. 'You guys…okay in here?' she added, surveying the cramped enclosure they had contained themselves within.

Hal leaned to the right, so he could see Rachel's face.

'Oh, hey Rach',' he said, trying to diffuse what must have clearly looked a little weird. 'Just, erm, you know, it's so sad. About Pete. We just needed to get away for a second.

'Riiiiiight,' said Rachel, not looking entirely convinced, on the basis she had eyes, ears, and more than a bare minimum level of experience when it came to human interaction. "Well, your drink's on the bar, see you in a minute?'

'Yup,' said Kara.

As Kara slowly but awkwardly shut the door in her friend's face, Hal and Kara dropped their fake smiles that they knew Rachel wasn't even remotely buying.

'We can't talk here,' said Kara urgently.

'I can't even stand *up* straight in here,' added Hal.

Kara scowled.

'Meet you tomorrow? Coffee in town?'

'Sure,' said Hal.

'Right. Bye then,' said Kara, straightening her dress out, opening the door and slamming it behind him.

Hal stood there in silence, wondering how long he needed to wait before he could reasonably exit the storage cupboard, trying to judge what the perfectly measured length of time was for a situation like this.

'Right. Good talk,' Hal whispered towards the space Kara had formerly been occupying.

After clucking his tongue to fill the sudden quietness, he decided five seconds was long enough, and exited the glorified wardrobe, gearing himself up to interact with a timeline that he was almost certain he didn't belong in.

CHAPTER EIGHT
Storm in a Coffee Cup

Saturday, October 6th, 2018, 10:59am

Hal met Kara outside the local coffee shop, and held the door open for her as she stepped inside. They didn't feel the need to fill silence with pointless chit-chat, and instead queued quietly until it was their turn to order.

They had chosen this particular coffee shop as it was central to both of them, and whilst deceivingly humble in size from the outside, the place was like a Tardis within. What it lacked in width it made up for in depth; the narrow entrance opening up to reveal plenty of nooks for private conversation beneath the post-modern art that lined the walls.

Hal fixed his gaze onto the glass shield that

protected the sugar-based cornucopia, and as he stared at the overpriced baked-goods he made a mental note to seriously consider eating breakfast from now on.

Kara ordered her skinny latte, and Hal ordered a full-fat equivalent. Everything was going swimmingly until the barista asked what size he wanted. He always froze when asked this question. His head told him to ask for a medium, but in his heart he felt conflicted over if he should instead be casting one of the three designated Harry Potter spells; Primo, Medio or Massimo.

He settled on a compromise.

'Accio *Medium*, please,' he said confidently.

'What?' the staff member asked, her expression not a million miles away from sheer boredom.

'He'll take a medium,' said Kara. '*This is why I never take you anywhere*,' she added in a playfully agitated whisper.

As they took their seats in a quieter section, they surveyed their surroundings to evaluate if they could talk without too many people overhearing. Kara slipped off her coat and slung it over a chair, an action which Hal mimicked, noticing that Kara was wearing an uncharacteristically monotone ensemble; a dark-green v-cut khaki shirt offering a negligible flash of colour against her black jeans.

His attention was unexpectedly drawn to a woman in her mid-twenties sitting several tables away, totally immersed in whatever entertainment she was indulging in on her expensive looking tablet. Her shoulder-length, vibrantly-purple hair covered the majority of her face, due to the angle she was sitting at, and cascaded down the back of a rather garish red leather jacket. But it wasn't the decidedly rebellious seizure-inducing colours she was sporting that held his attention. It was more the fact that even from the dimly lit corner she was occupying, and with half of her face covered, she looked incredibly familiar.

'Hey Kara, check out the girl behind you, don't you think she looks a bit like—'

Before Kara could turn to look, the woman jotted something down in the journal resting next to her coffee, hastily collected her things and promptly departed, running her fingers through her dazzling hair, turning her head away from them as she walked, making it impossible for them to see her face.

Hal blinked, shrugging off the nagging feeling that he had seen her somewhere before, finally indicating he was satisfied that the hustle and bustle would afford them a degree of cover, but it was Kara that actually got the ball rolling.

'So, I've been trying to reach Fearne all morning,' she said in a tone befitting of a conspiracy theorist.

'Yeah,' said Hal. 'After her speech yesterday, she's *clearly* feeling what we're feeling too. Any luck?'

It was no secret. Fearne had literally shouted that she believed Peter was actually alive somehow.

'That's just it,' said Kara, leaning in closer to him. 'She isn't answering her phone.'

'She's got a lot on her plate, to be fair.'

'Anyway, I did some digging into Peter's death, it turns out he was found murdered in a house a short distance away from–'

Hal pulled his phone out from underneath the table, the screen vibrant with life, and plonked it down in front of him.

'Settle down Nancy Drew,' said Hal. 'I've got Google too. Down the road from Fir Lodge.'

Kara shot him a look of disappointment. She had been rather proud of the information she had uncovered and he was totally stealing her thunder. Hal could tell she was hurt, and raised his hands apologetically, gesturing for her to continue.

She smiled and carried on.

'The guy who did it, Kevin Barker, is currently locked up.'

Hal knew this already, what with it being information that was in the public domain on the Crown Court website.

Hal took a sip of his latte, pensively mulling that over, then winced, tearing open a third sachet of sugar and pouring it into his cup. Kara shot him a disapproving look.

'What? I gave up smoking, I'm sure as shit not giving up sugar too,' said Hal defiantly. 'So, they have Jerry's owner pegged for this?' Hal thought about that, as a sadness befell him. 'What happened to Jerry?!'

'Oh, I did some Facebook stalking,' Kara said

happily, finally having some information Hal didn't. 'The owner of Fir Lodge took him in,' she added, pulling her own phone out, scrolling between applications for a few seconds, then turning the phone to face him so he could see a picture of Jerry at his new home.

'Top bloke that Danny,' said Hal, noting the feed on Kara's phone which revealed to him the man's profile.

'But here's the thing,' said Kara. 'I went through my own emails, and get this,' she paused for dramatic effect, which was somewhat dampened by the irritating whine emanating from a nearby baby in a pushchair a few metres away from them.

'You gonna tell me,' said Hal, 'or just stare at me until the CSI Miami theme tune kicks in?'

She looked at him with an expression laced with what Hal interpreted as *I don't know what that means* before dropping the bomb, and ultimately the mic.

'I gave a statement to the police after the incident. A statement I don't remember even giving, I might add…'

'Obvs,' said Hal, taking another swig of his latte.

'And something about it doesn't add up. Read it,' she said, sliding the phone across the varnished table.

Hal looked down at the screen and followed her instruction, reading her statement.

'My name is Kara Sanders. The following is a true account of the events that took place on the evening of August the 25th, 2018, at Pentney Lakes, Norfolk…'

Hal read about the events of Saturday the 25th, which recounted, beat for beat, everything that he already knew. Until he reached the last paragraph of Kara's statement, and a chill ran down his spine.

'Woah,' said Hal.

'I know right?!' said Kara, relieved that he had spotted the same inconsistency that she had. 'Ignoring the fact that I don't remember writing this at all, anything in particular seem notably screwy to you?'

Hal recited the exact line of transcribed dialogue that didn't ring true. In fact, it was nothing short of an absolute lie.

'*Peter must have taken Jerry back to his home. I was clearing broken glass from upstairs. Otherwise I would have offered to take him…*' Hal stopped reading out loud and looked up at his friend. 'That isn't what happened. *We* were the ones who took Jerry back.'

'Bingo. Which means—'

'Who says *bingo* anymore?' said Hal, entirely off topic.

'Which *means*,' said Kara, intentionally ignoring his attempted derailment of far more important matters, 'either I *lied* to the police…or my memories can't be trusted.'

'Which is impossible. Because I remember things going the same way as you do.'

'So why did I lie to them?' said Kara, starting to question not only her sanity, but her integrity as a human being. There's more. According to the records, Kevin claimed he was drugged prior to Pete's murder.'

'They must've run tests on him or something,' said Hal, basing his argument on old reruns of Diagnosis Murder and Columbo.

'They did. No traces of anything in his system. And it gets worse. How Pete was found…they think it ties in to huge back catalogue of murders dating back to the late-Nineties!'

'Holy crap,' he choked on his coffee. 'So, he was like, what? A serial killer or something?'

'Allegedly, yeah. But there's no way Pete died that weekend. Not when–'

'You, me, and possibly Fearne remember him leaving Fir Lodge alive and well,' said Hal, finishing her sentence.

She nodded. 'So, the real question is; why does everyone else believe it happened?'

Without warning, the door of the shop flung open, a rush of air bombarding them both, causing Kara's hair to flutter. An odd sound rippled through the coffee shop, shaking the cups on the tables, the glass stands nestled within the cabinet encasing the cakes, and the four walls around them. The sound was unlike anything they had ever heard before; In fact, it was more like the natural sounds around them were being sucked into a vacuum.

The universe, it seemed, had decided to answer her question personally.

CHAPTER NINE
Dancing with Yourself

5,840th Restart – Sunday, August 26th, 2018, 11:56pm

Malcolm found himself reminiscing over his short-lived victory. How he had traded the one named Peter's life to break the hold Harold, Kara, and time itself held over him.

His flawlessly executed plan once again coming undone.

There was only one way he could be here now; someone had changed the outcome of that night.

Harold and *Kara*…

Yes, he remembered now. His memories were as jumbled as his current thoughts these days.

Always shifting. Always *changing*. Reorganising themselves like a constantly shifting kaleidoscope.

They had ruined everything.

Again.

Malcolm recalled the implanted memory of seeing his own body being wheeled out on a stretcher. The blue flashing lights dazzling his out-of-phase eyes. And as his body crossed the boundary line of the Pentney Lakes, this new iteration of his time-travelling self was brought with it.

Brought here.

He stared at the sickly green reflection of the emergency lighting refracting off of the tantalisingly-thirst-quenching jug of water, which served as a mocking reminder that he wasn't able to drink, and for the 1,496th time a cover of the song "Dancing with Myself" drifted softly towards him from a nearby CD player, which had *kindly* been switched on by a nurse.

Whether this had *been* an act of kindness or a form of punishment, he couldn't be certain, though if it was the latter it was surely a torture he admittedly deserved. Little did she know that music was the lifeblood for time travellers such as himself.

It kept them anchored. Kept the mind sharp.

Too sharp…

He learnt a long time ago that the cover was performed by a member from the cast of an American TV show called "Glee", thanks to the helpfully face-down CD case beside the bed.

An album that had been playing on a continuous loop for the past three hours throughout the dead of night. His only salvation was that a restart was due in the next several minutes, and would abruptly put an end to the wailing. At least for the nine or so hours that would follow.

His analytical mind, combined with a near photographic memory, had afforded him a seemingly supernatural ability to track the passage of time. But, as a Restarter (a term he had long since made peace with using ever since he had heard Harold and the girl named Kara uttering the word) it was excruciating.

Every second of every minute of every day was catalogued in his mind, and even when he had *lost* said mind, the details of every second would slowly dripfeed their way back into his subconscious eventually. Only to be lost again with the arrival of the black fog.

He had spent countless years clawing his way back from the void of eternal damnation. The cruellest joke of all was that when he had finally broken free of the endlessly-rewinding thirty-three hours those children had trapped him in, he had ended right back where he started.

He remembered the *glee*…he winced at the use of the word, and adapted his inner-monologue accordingly, ensuring he made a mental note never to so much as think of using it ever again.

Malcolm remembered *fondly* how he had beaten the system. How, despite the odds, he had found a way to escape the invisible force field that ensconced the Pentney Lakes, vanquishing the self-declared Restarters at their own game.

But something had clearly gone wrong. Something had been changed.

And so it was that the universe once again consumed him, breaking his body down into billions of tiny fragments, before reassembling and discarding his essence back within the confines of acres of woodland. In Norfolk. Of all places.

He thought back to the events that followed. To his confrontation with the ones who refused to let him be. So many confusing encounters wrapped within paradoxes and sealed with a bow of impossibility. And, after it all, he found himself *here*.

Initially, he had experienced *relief*.

A sense of gratitude that he had reformed in a location he didn't recognise. Whilst the fluorescent lights that lined the ceiling had sent agonising beams of light into his corneas, once the vibrancy of his surroundings simmered down and he regained the superbly detailed intensity that a fresh restart afforded, he reasoned perhaps this was merely another challenge for him to overcome.

Malcolm had watched with pride as he looked down at his barely breathing body, being wheeled in on a stretcher, his legs and arms not only secured with straps, but also no less than *four* separate pairs of handcuffs. His arrival was heralded by a flattering abundance of trained professionals; eight police officers to be exact. Some of them armed.

He had chuckled at that. After all, in the United Kingdom, whichever way you painted it, that was a big deal. It meant you were not just a threat to others, but a threat to those that could protect themselves as well.

He was *death* incarnate.

Many years ago, he would have gone as far as to say a God…

But that was then and this was now and yet, somehow, *also* then, whilst paradoxically being tomorrow and yesterday all at the same time.

Malcolm closed his eyes and rubbed the sockets with his palms, violently running his hands through his thick black hair and shaking his head with vehement vigour. He sniffed a sharp intake of air, composing himself for what would come next, as the farcical narrative of the music once again crowbarred its way into this mind, igniting a melancholic sense of irony that was not lost on him in the slightest.

Well, let's sink another drink…because it will give me…time to think.

Malcolm sang along in his mind, barely concealing the fact that he was humming the tune out loud, then glared around the room; at the once tan-coloured flooring – now a slick black – that he knew must have smelled like disinfectant. At the empty vase on the window sill to his right, lacking the flowers that may have been there had he not burned every last friendship he ever had over the years (in some cases literally…) by becoming a brilliant, albeit definably psychopathic, murderer.

His eyes moved to his left, settling on the bed in front of him, the shadows of his past taking on a life of their own across the black bedsheets, swirling under the lights of the machine that were keeping his past-self from moving on. Oddly, said lights served as the only colour besides the security lighting amidst the impenetrable blackness and uniform blandness that had slowly possessed the room over time.

Day by day he had watched the colour being drained in tiny increments, coupled with an ever-thickening fog that seemed to feed on the warmth and life around him like a parasite fuelled by his own despair.

Realising he was losing himself to his thoughts again, Malcolm refocused his attention on the fluctuating hissing sounds of the iron lungs that kept him in what he knew to be a perpetual coma.

He was surely being kept alive solely so he could face justice for the crimes he had committed. Presumably, someone, somewhere was working on the assumption there were bodies to find. They must have known what he was capable of, as evidenced by the ankle braces and wrist straps that secured him firmly to the bed.

The hisses gave way to beeps and clicks, followed by the droplet of sustenance from the IV that, as its namesake suggested, travelled intravenously down a transparent tube and into his bloodstream. His eyes moved towards the closed door of his room, and at the armed officer standing just outside, visible through the inch-thick wire-mesh-lined glass. Being so close to his past self, he knew he *could* open that door, but also knew that it wouldn't do him any good.

The restart that had brought him here had seemingly decided he was too much of a threat; a restarting killer roaming the halls, potentially going on a rampage and murdering vulnerable patients…or worse, doctors and nurses.

Malcolm rationalised that the impact of killing those who worked in a profession that involved saving lives could cause untold pandemonium to the rivers of time.

That probably explained why the threshold of the room acted as his new Restart Point, much like the boundary line at Pentney Lakes.

He felt a pang of shame, and then anger. If that were true? If that were *really* the case? Then how was it acceptable for Ophelia to…to…

His mind ran off on a new tangent. A common occurrence for him now.

Malcolm sighed, letting go of his anger and suddenly feeling oddly nostalgic as he remembered those early years of restarting. When he was learning about how everything worked for the first time. A time of wonder. Excitement. Of plans that *went* somewhere. All of which had led him here.

His first mistake was assuming the same thirty-three-hour rule applied, and it took him a long time to realise no one was triggering a restart early. Once his paranoia subsided, he reached the logical conclusion that no one was intervening. This particular time loop was merely a twelve-hour cycle. Nothing more. Nothing less.

Eight years.

Eight years, relatively speaking, of being stuck watching his physical-self refusing to heal. It was an entirely new form of torture. With every second of progress his body made, all of it was undone every twelve hours, bringing him no closer to returning to the world of the living.

Malcolm stood up and stretched. The act did nothing for his muscles, which were currently a metre away from him lying on the bed before him and no doubt beginning their descent into atrophy. It was more the routine of doing so that helped solidify his resolve for what came next.

He walked towards his past-self, leaning over the body, and staring at his gaunt, ill-looking face, finally feeling truly ready to take this to the next level.

'What are you dreaming about I wonder…' Malcolm said to his comatose counterpart, the mechanical devices keeping his past-self alive responding with mechanical beeps and clicks.

The music triggered the return of a fleeting thought in his mind, which eventually coalesced to form a more coherent memory. It was taking him longer to form those now. He could feel it.

Something the rat-catcher had said. An evasive answer to a riddle that could have been little more than a desperate man trying to illicit the illusion of bravado. But it felt like more than that. Malcolm was astute and objective enough to know when a statement was laced with subtext or not. And those two simple words echoed amidst his thoughts once more.

"A team."

That's what the young man named Harold had said. But there were only two of them. Hardly what you could call a team. A *partner* maybe. But a *team*? Something felt off.

For the thousandth time, he replayed the moments over in his mind, thinking back to the seconds before he was forced out of existence in the previous timeline, an act which ultimately brought him to this place. He recalled that moment just as he was disintegrated at what he reasoned must have been at a molecular level, pressing pause on not only his life in the physical world but also his admittedly deteriorating mind.

"A team," he repeated, the blurriness of his thoughts gaining further cohesion.

And then it hit him.

A truth so obvious he was actually embarrassed it had taken him so long to figure it out. What he didn't know, however, was that this wasn't the first time he had reached this conclusion at all, merely the most recent instance of him remembering a long-solved problem. An answer which had driven him to this very idea in the first place.

Standing over his own comatose and utterly useless body, he chastised himself unfairly for forgetting his new goal. The fog was prone to stealing ideas right from under him.

Malcolm licked his lips and wondered if it could really be that simple.

If his comatose body was the one thing keeping him locked in time, in this room, reliving the same twelve hours over and over and over…

He placed his hand on the limp arm of his body-double, feeling the familiar sensation of a charge, not that it was strictly required. Malcolm was close enough to passively draw upon the temporal energy emanating from his body in the past. But it surely couldn't lessen his ability to interact with his surroundings by doing so.

Malcolm reached out towards and beyond the multitude of life-support devices, setting his sights on what lay behind them.

'I can't do this anymore,' he whispered, accepting that if this didn't work, he was at peace with it.

If he was right, he needed to get back to where it all began, and this was the only sure-fire way he felt he could achieve that goal. If he was wrong…well, better to be free and dead than to spend another second in this godforsaken hell of his own making. Either way, it would be progress.

It was then that Malcolm heard it; the familiar sound of rushing air. It had to be now, he didn't want time to steal the opportunity away from him, or worse, risk losing his mind again. A black static fog, which was somehow also viscous, swirled menacingly along the floor towards him.

He composed himself, not wishing to let that particular horror claim his focus, and continued reaching beyond the life-support network, which hissed in protest, still popping and clicking diligently. The thick mist seemed to gain speed around him, bridging the gap between the door and Malcolm's legs in a fraction of a second. Sensing he was on to something, he quickly pulled at the power cables, yanking them from the wall, then rolled over the end of the bed and poised himself, ready to jump.

The heart rate monitor chirped angrily as his physical-self began to flatline, just as the fog attacked his temporally-displaced torso, travelling up his arm and erasing his appendage from existence entirely.

Malcolm tried to scream in agony, but the pain was so unbearable he simply couldn't vocalise it. Instead, he compartmentalised the agony, regaining control of what was left of his out-of-phase body, as he jumped across the room, landing with a thud against the door to his prison.

The officer was speaking frantically into the radio attached to his chest, but it was all faint muffles and mumbles to Malcolm at this point. He had simply been here too long to hear the words of the living anymore, with the exception of that damn CD player of course.

Doctors and nurses flocked to the door, and

Malcolm pressed his temporally displaced body against it, the life that was ebbing away from his past-self still allowing him to retain enough of a charge to block their access. The mist grew denser, and shredded deep into his back, clawing at his tendons and bones, ripping through them effortlessly.

He released a guttural scream, as those outside the door managed to open it just an inch.

Malcolm glared at them, his eye sockets flashing violently with a familiar red energy, acting as an unseen warning to the doctors, to death, and to time itself.

'Release me!' he growled, in a voice that he didn't recognise. A voice that seemed to shake the room, along with the door, as the mesh glass began to crack, and those trying to enter the room recoiled in confusion, the released pressure on their side of the door causing it to close with a violent slam.

The police officer gingerly stepped closer to the door, shining a torch through the glass, and Malcolm growled again, this time causing the glass to shatter outwards. Malcolm thought he could see the flash of a blue garment behind the officer, being worn by a familiar face he couldn't quite identify, but the agonising pain he was experiencing filed it into a section of his brain that was, at best, reserved for mere afterthoughts.

And as his past-self left the land of the living, so too did his Restarter-self, time savagely ripping him to pieces, his mangled body collapsing on the floor, disintegrating like sand being sucked up by an invisible hoover until, finally, every single trace of Malcolm was gone.

It was in that precise moment, that Malcolm had achieved what no Restarter had ever done before; he had committed trans-dimensional suicide. The act creating a singularity in space-time so gargantuan, that it was a paradox only a Restarter could fix.

In fact, only two people in the entire universe stood any chance of undoing what he had just done.

There was just one problem. Harold and Kara were living in a new timeline. Their unique skillset not so much forgotten as erased entirely.

The "Restarters" didn't exist.

CHAPTER TEN

Little Coffee Shop of Horrors

Saturday, October 6th, 2018, 11:17am

The room was devoid of the natural chatter and clinking cutlery. The only noise that cut through the eerie silence was from the speakers above them, the jaunty jazz that had been playing becoming garbled and disjointed until, following an ominous crackle, the music petered out altogether for a brief second, suddenly being replaced with the sound of Glenn Miller's "In the Mood".

That alone was odd in itself, but not enough to cause such a sickening sense of foreboding between the two friends, nor the extremely disorientating wave of unexplainably mutual déjà vu.

As multiple timelines collided – each one vying for dominance – they found themselves confused as to why they were even in a coffee shop. Their reason for meeting momentarily elusive, as their memories were partially altered, before being returned to them.

'Kara,' said Hal, pointing behind her.

Kara turned around, resting an arm on her chair to balance herself, her jaw dropping as she drank in the sight before them; an elderly woman was pouring milk from a small jug into her giant coffee cup. Not in and of itself anything to be alarmed about. Hal and Kara's cause for alarm was more due to the fact that the milk was suspended between the cup and jug, not quite hitting the caffeinated liquid within, but not fully leaving the jug either.

They quickly realised that the effect they were witnessing wasn't merely localised to that woman alone; everyone around them was suspended in a state of frozen motion, seemingly as utterly oblivious to what was happening to them as they were completely unmoving.

'What's happening,' whispered Kara, as she stood up and walked to the woman with the milk jug and gingerly pushed her finger into the suspended dairy waterfall.

Her finger passed through without any more resistance than a trickle of milk should have done under the force of her touch, but as she pulled her finger back, the hole it had generated in the wall of white remained.

A river of fog began to spill from the front entrance of the coffee shop, under the legs of the patrons, and rose above the countertop, flowing up and over the baristas who were unknowingly indulging in an impromptu coffee break of their own from their daily duties.

Hal and Kara both experienced a simultaneous ice-pick migraine, causing Hal to grip his head with his hands in agony, with Kara being less fortunate and falling hard to her knees. An intense ringing noise filled not so much their eardrums, as it did the actual synapses in their brains.

Mercifully, the sensation dissipated as quickly as it arrived, and as the chorus of the song playing through the speakers began, the music seemed to rise in volume, signalling that the worst was yet to come.

And so began the first recorded example of what they would later discover to be a Global Restart Event.

*

The table Hal was resting his arms on was the first object to explode. Shards of wood erupted beneath him, oddly travelling along a horizontal trajectory, causing his arms to fall partially through the table. Inconceivably, time then proceeded to move backwards, as the table repaired itself, encasing – and consequently trapping – Hal's wrists in the most ridiculous form of handcuffs he'd personally ever seen.

'Erm, Kara,' said Hal, trying to pull his hands from the now solidified table. 'I've just been Jumanji'd. Little help?'

Kara moved closer, the insanity of the situation taking a temporary backseat as she felt around his wrists, and looked under the table. Hal's fingers were balling into fists then relaxing again, as if he was trying to force his way free, as she caught sight of an odd object attached to the underside of the reformed stockade.

'What the–' she began, automatically reaching out for the onyx-coloured shape, a blue light swishing across it indicating it was a device of some kind.

She was stopped in her tracks, as they both experienced another intense migraine.

As the pain slowly receded, Kara suddenly recalled flashes of a past life she, thus far, had no coherent recollection of. It felt like remembering a forgotten dream; flashes of blue, a lodge exploding, her head colliding with a kitchen cabinet…

She shook her head violently, in an attempt to cast out the distraction, the device no longer of interest.

'You feel that?' said Kara in a panicked voice.

'Gah,' groaned Hal, trying to fight the urge to vomit, knowing that doing so at this precise moment in time would add an unwanted grossness to his increasingly turbulent relationship with the universe. 'Yeah, flashes,' said Hal. 'Memories maybe?'

"More like dreams," he thought.

The elderly street magician behind Kara with the milk was the next to get the brunt of whatever on Earth was happening, as the jug she was holding exploded. Ceramic pieces flew outwards and upwards to the ceiling, which apparently had just been promoted to what now constituted as being the ground.

'Woah, woah, woah!' exclaimed Kara, as she too was pulled towards the ceiling above her. She clawed frantically at the table that was holding Hal hostage, but couldn't secure her grip, and landed with a sickly thud on the ceiling next to the shards of ceramic. Rolling onto her back, she looked down at Hal with an expression that seemed to suggest she was asking for help.

Hal shrugged his shoulders helpfully, as the woman in front of him suddenly became a magnet for the fog, which coiled around her, then set about dissolving her body like a malignant acid. The woman's body, becoming little more than ethereal sands of an hour glass, trickled upwards towards Kara's face, causing Kara to splutter. She attempted to hold her breath, turning her head to the side, as the woman below her disintegrated entirely.

Kara spat out what could be described as old-lady granules, which travelled a few centimetres away from her, then glided back up into her face. She fought the violent urge to throw up the contents of her stomach, knowing that doing so would result in an unfortunate gravitational boomerang effect.

'I just inhaled old lady,' said Kara grimly.

'I think they prefer the term mortality-conscious,' said Hal, in a display of misinformed political correctness.

'Why would they prefer *that*?!'

'I don't know Kar', older people can be funny like that. Did it taste like couscous?' asked Hal with genuine interest. 'It looked like couscous.'

Kara was about to offload a scowl, but it was cut short as gravity released its grip and she fell to the floor. She pulled herself up, slamming her fists onto Hal's table.

'We need to get out of here!'

Hal nodded in quick agreement, as the air electrified around them, and an arc of blue lightning shot across the room. They both ducked their heads down to avoid being struck by it, as the bolt of concentrated energy collided with the stationary body of a staff member, causing him to erupt into a billion shards of blue, glitter-like confetti.

'Must go faster, must go faster!' said Hal, in his best Jeff Goldblum voice, despite knowing his efforts would have been lost on his friend.

Though static in density, the fog moved onwards, marking new victims, as the lightning strikes became more frequent, erasing everything from coffee machines, the photo frames lining the walls, and randomly selected chairs and tables from existence without discrimination. A young girl, still frozen in the action of taking money from a customer from behind the till erupted into pieces, her arms flying savagely across the shop, before slowing down, then returning back to her torso making her whole once again.

'Kara, I'm parked down the road near my office. Take my keys, Grab what's in the boot.'

'What about you?' said Kara, her unwillingness to leave him here conflicting with her desire to stay alive.

'Just get *out* of here, I'll be fine!'

She nodded, realising that having the car running wasn't such a terrible idea, then made her way to the entrance of the coffee shop.

'The keys Kara!' groaned Hal, jerking his head backwards towards the jacket resting over the back of his chair.

'Right, keys,' she said, jogging backwards and rummaging around in his pockets until she gained purchase on them.

She ran down the narrow gangway back towards the door, but stopped in her tracks, as another ripple tore through reality, and yet another bolt of blue plasma appeared from nowhere. She dived over the counter to her right to avoid it, as it obliterated another customer.

Hal, meanwhile, had an idea, and stood up, the table weighing him down tremendously. Not for the first time in his life, he cursed himself for never making time for the gym.

'You okay Kar'?'

The wanton destruction resulted in a vast amount

of plates, cups and spoons to fall over her, which were now floating happily, caught between deaccelerated time and…somewhere in-between. She nudged a roaming plate that was floating past her face with her index finger, sending it spiralling off in a different direction.

'Still alive,' she shouted back.

Hal pulled the table up like a shield, and gingerly backed up towards the exit.

'By the power of Grayskull,' he mumbled, his voice shaking with adrenaline with each step, as his eyes darted around waiting for the tell-tale shimmer in the air that preceded an energy burst.

Finally, the air around him began to crackle. A small sound behind his left ear that was near impossible to hear, what with both the music and rustling wind attacking their senses, was all he needed. Using the weight of the table to aid him in spinning quickly, he faced towards the incoming barrage that was manifesting behind him.

Hal grinned, as if directly challenging the universe itself to a duel.

'Baa baa!' he sang just a little too enthusiastically, perfectly in time with the music, as a bolt of vicious lightning materialised from nowhere and shot towards him like a homing missile.

He brought the table up high above his head, digging his heels in, preparing to take the brunt of the force as it collided with the table. Shards of wood splintered outwards, slowly fizzling into nothingness, like blue-tinged newspaper on a burning fire.

A small rectangular object no larger than a smartphone landed with a clatter by his feet, looking notably scorched thanks to its run in with the bolt of lightning. Blue lights blinked half-heartedly around the curved edges of the device, until finally giving up altogether. Hal tapped the object with his foot, and it promptly disintegrated.

He didn't have time to wonder why it had been attached to the underside of the table, and instead focused on the immediate win; he was finally free. This seemed to anger the fog, which released another customer it was absorbing across the room, leaving only their torso and legs behind, as well as a hand suspended in the air holding the coffee cup they were drinking from, and made a beeline for him. It was an ugly site, the internal organs left exposed yet thankfully also cauterised.

Hal jumped up onto a nearby table, creating some distance from the floor, or rather the fog that was slithering across it. Nothing about it looked like it would do him any good if it touched him. Treating the floor as if it were lava, he jumped onto an armchair, then slid across another set of tables which would have tipped under his weight were they not frozen in time, and made his way closer to the exit.

"Dammit," he thought, feeling utterly gutted Kara hadn't seen him pull that off.

Another bolt of lightning shot out from a shimmering anomaly in the air, and he fell down into a nearby sofa to avoid its wrath, as it collided with a child in a push-buggy. The energy had a different effect on the baby, bringing it back into the present.

No longer frozen in time, the child began to cry, as another blast shot out and disintegrated the child, like granules of blue sugar dissolving into the coffee of infinity. With the child now gone forever, the pram exploded comically.

'Holy shit, that baby just exploded!' shouted Hal.

Kara had made progress, and was now standing at the door.

'If you're done taking a break on that sofa, let's go!' she yelled.

'Such a backseat…' said Hal, sensing there was another word that should have wrapped up that sentence. One which felt both alien and familiar to him all at once.

There was no time to dwell on that, and he pulled himself up, as tables, chairs, and a Bakewell tart exploded around him like proximity mines, crumbs and furniture debris suspended in the air around him.

Finally at the door, they slammed it closed behind them and took a moment, pressing their backs against the large windows situated either side of it.

The glass behind Hal exploded inwards, pulling him back into the coffee shop. A few seconds later he exited back out through the front door, dusting himself off and showing signs of more than a little embarrassment.

Kara chuckled at him, and he shot her a look

indicating they would never speak about that moment again.

As they looked out across the street before them, it was clear the incident they were experiencing was not localised to just the coffee shop, as arcs of lightning spewed out, indiscriminately atomising everything and anything that got in its way. Time, it seemed, hadn't just ground to a halt inside the shop; it had stopped everywhere.

'How is this possible,' whispered Kara in awe.

'Well, global warming just got real,' said Hal. 'Either that or CERN fucked up in a big way.'

'Why aren't *we* affected?' said Kara, her eyes wide with wonder.

He knew she was referring to the other people in the Little Coffee shop of Horrors they had just barely escaped from.

'I know just as much as you Kar'. I'm Jon Snow right now, I-'

'Know nothin'…she said, finishing his sentence, unaware it was even a reference.

'You watch Game of Thron–'

'Nope.'

'I need new material,' said Hal.

'You must recycle your jokes a lot if *I'm* starting to use them.'

He nodded guiltily, despite not remembering dropping that reference to Kara before.

'We need to get to my car,' said Hal urgently.

'Will it even *work* while all this is going on?'

'Good point.' He grimaced. There was no way of knowing if the engine would even start, what with reality caving in on itself. 'But it's what's inside it that matters.'

And off they ran. Past the countless mannequins that surrounded them, towards the only plan they currently had; reaching Hal's car before they were engulfed by the thickening whiteness that was closing in on them from all sides like a sentient tsunami.

CHAPTER ELEVEN

Raiders of the Lost Car Park

Saturday, October 6th, 2018, 11:17am

As Hal and Kara darted amongst the countless people still frozen in time, they made their way down a narrow alley and pressed their back against the walls of a cobbled archway, trying to catch their breath.

'What the hell is happening?!' panted Kara.

'Aliens, maybe?' offered Hal, equally short of breath. 'I *bet* it's aliens.'

Kara was about to laugh, but saw more than a flicker of seriousness in his eyes.

'Don't look at me like *that*! We don't know it's *not*

aliens.'

'It's not aliens, Hal.'

'What makes you so sure?'

'Because I'm not emotionally equipped to deal with *freakin'* aliens right now, that's what,' said Kara, her exhaustion at odds with the adrenaline coursing through her body. 'How far away did you park, anyway?!' she added, deciding to focus on something far more manageable than the possibility of an unexpected alien invasion, not entirely convinced she had much running left in her.

'It's a Saturday Kara, I parked at work!'

'That's miles away!'

'Don't be so dramatic. It's…*under* a mile away. Besides, I refuse to pay for parking when I can park at work for free.'

She was about to lay into him for being too tight to pay the ten-pence for weekend parking in the town centre, when they were both suddenly overcome with another crippling bout of nausea, which quickly evolved into yet another agonising migraine, forcing them to press their palms to their temples in the hopes of forcing away the pain, or at least to keep it at bay.

Forgotten memories of a past that had, up until now, been kept from them flooded into their minds, the pain clearly being caused by their brains receiving fragments of what felt like a year's worth of data all in one go. The recollections they were left with were jumbled and made absolutely zero sense to their frazzled cerebra. It felt like someone shouting information at them in another language they weren't even remotely fluent in.

The pain subsided, and they were once again able to communicate.

'Did you feel that?' asked Hal, causing Kara to shoot him a look of incredulity.

'No Hal, I just thought I'd copy you so I didn't feel left out,' she said with over-cooked sarcasm.

'Felt like we were back at…'

'Fir Lodge?'

'Yeah…' Suddenly he felt more desperate than ever to reach his car. He had merely *thought* he needed what was inside it, but now he *knew* it. 'We need to keep moving, we don't have much–'

The brickwork of the archway above them began to shake, and one by one, the bricks of the wall they were resting against were plucked from existence, reduced to tiny blue shards, a white fog filling the gaps where they once resided. A wisp of whiteness coiled around Hal's wrist and he felt an agonising burning sensation, causing him to snap his hand back quickly.

'Go!' shouted Kara, as their temporary safe haven was obliterated by an unseen force, revealing a tornado of mist above them that was pulling everything from cars, to shopfronts, to actual people into its ravenous epicentre. Despite having no way of knowing that they were actually in the heart of a global restart, they knew enough to know they needed to put as much distance between them and the relentless phenomenon.

*

They continued onwards, relying on their memory of the town's layout to get where they needed to go, as the landmarks around them were sucked into the vortex that was thundering above them. Or rather, *towards* them.

Their journey was made slightly easier, as entire buildings simply ceased to be, allowing them to run as the crow flew, rather than having to follow pedestrianised walkways. It was a hard habit to break, not having to be careful as they ran across the roads, but they quickly retaught themselves how to negotiate traffic in a timeless environment; namely, they didn't have to worry about it at all.

After running for far longer than would have been required, had Hal simply parked his car closer to the coffee shop like any normal human being would have, they finally hit the jackpot.

There was Hal's black car; its inanimate existence exuding heroic modesty, considering the vehicle was literally their ticket out of a storm that even Thor would've cashed in a sick day to avoid. Though, under the current lighting, it looked more like a midnight blue thanks to the crackling blue lightning that ricocheted throughout the clouds above them, giving their entire environment a terrifyingly oppressive blue hue.

Hal checked his pocket for his car keys, then

cursed loudly, remembering he'd given them to Kara.

'Keys, keys, KEYS!' he shouted, as a thunderous gust of wind blasted across them.

Kara reached into the pocket of her jeans, her jacket flapping wildly, as she searched frantically for the jagged objects, her heart sinking.

'Tell me you have the keys, Kara?'

'I…must have dropped them.'

Hal groaned as they reached the car and leant against it, catching his breath, seriously fighting the urge to tell her this was the exact reason why they weren't allowed to have nice things.

'It's okay. Not your fault. Not your fault. Brick!' he shouted, pointing behind her.

Her eyes followed the trajectory of where he was pointing, landing on the dislodged brick a few metres away. As she ran towards it, an arc of blue lightning flew up from the ground in front of her, surging into the sky and into the apex of the storm above. They had never heard a lightning strike happening in reverse before, and the backwards rumble that followed felt incredibly otherworldly.

'Okay, backwards lightning,' said Hal, laughing uncomfortably. 'That's a thing now.'

Kara continued onwards, grabbed the brick and lobbed it at Hal's rear windscreen like an Olympic shot-putter.

It bounced off the glass feebly, landing on the floor with a comical clickety-clack.

They looked at each other, and rolled their eyes in

unison, incredibly disappointed that real life clearly wasn't bound by the same rules as it was in the movies.

To make matters worse, the whiteness had them surrounded, now rolling in from all corners of the car park. One by one, cars were either sucked up into the oncoming storm, cut unceremoniously in half by reverse lightning strikes or, in an additional display of what the actual fuck, were simply atomised at the molecular level into billions of tiny azure crystals.

There didn't appear to be any method or order in which the world dismantled itself around them, and for the first time in his life Hal began to perceive reality itself as little more than a stroppy teenager being subjected to a revoked WIFI password.

'They kinda look like tractor-beams don't they?' shouted Hal, referring to the lights around the levitating cars.

'Okay, fine,' conceded Kara. 'We won't rule out aliens.

Hal picked up the brick from the ground and began smashing it into the rear windscreen, until the glass finally buckled under the pressure, albeit it only slightly.

'Maybe try the passenger windows?' suggested Kara.

Hal grimaced, realising that made more sense, and set about implanting the fresh tactic.

The glass of the rear passenger window shattered with little effort, and Hal reached over into the door to unlock it.

The tsunami of time seemed to become antagonised by this, speeding up its implementation of vehicular annihilation, the cars around them flipping and deconstructing themselves with an increased vigour, as if there was a giant prehistoric Megalodon swimming beneath the concrete of the car park, making a beeline towards the frantically beating hearts of the only two people it had left to devour.

'We are *so* gonna die,' said Kara nervously, as Hal continued to struggle with lowering the back seats to gain access to the boot of his car.

'You maybe wanna get in and give me a hand here, Negative Nancy?' said Hal, who hadn't seen the cars flipping behind his back, the path of destruction heading directly towards them.

'Oh for– you just push the button and pull the seats down Hal, stop making a meal of it!'

Kara opened the right-hand-side passenger door now that the central locking had been engaged, and did just that.

And there it was, in all its glory; a medium sized black backpack which, judging by Hal's smile, must have contained a harpoon specifically designed to take out the tarmac-churning Megalodon that Kara had created in her mind in such terrifying detail that she had even given it a name. She looked over her shoulder, past the front seats, through the front windscreen and out towards "Mr Waffles."

Hal crawled deeper into the recesses of the car

boot, seemingly wrestling with something that had been snagged, as the car shook violently.

'Erm, Hal?'

Kara stared in horror, as the front of his car began to break down into a blue sand-like substance, and she was once again reminded of the grains of an hour glass, pouring upwards in defiance of gravity.

Hal pulled his head back out from the boot, a small metal safe in his hands, as the sound of churning metal erupted within the cabin, the bonnet of the car being pulled at awkward angles by an unseen force, and flying off into the sky.

Hal and Kara shot each other a look, telepathically relaying a word that rhymed with "cluck", as the roof of the car peeled away like tin foil.

They both rolled backwards out of the car, landing hard on their backs, as the remainder of Hal's trusty vehicle finally gave up the ghost and surged up into the sky in hot pursuit of its roof.

'You think my insurance will cover that?' asked Hal, genuinely curious. 'Open this will you?' he added, throwing her the black lockbox as he buckled up what appeared to be a holster around his waist.

'What's the code?' asked Kara, suddenly realising she somehow had a pretty good idea what it would be, spinning the numbers to form a numeric code that inexplicably held significance within her subconscious.

'Zero, one–'

'–six, five. One hundred and sixty-five,' she repeated. "How do I know that?" she wondered, opening the lid of the box to reveal the contents within.

She raised an eyebrow, as her eyes were met with the sight of menacing metallic. Kara surveyed the gun, having never seen one up close before; knowing the chrome barrel would've sparkled under the sun, were it not for the natural sunlight being absorbed into the ever-expanding void above them, saturating their surroundings in a now dismal greyish monotone.

The weapon was beautifully crafted, the smooth metal sleekly connecting with the dark brown grip, flashes of gold revealing themselves from the side of a chamber that she assumed could be rotated. In its entirety, the bullet dispenser looked more than capable of messing someone's shit well and truly up.

'Who *are* you?' she asked, wondering how she was only just discovering her friend was the sort of person that kept a gun in the boot of his car.

He reached around the lid and retrieved the gun from the small lockbox.

'*Batman*,' said Hal, unable to resist, his voice full of gravel and his left eye full of wink.

'More like a crazy doomsday prepper,' she countered.

The sound of reverse thunder echoed above them, and they realised that the only thing more disconcerting than the sound of thunder working backwards was the sound of an echo retreating back to its point of origin. They stood back to back, as Hal brought the gun up in his left hand and unclicked the safety.

It was then that they realised that amidst their faffing, everything around them had been obliterated; the trees, the cars, the people…Hal couldn't help but shrug, noting that his office building had also been consumed by whatever this was. He smiled and gave a mini-salute, his way of saying goodbye to his overflowing in-tray and trusty desk. It felt oddly cathartic.

'So long, old friend,' said Hal.

'So long,' said Kara.

'I was talking to my desk,' said Hal, cocking his head towards her and shooting her a wry smile.

The thunder-strikes became more prominent, as the white fog swirled around them from every angle, until they were fully submerged within the mist.

They closed their eyes, knowing it was over.

Except, rather awkwardly, it wasn't.

They stood there for a moment, a wave of unbearable quietness enveloping them. Hal let out a half-hearted cough, the sort one usually reserved for when the small-talk had well and truly dried up and you needed to fill the void with literally anything.

The sound of a gentle fart filled the silence.

'Sorry,' said Hal.

'I hate you,' replied Kara, her chuckle betraying sincerity.

The deafening silence was replaced once more with the sound of rushing air. A sound that sent a chill down their spines, in the same way a war-time siren innately evoked an uncomfortable response to all those that heard it.

On that unfortunate note, Hal and Kara were mercilessly annihilated from the present, their respective futures stolen from them, like off-brand prizes being snatched up by the arcade claw-machine of the universe.

CHAPTER TWELVE
There's No Place like Home

166th Restart – Friday, August 24th, 12:02pm

The thunderous sound of air vacating an infinite echo-chamber, a blinding whiteness in every direction indicating that they were standing on the precipice of infinity, all of which ceasing suddenly, like someone pressing the mute-button on reality itself, the personification of eternal nothingness replaced with the blindingly vibrant light from the afternoon sun. A younger sun, being orbited by an equally younger version of the Earth.

A thousand tiny needles plucked at the synapses within their brains, bringing them to their knees, as the already-full cup of their memories overflowed with a lifetime of experiences, causing their short-term recollections to trickle over the edges of the metaphoric container that was their increasingly waning sanity.

Images, conversations and dark deeds all rearranging themselves in their minds to form a coherent narrative of the past. At least, coherent in a way that was like reading a book in reverse and reaching the first word after knowing everything that came after.

Each and every one of these sensations coalesced to form a singular, terrifying truth; Hal and Kara were back on the clock.

A sense of dread made unnecessarily more surreal on account of a wireless, vintage-looking radio sitting directly in front of them on the impossibly-bright shingle, belting out the 1955 classic "Mister Sandman" by a band Hal knew to be The Four Aces.

It felt odd to him that he could remember *tha*t, but not what he had ordered at the coffee shop thirty-or-so minutes ago. Which actually equated to six weeks from now. He shook his head, already pissed off by how much of a headache being a part of that conversation was going to be later down the line.

As the music continued to play out, Hal pulled himself up from the ground, and dusted himself down, before catching himself and sighing over the pointlessness of the habit. He turned to face Kara, who had done the same and was staring at the monolith of the past that loomed over them like an oppressive manifestation of literal, inescapable inevitability.

Fir Lodge.

Hal holstered his gun, which he had been gripping tightly before being pulled through the vivacious vortex, and took several steps forward, taking up position to Kara's left, and joined her in staring up at the building.

'How is this possible?' said Kara, her voice consumed by a terrified quiver that caused the last word to waver with an understandable mixture of both horror and awe.

'We planned for everything,' said Hal, his memories now fully-formed and his mind firing on all cylinders, now armed with the knowledge of all 165 of their previous restarts.

Will's red car pulled up on the driveway, as events of their stay began to play out from scratch. They watched, as Rachel and Jon came out to greet them, the retro-looking radio drowning out the music coming from the speakers of Will's vehicle.

'Radio's new?' added Hal helpfully.

'Where'd it come from?' her question becoming somewhat moot as Jasmine pulled up in her white car and drove into the radio, shunting it across the drive towards Hal and Kara's Restarter-selves and causing the music to end abruptly, interrupting whatever the hell it was that was powering it in the first place.

Hal squatted down and picked up the now-silent

radio, turning it over in his hands. 'It's in phase with us…' said Hal, matter-of-factly.

They both knew what that meant.

'Which means someone put it there,' said Kara. 'You sure it's not just because you're so close to past-you?' she theorised, as Hal's past-self stepped out from Jasmine's car.

Hal shrugged, stood up, lifting the radio above his head as if trying to win over a girl's heart like the scene from an 80's movie he barely remembered, and casually threw the radio towards his more-corporeal self, sniffing absently as it passed through his target without much of a to-do, before colliding soundlessly with the ground. The contraption's journey was brought to a halt as it struck Will's car.

'Nope, it's legit in *our* timeline,' said Hal.

'Huh. Which means–'

'We're not alone in this restart. Someone's trying to let us know they're here.'

'That could complicate things,' she said, with rightful concern.

'Bench?'

'Bench,' seconded Kara, and they made their way to what they fondly remembered as being their makeshift brainstorming war room.

As they made their way around the side of the lodge, and into the back garden, they were greeted by a confusing sight.

Peter and Fearne were occupying their bench, having an animated disagreement about something.

'Someone must have changed something,' said Hal. 'They shouldn't be out here yet.'

Kara nodded in agreement. 'Everything feels off Hal, can you feel it?'

He knew what she meant, assuming she was referring to an unexplainable anxiousness that was brewing deep inside his stomach.

'I mean, we're wearing what we were wearing in the–' Kara stopped. Where *were* they last? Was it a coffee shop? She was struggling to remember, as if that particular future was being erased entirely from the cannon of their actual lives.

'Give me your hand,' said Hal, and she dutifully obliged.

Blue sparks fizzled between them, and Hal relaxed a little. 'Okay, we've still got juice, at least our hoverboards will work on water.'

'What?'

Hal closed his eyes and inhaled a gentle breath, then exhaled through pursed lips, which helped to keep his unreasonable frustration at bay.

He was about to mention his backpack of swag, when he was startled by Peter, who had spun around on the bench and was seemingly addressing them directly.

'Hal? Kara?!' He jumped from his seat and began walking towards them with confusion.

The Restarters looked over their shoulders, naturally expecting to see their past-selves standing behind them, but were shocked to discover that wasn't the case.

And then it sunk in. The *real* reason Kara felt that something was off had been hiding in plain sight all along; Peter and Fearne were dressed in their fancy-dress costumes from the barbecue. A barbecue that was not scheduled to happen until tomorrow.

Hal noted that Fearne had discarded her blonde wig, her long brunette hair remaining suspiciously motionless amidst the breeze that was calmly causing the surrounding fir trees to sway.

Apprehensively, the golfer and Marilyn made their way towards the Restarters.

'You can *see* us?!' said Kara.

'You can see *us*?!' said Fearne.

'Guys, seriously,' said Hal. 'Let's skip this part. Obviously, we can see each other. The question we should be asking is *how*?'

Kara ran towards Peter and threw her arms around him. 'You're alive!'

'Kinda, I guess,' said Peter, trying to embrace the repelling nature of the blue energy that was radiating through them and making his neck go numb. 'Wait…when was I not alive?'

Thanks to the presence of their friends, Hal and Kara were forced to accept that this was not the past they had left behind. This was something else. Something much more complex.

Someone was changing their 165th restart and undoing everything they had achieved to free themselves. And that entity was more than likely responsible for changing Peter's future as well. Though why Fearne was here too was anyone's guess.

'Peter, Fearne,' said Hal addressing them directly with a serious tone in his voice. 'I need you to think real hard. What's the last thing you remember?'

Peter and Fearne exchanged a troublesome look, ending with Fearne nodding, as if giving Peter the go-ahead.

'We…went to look for you both last night,' said Peter. 'Jon mentioned that you had both set off to take Jerry home, but after a couple of hours you didn't come back. So Fearne and I–'

'–Went to look for you both,' interrupted Fearne. 'We knew you must've been close by, so we made our way up the road, calling out for you both…'

'We had no idea where to begin looking,' said Peter, taking over storytelling duties. 'Jerry must have heard us calling for you,' he added, explaining how the springer spaniel had run towards them, appearing from nowhere and barking for their attention. 'Jerry led the way back to another lodge and–'

'–Then we left,' said Fearne, an air of caginess in her voice that Hal and Kara wrote off as understandable stress.

The Restarters knew how frustrating it was on a first restart. Memories swirled in your mind, the full truth always just within your grasp, but ultimately being plucked away at the last moment.

'Hal, they came to look for us. You know what this means, don't you?'

'We didn't make it back,' said Hal.

'Make it back from where?' asked Peter.

Kara and Hal exhaled heavily, perfectly in sync with each other. They really hated this part. Explaining everything to a newbie was time-consuming, complicated, and not to mention potentially dangerous when you didn't know how someone was going to react.

'You guys are probably going to want to take a seat,' said Hal, noting that his past-self was speaking to Jon behind them, and would soon be commandeering the bench in front of them.

Peter's eyes lit up with curiosity as the second Hal appeared but, oddly, he didn't say anything.

Hal raised an eyebrow at Peter's apparent indifference, but was distracted by the sound of the hot-tub cutting out.

"That's…not right…" thought Hal, and shook his head to clear it. Refocusing on the task at hand, he gestured back towards the driveway. He wasn't keen on Peter and Fearne having to experience an echo of the past phasing through their unsuspecting bodies.

'Actually, let's take a walk,' said Hal.

The four Restarters made their way to the driveway, weaving through the cars. Kara stepped over the radio, finally becoming brave enough to answer the question she knew was on both their minds.

'It's *him*, isn't it? It *has* to be him?' Kara whispered to Hal, taking advantage of the moderate distance between themselves, Peter, and Fearne, who were bringing up the rear of their time-travelling entourage.

'Gotta be,' replied Hal, matching the volume of her voice.

The rules had clearly changed, and they had a pretty good idea of where to start in order to find out precisely what had gone wrong.

A small cabin in the woods, which a little dog named Jerry called home.

CHAPTER THIRTEEN
Conversations with Dead People
166th Restart – Friday, August 24th, 2018, 12:17pm

'So, where exactly are we going?' asked Peter, in the manner of someone who had just decided to tag along for an impromptu trip to the pub, as opposed to having just been disassembled at the molecular level and jettisoned off into the past via an intangible time machine.

'You're taking this pretty well, Pete,' remarked Hal, finding himself surprised by his friend's nonchalant attitude. 'Usually, the first question a Restarter asks is "what the hell is happening?"'

'Restarter?' said Peter, noting the odd terminology.

'That's what we call ourselves. I came up with it,' said Kara convincingly.

Hal sighed, but took the "Elsa" approach. There were bigger problems to contend with. Namely, how someone had pulled a Time Heist on them and decimated the space-time continuum, stealing their future out from the metaphoric bank vault that was "solidified time."

As Kara and Hal led the way to Kevin's home at a brisk pace, he recalled the jets of the hot-tub that had cut out. If this had truly been a fresh restart, the tub jets shouldn't have done that. It implied that more was going on than they could see. If the tub had been tripped, it meant it had been himself that had carried out the act in the past. And the only way that was possible was if–

'We're here,' said Kara, her words interrupting his flow of thoughts, and causing Hal's brow to furrow in slight frustration. He felt like he had been on to something, but the thought drifted away from him. 'What's the play?' she added, directing her question to Hal.

Her fellow Restarter shrugged. 'Go inside, see what the score is I guess?'

Peter and Fearne showed notable signs of reluctance. Having been brought up to speed on their new status quo, they had seemed to be taking Hal and Kara's explanation of what was happening to them at face value and entirely in their stride.

A little *too* well in fact.

It was reassuring to Kara to see them showing at least *some* signs of unease as they approached Kevin's home.

'I think we'll stay outside,' said Peter, a look of barely concealed fear on his face.

'I don't want to go in there either,' added Fearne.

'Why?' asked Kara, who was working on the assumption that Peter and Fearne had suffered the same fate as them, due to the two of them coming to look for herself and Hal on that fateful Saturday evening. If she was correct, the box-fresh Restarters wouldn't have held any direct memories of what happened during their final moments. That glum revelation would come to them *much* later, as Hal and Kara could attest to.

'Guys, you're coming,' said Hal, with an air of finality to his tone that was impossible to argue with. 'And stay sharp, okay?' He didn't want to admit that there was every possibility that it would take all four of them to make it out of Kevin's cabin if the person responsible for their being here was actually inside.

As they made their way up the driveway, Fearne and Peter bickered amongst themselves, allowing Kara to steal a moment with Hal.

'They seem off to you?' she said, as Hal reached the front door, which was incidentally open. 'Wait, should this be open?'

They both took a moment, remembering how

Kevin had been out on the Friday afternoon, and their many attempts at trying to get inside. It seemed like forever ago, and a few minutes ago all at the same time. It didn't help that their minds were still playing catch-up, as conflicting memories of multiple timelines wrestled for dominance, each stray thought eager to claim the championship belt that represented their true past.

Hal sensed it too. Everything was different. For a brief second, it felt like this was possibly the worst idea ever; if the man who had killed them was inside, there was no telling what he and Kara were dragging their friends into.

But then he remembered that they couldn't be hurt in their current state. Out-of-phase with time, they didn't feel hunger, or thirst, but most importantly of all they couldn't feel pain. At least not in the physical sense.

Hal found himself thinking back to the time he was flung against the wall of the sauna room next to Fir Lodge. And then there was the time he and Kara had been forced to jump from a moving vehicle, not even sustaining a single scratch. All the same, it was never a bad idea to exercise caution.

Reaching down to his holstered weapon, he unclipped the button that kept the gun in place, pulling it from the black mesh that was keeping the business end of the weapon away from causing harm.

The slab of metal weighing heavily in his hand, he rested his gun-toting wrist on his right forearm, mimicking the way he recalled Jack Bauer brandishing a weapon, and aimed the barrel inside the doorway.

'Good call,' said Kara.

And with that, they stepped over the threshold.

*

'Where did you even *get* that thing?!' whispered Kara. Guns were not something easily acquired in England.

'Does it really matter at this point?' said Hal, moving his way through Kevin's living room, and jerking the gun towards the corners of the open space, trying to look professional, but ultimately looking utterly ridiculous.

'Do you even know how to use it?'

Hal could feel her smile burning into the back of his neck.

'Sshh,' said Hal, skillfully dodging the question. In fairness, he had actually thought he'd heard something, and balled his right hand into a fist in the same way Navy Seals would often do in the movies; the universal instruction issued when a leader of an infiltration team needed everyone to remain perfectly still.

Kara, of course, ignored him entirely, and continued walking past him, causing a knock-on effect of Peter and Fearne doing the same.

Hal began to sigh, not allowing the non-air to completely leave his lungs due to hearing another sign they were not alone; the faintest sound of a muted cough.

The dark-blue basement door was open, too. Another indication that events were not playing out like they had done in every other of their 165 restarts that had preceded this one.

Kara stared down the dark staircase, the dim light of the afternoon sun affording her the bare minimum of illumination on what was waiting for them below.

'Gimme the gun,' said Kara, reaching her right hand over her shoulder, not taking her eyes off of what lie beneath them.

'What? No, it's my gun.'

'Oh for…stop being so precious about it. Give me the thing!'

Hal grumbled, but reluctantly obliged.

'Be careful with it, it was expensive,' he mumbled sulkily. Despite her facing away from him, he could tell she was rolling her eyes at his request. 'I should probably mention, it's not quite–'

'Shh,' said Kara.

And they descended into the chasm below, Kara taking the lead, followed by Hal, with Peter and Fearne bringing up the rear.

*

Kara treaded lightly, proceeding down the wooden staircase one tiny step at a time, aiming the gun into the poorly lit void of the basement beneath her, as additional memories flooded back to the forefront of her mind; the sight of the surrounding worktops filled with either half-started or half-finished projects, the walls lined with various tools and trinkets…as she peered over the banister she saw their trusty friend; the box of screws that were instrumental in aiding Kevin's escape from the small room to her left, not yet moved into the position they needed to be, the door of said room currently closed for business.

She froze in place, as her eyes landed on an inconsistency to her surroundings that greatly overshadowed open doors and rogue radios, whilst also explaining the breadcrumbs they represented.

There, in the centre of the room, existed something that shouldn't have been there at all, as their ears filled with the sound of boisterous clapping. Rhythmic in speed, and deliberate in delivery, each audible emanation bounced off the walls around them as if they were occupying an echo chamber, the acoustic paradox made possible due to the Restarters being seemingly in-phase with the entity that was emitting them.

'Oh God,' said Hal, as horror took hold of him.

'That's impossible…' said Kara.

A familiar arc of electricity flowed through them both, fuelled by the crippling shared fear they felt in their hearts.

'We need to get out of here,' said Hal, the fear in his voice spilling out into the room as the clapping slowed in speed.

The man remained seated, finally ceasing his incessant clapping, and spoke.

'You both took your *time*,' he said, the seemingly causal colloquialism of his statement laced with dramatic irony, flashing his shark-like white teeth at them as he offered up a knowing smile.

The electricity surged between Hal and Kara once more, as if it were an involuntary reflex. Or, more aptly, a defence mechanism.

Malcolm raised his hand, as if to signify they could calm down.

Peter and Fearne took an instinctive step backwards, expecting Hal and Kara to turn tail and run. But, despite their shaking shoulders threatening to betray the fidelity of their resolve – which Peter assumed must have been brought on by adrenaline – Hal and Kara stood firmly in place.

All four of them remained as motionless as marble statues, as the man in the seat stood up, the chair of the past refusing to creak under his displaced weight, the out-of-phase wooden furniture continuing onwards through time, entirely unburdened to begin with.

He was just as they remembered him; his immaculately pressed white long-sleeved shirt, sleeves rolled to a perfectly-considered equal length, complemented by his ghastly, jet-black rubber apron, which covered the top half of his black work trousers. Brown, weathered work boots finished off the look, proving that when it came to killers, less was apparently more. If Malcolm's goal was to blend in to his surroundings, only the apron would have generated a red flag if they were to have encountered him out in the wild.

Malcolm continued to direct his grin at the four of them, feeling relieved that after all his patience, preparation and implementation, the desired result had finally led to fruition.

And then, for the first time in recorded history, five murder victims were presented with a once in a lifetime chance; the unique opportunity to speak directly to their respective killers *after* their deaths.

At least, that *would* have been the case.

Instead, Kara pulled the trigger.

CHAPTER FOURTEEN
I Know What You Did Last Summer
166th Restart – Friday, August 24th, 12:21pm

For all the false-charm he possessed, Malcolm hadn't engaged in an honest discussion in a long, long time. Decades even. Whenever he spoke, it was always a means to an end. Lure a person here, get them to trust you enough to go there, getting them to reveal a personal truth before draining the life from their body with his bare hands. That sort of thing.

The result of this was that he found himself a little lost for words now that his quarry had finally arrived. Thankfully, this awkwardness was quickly done away with, as the bullet traversed the distance between the shooter and her target in an instant, penetrating not only Malcolm's black apron and the starched shirt beneath, but also his flesh, the slug embedding itself into his body mere inches from the killer's presumably cold, black heart.

The unexpected act of being shot at broke not only the ice, but also erased the need for small-talk, as Malcolm's head flew back wildly in shock as the bullet struck him.

Kara pressed gently down on the trigger a second time, but Malcolm was ready, dodging out of the way as everyone else covered their ears at the sound bellowing from the firearm.

The second bullet whirred past Malcolm's right ear, ricocheted off the wall behind him, then headed off at an unpredictable angle, ultimately refusing to entrench itself into anything. Instead, the bullet eventually ran out of steam and fell to the floor, leaving the room entirely unharmed.

Hal reached towards Kara and pushed the gun upwards towards the ceiling.

'Woah, woah, woah, nice shooting, Tex! What are you doing?!' Hal shouted, a little louder than was socially acceptable due to the slight ringing sensation in his ears.

'He killed us, Hal!' shouted Kara incredulously, wondering why she was even being asked the question.

'I know, I mean I was there too. I get it, I do,' said Hal earnestly, 'but as much as I hate to admit it, we might just need this nutcase. At least for a little longer so he can tell us exactly what he's changed.'

'Very good, Harold,' said Malcolm, a slight growl of irritation escaping from him. 'Smart boy.'

'Feel the room, douchebag. Or I'll shoot you myself,' replied Hal, realising that he didn't actually know the man's name, and that it was clearly an empty threat. He turned back to face his friend. 'Besides…it's not real!'

'What?' said Kara.

'The gun. It's just gas powered, shoots metal pellets.'

'It sounded real enough?'

'Yeah, the hammer connects with gunpowder caps when you fire. You thought I'd managed to score an actual gun?!'

'Why didn't you tell me?!' she said angrily.

'I tried! But you were all like "give me the gun, Hal",' he said, doing an impression of Kara that wasn't at all flattering.

'That's not how I sound!'

'Little bit naggy…' he added bravely.

Kara sighed, then reluctantly lowered the weapon.

'Okay everyone,' said Hal, addressing the room and eager to put an end to the pointless debate over the gun that wasn't, strictly speaking, of any real use. 'Let's all just agree to not kill each other for a few minutes. Assuming we even *can* in this state. You on board with that plan, Dexter?' he posited, speaking directly to Malcolm, who merely nodded, pressing gently in the general area where the pellet had connected with his chest as if trying to dispel a case of heartburn, before holding up his hands in a symbolic gesture of peace. 'Let's start small, what even *is* your name?'

Malcolm stood up slowly, perfectly resisting the desire to wince in pain, and not needing to dust himself down. He had put an end to that habit, what with abhorring procrastination and knowing it was a waste of time in his out-of-phase state, but still took the opportunity to adjust his thick rubber apron.

Lowering his hands, he sat back down on the chair, realising it would make him appear less imposing, given his size.

'Of course,' said Malcolm. 'How rude of me. In all this time we've never been *formally* introduced, have we…'

Peter was whispering something frantically to Fearne, who was nodding in agreement. Kara noticed, but didn't shoot them more than a cursory glance through fear of taking her eyes off the killer seated before them. She knew as well as anyone that one second was all it took.

'Guys, calm down,' said Hal, sensing the sudden rise in agitation between the newly recruited Restarters and attempting to reassure them. 'Everything's under con—'

'We need to get *out* of here,' said Peter. 'Now.'

'Come now, *Peter*,' said Malcolm, his enunciation of the last word laced with barely-concealed meaning.

'We *all* have a lot to talk about. Wouldn't you agree, *Fearne*?'

Hal and Kara noticed the same inflection when he mentioned Fearne by name.

'We get it,' said Hal, reasoning that their murderer was trying to prove a point. 'You've been stalking us for God knows how long, unseen and unheard. You have our names, big whoop.'

'Oh. That makes sense. They don't *know* do they?' said Malcolm, addressing the two newbie Restarters standing behind Hal and Kara.

'Shut up!' said Peter.

'You haven't *told* them yet…' Malcolm barked a laugh, which was utterly fake and clearly purely for dramatic effect.

'Malcolm,' said Fearne. 'Don't do this...'

Malcolm extended his arms, palms upwards, as if showcasing how Fearne herself had just proven his point for him. She covered her mouth, as if doing so would cause the words to retract, redact, and disappear from the memories of all those around her. Which, of course, worked about as well as could be expected. Namely; it didn't.

'Wait,' said Kara, addressing Fearne with suspicion. 'How do you know his name?'

'Yes, Fearne,' said Malcolm, standing up and indulging in a stretch, more for the look than any real necessity. 'How *do* you know my name?'

The silence, taking a turn towards the oxymoronic, was deafening.

'It seems your *dearest* friends,' continued Malcolm, revelling in the drama, 'haven't been *entirely* honest with you *Harold*. Nor you, *Kara*.'

The Restarters winced, a sickly feeling filling their stomachs. It felt incredibly unnerving hearing their killer saying their names out loud, though this did little to stop the man from delving deeper.

'Why don't you tell them about the "Repeats", Peter? No? Fearne? Perhaps you'd like to take a…stab at it?' Malcolm chuckled at his own joke. 'Very well,' he added, speaking for them and addressing Hal and Kara. 'You see, you weren't the only ones to be trapped inside a time loop.'

'What's he talking about Peter?!' asked Kara, her world beginning to shatter.

'Hal, Kara,' mumbled Peter, 'you *have* to understand, there wasn't anything we could do!'

'No…' said Hal, feeling a gap in the pit of his stomach. One that always preceded just before a terrible truth was released into the world, like a tidal wave of destruction pulling everything he thought he knew about anything into question.

'Yes, Peter. What am I talk–'

'Shut UP, Malcolm!' the four Restarters shouted in unison.

'Whatever it is,' said Hal, 'it can wait. We're–'

'It all began when–' began Peter.

'Pete mate,' said Hal. 'I'm super stoked to hear all about it, but now's not the time, we've–'

'—we first arrived at Fir Lodge and—' continued Peter, causing Hal to realise he wasn't succeeding at stopping his flow.

'Okay, so this is happening, we're doing this *now* then?' said Hal talking over Peter, who was evidently determined to wear his inner-monologue on the outside, where it didn't belong. 'On the stairs. The only thing keeping a serial killer at bay being my fake as shit gun. One that *Billy the Kid* over here has already blown two out of the only six rounds we have.'

Hal cut in before she had time to scowl.

'Kara, if you know of a way to pull the plug on Peter's "Wonder Years meets Scrubs" interlude, now's the time to work your magic.'

He took a seat on the step he was formerly standing on.

'In fairness,' said Kara, 'we wouldn't even be having this conversation if you'd gone to a *real* gun shop instead of eBay.'

'That's a *replica* Colt Python you're holding!' said Hal, deeply hurt.

'Wait,' said Fearne, interrupting them all. 'Did you say *serial killer*?!' Fearne glared at Malcolm, who shrugged like the sort of selfish bastard who had just finished the last of the Coco-Pops and put the box back in the cupboard with no regard for the next person who may have desired breakfast.

'What Peter is *trying* to tell you,' said Malcolm, his smile wide and almost crackling with the power his next words would contain, 'is that you were *not* the first Restarters.'

Malcolm's words hung in the air.

It was the most dangerous type of lie; one that was tinged with just enough potential truth to cause utter ruin to all that heard it.

'That's not possible,' said Hal, refusing to accept that this was anything other than an incredibly clever mind-game. 'You're lying. Tell him he's lying, Pete.'

But as Hal turned to face his friend, he could tell instantly that there was far more to Malcolm's revelation than just hollow words.

'Yes Peter, tell them who was really responsible for their deaths.'

'Fearne?' said Kara, her face begging for her friend to end this nonsense, but Fearne merely stood there, fidgeting with the seam of her flowing white dress.

Peter sighed, his heart heavy. He looked at Hal and Kara, tears trickling down his dark cheeks, then placed a hand on Fearne's shoulder, gripping it tightly, letting go rather quickly as blue sparks repelled them apart.

'I'm so sorry,' said Peter falling back into a sitting position on the top step of the staircase, seemingly overwhelmed by the undying truth that refused to remain buried; that it wasn't Malcolm who had killed Hal and Kara.

It was Peter himself that was responsible for the death of two of his closest friends.

CHAPTER FIFTEEN
A Snap, a Crackle, and a Pop
166th Restart – Friday, August 24th, 12:28pm

The dust danced across the diagonal shard of concentrated sunlight that poured in through the small window situated behind Malcolm, clipping against the killer's shoulder, motes swirling in a hypnotically rhythmic pattern, like gravity-defying grains of artificial snow occupying a lopsided snow globe, living out their existence in a way only the universe could predict.

Or a Restarter. Who had unconsciously watched the same particles over a multitude of timelines, gifted with the innate knowledge of knowing when each one would dip, careen off course, or simply roll perpetually into infinity, never actually making any progress towards any kind of goal other than simply existing for the sake of it.

Hal could relate, such was the current futility he too was feeling. Always moving forwards, but somehow eternally stuck in place, the end of his journey through time seeming more like a cruel joke than an existence that served any real purpose.

They were less than an echo. They were those same motes of dust personified…mere thoughts on the wind…

Kara, meanwhile, was feeling considerably more attached to the present moment. Their initial sense of security and illusion of having the upper-hand having quickly dissolved, the Restarters now found themselves well and truly in over their heads.

Despite their numbers, and Malcolm's apparently calm and amenable demeanour, the fact remained that they were in real danger. Every second they spent here accentuated that fact.

The gun in Kara's hand shook a little, as she struggled to steady her nerve at the prospect that she was currently inside a shark cage with a great white, armed with little more than an admittedly impressive-looking party-popper.

'Hal,' she whispered. 'We need to get out of here. *Now.*' There was too much information to unpack, they needed to put distance between them and the unpredictable man before them in order to regroup and form a plan.

'Well,' said Malcolm, directing a sickly smile solely towards Kara, sensing the penny had very much dropped and that, finally, she fully understood the gravity of the situation.

He found it hard to dismiss the sense of elation he felt knowing that, even after all this time, he could instil that level of trepidation in another living, breathing individual. But he temporarily left his ego at the door to continue.

'This has been positively enlightening hasn't it?' the killer cooed. 'We've learned some things, grown better acquainted and, in such a short time, you have already managed to find yourselves *betrayed* by the *very* friends you hold most dear. Quite an achievement.'

'You're very chatty for a man who was defeated by two of the people in this room,' said Kara quietly, cocking the gun once more, despite them both knowing it wasn't as dangerous a firearm as its convincing appearance insinuated.

Malcolm's smile dropped, and his features hardened. He stood up, and somehow managed to almost fill the room, allowing his tall frame and flexing muscles to truly dominate their surroundings.

'You would do *better*,' said Malcolm, his words thick with disdain and malice, 'to show me some *respect*, little girl.'

Kara scowled, not wavering in her resolve, her upper lip arcing to return a volley of equal hatred.

'May I remind you,' said Malcolm, eager in his

pursuit of reiteration, 'that *skulking* around in the shadows, relying on a hitherto unparalleled level of invisibility does not make you *brave*. Nor does it make you heroic. What it makes you…is *cowardly. Invulnerable.* There was no risk involved, and certainly no power in what you achieved.'

'What is *with* you? Nobody talks like that,' said Hal, returning to the present and shooting a patronising look towards Malcolm. 'I think the auditions for the sequel to The Princess Bride are taking place in the venue next door, but your Vizzini impression?' Hal brought the pincered fingers of his hand to his mouth, then allowed them to burst open dramatically with a kiss that signified the essence of the term "Magnifique", sending it on its journey towards Malcolm's general vicinity.

Unbeknownst to Malcolm, Hal kept his right hand behind his back as he did so, gesturing for Peter and Fearne to get their heads back in the game and back the hell up the stairs which, in their mutual misery, they were unintentionally blocking. It was their only escape route, and Hal and Kara could both feel the conversation was about to curdle like last week's milk.

'Wait,' said Peter, a look of awe replacing the sadness on his face for a split second. 'You beat it? You beat *him*?'

'Yes Pete,' said Hal. 'We found our way to beat this thing without having to *kill* any of our friends in the process.'

The colour drained from Peter's face, his momentary look of awe switching to one of intense shame.

'I mean…' began Kara, 'we didn't kill *tha*t many of you anyway…'

'Not helping,' said Hal, noting her shoulders shrugging from his viewpoint behind her.

Malcolm closed his eyes, taking a deep breath. This was not how he had intended this interaction to go. He needed to calm himself. But the flagrant disrespect of the two time-travellers before him had reignited emotions within him that he had truly thought were extinguished.

'You did not defeat me,' Malcolm eventually whispered, and his voice notably more measured. His eyes shot open and he noticed that three of the four Restarters before him were retreating up the staircase of the basement. He smiled, knowing it didn't matter. 'You actually presented me with a gift…' he added, with more than a hint of ambiguity in his words.

'Uh huh,' said Hal, continuing his attempt to distract the man, and placing his hand on Kara's shoulder, the spark of the connection flooding her system like an alarm bell as he whispered solely to her. 'Time to fly, flutterby.'

Kara nodded, keeping the gun trained on Malcolm, and began her own backwards ascent.

'Leaving so soon?' said Malcolm, like a grandparent realising their relatives were getting ready to bail a mere thirty minutes into the hour they had promised, outstretching his arms as if inviting them to partake in a deadly bearhug to finalise their goodbye. 'Well. How rude. Alas, we have more urgent matters to discuss. I mean you no harm, quite the *opposite* actually.'

'Yeah…' said Hal, 'you'll have to forgive our reluctance to accept that at face value, given that you killed us…what's the tally again Kar'?'

'One-hundred-and-sixty-five times' added Kara.

'Wasn't it one six four?' whispered Hal.

'No, we beat him on the one-sixty-fifth, but you're forgetting the first time, before the restarts.'

'Oh, yeah.'

'If you're quite *finished*, perhaps we can begin?' said Malcolm. 'As I've already said, I mean you no harm. That is to say, this current *incarnation* of me means you no harm.'

He raised his hands above his head and gestured downwards to draw attention to his imposing frame.

'*This incarnation*?' repeated Kara, sensing Malcolm's words were once again dripping with subtext.

'Well, yes,' said Malcolm, clearing his throat with a cough and showing signs of mild embarrassment and awkwardness. 'I've been thinking how best to convey the new status quo of which you are now occupying. I *could* talk you all to deat–' Malcolm winced, and corrected his unfortunate metaphor by charging ahead as if it hadn't happened. 'But, in the interest of saving time, I've decided it best to just *show* you.'

Malcolm raised his right hand and brought his fingers together, as if he were utilising invisible chopsticks. 'You may want to…hold onto something.'

And with that, Malcolm's eyes lit up with an electricity that Hal and Kara both recognised instantly as being Restarter energy. With one subtle difference; the electricity was a heinous looking blood-red.

'Ohh,' said Kara, taking a step backwards towards the door above them. '*That* can't be good,' submitting her entry for the understatement of the year awards, feeling fairly certain it would outdo Hal's former entry which he had informally submitted during their last restart cycle.

'Jeez, Peter! Will you piss off out of the bloody doorway already!' shouted Hal, but it was far too late.

Malcolm took a deep breath and lunged towards them. Closing the distance in a heartbeat, he reached out and grabbed Kara by the wrist with one hand, and clicked his fingers with the other, performing a perfectly executed snap. A crackle of the same red electricity erupted from his fingertips, generating a blinding flash to the four Restarters who were haplessly pushing and shoving each other on the stairs of the basement, inadvertently connected like a human daisy chain.

The action seemed to summon the sound of rushing air, the kind that usually signified a restart was on its way, though the sound was moderately less intense than usual, and the room began to warp around them, bulging and contracting as invisible strands of a reality-bending aftershock pulsated and shifted, rippling with such intensity that it took all Hal and Kara had not to fall to their knees to support themselves.

It was a sensation of vertigo reminiscent of their first ever Restart.

Peter and Fearne were not quite so fortunate, the stair rail beside them the only thing preventing them from tumbling down the stairs. Both Hal and Kara noticed the shards of the afternoon sun that had previously cut across the room, but were now rapidly accelerating, juddering erratically as if they were watching a time-lapse of a setting sun. One which was eventually replaced with moonlight.

And then, with a pop that made everyone in the room stretch out their jaws as if they were all on an airplane that had just ascended too quickly, the ripples dispersed into nothingness, the four of them entirely unaware that everything they thought they knew about Restarting was just the tip of the blood-soaked iceberg.

CHAPTER SIXTEEN
Bullet Time

166th Restart – Saturday, August 25th, 8:09pm

'Did you just…*Thanos* us?' said Hal, thankful that vomiting wasn't possible in his out-of-phase state and feeling like a mass of water that had been poured from one container to another. 'What the hell just happened?!'

'I fast forwarded the current restart,' said Malcolm, in a display of un-Malcolm-like modesty. 'Bringing us all closer to the end of the thirty-three-hour loop.'

'Wait, you can *do* that?' said Kara, twisting her wrist out of his grip.

'We *all* can,' replied Malcolm, his expression more than a little puzzled. 'Surely you know this?'

Hal and Kara shifted awkwardly, unable to hide the fact that they most certainly did *not* know this.

'How did you get anything done?!' asked Malcolm, staring in disbelief.

'We just... waited for the cycle to end, then tried again,' said Hal, neglecting to mention their discovery of the Restart Point, not seeing the sense in showing their entire hand so early in the game.

Malcolm laughed, producing a noise not entirely unlike stones churning in a cement mixer.

'Wow, someone's been practicing their evil laugh,' noted Hal.

'What?'

'It just came across as a bit rehearsed is all I'm saying.'

'Regardless, I am not the man you remember,' stated Malcolm. 'I've changed at lot since we had the displeasure of stumbling into each other's lives.'

'Somehow I doubt that,' said Kara.

'In time, you'll see just how much,' Malcolm muttered, his words coming across more like a threat than a promise. 'Until then, I need you to understand what we're up against.'

Malcolm returned to his chair and fell into it.

'There is no *we*, Malc',' said Hal, shutting down that particular pronoun immediately.

The killer smiled weakly, unwilling to allow the young man to ruin his rhythm. 'The *Restarting* version of myself you left behind has grown quite proficient in altering time. Unfortunately, he is also teetering on insanity.'

'I'd say you base-jumped off that ledge a long time ago.'

Malcolm ignored Kara's dig. They had no idea how hard it was to exist without human interaction. Even for someone of his solitary preference. 'Today is the day his ambitions ultimately *matched* his desire.' Both Hal and Kara clocked his use of the past tense. 'He is attempting to alter time in such a significant way that, well, you really should see it for yourselves. Today is a very big day for my past-self.'

'Let me guess,' said Hal, 'you finally figured out how to reverse what Kara and I did to get ourselves out of here.'

'No, that came much later,' said Malcolm cryptically. 'There are some things you need to understand about me. About *all* of us. But I've ascertained this is the most effective way for you to understand what's at stake. There is a version of me at Fir Lodge, right now. And his goal is simple; to prevent Peter from entering Robert's room. If Peter doesn't enter, it will be he and he alone that returns the dog to this place,' said Malcom, gesturing outwards to the room around them. To Kevin's home.

Malcolm explained to them how his past-self had spent years occupying Hal and Kara's last restart, and that after countless failed attempts at gaining freedom, all roads had led to what happened in the next thirty minutes.

'And that,' said Malcolm finally, 'is why I've brought you together. To stop that from happening. Succeed in your task, and we'll have all the time in the world to talk about what comes next.'

'Bullshit,' said Peter. 'That *is* bullshit right?' he whispered to Hal.

Hal honestly didn't know, but if today really was the day that Malcolm changed history, and they really could prevent Peter's death, prevent his *funeral*…Hal noticed Kara wincing in pain.

'Ice-pick headache?' asked Hal, as he pressed his chest to fight away the feeling of a trapped nerve being plucked deep within him.

They shared a knowing look, both turning to face Malcolm, who tapped his wrist as if to emphasise their window of opportunity was dwindling.

'We'll be back. Don't go anywhere,' said Kara.

'I'm counting on that,' said Malcolm smugly. 'You know where to find me. Oh, and one piece of advice, because I really *am* rooting for you, *truly* I am,' he added, his words sickly sweet. 'Remember, you won't be able to see the time-travelling version of myself of the past, you're still out-of-phase with him.'

'Yeah, yeah,' Hal shot back over his shoulder. 'Thanks for the heads up, Jafar.'

'Aladdin?' whispered Peter.

'Got it in one Iago,' implying Peter was the pet parrot in this scenario.

'It's not what you think, Hal,' began Peter, eager to absolve himself.

'Save it,' said Hal sourly. 'With any luck we'll send you hurtling back to the future and we'll all forget this ever happened anyway.' Hal knew that was a longshot, but hoped that meant it was also a potential possibility.

On that salty note, the four of them exited the basement.

*

Hal noted the clock on Kevin's wall as they emerged into Kevin's living room, deducting the four minutes, remembering the clock ran fast.

'8:14pm,' he said, informing his fellow Restarters. 'That doesn't make sense, Malcolm should be *here* right now, in the past, ready for when our past-selves arrive.'

'Maybe he *has* changed everything,' said Kara.

Fearne had a more pertinent question. 'Why are we even entertaining this?'

'Because something feels off,' said Kara. 'Just trust us, this is kind of our thing.'

Peter and Fearne shared an awkward glance, which Hal pretended not to notice, and the four of them set off to Fir Lodge, to see what kind of chaos Malcolm's past-self was unleashing.

*

Malcolm returned to his seat, staring up towards the doorway at the top of the basement staircase, giving his guests just enough time to leave, before finally giving in to the gasp that had been dying to escape his mouth ever since the projectile had entered his chest.

He yanked off his apron, revealing a blood-stained shirt, and pressed against his chest where the stainless-steel ball-bearing resided, grimacing at the pain it caused. Ripping his shirt open to inspect the damage, he took a deep breath, and reached into the hole the pellet had created. After a few failed attempts, he finally managed to gain purchase on the bullet with his fingernail, and slowly pulled it out from the wound, bringing the bloody object up to his eye-level for inspection.

Rolling it between his index finger and thumb, he stared in bemusement at the trail of blood each roll left behind. The rules that governed this world between the living and temporally-displaced dictated that, in their current form, they were unable to cause direct physical harm to anyone in the past. The one exception being what Hal and Kara had achieved on the night of his true death. Nor could Restarters feel pain or sustain injury whilst out-of-phase. Or so they had assumed. But Malcolm knew differently. And now possessed evidence to the contrary, both in the form of his perpetually-shifting memories, and by the presence of a spherical token that verified it wasn't *just* the past that could be changed.

He flicked the tiny bullet over his shoulder dismissively, into the shadow-filled corner of the room, now the sole keeper of a remarkable secret; whilst they may not have been able to directly harm the living, they were more than capable of harming each other.

CHAPTER SEVENTEEN

Restarters Assemble

166th Restart – Saturday, August 25th, 8:24pm

'Guys, maybe we should talk about this?' said Peter, increasing his speed to match that of Hal and Kara's, who were leading the way.

'What's to talk about?' said Hal, not showing any sign of slowing down. 'If this is what led to your funeral, we can stop it from coming to pass. We jump in, change the events that lead you to going to Kevin's alone, and end this madness here and now.'

Kara didn't seem so sure, which grabbed Hal's attention enough for him to mention it.

'You okay, Kar'?'

Kara slowed down, stopping to think.

'Pete may have a point, Hal. What if this is exactly

what he wants us to do?'

'What difference does it make what *he* wants?' Hal argued, slowing down and walking backwards. 'If we change this moment, Peter's funeral will never happen.'

'Assuming this is what causes that at all. I'm just saying maybe we should take a moment to think about this. We don't know what's waiting for us back at Fir Lodge. It could be a trap.'

Hal stopped his poorly executed moonwalk, noticing his three companions had come to a halt, unable to ignore how right she was.

In all of the excitement, he hadn't stopped to consider how he was not only running head-first into a chain of events he knew nothing about, but was also ready to change them at the flip of a coin, based on little more than the information he'd been told by the *very* person who had set them in motion in the first place.

He took in a deep breath, releasing it slowly. 'You think we shouldn't?'

'I think we shouldn't just run blindly into this based solely on *Malcolm's* word.'

Hal turned his attention to Peter, remembering he alone possessed the answers they all needed, locked away in his own memories. 'What do you remember? After what Future-Boy did, you must have inherited the restarts? What happened?

'I…don't remember,' said Peter feebly.

'How can you not remember?' Kara challenged.

'I just don't, Kara! It's not something I have any control over!'

And it was true. Peter held no memory of this altered timeline, or of Malcolm killing him off and sparing Fearne. And least of all a chain of *repeats* where he was left alone to fend for himself. In fact, the only repeats he had any recollection of were the ones he shared with her.

'Urgh,' said Hal, gripping his hair in his hands before looking back up at them wildly, not for the first time reminding himself how much he hated time travel. 'Okay. Then we put it to a vote. All in favour of changing this moment to free Neville-Longbottom-sans-Remembrall here from his solo restart chain? Raise a hand.'

Hal raised his own, followed almost instantly by Fearne.

Peter seemed unsure, but raised his hand slowly all the same, voting in favour also.

Kara held fast, blinking repeatedly, as if running the numbers in her mind, still unsure if this was the right call.

'It's decided then,' said Fearne. 'We go save Peter.'

Hal ignored her, speaking directly to Kara as if they were the only people present.

'No, this is a *Restarter* vote. If Kara is out, we're bailing.'

'What?!' said Fearne angrily. 'How is *that* fair?'

Hal rattled off his response without so much as a

glimmer of hesitation. 'Because every decision we ever make is to save people! Build a bridge and get over it.'

'That was harsh,' said Peter.

'Kara,' said Hal ignoring all but her. 'Tell me what you want to do, and we'll do it.'

Kara looked into each of their eyes, searching for an answer. For a hint of guidance from the universe. *Anything* she could use to make an informed decision, before accepting one would never come. She straightened up, breaking free from the trance of indecision that shackled her.

'What the hell,' she said finally. 'Let's go save Peter.'

*

They ran as fast as their legs could carry them which, as it transpired, was pretty damn quick considering their energy was infinite, their lack of physical form preventing their exertion from leading to fatigue.

'I forgot how easy it was to keep going here,' said Hal happily.

'I know,' said Kara. 'It's almost as if I haven't bailed on going to the gym for the past two months.'

Approaching the driveway of Fir Lodge, they realised they were behind schedule, as Jerry darted across from them in a sharp right turn, the sound of shingle clacking beneath his tiny paws. A delay no doubt by design of the once and Future Malcolm, who had sent them on this half-baked quest.

Each of them sensed that this little test he had

engineered was designed solely for them to fail. That was the point, surely? To emphasise the futility of it all. Making them not only need his help, but to *want* it too.

Turning sharply, they rushed the last corner, finding themselves confronted with an incredibly odd sight.

'Erm, guys,' said Kara. 'Why is there a *Malcolm* on the roof?'

Sure enough, crawling on all fours like a mid-life crisis version of Spider-Man, knees faintly grazing against the tiles and emanating small, barely noticeable clicks and clacks, was Malcolm.

The four Restarters slowly weaved between the cars on the driveway, utterly mystified by what the bulk of a man was trying to accomplish. It was utterly surreal, seeing him behave this way.

'You okay up their chief?' shouted Hal, not sure on what else he could say. Anything would have sounded stupid.

The man ignored him, and placed his head face down onto a slate.

'I don't think he can hear you,' said Fearne.

'Yeah, I got that vibe,' said Hal dryly.

'So which Malcolm is that?' asked Peter. 'The one we just spoke to?'

'My money's on it being the real deal,' theorised Kara. 'I mean, you could hear him moving across those tiles. If he was a Restarter, he'd have been silent.'

"Smart," thought Hal, glad she was with him.

The thought of having to explain the rules of Restarting from the top felt like an exhaustive proposition. Then he corrected himself, remembering Peter and Fearne weren't as new to all this as he and Kara had initially suspected.

'Okay,' said Hal, getting the show on the road. 'So, forget about *Malcolm The Barbarian* back at Kevin's. He's sitting this one out. Which leaves *Fiddler on the Roof Malcolm* up *there*…taking his nap. That means we've got one more Malcolm to worry about. He's in here somewhere; we need to get to Rob's room, and make sure that door stays open so Peter doesn't end up taking Jerry back on his lonesome. Got it?'

Everyone nodded.

'All righty-roo,' said Kara, shooting a smile of determination at Hal. 'For Rohan, then.'

Hal couldn't bear to sully her call-back to their last successful restart, deciding to let her words hang in the air without further explanation.

*

They bypassed the front entrance and made their way in through the rear garden, nothing preparing them for the sight of seeing their friends interacting. Drinking their drinks, Robert – as always – in the hot-tub…everything appeared both familiar and new all at once.

To Kara, it felt like interactive nostalgia; as if she were drifting through her own memories. A passenger, travelling in the slipstream of her own history. It was intoxicating, and for a moment she thought she might just abandon this mission altogether and hang out with her chosen family, contemplating how she honestly didn't know if she would ever get to see them again. At least not in any tangible way that counted.

She shook the fuzzy notion from her mind, remembering why she was here; to make sure all of them lived long enough to have a future at all. Daydreams of the past wouldn't bring any of them closer to that goal.

And then, looking into the hallway from the rear garden, she saw it. They all did.

Peter's past-self attempting to open Robert's bedroom door, and the door slamming shut from the inside, the faint flicker of a single grain of red electricity passing through it as it did so.

Hal and Kara didn't waste any time, immediately locking arms and running to the bedroom door.

'Peter, Fearne,' shouted Kara, 'we need this door open, now!'

Their friends joined them, the blue energy sparking more savagely than Peter and Fearne had ever seen before. Except for that one time, when they–

'Okay Pete,' said Hal, unknowingly pulling his friend back into what could loosely be described as the present. 'All hands on-deck. Let's send this sucker packing. Time to touch yourself.'

His friends stared at Hal with confusion, though Fearne's face in particular edged more towards the side of a giggle.

*

The door handle rattled, as it always did, and Malcolm envisioned the energy building from his core, channelling it into his hands.

With a creak, the door began to move inwards, as Peter's alive-self tried to enter, and Malcolm gritted his teeth, focusing all of his hatred into something he could use; a power source that would act as a key to finally freeing him from this place. The door slammed shut under his force, preventing Peter from entering.

Malcolm heard the young man from the other side of the door mumble a quizzical hum of perplexed confusion.

He was done in this place. He felt *saturated* by it, as if the moronic banter of those residing in Fir Lodge were somehow infecting him with their banality. The door handle quivered again, and Malcolm growled, as the door began to give way under his ever-depleting charge of residual energy.

But the door creeped ever further open, as he heard the golfer speak.

'Rob, you in there, mate? I need to borrow your charger!'

Images flashed through Malcolm's mind, fuelling his anger further, haunting his sense of self; one image in particular, of a young rat-catcher and his orange secretary.

Malcolm screamed, giving it his all, but the door remained firmly in place, refusing to close.

'Close, damn you!' shouted Malcolm.

And then he saw it. A shimmer at first, occupying the space between the crack of light between the door and the frame, like a brief refraction of light creating a fishbowl effect, warping the molecules that made up the very fabric of reality. But the shimmer expanded, popping without warning and showering him in an energy that peppered his face with an odd burning sensation in a way that he imagined acid rain would feel like against mortal skin. Or, perhaps, how he imagined the acid must have felt when he poured it on his victims, when he was feeling in a particularly inventive mood.

Suddenly, Malcolm knew there was more to this than he could perceive.

Was it possible? Had they found their way back? Eager to torment him further. To rub salt in the wound that served as his unwilling incarceration?

'How are you *here*?!' he snarled, talking to ghosts he couldn't see, his eyes igniting with a reinvigorated red electricity that would've filled the dark room, had light been able to reflect from between Malcolm's present and the pocket dimension of the past.

He was so preoccupied with the how, he hadn't even noticed that time had literally stopped. It was the hue of the room that made him realise. A colour that plagued the dreams he was unable to have thanks to the sleep he could no longer indulge in.

A colour he had fostered an irrational hatred for.

That colour, of course, was blue.

*

Peter's hand was phasing through his past-self, effectively super-charging the four of them, unexpectedly causing time to slow to a crawl, eventually grinding it to a halt altogether. At least, that's how it appeared to them.

'You g-guys are gross,' said Hal.

'To be f-fair,' said Kara, her teeth chattering and making it all but impossible to hold back the laughter, 'you co-could have ph-ph-phrased it b-b-better…'

'I ha-hate you all,' said Hal, his mutual laughter betraying the sentiment.

*

Malcolm realised he was beat. He was able to draw off scraps of energy from the other side of the door, but the wood oddly seemed to provide enough of a barrier to prevent him from recharging himself, and the red energy within him eventually dwindled to nothing. His connection to his alive-self lying flat above him on the roof giving little in the way of support.

He had just enough time to wonder if the physical version of himself he had stationed on the roof had gone AWOL and left his post, as the door flung open. Reality began to stabilise, and the flow of time returned to normal, as a blue lightning bolt shot across the doorway, erasing any doubt he may have had that Harold and Kara were responsible for this.

Even though they were gone, free from this place, they had still managed to find a new way to interfere.

Peter's past-self entered the room, grabbed a phone charger, then found himself pressed against the bedroom wall, as blue electricity filled his eyes, just as it always had. Not that Malcolm was looking. He was staring at the doorway, a look of thunderous rage on his face. And with that, he clicked his fingers, speeding up the flow of the current Cerebral Reversion, leaving the phantom-like intruders behind him to enjoy their little moment, having ruined what *had* been a perfect plan.

*

'Bangarang!' shouted Hal. 'And *that's* how it's done! Up top!' he added, holding his hand up to Kara for a high five, which she responded to with customary reciprocation, a dull crackle repelling her palm.

'Up…top…' said Kara, almost more as a question than a bookend, in shock that it had all ended so quickly. 'That was…*easy*, all things considered.'

In that moment, Restarting suddenly felt a lot like riding a bike to Kara; the two of them representing a fluttering playing card wedged in the spokes of time, emanating flutterby effects instead of nostalgia.

'So, what next?' said Hal, rubbing his hands together. 'Shall we go save the dinosaurs? Or we could go and talk Clooney out of making Batman and Robin? It'd be nice to give something back to the universe, don't you think?'

Kara heard a voice that, even after all this time, still sounded alien to her, and it took her a second to realise it was because its point of origin was a duplicated version of her own voice-box.

'Looks like we're about to take Jerry home,' said Kara, eavesdropping on the words being spoken by her alive-self.

'And we know we *nailed* that part' said Hal, recalling the intricacy of their 165th restart. 'Which means we're done here. Everything's back to normal.'

'Anyone else think that was…I don't know, a little *too* easy?' said Fearne, but her words fell on deaf ears. Literally, as it turned out, due to the sound of rushing air flooding their out-of-phase eardrums.

But, for once, it didn't signal defeat. It sounded to the four of them much more like something else.

It sounded like victory.

CHAPTER EIGHTEEN
The Three Malcolms

167ᵗʰ Restart – Friday, August 24ᵗʰ, 12:02pm

The first thing Hal and Kara noticed was that the aforementioned victory was of the short-lived variety, as they reappeared outside Fir Lodge in a fresh restart to the unsettling sound of "Mr. Sandman", which was once again blaring from the inexplicable radio occupying the space in front of them.

Realising he was brandishing his gun, which had re-materialised in the exact position it had been when they first arrived here, Hal once again dropped the weapon into its holster

'Ummm, Hal, why are we back here?' said Kara.

'I don't get it,' he replied. 'We beat him. Undid

what he changed, we should be back sipping lattes right now.'

'Of course. Because that would be far too easy, wouldn't it,' said Kara sourly. 'Bench?' she suggested.

Hal nodded, confirming that the motion had been carried to adjourn to their make-shift war room.

As Hal and Kara made their way into the rear garden, they remembered Peter and Fearne were occupying this restart with them.

'You guys too huh?' said Hal, more than a little confused.

'Looks like it didn't take,' said Peter, stating the obvious.

'This doesn't make any sense,' said Kara.

'Okay…okay,' said Hal, the cogs clearly starting to turn in his brain, slipping off his backpack and emptying the majority of the contents onto the table, ensuring that one item in particular remained nestled safely within the bag out of sight. He flicked several of the objects out of the way, looking for something in particular.

As he did so, his three friends sat around the table, staring curiously and trying to make sense of the items he deemed worthy (albeit sub-consciously) to bring back with him through time.

Several snacks in the form of energy bars, two bottles of water, two cans of a popular brand of energy drink, an A5 sized notebook and some heavy-duty adhesive tape were visible at first glance. Amidst all that were photos of Jess, his dog Shelby, and pictures of their initial stay at Fir Lodge, featuring all of their friends. A closer inspection revealed a leather wallet, a small box of what appeared to be cigarette filters, a flip-top silver lighter, a packet of chewing gum and bizarrely, hidden beneath it all, a bright pink rubber duck.

"Correction, *flamingo*," thought Kara, utterly beside herself with confusion.

'Were you planning for a trip through time, or a *stag* do?' asked Kara, genuinely curious.

Hal scowled at her.

'Dammit, where is it?!' said Hal, returning his attention to his bag and rummaging some more, until finally gaining purchase on what he was after, pulling a black biro from the bag. 'Pass me the notepad would you, Judas?'

Peter, balked, but chucked Hal the book all the same.

Hal took a deep breath, grabbed one of the energy drinks, pulled the tab in one swift motion and proceeded to down the entire can.

'Hal,' began Kara, but her friend simply raised his hand, extended his index finger as if asking for a moment.

As he necked the remainder of the contents, he crushed the can and threw it over his shoulder, releasing a satisfied gasp, despite there being little in the way of carbonation in the can of caffeine-infused, potential-diabetes-inducing beverage. Reaching for his trusty filter box and lighter, Hal plucked a cigarette from the container and lit up his first smoke in six weeks.

'I thought you quit?' said Kara, a look of disappointment on her face.

'I'm dead, it doesn't count,' he joked, noting that everyone was staring at him disapprovingly. 'Wow, tough crowd.'

Hal's past-self was talking to Jon by the hot-tub, and Hal swiped his arm across the picnic table, guiding all of the objects back into his bag. 'We're on the move, let's roll,' said Hal, leading the way deeper into the rear garden and sitting down on the grass, waiting for them to join him.

'Are you done?' said Kara.

'Yup. I think I know what just happened, but you'll need to bear with me, because this shit is about to get complicated. We're talking *Pre*-New-52-DC-Comics-continuity complicated.'

'I don't know what that means…'

'Nobody here does,' said Hal reassuringly, scribbling in his notebook vivaciously. 'So, I think we just experienced a convergence of multiple timelines. By killing Malcolm on our 165 restart, we miiight have just given him the keys to a time machine.'

'Not out brightest move,' said Kara. 'We created a bloody Restarter.'

'Worse,' said Peter earnestly. 'Some kind of…*Dark* Restarter.

Hal blinked, clearly wrestling with sticking to his guns about being mad at Peter and wanting to commend him for coming up with such a spot-on title.

'That…is surprisingly not terrible. Good shout, Pete,' he said finally, recalling the moment when he flicked Malcolm the bird after they defeated him.

It had been a pretty glorious sight, seeing Malcolm's face as he walked up the stairs of Kevin's basement, utterly unaware at that point they were cursing the killer to an eternity of restarts.

'A sort of…*Malcolm 2.0*,' said Kara, unable to think of a better term. It seemed to do the job.

'Exactly,' said Hal with a smile. 'He's had God knows how long to change things, reliving our 165th restart over and over. And, somewhere along the line, he's figured out how to move his *living-self* away from Kevin's place.'

'How did he manage that you reckon?' asked Kara.

'We'll need to ask the man himself on that one,' said Hal glumly. 'So, Malcolm 2.0 was there at Fir Lodge, pulling the strings of his alive-self.

'Malcolm 1.0,' said Peter helpfully, eager to contribute to the conversation, sensing he might be on the right path to winning his way back into his friend's good books.

'Nobody likes a kiss-ass, Pete,' said Hal, returning to his curmudgeonly mood, still reeling from the weight of Malcolm's revelation that Peter and Fearne had betrayed them. A fact they would need to discuss at some point.

'Think of it this way; there's the past versions of us,' said Hal, eager to break things down. 'Alive and well on Friday the 24th of August. There's also a version of us on our last run of restarts, changing time to free ourselves. And then, there's the four of us right here and right now, a *third* copy of ourselves occupying the same space, but contained within separate pockets of time.'

'What about the future we came from though?' asked Kara. 'Are *they* still there? That version of us? Alive and kicking?

'I think it's safe to say that timeline is toast.'

'Well, that sucks,' said Kara. 'Although, at least that means Peter's funeral hasn't happened.'

'I still don't get why I don't remember that?' said Fearne. 'If I was dragged from the same future as you, I mean.

'You've got me there,' conceded Hal. 'But at least we can work out how many Malcolms we have to contend with.'

'Same as us, you think?' said Kara.

'I'd say so,' agreed Hal. 'There's the Malcolm of the past from the 24th of August, still alive and being all *murdery*, then the second Dark Restarter version of himself we created…'

'The one we just stopped from sending Pete to the slaughter?' said Kara.

'Right. All the fun of a vanilla serial killer, but with access to the same sandbox of thirty-three-hours we had access to. What I can't figure out,' said Hal, his brow scrunching, 'is this *third* version of Malcolm. Where the hell did he come from?'

'Well, according to him, he's claiming to be from the future.' said Peter.

Hal wasn't so sure.

'So, there's the original timeline,' began Hal. 'Before all this started, Timeline *Prime*. Then what happened to you and Fearne…we'll call *that* balls up Timeline Alpha.'

'Hal, I–'

'We'll *get* to that Pete. Then the new timeline. Everything was peachy, apart from the part where Malcolm killed us and we started Restarting, right?'

The three Restarters shrugged in unison.

'We'll call that Timeline Beta. So, Kara and I go back in time, we begin Restarting. 165 restarts later, we change our destiny and escape, sending us back to a brand-new future,' the intensity of his scribbling bolstered by an enthusiasm brought on in part by the novelty of having actual writing equipment at his disposal.

'Timeline Charlie then,' noted Kara. 'But when we made it home, we didn't remember any of it.'

'Yeah,' frowned Hal. 'I guess because *time travel* or something. Nothing to remember if it didn't happen, I guess?'

'But it *had* to happen for it *not* to happen?' said Kara, a headache forming.

'Yeah, let's not get caught up in that,' Hal deflected, not wishing to draw attention to the reality of him not being in any way proficient when it came to *actual* quantum mechanics. 'So, a glorious new timeline is born. Kevin is saved, we're saved, Malcolm is deader than disco.'

'Who's Kevin?' asked Fearne.

Hal gawped.

'Seriously? You guys are like the *worst* time-travellers ever. Anyway, jump to six weeks from now, Peter is erased from the present; and boom!' said Hal, miming a dramatic explosion with added sound effects.

'Malcolm gets sent back through time and inherits our restarts,' said Kara, finally getting a good grasp on their current dilemma. 'Then, having access to an infinite amount of do-overs to get the job done, he finds a way to stop Hal and I from even reaching Kevin's, resulting in Peter taking Jerry back alone?' she surmised.

'I think we're cracking this nut! That's it,' said Hal, glad he was making sense despite Peter and Fearne still looking completely lost.

A new memory was forming in Hal and Kara's mind which corroborated this theory. A memory of seeing the entrance doors to Fir Lodge close before they could set in motion their plans on their 165th restart. But now that they'd changed those events, their memories were shifting back again, as the new timeline they had created took hold.

'Creating a fourth timeline,' said Peter, sort of getting his head around it.

'So,' said Hal, picking up momentum, 'We're living happily in a new future of our own making, Dark Restarter-Malcolm kills Peter, changes the future—'

'—and frames Kevin for Peter's murder whilst he's at it!' added Kara, remembering her Velma-like Googling back in their now-erased future. 'But if Malcolm escaped the restarts, why is there a version of him from the future? Still here, at Fir Lodge?'

'And on top of that,' said Fearne, eager to address a huge plot-hole in Hal and Kara's rambling, 'none of this explains why *you're* both here, or *me* for that matter.'

'Good point,' agreed Hal. And she was right.

If past-Malcolm had indeed altered time so Peter was his only victim, something else must have occurred for Fearne, Hal and Kara to wind up back where they started. Not to mention the mystery of a Future Malcolm.

And then it dawned on Hal. Another part of the puzzle slipping into place.

'Maybe…maybe we're not *in* The Dark Restarter's *final* restart?' posed Hal. 'Future Malcolm said it himself, when we asked him when he figured out how we beat him the first time. What was it he said?'

'He said *that* happened much later,' said Kara. Everything had moved so fast since they got here, but she had picked up on at least that much.

'That was it,' agreed Hal. 'Wherever Malcolm has brought us, I'm fairly certain it's early on in past-

Malcolm's restart chain. Based on all that, I'd wager the four of us and Future Malcolm are existing in a fourth timeline…' said Hal, wrapping up the minutes for their team meeting on his notepad with an exaggerated underlining, before spinning the book around and chucking it on the ground between them to show them all. 'Well, fifth, if you count what you two did before Kara and I got caught up in this mess.'

The writing was hastily written in a style that drew immediate comparisons to a chicken that had walked through some ink and inadvertently across some paper:

> **Timeline Prime** – *Arrive at Fir Lodge.*
> **Timeline Alpha** – *Peter and Fearne ruin our lives.*
> **Timeline Beta** – *Hal and Kara Restart.*
> *Kick Time's ass! #Timepolice*
> **Timeline Charlie** – *Dark Restarter Malcolm changes future. Kills Pete. Karma. Hal and Kara survive. (Because awesomeness.)*
> **Timeline Delta** – *Whatever this thing currently is.*

Fearne scowled at the crude little diagrams in the margins. Notably the one of Peter and her, holding what appeared to be boat paddles, carrying out the act of pushing Hal and Kara into a portal situated next to a sign that Hal had handily labelled as "Welcome to Shit Creek."

'You spent that whole time with the notepad,' said Fearne, 'and *this* is what you've came up with?'

'Oh, I'm *sorry*,' said Hal, showing the signs of someone who was clearly not sorry, 'how's *your* thesis coming along, Fearne?

'I was expecting, I don't know…' she replied, somewhat lost for words. 'I guess, at least *some* mathematical formulas or something.'

'I feel like you're missing the point.'

'And I feel like you messed up Peter's strong jawline,' retorted Fearne. 'It's like a seven-year-old popped on a blindfold, got drunk on cough syrup and tried to finish his homework on the bus ride to school. During an earthquake.'

'In fairness, I put all my energy into nailing the picture of you stabbing Kara and I in the back. Which I feel is reflected perfectly. What do you think, Kar'?'

'Oh no, don't you drag *me* into this, if you two want to thrash it out, be my guest,' said Kara, clearly wishing to remain neutral until she possessed more facts on *that* particular time-bomb.

'So,' said Peter, intervening in the hope of diffusing the apparent hostility that was forming between Fearne and Hal. 'Five timelines, huh?'

'That's my best guess,' said Hal, seeing what Peter was trying to do, and not wishing to fight him on it. 'And three Malcolms. Based on all the information we have.'

'So, what do we do now?' Kara's brain felt fried by the prospect of the three Malcolms that were the personification of the past, present and future. She struggled to balance her life when there was only one clock to worry about, yet here she was, apparently in a fifth iteration of an entire universe.

'I...honestly? I have no idea.'

Hal didn't see the benefit of sugar-coating it, realising they were at the total mercy of whatever had brought them here. They were so balls-deep lost in time that there wasn't a watch in the entire universe that could even begin to tell them *when* the hell in time they actually were. Luckily, they didn't need a watch. They just needed a *person*; the only man who knew for certain what the future held.

Before they could go down that rabbit hole, however, there was still one huge omission from the dizzying list of timelines they had mapped out. One involving the small matter of Peter and Fearne. A timeline that allegedly not only predated Hal and Kara's initial trip through time, but had directly caused it in the first place.

'We can't go any further into this half-cocked,' said Hal. 'I think it's time you told us everything.'

All eyes resting on him, Peter took an enormous deep breath and exhaled slowly, eventually encroaching beyond the territory of what was socially acceptable in terms of exhalation duration, as he stalled for time.

'Okay,' said Peter, searching for the courage he would need to tell his side of the story. 'This is what happened.'

CHAPTER NINETEEN
Living for the Weekend

Timeline Prime – Saturday, August 25th, 2018, 8:35pm

Peter felt a subtle vibration against his leg, and reached into the right-hand pocket of his grey golfing trousers, his fingertips making contact with one of the curved edges of his phone. Pulling the device from its resting place, and holding it parallel to his hip, he looked down at the screen.

The features of his face danced across the black mirror, reflecting a man in his late twenties. It was the general consensus of his friends that he had a facial structure that would age gracefully, not that they ever told him that of course. Peter's meticulously maintained designer stubble defined his already attractive cheekbones, and his piercing brown eyes simmered with intensity even whilst indulging in the mundane task of checking his phone.

As the familiar fruit-shaped logo disappeared from the display, all of this was lost on Peter, who merely noted the reflected look of disdain and mild irritation adorning his face. He raised the phone closer, using the opportunity to fuss with the front of his already perfect hair, running his fingers through it, the rogue strands effortlessly returning to their correct and proper place. Whilst in Rome, he also stole a glance at his complexion, not that his regularly moisturised skin ever suffered from such trivialities as dehydration. One of the more endearing things about Peter was that he wasn't vain, he was just innately, obliviously, easy on the eye.

'Bastard,' said Peter, realising he'd need to find a charger.

He left Will and Jon to their game of pool and began his pursuit of a means to charge it, knowing that neither he nor Fearne had remembered to bring one. As he made his way through the hallway that led to the rear garden of Fir Lodge, he noticed Hal slipping into his own room, and called out to his friend.

'Hal mate, can I borrow your charger?'

Peter heard a somewhat mumbled response that sounded like a disappointing "no", followed by the suggestion that he should try asking Robert.

'Urgh,' mumbled Peter. 'Will do.'

As Peter made his way down the corridor, he pressed gently against Robert and Daisy's bedroom door, clearing his throat a little to announce his presence. Noting the light was off, he felt it safe to enter without making more of a thing of it.

The exterior lights that illuminated the hot-tub and rear garden offered little in the way of cutting through the darkness of the room, but the refracted light glistened back at him from a silver object that had been discarded on the top of a suitcase, which he immediately recognised as the buckle of Robert's Santa Clause belt.

'Gotcha,' said Peter, as he leaned over the case and acquired visual confirmation of the white plug and charging cable nestled happily into the plug socket behind what he reasonably deduced to be Robert's bed.

Grabbing the lead, he shoved it into the charging port, placing his phone onto a bedside table, waiting idly for the tell-tale sign of the charging symbol to adorn the screen, then span around happily, proceeding to head back out to the party, before suddenly feeling a little out of sorts.

Peter surveyed the humble room with nonsensical suspicion, his eyes adjusting gradually to the darkness, as a sudden bombardment of both oppression and anxiety formed a heady mix within him that felt an awful lot like claustrophobia. It was as if the world was closing in on him, his mind adamant that it knew this particular room far better than he should, for reasons he couldn't quite rationalise.

Having no way of knowing he was actually experiencing the onset symptoms of temporal dysplasia, due to having no prior point of reference to define the sensation, he simply shivered the shiver that often accompanied the prospect that someone had just walked over their own grave. Eager to shake the malevolent feeling, he left the room, pulling the door closed behind him.

As Peter burst forth into the much more adequately lit hallway, his ears were met with Greenbaum's "Spirit in the Sky", which seemed to be blasting from the living area above his head. Suddenly, Hal bumped into him, making his way into the rear garden and clearly not looking where he was going.

'Sorry dude! Didn't see you. Any luck?'

'Huh?' replied Peter, still feeling a little bit out of sync with the world.

'Did Rob have a charger?' said Hal, expanding on what he had wrongly assumed to be the obvious.

'Oh, yeah, thanks. Have you seen Fearne?'

'Upstairs I think,' shrugged Hal. 'Catch you in a bit!' he added, excited by the prospect of sneaking in a not-so-secret cigarette as only an addict would.

'Sure thing,' said Peter, making his way back into the communal area where the pool table resided.

Out of the corner of his eye, he saw an odd shape through the window of the double front entrance doors to the lodge, and called over to Will and Jon who were still playing pool.

'Lads, that dog from earlier is back.'

From the floor above, Fearne eased her way past Stacey and trotted down the central staircase, removing herself from the embarrassing situation of the champagne flute she had just knocked over, knowing she'd just get in Daisy's way if she stayed.

'Aww little doggy!' said Fearne, full of the loaded coos that sent a streak of panic through Peter whenever Fearne showed even the remotest indication that she was broody for small animals or, more concisely, *babies*. 'Let him in, let him in!'

Peter opened the door and Jerry sauntered inside, sniffing the pair of them before making his way to the two men playing pool, until eventually trying his luck and trying to make his way up the stairs.

Daisy called out, ordering them all to keep Jerry away whilst she cleared up the broken shards of glass, as Kara seized her opportunity to give up on cleaning duties, reasoning that Daisy and Stacey both clearly had it covered.

The top of the stairs was entirely unobstructed now, allowing free passage for Kara to descend, so she swiftly grabbed her glass of Southern Comfort and headed down them.

As she joined Peter and Fearne, she too fussed over Jerry, who rolled over to present his belly to her, eager for some attention.

'Naww, hey Jerry!' said Kara. 'What should we do

with him?'

Jon, meanwhile, was clearly losing at pool to Will. Badly. And he chimed in, willing to do anything to free himself from another defeat.

'Didn't that Kev guy say you just have to tell him to go home?' said Jon, preparing to ditch his pool cue. 'Here, let me try...'

'Don't think so, mate,' said Will. 'You're not getting–'

'–out of this *that* easy...' whispered Peter, the volume of his utterance cloaked by Will saying the words at the exact same time.

'You okay, Pete?' said Kara, noticing how he appeared to be zoning out a bit.

'Fine,' said Peter, partially snapping out of it.

After several failed attempts at instructing Jerry to return home, Kara put into words what she, Fearne and Peter were all thinking.

'Yeah, that's not working. Shall we just *take* him home?' she suggested, knocking back a large swig of her whisky-mixer. 'Can't be that far.'

'You're okay hun, we'll take him,' said Fearne. 'Right, Pete?'

Peter was staring up at the stars, a million miles away from the two ladies standing next to him.

'Peter!' repeated Fearne, nudging him in his ribs.

'Huh?' he said, quickly resorting to his tried and tested response when he had been ignoring his girlfriend. 'Sure sweetie, definitely.'

'Did you even hear what I said?' her tone playfully

suspicious.

In times like these he found it prudent not to hesitate, and surveyed the things in his immediate vicinity in the hope that combining the words might form a coherent sentence that held relevance.

'Jerry,' he said, looking down, 'lodge,' he added, looking behind him, '...Kara?' he said finally. "Nailed it," he thought.

Fearne sighed, and grabbed his arm. 'You're *very* lucky you're pretty,' she said jokingly. 'Wait, do we know where he lives?'

'Check his—" began Kara.

'—don't bother,' said Peter. 'I know the way,' he added creepily.

Kara and Fearne exchanged a look that seemed to show they were both aware of how weird Peter was acting, resulting in Kara turning around and heading back inside whilst taking another sip of her drink, more than a little glad that none of that was her problem.

'What is *with* you tonight?' asked Fearne, as they walked down the shingle driveway of Fir Lodge. 'Have you been drinking Jon's cocktails? I told you not to drink too much of them, I swear I caught him putting pasta sauce into one of them…'

Fearne's torrent of questions eventually faded into nothingness, as the two of them headed out into the darkness of the woods with both Jerry and, bizarrely, Peter leading the way.

CHAPTER TWENTY
The Stowaway

Timeline Prime – Saturday, August 25th, 2018, 8:52pm

As Fearne walked alongside Peter, she was beginning to find it hard to determine if they were following Jerry, or if Jerry was following *them*. Peter was unusually quiet, but as another lodge sprung into view, whatever it was that had him so preoccupied slowly began to bleed into her own mood as well.

There was an eerie sense of foreboding in the humid air, which generated a shiver deep within her. Her white dress rippled in the barely-present breeze, and Fearne felt more like she was gliding across the road they were traversing, as opposed to taking it step by step. The fresh air was clearly coercing with the admittedly excessive amount of alcohol in her system, and she had to consciously shake her head in order to keep the fogginess at bay.

Peter had apparently adopted the same ethos to their impromptu walk in the pale moonlight, shaking his head and reverting to his actual personality in an instant.

'Eesh, I think we're here,' he said, with more than an ounce of relief.

'Are you okay?'

'I'm fine hun, promise. You're right, must be Jon's cocktails. I kind of hit them hard over dinner.'

Peter leant down to check Jerry's collar. 'This must be the place,' he added, raising a perfectly maintained, yet undeniably manly eyebrow at the humble lodge before them.

"More of a cabin, really," he thought.

'Well that's not creepy as shit,' said Fearne, the lack of any lights beyond the open door sending off all kinds of red flags.

She calmed her nerves, realising she was being somewhat over-zealous. After all, it was just an empty cabin in the woods, and this was Norfolk. Not exactly prime real-estate for netarious goings on.

Peter laughed heartily, immediately putting her at ease in a way only he knew how; he had an innate skill of being able to calm her concerns without making her feel silly. She loved him for that.

'Yeah, doesn't look great, does it. In you go doggy,' said Peter, flapping his hands effeminately in the direction of Jerry's home, as if forcing a flow of air would be enough to egg the spaniel on, dropping his head dramatically for effect and staring at the ground between his feet when, predictably, Jerry failed to play ball.

'Babe, what even *was* that weird hand-flap thing you just did?' said Fearne, her eyes judging him with a playfully delivered partial squint. 'I swear, I'm banning you from any more rewatches of La La Land when we get home.

'First off, La La Land is *life* Fearne. It's a cinematic masterpiece. But I'll chalk up you thinking I remind you of Ryan Gosling as a win.'

'Oh yeah, that's *clearly* what I meant…'

'Secondly, you're welcome to give this a punt?'

Fearne hurtled a pair of daggers towards him in a loving act of amused defiance, and walked up the small driveway towards the rectangle of blackness that made up the doorway, her white heels clacking against the pathway tiles that were all but concealed beneath years of weathering, coupled with the natural dirt generated by the forest. She accentuated the movement of her hips as she did so, knowing it drove him wild, and that he'd backed himself too far into a corner of pride to be able to mention it.

Fearne stopped at the door and looked over her shoulder, the swift action causing her long brunette hair to cover the right-hand side of her face.

'You coming?' she said daringly.

She could just make out the smirk beneath his ridiculously-expensive designer golfing cap, which was casting a shadow over the contours of his jawline. It always amazed her how he genuinely seemed to believe she had no idea how much he spent on that crap.

Placing her right hand on her waist, Fearne straightened her posture slightly, just enough to match his irritatingly inherent smoulder. She called out for Jerry, and stepped into the dark, the springer spaniel treading gently, and slowly following her inside.

Realising she had him over a barrel, Peter sniffed in some of the night air and exhaled an over-the-top sigh, then retraced the path his heroic partner had mapped out before him, his athletic frame being the third living entity to be claimed by the gloomy threshold of the doorway that evening.

And, indeed, for that particular timeline.

*

Peter felt uncharacteristically unnerved. He wasn't afraid of the dark, but the unfamiliar environment, coupled with the sudden sound of an unseen radio hit home the fact that they were both technically trespassing. He didn't know who was singing, but after a few seconds managed to gather the song was probably called either "Man comes around" or "Hear the trumpets."

He'd seen enough movies for his over-active

imagination to reason that if the owner was home, he was probably within his rights to shoot them dead.

It was then he felt the blades carve through his eyes; blades of amber light surging from the bulb above them, as Fearne hit the switch behind him. She was lurking behind the frame of the door like a malevolent wraith, clearly chuffed that she'd caught him off guard.

'Found the light,' she said innocently, as Peter pinched the gap connecting his tear ducts with his right forefinger and thumb.

'Super,' he drawled.

His eyelids blinked open, and he drank in the room.

An old-fashioned radio that he was seeing for the first time was the first object to catch his eye; consisting of cream-coloured panelling connecting the metal grills that housed the speakers, several burgundy dials protruding from the unit, with a handle of matching colour tucked down behind it neatly.

"Definitely *Man Comes Around* he thought, as a singer that sounded to him like Elvis in his later years continued to serenade them.

'No one's home,' said Fearne, calmly dispensing a rhetorically-saturated list of things he could make out for himself. 'Well, we should go, Jerry's safe now and we're missing the party!'

Peter nodded several times, as if each dip of his head signified that he was ticking off all of the above, then made his way to the front door, grinding to a halt when he heard Jerry whining and sniffing at a bedroom door.

'I think he wants to get in there?' said Fearne. 'Shall we open it for him?'

Peter shrugged as he approached Jerry and reached out for the handle, which turned in his hand with little fuss, before pulling the door towards him.

He flinched, as a sharpness cut across his skin.

A breeze surging forth from the basement below had collided with his arms, seemingly caused by the vacuum he had created, and he realised that the bedroom was actually a basement.

Without warning, Jerry bolted through Peter's legs and down the stairs into the darkness below, growling angrily.

'Shit,' mumbled Peter. 'God knows what's down there, we can't leave the poor doggo in a basement.'

'Just leave the door open for him,' reasoned Fearne. 'He can come back up when he's ready.'

Peter let go of the handle and turned his back on it, ready to walk away, as Jerry's growls grew louder, accentuated by an angry bark. 'He's worked up, I should probably go get him.'

'Be careful,' said Fearne, not offering him the counter-argument he was hoping for.

'Relax. I'll be *right* back.'

*

After waiting impatiently for several minutes, the singular noise of Peter navigating multiple floorboards evolved into what sounded like him tripping over something and causing all kinds of havoc.

"Beautiful, but clumsy as ever," thought Fearne, the inanimate objects he'd somehow managed to knock over bouncing around beneath her.

She could hear Jerry growling at him and, deciding her dearest Peter had clearly been the cause of some form of self-imposed mayhem, she descended the staircase in search of him.

Fearne scanned the room, her eyes resting on the far corner, the swaying light bulb above causing countless shadows to frantically dance around her, casting just enough glow for her to see Peter's quivering legs, which were oddly being supported by the mere tips of his expensive astro-turf golfing shoes.

As the swaying bulb lit up the left-hand side of the room, Peter was once again cast into darkness, until the pendulum of illumination made its return journey. Fearne's vision was obscured by a huge mass of darkness, which she realised all too late to be the silhouette of a large-framed entity. The blackness obscured Peter from her line of sight, as her eyes caught glimpse of a sliver of silver, which moved diagonally with such speed that it seemed only to exist between blinks.

Fearne felt a sharp bee-sting like pinch in her throat, and instinctively brought her right hand up to her neck to see if she could feel what had grazed her.

To her horror, she felt the skin of her neck opening up like a second mouth, as liquid drenched its way through her fingers. The swinging bulb returned for an encore above her, and she looked downwards to her chest, noting how her beautiful white dress was slowly transforming into an ever-expanding pitch black.

She called out for Peter, her voice a hoarse whisper that became a sickening gurgle of panic, as she fell to her knees into the pool of blood beneath her.

"*My* blood," she thought, before being overwhelmed with dizziness and passing out in an undignified heap on the cool basement floor.

*

Peter was still reeling from having nearly been suffocated by the man he had, in typically British fashion, just *apologised* to for disturbing, the swirling black lines that filled his vision slowly receding from whence they came now that precious oxygen was returning to his body via the desperate gasps he was making. Gasps he *needed*, in order to restock the supply his body required in order to stay alive.

Pulling himself up into a kneeling position, he instantly resented his reacquired ocular clarity, as he saw the murderous monster slashing across his girlfriend's throat. As she fell to her knees, her face was lit up by a brief streak of light from the bulb above, eyes wide, her white dress a horrifying crimson.

Jerry's hackles were up, and he barked angrily at the monster between them, positioning himself between the two men.

Peter wanted to scream, but thankfully a subconscious act of self-preservation grabbed the steering wheel of that particular decision-making process and prevented him from doing so. Instead, he simply shook with terror, his jaw wide, as he enacted the process of yelling without generating any sound at all. His whole body shook with such intensity that it seemed to generate an audaciously fervent energy that managed to reverberate through the floorboards beneath him and even made the bannister rail behind him shake.

Peter attempted to control his own body, if only for a second, realising that his utterly forgivable descent into torturous despair was causing tremors that would surely show up on the monster's built-in Richter scale sooner or later. Peter's preference, if given the choice, being the latter of two evils.

The man and Fearne were at the base of the stairs, blocking Peter's only route out from this vertical slice of hell. The only way for them both surviving was for him to escape. To get help. Maybe then–

"Oh God she's *dead*, I've *lost* her, how did this–" he pulled the plug on those thoughts.

If he could just make it up the stairs, he could get help.

Fearne would be okay.

She *had* to be okay.

Peter reached out to the counter to his right, using it to pull himself up. He was on his feet like a panther, and felt the reassuring shape of an object beneath his splayed fingers. Allowing his hand to curl around the object, Peter clutched it as if it were the rip-cord to a parachute he had to pull at exactly the right moment to avoid imminent death.

And then, his body filled with adrenaline, as he surged forwards towards the man, whose muscular shoulders were rising and lowering slowly, his head craned down as if surveying Fearne with…what? Sadistic *pleasure*? *Regret*? Peter didn't have time to stop and ask, as he pushed into the hulking body of the man who was still facing away from him.

Rather embarrassingly, their attacker didn't move a single centimetre under what Peter had gauged to be a significant amount of sheer force on his part.

An irritated huff of exhalation escaped from the killer's mouth and nostrils as he spun around, bringing the knife he was holding in a downwards arc that was surely more than capable of cutting through Peter's brain like a machete passing through a head-shaped watermelon.

"Watermelons are already kinda head-shaped. Don't overthink it," he overthought.

Peter closed his eyes, holding up the object in his own shaking hands as if it afforded him a single iota of protection, as an incredible force pushed down against his now-burning muscles, causing his arms to ache terribly.

Gingerly, Peter opened one of his eyes expecting to see, well, nothing much at all given that he should have been dead.

Instead, he was greeted to the ridiculous sight of a ferocious-looking man who was staring back at him with incredulity.

They shared the moment together, both standing there experiencing a rather definitive example of awkwardness, as Peter realised the rusty barbecue fork he was clutching onto for dear life was halting the blades progress mere inches above his head, caught between the V-shaped prongs, and being kept at bay by Peter's slowly diminishing strength.

The beast stared at Peter with eyes that seemed to be completely black, which Peter told himself was surely just due to the poor ambient lighting. His opponent's shark-like teeth remained clenched, as Peter cocked his head a little and shot him an embarrassingly apologetic smile.

Peter stepped backwards, his arms now fully outstretched, and allowed the man's sheer power to win the unexpected instance of Priori Incantatem, pulling the barbecue fork downwards and away from his attacker.

Exploiting the brief reprieve he had been gifted with, Peter span on his heels, moving backwards as he did so, and was granted a once in a lifetime opportunity; the stairs were now open to him.

He didn't waste a single second, running towards them and taking three steps at a time.

With surgical precision, Malcolm poked his blade through the spokes supporting the bannister rail, severing what Peter assumed was his Achilles tendon, as the sound of a sickening snap rippled through his entire body, making him want to vomit. Peter fell to his knees as the agony took hold, his shins cracking audibly against the edges of the steps that were meant to be his salvation, and quickly used his elbows to crawl his way to safety, the thin slit of L-shaped light seeping in around the basement door above him appearing to be a million miles away to him now.

"Might as *well* be," he thought defeatedly, as a hand clasped around his ankle, the fingers of which digging into his frayed flesh and clamping into him like a vice, the tendons flaring under the pressure and causing the black spots to seep back, robbing him of his ability to see.

He brought up the barbecue utensil and thrust it behind him, not daring to look back, fear taking hold of him as it failed to connect with anything. He tried again, and this time he felt it plunge deep into something, like a pronged fork coasting through a freshly roasted chicken. Notably *un*-roast chicken-like, however, the action resulted in a guttural growl that filled the tomb behind him.

Clambering onto his one good leg, Peter hopped the last few steps and reached out for the door in front of him, fumbling for the doorknob, which mercifully met his hand as he pushed through it. The door creaked open, humming with inanimate encouragement, Jerry's barking reaching fever pitch, growing increasingly louder and more frequent, until a sickening whimper echoed below him, and the barks ceased.

Peter fell forwards into the living room, not having time to take in how normal and comforting the room appeared, his eyes darting in frantic desperation towards the front door of the cabin from hell. He made a snap decision, realising he wouldn't get very far in his current state, noting the trail of blood pulsing from his ankle, as his ears were greeted by the music emanating from the nearby radio.

Accepting that this would be his final stand, he limped towards the retro device, lifting it from the cabinet it was resting on, hoping to use it as a weapon, just as he felt metal tearing through his shoulder, causing him to fall backwards, pulling the radio with him, and falling onto his back, the radio clutched to his chest. A flicker of steel filled his vision, as the blade followed through, embedding itself into his eye socket, killing him instantly.

*

In that moment, outside the perceivable realm of human consciousness, reality splintered, and a static fog hummed to life, awakening from its slumber. It was everywhere and nowhere, existing between the fabric of space, time, and every dimension in between, summoned to fill the void that had been created.

This force knew nothing of life, or of death, nor

did it care for either. It simply travelled to where it needed to be, like a sea of power trying to refill a chasm that had appeared in the centre of an ocean.

As the fog made its way through the ages, a stowaway latched onto it; a colourless energy of unknown origin, that occupied the farthest recesses of the cosmos, living within the hearts of dying stars, dancing through the inhospitable and treacherous apex of the nameless singularities that twisted and contorted through the tunnels of time. A lonely ouroboros, imbued with the transferable ability to change the very course of fate itself.

Had Hal been present, he probably would've named it Dave.

Free from the confines of existing in a dimension that didn't have a need for colour, the lightning-like power adopted a form more befitting of its new environment.

The intangible passenger crackled and contorted in protest, shifting in appearance, seemingly unable to decide on if it wanted to be red, or blue.

Hal's choice notwithstanding, had the hitchhiking electricity been capable of taking a name, it would have translated into that of a single word.

Destiny.

CHAPTER TWENTY-ONE
Restart Zero

Timeline Prime – Saturday, August 25th, 2018, 9:07pm

Fearne waited for Peter to hop over the threshold before closing the front door of Kevin's lodge behind them, dusting off her hands to signify a job well done, and they set off back towards Fir Lodge.

She skipped quickly to close the distance between them and reached out to hold his hand, only to be repelled from him due to an unexpected static shock.

'Ouch! Did you see that? Actually saw a *spark* there!'

'Must be my magnetic personality,' said Peter, dispensing what he hoped was a charismatic grin.

'A personality that repels women, you mean?' said Fearne, failing to hide her own smile under the dramatic sigh she made to emphasise her disapproval at his terrible joke.

'You're a mean drunk.'

'You know, you saying that...this walk really must've cleared my head,' said Fearne. 'I don't feel nearly as drunk as I did when we left.'

In fact, as she took a deep breath and stared up at the sky, Fearne realised she was no longer intoxicated at all, the thought evaporating as the beauty of the sight above her filled her soul; a billion blinking lights shone down on her from the heavens, impossibly vivid in their clarity, as if she were looking at them through a powerful telescope.

'Will you look at that sky,' she said, exhaling sharply, completely mesmerised by it.

Peter let out a short whistle, equally impressed. 'I don't think I've even seen the moon in that much detail. It's the second most beautiful thing I've ever seen.'

'What's the first? A full bucket of balls at the driving range?' replied Fearne, not willing to let him score a win so easily.

'You know I meant you,' said Peter, looking directly into her eyes, which seemed a far deeper brown than usual. Amplified in depth, almost…

Fearne glared playfully, the redness in her cheeks betraying the prospect that his words didn't affect her.

As they made their way up the driveway of their temporary home away from home, a sense of unease grabbed hold of Fearne, who failed to realise it was brought on by the sound their footsteps were refusing to make against the gravel. Of course, they had no reason to suspect that it was the universe trying to offer them their first heads up that everything was very, very wrong.

Fearne walked towards the glass-panelled double entrance doors and reached out for the handle, which refused to budge under the force she was expending.

'Ah, your greatest nemesis. Doors,' jibed Peter, now standing alongside her.

'Bloody door's locked,' said Fearne, with the tone of a surly sailor. 'And if you're referring to the time I locked your keys in your car, it could've happened to anybody!'

'Never happened to me,' said Peter, checking the door himself and quickly changing the subject upon discovering the door really was locked tight. 'We've only be gone like, what? Twenty minutes? There's no way they would have locked us out...' but his certainty wavered, as he too struggled a second time to make the handle so much as wobble.

He tapped gently on the window in an attempt to get either Hal or Jon's attention, who were both playing a game of pool. 'Back door it is,' he said, finding it weird that neither of his friends would so much as look up at him. Giving up, he set off towards the rear garden via the side access.

As Peter entered the rear garden, Kara sprung up in front of him.

'Oop! Sorry Kara!' said Peter apologetically, having nearly taken her out.

She ignored him entirely, dropping a towel and climbing into the hot tub armed with a fresh glass of Southern Comfort and Coke.

'Okaaay…'

'What's up?' asked Fearne, pulling up next to him.

'Oh, just Kara, she totally just blanked me.'

'I'm sure you just imagined it babe. Let's go inside, I could use a drink!'

'Figures,' mumbled Peter, causing her to nudge him in the ribs, and they made their way inside.

Gradually, Fearne began to notice her vision becoming partially obscured by a static mist that was slowly but surely thickening in density.

'What's up with this stuff,' said Peter, flapping a hand in an attempt to dispel the oddly unmoving and entirely intangible whiteness.

Things grew stranger, as everyone they came into contact with ignored them, until eventually Peter started to wonder if their friends were playing a prank on him. Stopping at the pool table, Peter reached out to place his hand on Hal's shoulder, his fingertips stopping a mere millimetre away from Hal's boiler suit, as a faint rumble of thunder rang out above the lodge, causing him to hesitate.

"That's not right," thought Peter.

The sky had been notable for its absence of

clouds a mere moment ago – a thought he had little time to voice – as his senses were assaulted by the sound of a tremendously powerful rush of air.

He looked to Fearne, who was scanning their surroundings, ears covered, eyes fixed firmly open.

The fog thickened around them, and Peter nodded towards the communal staircase. Fearne cracked his code, realising he was suggesting they get to higher ground, knowing the doors behind them were locked.

But as Peter began to ascend, Jasmine blocked his path. He tried to ask her what was happening, to warn her not to go downstairs. That it wasn't safe. But his words fell on ears that either chose not to hear him, or more terrifyingly, *couldn't*. Jasmine sauntered down the steps, entirely unfazed by the unfolding chaos around her, as Peter pressed his back against the banister to let her pass, and she swirled away into nothingness, erased by the mist.

The relentless cacophony of thunderous wind conspired earnestly with the impenetrable fog, which filled the ground floor like a rising tide of pristinely-white lava, and for a moment Peter felt almost certain it was coming for him specifically.

'Come on,' he shouted, the shrillness of his words muted by a world that was slowly disintegrating around him.

Fearne didn't need to hear him to *hear* him, and made her way up the staircase.

They were greeted by yet more fog, which spilled

in from the windows of the upper-level, across the kitchen counters and proceeded effortlessly on its mission to consume them, pulling them both apart, the fragments of their former-selves now blue dust on a non-existent wind, converting them into something far beyond what they could initially comprehend;

The first two individuals ever to be sent back through time at Fir Lodge.

CHAPTER TWENTY-TWO
The Repeaters

Timeline Alpha – 7th Repeat – Friday, August 24th, 2018, 12:02am

'This is incredible,' said Peter, as they re-materialised into their seventh repeat.

A term Peter had initially tried to sell to Fearne in the following way; namely by pronouncing it as "Re-Pete." But his partner was having none of that. And so, whilst she allowed him to refer to what was happening to them as "repeats", it was under the *strict* proviso that his name was not a part of the equation.

They had been spectating on their friends for seven repeats now, and Peter genuinely couldn't understand why his significant other was equally averse to naming themselves as if they were a superhero team.

'What's wrong with calling ourselves The Repeaters?' said Peter, throwing the retro-styled cordless radio over his shoulder, clearly not seeing a problem at all. He had no idea why he started every new cycle holding that thing, but without fail it was pressed between his chest and arms, every time they reformed.

Even more confounding was that, despite being unplugged from the mains, music blasted through the speakers upon each new arrival into what they now knew to be their own shared past.

Peter had spent time fiddling with the back compartment, gleaning that the device did at least appear to have a backup power source, thanks to the presence of six D-sized batteries. What he couldn't figure out was how the time-travelling-music-dispenser was somehow broadcasting what was clearly a radio signal.

He'd spent a solid twenty-or-so hours mulling that one over. How a radio receiver could pick up anything at all in their shared state was mind-boggling, but why the batteries retained their power long enough to allow for a solid one-minute-and-twenty seven seconds of uninterrupted music before dying completely, he had no idea.

Unbeknownst to Peter, the point of re-entry into the timestream brought with it a gift. One that took the form of a spike in residual energy, which transferred from his body and into the radio clutched in his grasp. Not enough to power a lithium battery of a smart-phone by any means, but just enough to send a charge into the more conventional cathodes and anodes of the batteries of old, allowing for the build up of electrons to serenade them with a song.

Always the same song; "Mr. Sandman."

Always eerie as hell.

Always fizzling out into nothingness before the song itself could finish.

'Because, honey,' began Fearne, for what felt like the one-hundredth time, 'it makes us sound like we're in a tribute folk band. And that is not as cool as you think it is. Nor is it how I want to be remembered once we get back.'

'We've re-Pete'ed, what? Seven times now? And—'

'Just stop.' said Fearne.

'What?' said Peter with as much innocence as he could muster.

'You're *doing* it again.'

'Doing what?' he said guiltily.

'Adding emphasis to the *Pete* part in *repeat*. Stop it.'

'Why are you so against that?'

'Babe, I love you. You know this. But so help me God if you call it Re-Pete'ing again I'm going to beat you to death with my stiletto.'

Peter fell silent, lamenting over how relationships could be challenging at the best of times. The way the person you live with chews their cereal, as if channelling the spirit of a cement mixer that has an inability to break down cornflakes, so just churns them over and over into infinity whilst you sit their nursing your passive aggression, stealthily turning the volume up on the TV in the tiniest of increments, taking comfort in the sweet release that will only come in four and half minutes when they finally finish the bowl and exorcise the industrial-machinery-demon that has claimed their soul for the malevolent end of breaking your own spirit for no other reason than because it can.

For example.

But there was something about time travelling together that not only highlighted these minor gripes, but also amplified them. Indeed, a fact both Peter and Fearne were quickly realising was that having only each other to talk to and interact with was not quite the holistic honeymoon either of them could have predicted.

Of course, it *was* fun at first. Downright adorable, in fact. Getting to spectate on their friends living out their lives. It was extremely eye-opening too, seeing how people acted when they believed they weren't being watched.

Case in point; Peter really didn't have Will down as the sort of man that would spend so much time rummaging within his nostrils, eager to acquire the rare nose gold that occupied the caverns within.

Whereas Fearne had always wondered how Daisy acted when she wasn't in a group environment.

Robert's wife was always so positive and happy,

giving the best advice to those who needed it. Fearne had almost expected her friend to perhaps have the mouth of a dock worker behind closed doors, possibly knocking back secret cigarettes and vodka shots. But, rather disappointingly, Daisy was every bit as wonderful to her husband when no one else was watching at all as she was when they had company.

Jerry wandered past them, then cocked his ear, turning on the spot to face them.

'Eek, hey Jerry!' said Fearne, cooing enough to make Peter recoil at the thought of the inevitable parenting that was edging ever closer.

Responding to his name, he ran over to them, his tail wagging enthusiastically.

'Wait, what's happening?' said Peter, as Jerry pounced on Fearne and began licking her out-of-phase face, each lick generating lashings of electrical energy that sparked across her skin.

'Oh no!' said Fearne, in quick realisation.

'How is that possible? We can't interact with anything or anyone here!' said Peter, utterly confused.

They had yet to figure out what had caused them to become trapped within their time-loop, the memories on the lead up to their deaths unhelpfully locked away behind a mental block that would only crumble when they were sub-consciously, and emotionally, capable of comprehending it.

It was a mercy, in this instance. For if they were aware of what had brought them here, they would have also been forced to deal with the truly awful implications of Jerry being in-phase with them; that during their last stand with their murderer, Jerry had tried to aid in Peter's escape up the staircase of Kevin's basement. That in doing so, he had put himself in the firing line of Malcolm's fury. And so it was that Jerry had become the first dog in the entire universe to become a time traveller.

A canine Restarter, or in this case, a spectating *Repeater*, that had suffered the same fate as Peter and Fearne.

CHAPTER TWENTY-THREE
The Curious Case of the Dog in the Timeline

Timeline Alpha – 49th Repeat – Saturday, August 25th, 11:27am

Having Jerry as a companion brought with it certain perks; for one thing it was far more difficult to fall into a cycle of despair over the futility of their new existence when they had his well-being to consider and, slowly but surely, the needs of the tenacious Springer spaniel superseded their own.

They played with him regularly, gave him their undivided attention in an attempt to distract him every time he tried to drink from one of the many water sources the three of them had encountered, as he was forced once again to lay down in defeat, huffing with frustration.

'Poor little guy, just can't draw a sip,' said Fearne, kneeling down on the ground next to him and ruffling his ears, the crackle of blue sparks causing his tail to wag rather than distressing him.

'Makes me glad I haven't felt thirsty the entire time we've been here,' said Peter, not for the first time wondering why on Earth that was.

They had been watching their friends from afar, and were currently following a handful of them as they embarked on their woodland walk. Having stopped to tend to Jerry, they took the opportunity to take stock of what they had observed on their latest attempt at fusing together the multitude of puzzle pieces, which made up the entirety of their thirty-three hours of repeating time.

Their friend Will was currently lamenting how they had hit a dead-end, and would need to double back on themselves in order to make it back to Fir Lodge.

'I've been thinking,' said Fearne, as Jerry ceased feeling sorry for himself, stood up, and shook out his body from nose to tail, before waddling off to sniff only God knew what. 'This thing we're caught in?'

'Repeating, you mean?' said Peter.

Fearne had finally given in and allowed Peter to refer to themselves as *Repeaters*, but it still wasn't growing on her in any substantial way.

She was honestly just tired of having to come up with new ways to describe their activity within the bubble of time they were imprisoned in.

'Suuure. Yeah, that. Something must have caused it. This can't all be random.'

'We've spent tons of repeats going over this,' Peter replied wearily. 'It always happens the same way; we drop Jerry off, return to the lodge, the creepy fog rolls in, and boom. We're right back where we started.'

"Restarted?" he thought. "Nah." Repeated was better.

'Exactly. Which indicates that whatever sent us back here happened before we returned to the party.'

'We've retraced our steps multiple times,' pointed out Peter. 'If there was something else to it, we'd have seen it by now.'

'I don't…' something was blocking Fearne from thinking clearly. As if she knew the answer to that question, but was somehow unable to articulate it. Every time she came close to forming a coherent thought, her mind drifted. 'Is it me or is it getting harder to concentrate?'

'Yeah, now that you mention it,' said Peter. 'Also, is it my imagination, or is it getting harder to focus on what the gang are saying?' he added, referring to their friends.

She'd noticed it too.

In fact, it was just another thing on a very long list of issues that were gradually filling her with a mentally debilitating sense of trepidation.

For example, Fearne couldn't help but notice the saturation that had occurred in the short time they had been away since this repeat and the last. As if someone had removed the Instagram filter on their lives and dropped the overall hue by a drastic percentage. Their last repeat had definitely been more *Mayfair*, colour wise. In stark contrast, this new loop they had entered into was more...

"Hudson," thought Fearne happily. God, she missed her phone.

Before she was stuck inside the weekend that refused to end, there was not an hour that went by when she wasn't either scrolling through her social media feed, or applying a carefully tweaked filter to a photo of the two of them. The withdrawal was accentuated by the inherent boredom that came from not being able to interact with anything in the physical world. All they had with them was the retro cordless radio that Peter was clutching every time they started over.

"Start-Over," she thought. That sounded marginally better than repeats.

*

After a short while, their canine cohort decided it was time to lead Peter and Fearne away from the woods and back the way they came.

He had taken them under his wing ever since he had discovered they could see him. It had been driving the poor dog crazy for his first handful of trips back through time; unable to interact with anyone, especially his dad. Despite the fact he had no real comprehension of the passage of time, Jerry had felt constantly burdened by his ineffectual attempts at falling back in-favour with the humans at Fir Lodge. He had tried all manner of things to make it back into their good graces, hoping to regain his status of being a good boy.

That had all changed on his fourth trip into the past. Just as he was starting to suspect that he was, in reality, a bad dog – as if he were being punished for a crime he could not remember committing – the humans were having another meeting and eating food. He really couldn't believe his luck at how predictable this group of people were when it came to when they ate.

It had taken Jerry a while to find his way back to them, what with not having the advantage of his sense of smell, which had only recently become unreliable. Instead, he had to focus on actually learning the way to where the food would be.

However, as his dad had often told him, he was a clever boy, and had mastered the route much faster than even he would have expected, were it possible for Jerry to quantify such an arbitrarily redundant musing as "trial and error."

He simply repeated a task until it yielded results. Or it didn't.

It was only when he entered the garden and saw another dog just like him, breaching his territory without so much as a customary sniff that he'd had enough. Not even a sign of bowing in submissive appreciation.

That annoyed Jerry, and he decided he could not stand for it.

He ran at the dog and barked for attention, entirely unaware that he was barking at his past-self, what with never having seen his own reflection in three dimensions before. Jerry's past-self was immediately aware of his presence, and after scoffing a sausage given to him by a woman he would later understand to be called "Ra-ra", he sauntered off to give his time-travelling self some space.

Jerry the Restarter had tried and tried to eat the scraps of food that had fallen beneath the picnic bench, until eventually realising his attempts were pointless.

It was during this futile endeavour that he first caught wind of a new scent; one that smelled like rain and thunder, two things that usually put him on edge, but in this instance had led him to the only two humans that could see him; Peter and Fearne.

After three more jumps back into his own past, he had finally managed to track them down. And now, here he was, weeks later, still teaming up with the only two people he could sense and smell in the same way he could when he was alive.

With a jolt, Jerry was pulled from his own doggish thoughts as he realised they were approaching his home. Jerry felt a surge of discomfort, for reasons he couldn't quite rationalise. Partly, because he was a dog, but equally because his long-term memory was uncharacteristically shrouded by a feeling of confusion. He knew he should be rushing home to see his dad, who would surely be worried about him. But something was repelling him from that place, as if a crow-scarer resided within the humble lodge, waiting to generate a huge bang if he so much as thought about returning. Or worse, a handsy child with jam-covered fingers eager to ruin his day by making his coat all sticky.

Jerry shuddered at the prospect of that.

He adjusted the route he was taking, and gave the lodge that was once his home a wide berth, drawing the attention of a very astute Fearne.

*

'That's the second time he's done that,' noted Fearne, as she observed Jerry dodging out of the road to stay away from his home.

'Hmm,' said Peter absently, wondering if he could influence any of his friends to put the footie on this afternoon.

They had learnt that the power of suggestion seemed to result in a feedback loop of sorts; if he said the same words over and over enough, sometimes his past-self would repeat them back in the past as he uttered them. But with two words being his record, he was trying to determine the best phrase to utter in the hope it would lead to a tangible decision being made. "Football on, maybe?"

'Pete, have you been listening to a word I've been saying?'

He turned around to face Fearne, who had stopped and was standing several yards behind him, now outside Kevin's lodge.

Jerry, meanwhile, was hunched down in the long grass on the opposite side of the road to them, having none of what he assumed was going down.

'Of course?' he said, knowing full well this was a trap.

Regrettably, the rising in his voice coupled with the end of his response sounded suspiciously like he was asking a question, rather than stating a cold, hard fact.

'Oh Lordy, Peter.'

Fearne ran a hand through her long brunette-coloured hair, utterly crushed that even when she was the only other person on the entire planet that he could interact with, he had still managed to find a way to not listen to her.

He tried to disarm her with his trademark smoulder, but Fearne couldn't be bought.

'Don't you give me that look,' she said, the dimples in her cheeks, as always, betraying her attempt at conveying true anger. 'I *said*, what if we've been thinking about this all wrong? What's the one thing you come back with every time a repeat is triggered?'

'You?' said Peter, trying his best to regain ground, but ultimately still being the worst at paying attention.

'Yes Peter, ten points to bloody Gryffindor for stating the obvious. I meant *besides* Jerry and me.'

'Oh, the radio!'

'More specifically, the radio from Jerry's place!' she said, mimicking the build-up just like she recalled Hal did whenever he geared up towards a mic-drop moment.

'So, you're saying we should put it back?' said Peter, still rather lost.

'What the fu–? No! How would that even remotely…' she took a breath and exhaled sharply. 'I'm *saying,* that whatever happened to us may have a connection to this place. I say we spend the remainder of this weekend here!'

Seeing no reason other than the rambunctious shiver that ran down his spine and filled his stomach with dread, Peter reluctantly agreed to Fearne's proposal, unaware that this decision would send ripples across time that would come back to hit them like a tidal wave when they finally reached the shore that represented their future.

CHAPTER TWENTY-FOUR
The Lake of the Damned

Timeline Alpha – 486th Repeat – Friday,
August 24th, 12:02pm

They landed abruptly into a fresh loop, as Peter clutched on to the memory he was replaying in his mind prior to the previous thirty-three-hours coming to their natural end. He had been running over the events they had witnessed all those repeats ago.

Even now, knowing what they knew, having seen it with their own temporally-discombobulated eyes, it didn't seem real. Like watching someone else's lives play out. Literally, it turned out, to the bitter end. Seeing their own deaths had given Peter nothing if not a darker sense of humour.

He shook away the already-fuzzy memory, pulling himself back to whatever constituted the present. After a relentlessly tumultuous fling with the harsh mistress known as "trial and error", the Repeaters had at least discovered a powerful secret that lurked within their own fragmented consciousness; a ferociously versatile energy that imbued them with a monumental amount of leverage against the rising tide of their circular nightmare.

They had initially dismissed the short bursts of static shocks they continually experienced when connecting with each other in their own past, incorrectly assuming it held no purpose other than to keep them exactly that. *Apart*. But they eventually stumbled across the game-changing side-effects that prolonged contact afforded them.

During a particularly dismal repeat, they had broken down, collapsing in each other's arms as their memories began to fail, finding themselves truly on the cusp of being swallowed up by the ruthless timestream that held them captive. This sadness had led to a passionate embrace between the two of them; one fuelled by both their undying love for one another, and their intense will to rebel against the backwards laws of physics of what they understandably presumed to be the afterlife.

The resulting surge of feedback had changed everything and, for the first time, they experienced an invigorating sense of hope. The colours of their bleak surroundings had been restored, *returned* to them, the sun once more collided with their skin and allowed for the sensation of heat to warm their previously moderated body temperatures, and their friends even came back into focus, no longer the shadowy echoes they had devolved into. Even the faint smell of flame-grilled burgers and sausages filled their noses once more, reminding them of what it felt like to be hungry for the first time in what they had, at the time, worked out to be several months.

They learnt that they could move small objects, and in some instances even larger items, as long as they remained in close proximity to their past-selves.

It was glorious.

Until it wasn't.

Over time, the power faded, as did their memories of one another. And suddenly, they found themselves faced with a new problem they didn't even know they were fighting; after all, what good could come from the knowledge that sustained contact was the key to engaging with the past, when the person sitting opposite you had become a total stranger.

As the fire of their love for one another was doused by the oppressive fog which clouded their minds with each jump back into the past, those feelings transcended into unadulterated confusion.

They recognised that they were significant to each other, and the music playing throughout their time-loop afforded them brief respite; like air pockets in the heart of a cave that gave them a chance to remember what they meant to one another all over again.

But sure enough, those moments became more and more fleeting, and they would often wander aimlessly throughout their repeats, sometimes ending up deep in the woods, far away from music, their thoughts and shared connection growing ever more tenuous.

And so it was that they found themselves re-materialising into yet another repeat of days gone by, as Peter took advantage of the brief charge that ran through their veins every time they were hurtled back to the beginning of their journey.

He clutched the radio he had reappeared with, and reached out for Fearne's hand before she had a chance to object. The contact fizzled between them, and he looked deeply into her beautiful, brown eyes.

'We're getting out of here' said Peter, a grim look of determination on his face, one greatly accentuated by his strong jawline, which was made all the more prominent thanks to the way he was clenching his teeth.

'How,' said Fearne, her voice barely a murmur.

'Through the forest. We'll keep going until we're as far away from this place as possible.' He lowered his voice and moved closer to her. 'To somewhere not even time can catch us,' he muttered, as if it made a difference.

Fearne became excited. She had a faint memory that she possessed vague evidence this would never work, though she couldn't remember precisely how or why she knew this. She blinked the thoughts away, intoxicated by the prospect of freedom, and instead agreed with…

"Peter, his name is Peter," she said to herself sternly, the charge between them keeping the integrity of her mind afloat in the sea of haziness. A lake that was lapping over the sides of the dingy which represented her consciousness, threatening to capsize and flip them into a deeper purgatory.

'Let's go,' she said, and they shared a mischievous smile.

This would work.

She knew it.

*

Not wishing to waste a single second, Peter and Fearne ran towards the grey haze of what was once Will's red car, treading lightly on the bonnet, onto the roof, and over the rear of the car, their feet hitting the shingle of the driveway without so much as a single crunch.

'Yeah, these have to go,' said Fearne, kicking off her stiletto heels as she remembered, albeit for a second, that she wouldn't feel pain by running barefoot.

They set off again, their pace brisk, running along the road at first, waiting for an opening in the surrounding woodland, due to it offering the least resistance. They passed lodges they didn't recognise, and flew past the humanoid shadows that they knew were once the fully-defined tenants of their own history. They could feel the charge building between them, splashes of arcing blue energy spitting from their interconnected hands like oil hitting a naked flame.

Their own thoughts intermingled, and they telepathically agreed to channel that energy into their increasing momentum, not wishing to waste it on repairing their fractured recollections. They had a singular goal; escape.

They were travelling so fast through the thickets, trees and foliage that they didn't even so much as glance at another horizontal shadow that had become clearer than the rest, thanks to their self-restoring residual charge. A tall, dark man that was unloading various folders and items, including unseen syringes filled with green liquid, into a nearby shack. Nor would they have understood his significance due to their current cognitive dissonance.

They traversed steep inclines, burst through numerous clearings, vaulted over rocks and vehicles and fences, cutting through the Pentney Lakes like a lightsaber through Darth Maul, until finally, they reached their last hurdle; an expansive lake that stretched out all the way into the perceivable horizon.

They glanced at each other, understanding that this was the last test, the last obstacle keeping them from vanquishing whatever it was that was keeping them here. In order to escape the laws that governed them, they would need to break the rules. They would need to stop thinking like they were alive, and start fighting like their souls depended on it.

They would have to swim.

They jumped as one into the water, preparing for the longest swim either of them had ever attempted. The water remained undisturbed, their invasive presence causing not so much as a ripple.

Curiously, as they waded further in, their actions were devoid of aforementioned wade. They were simply walking, as the water level rose to their waist, then crept slowly up their chests, like a holographic simulation of what water used to be.

Fearne took a deep breath, and pressed onwards, as she stepped further into the lightless murkiness, and the water level reached her nostrils, before engulfing her head. She panicked, her eyes widening, finding herself involuntarily flapping her head from side to side, trying to regain buoyancy. Despite her temporally-compromised mind, she still possessed a deeply innate muscle memory, knowing that she could not breath underwater.

In her panic, she completely forgot that all she needed to do was go back the way she came. That the rising tide would not engulf her if she walked her way back across the riverbed. She waved her arms frantically, trying to part the water surrounding her, unable to reconcile in her mind that the water was little more than an illusion. But the oppressive fathoms harboured an uncertainty that grew exponentially with each passing moment.

With her vision obscured by the watery haze, her other senses became heightened, her fear of drowning flooding her body with an incredible blast of blue energy. It was then that she felt something grab her hand, and she flinched as it pulled her forwards, before hearing a familiar voice in her head, who she knew to be Peter.

"It's *okay*,' the voice said soothingly. "We can *breathe*."

She relaxed, and opened her eyes, realising that against all odds, she trusted the voice with every fibre of her being. Fearne gasped for air, expecting her lungs to fill with the submerged plant life and green hued river water, her body instead filling with something far less life-threatening; *relief*.

They moved through the darkness, not wanting to push their luck by talking, steeling glances at the unsettling visuals of sunlight dancing across the water above them. Slowly, as the fear ebbed away, it became fascinating. They were viewing the world from a perspective no one had ever witnessed before.

They picked up their pace, unimpeded by the water. In fact, it felt identical to running on dry land, due to the silt of the riverbed refusing to give way under their out-of-phase weight. The only notable difference arriving in the form of a large carp, that appeared from nowhere and passed through both their faces, along with schools of smaller fish which proceeded undeterred through their bodies.

And then they heard it; the sound of rushing air.

A truly soul-destroying notion filled Fearne's mind, as she remembered precisely how she knew this wouldn't work.

Though they had never taken this particular path, they *had* done this before. Different routes, different paths, but it all ended the same way. As they reached an unmarked point in their journey, the fog always caught up to them.

She gasped, not for air, but in horror, her eyes filling with tears of desperation as the memories of every single repeat came flooding back to her in a way the water that surrounded her never could.

Peter and Fearne hadn't merely dabbled with this plan several times. They had already tried it two-hundred and *sixteen* times.

As their two-hundredth-and-seventeenth attempt was slowly but surely obliterated by the static fog, she knew it did so with a singular purpose; to whisk them away from the lake.

A lake of the damned.

To send them back to the beginning of their thirty-three-hour time loop.

With a heart as broken as her mind was fractured, she collapsed on to the river bed, bringing her knees up to her chest, and wept until she *too* was atomised, and sucked back into hell.

CHAPTER TWENTY-FIVE
Sins of The Past

795th Repeat

After just shy of eight-hundred do-overs, the reluctant time travellers were mere echoes of their former selves. In truth, they had lost all recollection of exactly how long they had truly been there.

Their memories were shot to hell, and it took virtually all they had just to remember their own names, let alone each other. Mistrust and suspicion had resulted in the Repeaters wasting many of their chances to set things right.

Today was one of those mornings.

They sat there in Fir Lodge, glaring at each other. Both trying to ascertain the hidden agenda of the other. What was once a hyper-realistic ocean of colour was now an immaculate, white hellscape, dust motes around them falling like snowfall, swirling back into the air whenever they reached out for them, unable to settle. Every item in the lodge had lost detail, now mere shapes that resembled the things they actually were. The place felt more like a pristine sanatorium now, rather than the holiday retreat it once was.

Shadows of people they almost remembered as being real wandered the halls like mumbling spectres, reliving their history, completely oblivious to the presence of the two of them, who were little more than ghostly spectators of a past that had no desire to include them.

Suddenly, noise erupted throughout the lodge; a deafening assault to what remained of their consciousness that initially terrified them both. The sound of rushing air flooded their eardrums, coupling with the sound of an other-worldly gong which exacerbated their mutual confusion.

For a brief moment, their senses were bombarded by a disembodied hovering noise, reminiscent to that of an alien spacecraft, which sounded as if it were potentially descending upon them, ready to end this eternal torment and release them from the purgatory that they were indefinitely detained in, like the waiting room of an unstaffed doctor's surgery, or the queue of a post office.

An ethereal cheering emanating from an unseen

crowd followed, unsettling them further, leading them to the alternative possibility that they were the unwilling participants in some form of Truman Show-esque social experiment.

And then they heard syllables, which slowly evolved into words, and then matured into sentences, until, eventually, their minds deciphered what was happening.

Music.

It was music! The man recognised the voice as being that of Michael Jackson. The woman, meanwhile, recognised the track itself as being "Dirty Diana." Their mutual suspicion and inexplicably misappropriated hatred drained away from them, their cerebral synapses permitting them once again to see each other for who they really were. At least to the point where they knew they could trust one another.

The unexpected distraction cut through the tension that was lingering between them like a serrated blade. A metaphor that seemed ironic, though Peter struggled to remember exactly why.

'Jesus, that was a long one!' said the woman. The man couldn't quite remember her name just yet.

'Yeah, how long were we out, do you think?' asked the man. 'Hours?'

'Felt like days.'

They both took a deep breath, shaking off the aftershock of a fight they couldn't remember having.

'We can't go on like this,' said the man. 'We can't even work together anymore,' he added, remembering the sense of self-imposed isolation they had both been indulging in for the past goodness knew how long.

The woman hesitated, as his name took shape in her mind, finally revealing itself to her once again.

'Peter,' she said. 'I love you. You know that, right?

'I know...*Fearne*,' said Peter, hoping his memories hadn't betrayed him and that he'd gotten her name right. He placed his head into his palms, rubbing his sockets firmly, then looked up at her, knowing once more who the woman sitting in front of him truly was.

A tear rolled down the dark skin of his face, as the devastation that he had almost forgotten her again sunk in.

The music afforded them an additional bonus, as the entirety of their memories began drip-feeding back into their minds.

'We need to get out of here,' said Peter. 'Maybe try to leave again?'

'What's the point. You know it just leads to another...*reset*.'

Another bout of funnelled air filled the room, and the Repeaters recoiled reflexively. It was far more visceral than the music, evoking a sense of stomach-churning dread that they gradually recognised as the harbinger of a repeat; the phenomena Fearne slowly remembered as being what they were currently the slaves of.

'That can't be right,' said Fearne. 'It's not dark

yet…'

As they covered their ears, preparing themselves for their inevitable journey back thirty-three hours into the past, they were instead greeted by the presence of a tall, muscular man, who materialised at the top of the communal staircase.

The man brushed away the imaginary dust from his trousers and approached them in the communal living area.

Fearne hopped up off of what she had forgotten was her favourite sofa and stood next to Peter, who remained seated, but leant forward protectively.

'No need to be afraid,' said the man. 'I've been watching you for some time. Quite the pickle you're in,' he added, grinning from ear to ear.

'You can *see* us?!' said Peter, a duality to his tone that revealed both fear and relief. It had been so long since they had been able to speak to anyone but each other.

'See you, *hear* you, but most importantly of all, I can *help* you,' said the man. 'I'm just like you. Travelling through time, trying to find my way home. Say, you wouldn't happen to know what day it is, would you?'

The question, as intended, threw both Peter and Fearne on the back foot. Instead of questioning their impossible guest, they found themselves engaging with him in conversation. They had no way of knowing this was one of the man's "go to" diversion tactics when marking a new target; lure them in with banality. After all, time traveller or not, human beings were conditioned to abide by simplistic social cues. It had been a challenge for him, a sociopathic outsider, to learn how to manipulate that.

'Saturday. I think,' said Fearne, not entirely sure the information she was providing was accurate.

'Splendid,' said the man, clapping his hands together loudly, the sound distracting them once again like a well-timed magician's flourish. 'That means we can do this tonight, if we play our cards right. Maybe one or two tries for good measure, depending on how well we work together.'

'Do *what* tonight?' said Peter, wholly lost.

'Why, *escape* this place, of course!' said the man. 'My goodness, I haven't even asked you your names. How rude of me,' he said, extending his palms towards them in an open gesture, implying the friendly transparency of camaraderie.

'Fearne. And this is Peter.'

'You seem like a wonderful couple. You *are* together, I assume?'

They nodded in unison.

'And who are *you* exactly?' said Peter, softening his tone, entirely sucked in by the man's charm.

'I go by a few names,' said the man. 'But to my friends…well, they call me Malcolm,' he added, taking several strides towards Peter, and extending his hand.

Peter followed suit, and recoiled as the energy surged between them, ripples of blue and red energy arcing between their hands as they shook.

As they pulled apart, Peter felt notably drained, his mind foggy once again.

'I've never seen the energy go that colour before,' said Peter, genuinely excited despite his tiredness.

Any change to their routine at this point was a welcome one.

Malcolm smiled, baring his predatorial teeth, the sudden danger Peter was in entirely lost on him. Unbeknownst to this younger, greener – in terms of time travel at least – version of Peter and Fearne, this was not the Malcolm from either their past or present, but the version of Malcolm from their soon-to-be future. The Malcolm who would later bring both Restarters and Repeaters together. But before he could do that, there were things that needed to be done. Events that needed to be set in motion. And Restarters that would not be born at all until he fixed this particular wrinkle in time.

'Oh, there's a *lot* about this place you don't know,' said Malcolm reassuringly. 'Come on then, no time to waste. Follow me,' he added, turning around and heading back down the communal staircase.

As the two of them watched him make his way down the stairs, Peter leaned in to Fearne.

'I have a really good feeling about this, Fearne,' he muttered, in a hushed undertone.

Fearne, on the other hand, felt the complete opposite, as a rogue memory attempted to force its way to the forefront of her mind. She couldn't shake the feeling they had met this man before. Like the memory of a memory of a dream. Unfocused, fragmented. But in her current state, out-of-phase for however many years it had been, it was simply beyond the realm of her capabilities to remember just how important that information was to them.

*

'It's done,' repeated Peter, echoing his thoughts by presenting the words to his cohorts.

Malcolm grimaced. He was losing them. It felt like trying to herd cattle into an invisible enclosure. One that regularly vanished and reappeared elsewhere between blinks.

Why he alone was able to maintain his own focus was a mystery to him. He had travelled more than either of the young couple standing before him, whose minds were becoming increasingly afflicted by the addling after-burn of reductive amnesia. The pride within him made him reason it was his sheer *will* that kept him grounded, though he knew deep down – and from first-hand experience – that this character-trait alone would not have kept him from falling foul of the insidious fog.

In the end he suspected that it had more than a little to do with the manner in which he had cut the tether to his present and future, by turning off his own life-support at the hospital.

Malcolm placed a heavy hand on each of their shoulders, creating a bridge between them, one that was illuminated by both the red energy that flowed through him and small splutters of the remaining blue energy within the meek individuals he was trying to wrangle.

'We are far from done, Peter,' said Malcolm, his voice forceful yet somehow calm, as if articulating the words would assist Peter in his rapidly decreasing ability to process them. 'We have rearranged the board to aid our escape, but there is one more crucial component for us to implement.'

Fearne remembered now, infused by the energy she was siphoning, thanks to the connection to Peter and their self-proclaimed saviour. The sun-drenched garden making the blades of grass look like a flowing ocean of gold water, as they were flicked by the cool mid-morning breeze.

She felt drained again, stealing a glance to her shoulder, seeing the red energy spiralling savagely, and realised all too late that they had placed their trust in a man who almost certainly possessed a more convoluted agenda that he was willing to share with them.

But as she looked upwards and into the eyes of Peter, who was gazing back at her with moistened eyes of sadness, she made a choice; she knew how far she was willing to go in order to return to the world of the living, to a time where she could once again hold him in her arms.

'To the end and back,' she muttered, a single tear running down her cheek.

*

They moved quickly, as Fearne rushed up the central

staircase of Fir Lodge, waiting for her instructions. Meanwhile, Peter and Malcolm headed into Robert's bedroom.

The two men waited patiently, standing there in the dark, utterly silent, arms interlocked, until Peter's past-self finally entered the room, on his predetermined path of seeking a phone charger.

Malcolm closed the door behind the Repeater's past-self as he entered, and they edged as one towards the living, breathing version of Peter.

'Now,' said Malcolm, barking the order.

And together, they plunged their free hands into the brain of Peter's living facsimile, red and blue energy spiralling wildly from the connection.

Peter's alive-self took a step forward, seemingly trying to fight against whatever unseen force was assaulting his physical form.

Drawing on both the energy being produced by his contact with Peter's time-travelling self –which held considerable potency, given the proximity the two Peter's were currently sharing – and his own brand of equally powerful, red-coloured energy, Malcolm pushed the Peter of the past against the wall.

It was working.

"Just a little longer…" thought Malcolm.

Malcolm noticed a flicker of blue light to his right, dancing just outside the realms of his peripheral vision. A mere glimmer, but it signified something more…they were being watched. Someone was spying on them, invading their realm of existence.

The flicker of blue took on a more prominent shape; that of two jet-black bodies.

Malcolm had come too far to allow an unexpected intrusion to ruin everything, so he leaned closer towards the wisps of blue light, hoping it would scare whatever, or *whoever*, it was back to whence they came.

His vision was suddenly filled by the arrival of two featureless entities. Their forms began to take a more stable state, and Malcolm turned his head slightly, facing Peter's alive-self once more.

"There you are," thought Malcolm, as he saw an additional two arms come into focus. Arms that were also reaching into Peter's body.

Peter's alive-self spoke, though it was impossible to tell if he was talking to Malcolm, to his time-travelling self, or to the two intruders, as he muttered but five broken words;

'Ha-Hal? Karrr? M-my f-ft. Mist…'

Malcolm knew what he was doing here would lead to Harold and Kara inheriting the restarts of Peter and Fearne, but their presence here, between phases was unexpected. Had they found a way to traverse through The White Lodge? Surely not. Though it was a concern.

Malcolm peered closer, reducing the gap between his own face and that of the Restarters. It seemed to do the trick, as the humanoid black shapes vanished. If they could travel between the timelines like he had mastered then–

'What's *The White Lodge*?' asked the Repeating

version of Peter.

Malcolm froze. This was his first time encountering the inherent degree of telepathy between time travellers. A by-product that occurred when the temporally-afflicted connected for any length of time. In this case, the connection between Peter, his past self and Malcolm had apparently led to an irksome transference of thoughts.

'It's nothing,' lied Malcolm. 'We're done here,' he added, noting that the intruders had vanished.

He signalled to Peter that he could pull away from his physical form.

'Now, if you'll excuse me,' said Malcolm curtly, 'I need to assist Fearne.'

*

Fearne waited impatiently, wringing her hands with anxiety.

For a moment, she wondered if Malcolm would show at all, as he bounded up the stairs just in time, striding towards her like an army general. Fearne's focus was bolstered by the music filling the room, the catchy beat of "Spirit in the Sky" laced with irony, as the lyrics hit her hard.

Malcolm grabbed Fearne's arm and nodded, signalling for her to mimic his action of thrusting his hand into the head of Fearne's alive-self who promptly became dizzy, falling forwards towards the staircase. Stacey caught her just in time, and escorted her temporarily-dazed friend to one of the communal sofas.

And with that, the deed was done.

Peter and Fearne departed through the rear garden and kept walking, needing to distance themselves from the music that kept them anchored to their memories, eager to forget that in order to escape their damnation, they had made a deal with the devil. That the price for their freedom was as devastating as it was simple; they had sacrificed the lives of two of their closest friends, sentencing them to a death they wouldn't see coming, and could do nothing to stop.

For a brief moment Peter wondered if those two friends would have to make the same trade for their own freedom. Would they have been able to find another way? Another solution? Or would they *too* sentence people they loved to an eternal nightmare?

He knew that together they…that *he*…what were their names? He couldn't remember. The fog was coming, and they were standing too far away from the music inside the building behind them to fortify their senses. Despite the wave of temporal dissonance, the side-effects he was experiencing did little to combat the burning sensation he felt in his throat.

The two spectators watched the events unfolding before them from a distance, everything playing out in the same order it always did, hoping they had done enough. The young man looked over to the woman standing beside him, a stranger to him once again…and yet, at the same time…somehow not. Her presence was simultaneously a comfort, and a horrifying reminder that everything was wrong.

He blinked to release the tears that were building up in his eyes, like a wall of doubt, blurring his vision. His throat burned with regret, for a sin he could barely remember, one that he also had no desire to clutch on to any longer.

Why did his throat hurt? What was he upset about? Who was the woman walking beside him?

And as his body disintegrated, it felt like he was falling head first into a bottomless ocean of white mist; a fog paradoxically static, yet seemingly shifting with a life all its own.

It suffocated him like a pillow being pressed against his face, preventing him from drawing breath.

As he tried to lash out at the force pressing down on him, he realised he no longer had arms with which to do so. Until, finally, there was nothing but the sweet release of darkness.

CHAPTER TWENTY-SIX
The Offer

Timeline Delta – 167th Restart – Friday, August 24th, 12:48pm

Hal and Kara sat there in silence, unpacking all of the information Peter and Fearne had just unloaded onto them, both with a look on their faces that seemed to say they were sorry they'd asked.

'But instead of returning home, we found ourselves back here,' mumbled Peter. 'Then you guys showed up. We didn't know what was happening...so we just…'

'Ran with it,' said Fearne. 'Until we had a better understanding of what we were dealing with.'

Kara and Hal remained silent.

'Say something, *please*,' said Fearne, unable to handle the prolonged stares of judgment.

'All this time…' said Kara finally.

'…It was *you* that brought us here,' said Hal quietly. '*Trapped* us here. Left us to *die*.'

'It's not as simple as that,' said Fearne defensively.

'I mean, it kind of *is,* though,' said Hal angrily.

'Hal, we didn't know what we were doing until it was too—'

'I can't even look at you both right now,' said Hal cutting Peter off. 'If you're asking me to feel sorry for you, magic 8-Ball says *not bloody likely*. The only one I feel sorry for is poor Jerry!'

'Kara?' said Fearne, hoping her friend could understand.

But Kara was equally lost for words, clearly unable to process the huge bomb of knowledge that had just been dropped on top of them.

'Let's…we need to talk to Malcolm,' said Kara, eager to dodge further questions. '*Future*-Malcolm,' she added, in an attempt to snap Hal out of his thousand-yard scowl.

'Yeah.' said Hal distantly. 'Sure.'

*

Armed with the full picture on exactly what Peter and Fearne had done to escape their incarceration, they silently marched to Kevin's home, where they hoped to find the once and future Malcolm.

The Restarters were relieved to find him sitting in

the same chair, waiting patiently.

Malcolm wasted little time, seemingly oblivious to the tension radiating between the four potentially-former friends.

'I must admit,' said Malcolm happily, 'I didn't think you'd succeed on your first attempt. Bravo.'

'Save the kudos, Kujo,' said Hal, needing answers more than he needed false praise. 'Why are we still here? We played your game, restarted the past. How are we even *talking* right now?'

'All in good time,' said Malcolm, clearly revelling in the power he had over them. 'Saving Peter was just the beginning. That was the day I was meant to escape from this place, but we're now occupying a restart unlike anything we have encountered before. Something of a blank slate, as it were.'

'What are you talking about?' said Peter.

'As I said before,' said Malcolm, pointing towards Hal and Kara, 'the two of you escaped after – how many restarts was it?'

'One, six, five,' said Kara through gritted teeth.

'Ah yes,' said Malcolm, as if he didn't already know that.

And so, it began, as Malcolm filled them in on every facet of his *own* journey.

How he had been defeated by Hal and Kara no less than thirteen years ago, relatively speaking.

What followed after that fateful encounter came to be known to him as The Dark Days; after they had vanquished him, he had spent two of those years reliving their 165th restart over and over, focusing squarely on revenge. It had proven to be a fruitless pursuit, however. One that had ultimately resulted in him having to make peace with the fact that he would have to let the two Restarters go.

His shift in focus led to a revelation; by concentrating on a more realistic goal, that of *escape* from the endless loops in time, he was able to act far more productively. Especially once he had deduced how being dislocated from time came with some unexpected new abilities. Most potently of which, after many restarts, was the discovery of being able to communicate with his alive-self, albeit indirectly at first.

'You found a way to communicate with yourself in the past?' said Hal, barely able to hide how impressed he was by that. 'How is that even possible?'

Kara thought back to when she had witnessed the first evidence of this being *more* than possible, during their 165th restart.

The Big One.

She had casually uttered "go team" to herself, and her alive-self had mimicked the exact same words. Kara had thought little of it at the time, what with everything being on the line, and there being far more pressing matters to contend with.

Was it really that much of a stretch for Malcolm to have made the quantum-leap to perfect this method of cross-phase communication? It suddenly all made sense to Kara.

'He's relying on the repetition of it all,' she said. 'Using the restarts as a tool to communicate his thoughts through time, all the way into the present! Or past. You know what I mean. Malcolm 2.0 is manipulating Malcolm 1.0! That's how he's changing everything.'

'That is…*exactly* right Kara,' said Malcolm, realising he had grossly underestimated her. 'Though the consequences are far more dangerous than my Restarter-self is willing to admit. By attempting to control his alive-self in the past, he is unwittingly creating a *feedback loop*, preventing my considerably more-corporeal self from forming new thoughts of his own.'

'You mean *alive*-you can't make decisions of his own anymore?' asked Fearne.

'Not whilst my Restarter-self is there, like the proverbial devil, resting on my own shoulder, no. I surmise this is one of the discerning factors that has resulted in my being comatose in the present.'

'Wait, coma?' said Peter, confused already.

'Patience,' said Malcolm, and he continued with his story. 'In the additional two years that followed, I finally succeeded in changing the course of events of your 165th restart by trading Peter's life for the two of yours. Destiny returned me to a new present, with no memory of this cursed life.'

'That explains the funeral,' Hal mumbled to Kara, who nodded gravely. "But not the coffee shop," he thought, slowly sliding off his backpack enough to retrieve his trusty notebook, whilst Malcolm surged onwards.

Time, it seemed, had changed around them to account for the changes Malcolm had made by sacrificing Peter.

'But, alas,' said Malcolm, his words heavy. 'It didn't last. I found myself back here, in these wretched woods. I had no idea back then that my return was instigated by my own intervention here today.'

'When you sent us to save Peter just now,' said Hal, piecing it together. 'You changed your own future. Why?' he added, confused by why anyone would return here by choice.

'I was stuck. What we have changed today will eventually result in all of us escaping. That version of myself included. But...I will awake in an Intensive Care Unit on the most elusive of days for those of our…ilk. Sunday the 26th. You think 165 restarts is bad? Try thousands. Eight years, Harold. In twelve-hour chunks. Inside a single room. In the end, I will then pull the plug on my own life support.'

Left comatose, a new anomaly in space time had manifested that day, trapping him in another time-loop reserved just for him. And for a further eight, bitter years, he waited. Defeated, shamed, Malcolm was left with nothing but a cup of anger and a side dish of damaged pride, doomed to spend an eternity staring at his own fragile body.

It was torturous, knowing the body before him

would never wake from its vegetative state. For him, his hospitalised time-loop triggered automatically every twelve hours, meaning that every twelve hours of healing his body went through was undone with each new restart.

The horrifying truth had dawned on him quickly; he could never recover.

As the black fog had thickened, and the red energy within him faded, he explained to his captive audience how he eventually forgot who he was entirely. Everything that drove him faded away. Even his years of murdering the innocent felt less like reality, and more like fever dreams. But one singular desire remained; freedom.

'Black fog?' asked Peter.

'Yes, the fog that claims you when it's time to start over,' said Malcolm, as if he were explaining something as obvious as how online shopping worked.

The four Restarters shifted uncomfortably.

'Out with it,' said Malcolm impatiently.

'Well,' said Peter, clearing his throat awkwardly. 'It's just…well, the fog is always *white* for us, right guys?' he said, directing his question to Hal and Kara, suddenly worrying he had made the assumption for the four of them based solely on his and Fearne's experiences.

'Yeah,' said Kara. 'I guess serial killers get a different package than us mere normal folk.'

Malcolm pursed his lips, clearly intrigued. He had

heard Peter and Fearne discuss the white fog during his time with them, of course, but had never outrightly confronted them on it.

It seemed of little importance now, as Malcolm moved on to how the eight years he had spent within the confines of that hospital had far more pressing, unprecedented side-effects.

Being separated from his physical body allowed the imbalances in his perception of what was real, and what was not, to go full circle. Eventually, as the trauma from his younger years faded into nothingness, he was finally able to view his life from a unique perspective. One that was far more objective and rational.

All of this ultimately led to the bold masterstroke of switching off his own life support. Sending a third Malcolm, one from the future, back into the past. Free to explore their shared bubble of time entirely without limits.

'What do you mean, *without limits*?' asked Kara.

'Without *boundaries*,' said Malcolm, simply. 'Unseen and unheard unless I specifically chose otherwise, but ultimately being unable to affect any of my surroundings. Unless connected to another Restarter, of course,' he added, stealing a glance at Peter, who broke eye-contact immediately.

Malcolm became a phantom, tethered only to the thirty-three hours of perpetuated time; to when his physical form had first arrived at Pentney Lakes. Though his transcendence still held caveats.

'Despite my best efforts, I cannot travel further back in time than the 24th of August 2018. Nor can I travel forward further than Saturday the 25th, up to the very moment Hal and Kara here *killed* me in the real world for the first time.'

'Hang on, what do you mean, *killed* you?!' said Peter.

'Wait,' said Hal, the cogs turning and ignoring the totally skewed use of the word "killing". 'Why can you only go as far as Saturday?'

Malcolm looked at him strangely, as if Hal had missed all of the most important details and was honing in on something utterly irrelevant.

'Don't look at me like I'm honing in on something totally irrelevant,' said Hal, understanding his glare with perfect clarity. 'If you wound up in a hospital on Sunday, getting trapped in a whole new restart chain, why are you stuck here and not there?'

Malcolm shifted his weight from one foot to the other, clearing his throat as if wanting to change the subject.

'Oh, come on,' said Hal in utter disbelief. 'You've been back here, what, a whole *year*? And you've never once tried to go further?'

'That,' said Malcolm defensively, 'is when the restart triggers. Every time,' he added, thinking both backwards and forwards to the day he had technically taken his own life by switching off his life support. He had no desire to ever revisit that point in his life. 'My time there changed me. I am not the monster I once was.'

It was all incredibly convincing, with one minor exception;

'So, you're saying,' said Fearne, 'that the time you spent in solitary confinement has left you, what's the word?'

'You're saying you're *reformed*?' said Kara, equally unconvinced.

'Yes. I suppose I am,' said Malcolm. 'I thought that would have been evidenced when I helped you save Peter's life?'

'That's…a *lot* to ask of us Malcolm,' said Hal. 'To *accept* at face value, I mean.'

'Well,' said Malcolm matter-of-factly, 'fortunately for all of us, you don't *have* to accept it. The only part of this that holds any real importance is that I, and I alone, know what's going to happen next. And you're going to need my help.'

'This should be good,' said Hal. 'Why?'

'Because a *battle* is coming, Harold.'

'Don't call me Harold.'

'A battle between the past version of myself,' said Malcolm, ignoring him. 'A fight you cannot possibly win. And I am offering you my help so that you may survive it.'

'And why would you do that?' said Peter.

'I have a theory on how I arrived at that hospital,' said Malcolm. 'The only logical explanation for how I broke through into Sunday is that something happened after you defeated me for the first time, when you reached into me and stopped my heart.'

Hal and Kara shifted uncomfortably. It would be harder for them to take the moral high ground with Peter and Fearne now that this particular cat was out of its respective bag. They could feel the glares shooting towards them, and mutually refused to meet them.

'Maybe we didn't actually…' Hal mimed the act of drawing an imaginary knife across his own throat and made a high-pitched noise reminiscent of a duck trying to perform the sound effect of paper being torn, '*do you in* after all?'

'I have revisited that moment countless times,' revealed Malcolm. 'That is to say, I witnessed my *murder*. And besides, my past-self running amok is proof enough that you took my life. Not very smart. Poor Kevin, left to rot in that storage cupboard.'

Hal and Kara shared a sideways glance and smiled.

'Tsk, tsk, tsk. Not very heroic, laughing at the dead,' said Malcolm.

'Agreed,' said Kara. 'Lucky for us, he didn't die.'

This clearly caught Malcolm off guard, and it felt good to possess knowledge he didn't have.

'Yeah, we totally saved him,' chirped Hal. 'I don't want to say you're the worst serial killer ever, but…'

'You literally are,' chimed Kara.

'How did you…remarkable,' added Malcolm, with barely-concealed wonder. 'How?'

'Time heist,' said Kara, as if it was the most

obvious thing in the world. 'Keep talking.'

Malcolm glared, then smiled, realising yet again that she was smarter than he gave her credit for. Her reluctance to provide him with such crucial information meant that he would really need to up the ante to win her trust.

'That's as far as I've ever reached,' said Malcolm. 'The fog claims me shortly after. However, before I am whisked away, there's a faint flicker above the chest of my dead body. It's the reason I brought us all together. It was—'

'Yeah, about that. How *did* you bring us back here?' asked Hal, interrupting him without remorse as he drew a sharp line across the page of his notebook.

'Hal's got a point, Peter's funeral is one thing,' said Kara, stealing a glance at Hal's notepad trying to decipher his scratchy handwriting, but giving up. 'It makes sense that something as big as that could change our future into a world where Peter was dead. But it doesn't explain what caused a coffee shop to explode. You basically Restarted the entire world around us. What else did you do?'

'I didn't *do* anything' said Malcolm. 'I don't know what was changed to warrant *your* return, or of the coffee shop of which you speak. I merely brought Peter and Feanie into phase with you once I spotted you.'

Hal and Kara sensed there was way more he wasn't telling them, but with no way to prove it, they had little choice than to accept that at face value.

For the time being, at least. Whatever that even meant anymore.

'As I was saying,' continued Malcolm. 'Before my restart chain ends, there's a flicker of *blue* electricity. And, seeing as how my *particular* brand of *Restarter energy* consists more of…the *claret* variety, that can mean only one thing; I am revived at a point beyond our thirty-three-hour time loop. At least, long enough for me to reach a hospital.'

'Paramedics maybe?' suggested Kara.

'Unlikely,' posed Malcolm. 'Who would have called them? My working theory is that someone came back, somehow managing to restart my heart.'

'And you think,' said Peter, 'that it was *us*?'

'No, Peter,' said Malcolm, 'I think it was the two of *you*.'

He stared at Hal and Kara.

'Hate to break it you to Malc',' said Hal, 'But Kara and I vanish after our thirty-three-hours are up. No matter what gets changed, no matter what phase we're in, after just gone 9pm…'

Hal enacted the action of a smoke bomb being dropped, adding a wonderfully delivered matching sound effect to indicate the ceasing of their existence.

Kara saw Hal's point. 'There's no way either of us can resuscitate you after we…*take you down*. Everything after that point is set in stone.'

'Clearly we find a way to break that rule,' said Malcolm, never one to allow such a thing as a pesky temporal constant to stand in his way. 'You understand now what I need of you. I need you to restart my heart when that time comes. After you have *stopped* it, of course.'

Hal and Kara looked at each other, wondering if they should break the news to him about why his plan was so awful. It wasn't just the laws of time they would have to break either. It was something much more grounded in the real world. Eventually, Hal nodded, giving Kara the go ahead with a "why not" kind of shrug.

'There's a huge flaw in your plan you haven't accounted for…' said Kara.

Malcolm looked confused. Incredulous even. As if that were impossible. He had dedicated an entire year of his life to this plan, and was certain he had accounted for everything.

'What are you talking about,' he said snappily.

'I'm sorry Malcolm, but even if you *are* as coherent as you claim to be, eventually that version of you in the coma may wake up, with no memory of any of this. It'll just be business as usual for you.'

'Kara's right,' said Hal. 'When we made it out, we didn't remember any of this. You said it yourself, neither did you.'

'That is a risk I'm willing to take,' barked Malcolm, taking precisely half a nanosecond to mull that over, his calm façade dropping to reveal more than a glimmer of his true nature.

'And one *we* simply *can't* take,' added Kara.

'But you've already taken that risk. I'm living

evidence that you restarted my heart!' Malcolm countered.

'I'm no doctor,' said Kara, 'but even if we *could* hold off a restart long enough to revive you, there's no telling what damage that could cause to your physical body. The implications would be…well, I have no idea. But my prognosis would be *not bloody great* is what I'm saying.'

'Wait, I need to get my head around this,' said Hal. 'So, you've done *all* this,' he added, raising his hands as if to encompass the room. 'You changed our 165th restart, offering up Pete here as a sacrifice, then escaped the restarts entirely. Then found yourself in some kind of …*restarting hospital*. You then *killed* yourself at said hospital, nipped back and helped Peter and Fearne trade their lives for mine and Kara's?'

'That is correct,' said Malcolm. 'After reviewing multiple timelines I discovered that without my help, they would never have changed time to bring you to the beginning of your journey in the first place.'

'You can travel *between* timelines?!' said Kara, her mind blown.

'It's…complicated,' said Malcolm, not eager to get into that just yet.

'Oh, you can put a pin in that bullshit,' said Hal, not wishing to get thrown off trajectory for what he felt was an important summary. 'So, you *recruited* the four of us…now you want to help us defeat a version of *you* from the past, in an upcoming punch-up, with no idea of how Kara and I's past was changed for us to be even *having* this conversation right now…all in the hope it will finally set you free permanently?'

'Set *all* of us free, Harold. Once and for all. My offer is simple; allow me to help you survive the oncoming onslaught my past-self is threatening to rain down upon you. All I ask for in exchange is the small gesture of restarting my heart when the time comes so that I can become the man in front of you now.

Malcolm stood up and offered an open hand in the direction of the baffled Restarters. An offer that was soon to be solidified in time as a temporal constant, with the utterance of ten words that threatened to take their lives down a path they never could have predicted in a million restarts;

'So, what say you, *Restarters*? Do we have a deal?'

CHAPTER TWENTY-SEVEN
The Fault in our Time Zones

167th Restart – Friday, August 24th, 1:17pm.

It took Hal and Kara an exorbitant amount of time before they could form a full sentence, due to being doubled over in utter hysterics as they laughed deliriously in the face of both Malcolm and his utterly-insane offer.

'Hahahahaaaaa! He-he wants a—' tried Hal, still not nailing it, until eventually he grew quiet for a moment, letting the preposterousness of the situation sink in.

'T-truce!' spluttered Kara, her sides splitting once again and sending her into an endless cycle of giggles which, in turn, set Hal off again.

'Th-that's your play?' said Hal, totally in stitches.

'There's no need to be so rude,' said Malcolm, in the manner of a man being brutally scrutinised in a job interview that, up until now, he thought had been going rather well.

Having spent a long time on his speech, he felt it was more than passable. *Good*, even. Clearly his efforts had been wasted on the cretins before him.

'No!' said Hal finally, wiping the tears from his eyes and cheeks. 'No chance. No way. Never going to happen, Malc'!'

'Hal, maybe we should listen to him,' said Peter, the gravity of saying no to a man such as this crashing down on him like an anvil of life-changing destruction. 'If even half of what he says is true—'

'Oh, *there's* a surprise,' said Hal, his good mood being quickly nullified by yet another elephant in the room let loose by Peter, who seemed determined to turn Hal and Kara's life into an elephant-only menagerie. 'We're team *Jacob*, and Peter's Team *Edward*.'

'What's *that* supposed to mean,' said Fearne, her temper flaring at the loaded pop-culture reference.

'I *think*,' said Hal, 'you know *exactly* what that's supposed to mean,' his words cutting through her like one of the collector items that were surely mounted on the walls of wherever Malcolm actually called home.

'No,' said Peter, 'it's *more* than that. If *this* version

of Malcolm helped us escape our repeats…'

The room fell silent, as Hal debated the ramifications of that.

'Is that really true?' said Kara, praying it wasn't.

'It is,' said Malcolm, setting fire to said prayer before it had a chance to take flight.

If that truly were the case, and they didn't accept his offer, this very version of Malcolm from their shared future would be unable go back and help Peter and Fearne to free themselves from their restarts. Meaning Peter and Fearne would never have escaped their purgatory.

'But if you don't break your restart chain,' said Kara, addressing Peter and refusing to adopt their time-traveller terminology, despite the seriousness of the situation dawning on her, 'Hal and I will never inherit the restarts in the first place!'

They had not only seen a glimmer of this potential future, they'd lived in a similar version of it for the past six weeks. Or was that six weeks from now? Kara decided not to dwell on semantics.

The four of them stared at each other in silence, none of them wanting to be the one to admit they had been well and truly backed into a time-travel-tinged corner.

'You clever bastard,' said Hal, staring at the man claiming to be from their future. The fact they were still here in this very moment proved they were destined to say yes.

They had no choice.

Their entire existence hinged upon their collaboration. 'He's just Act 3 Prisoner of Azkaban'd us!'

Hal once again took to his pad, amending his list to incorporate how not helping this version of Malcolm would have a knock-on effect to the previous timelines he had mapped out, passing it to Kara.

> **Timeline Prime** – *Arrive at Fir Lodge.*
> **Timeline Alpha** – ~~*Peter and Fearne ruin our lives.*~~
> *Future Malcolm shows Pete and Fearne exactly what to change to ruin our lives.*
> **Timeline Beta** – *Hal and Kara Restart.*
> *Kick Time's ass! #Timepolice*
> **Timeline Charlie** – *Dark Restarter Malcolm changes future. Kills Pete. Karma. Hal and Kara survive. (Because awesomeness.)*
> **Timeline Delta** – ~~*Whatever this thing currently is.*~~
> *The four of us stop Dark Restarter Malcolm from killing Peter, bringing Dark Restarter back into his restart chain. He must reach the hospital or Timeline Alpha is toast.*

'Oh…' Kara's eyes widened. 'Oh, that *is* clever. If we don't get the version of Malcolm we just stopped from killing Pete to the hospital at the end of all this, and it erases Peter and Fearne's chain of restarts…'

'We'll be torching Timeline Beta. All 165 of *our* first run of restarts!' confirmed Hal, relieved she understood. 'Which means no Malcolm 2.0 timeline.

And, just for good measure, the timeline we're *currently* in would get wiped as well. We wouldn't even be having this debate right now.'

'None of us would,' said Fearne, grasping Peter's point now that it had been explained in greater detail by Hal.

In truth, Peter really hadn't considered the long reaching effects of his initial observation. His mind blown by how one man could be causing so much chaos.

'Am I saying "timelines" too much?' Hal whispered to Kara, suddenly feeling self-conscious about the matter.

'A little,' she confirmed, causing Hal to nod apologetically, taking her constructive criticism on board.

None of them seemed sure on if Future Malcolm's plan was pure genius, or pure blind luck.

But one fact was clear; they needed to make sure Malcolm made it to that hospital on Sunday the 26th of August. A point in time none of them could physically reach.

Malcolm stood there, arms crossed, stone faced, the hint of an irritating smile lurking beneath his left cheek, despite not knowing precisely what that meant.

'Okay,' said Hal, forced into changing his tune. 'First off, "Repeats" is never going to be a *thing* Pete, so stop trying. Secondly, even if we *wanted* to stop Malcolm 2.0, that version of you is literally running around in a completely different phase to us. We stopped him, remember? Now he's out-of-phase *and* in a brand-new restart groove.'

'Yes,' confirmed Malcolm. 'That was intentional. I thought it prudent to allow you all the necessary time to acclimatise, rather than dropping you all in at the deep end and forcing you to face my past-self head-on.'

'How thoughtful,' drawled Kara.

'In order to stop him,' continued Malcolm, ignoring her jab, 'from causing any more damage to time, we have to take him *off the board* entirely.'

'But how do we fight something we can't see?' asked Peter. 'Let alone interact with?

'There is only one way,' replied Malcolm. 'We must bring ourselves into phase with him on a quantum level.'

'Neat idea,' said Hal, rubbing the stubble of his forever-unchanging five-o'clock shadow, an idea clearly forming. 'But it's not like tuning a TV, we're occupying different dimensions, Malc'.'

'Please stop calling me that.'

Hal smiled, and Malcolm grimaced, knowing that Hal would forever call him that from here on out.

'The fault in that concept is…the fault in our *time* zones. We're in different phases,' continued Hal. 'Which is exactly why we couldn't see Peter and Fearne whilst they were here before us, ruining *our* lives.' His words caused both Peter and Fearne to wince. 'I don't know if that's even possible.'

'You are not listening, I have told you already that

it *is* possible….' said Malcolm, revisiting his bold claim of traversing between timelines. 'When I showed Peter and Fearne the way to trade their lives for yours.'

Peter and Fearne flinched, each feeling like Malcolm could have chosen a better way to word that.

'*Timelines* maybe,' said Hal, his eyes forming a squint of scepticism. 'But between phases?'

'I'm still not sure I'm buying that,' said Kara, wondering what the next bout of lies would bring to the conversation.

'It's how I brought the four of you together,' said Malcolm, his glare burning with truth. For all his swagger, his past-self had never managed to kill all four of them in one timeline. 'I had to step between two separate timelines to bring you all here.'

'So, you know how he did it?' asked Kara. How past-you restarted the past somehow, and brought us back here?'

Malcolm stared at them, seemingly weighing up his options, deciding if telling them how Hal and Kara had ended up back here would serve his own needs. In the end, he huffed, and spoke.

'It is…complicated,' said Malcolm, apparently eager to embrace that cop-out as his new favourite term.

Hal had no doubt it was clearly an understatement.

'You're overthinking it, Sinestro,' said Hal

irritably. 'It's a simple question with an answer you must remember. It's your own damn past'

'It does not matter what my past-self changed,' countered Malcolm, 'given that it will come undone when, and *only* when, we defeat him.'

It occurred to Hal that Malcolm was probably being intentionally evasive on detailing the exact point in the past his younger self had meddled with. But he assumed it must have been a pivotal moment during the restart that changed everything; when Hal and Kara had vanquished their foe.

After all, keeping that information off the table and out of their reach would prevent them from attempting to change the outcome of the new timeline Malcolm was trailblazing. Assuming they *could* even fix the mess that the killer had already made.

'Fine,' said Hal. 'Keep your secrets. It's not like we can change it now anyway.'

'That still doesn't explain *these* two,' said Kara, throwing a thumb over her shoulder towards Fearne and Peter. '*When* exactly did you drag them from?'

'So,' said Malcolm, eager to change the subject. 'Now that we've covered that my past-self has been existing in your 165th restart, altering and perverting it to his own ends, *that* is where we need to go.'

'Again, how?' said Kara. 'We're locked in…damn, what are we even on now?

'We've been here for two restarts now,' said Hal helpfully.

'Right. So how do we travel from *our* 167th restart to our 165th?'

'You've answered your own question,' confirmed Malcolm. 'We must cross *between* restarts to reach him.'

'That's not how *The Force* works?!' said Hal, doing his best Han Solo impression, and causing Peter's eyes to light up with mild nostalgia. Peter and Hal always saw those films together. He wondered if they ever would again.

'What *Force*?' said Malcolm, causing Hal to roll his eyes.

'*Restarts*, Malcolm. That's not how *Restarts* work,' said Hal, draining all the fun out of the reference so that the murderer could grasp his point. 'They play out consecutively. That means *in order*. You can't just bounce between different ones on a whim. Unless you've got a Stargate in your pocket you haven't told us about?'

'That's not how a Stargate works, is it?' muttered Peter.

'Holy shit, Pete…really?' said Hal incredulously. '*Now's* the time I get called out on the semantics of interplanetary wormholes?'

'The White Lodge,' said Fearne, her voice barely a whisper.

Malcolm grinned, baring his teeth as if they were an armoury of daggers.

'What the hell is *The White Lodge*?' asked Kara.

'It's easier if I just show you,' said Malcolm.

Hal shot out a sharp puff of air from the corner of his mouth, finally understanding how annoying it was when someone did that, feeling bad for all the times he had done the very same thing to Kara.

CHAPTER TWENTY-EIGHT
Where We're Going…

167th Restart – Friday, August 24th, 2:12pm

'So, let me get this straight,' said Hal as they made their way to the boundary line of the Pentney Lakes. 'Not only can you fast-forward through a restart, you've found a way to manoeuvre *between* them too?!' It sounded incredibly unlikely to Hal that this was an actual thing.

'Yes,' said Malcolm, not bothering with egotistical exuberance.

'And the key to that, is accessing this *White Lodge*?' said Hal for what was at least the tenth time.

'Correct,' confirmed Malcolm, his patience thinning.

'This sounds *so* made up that it's just crazy

enough to be real,' said Hal, crossing his arms and staring up at the afternoon sun, not trusting their inadvertent ally one iota.

'I assure you, it's quite real,' said Malcolm.

'And *you've* both seen this place?' said Kara, directing the question to both Peter and Fearne.

'Only briefly,' mumbled Peter. 'We travelled through it with him to get here I think, but it's hard to remember *when* that was exactly,' he added, noting how it oddly felt like forever ago. 'The first I heard of it was…I…it's hard to explain.'

'Is that because it involves telling the truth?' said Hal with an impressive level of snarkiness.

Fearne shot Hal an indignant glare, but her expression softened when Peter smiled at her, indicating it was okay.

'I heard it in Malcolm's thoughts,' said Peter, deciding to just go all in and be done with it. After all, was it really that crazy a prospect? Not so long ago, time travel seemed equally impossible. Yet here they were, doing exactly that. 'Whilst we were connected, right after we trapped past-me in Rob's room and–'

'Betrayed us?'

'We didn't betra–' began Fearne.

'Hal and I have experienced that sort of connection before,' said Kara, cutting all of them off. 'Reading thoughts. It checks out.'

It was true. They had done just that right before defeating Malcolm on what they had wrongly assumed to be their final restart. As the Restarter energy thrummed between them, their minds had unified, albeit temporarily.

'So, Skeletor,' said Hal, addressing what was clearly a mainstay addition to their rapidly-expanding team. 'Assuming this isn't just one of your tricks, how did *you* even find it?'

'Does it really matter?' asked Malcolm, conscious of how much time it was taking to bring them up to speed.

'I feel like it's a pretty important part to leave out, yeah,' said Hal, but decided to let it slide for the time being. He sighed, resigning himself to becoming a version of himself that was willing to accept the impossible, if only for the sake of argument.

Hal missed the days when he and his brother Alex would spend hours geeking out over situations such as this. When they were only hypothetical.

"The days when it wasn't real," he thought.

'Right then,' pressed Kara, taking the wheel of the crazy-boat for a second. 'Assuming this is a thing, how do we access this *White Lodge* of yours?'

'We go through the barrier together,' said Malcolm, extending an upturned palm towards the Restart Point.

'That can't work. If we walk through that, it'll just trigger a restart and we'll be right back where we started.'

'For you, Kara, yes,' agreed Malcolm. 'But not if we go together.'

The basis for the discovery of this fact was

evidenced by the presence of Peter and Fearne, the first two entities he had successfully brought back with him.

Hal was about to ask why the Restart Point didn't work the same way for Malcolm as it did for them, but was beaten to the punch by Malcolm himself, who explained exactly how death *after* death had changed him.

That by switching off his own life support whilst occupying a restart, his ability to use the Restart Point in quite the same way had seemingly been revoked.

Hal shuddered, as he remembered the time he had broken his own jaw by hitting his alive-self. Would he have shared the same inability to trigger a restart, if he had hit just a little harder? If Hal had effectively killed *himself* in the past whilst trapped in an out-of-phase state?

He didn't want to think about the consequences of that.

'Okay, Mighty Max,' said Hal. 'Enough telling, more showing. Pop on your red cap and let's do this thing.'

'We'll need to take two trips,' said Malcolm, throwing a last-minute curveball. 'It's too risky to all go through at once.'

'Of cooourse it is. And why's that exactly?' asked Kara, not liking the sound of that one bit.

'It may draw…unnecessary attention,' said Malcolm, with a level of ominousness befitting the last soul-survivor of an abandoned space-station tasked with exporting a large quantity of face-huggers.

'From what?!' said Fearne, her memories, as foggy as they were, refusing to kick up any indication that there was anything but endless whiteness where they were going.

Malcolm grew silent, his face impenetrably unreadable.

'From *what* Malcolm?' said Kara, repeating Fearne's question.

Malcolm swallowed, for once in his life somewhat lost for words. 'Where we're going–'

'–we don't need roads!' blurted Hal, interjecting with excitement. 'Please say roads!'

'You are a very odd man, Harold.'

'Says the man wearing an apron.'

'I was *trying* to say, there are things beyond our ability to comprehend,' said Malcolm, choosing to ignore the Restarter entirely.

'Vague much?' said Kara.

'Just stay close to me. And do *exactly* as I say, understand?'

'Not really,' said Peter.

'Are you ready?' asked Malcolm, addressing them all.

'Not even a little,' said Fearne.

'Then let's go. I'll take Peter and Kara first, then come back for you and Fearne,' the former killer proposed, shooting a look at Hal with uncharacteristic chirp.

'Absolutely no chance in hell,' said Kara without

hesitation. 'Hal and I go together or not at all.'

Malcolm stared at her, his good mood extinguished, and his glare narrow, as if fighting an innate urge to murder her on the spot right then and there for her insolence, before gruffly conceding with a barely formed word of agreement and extending his hand.

'Try not to stab me,' said Hal, as he took the allegedly-reformed murderer's hand, instantly feeling drained, and quickly pulling away from the harrowing handshake. 'What the hell, Malc'?!'

It was entirely unlike the energy spike he usually received when he connected with Kara. Rather than charging him up, it had the complete opposite effect; hoovering up Hal's internalised power like an unleashed Dementor sucking happiness from a room.

'What is it?' said Kara.

'See for yourself, *Henry the Hoover* over here is hogging the blue!'

Kara reached out for Malcolm's still-outstretched hand and connected with it, blue and red sparks spiralling wildly between them. She had to admit, it wasn't the same as when she connected with Hal, but it wasn't as bad as she was expecting. It was tolerable, at least.

'Stop being a baby,' said Kara with a wink, causing Hal to stomp closer and interlock his arm on Malcolm's opposite side in defiance.

He noted that with Kara in the mix, the sensation of being drained didn't seem quite so bad, and wondered if perhaps he had imagined it.

With that, Hal and Kara, with Malcolm in the middle, each linked their arms, creating the surreal image that made them look like the best of friends.

Fearne noted that it looked a lot like they were both supporting a drunken friend on a pub-crawl gone wrong. The only thing that shattered this illusion was the arcing red and blue energy that hummed between them, forcibly trying to repel them apart.

They maintained their connection, Hal and Kara utterly sceptical that anything would happen at all besides an inevitable restart, certain that Malcolm was luring them into an elaborate hoax. "Or worse," thought Kara, "a trap."

'Right then, let's go see the Time Wizard,' said Kara, hiding behind a passable forgery of bravado, as they stepped over the boundary line and into the portal that served as a Restart Point, a look of approval appearing on Hal's face, as each of them shattered into billions of tiny blue and red shards of energy.

ENIN-YTNEWT RETPAHC
The White Lodge

R.I Timestamp Error: Recalculating...

System Error. Timestamp Failure.

The red and blue energy thrummed between the three of them, forcibly trying to repel them from piercing through the fabric of space, time, and all the other bits and bobs that kept reality ticking over, so that those who were still alive could drink their morning coffees, instead of forcibly being made to undrink them.

After all, there was a reason people left for work, instead of leaving for bed, so that they could feel unrested during their stay in an ocean of traffic that travelled backwards all the way to their hungry in-trays, which insatiably demanded their owner's daily grind be undone. Not least of which being that it would have made for terrible small-talk, having to tell someone about the day you were yet to have, yet somehow had already lived through.

"Or something," thought Hal, lost in the chasms of his daydreaming mind.

Of all the places they shouldn't be, it seemed the universe was particularly intent on preventing them safe passage to what lay beyond, until eventually it relented under their combined power.

To Kara, it felt as if she was passing through a mesh like veil, or forcibly pushing her body through an enormous rubber balloon.

Hal, on the other hand, was wrestling with his own descriptive terminology, his imagination igniting within him a terrifying fear, convincing him that he was pushing his face through a century-old amalgamation of approximately one-billion-and-forty-eight cobwebs.

As the colour was pushed to the outskirts of their vision, their eyes were greeted with a familiar sight; an entire world laying ahead of them, seemingly contained within the heart of a marble, as if they were looking through the wrong end of a dodgy telescope. A world of immaculate and pristine whiteness, that gave their approaching destination an eerily clinical looking makeover.

Malcolm looked at the sorry souls either side of him, then yanked them rather unceremoniously into the great white yonder.

And with that, they were through.

Hal was frantically rubbing his face, trying to wipe away what he was certain was a particularly nasty cobweb, spitting repeatedly, as if the intangible barrier had somehow adhered to his lips.

'Is it off me? Is there anything on me?' said Hal, his voice more than a notch beyond overtly high-pitched.

'There's nothing *on* you,' growled Malcolm, failing to even remotely cloak his complete lack of empathy, his words a constant reminder to them that they were only here because he needed them, not because he wanted them to be.

'You're fine, Hal,' said Kara reassuringly, helpfully attempting to ease his mind by dusting off his shoulders in a show of solidarity. Barely-visible sparks bounced off his shoulders, presumably thanks to Malcolm having stolen his charge like a hungry hippo let loose in a marble storage facility.

With the drama of interdimensional travel behind them, they at last had the opportunity to drink it all in; a world between worlds, existing outside of time itself. Just as Malcolm had promised.

Only his description did it little justice.

White particles circulated around them, like self-conscious snowflakes that fluttered as close as they could possibly get to the three of them, but dancing away before making contact with whatever phase their bodies were currently in.

Kara extended her palm, hoping that the ethereal grains of the hourglass they were occupying would grow brave enough to land on her, but the quantum-entangled motes of dust spiralled away from her outstretched paw as if sensing her ploy, and swirled off in a seemingly random direction, eager to retain their freedom.

'You have to hand it to *Vigo The Carpathian* over here,' said Hal, casting a thumb over his shoulder in the direction of Malcolm. 'He *really* knows how to undersell an alternate reality.'

'It's not an alternate reality,' said Malcolm abruptly, 'it's a space between time.'

'Like a truck stop?' said Hal innocently, intentionally playing dumb to wind up their guide.

'No, nothing like a....' Malcolm closed his eyes, and took a deep breath, as Hal and Kara shared a mischievous smile.

Hal swatted at a flurry of simulated snow, sending a gaggle of flakes into disarray, repelled by his body like he was an opposing magnet that gave them little choice in the matter.

'What's with the snow?' asked Hal curiously.

'I have no idea,' said Malcolm, not wishing to mention that he always perceived it more like ash; a remnant from the eruption of the volcano that represented his long list of historic failures.

Hal and Kara spread out, unable to resist the urge to explore.

They were in an identical recreation of Fir Lodge.

Identical in size, layout, and décor anyway. Notably, the lodge was entirely empty, with not a single person but the three of them roaming its halls. The balls on the pool table looked as if a game was underway; two pool cues suspended in place, one upright as if magnetised to the floor in a vertical position, implying an unseen individual was using it to prop themselves up whilst waiting for their turn to arrive. The second cue was suspended in mid-air, hovering motionlessly, an unseen echo seemingly halfway through taking a shot of their own.

The tip of the stick rested several millimetres above the blue baize cloth of the table, and despite being static, somehow managed to look as if it were poised for the motion that would follow, once the person wielding it was ready to proceed. Which was unlikely, as that person was presumably entirely out-of-phase within this particular slice of frozen time.

Hal slowly made his way down the corridor, past what was once his room, oddly drawn to Robert's digs at the end of the hall.

As he arrived at the door, he reached for the handle, feeling with certainty that answers to a very particular question resided behind it.

There was a power behind the door. He could almost feel it.

Something vibrating with a temporal energy the likes of which even he had not encountered before.

Hal's body shook, as he felt a large hand on his shoulder, and out of the corner of his eye he could see muted red sparks pinging from where Malcolm had made contact with him.

'I wouldn't go in there if I were you,' warned Malcolm.

Hal scowled defiantly, but eventually nodded and followed his instruction all the same.

The two men made their way back to the communal lower level, and Hal panicked, realising Kara was nowhere to be seen. How long had he been at the other end of the lodge?

The thought brought with it larger concerns; his perception of the passage and flow of time as he knew it felt…a lot like being drunk. But the shit kind of drunk. The kind where you know you shouldn't spark up a conversation about The Last Jedi in the urinals, but you do it anyway.

'Kara!' he shouted, his voice echoing up the staircase in front of him, the reverberations bouncing back towards him in reverse, as if the focus of the returning imitation of his own voice peaked with the first syllable, and faded into nothingness as he uttered the second part of his friends first name. An echo in reverse.

He shouted her name again, adding extra emphasis on the "K", but the final "A" was once again all but hollow.

Hal sprinted up the stairs and sighed with relief, as Kara was walking in circles around the kitchen island that housed the cutlery, focusing intently on a four-inch-tall glass that was suspended mid-tilt, the contents of which a gross-looking black, with a viscosity reminiscent of melted candle wax. A grey straw jutting out from it daring those that found themselves here to take a slurp.

Kara was mesmerised. She knew when this was.

'I think,' she said, choosing her words carefully, as if pulling them into this realm would provide a rational explanation for her thoughts, 'that's *me*. Holding that glass.'

Hal looked confused, but knew better than to snuff out a ridiculous concept. In his experience, the more preposterous the idea, the more likely it was to be a game-changing fact in this barmy old paradoxical sarcophagus they were forced to call home.

Instead, he waited for her to continue.

'I think that's me, drinking the Bloody Mary I made.' She thought back to that moment, which felt like an eternity ago; how she had made the drink to combat the hangover that had been sent her way via next day delivery, courtesy of mother-nature herself. 'Which would make this...'

'Saturday morning,' said Hal. 'Except there's a pool game going on downstairs between Casper and the mum from "The Others" that would indicate it's actually Saturday *evening*,' he noted, his mind a complete jumble as he tried to shake off the nausea being brought on by his inexplicable drunkenness.

Kara extended her hand and pointed a finger, reaching out to touch the stick of celery that wasn't a straw as Hal had first deduced, white particles of ashy-snowflakes spinning wildly to avoid her.

As her finger made contact with it, a sizzle of white energy caused her to recoil, the glass falling to the wooden table, the wax-like contents taking on the form of an oozing liquid instead, traversing across the wood, dripping over the edge, the droplets taking forever to reach the floor.

Kara kneeled down and placed her right palm under the slowly progressing droplet of vodka-laced tomato juice, which looked more like black coffee in its currently colourless hue. The droplet collided with her hand then, as quick as lightning, ascended back up the table, the contents retuning to the glass in a flash, culminating in the glass itself once more hovering above the central wooden island.

'Was that deliberate, Sabrina?' said Hal, wondering if she had actually willed that to happen.

'Nope. And I'd gladly be a witch if it meant I was still in my teens,' said Kara, pushing herself up from her kneeling position and dusting off her hands, the action generating faint claps that also echoed in reverse. Hal beamed at her, and they shared a look that signified a nineties-endorsed high-five.

'Where the hell are we, Malc'?' said Hal, turning to face the man who apparently knew everything, but seemed adamant to tell them nothing.

'Fir Lodge, Harold,' he replied smugly.

'You're the worst. You know that, right?'

'And *you* are asking the wrong questions,' said Malcolm enigmatically.

'Okay,' said Hal, mid eye-roll, 'then *riddle* me this, Batman; *When* are we?'

'Better,' said Malcolm, clearly revelling in the theatrics, and extended his arms, gesturing outwards to their surroundings. 'We are in *every* moment, in-between every*thing* that *ever* happened during your time here.'

Kara frowned. 'What? You mean all thirty-three-hours-and-change are happening…all at once?'

'You're not thinking big enough, Kara,' said Malcolm.

Kara cringed at hearing him say her name. 'Gross. Can you just…*never* say my name ever again please?'

Malcolm smiled, as if trying to increase her discomfort, but Kara just raised an eyebrow as if to indicate she wasn't even remotely threatened, and his smug demeanour evolved into a furrowed brow, in a way only an apex predator who was losing his touch could fully appreciate.

'Oh…oh wow,' said Hal.

'Oh, come on Hal, don't be *that* guy,' said Kara, who could tell he was blatantly gearing up for one of his patent-pending overly-dramatic reveals.

'Be *what* guy?' said Hal innocently.

'I can tell you're about to Obama this thing,' added Kara, more than hint of a smile creeping onto her face.

Hal stood there, clicking his fingers at his side, the action generating the sound one would expect, only audibly manifesting backwards by the time it reached her ears, throwing her off balance a little. He then began to fidget further, shifting from foot to foot, until she finally caved and sighed at him, hung her head in futility, and half-heartedly fired a pretend bullet from her fingers for him to let slip the theory he was clearly dying to share.

'I don't think he means just the time we spent here whilst we were in-phase…' said Hal, looking over at Malcolm as if seeking reassurance that he was on the right track. Malcolm's nostrils flared unhelpfully, so the Restarter decided to just run with it. 'I think…he means *every* moment. Every *restart*, every *possible* outcome, it's all happening in the same moment we're currently occupying!'

'Very good,' said Malcolm.

'Which means that this isn't just a snapshot in *time* Kara, this is the crossroads that connects *all* of time. We're in a freakin' *pocket* dimension!'

CHAPTER MALFUNCTION
Pocket Full of Sunshine

R.I Timestamp Error: Recalculating…

System Error. Timestamp Failure.

'A *what* now?' said Kara, wondering how her life had become so filled with terms such as Pocket Dimensions.

'It's like a Fir Lodge Nexus!' said Hal.

'Please don't make me say "what" again Hal,' said Kara, growing increasingly frustrated by all of the made-up things she was being told were real of late. She was getting closer to the point of just sitting this restart out altogether.

'You know, like in Star Trek Generations? Picard? Kirk? Riding *horses* for some reason. Back me up,

Voldemort!'

Malcolm grumbled something unintelligible under his breath.

'In his own idiotic way, he's right,' said Malcolm in begrudged agreement.

Malcolm regaled them on how he had discovered this nook in reality. That upon ending his own life at the hospital, he had not freed himself as expected. He had, instead, re-materialised in a place between places. An identical recreation of Pentney Lakes, with what initially appeared to be one discernible difference; it was devoid of any other colour but white. For weeks – or perhaps months, it was impossible to know for certain – he traversed the landscape, until he began to notice that time was indeed free-flowing. The landscape would shift, and shadows would flutter in and out of sight. Eventually, he reasoned these were echoes of the past, re-enacting their own histories, entirely oblivious to his presence.

He had latched on to one such shadow, drawing on its miniscule amount of energy, refusing to allow it to vanish, his fingers drifting through the silhouette, until he found enough energy within himself to truly dig his claws into it. And when the apparition had finally disappeared, it had unknowingly pulled Malcolm along for the ride with it, bringing him back in-phase with a far more vibrant point in time.

It was purely by accident, during one of his attempts to pass through the boundary line, that Malcolm realised doing so no longer triggered a fresh restart for him. Instead, passing through that barrier brought him back to what he began to refer to as simply The White Lodge. Allowing Malcolm to try new shadows, taking him to new destinations, which he eventually realised were entirely separate restarts.

'This is so awesome,' said Hal, who was beaming with excitement. Never in his wildest dreams would he have imagined he would be witnessing something so fantastical, getting to see with his own eyes a pocket dimension that connected all of time. 'Can we go check the garden?' he said excitedly, eager to see more interactive dioramas of his own past.

'Fine,' said Malcolm. 'But we don't have much ti–' but Hal was already long gone.

Kara caught an uncharacteristic look of fear creeping across Malcolm's face, as he arched over the banister of the stairs, as if looking for the early warning signs of…something, watching as Hal jumped down them three at a time.

'What's got *you* so spooked?'

'It's nothing,' he lied.

'Whatever,' she said, following Hal down the stairs.

*

Having made it to the rear garden area of The White Lodge, Hal found himself fixated on what appeared to be a game of temporally-isolated beer pong; the grey cups with white trim angled oddly, clearly on the precipice of being knocked off by the floating white balls that were locked in time and suspended mid-flight above them.

Beer bottles and wine glasses lined the perfectly-white picnic benches behind him, some glasses raised and hovering, as if they were being held by unseen hands, which of course they were.

Meanwhile, Kara had become distracted by the game of pool that Hal had mentioned earlier, the floating pool cues vanishing, then reappearing in an instant, now in different positions. She reached out to one of the cues, touching it with her fingertip, and the cue sprang to life, potting one of the balls, then froze in time once again when she pulled her hand back warily.

'Ha, this *is* pretty amazing!' said Kara, noticing that Malcolm was now standing on the white shingle of the driveway, and went out to join him, weaving through several white cars. She glanced inside the vehicles as she did so, observing the pristine white interiors and unreadable number plates, due to the writing on the registrations being, well, as white as the plates they were printed on.

'What are you looking for?'

'Our destination…' said Malcolm curtly. 'There! Do you see it?'

She couldn't see anything, thanks to the white sky and white trees which merged seamlessly to form an almost invisible horizon, looking increasingly like a blank canvas which only contained three-dimensional depth as you moved through it.

'We need an *anchor*,' said Malcolm, pointing into

the featureless, fog-filled forest.

And then she saw it; wisps of red energy, that twisted and contorted until finally forming into a humanoid shape, energy flowing through a disembodied central nervous system that was gliding across the ground.

'What *is* that?' asked Kara, staring in apprehensive awe.

'Me. Or, rather, a past version of myself. That's who we need to lock onto, in order to align ourselves with his timeline.'

'And that will put us in phase with the version of *you* we need to stop?' asked Kara. 'Can he see us?'

'That is correct. And no,' added Malcolm reassuringly. 'He cannot see us.'

'Well, that's a relief.'

'We need to find Harold, I'd prefer to leave sooner rather than later. You keep an eye on my past-self for me, would you?' said Malcolm, setting off to locate their wandering colleague.

'Sure, I guess.'

*

Hal came back in through the rear entrance of the lodge, having had enough fun witnessing the reality-bending re-enactments playing out before him out back, but once again found himself stopping outside Robert's room, remembering Malcolm's clear instructions not to go inside.

'To hell with that,' said Hal.

If Malcolm didn't want him going in here,

chances are it was because it held answers he didn't want either he or Kara to possess.

Hal gently pulled down the handle, and pushed the door inwards, wincing at the sound of a deafening creak playing out in reverse.

'Oh god,' said Hal, as horror took hold of not only his body, but also his breath, causing his heart to pound.

A shiver rolled through him, as fifty or so faceless shadows – no *not* shadows, they had more substance than that – with skin as slick as oil, stood staring at the corner of the room. Hal realised that the creatures appeared to be focusing on the exact point where Peter had been pressed against the wall on the evening before their first death.

'What the fu–' muttered Hal, his involuntary whisper bouncing into what passed for the ears of the creatures.

The place where their ears *should* have been shimmered, like a small pebble being dropped into a cup of oily water, undoubtedly detecting his presence. Hal assumed these must have been the shadows Malcolm had mentioned; the ones he used to travel between timelines. Only they weren't at all like Malcolm had described.

They were solid. And not in a "willing to help you move house" sort of way.

Hal swallowed hard, hoping against all odds that maybe, just maybe, they weren't in phase with him. But that hope was immediately crushed by the bulldozer of bullshit that was the Callaghan Luck.

The horrific, faceless silhouettes span around in unison, their combined movement generating an amplified sound of a single synchronised footstep.

Hal slowly stretched an arm out towards the handle of the door, eager to close it to lock the monsters inside. He stopped himself, his hand halting just before it reached the door handle, as each of the fifty androgynous beings before him mimicked his action, their arms now extending towards him.

He felt a prickle of electricity against his cheek.

'Ouch', said Hal, feeling a pinch of pain.

The creatures repeated the word in reverse, generating a noise that sounded far too much like a crescendo of the word "chew" for Hal's liking. He watched in transfixed awe as the spark on his cheek slowly pulled away from him, all the way to the outstretched fingers of the nearest jet-black lifeform before him. As the energy connected with whatever the hell it was…

"He? She?" To be honest it became a moot point to Hal at that moment in time.

Regardless, as the blue spark of Restarter energy connected with *it*, the beast flicked its head back, squealing deliriously. The surrounding creatures huddled towards their brother or sister or significant other, seemingly desperate to absorb the scrap of energy Hal had unwittingly just fed them.

Realising the energy had now dissipated, the creatures slowly reasserted their eyeless gaze back towards the face of the Restarter, who was still standing on the threshold of the doorway.

'Nope', hummed Hal, quickly leaning in towards the door and pulling it closed.

He heard the beasts within collide against it, bashing furiously from the other side, each of them squealing and clawing, desperate to dig their knife-like talons into Hal's self-described "too pretty for prison" flesh.

'Malcolm!' shouted Hal, as he was momentarily overpowered, the bedroom door being yanked away from him from the inside, creating a small gap that was just wide enough for sharp fingers to reach through. The nails dug deep into Hal's hand, and he felt the weakening sensation of Restarter energy being drained from deep within him. Not dissimilar to how he had felt when making contact with Future Malcolm for the first time.

But much, much worse.

'Oww! Piss off, Slender Man!' snapped Hal, regretting the reference and making himself shudder once again.

'*Malcolm!*' he called again.

Both Kara and Malcolm ran down the hall to him.

'What did you *do*, boy,' growled Malcolm.

'Settle down, Kratos, I didn't *do* anything.'

'Hal,' said Kara, suddenly feeling incredibly exposed, this Fir Lodge not feeling even remotely safe for them any longer. 'What's behind that door?'

'Erm, if I said like a hundred Time-Demons

and/or vampires that can suck Restarter energy straight out of your body like you're a milkshake, would you freak on me?'

'Are they alien looking things without faces that walk like stop-motion puppets?'

'Wow,' said Hal, surprised by her spot-on description. 'That was *oddly* specific. Also, can we ban the use of the word "puppets"? You just made them sound way creepier than…wait? You've seen them too?!'

'You *could* say that,' said Kara, taking a step back from the door to the right of the three of them, her voice shakier than he'd heard it in a while, as she pointed behind him.

He spun around, adjusting his grip on the door handle so as not to give the ghouls inside the chance to break out.

His fears were multiplied, as he was greeted by the spirit-crippling sight of hundreds of the creatures, each working their way towards the three time travellers, edging ever closer with inhuman, jerking movements across the artificial-snow-like grass.

'Malcolm, I have a confession to make,' said Hal.

'You went insi–'

'I went inside.'

'Into the room I specifically told yo–"

'Told me not to go into, yeah.'

'What do we do?!' Kara's voice was full of panic as she looked back up the corridor that led to the central staircase of the lodge, making sure they weren't about to get boxed in by the SWAT team from hell.

'We run,' said Malcolm. 'Come with me if you want to live.'

Street Fighters

R.I Timestamp Error: Recalculating…

System Error. Timestamp Failure.

Malcolm and the Restarters burst forth from the entrance doors of Fir Lodge, not having time to take in the fact that if they were they living in the 1950's, that would have made for a great band name, and instead bolted between the cars on the driveway, reaching the connecting main road in a flash.

'Which way do we go?' said Kara, risking a glance over her shoulder and seeing the army of oily creatures caught in a bundle, trying to force their way past each other through the doors, the bottleneck granting the three of them a precious few seconds to think.

'This way,' barked Malcolm, choosing the path most travelled; the one that led them back towards Kevin's lodge.

'Okay, level with me,' said Hal, matching Malcolm's pace. 'Was that a Terminator 2 reference back there, or just purely accidental?'

'Focus,' Malcolm grunted, his eyes darting around as if searching for something.

'What are you looking for?' asked Kara.

'A way out of the mess Harold has made. I *warned* you not to go in there!'

'Are you kidding me right now?' said Hal defensively. 'Only in the most obtuse way possible! Why not just open with "Hey Harold. Don't go in that room. It's totally full of Time Vampires that want to kill you real good!"'

'Where are you getting this *Time Vampires* thing from?' said Kara

'You wanna stop running and rename them?'

'Fair point. Hard pass,' she replied, noticing Malcolm had halted to a stop.

Hal and Kara, now a good ten strides away from him, turned to face the man.

Malcolm was frozen in place, as the sight of the temporally-challenged vampirically inclined beasts bounded towards them at a pace more akin to a gallop than a canter.

'Erm, Malc, the *Cullens* are still chasing us!'

shouted Hal. 'Why are we stopping?'

Malcolm pointed towards the glowing red fairy lights of a central nervous system floating between some trees less than one-hundred-yards-or-so in front of them.

'That's where we're heading,' said Malcolm. 'We just need to grab onto him and–'

'Roger that,' said Hal, darting towards the light show.

'Not *yet*,' shouted Malcolm, grabbing Hal's arm and nearly dislocating the Restarter's shoulder in the process.

'If ever there was a *yet*, now would be that time, Malcolm,' said Kara, the gap between them and the vampiric demons decreasing at an alarming rate.

'Do you want to emerge standing directly next to him,' snapped Malcolm. 'Losing the only advantage we have in the process?!'

'If it's a choice between us three versus one you,' said Kara quickly, 'and us versus all those *Demogorgons*, I choose the former!'

'Aww, you watched it?' said Hal.

'Everybody has, Hal.'

'Yeah, but still. You never watch anything I recommen–'

'Will you both be quiet?!' their incessant rambling making it incredibly difficult for Malcolm to focus. 'We don't have much time before it–'

The red energy disappeared in an instant, removing the choice from the table.

'Damn you both,' the killer shouted, despite it not really being anyone's fault.

'Where'd he go?!'

'The timelines move in cycles, Kara,' said Malcolm, trying desperately to decide on a course of action that wouldn't result in them being killed. There was no telling what would happen if they died in this place. Or if they even could. He was testament to the fact that there were indeed fates far worse than the simplicity of death. 'Come on, we need to keep moving.'

'Cycles?' repeated Hal, as they ran. 'Tell me you don't mean chronologically?!'

'No,' said Malcolm. 'We will not have to wait the full 165 cycles. They're random. Some restarts last minutes here, others last hours…' he added, clearly haunted by the memories of first-hand experience.

'And those things?' said Kara, as they all turned a sharp corner and reached a crossroads, coming face to face with another hoard of the creatures.

'Bollocks,' said Hal, 'they're bloody flanking us!'

Malcolm ordered them to move once again, and they set off down an alternate route, eventually reaching a fenced off area.

'I have no idea *what* they are,' said Malcolm, vaulting over the fence, with Kara following suit, leaving Hal to scramble frantically, unable to hoist himself over.

One of the wooden fence-panels blasted apart, sending Hal onto his back.

It took him a second to realise Malcolm had kicked a hole in the fence. It wasn't much, but it was just enough for Hal to squeeze through, which he dutifully did. The splintered wood grazing against his cheeks as he slid himself between the panels, forcing him to direct his gaze back towards the oncoming hunting party.

Hal froze in fear, they were nearly on him.

It was over.

This really wasn't the way he had hoped to go out; wedged between a fence, consumed by *Time Vampires* in the heart of a pocket dimension with a whole season of Jessica Jones sitting on his to-be-watched list.

He felt a surge of pain grip his shoulder as the blade-like fingertips dug into him, causing him to clench his jaw down hard as he was dragged from in-between the vertical stockade of Malcolm's making.

He closed his eyes, waiting for the real pain to come, then opened them to see that Malcolm had pulled him through to the other side of the barrier, and to temporary safety.

'Thanks,' said Hal, as the monsters flew into the fence, clambering over each other in an attempt to reach the three time-travellers.

'Don't get sentimental,' said Malcolm, extending a hand to help him up. 'You're no good to me dead.'

'Sooo, should I cancel those Ed Sheeran tickets, orrr?' said Hal, accepting the offer of the killer's extended hand and returning to a less embarrassing, notably more upright plane of existence.

Malcolm replied with an agitated grumble, and they set off through the large garden they now found themselves in.

*

As they ran past what appeared to be a game of badminton, Kara swiped at a levitating shuttlecock as if it were a bothersome fly.

'Oh look, these guys have formed a badminton!'

Hal laughed, remembering their friend Jon's ridiculous way of describing the particular sport.

His adrenaline-fuelled delirium was cut short as they reached the end of the garden and were greeted by yet another fence, made all the more unclimbable thanks to the ancient fir trees situated on the other side, forming an extra layer of un-traversable bullshit.

'Fuck,' said Kara.

'Hey,' said Hal, 'think you can *Hulk Smash* through this one too?'

'Unlikely,' grumbled Malcolm.

'Yeah, sun's getting *real* low, to be fair.'

And then, like rock stars at their own gig who had foolishly decided to keep it real by using the regular, communal portable toilets at a festival, they found themselves boxed in and surrounded by their fans.

Unlike an aforementioned rock star, Hal pulled his gun from his holster and aimed it into the crowd before them, firing off a warning shot that hit one of the creatures square in the chest.

The pellet dissolved, as if melting amidst a pool of

acid, fizzling away into a faint blue wisp. The Time Vampires however, remained entirely undeterred.

Hal huffed, resigned to the fact that things were about to get messy, and was about to say it was worth the literal shot, as one of the monsters squealed like a werewolf howling at an invisible moon, apparently giving the green light to his surrounding brethren that it was feeding time.

'Well, at least it can't get any worse,' said Kara.

Their attention was drawn away from the hoard, thanks to the sound of a savage growl that made them flinch.

Guttural.

Feral.

Primal.

Standing there in the darkness at the side of a building to their right were two canine-esque beasts, hackles raised, chests heaving, and deformed jaws baring razor sharp teeth.

Hal and Kara shot a look towards Malcolm, who held an expression that seemed to waver between exhausted acceptance and resentful indignation.

'Kara,' said Hal, slapping his cheek with incredulity.

'Yeah?'

'You suck.'

'Defend yourselves,' muttered Malcolm, ripping of his apron and discarding it on the ground.

*

The three interlopers found themselves swarmed

from all sides, from both humanoid and hell-hound varieties alike, as Kara felt countless hands clawing into her flesh, scraping trails of blue sparks along her skin.

'How are we feeling this?!' screeched Kara in agony.

'I guess,' growled Hal through gritted teeth as he wrestled with his own pain threshold. 'The White Lodge is Krypton! And we ain't so *super* here!'

The more energy the creatures drained from them, the more defined their features became, their once spoon-like faces now full of jagged teeth that bit into her, as the hollow, empty eye sockets stared back at her without fear or remorse, the central nervous systems of the beasts lighting up with a vibrant blue with every successful slice.

The chronologically-distorted vampires continued to leach the energy from the very cores of the three Restarters, ruthlessly drawing power from them, as if doing so would make them whole again and bring them to a state of existence closer to the three people invading their world. But with each slash of their sharp fingers, no matter how much power they successfully drained, the effects were merely temporary.

Once the transference of electricity had dissipated, the eerie blue glow that emanated from their frail forms vanished, and the creatures who had been fortunate enough to experience a mere taste of a universe beyond their own grew wilder, even more savage, like a candy crush addict who reasoned that their next attempt would truly free them from the current level they were trapped in, taking them to somewhere new and infinitely more rewarding.

'Hal,' shouted Kara, struggling to be heard over the horrific squealing and stabbing sounds.

'Mmmhere,' he said, his voice a mere muffle.

She could see his hand grasping at nothing amidst the swath of oily blackness that had engulfed them, and reached out for it.

'Happy thoughts!' she shouted, a crackle of energy surging between them as she made the connection.

And she closed her eyes, getting her zen on.

Images floated by in her mind's eye; flashes of Greg, of her dogs. Her *wonderful* dogs. That super-cool Green Lantern ring she'd been after for years that she found on eBay and…that was the one. The thought that was not her own. A thought that meant she and Hal were entirely in tune.

She focused on that, allowing herself to drift into the memory, then opened her eyes, ready to hit the gas and unleash the thunder.

*

The garden was filled with the sight of flailing creatures, which were thrown into the air by the impact of Kara and Hal's energy blast, freeing Malcolm from the humanoid beasts that were leaching away his consciousness, and the wolf-like monstrosities that were gnawing at his ankles.

He growled savagely, grabbing an oily attacker by

its throat, the connection feeding the vampiric aberration with his dwindling reserves of red energy, revealing a snapping maw of human-like teeth.

Malcolm threw the creature aside and proceeded to unleash a beat down on the face of the next feral animal that felt lucky enough to try its luck, smashing his fists into the unfortunate face belonging to the lost soul of the damned.

Hal and Kara dragged themselves up, their eyes glowing with the slowly degrading shimmer of Restarter energy.

'Hadouken!' remarked Hal, dusting himself down.

'Time to move,' said Kara.

'Umm, I'm not sure if he's ready yet,' said Hal, directing her attention towards Malcolm by throwing his thumb over his shoulder.

'You,' said Malcolm in-between brutal punches, 'dare,' he added, literally ripping an arm from one of the creature's sockets, 'touch' definitely leaving a mark on another, 'me?!' he growled, his voice thunderous, seemingly refuelling his own brand of Restarter-sauce direct from the source.

'I think you got him, Drago,' said Hal, eager to create some distance between the reanimated corporeal cadavers that were already returning for another go, clearly being drawn by the seemingly rekindled energy the three of them had tapped into, like moths to a blowtorch.

Malcolm landed several more punches, then seemed to come to his senses, staring back towards the Restarters.

'Reformed, huh?' said Kara dryly.

Malcolm threw the creature that was frantically kicking its own legs, being held up by the killer's unbreakable grasp, his eyes slowly returning from a fiery-red glow to his usual, equally-unsettling, murderous glare.

No words were needed, it was time to go.

With the entirety of the mob now contained within the garden they were occupying, they made their way back through the fence that was now unobstructed, the gap initially made by Malcolm now considerably wider thanks to the stampede created by their attackers.

They caught sight of a gliding shadow, one which was seemingly going about its business in another timeline entirely.

'Hold onto me,' said Malcolm, waiting for them to do so before he reached his hand out into what was little more than a glitching silhouette, as if he were fishing for something to latch onto.

Nine agonizing seconds later, like an expert lockpicker attempting to tumble the mechanism contained within a particularly dastardly padlock, he smiled darkly, then grabbed on harder to his quarry.

The creatures behind them were almost on them, and as one attempted to latch on to Kara's shoulder she pulled herself closer to Malcolm out of instinct, wincing in expectation of the pain that would surely follow.

Instead, they heard the oddly comforting sound of rushing air, and Kara realised it wasn't a lock Malcolm was trying to crack, it was a key he was trying to *turn*.

She clenched her eyes shut, as they were once more dragged back through the fields of time, to a place far away from The White Lodge. A world where neither the stench of decay, which bled from the bodies of forgotten souls, nor the guard dogs of the underworld could reach them.

Back, she hoped, into the light.

CHAPTER THIRTY-TWO

The Gunslinger and The Locksmith

R.I Timestamp Recalibration Error:

Restart Unknown

D azzled by the afternoon sun of whatever restart they were now occupying, the three time-travellers felt a distinct sensation of pressure as their bodies were ejected from the pocket dimension with a ferocity that implied wherever they had just been was truly glad to be rid of them.

They were greeted by the sight of a woman they had never seen before, who hummed an unfamiliar tune as she proceeded to discard a large black sack of rubbish into a wheelie bin which was camouflaged by a wooden enclosure, surrounded by thoughtfully planted hedges.

'When are we?' gasped Hal.

'And *where* are we?' added Kara, equally discombobulated.

Hal looked behind him and saw a familiar fence, once that had previously been kicked in by Malcolm, and made wider by the onslaught of hundreds of oily demons, but was now inexplicably repaired. "Because *time travel*, he thought, shaking his head slightly amidst a suitably awe-struck smile.

'It is…difficult to say for certain,' mumbled Malcolm.

'You have no idea do you,' said Hal, his words goading the killer into embracing the truth for once.

'It's not an exact science Harold,' Malcolm replied gruffly, 'unlike your petulance.'

'I thought the plan was to lock-on to a particular version of you?' said Kara.

'It was,' confirmed Malcolm. 'But given the immediacy of the…Time Vampires–'

'Ha!' said Hal happily. 'I made a serial killer say Time Vampires!'

'–I thought it *prudent*,' continued Malcolm, ignoring Hal's childishness, 'to take advantage of the hand we'd been dealt.'

'So that was just a random Time Echo you latched onto?' said Kara, in no way complaining. She was honestly just as relieved as the rest of them to be out of that doomed netherworld.

'What do you mean by "Time Echo"?' asked Malcolm, unfamiliar with the term.

'It's what we named them,' said Hal, rapping a knuckle against the now-repaired fence.

Malcolm stared blankly, clearly needing further clarification.

'On one of our later restarts,' said Kara, recalling the encounter, 'we sort of…*broke* time a bit.'

'Of course you did,' said Malcolm, the mere hint of a smile curling his top lip.

'Anyway,' she continued, 'things kind of escalated. Echoes started popping up left, right and centre. Versions of us from different phases. Some that hadn't even…'

Kara stopped short, recalling one Time Echo in particular; wearing a brown leather jacket, and brandishing a gun.

Hal pulled his attention away from the remarkably unremarkable fence, and turned to see why she had stopped talking.

'You okay, Kar'?' he asked her, concern in his eyes.

'Yeah. Fine,' she lied, trying not to look at the gun holstered to his side or the brownness of his jacket. And wondering who the hell he would have to pull a gun on before their time here was spent.

'I know nothing of the…*Time Echoes* of which you speak,' said Malcolm, rousing her from her private thoughts, but sensing there was something resting beneath the seemingly trivial facts within her words, 'though I imagine the same rules apply. During each cycle at The White Lodge, echoes of the past present themselves as shadows. They act as doorways to the many restar–'

'You mentioned that already,' said Hal. 'Nice work getting us out of there.'

'You are welcome.'

'Gah,' shuddered Kara. 'How do you manage to make even basic small-talk creepy?'

Malcolm shrugged, and shot her an ugly grin.

Kara bristled, and was about to ask him what the hell they were going to do next, when Malcolm pre-empted the question.

'You two head to that lake over there,' he said, pointing to the wide expanse of water situated behind them. 'Stay out of sight until I return.'

'And where are you off to?' said Hal suspiciously.

'I have to return for the others. Or have you forgotten about them already?' he chided.

'Of course not!' balked Hal, though in fairness, in all of the death-defying excitement he almost sort of kind of had. 'I just meant you're going back for them now?! With all those…*things* waiting there for you?'

'Hmm,' hummed Malcolm, making it evident he wasn't fully buying Hal's act, but allowing it to slide. 'I will be fine, but we need to regroup before making another attempt, lest we risk losing your colleagues.'

'Another attempt?' said Hal, not following.

'We missed our window when we lost the anchor

of my past-self,' said Malcolm, presumably referring to the floating central nervous system of a notable red disposition. 'We were lucky to find this woman to latch onto,' he added, as the lady walked away from the bins and back into the building that may or may not have been her home. 'But the chances of this being your 165th restart, let alone us being in-phase with the specific restart my past-self is occupying is…'

'Slim?' guessed Kara.

'Quite.'

'Dammit,' blurted Hal, knowing that would mean only one thing; they would have to return to The White Lodge to try again. The thought was less than appealing, and felt a lot like they would be pushing their luck.

Malcolm, meanwhile, was fairly confident he could locate Peter and Fearne having only made one jump between timelines, but felt less so attempting to navigate his way back to them by indulging in another. The search for his past-self could wait.

As he prepared himself for the long walk back to the Restart Point situated at the edge of Pentney Lakes, he grimaced. How far had he fallen? Reduced to little more than an interdimensional taxi driver.

'You can't go back there, Malcom,' said Kara, alarm in her voice. 'Those things will swarm you!'

'Is that *concern* I detect?'

'We literally couldn't care less,' said Hal, 'but you're the only one that can Nightcrawler your way around timelines.'

'Oh...well…yes,' said Malcolm, realising he would still need to work on gaining their absolute trust. 'You needn't worry. As I've said before, time works differently there. Hours will have already passed. Perhaps even months.'

With that, he departed, leaving Hal and Kara alone, and arguably stranded, now prisoners in a vertical slice of residual time. Seeing few other options, they slowly made their way to the nearby lake, eager to take a well-earned breather.

*

'What's on your mind?' said Kara, noticing the troubled look on Hal's face as they walked.

Hal appeared to show signs of hesitation.

'Oh, come on Hal, if we can't talk to each other we really *are* screwed.'

'It's probably nothing.'

'You've always been good at making something out of nothing,' she quipped.

Hal shot her a raised eyebrow, and she winked to let him know she was kidding, which was apparently all it took to put him at ease enough to make him spit it out.

'It's just, how did we generate that much power back there? We were nowhere *near* our past-selves…'

'It's not the first time we've pulled that much out of the bag,' noted Kara, recalling the notable occasion they had managed to stop Malcolm's actual heart when push had graduated to shove.

Hal pulled a face.

'*Again* with the face. What?'

'I don't think *we* did anything Kar', I think...that was all you just now.'

'Nah, it was both of us,' said Kara, dismissing the notion. 'Maybe we were just...I dunno, closer to the *source* whilst we were in...wherever the hell we just were.'

Hal wasn't so sure. The more he thought about it, the more he realised it had felt like he had just been drawn upon by Kara as a sort of energy boost. Something felt off to him; if they were so close to this *Restarter energy source* Kara had mentioned, why were those Time-Vamps chomping at the bit just for scraps of the stuff. It made no sense.

To add a further layer to his unease, amidst the pile-up of oily bodies, he was certain he had seen a flash of red. At first, he had reasoned that perhaps Malcolm had generated it. It was certainly hard to tell up from down, whilst they were crushed beneath the bundle of chaos. But now he wasn't so sure...

'There's one thing I *am* sure of, though,' said Kara, as if reading his mind.

'Hmm?'

'Remember that Time Echo you were crushing on when we broke time? With the gun and leather jacket?'

'I wasn't crushing on anyone, he just looked badass is all. I'm comfortable enough in my sexuality to appreciate a cool looking–'

Kara stared at him, a look of amusement on her face, as the penny dropped.

'Wait…' said Hal, resting his left-hand on the grip of his holstered Colt.

'Theeeeere it is,' said Kara, seeing that he finally understood.

'Woah.'

'You're damn right, woah.'

'Why didn't you mention it earlier?'

'Didn't see the benefit of letting Malcolm know everything. At least, not until *we* knew what it meant.'

The revelation hit him like a brick.

'But that would mean…you and I were always destined to come back here?' reasoned Hal. There was no other explanation.

Which led to a more pressing question; who exactly in the future was he aiming the gun at?

*

There was nothing Hal and Kara could do whilst they were waiting for Malcolm to bring Peter and Fearne into phase with whatever restart this even was, so they waited as instructed along the outskirts of the forest in an attempt to stay out of sight. They knew there was a slim chance the Dark Restarter was roaming the area, and didn't want to risk bumping into him before they had a chance to formulate a plan.

Hal set himself down on the ground, resting his weight on his elbows, revelling in the first moment of silence since they arrived back in the past. He retrieved the two cans of energy drink from his backpack, delighted to discover they *too* had been restarted, and raised his eyebrows to Kara.

She nodded, and he chucked her a can, before cracking one open.

'Seriously Hal, I can't stress this enough, great shout on the bag!'

'Thanks, that panned out pretty well, right?' he said.

'I've got something to show you,' said Kara, placing her can of drink down for a second and reaching into the jacket she had discarded by her side.

She rummaged in one of the internal pockets, before retrieving a pair of spectacles and a magnifying glass, handing them to Hal.

'I don't know why, but I've carried them everywhere with me since our trip to Fir Lodge.'

'I guess now you know why,' said Hal with a chuckle. 'It's like you were trying to tell yourself something.'

'I guess so,' said Kara, picking up her drink and pulling the ring of the can. She took an enthusiastically deep gulp of the fizz-less beverage, realising that she too had taken up some interesting hobbies once she had returned to their present.

'You know,' said Kara, 'I bought a "lock-picking for dummies" book when I got back.'

'Why?' chuckled Hal, handing back her time-travelling knick-knacks.

'I guess due to being stuck inside that storage

room in Kev's basement with *you* for the best part of thirty-three hours. Never again.'

They laughed, and each took a sip from their cans.

'Fair point. You any good?'

'I managed to pop a few locks, yeah.'

'Sick,' said Hal approvingly.

All he'd really achieved was discovering where to buy rubber-duck-style flamingos.

They sat there, lying on their backs, as Kara fiddled with the ring on the can, slowly weakening it until it snapped with a satisfying "tink", before continuing to chug the drink like it was air, until the container was finally empty.

'Not bad,' she said finally. 'Why are you smiling? It's weird. Stop it.'

'I've just missed this, that's all,' said Hal. 'Not the *dying* part obviously, but us, working a problem. The Restarters, solving crimes in time.'

Having polished off the final droplets inside the can, she looked around for a bin to recycle it, then realised that didn't matter, remembering it would vanish on the next restart.

'So, what's the play?' Said Kara. 'You all in on Malcolm's plan?'

'Peter and Fearne seem on board,' said Hal, nursing his own drink as if it were a fine whisky.

'I don't care what *they* think. I only care about what *you* think.'

'I think...he's gotten us this far,' said Hal.

'That he has...' agreed Kara the words loaded with subtext. 'He seems different. Less…'

'Murdery?' said Hal, and Kara nodded thoughtfully.

'It feel odd to you?' she said. 'That *that's* the new bar for the people we do and do not trust, these days?'

'Their ability to resist the urge to drive an axe into our back?' clarified Hal. 'A little.'

'We could go our own way? Bail on…' Kara could see Hal was trying his utmost not to burst out into song. 'You're singing Fleetwood in your head aren't you…'

'No,' Hal lied.

Kara squinted suspiciously and smiled. 'Liar.'

Hal shrugged unapologetically and allowed her to continue.

'We could bail on all this. Fly solo, and solve this thing ourselves?'

Hal thought about that. It did have a certain appeal. With the exception of one or two major issues.

'And have not only three Malcolms to worry about, but also two rogue Restarters knocking around?' said Hal, voicing his concerns.

'We've survived worse odds,' countered Kara.

'Have we though?'

'Not really,' she admitted, pursing her lips, as if wrestling with another question. Hal gave her the time she needed. 'Are you really as mad at Peter and

Fearne as you make out?' she asked finally.

'Are you not?'

'Of course I am, but…you seem extra-pissed.'

'Honestly?' said Hal, exhaling slowly. 'They did what they had to in order to survive. And by the sounds of it, they were here a lot longer than we were. Who knows what lengths we would have resorted to in the end. Doesn't mean I'm not going to give them a hard time for a while though. We've earned that much.'

Kara nodded.

'Back to Malcolm for a sec',' said Hal, reaching the only conclusion that seemed the most logical. As much as they hated to admit it, they had little choice but to work with him. At the very least, his quantumly-charged bus pass has been worth its weight in gold thus far. 'I say we keep our eye on him. First sign of a murderous relapse, we make our way to the Restart Point and ditch him.'

'He's hiding something.'

'Oh, no doubt. He's hosting a freakin' Easter egg hunt of truth eggs all over the entirety of the Pentney Lakes.'

'You think it was Future Malcolm that brought us back here? Restarted our past? Or Dark Restarter Malcolm?' asked Kara.

'Whichever one of them it was, Future Malcolm would remember it either way. Which means he's blatantly lying when he says he doesn't know.'

'What if it wasn't either of them?' posed Kara.

They sat there silently pondering that. If that were the case, it meant there was another variable messing with their past. Potentially another Restarter entirely.

'I've actually been thinking of a way we can find out for sure…' said Hal.

Kara leaned in, eager to hear what was sure to be an interesting Time Heist in the making.

As he explained his idea, she chuckled. It was perfect. And just crazy enough to work.

'That'll take time,' she said eventually, having both thrashed out the kinks.

'The *one* thing we have,' said Hal simply.

They clinked their empty cans together in agreement on that, and laid in wait for the return of Malcolm, Peter and Fearne.

CHAPTER THIRTY-THREE
Someone that I used to Know
Restart Unknown – Friday, August 24th, 2018, 4:01pm

The minutes, as they were prone to do, had turned into hours, and both Hal and Kara were getting antsy.

Kara was feeling notably safer, knowing that they were in a bog-standard restart which, if Malcolm was to be believed, was little more than a rerun from their own past. One which would run its course without incident, so long as they didn't wade in and mess it all up. All they had to do was sit still and not interact with anything or anyone.

A necessary requirement that quickly became boring for the two of them.

Kara excused herself from Hal's company, who insisted she not wander too far. Neither of them wanted to bump into Malcolm's murderously marauding past-self before formulating a solid plan of attack. Or worse, versions of their Restarter-selves who were undoubtedly still working their way up to their 165th restart, believing their actions would eventually end their time-loop once and for all.

She thought about that, as she took a stroll deeper into the woods, finding herself equally keen on taking advantage of the opportunity to be alone with her own thoughts.

After a short while, she found a nice familiar spot; a wooden log that overlooked the lake. She took a seat, smiling at the significance of the location.

Remembering how they had been following Kevin, but got side-tracked by the beauty of the lake. It may have been the fog messing with them, but she personally remembered it less cynically.

Through all their adventuring, it had been a true moment of simply allowing the picture-perfect lushness of their surroundings to wash over them. It had made them feel normal. Just two friends hanging out, without the worry of time, space, or the cyclical continuation of their untimely deaths, that would play out indefinitely if they simply stopped chasing the answers that, back then, seemed eternally out of reach.

Not that they were that much more the wiser now, of course.

Kara sighed, contemplating the many ways in which The Dark Restarter could have changed their past to bring them back here. Each one more outlandish than the next. If indeed it was *that* version of himself that had done so at all…

It was during one of these ruminations that she heard the rustle of leaves behind her, and she span around quickly, like a ninja responding to the tell-tale flutter of an impending dagger. And there, standing before her, beneath an archway created by nature itself, thanks to two incredibly thick interconnecting tree branches, was Hal.

Her friend dusted himself off and looked directly at her, or rather, *through* her. Glancing down at what Kara presumed was a watch, she saw him bring his wrist closer to his face, as he twisted the rotating bezel and whispered gently into his own arm.

'Okay Iris, I'm going for minimal contamination, wake me up when it's time to *go* go,' said Hal, seemingly unaware of Kara's presence. A voice emanated from the watch, as the circular dial lit up in a vibrant blue.

'*You should leave immediately*,' said a female voice that seemed as articulate as she was keen to enunciate. '*As I advised. Before you ignored me and came here anyway.*'

'Don't you *sass* me, Iris,' said Hal. 'This is a *temporal constant*, just like the bar in London. Probably.'

Kara, still invisible to him, noted how he muttered that final word with a lack of conviction.

'*You mean the bar fight,*' said Iris, her tone dripping with sarcasm. '*Which could have been avoided, had you just listened to—*'

'Mute,' said Hal abruptly, causing the dial to flash angrily, before settling back down to a gun-metal grey.

Hal reached into the pocket of a black leather jacket she'd never seen him wear before, retrieving a ridiculous pair of nerdy specs that more than a little reminded her of the ones she had worn to finish off her Velma costume. He popped them on, then pressed gently against the left-hand side of the frame, the transparent lenses instantly becoming opaque with a wild blue hue.

Hal continued to press the frame of his glasses, breathing deeply through his nose as the lenses flickered in tandem with his touch. 'Nope…nope…*still* nope.' He huffed in frustration, each utterance of the same word becoming snippier.

'Hal?' said Kara, standing up and walking towards him, surveying his attire; dark blue jeans that looked like they needed an iron, a pair of worn brown boots, and a black t-shirt emblazoned with bright neon blue numbers and letters that read "88MPH". She noted that they were printed in a font that had an eighties sort of vibe to it. All of which solidifying the chilling realisation that this was not the same version of her friend from the here and now.

Finally, his eyes were apparently met with what he

was looking for.

"There she is! Kara!' said Hal, making her jump, as he ran towards her and attempted to give her a big hug. Regrettably, he passed straight through her, and span around on the spot looking more than a little embarrassed. 'Right, bollocks, schoolboy phase-fail.'

'What's…happening right now?' asked Kara, forgivably confused.

'Wait, hang on,' said not-Hal. 'Can't hear you, it's a whole thing,' he added, this time reaching into the pocket of his jeans to retrieve a small, black coloured object, which he jammed into his ear, pressing the frame of his glasses for a second time.

'Hey!' said Hal. 'Sorry, forgot to pair them up. What was that you just said?'

'Hey…I said what's going on?' replied Kara, growing a little impatient with all his faffing. She took comfort in the fact that some things clearly never changed. Whatever was happening, this seemed like his first time at it.

'Oh, sorry, we're not in-phase with each other right now. You can hear *me*, but I can't see or hear *you* without *these* things,' he said extending a finger of his left hand and running it in circles in the direction of his glasses and ear piece, like a cowboy spinning an invisible pistol.

Kara stared at him, the backdrop of the lake now behind him.

'Are you really here?' asked Kara. It seemed like as good a question as any.

'Are *any* of us?' said Hal, shooting her a warm smile that failed to hide the tiredness lurking in his eyes.

She couldn't decide if he was making a joke to lighten the mood, or if he was hiding *behind* one to conceal an ugly truth. Knowing him the way she did, she'd put money on the latter.

'You're looking...*well*,' she lied, his usual five-o'clock shadow having grown out dangerously close to being regarded as a full beard, his hair far longer than she'd ever seen it. Still short, but very unkempt. 'You want to fill me in, here?'

'Right. Yeah. Of course,' said Hal, clearly trying to find the right words.

She walked past him and sat back down on the log, knowing full well he was gearing up for a classic Hal-branded ramble. 'I'm...well, from the future. *A* future I should say.'

'You. Right now? You're from the future?!' It seemed obvious as soon as he said it. 'How is that possible?'

'Oh, you know. The usual; life, death, tequila...and time travel.' That seemed to make him chuckle for some reason. 'To be honest, it...feels like a story for another time. Or *from* another time, as it were.'

'Urgh,' grimaced Kara playfully. 'I can only *imagine* how long you've been waiting to bust that one out.'

'I just came up with it now,' said Hal earnestly.

'Liar,' she said, shooting him a knowing smile.

'Ha. It's really good to see you Kara.'

'How *is* the future? Tell me we beat this thing!'

Her voice was full of hope, which she reasoned wasn't unwarranted. After all, if he was here speaking to her, it surely meant they had made it back.

'The future's okay,' said Hal breezily. 'I meeeean, the zombie outbreak set us back a bit. But at least Avengers 4 had a terrific ending!'

'Wait, seriously?!'

'Yeah, I know right, I was surprised they stuck the landing on that too. So much hype,' said Hal, his eyes glazing over at the fond memories.

'I hate you,' said Kara, realising he was joking.

'Anywhoooo, I can't tell you any more than that, but something's going to happen. When it does, I need you to focus on *one* thing, okay?'

'What's going to happen?' asked Kara.

'I can't say,' Hal replied cagily.

'Okay, *when* is it going to happen?'

'I...can't say,' he said again, his brow furrowing with frustration.

'Are you *kidding* me right now?' said Kara, noting a fleeting reflection of herself in the lenses of Hal's glasses. An outline that seemed incomplete, as if she was made up of fluctuating lines of a vibrantly blue neon.

'All I can tell you is that you need to go *big*. Bigger than we've ever gone. We're talking *Full Blue*. I won't be able to lock on unless it's big.'

'Full blue?! Cryptic much?' said Kara, her voice

peppered with a drollness that caused Hal to laugh.

'Sorry, but I'm sorta breaking *every* rule in the book just by *being* here. Oh, there's *one* more thing.'

'Shoot,' said Kara, quickly coming to terms with there being no point in asking this time-travelling Columbo any more questions.

Hal hesitated, as if he were weighing up whether he had already said too much. But eventually, the Hal she knew won the internal battle.

'I'll *never* stop looking. *Ever*. Understand?'

'Not really,' said Kara truthfully.

'Say it,' he pressed.

'Say what?'

'What I just said.'

'You'll never stop looking. I get it. Jeez.'

'Also, and I know it sucks, but don't tell *past-me* anything about what we've just talked about, okay? That's *incredibly* important,' his eyes suddenly full of worry.

'What *have* we just talked about?' said Kara, genuinely unsure.

'Exactly.'

The watch around Hal's wrist began to beep, the screen glowing a worrying red, which he responded to by pressing the screen and killing the alarm. Presumably, she reasoned, it was signalling him that it was time to leave.

'Okay Kar', close your eyes.'

'Why?'

'Because time travel and *reasons*, Kara. Just trust

me.'

'Fine,' she said, closing her eyes and crossing her arms, as well as blowing a stray strand of hair that was dangling from her fringe in pathetic rebellion.

She felt a presence leaning in close to her as her friend from another time whispered three nonsensical words into her ear.

'Follow the flamingo,' he said.

A parting gift to remind her he was definitely the real deal and not an echo. His dumb sense of humour still very much intact.

'Oh, come *on* Hal, you–' but upon opening her eyes, she realised he was gone.

'Who were you talking to?' said Hal, who had approached her silently from the left and was standing directly behind her.

'Gah!' she screamed, noting that this was her Hal. 'What the *shit*, Hal?!' she said punching him hard in the shoulder, blue sparks exploding from the contact and making him stagger backwards. 'You scared the *crap* out of me, sneaking up on me like that.'

'I wasn't sneaking,' he said, rubbing his arm. 'It's not *my* fault I can't generate sound when I walk.'

'Dick.'

'What's got *you* so spooked anyway?

'No one,' said Kara, instantly correcting her course. 'Nothing.'

'Uh huh, Are you *sure* you're okay? You look like you've had a run in with a boggart or something.'

'I understood that reference,' said Kara, forcing a

chuckle.

'Finally!' said Hal. 'Maybe you *are* human after all!'

'Yeah,' she replied, her mind clearly somewhere other than the present.

'Because, I'll be honest. I was legit starting to wonder. Come on, we need to get going,' he added, not utterly convinced Kara was being entirely open with him, but respecting her space all the same. 'Hannibal Lecter just popped up with Pete and Fearne.'

'Uh huh,' replied Kara, looking back over her shoulder hoping to catch a glimpse of the future iteration of her friend, the ominous nature of their conversation feeling more like a dream with each passing moment.

And with each step she took, the memory slipped further and further away from her.

CHAPTER THIRTY-FOUR
The Flutterby Conundrum

Restart Unknown – Friday, August 24th, 2018, 4:11pm

'You guys took your sweet time,' said Kara, eyeing Peter and Fearne with notable suspicion.

'Yeah,' said Hal with equal mistrust. 'What happened? Did the three of you stop off for a quick killing spree before coming back?'

'How many times can we apologise?' said Peter, as diplomatically as he could muster, though the constant attacks and jokes were wearing real thin real fast, and his tolerance for Hal's anger had all but been expended.

'The amount of time you were gone, surely you had time to burn down the odd orphanage or two?' said Hal, refusing to relent.

Fearne dispensed a dagger-like glare at the Restarter, and seemed to inhale enough breath to fuel a tornado of retaliation, before Malcolm stepped in to explain their absence.

'As you saw yourselves, during our foray along the *precipice* of *infinity*, it is not an exact science. I had trouble locating the two of you Harold, nothing more,' Malcolm's words offering little in the way of warming the frost between them, eliciting a feeling deep within Kara that made her wonder if dividing them all had been his intention from the very beginning.

'So, which repeat,' began Peter, before feeling the room and adjusting his lexicon. 'Sorry, *restart*, are we in right now?' He'd sensed pretty early on that "Repeats" was not going to catch on, and when Malcolm adopted the term Restarters, that was pretty much the last nail in the vernacular coffin.

'We couldn't tell you,' said Hal sourly. 'We haven't ventured back to Fir Lodge to check. We were waiting on you.'

'Well, let's get going then,' said Fearne coldly, marching away from them down the road, with Hal following in hot pursuit.

'Is this a bad time to tell them that's the wrong way?' Kara whispered to Peter.

'Most definitely.'

*

After a diplomatically orchestrated course correction, and some considerable sleuthing later, the once and future Velma, Ghostbuster, Pro-Golf Player and Marilyn Monroe had all managed to ascertain this particular restart appeared to be somewhere not even remotely close to the 165th time-loop of Hal and Kara's first adventure that they had hoped for, which Malcolm convinced them was actually a good thing.

Before they made another attempt to phase with his past – and considerably more murderous – self, he proposed that they should probably use the opportunity to prepare for what would surely be a dangerous first contact.

They knew that in order to reach their target, they would eventually be forced into returning to The White Lodge, where Malcolm would then have to search for the red-coloured anchor that represented his former self. It was Malcolm's hope that they would then be able to latch on to a nearby echo of the past, hopefully generating some distance between the Restarters and Malcolm's darker persona.

After all, Future Malcolm had no intention of allowing his past-self to know he was working with the four of them, given that it could have, as he put it, "disastrous repercussions in terms of cause and effect."

'I don't get it,' said Peter. 'Why don't we just send Future Malcolm here to go and take care of this *Dark* version of himself?'

Having calmed down a little, Hal and Fearne had reverted to a far more amicable level of passive-aggression towards each other. This was, in part, a direct result of returning to Fir Lodge, and getting to relive (albeit vicariously) the highlights of Rachel's thirtieth birthday party.

'Did you see that?' said Fearne excitedly, watching as her past-self and past-Stacey completely destroyed Jon and Gavin at a round of beer pong. 'We really smashed them at that!' she continued, watching as her alive-self removed the blonde wig of her costume and swished her brunette hair with a sturdy rambunctiousness.

'I cannot attack this…*Dark Restarter* as you call him, head on,' said Malcolm, immediately quashing the idea.

'I can't see why…wait? What did you just say?' said Hal, Spider-Sense flaring.

'I said I can't confront him head on,' said Malcolm, growing impatient at having to repeat himself.

'Not that,' a look of suspicion rolling across Hal's features. 'I don't recall any of us calling past-you a Dark Restarter,' his brow furrowing and immediately doubting himself.

Had they said it? Perhaps in passing? So much had happened, it was virtually impossible to keep track. But the niggle clawed at his thoughts all the same.

'You must have,' said Malcolm simply.

'Preeetty sure we haven't,' agreed Fearne. 'What about when you were at The White Lodge?'

'Nope,' said Kara.

'I must have just made the leap,' said Malcolm weakly.

'I guess,' said Peter, who admittedly *had* been putting extra emphasis on the word "dark" an awful lot.

'Then I merely assumed that is what you went with. Am I mistaken?'

The four of them shifted awkwardly.

'Well then, clearly you're not all as creative as you *think* you are Harold,' the killer noted.

'In my defence, Pete came up with it,' said the Restarter, throwing Peter under the bus.

'Well, Peter,' said Malcolm coldly. 'I don't care much for the term.'

'Fill in a complaint form,' said Kara. 'I'll make sure it gets filed into the correct receptacle. It's the one that sits under the desk.'

'You know, where the trash lives,' said Hal, giving Kara a high five.

As the smattering of blue sparks evaporated, Malcolm let out a sigh, secretly berating himself for making such a stupid error. In the end, he decided to go easy on himself. He had a lot on his plate.

'Juvenile *labelling* aside, I do not remember it happening,' said Malcolm matter-of-factly, subtly steering the conversation back to Peter's suggestion of sending his future-self to take care of his younger, darker, restarting incarnation. 'Therefore, we must have determined a reason not to take that approach.'

'Well that's *convenient*,' said Peter, still smarting over the assassination of what he felt was a totally solid Bad Guy name, watching longingly as Hal retrieved a bottle of water from his backpack.

'Kylo Ren's right,' said Hal, referring to Malcolm as he popped the screw-top lid off of his drink.

Noticing Peter's apparent desire for some water, Hal smiled at his friend and grabbed the second restarted bottle, lobbing it to him as if it were a hydration-themed peace offering.

None of them felt thirst here, but there was something oddly comforting about holding an object that was in-phase with them. They were beginning to realise that there was a lot to be said for the nostalgic act of simulated refreshment.

Flicking the lid of his metal lighter, Hal lit up a cigarette, took a drag, then stubbed it out and discarded it, determined that he was done with the things. Ordering his thoughts, he dropped his theoretical musings on them all.

'Flutterby Effect,' Hal blurted, causing a smile to run across Kara's face.

Actually, his emerging idea had more to do with an Infinity Loop Paradox, but he knew the former terminology would make Kara happy, which was far more important to him than technicalities.

'What's a…Flutterby Effect?' said Fearne.

Kara told them, once again breaking down why "Flutterby" was a much better name for the colourful insect that "butterfly" ever was.

'Malcolm can't just zip backwards and take himself out,' said Hal, finally getting to the meat of the matter. 'Assuming he could even win–'

'Obviously I could,' said Malcolm proudly, as if it were a given.

'Uh huh, sure you could big guy,' continued Hal, smiling at Malcolm's touchiness and adjusting his word use. 'When ol' *Stabby-McStabberson* wins then, and successfully subdues himself, his past-self won't go on to do all the things he's already done.'

'Sound like a win to me,' said Peter.

'Oh, it would be,' agreed Hal. 'In the short term. But sooner or later, time will catch up with them both. If Dark-Restarter-Malcolm doesn't do the things he needs to do to finally become *this* Malcolm,' reasoned Hal, pointing towards the fifth member of their party, 'Future Malcolm will have no reason to be here. All that would come undone.'

'Meaning Future Malcolm would what? Disappear?' said Kara, well and truly getting it.

'Yahtzee,' said Hal, gulping down some lukewarm water.

'So,' said Fearne thoughtfully, '*Our* Malcolm vanishes. Then what?'

'My best guess? Everything restarts again,' said Hal. 'His past-self will continue on with his plan, which in turn will lead to Future Malcolm coming back to stop him. With the added bonus of having potentially zero memory of his previous attempt, trapping them both in an infinity loop.'

'Like the snake eating its own tail?' said Peter.

Hal shot-clucked his tongue, his hand shooting off an imaginary bullet of agreement.

'So, it has to be us,' said Kara. 'We have to be the ones to stop all this.'

'Which brings me to something I want to discuss,' said Malcolm. 'Even with the four of you, your chances of killing my past-self are…minimal.'

'Woah there, Agent 47,' said Hal, 'no one said anything about *killing* anyone. Besides, that's not even possible, we're invincible here.'

Malcolm hid his smirk perfectly. 'Leaving him *alive* will allow him to continue his work. It's too much of a ris—'

'We'll find another way,' said Kara, her words simple, and clearly non-negotiable.

'If we could capture him,' reasoned Peter, 'maybe we could try and convince him to work *with* us?'

'That will never work,' said Malcolm.

'It might,' said Fearne. 'I mean, you're working with us now…*aren't* you?' her words laced with an insinuation that he may have something to share. An agenda perhaps, indicating this was all for show.

'This is different,' said Malcolm. 'I am not the same man now as I was back then. You don't understand how he sees you.'

'How *does* past-you see us?' Hal straightened his

posture, eager to gain some insight.

'To him you are hapless children. Old enough to be extinguished, of course. A rat-catcher and his orange secretary–'

'What?' exclaimed Kara. 'Why am *I* the secretary? You sexist piece of shi–'

'Settle down,' said Malcolm. 'I had no way of knowing your names, nor did I know you were wearing…costumes. I am many things, but when it comes to gender, I do not discriminate,' he said darkly, sending a loaded smile towards Fearne, which caused her to shudder.

Kara conceded, but still looked huffy.

'Rat-catcher?' asked Hal. 'You've never seen Ghostbusters, I take it? Don't you ever just take a "me day" and catch up on some movies? Pop the knives away, go for a nice walk, head to the beach?'

'Do I look like a man that would be interested in such pursuits?'

In truth, Malcolm had seen that film. He just preferred not to admit he'd missed such a simple detail. Given his line of work, that was what Millennials referred to as an "epic fail."

'You look like a man who could do with a good spa day to be honest,' said Kara.

'Regardless, it would be wise for us to prepare for some worst-case scenarios. I would be willing to train you.'

'Train us in what?' said Peter.

'To survive, of course,' said Malcolm. 'More

specifically, how to survive *me*.'

The four Restarters looked at each other, the absurdity of the offer weighing heavily on top of the silence like a layer of congealing custard on an unrefrigerated trifle.

'Why not,' said Kara eventually. 'And whilst you're at it, you can show us how you fast-forward through a restart too.'

Malcolm smiled as he stood up, and adopted a predator-like posture, reminding them all how tall he actually was, not to mention how imposing his presence could *truly* be when he switched it on.

Each of them realising that if they ever did have a run in with the serial killer's darker, Restarting-self, maybe running away would be their best, or perhaps *only* chance of survival.

CHAPTER THIRTY-FIVE
Wax On, Wax Off

Restart Unknown – Saturday, August 25th, 2018, 6:01pm

After spending the lion's share of their current restart sparring with Malcolm at the far end of the rear garden of Fir Lodge, Hal was reminded of the time he had attempted to learn to juggle. There were some skills his poor sense of coordination couldn't assimilate, and fighting was clearly on that list.

Hal had started their training with eager enthusiasm, dazzled by the prospect of learning how to defend himself. But, from the moment Malcolm had discarded his apron and rolled up his sleeves, the

Restarter's good mood had gradually been eradicated, as Malcolm laid a hefty beatdown on him, and once again he found himself face down in the dirt.

'How do you fast-forward like that,' said Hal, brushing off the non-adhering dust.

Malcolm was taking great pleasure in displaying a rather delightful bonus to being able to travel forward in time within their existing restart. Every time Hal went to throw a punch, Malcolm would pop out of time, leaving Hal standing there, alone and confused, before arriving in Hal's future, continuing his onslaught with savage efficiency. 'How can I fight *back* if you keep jumping into the future?' said Hal irritably. 'It makes you near impossible to keep track of.'

'I just focus on *when* I want to be,' said Malcolm. 'And the world speeds up,' he added for good measure, as if he were explaining his preferred method of making toast, and not spontaneously-activated teleportation via the medium of quantum-entangled wormholes. 'I slow my breathing as I enter a point in time I want to occupy, and that period of time comes into focus, then I can pull myself back into phase with a fair amount of precision.'

'Yeah, well,' grumbled Hal, 'I can't catch a Golden Snitch.'

'I got that one!' Kara squeaked happily. 'Wicked fast? Damn near impossible to see!'

'Nerd,' joked Hal in fake beratement.

'You know,' said Kara, 'I think…we did it once

before, back before we knew what happened to us. We fast forwarded to the moment before our death.'

'Hmm...'

He remembered it well. It was the day they had truly seen the horrors that had befallen them, and the cause of what had sent them hurtling back into the past in the first place. 'As well as that, we moved from Fir Lodge all the way to Kevin's in a heartbeat.'

'There you are,' said Malcolm. 'At first, I could only move forward through *time*, never through *space*. I would always reappear in the same place I was previously occupying. But with practice…'

Hal and Kara thought about that. They had learnt so much over the handful of months during their tenure as Restarters…but Malcolm had spent years here.

Unbeknownst to one another, they felt a shared pang of concern over that.

Over what *else* he was capable of…

Hal nodded thoughtfully, before returning his focus back to the inevitability of constant failure.

*

'This is pointless,' he said eventually, having just pulled himself up off the dirt for what felt like the millionth time. It felt a lot like Malcolm was focusing far less on actually training him, and far more on using the whole thing to beat ten tons of crap out of him.

'It is only *pointless*, if you continue to whine and fail to learn what I'm teaching you!' his tutor responded, equally frustrated. They needed to learn this. But at this rate it would take him years to bring Hal to a level where he could defend himself for longer than a split-second.

'I don't remember Mr Miyagi being such a grumpy wanker,' Hal jibed.

'Well, perhaps this Miyagi you refer to had a better student.'

Hal balked. 'Seriously? Karate kid? You've *seen* The Karate Kid, right?'

'I have not.'

'Kara? Tell him, will you?'

'I mean, I've *seen* it, but couldn't tell you any of their names,' said Kara, sitting on a nearby log and gulping down some restarted water.

'What is *wrong* with you pod-people?' said Hal.

'*Pod* people?' questioned Kara, in a blatant attempt to wind him up further.

'I hate you all.'

'Again!' demanded Malcolm.

'I'm out, your turn Kar',' said Hal, nursing what felt considerably like a broken rib, despite the fact his body shouldn't have been able to sustain actual damage.

'We are not done,' said Malcolm, refusing to let him duck out.

'I *feel* done…' said Hal, gingerly applying pressure to his ribs, which throbbed with a dull ache, reassuring him that he was perhaps merely imagining the pain.

'He will approach you quickly,' said Malcolm, pacing impatiently, eager to impart wisdom. 'Without hesitation. His goal is to finish you before you have time to even begin fighting back. Do not try to reason with him, do not show mercy, and most importantly of all…and Harold, I'm talking directly to *you* here. Do. Not. Talk. To. Him.'

'Why are you singling *me* out?'

'Because, Harold, you like to act like you're in a movie, trading quips, whilst he will only be interested in trading successive blows of a blade to your flesh. Drop the ego, drop the flair. You *must* take this seriously. Your life will literally depend on it.'

It was hard to take the man seriously, given that the makeshift blade he was currently brandishing for emphasis was actually a small, rubber flamingo.

'Yeah, about that,' said Peter. 'You say past-you somehow managed to bring a knife back with him into the past?'

'Just one,' said Malcolm.

During their training he had recounted to them all how, as his body had fallen to the floor after Hal and Kara's handiwork, the back of his hand had been resting against the hilt of the dropped blade.

It was just enough of a connection to send the knife back in time with him, however it had taken Malcolm many a restart before he realised there was a tangible blade at his disposal. As he re-materialised into the past, the blade inexplicably reformed in Kevin's basement; his final resting place. Malcolm had only stumbled on it by accident when he noticed the familiar weapon existing far too early in the timeline, whilst searching Kevin's home for answers.

He remembered licking his lips, frightened to reach out for it in case it was a cruel mirage; a joke at his expense. The joy he experienced when his outstretched shaking fingers wrapped around the hilt was palpable…

'And you're saying this knife reappears at Kevin's every restart?' asked Peter curiously.

'Yes,' confirmed Malcolm. 'My past-self is forced to head out and retrieve it every time. Twenty-nine minutes wasted on each new Cerebral Rever…*restart*.' It was an awful lot of work, having to run such a menial errand of collection each and every time.

'That's a bit of a game changer isn't it,' noted Kara. 'I mean what happens if he stabs us whilst we're…out-of-phase like this?'

It was a valid concern. From watching Hal and Malcolm's sparring session, they had established injuries did not seem to take hold in the same way as they would have in the present, though there was no telling what affect an in-phase knife would have on their bodies.

'Whilst it is unlikely,' posited Malcolm, 'that the blade could cut into us in our current state, it would be advisable to not test the theory.'

"A *ropey* theory," thought Kara.

A sentiment the others apparently shared, judging by the crumpled noses of her friends. His words didn't exactly succeed in filling any of them with much confidence.

Peter seemed to be the only exception, the cogs of his mind clearly churning, as if mildly intrigued by the prospect of their inherent invulnerability.

Not for the first time, Kara wondered if Malcolm was intentionally withholding vital information from them all.

'The only advantage you will have,' said Malcolm, returning to the matter at hand, 'is that he will not be able to foresee that I have trained the four of you. That, effectively, *he* has trained you. But he *will* adapt. You'll get three attempts, maximum. If any more time passes, it will be over before it's begun.'

'You must be a real hoot at parties,' mumbled Hal, as Malcolm popped out of time, leaving only a loud snap in his wake, a short rush of air flooding the space the killer was previously occupying like a shawl of unseen piranha.

'Dammit,' said Hal, knowing what was coming next, as Malcolm reformed and punched him hard in his kidney.

*

'I've been thinking,' said Hal, watching as Peter took his turn at being punched repeatedly by their surly tutor. 'You mentioned you could travel anywhere within the confines of the restart cycle?'

'Correct,' confirmed Malcolm.

'By that logic, there must be a way to reach Sunday, then?' said Hal, the cylinders of his mind clearly whirring at full speed.

'We've been through this,' said Malcolm, his back to Peter, who took the chance to run at him.

Malcolm cocked his head to one side, and popped out of time for a second, causing Peter to come in hot. Peter ran through where the man had just been standing, his momentum carrying him forward, as Malcolm popped back into phase and shoved him hard from behind, sending Peter face first into the thankfully-harmless gravel.

Having waited for Malcolm to return, Hal continued.

'When you ended up at the hospital. You effectively broke out of this loop we're all in.'

'I cannot travel further than the thirty-three-hours. Sunday was nothing more than an anomaly.'

'Eight years isn't an anomaly though, is it?' noted Kara.

'Right?!' agreed Hal. 'That's like…many-omalies!'

'Even if I could, what would be the point?' said Malcolm irritably. 'There's nothing there but the hospital room. Even if I could go back there, the Restart Point is just outside the door. And I can't manipulate *myself* to leave the room to extend that, what with myself being not only comatose, but physically *chained* to a bed.'

'Yeah,' said Peter, his voice temporarily muffled due to his face being pressed into the ground, 'but that was before you topped yourself. I think what Hal's saying is, what if you're not bound to that room like you were before?'

'Peter gets it!' said Hal, remembering once more why he loved Peter. 'I'm saying, what if time isn't *looking* for you anymore? What if you could fast forward to Sunday and *leave* that hospital room.'

Malcolm stared at Hal, raising his hand as a signal for Peter to stop their training. Peter nodded into the dirt with what Fearne interpreted as being pleasant relief.

'You said it yourself,' said Hal, now pacing in small circles around Malcolm, eyeing the man up like a Kingsman tailor taking guesstimates on measurements for a new suit he had been tasked with making. 'You can't trigger restarts anymore when you cross a Restart Point. What if The White Lodge is just the beginning? Another piece of the puzzle?'

Kara pulled herself up from the grass, realising this was the start of what they had talked about earlier. 'Another nexus at the hospital you mean?'

'Exactly!' said Hal. 'You could check out what affect our actions in the past are having on that Sunday. Maybe take a peek on how what we're doing here is affecting our present.'

Malcolm couldn't help but marvel at the boy's imagination. It was as if he possessed a remarkable intellect that evidenced a deep understanding of fourth-dimensional physics, whilst at the same time stumbling across such musings purely by sheer luck and a refusal to be beaten.

'Fast-forwarding that far…' mused Malcolm,

opening his thoughts to the rest of them, '…beyond the end of these thirty-three-hours? Into my second set of restarts…it would take a tremendous charge of power to reach across time in such a way.' He hadn't told them how much it actually drained him every time he jumped even a few hours. 'Though even if we were to succeed, I doubt there's much coverage of how the four of you are doing in a Norfolk hospital.'

The serial killer had a point.

'I, erm, have an idea on how you could…generate that kind of energy…' said Fearne, startling them by her sudden desire to enter the conversation.

'Fearne, I don't know if–' began Peter, an uncharacteristic look of embarrassment flashing across his face, equal in intensity to his trademark smoulder.

'Well...' she continued, ignoring her partner's plea. 'On one of our early repeats, sorry *restarts,*' she added, amending her terminology to eradicate Hal's scrunched nose of displeasure. 'We ahh...how do I put this?'

Fearne flushed red with mild embarrassment and brushed a rogue strand of hair behind her ear, seemingly unable to make eye contact with Hal, Kara, and especially Malcolm.

'No one was around, and we just thought, what's the harm, right?' said Fearne, shooting a loving look at Peter, as if remembering a very specific moment that made her feel fizzy in ways only Peter ever could.

'I'm not following?' said Hal, utterly lost by

whatever subtext he was meant to be understanding.

'Oh God, please stop talking,' said Kara, addressing Fearne, sensing where this was going.

'Plus, ya know,' said Peter, deciding to embrace the moment in an attempt to look nonplussed and masculine. 'It's not like anyone could *see* us.'

'Kind of made it feel more dangerous,' agreed Fearne, staring straight into Peter's eyes. 'Being in the middle of the living room like that. More risky. When–'

Hal looked from Fearne, to Peter, then back again, wondering why they were acting as if they were currently alone right now and sharing what was clearly some kind of intimate look of...

'Oh,' said Hal, realising what they were talking about. 'Ohhhhh...'

'There was something about being in that moment together,' said Fearne, wrapping her arms around herself and giving off a little shiver, as the memories replayed in her mind. 'That...well, the blue energy spiked, and kept us charged for *hours* after.'

'You had sexual intercourse?' asked Malcolm, as unfazed emotionally as he was un-phased physically.

'Okay, first off Malc',' said Hal, 'you're banned from using those words for the duration of our time here. Second of all, that's swell Fearne, but clearly that's not an option for Kara and I!'

'Yeah,' agreed Kara. 'I think we'll just take the long way around and charge ourselves the old-fashioned way, thanks. Ya know, without the need for a cigarette afterwards.'

'Man, I could really go for a cigarette right now,' said Hal casually.

They all stared at him.

'Not for *that* reason!' he said, as the motivation behind their questioning glares sunk in. 'Get your heads out of the gutter guys!'

Everyone but Malcolm laughed.

'If it would expedite the process…' began Malcolm, apparently weighing up the potential usefulness of such a tryst. His words generating a face-palm from both Hal and Kara.

'Malcolm,' said Hal, 'you're benched, mate. Go sit over there and think about what you've done.'

*

After twenty hours straight of receiving an onslaught from Future Malcolm, Hal knew for certain that he would be aching all over, were he not out-of-phase with the physical world.

Malcolm was reluctant to merge into the timeline that his past-self was occupying until the four of them were ready, but Hal had finally convinced their guide that enough was enough. He argued that they had learned all they could about their new status quo for the time being, and that spending any more time going over old ground would become *wasted* time, once the fog grabbed hold and started draining the finer details of their memories.

Reluctantly, Malcolm agreed, on the understanding that they would revisit their training when they had the free time to do so, and they split off into groups preparing for the journey ahead.

Malcolm was sitting, legs crossed, in the middle of the road far away from the others, watching the last rays of sunlight retreat into the horizon above the trees either side of him, as Peter appeared behind him.

Despite not hearing any footsteps, Malcolm grinned at the road ahead, not needing to turn around.

'Something on your mind, Peter?'

'How did you know it was me?'

'Occupational hazard,' said Malcolm, his words an icy reminder that sneaking up on the man would be nigh on impossible.

'I wanted to ask you–' began Peter.

'How are you feeling?' said Malcolm, cutting him off.

'What?' the question coming from a man like Malcolm. confusing him. Peter stared at the back of the killer's head, trying to look through the thick black hair as if it would hold answers as to the meaning of the question.

'It must be hard,' said Malcolm, still facing away from the Restarter, 'Trying to get your friends to understand why you did what you did to them?'

'They'll understand eventually,' said Peter, shifting uncomfortably, and attempting to kick a stone, which traitorously refused to budge under his out-of-phase foot.

'You had no choice but to *betray* them Peter,' said Malcolm, turning his head around and making eye contact with him. 'It was you or them. There's not a single person on Earth that wouldn't have done the same.'

Peter's head was lowered, the late evening shadows shrouding his chin beneath his golfing cap.

'Yeah. Except Hal and Kara. They never would have done that. They would have found another way. They *always* find another way.'

'They talk a good game,' conceded Malcolm, his voice soft and reassuring, 'but had their plan to stop my heart failed, what would they have resorted to then? How *far* would they have *truly* gone when they ran out of options like you and Fearne did?'

The silence drifted between the two men until, finally, Malcolm broke it.

'What did you come here to ask me?'

'The knife,' said Peter. 'Where *exactly* did you say it appears on a fresh repeat? *Restart*,' he corrected.

'I didn't. For what it's worth, I prefer "Repeats", by the way. Far more concise.'

'Where does it *appear*, Malcolm?'

'You wouldn't be planning on doing something stupid, would you Peter?'

'Are you going to tell me or not?' said Peter, raising his gaze and meeting Malcolm's, a grim look of seriousness etched across his attractive face.

Malcolm shrugged, then gave Peter what he wanted.

'Basement. Right-hand side of the room. Between the staircase and the worktable.'

'Thanks.'

And with that Peter left the man in peace.

Malcolm turned his head back to face the road ahead. Having traversed it so many times, he knew exactly where it led to, and he'd never felt more satisfied.

Raising his hand to the exact spot where Kara had shot him, Malcolm pressed firmly against his chest. The buttons of his shirt had naturally repaired themselves, his restarted body miraculously healed, but he held onto the memory of the damage it had caused.

He was glad that the blood on his shirt had also vanished, following the restart after the shooting – there was a surprising amount of it for such a small ball-bearing – otherwise he would have needed to continue wearing his apron to conceal it. He knew that would have drawn suspicion at some point.

Thankfully, not one of them suspected that the Restarted weapon had caused him any harm at all.

CHAPTER THIRTY-SIX
The Time Traveller's Knife

R.I Timestamp Error: Recalculating…

System Error. Timestamp Failure.

Not wishing to find out what happened to them if they allowed the next restart to swoop in, they agreed it best to leave before time came looking to reclaim them.

This time around, Malcolm had taken Peter and Fearne through the barrier to The White Lodge first. Giving the alternate Fir Lodge a wide berth, they eventually caught sight of their quarry; a curling red energy that flowed forwards, complimented by inexplicable black wisps, which flowed backwards against the flow of redness, shimmering sporadically, as if holding its own unique element of self-perpetuated fuel.

It was a sinister looking electricity, seemingly being siphoned from an unseen and altogether darker dimension. A central nervous system floating lazily towards a goal only Malcolm knew for sure.

'So, what do we do?' said Peter nervously. 'We don't want to just appear right next to him, do we?'

'Indeed,' said Malcolm. 'Once through, I'll slow down time for the three of us. If we're lucky, a few seconds for us will be like an hour for him. Plenty of time for us to forge some distance between him.'

'You can *do* that?' said Fearne, not really buying it.

'It's no different from jumping ahead within a restart,' said Malcolm, his certainty instilling unexpected reassurance within Peter and Fearne's minds. 'I'll just need to concentrate, and I'll need you to give me a boost. Do not let go of me until I say.'

'If you say so,' said Peter.

Malcolm extended his elbows, as if he were about to perform a ridiculous chicken dance, and they interlocked their arms. Without fanfare, Malcolm reached deep within the swirling red tendons of his past self, fishing for something substantial to latch onto, until he eventually found the anchor he was looking for.

'Here we go,' he said, as the sound of swooshing air filled their eardrums, the whiteness of their surroundings falling away, slowly replaced by colours of a far more vibrant variety.

With a violent hiss, the air around them was sucked away, and the three of them were greeted by the sight of a duplicated Malcolm. The Malcolm of their past.

The Dark Restarter.

Future Malcolm concentrated, and the Restarters either side of him felt a slight vibration, as Future Malcolm drained all the power he could from them. To Peter and Fearne, it didn't feel all that different than the sensation of connecting with a Restarter, with one exception; the sparks generated by the trio's contact felt as if they were being drawn towards each other, rather than the usual experience of being repelled from one another.

*

The Dark Restarter span around, certain he had been approached by someone. Which was impossible, considering he was out-of-phase with everyone and everything.

Nevertheless, he knew he was being watched. He had a gift for sensing things like that. Something of a vocational necessity, thanks to his lifestyle choices.

He stared out at the open road in front of him, the afternoon sun lighting up the path before him. Entirely unremarkable in every conceivable way.

His eyes narrowed, as if searching for a tell-tale shimmer, a flicker of blue, perhaps…anything to indicate that an unwanted rat-catcher of orange secretary were utilising some form of trickery to hide themselves from him.

But there was nothing he needed to be concerned about. He smiled, then relaxed the muscles around his eyes, before turning back to the task at hand. He had an errand to run. The same errand he ran every Friday afternoon. One that began at precisely 12:01pm. Today was no different.

*

'He's leaving,' said Fearne, no longer feeling the need to wince, as if doing so granted her some form of ridiculously illogical invisibility. 'It's working!'

Once Malcolm's past-self had truly left their field of view, Malcolm instructed the two of them to let go of him, the act pulling the three of them back into true phase with the timeline they had been striving for, and the one the Dark Restarter called home; Timeline Charlie. A point which, for all intents and purposes, now served as the Restarter equivalent of "The Present". For everyone except Future Malcolm, of course.

Hal and Kara's 168th Restart.

Peter and Fearne's 798th Repeat.

The Dark Restarter's 1,063[rd] Cerebral Reversion.

And just another day for Future Malcolm, what with him having ceased the arbitrary task of keeping count long ago. Though, if anyone *had* been able to quantify the combined total of every thirty-three-hour and twelve-hour restart he had endured, it would have been labelled as 7,130 loops in total.

Instructing the two of them to return to Fir Lodge and for them to await further instructions, the

Malcolm from their future made his way to the Restart Point, which would lead him back to The White Lodge, and in turn to Hal and Kara.

*

'All I'm saying is, there's *still* the matter of finding enough lemons to begin with,' said Hal, finishing their conversation.

Malcolm groaned, feeling like he'd just escaped from the confines of a small car after a seven-hour car journey driving in circles around Milton Keynes with the most talkative man on the planet.

Fearne jumped in surprise, given that it had only been eight minutes or so since Malcolm had departed, and the three of them had sprung up right next to her in the rear garden of Fir Lodge.

'Oh, hey Fearne,' said Kara chirpily.

'Oh thank god! Something happened! Wait, how did you get here so quick?' asked Fearne, utterly confused. 'I've only been here a few minutes.'

'Really?' said Hal. 'That's cool. It's been several hours for us. We totally bailed on looking for Swirly-Red See-Through-Malcolm-2.0, and just decided to lock onto you and Pete instead.'

It had been considerably easier to lock-on to two blue echoes in time, with Dark Malcolm proving to be as elusive now as he ever was all that time ago in their initial one-hundred and sixty-five restarts.

'Where *is* Peter anyway?' said Kara, turning on the spot and scanning the area around her.

'That's what I'm trying to tell you!' said Fearne

anxiously. 'He said something about going to make it *right*, something about getting a head start? "*Taking a piece off the board*" were his exact words. I told him not to leave me. That we needed to wait here so you could find us. But he told me to wait here and, and–'

'Did he say where he was going?' said Hal, worried by the thought of his friend waltzing around on his own, now that a very real threat was also occupying the same phase in time as them.

'Nothing!' said Fearne. 'I should've gone with him, but he told me it was a surprise and…'

'A piece off the board?' said Kara. 'What could he mean by that?'

Malcolm grimaced.

'What is it,' said Hal.

'It's probably nothing…' said Malcolm, with a look of uncertainty on his face. 'But before we left, he was asking me an awful lot of questions about the knife.'

'What knife?' said Kara. 'Not *the* knife?!'

'I must admit,' said Malcolm apologetically, 'I thought nothing of it. You don't think he's…he wouldn't be stupid enough to try and retrieve it, would he?'

'Why would he *do* that?!' exclaimed Hal.

'Oh, I don't know Hal,' said Fearne aggressively. 'Maybe because you haven't stopped *blaming* the two of us for *betraying* you since you got here?'

'Are you *seriously* blaming me right now?' said Hal incredulously. 'I wasn't even occupying the same timeline! And even if I *was*, I'm not responsible for your damn boyfriend. And if you were so worried, why didn't you go with him? Like a normal, actual human being?!'

'Guys,' said Kara softly.

'I'm sick of your bullshit, Hal,' said Fearne, letting rip. 'The *perfect* hero, a time travelling *superstar* that knows everything! Except you *don't* know everything! You don't *know* how much it kills us to know a decision we made led to you and Kara getting stuck here!'

'Guys!' shouted Kara, punching Hal in the shoulder and shocking him out of whatever comeback he was formulating. 'Pete needs us right now. If he's gone to Kevin's…'

'The Dark Restarter might reach him before we do!' said Hal, suddenly realising what was at stake.

The three Restarters set off at a sprint, noticing they were one short.

'Malcolm! Come on!'

'My past self cannot know I'm here, Kara,' said Malcolm. 'It's the *only* advantage we have.'

'Fine, whatever,' said Kara angrily. 'Come on, let's go.'

*

Peter entered Kevin's lodge, entirely unaware that the front door shouldn't have even been open like it was, and made his way deeper inside, his sights set on reaching the basement door.

A familiar tune, which he recognised as "The

House of the Rising Sun", filled Kevin's living room as he slipped through the gap of the paradoxically ajar basement door, and slowly descended the stairs to the storage area below. Another unacknowledged warning that things were not as they should be.

That the past had been changed.

But he continued onwards, having no way of knowing that was the case.

The Repeater-turned-Restarter scanned the basement, which was surprisingly well lit thanks to the small rectangular window several feet ahead of him, cascading beams of pure sunlight that oddly refused to refract off a notably silver object. Ignoring the shadowy corners of the room, he hopped down the last two steps and pushed off from the wooden banister rail, stopping just short of an incredible sight; an object travelling through time, eternally out of reach to everyone in the universe but him.

A time-traveller's knife.

An object that could potentially not only turn the tide in their favour in their upcoming confrontation with the Malcolm of their past, but also one that could change the group dynamic for him, Fearne and his friends. He imagined the scene that would surely play out upon his return. Regaling them all with his fool-proof idea on how he had cheated the system.

How by retrieving this weapon before The Dark Restarter could get his hands on it, they would be levelling the playing field. Even if the knife couldn't hurt them, it was evidently important enough to

Malcolm to come back and retrieve it every time he restarted. At least, that's what Future Malcolm had said; how inconvenient it had been, having to run that errand every thirty-three-hours…

He wondered, briefly, why it was so important to the killer. Maybe it held great sentimental value? Like Negan and his barbed baseball bat. Or perhaps he just felt naked without it. Whatever the reason, presenting this to Hal and Kara would show he was sorry. That he could *contribute*. That there was more to him than the mistakes of his past, and that he was still the friend they remembered. Someone they could trust.

The music continued from the floor above him, his heightened senses thanks to his recent realignment with a new timeline reigniting that box-fresh Restarter feeling.

He smiled, noting that the song he could hear was a suitably badass enough soundtrack to such a defining moment. And for the first time since he had re-joined Hal and Kara, for the first time in *years* in fact, he truly felt like himself again.

He reached down, allowing the sense of anticipation to get the better of him, as his fingers brushed against the curved hilt of the menacing-looking serrated treasure.

Peter guesstimated that the blade itself was roughly eleven inches in length, well and truly long enough to pass all the way through someone matching his athletic frame. Scanning the length of the blade from hilt to tip, his eyes rested back on the former; which added an additional five-or-so inches in length to the weapon. Made from a sturdy-looking wood that was silky smooth to the touch, divided from the business end by a curved metal hand-guard made of the same material as the blade.

The weapon ended with a stylishly curved pommel that Peter suspected a professional could probably take advantage of when needing an extra bit of leverage, as they pulled the knife out of whatever was unfortunate enough to be on the receiving end.

Wrapping his hand around it, he picked up the object and brought it closer to his face, resting the sharp end on his fingertips, eager to inspect it. It seemed like an awful lot of fuss for something – in his hands at least – so mundane.

He buckled his swash, swishing it in the air in a diagonal swipe, like a pirate testing the balance of a new sword at the blacksmiths, or wherever it was pirate's obtained swords. He had about as much knowledge on the specifics of that as he did cares in the world right now, which made it all the more ironic when the sliver of metal, barely longer than an inch, popped out from the inside of his hip.

He stared down at it, bemused, as blood began to engulf the foreign object lodged deeply in the side of his own body, reaching out to it with his free hand, still clutching what was now a blade of his very own.

Peter flicked the protruding arrow-head-sized triangle of metal, and his curiosity quickly evolved into horror, as it retreated back inside him, making him feel dizzy, and eager to reach in after it to drag it back out.

None of this was rational of course, but he was yet to piece together the whole picture. With relief, the metal object popped back into view, this time bringing with it a distinct burning sensation, as if it were white hot.

As the enormous arm wrapped around his neck, he momentarily drifted out of consciousness, noting how the black spots filling his vision were laced with both blue and red sparks, each looking incredibly beautiful, in their own unique way.

That was the funny thing about a dying mind; it always managed to recalibrate the senses to see beauty, instead of what was really there.

CHAPTER THIRTY-SEVEN
Death of a Restarter

168th Restart – Friday, August 24th, 2018, 12:18pm

The Restarters flew through the front door of Kevin's lodge and made their way straight for the ominously-open basement door, making Kara the first to witness the horror within.

There stood Peter, held firmly in place by Malcolm's past-self, red sparks drowning out the splutter of blue, as the energy ebbed away from their friend.

Malcolm turned his attention to his new guests, pulling the knife from his captive's torso in a sudden, sickening motion.

'Peter,' whispered Kara, 'no...'

'I hadn't expected an audience,' said the Restarting-Malcolm of the past, clearly delighted. 'Not usually my standard *modus operandi*, but I'm willing to make an exception,' he added, allowing the blade to dance within an energised beam of dust-mote-laden sunlight, and grimacing as the light of the Earth's Sun refused to refract against what would surely have been glistening blood. Instead, Peter's lifeblood looked rather dull and boring to him. 'Given our *history*.'

'It's okay,' gargled Peter, claret spewing from his mouth, his kind-hearted smile at odds with his blood-soaked teeth 'Re…Restarter, remember?' he said, shooting them all a wink that he immediately regretted, as a burning fire coursed through his veins, causing more redness to pump from the gash in his side, his red golfing shirt turning black like blotting paper…a Rorschach test gone horribly wrong. In that moment, Kara thought she could see the outline of a butterfly amidst the ever-expanding ichor.

'He keeps saying that,' said the Dark Restarter, his face one of perplexed curiosity.

'Let him go,' said Hal softly. '*Please.*'

Fearne was last to make her way through the door. Eyes widening, her hands flung to her face, as she let out a piercing scream that caused both Hal and Kara to wince, their taught nerves snapping under the shrillness.

'Ah, the lover turned widow,' said Malcolm. 'I've been watching you all for quite some time,' he added, his face scrunching up as if he were running a complicated maths equation through his mind. 'For four years now,' he said, his expression returning to one of overt maliciousness, finally at ease that his memories had yielded an accurate result. 'There's nothing I don't know about you. How does it go?' Malcolm pondered, running off at an apparent tangent, the energy he was draining from Peter revitalising his fractured mind. 'For never was a story of more woe, than this of *Fearne* and her Romeo…'

He plunged the blade back into Peter, causing him to judder uncontrollably, the hideous tip of the blade reflecting the red energy past-Malcolm was utilising.

'Fearne, get to the Restart Point,' said Kara, all business and no filler. 'Now, Fearne!' she ordered.

But Fearne remained firmly in place, frozen with terror.

'There you go again with this *Restart* nonsense,' said Malcolm. 'Please elaborate. I should add, it's not in my nature to ask twice,' his smile dropping to an expression that was as serious as a bullet to the brain.

"Or a blade to the gut," thought Hal.

'Oh! No, don't tell me…is that what you *call* yourselves?' said Malcolm disdainfully, letting out his most impressive fake laugh yet. 'How precious.'

'What have you done,' whispered Kara.

'In my defence,' said Malcolm, admittedly perplexed, 'I had no way of knowing this would happen. I mean, honestly, the *memory* of a knife being able to affect us so…*tangibly*. It begs the question though, doesn't it?'

Kara knew immediately what question he was referring to. She prayed she was wrong, worrying what it said about her as a person that she reached such a conclusion so quickly.

'Well, now we know we can *bleed*. But can we *die*? In this place, I mean,' said Malcolm, apparently having a conversation with himself. Something he was more than proficient at these days.

He released his grip on Peter's neck, using his partially-free hand to gesture at their surroundings, steering Peter with the knife that was still in his side. 'What do you say, *Restarters*?' he added, in pure mockery. 'Shall we find out?'

'I will *end* you,' said Kara, reaching to Hal's side and pulling what was slowly becoming the communal gun from its holster.

She cranked back the hammer and took aim, scorching the man with her look of conviction.

'Little echoes,' whispered Malcolm, 'messing with things that you can't understand, and hoping *toys* can save them.'

Kara flinched at the word. There wasn't much that got to her, but she hated the thought of being nothing more than a Time-Echo. More than anything, it was her greatest fear; to not be real. Just a shadow. To not be the *true* version of herself.

Did he know the gun was fake? It seemed unlikely. But it was possible.

She quickly shook off the self-doubt and regained control, noting that his seemingly brave words had been betrayed by a tell; he had taken a step backwards, bringing Peter with him along for the ride.

The Dark Restarter stole a glance towards the room to his right, the one that would soon house Kevin. If that was even a thing in this nightmarish timeline anymore. Clearly, he'd moved on to loftier goals.

'Something wrong, *Kara?*' said Malcolm, probing further, as Kara realised she had been incorrect, and that this version of Malcolm using her name was far worse than him referring to her as an echo.

'*Echoes* of the past got your tongue?' the killer purred. 'Perhaps I could help you with that?' he added, pulling the blade out of her friend and pressing the edge of it against Peter's neck, the jagged edges of the knife catching his skin and leaving behind a trail of rivulets which ran down his throat.

That word again.

"Dammit," she thought, hating that he'd seen her flinch at its usage the first time. "Just a bit more," thought Kara, knowing that a gas propelled pellet to the forehead would surely give them a second to turn this all around.

But Malcolm was no fool, and ducked his head behind Peter's like a blood-curdling game of peek-a-boo, using their friend as a human shield.

Kara cursed under her breath, knowing that she couldn't risk firing a round without a clean shot. If she missed, Malcolm would know the gun was for show, and would clearly waste no time in demonstrating his skills with his considerably more dangerous weapon.

Hal sensed what she was trying to achieve, and brought on the big talk in the hope it would afford them a distraction.

'Hey, Jigsaw, hate to be the one to tell you this, but you brought a knife to a gun fight,' he said loudly, hopping down the steps theatrically, as if he hadn't a care in the world, attempting to draw the killer's attention away from Peter for just a second.

It's all they needed. A single second. Was it so much to ask for? After all the hours they had been gifted?

'How bout we take a rain check on all this and you can try again tomorrow. Sound good?'

'You mean, we all just walk away?' said Malcolm, lowering the knife.

'Exactly that. Besides,' said Hal, leaning on the banister as if he were having a casual catch-up with an old friend. 'We're from the future, man. We know how this ends. So let's call it now, save ourselves a bunch of aggro.'

'Your friend talks too much,' said the killer. 'This one is on you *Harold*. Remember that, Fearne. That it was Harold who did this.'

'Malcolm, no!' shouted Kara, her words doing nothing but generating a savage smile from their adversary, as he locked his eyes onto hers, clearly wishing to make the moment more intimate.

It all happened so fast; Malcolm spinning Peter to face him, sliding the knife into his chest, twisting the blade clockwise, then counter clockwise, pulling the blade back out, the serrated edges surely catching on Peter's internal organs, shredding them beyond repair.

Kara, in too much shock to fire, dropped the gun and ran at him, eyes blue and teeth bared, growling ferociously, as Malcolm ducked into the room to his right. Hal, meanwhile, was on Peter in an instant, catching him in his arms before he could hit the ground.

The Dark Restarter barked a laugh through the door, attempting to pull it closed behind him, the energy he had absorbed from Peter refilling his out-of-phase tank.

Kara placed her hand between the door and its frame, preventing it from shutting fully, forgetting for a moment that being out-of-phase with the wood spared her from experiencing pain.

Not having time to be thankful for that, she used her arm as leverage to open the door. But her ears were greeted by the sound of a sharp popping sound, and her heart sank, as her eyes were met by nothing more than an old sheet covering a shoddy coffee table, dog treats on a metal shelf, and old paint tins.

Malcolm had clearly fast-forwarded into their current restart, and in doing so, had escaped to safety.

'Dammit Pete,' said Hal, as his friend's blood spread rapidly across his hands and clothes. 'What were you thinking, mate?'

'Wanted... make it right,' said Peter, the colour draining from his dark skin. 'Prove...you could trust me,' he added, his eyes rolling back into his head, the sparks between them both growing weaker and less vibrant by the second.

'We need to stop this blood,' said Hal, pulling of his jacket and t-shirt, ripping the latter to make what he hoped was a tourniquet. 'Fearne, Kara, I need you both. We need to put pressure on it or...or something. On the wounds.'

Was that how you did it? Hal had no idea. He was so far out of his depth he may as well have been in a different timeline from Peter altogether.

'Frrrnnn,' said Peter, his eyes spinning back around with Fear. 'I'm s-sorry. My f-fault.'

'You stupid bastard,' said Hal. 'Don't you *dare* die on me, you're making me look like a right dick here!' he added, trying to keep the mood light in the hope it would keep his friend coherent.

Kara was there in a flash, using Hal's shirt to stem the flow of blood, as Fearne fell down beside her boyfriend and began stroking his hair. She whispered something to him, needing him to know something important. Something he could take with him to the grave.

Peter smiled, Fearne's words clearly a comfort, and he looked upwards into her eyes, his voice barely that of a whimper as he spoke. 'Fog's here,' he said, as the last drop of life left his eyes.

They looked around, but saw no evidence of any fog, nor the sound of rushing air. They assumed the blood-loss was making Peter hallucinate, until Fearne jerked her hand away from Peter's forehead.

It didn't take long for Hal and Kara to see why she had recoiled.

Tiny amounts at first. Small granules of blue energy rising into the air, like grains of sand being coerced upwards into nothingness.

Peter's body was disintegrating.

Within seconds, there was nothing left but silence, as the seriousness of what had just happened truly dawned on them.

Peter wasn't just dead.

He was gone.

CHAPTER THIRTY-EIGHT
All Flights are Cancelled

168th Restart – Friday, August 24th, 2018, 12:42pm

They mobilised quickly, knowing that Peter's only hope rested in them triggering a restart.

It took a fair few attempts to convince Fearne to come with them, her reluctance to leave Kevin's basement fortified by her belief that he could materialise at any moment, and she didn't want him left lying there on the cold floor wondering why she had left him.

Eventually, Kara had managed to convince her that the fastest way to bring Peter home was to bring an end to the fastest example of a restart turning south since...no, this was definitely the quickest balls up they'd ever been faced with.

The only thing Hal and Kara were certain about was that they needed to restart the past in order to provide Peter with a fresh future.

'Where the hell is Malcolm?' barked Hal, as they ran towards the portal that resided at the boundary line.

Kara knew he meant *their* Malcolm. The Malcolm of the future.

What she didn't know was the answer to that million-dollar question, though she suspected his reluctance to show himself was due in no small part to the monumental loss the team had just sustained. Kara lowered her voice so that Fearne couldn't hear, before addressing the more immediate concern that was surely on all of their minds.

'Do you think this will work?'

Hal knew she was referring to their working theory that a restart could bring Peter back to them, which was actually less of a theory and actually more akin to a Hail Mary.

'It has to,' he muttered simply, his hushed tone equal in volume to that of his friend.

*

As they reached the boundary line, Hal stopped several metres short of the invisible line that would trigger Peter's resurrection, gesturing for everyone to do the same.

'Why are we stopping?!' shouted Fearne, angrily

wiping the remnants of tears from her face. She refused to mourn that which was due to return to her in just a few short steps.

'I hate to say it,' said Hal, trying to choose his words carefully, 'but we can't leave without Future Malcolm.'

Fearne shot him a look of disbelief, her eyes screaming "why the hell not." A thought she was about to vocalise, before Kara intervened.

'Hal's right,' said Kara. 'If we jump without him…'

'We're all in-phase!' shouted Fearne. 'He can find us on the other side. Assuming he dares to show his face after what he's done to us.'

'He has a lot to answer for,' agreed Hal, 'but we have no way of knowing if he knew that would happen to Peter.' The words seemed false in his mouth. This was their Malcolm's past after all, which meant there was a very good chance he had full memory of his past-self committing this heinous act. Unless…

His thoughts were prevented from reaching completion as Fearne pushed past Hal and Kara and ran towards the Restart Point.

Shards of blue erupted as she connected with it, like a mirror that had been struck by a hammer, only the fractures were represented by hundreds of thunderbolts which spread across the point of impact, and outwards across the boundary line, like temporary cracks in a wall none of them could see. Cracks that eventually retraced their steps and flowed back to the epicentre, dissolving into nothing, as if they had never been there to begin with.

'No,' said Fearne, smashing her fists against the flawlessly transparent wall obstructing her path, generating yet more cracks of electricity which spread upwards and outwards, revealing the hints of just how far the barrier extended. 'No, no, NO!'

The three of them stood there in awe, having just been subjected to a sight none of them had seen before; an invisible force-field. One apparently shielding the Restart Point and what lay beyond the boundary line, preventing them from triggering the restart they so desperately needed.

A literal manifestation of the time bubble that seemed adamant on containing them.

'That's…not possible,' said Hal, extending his left hand and pressing it gently against the glass-like barrier.

As his fingers connected with it, small fractures of blue energy spread outwards from where his hand was resting. He felt the blockade resonating under his touch, as if were vibrating at the exact same frequency as his out-of-phase body.

Hal balled his hand into a fist, and hit the barrier with more force, causing the lightning-blue cracks to spread wider and more intensely, eventually working their way backwards to the source of contact, before repairing themselves and returning to an entirely transparent view of the road ahead.

'Why can't we pass!' said Fearne, tears threatening to coat her cheeks once more. 'Peter needs us!'

Hal looked over his shoulder to Kara, whose eyes were wide with equal bewilderment.

'I...don't know,' said Kara. 'We've never been locked out from a Restart Point before.

'Wait,' said Hal, 'it's got to be Malcolm. *Dark Restarter* Malcolm, I mean. What if he didn't just disappear, what if he fast-forwarded.'

'You mean, jumped forwards into this restart?' said Kara. 'Can he do that yet?' Their Malcolm hadn't actually mentioned *when* he had learnt that parlour trick. 'That *would* explain how he managed to pull that Houdini in the basement,' she noted, kicking herself for not thinking of it sooner.

'Yeah,' agreed Hal. 'Makes sense. But it's bigger than that. If he's in the future of this restart, it's possible we've been locked behind this force-field until we...catch up with him.'

'Why would it matter *when* he is right now?' said Kara.

'Because,' said a deep voice from behind them, cutting into Fearne's soul like a laser etching its way across glass, 'for all the ways in which this place bends how we perceive this reality, there is but one constant,' said Malcolm.

For a brief moment they all assumed it was their dark enemy, returning for another onslaught, but the man's expression somehow eradicated that notion.

Before any of them had a chance to breathe a sigh

of relief and react to his unexpected return, he finished his explanation.

'Time always moves forwards,' said Malcolm. 'Each restart has a beginning and an end. And if my past-self is occupying a point in time that is ahead of *us* in this thirty-three-hour cycle…'

'All flights are cancelled,' said Hal, the realisation of what Malcolm was telling them finally made clear thanks to an inconvenient truth; their portal privileges had been revoked for the simple reason that they couldn't trigger a restart whilst another time-traveller was occupying the future of the same timeline as them.

'He wouldn't even need to be *that* far ahead,' reasoned Hal. 'I mean, even if he was a single minute ahead of us…'

'We'd never make up those sixty seconds and catch up to him,' said Kara.

'Correct,' said Malcolm. 'That would be enough to lock you out of restarting the time-loop. He's occupying a future you have yet to reach.'

'I hate time-travel,' said Kara glumly.

None of that mattered to Fearne, of course, who erupted with arcing blue energy at the sight of the man who had killed Peter, her long brown hair swirling in the air, defying gravity.

'Fearne, wait!' shouted Kara.

But she couldn't hear them, or didn't want to.

Instead, she flew towards Peter's killer, grabbing him by the throat, the connection between them generating red and blue sparks that were almost as wild as Fearne's eyes.

What really caught them all off guard, however, was how she managed to summon the strength to throw Malcolm off his feet, sending him skidding several metres across the ground, the stones beneath him shaking impossibly.

'I'll kill you,' screamed Fearne, with such intensity that her voice seemed to generate a clap of thunder. 'I will *fucking* end you!'

CHAPTER THIRTY-NINE
Seeing Red

168th Restart – Friday, August 24th, 2018, 12:46pm

Kara and Hal each grabbed one of Fearne's shoulders, their entire state of being suddenly flooded by an overwhelming concoction of emotions; soul-crushing sorrow, coupled with a debilitating sense of despair, that was overridden by the unmitigated hatred they felt towards the future incarnation of their lover's murderer.

It was so all-consuming, so laser-focused, that it took them both a moment to realise they were simply channelling Fearne's emotions in their rawest form.

Ripples of crackling energy surged between the

three Restarters, slivers of menacing red fizzling amidst the blue, swirling in and out of phase around Fearne's clenched fists, as if daring her to draw upon an entirely different type of energy. One without limits. One that could give her everything she wanted.

The revenge she craved…

'Th-this isn't you,' stammered Kara, in a desperate attempt to pull her friend back from the brink of vengeance.

'Get your damn hands off me,' shouted Fearne, a simple shrug being all that was needed to send both of her friends flying backwards, repelled by the conflicting energy being generated between the three of them, terrifyingly amplified by Fearne's intense emotional state.

Hal and Kara landed hard, rolling several metres along the ground, each feeling unexpectedly drained of strength and focus.

'You feel it, don't you,' said Malcolm, on his feet once more, but not retreating.

For all the knowledge he possessed, this was now his present, and he had no way of knowing for sure what was about to happen. No memories to draw upon, no cheat sheets. All he had to work with was the here and now.

It was surprisingly invigorating, like being alive again for the first time in forever. 'The power at your fingertips, begging to be drawn upon.'

'What are you talking about,' shouted Fearne, ignoring the hue of red that flickered across her vision, unbeknownst to her illuminating the tears that were streaming down her face.

Like droplets of blood, thought Malcolm fondly. 'The red,' he said, his voice chock full of gravelly wonder.

Hal, meanwhile, had managed to drag his weakened body closer to the Restart Point, pressing his palm against the invisible barrier, a sense of relief flowing through him as his fingers drifted over the boundary line. He watched as his hand began to disintegrate into blue shards, but not for long, quickly pulling his hand back and feeling thankful that his hand had been returned to him fully intact.

"Finally," he thought, realising this could mean only one thing; the Malcolm of the past had clearly caught up with them, in turn reopening the rift in time. The Restart Point was once again open for business.

'Go!' yelled Kara, seeing what her fellow Restarter had discovered and barking her approval.

Hal didn't waste a second, pulling himself up and all but falling through the portal, the world behind him breaking away into nothingness. As he entered a state of freefall, the sense of weightlessness overwhelmed him, sending them all back to a place where they could fix this mess, or at the very least a place where Fearne and Malcolm could be separated until Fearne cooled off.

And maybe, most importantly of all, a place where Peter was alive.

*

Now that Future Malcolm had ceased pulling the strings on precisely when and where he wanted Hal and Kara to be, both of them experienced a more traditional re-entry into the past.

This was technically their first proper restart since Malcolm had brought them into phase with his murderous past-self, and the two Restarters were relieved to discover that the timeline they had crowbarred their way into had seemingly accepted them as part of the furniture, placing them once again on the driveway outside Fir Lodge.

Thankfully, Malcolm was nowhere to be seen, and they assumed that he too must have been jettisoned off to his own point of Restarting-origin.

Hal holstered his gun, which was once again inexplicably in his hand despite Kara having discarded it on Kevin's basement floor in another reality entirely, and felt a pang of concern at that; did that mean that Malcolm was currently standing next to his past-self right now? That would be…potentially problematic.

Kara was about to head into the garden behind her, where she assumed Fearne would be waiting, when the area of space where Robert's car was soon destined to occupy began to shimmer erratically. It was in that moment that both she and Hal were gifted with a unique perspective; witnessing from a distance exactly how it looked when a Restarter materialised into a fresh restart.

The shimmering particles made way for a crackling of what could only be described as amplified static electricity, as blue grains of energy appeared from nowhere, dancing lazily like drunk and disorderly fireflies.

The sloshed manifestations of temporally-charged lights gradually began to swirl with greater enthusiasm; some sailing past each other like busy commuters not wishing to engage in conversation, merely tipping their hats with a "how do you do" demeanour, whilst others collided more forcefully.

Exploding upon contact, these rogue particles multiplied with gusto to create even more blue light, until the sound of rushing air filled the vacuum being created before them, the aforementioned static electricity funnelling through invisible channels to form the faint outline of a central nervous system.

For a moment, Hal and Kara feared the tornado-like sound was heralding that they were being rejected by this timeline, and that maybe they were about to be sucked back into the timestream, sent hurtling to wherever it was aberrations such as them called home.

But it soon became obvious that the angry, self-contained storm merely signalled the arrival of a Restarter, as Fearne was pulled into chronological alignment with the two of them.

Peter was very much conspicuous by his absence, as Fearne effortlessly nailed a time-traveller landing and spun around on the balls of her high-heeled feet.

Catching sight of Hal and Kara, she walked

towards them, giving them a look of desperation, which they acknowledged with mutual expressions of fear-tinged confusion. None of them seemed to be able to ask the question that mattered, not that the three words were needed to give the question itself the life it needed to exist;

Where was Peter?

Kara and Hal exchanged a shared look of anxiousness. They were working on the assumption that triggering a restart would bring Peter back to them. But the truth of the matter was that they honestly had no idea what happened to a person if they were killed whilst out-of-phase with time.

To add insult to mortal-injury, Robert had pulled up outside the lodge, and Fearne and Peter's past-selves exited the car.

Fearne jogged ahead of her doppelganger and reached a quivering arm out to the Peter of the past, tears filling her eyes as her arm passed straight through him.

In that moment, she knew. *Her* Peter was truly gone.

*

The three Restarters took up residence on the patch of grass that ran parallel to the front driveway. Whilst they were ridiculously exposed, it offered a relatively solid vantage point; not only could they see all the way along the rear access of the lodge into the garden itself, but a quick glance to their right allowed them to see a reasonable distance into the road that led to

Kevin's.

Their makeshift war room kept them visible enough for Future-Malcolm to see them, whilst also offering as much of an early warning system to past-Malcolm's inevitable arrival, giving them plenty of time to run if needed.

Kara heard her own playful scream billowing over the roof of Fir Lodge, realising that Jerry must have just made his appearance. She knew their timeline well enough to know that meant it was approximately 3:30-ish on the Friday, meaning they'd been waiting for *their* Malcolm for over three hours now.

'Maybe he didn't make it back?' suggested Kara.

'Maybe he knows what's waiting for him if he does,' said Fearne savagely.

'Maybe he's fighting with his past-self?' mused Hal.

'No way,' said Kara. 'You know how obsessed he is about not interacting with his past-self.' Kara pulled her best grumpy face, and lowered her voice, mimicking Malcolm. '"I don't remember it *happening* that way, therefore it *can't*, I'm the *master* of time, I know all." Blah, blah, blah.'

Hal laughed, and even Fearne smiled, though caught herself and ceased doing so just as quickly.

'Yeah,' agreed Hal. 'I know he sees himself as the literal manifestation of a Zoltar machine,' he added, referring to the iconic fortune-telling contraption. 'But what if he didn't have a choice?'

'How'd you mean?' asked Kara.

Hal elaborated, reasoning that if *they* had sprung up where they always had on a fresh restart, it stood to reason that Malcolm had too. Only now there were two of them, occupying the exact same point in space and time.

'Well we didn't splice into old restarting versions of ourselves,' noted Kara.

'Because those versions of us in our 165th slam dunk of awesomeness are in a different phase to us,' said Hal. 'Dark Douchebag is in-phase with Slightly-Less-Dark-Douchebag.'

Hal was just rounding off his theory that they all needed to prepare themselves for the possibility Future Malcolm might just have been reduced to a pile of gross-looking goo, when Jerry wandered over to a flower pot situated by the rear corner of the lodge, which he proceeded to sniff with interest.

'Oh man,' said Hal excitedly. 'That's precisely where we were standing on our first ever restart, remember?'

Kara smiled nostalgically, then raised a quizzical eyebrow. 'How is he still sensing us standing there?'

'I guess, for Jerry, it's still the first time,' reasoned Hal.

'I remember him walking over and playing right where we're sitting now…' said Kara, her eyes lighting up at the prospect that she was about to become a self fulfilling prophecy. 'Watch this,' she said, knowing Hal would surely get a kick out of this, and whistled warmly to get Jerry's attention.

Sure enough, Jerry's ears twitched again, and he bolted towards them, sitting like the good boy he was, before rolling onto the grass between the three of them.

'No waaaay,' said Hal, his mind suitably blown.

'Yup,' said Kara, as if she'd just delivered casual small talk as opposed to taking a pliable moment in time and solidifying it as a temporal constant.

She ran her out-of-phase fingers across Jerry's upturned belly, his tongue hanging out to one side, enjoying the attention as always

'We were here all along,' said Hal, utterly mystified by the ramifications of that.

'That's a good sign, right?' said Kara optimistically. 'It means we're right when we're meant to be.'

Hal shrugged. It certainly seemed like a good sign. On their first ever restart, Jerry had been drawn to their Restarter-selves when Hal had let out an unintentional whistle of amazement. Shortly after, Jerry had lost interest, trotting off to where they were currently sitting in what constituted as their perception of the here and now.

To Jerry, it was like walking from one Hal and Kara to another. On the flip side, they were indirectly interacting with their first ever restart all the way from their 169th.

It was a sobering thought; they weren't just changing the future, they were simultaneously building what was always destined to be.

'Hate to tear you two geeks away from whatever *this* is,' said Fearne sourly, 'but there's a Malcolm making his way over to us.'

They turned their gaze to the road that ran alongside the lodge, causing Jerry to stir and continue on his path, sensing the attention he had been enjoying had come to an end.

Malcolm strode towards them, undoing and discarding his black apron onto the ground, his hands held high as if signalling he meant them no harm.

'Could be a trick,' reasoned Fearne. 'Malcolm 2.0 pretending to be 3.0?'

'Except the Dark Restarter doesn't know a future version of himself exists,' countered Kara. 'I think this is *our* Malcolm.

Whichever version of Malcolm this was stopped short, and waited on the edge of the driveway before breaking the silence. His tone told them everything they needed to know in order to carbon-date him.

'We have a lot to discuss.'

CHAPTER FORTY
The Restarter who Knew Too Much

168th Restart – Friday, August 24th, 2018, 3:59pm

Malcolm had delivered a thrilling recap of where he had been for the past three hours, quashing Hal's theory that he had reappeared next to his past-self, as he described the odd limbo he had found himself in; a space *between* restarts, not unlike The White Lodge, where he presumed he had been kept on retainer, whilst time itself wrestled with the decision on what to do with him, and where to send him.

Eventually he found himself whole once more, or as *whole* as any of them could truly be in their current state, in a seemingly random location near the boundary line.

Hal, however, wasn't buying it.

'Cool story, bro. But it doesn't take three hours to walk back here,' he said, staring with that look of a man trying to ascertain who in the room was responsible for letting rip a drive-by bout of flatulence.

'I have only just reformed, and this was not my first stop,' said Malcolm irritably. 'I assumed you would be at Kevin's. I also had to ensure I didn't run into my past-self along the way.'

'I personally don't care *where* you were,' said Fearne, her patience all but extinguished. 'I only care where Peter is now!'

'Fearne's right, what the hell is going on,' said Kara. 'Where's Peter?'

'I…do not know,' said Malcolm truthfully.

'You knew this would happen,' said Fearne, her eyes glistening once again. 'And you did *nothing* to help us change it,' a blue energy sizzling around her body, desperate to be released.

'If only it were that simple,' said Malcolm, his face not giving anything away, but more importantly not showing a single flicker of remorse.

'Actually,' argued Hal, 'it literally *is* that simple. You knew your past-self would do this, because it's your own freakin' past!'

'Our arrival here has evidently led to a deviation in my timeline,' said Malcolm. 'He is free to make new choices based on our actions.' He saw the doubt in their eyes, and breathed in through his nose, deciding to try a different approach. 'Though my memories do eventually adapt,' he conceded. 'Honestly, I don't think even he expected to take things that far. At least you see what's at stake now. How far gone I was at this point in my time here.'

'Past-you is a monster,' said Kara, slinking back down onto the grass.

'*You're* the monster,' said Fearne, standing up and staring down on him.

'I was,' conceded Malcolm, before correcting himself. 'I *am*...but that's not what I want to be anymore.'

'You don't just get to *choose* just because it's *convenient*,' said Fearne. 'You can't wash away the fact you killed him with just words, Malcolm.'

'That is not—'

'You can't be buying this crap-fest?' said Fearne, cutting Malcolm off and opening up the question to Hal and Kara. 'What the actual *hell* are we thinking, trusting this...this…Dark Lord of bullshit. He's literally killed all of us once already!'

'So have you,' said Hal. 'But we trust you.'

Fearne's jaw dropped, unable to formulate a response, and an awkward silence filled what felt like the entirety of the Pentney Lakes. All that was missing was an awkward cough or a tumble weed.

Kara settled on the former.

'Fearne, I'm sorry,' began Hal, trying to pull the words back into his mouth, but finding that there was no room for them *and* his foot. 'I didn't mean it to come out like tha–'

'*Fuck* you, Hal,' she said simply, her words more cutting and absolute than anything the Malcolm of their shared past had at his disposal.

She stormed off, utterly done with the lot of them.

'Too much?' said Hal, seeking reassurance from Kara.

'I mean, I don't want to undersell it…' said Kara, before pulling herself up.

'It felt like too much,' sighed Hal.

'Let's just say, if "much" was a liquid …you just drowned everyone in a ten-mile radius,' said Kara, heading off after Fearne to try and fix what was slowly evolving into an irreparable disaster.

Watching the two girls leave, Malcolm stood up and stretched.

'And where the hell are *you* going?' said Hal, realising that their team of four had left him flying solo.

'To check the perimeter. There's no telling where I am right now. Or when he will strike.'

"Great," thought Hal. "Just perfect."

*

Kara caught up with Fearne just in time to catch her wiping the cheeks of her face.

'Fearne,' said Kara. 'He didn't mean for it to come out like that. We're all at a loss for what to do right now, and Malcolm may just be our only hope.' That sounded familiar to Kara, and she suspected she'd just made a reference that Hal would have picked up on. She loved that about him, not that she'd ever tell him that. Or say it out loud to anyone. Ever.

'This isn't *about* me!' she shouted, before reining her emotions back in. 'I just...we fell for his act before. And look where it got us. No good can come from working with this guy, Kara. I'm telling you, as soon as he gets what he wants, at *best* he's going to bail on us. *Hard*. At worst? He's going to get us all *killed*. You know that, right? Peter was just the start.'

Kara gave that some thought, choosing her next words carefully.

'I really don't think that's true, Fearne. At this point, he has *just* as much to lose as we do. He needs *us* more than we need him.' Kara could sense Fearne was a millisecond away from producing a counter-argument, so she continued onwards before she had the chance. 'That said, I *hear* you. I'm *listening*. If Malcolm so much as hints at a hidden agenda, I'll drop him. The three of us will take him down. And he won't see it coming if he thinks we trust him. So, work with me on this okay? We...can't do this without you. We *need* you. And I...need my friend.'

Fearne went quiet, unpacking Kara's words, scanning the sincerity on her friend's face.

Kara's eyes burned with conviction, and Fearne

realised that was good enough for her.

'Okay,' she decided. 'We'll do this your way. Just...promise me you and Hal won't get sucked in by all his lies? That you'll be careful.'

Kara snorted playfully.

'Hal and I are *never* careful,' she said, shooting Fearne a wink. 'We can't help ourselves, to be honest. We're basically time-pirates.'

Fearne rolled her eyes.

'You're starting to sound like him. You know that, right?'

'I know this,' said Kara, and they shared a warm smile.

They both felt it; a fleeting moment where it felt like the old days. Where their lives were filled with far more mundane distractions, like paying bills and trying to avoid clip-boarders on the high street that were trying to induct them into surveys that no one on earth actually read the results from.

'Come on, let's get back, okay?' said Kara, whilst the warmth of their shared solidarity still lingered. 'We need to get a plan together, and I don't feel comfortable leaving Hal and Malcolm alone.'

As they departed, retracing their steps back to Fir Lodge, Future Malcolm stepped out from behind a nearby fir tree, having heard everything they had said to each other.

He growled to himself, the cogs turning in his mind, realising that he would need to expedite his plans.

They were *so* close now, and there was too much at stake to allow Fearne to foil his meticulously-orchestrated calculations.

She would need to be dealt with, before she derailed his only chance of escaping this wretched place.

CHAPTER FORTY-ONE

Jurassic Dark

168th Restart – Friday, August 24th, 2018, 8:09pm

As the sun set on yet another Friday, they remained within the confines of Fir Lodge, watching the shadows that ran across the hedges surrounding their perimeter for any signs of movement, all of them on edge.

With the exception of Malcolm, that is, who seemed entirely unperturbed by their very real concerns.

It made the three Restarters immensely uncomfortable that he wasn't showing even the remotest display of worry. His singular reason for which being that if his past-self decided to strike, he would remember the decision being made. Fearne pointed out how well that theory had borne fruit following what had happened to Peter.

'You know,' said Hal, determined to lighten the mood, 'I thought there'd be more dinosaurs in your dinosaur park.'

'I don't follow,' said Malcolm.

'It just makes no sense. 'There's been no sign of the T-Rex. What's his next play?'

They all felt it. Each and every one of them, except Malcolm apparently.

It was as if the well-lit Fir Lodge was a life-raft, and they were being circled by a shark they knew was there, waiting for the monster to strike and finish them off for good, but unable to predict exactly when, or from what side.

'I've been thinking about what happened,' said Kara, a thought occurring to her. 'I thought you said there was only one knife?' she said, referring to the knife Peter had attempted to retrieve, and the knife Malcolm's darker-self had used to kill their friend.

'Clearly,' drawled Malcolm, 'he has found another.'

'And you just conveniently forgot that part?' asked Fearne, challenging him.

'Apparently, the past is far more fluid than any of us could have accounted for,' contested Malcolm.

'Yeah, sound theory,' said Hal. 'Except there's one problem with that, John Connor; if *he* found a second knife that means *you* found a second knife. A fact that has to be nestled safely in your own damn memories.'

'I don't know what you want me to say,' said Malcolm with notable tiredness.

He wasn't used to engaging in so much conversation. He would talk *at* his victims all the time, but all of this two-way communication was leaving him more than a little exhausted. 'There is one knife, the knife I died with. I know not of the second, nor its origin.'

They sat there quietly, as the trees rustled under a soft evening breeze, anticipation that would have caused their combined muscles to tense, were they in-phase with the mortal realm.

As the small talk eventually crumbled beneath the oppressive weight of the phantom that stalked them, each of the rag-tag bunch of time travelling renegades shared an unspoken sense of relief that they didn't need to sleep whilst in their current form.

In fact, what was once a disconcerting side-effect of Restarting had now become something of a huge advantage. For one thing, they didn't need to assign shifts, or take it in turns to keep watch. For another, the fog remained mercifully at bay, thanks to them being so early on in their newly-inhabited restart chain. The downside was that the four of them were burdened by their heightened senses, and as the lights within and around Fir Lodge flickered off in staggered patterns, they were left with only each other and their own thoughts for company.

Fearne had broken away from the group, resting her chin on her knees and locking her arms around her legs, staring relentlessly at Malcolm, who pretended not to notice. Just far enough to remain excluded, but just close enough to be able to rally if the situation took the dark turn they all knew it would, sooner or later.

But as *sooner* was replaced by the tenacity of *later*, and a new dawn took hold on a very familiar Saturday, it became clear that the shark of the past was regrouping. Their unexpected presence had thrown a considerable number of spanners in the works, and each of the Restarters now represented a multitude of variables that would need to be studied and observed, before they could be eliminated.

Kara was the first to speak, her voice a hoarse croak after remaining silent for so long.

'We can't stay here,' she said, standing and stretching, despite her out-of-phase muscles being incapable of seizing up.

'I agree,' said Malcolm. 'We would do well to find a new location from which to operate, one that my past-self cannot foresee or predict.'

Fearne snorted, continuing to burn her stare into the back of Malcolm's head. 'I'm not going anywhere. I'm staying right here for when Peter returns.'

The remaining two Restarters and Malcolm shared a concerned glance.

'I can see you glancing at each other,' said Fearne. 'You could at least *try* to hide the fact that you think

I'm crazy.'

'We don't think you're crazy, Fearne,' said Hal in a tone that he hoped she would find soothing as opposed to patronising. 'It's just…we can't go on like this. Waiting for The Big Bad to make his move. He's got us in a Schrodinger's box here.'

'That was…well executed,' said Malcolm, actually showing an expression of impressed respect.

'And you'd know *all* about that wouldn't you,' snapped Fearne. '*Execution*, I mean.'

Fearne stared at the three of them.

"Team Malcolm," she thought, with a bitterness that forced itself upon her to the point where she thought she might be sick.

Fearne wondered how two of her closest friends, people she trusted, could be so blind. Be so drawn in by the man's deceptions. She felt truly alone. Like she'd lost whatever measly shred of control she had over the world around her.

If they couldn't see it, it would be up to her to protect them. She would bide her time until Malcolm least expected it, waiting for her window of opportunity. And upon the first glimpse of that window, she would force it open and strike, ending his miserable excuse for a life.

'Fine,' said Fearne, standing and walking towards the weary time travellers that were under the killer's thrall, adopting a light-hearted tone that she hoped would illicit the impression she was on-board with them. 'Where do we go from here?'

Hal hummed a tune, unable to help himself.

'I swear to God,' said Fearne, 'if that's a Star Wars reference or some shit, I'm going to slap you, Hal.'

'Of course not!'

'Well come on then,' said Fearne taking charge and storming off, shouting her last thoughts on the matter over her shoulder. 'Let's go find us a place to figure crap out.'

'*Was* it Star Wars?' asked Kara.

'Buffy. Once More with Feeling.'

'Urgh,' grimaced Kara, walking away from him and catching up to Fearne. 'Sorry I asked.'

'What the hell's wrong with *Buffy*?' replied Hal, running to catch up with them.

Malcolm groaned, his social anxiety flaring at their bickering, making him wonder if it would just be easier to kill them all now and be done with it.

Without warning, far earlier than expected, a swirling wind engulfed them, shattering the sleepy backdrop with its intensity.

'*Now* what,' barked Fearne, struggling to be heard over the thunderous bombardment.

'Malcolm, what's happening?' shouted Kara.

'I think–' began Malcolm, rudely cut-off in his assumption as they were all vaporised.

CHAPTER FORTY-TWO
Fight Club

169th Restart – Friday, August 24th, 2018, 12:01pm

As their bodies reconstructed themselves into a brand-new restart, Kara realised what must have happened.

'Oh c'mon, Evil Malcolm crossed the boundary line?'

'What's the point in that?' said Hal, equally confused.

At best, it served as little more than a mild inconvenience.

'Right? What a pric–' but Kara's cursing was halted, as Hal interjected.

'Hang on. Might as well wait a minute for Fearne.'

In truth he just couldn't be arsed to have the same conversation twice.

As he counted away the fifty-or-so seconds, Fearne re-materialised with a crackle and a snap, a few feet away from them in what was clearly her designated spot of re-entry.

'What's hap—'

'Dark Malcolm. Triggered a restart, we think,' said Kara, helpfully bringing Fearne up to speed.

'Why?'

'Because he can I 'spose,' reasoned Hal. 'A show of power, maybe?'

'Or, more likely,' said Kara, trying to think like the thorn in their side would have, 'he just didn't want us having the chance to change anything. At least, nothing that could stick.'

Hal gave it some thought. It made perfect sense. The Dark Restarter was outnumbered, with no way of knowing how far in Hal and Kara both were restart wise. He may have been a force to be reckoned with, but they had beaten him before. What they lacked in physical ability they more than made up for in time-travel shenanigan-smarts. It stood to reason he wouldn't risk allowing them to beat him from the time-travel angle.

'Maybe it was a one off?' suggested Fearne. 'So many of us being here, maybe it caused time to wig out or something.'

'That's not how Restarting works,' said Hal.

'Oh, I forgot you were the *expert*,' Fearne replied like a speeding bullet, a direct shot to his ego that was so sour and laced with subtext it was borderline alcoholic.

'You want a flask for all that sass you're carting around? I just meant—'

'Can you two cut this shit out?' said Kara, finally losing her cool. 'I'm trying to think, and it's like I'm babysitting the world's worst toddlers.'

That shut them up. Kara rarely, if ever, spoke to anyone like that.

'*Thank you*,' she said, breathing in deeply through her nose, finally able to organise her thoughts. 'Okay, let's wait for Future Boy to get here, maybe he'll have some new memories of what went down. Or at least of what his new agenda might be. Or, old agenda. Whatever. You get me.'

'I get you,' said Hal.

'Kiss ass,' muttered Fearne.

*

'He's just stalling,' said Malcolm.

They had settled on an open expanse of land that was lush with grass in the winter, yet currently barren thanks to the weeks of summer sun that had been beating down upon it, the outskirts surrounded by a thick barrier of dense fir trees.

Their new choice of locale was simple, but effective; far enough away from not only Fir Lodge, but both Kevin's *and* the Restart Point. The open space also granted them adequate room for Malcolm to train them in the ways of, as Hal had described it, "The Path of The Dark Ninja."

It had taken them an hour to find it, making it just under two hours since Malcolm had returned to them, and both he and Kara were engaging in a sparring session. Fearne and Hal, meanwhile, were spectating from the side-lines and showing clear signs of boredom.

'Stalling for what?' asked Fearne, who was lying flat on her stomach, idly allowing her legs to sway behind her, chin resting on her hands, whilst Hal was being a little more creative.

Having placed two now-empty water bottles, two energy drink cans and his rubber flamingo on the log Kara had called dibs on as "her seat", he was taking practice shots with his wannabe Colt Python. The sound of compressed air being channelled through the pistol did little to give away their position, thanks to him having the foresight to remove the caps that generated the impressive sound of banging. As Hal took another three steps closer to his targets, cursing under his breath having missed all three, he gave it another go, as Malcolm spoke.

'I remember needing time to get my bearings,' said Malcolm, his memories slowly contradicting his own past thanks to the arrival of the four of them. Or so he claimed. 'Though my past-self has yet to settle on a definitive course of action to thwart you—'

'Nobody says *thwart* anymore, Malc',' said Hal.

'Would you rather I said *kill?*' a crease beneath his

eyes indicating a smile was threatening to show itself.

'Thwart is fine,' Hal conceded, before allowing the hint of his own smile to get lost amidst an eye-roll, turning his attention back to missing yet more targets in his make-shift shooting range.

'My point being, we can probably expect more impromptu restarts whilst he makes his decision on how to deal with you. Once he's settled down, we can devise a plan to stop him. For good,' added Malcolm, bookending his thoughts with a wax seal of conviction.

'What's next?' said Kara, returning her attention back to Malcolm's training, feeling like they were going over old ground with the current sparring arrangements.

The *exact* same ground as it turned out. Malcolm had been oddly regimental about making her repeat the same moves, over and over again.

Malcolm hesitated, as if unsure on how to word his next sentence.

'Very well. I wish to teach you…one move in particular,' he said finally. 'Attempt to stab me.'

'With what?' said Kara, more than a little bemused by the proposition.

'This will have to do,' said Malcolm, walking quickly to Hal's fairground attraction and picking up the ever-faithful rubber flamingo, passing the prop to Kara to use as a makeshift knife.

'Hey,' moaned Hal. 'Don't steal my targets!'

'They are only *targets*, if you actually stand a *chance*

at hitting them, Harold,' said Malcolm dryly.

'Meww meww target mew mew mewmold,' Hal mimicked under his breath in a high-pitched tone that was drenched in mockery.

'What was that?' said Malcolm, knowing full well Hal was taking the piss.

Hal merely aimed the gun at the man from their future, making a clicking noise with his tongue, topping it off with a wink.

'Hmm,' Malcolm grumbled, before splitting the out-of-phase air with two curled fingers, egging Kara on to begin.

Kara smiled, and struck out at Malcolm, her intention apparently to imbed the flamingo into his chest as if brandishing Excalibur itself. He grabbed her wrist effortlessly, red and blue energy manifesting between them, causing their arms to hum with a soft vibration.

'Now push the blade closer to my chest,' he said, somehow refusing to allow himself to stammer.

He still couldn't make sense on how much more difficult it was for him to drain her of her Restarter energy. With everyone else he had encountered, it was an instant transference. But with Kara…

'I c-can't, you're t-too strong!' she said weakly.

'Strength means nothing in this place!' said Malcolm, all but spitting the words into her face, their close embrace making it all the more personal. 'When will you *children* learn that–'

'Hey, Evil Morpheus,' said Hal, noticing how

Malcolm was losing his cool and getting a bit too close to Kara for his liking. 'Dial it down a bit, yeah?'

Malcom sighed, then apologised, tempering his anger but not wishing to discard the lesson he so desperately needed her to learn.

'Even when your adversary is stronger that you, there is always one more card to play. In the heat of the moment you must commit to a singular course of action. It's hard to think under pressure. So, if the blade can't move forward...'

Kara brought up her free hand, applying more pressure on the "hilt", but it made little difference, as Malcolm added his own free hand to the mix to bolster his right elbow.

'It doesn't make a difference,' said Kara, still not getting it.

'So, what does that *tell* you? If two hands don't change the outcome? What does that mean?'

'I...' she released her second hand from the hilt that was actually the arse-end of a flamingo, making sure to continue pushing her strength into it. 'Oh...' she said, finally understanding.

She dropped her left hand to her side, accepting it as a useless appendage that had nowhere to go and nothing to do.

Malcom grinned, and nodded ever-so-slightly. He could see the light bulb pinging to life in her eyes.

She brought her free hand up to waist-level, then released her grip on the flamingo, causing it to fall to the ground, the dirt beneath them refusing to budge under its negligible weight due to its lack of relative substance.

'Again,' said Malcolm, breaking form and taking several strides away from her, not even bothering to face her.

Kara grinned, picked up the flamingo, and ran towards him, releasing an Amazonian-like war-cry.

*

Friday passed in a rather uneventful manner.

Malcolm's past-self had not blessed them with his presence, nor had he triggered another early restart, resulting in the Restarters feeling unexpectedly relaxed. Even Fearne seemed more talkative, despite the fact the second fresh jump into the past had not returned her beloved Peter to her.

Kara had decided to take a break, much to Malcolm's disapproval, indulging in a spot of entirely inconsequential sunbathing; her retained charge from training with Malcolm allowing her the rare treat of feeling the heat of the afternoon sun across her bare arms. Something that shouldn't have been possible, given that their sparring should have drained her, not recharged her.

Not that Malcolm had shared that observation with the others, of course.

Sparring with Malcolm had allowed Kara to witness the red energy he was utilising in much greater detail, and it filled her mind with questions as she remembered all of the little details; a curling red energy that flowed forwards, complimented by barely-perceptible black wisps, which flowed backwards towards Malcolm's outstretched hand, shimmering sporadically, as if holding its own unique element of self-perpetuated fuel. It was a sinister looking electricity, seemingly being siphoned from an unseen, and altogether darker dimension.

It was during this moment of solitary reflection, as the faint voices of Hal and Fearne reached her ears, drifting across the expanse of the clearing they had set up shop in, when *their* Malcolm approached her. She steered her focus away from yet another argument her friends were engaged in, focusing entirely on the man before her.

'Kara, I need to speak with you,' said Malcolm, a hushed tone to his utterance of the words, as he shot a glance over at Hal and Fearne to make sure he was definitely out of earshot.

'What is it?' said Kara, her voice a combination of dismissiveness and implied suspicion.

'You and I…we see things very similarly…'

'Whatever this elevator pitch is,' said Kara sarcastically, 'it already needs work.'

'Yes, well, what I meant by that is we are very alike.'

'I'm nothing *like* you, Malcolm.'

'That's certainly a matter of perspective isn't it?' his narrow eyes clearly leading to whatever point he was trying to make. 'After all, we've *both* killed, haven't we?'

And there it was, just as she predicted.

His angle.

Kara wasn't willing to play this game. She knew he was a master manipulator. If nothing else, his past with Peter and Fearne was evidence enough of that. She was starting to understand how he had managed to lure past victims into a simulated trust for his own evil agendas, before eradicating them with his mastery of whatever Batman-esque fighting prowess he was now trying to impart on them.

'How many times, Malcolm?' said Kara, her words tired and forced, as if having to reiterate the point was sucking the very life out of her. 'There's a huge difference between acting in self-defence and murdering for the sake of it.'

'Yes, there is. Which is why you need to hear what I have to say.'

'Urgh,' she grumbled. 'What then.'

'When the time comes, if Hal cannot do what must be done, you must take *charge*. You *must* finish this.'

'Hal and I have got this covered. We'll talk *Dark-you* round into seeing the bigger picture. And prevent you from causing any more harm to anyone.'

'That won't be good enough, and you know it. There's only one way to stop him.'

'Stop *you*, you mean?' corrected Kara.

'Semantics aside, there is only one course of action that will yield a long-term result. Like we saw with Peter…'

'Don't you *dare* say his name,' snapped Kara,

sitting upright, her eyes flooding with blue energy.

Malcolm took a step back.

'You truly are remarkable, Kara,' said Malcolm, marvelling at the ease with which she could draw upon celestial energy simply via an impromptu emotional response.

Kara took a breath, calming herself, and the flaring of energy retreated.

'You may serve a purpose to us right now, but make no mistake,' warned Kara, squaring up to the bulk of a man, 'the moment you outlive your usefulness? This *alliance*? This *truce*? *Whatever* you want to call it. It's over. Once we correct the shit-storm you've brought down on us, you will be dust. Less than dust. There'll be no need for you to be here. You'll be little more than an echo on the wind that we won't even remember on the other side.'

'I am different now, you must know this,' he said, attempting to interject, but realising her tirade of a rant was impenetrable.

'I'm not done!' said Kara, nostrils flaring. 'You want salvation? Vindication? I don't buy any of the crap you're trying to sell. So, do your part and keep your grooming pep-talks to yourself? You get me?' said Kara breathlessly, standing up, walking past him and barging his shoulder hard, sparks of blue and red emanating from their moment of contact, and fizzling into nothingness in the ever-growing space between them, as she tried to put as much distance between them both as possible.

'That's the spirit,' whispered Malcolm, rubbing his shoulder and noting that there were far more red sparks than there were blue, as his ears were greeted by the sound of rushing air.

'Of course,' he said, releasing a sigh of irritability as his past-self chose once more to meddle with his own future.

Malcolm smiled, armed with the knowledge that delaying inevitability was little more than a band-aid. One that would eventually lose its ability to adhere to the skin of the soon-to-be mortal wounds time itself was destined to inflict.

CHAPTER FORTY-THREE
A Glimpse of the Future

178th Restart – Friday, August 24th, 2018, 4:02pm

The fistful of premature restarts that followed seemed to be devoid of a pattern. Malcolm knew this to be by his own twisted design of course, remembering how he had indeed chosen them at random.

Some days, the Dark Restarter allowed the interdimensional interlopers to reach the late afternoon of Saturday the 25th of August, and others giving them less than an hour in Friday the 24th.

Despite his words of reassurance that it would settle down, a further eight restarts had now passed, and everyone but Malcolm was sick of it.

And still, no sign of Peter.

Whether it was through boredom alone, or the fact that Fearne had once again become worryingly quiet, Hal suddenly felt the urge to revisit a concept that Malcolm had, until now, felt certain to be discarded.

'I've been thinking.'

'May God have mercy on us,' said Malcolm in false prayer.

'It couldn't hurt to at least try jumping to Sunday.'

'Harold, how many times. It. Will. Not. Work.'

'Maybe you just need a boost,' pressed Hal. 'If we get close enough to our alive-selves, we could really give it some oomph.'

'Besides,' said Kara. 'If you jump ahead in this restart, won't it lock your past-self out? From using the boundary line, I mean?'

Malcolm stared at her blankly. She was right, of course.

'Fine,' said Malcolm, unexpectedly. 'If only to bring an end to the matter once and for all.'

And with that, they made their way back to Fir Lodge, reasoning that Hal, Kara and Fearne could generate a far more effective surge of energy by remaining as close to their alive-selves as possible.

*

Once inside the lodge, using the communal living area as their anchor point, Malcolm held out his hands, each of them being taken by Hal and Kara, red and blue sparks filling the air around them, all of which entirely invisible to the living.

Fearne seemed reluctant, her arms crossed, and her pose guarded.

'It'll need all of us,' said Kara softly.

Begrudgingly, Fearne stepped between Hal and Kara, completing the circle so they could initiate what felt an awful lot to Fearne like an ill-conceived séance of stupidity.

They had already discussed what the plan would be on the walk over; drawing upon their respective power, Malcolm would let go of their hands in the hope the energy would be enough to catapult him beyond the realms of their existing restart loop. If it worked, they would effectively be sling-shotting him into Sunday the 26th of August, where his second cycle of restarts had begun, and his comatose-self presumably still resided.

He broke contact with them, disappearing with the familiar ruffle of a heavy-set ground sheet being shaken out, leaving the three of them behind.

*

Malcolm flew through their current restart, his eagerness to reach the end fuelled by the knowledge that the act of doing so locked them all out from using the portal on the boundary line.

He wasn't fond of leaving them so vulnerable. Or, more honestly, to allow them to make any hasty decisions without his say so.

The world passed him by, as Hal, Kara and

Fearne moved around him, talking too fast for him to hear, as if their lives were running on fast-forward which, of course, they were.

The night retreated, and was replaced by the morning light of Saturday morning, as the occupants of Fir Lodge sped through their daily routines.

Hal's considerably-more-alive-self searched drawers for a spoon for his coffee, whilst alive-Kara inhaled the Bloody Mary she had mentioned during their trip to The White Lodge. Crumpets popped from a nearby toaster, vanishing just as quickly as they were consumed with equal veracity by Daisy and Jasmine alike.

He needed to go further.

Faster.

He closed his eyes, allowing his sense of self to be transported to the moment he knew he could not cross; that of Saturday evening.

The night of his first death.

When he opened his eyes, he was amazed to see that he had travelled beyond 9pm, the hands of the wall clock to his left spinning wildly.

10pm.

11pm.

The furthest he had ever been, the remarkable sight filling his body with adrenaline.

But he could feel himself being tugged, the lasso of time eager to ensnare him. Malcolm fought against it, clenching his fists to summon as many extra seconds as he could, as a darkness slid across the floor, lapping at his legs, yet seemingly unable to sink its tendrils into his body; snake-like coils of dark matter that seemed to grow frustrated by their inability to gain purchase on him.

He looked up to the ceiling, gritting his teeth.

And then, for the first time in his entire life, the darkness he was so accustomed to was gone. Replaced with something else...something altogether new.

Not like the whiteness he had experienced at The White Lodge. No, he found himself dazzled by the intensity of the sun he was staring into, as if the contrast setting of the universe had been turned to its maximum output level.

He lowered his head, discovering it wasn't a sun he was staring into at all, but a fluorescent light bulb. The type most commonly found in–

'A hospital,' he muttered in hushed awe, as if saying it any louder would draw unwanted attention from whatever force it was that governed the now duplicated planet, the speck of dirt his existence represented on a cosmological level at odds with his innate sense of self-importance.

It *was* remarkable, though. A day unlike any other.

He had made it to Sunday.

It was hard to put into words the sense of elation he felt. After being a prisoner of the same thirty-three hours of time for so many years, it was utterly intoxicating to be somewhere else.

Anywhere else.

He chuckled deliriously, the sound catching in the back of his throat before escaping between his chattering teeth as his shoulders convulsed at the absurdity of every detail.

But his shaking shifted from humour to alarm, as he fell to the floor, his body hitting the ground hard, until he was once again surrounded by darkness. A blackness that would have been smirking, having successfully entrenched its claws back into him, a warden returning the handcuffs of damnation to its wily prisoner.

He was back at the beginning.

Back in the room he *always* restarted in.

Returned against his will.

Back to the Pentney Lakes.

*

'Told ya,' said Hal smugly, finally holstering the gun that had reformed in his hand as it always did, the four of them having regrouped in a brand-new restart.

'A second spent in the Sunday of our future does not constitute a success,' said Malcolm icily. 'Nor does it hold any quantifiable value.'

'Leave it to you to turn a roaring success into a Shakespearian bloody tragedy,' joked Hal.

'Hal's right, this is kind of a big deal Malcolm. It shows it's *possible*!' said Kara excitedly, following Hal's lead. 'Now we just need to find a way to extend the time you spent there…'

'I don't see how any of that–' attempted Malcolm, but there was no stopping Hal and Kara when they were on a brainstorming roll.

'Kara's right,' said Hal, following the trend. 'If we can master that…send you into the future to determine if the changes we're making in the past are having a positive impact…'

He didn't need to finish. It would mean they could effectively proof-read every big decision as they were making it.

'I…' began Malcolm, his heavy frame wobbling erratically, causing him to fall to his knees.

'You okay there, drunky?' said Hal, not showing any indication that he was going to help the man up.

'Memories,' said Malcolm, bringing his palm to his temple, pressing firmly against it, as an ice-pick headache surged through his brain. Flashes of barely-remembered thoughts fighting for his attention, trying to make room for themselves in an already full to the brim mind.

'*New* memories?' said Hal in excitement.

Malcolm nodded, his face unnaturally pale.

'Finally!' said Hal. 'What's the Dark You planning?'

'Risks everything,' sputtered Malcolm, wanting to vomit, but blessed by Restarter perks. 'We have a problem. My past-self, he's *leaving* in a few hours.'

'You mean leaving his hiding place?' asked Kara.

'No, leaving the lakes entirely,' replied Malcolm shakily.

'That's impossible,' scoffed Hal. 'There's no *way* he could cross the boundary line without triggering a restart. Not without…'

Malcolm stared at Hal, relieved that he understood.

'Are you kidding me? He wouldn't, surely?'

Malcolm glared at the three of them, as if the answer to that was obvious.

'How do we stop him?' said Hal, Fearne utterly lost and Kara suddenly getting it.

But for all his intelligence, all of his knowledge pertaining to his own future, he was at a complete loss. His past self was operating to an agenda that had been instigated by their arrival, demonstrating a level of free will that Malcolm himself could never have predicted. For once, he didn't have the answers.

For the first time in years, he felt frozen. This was not supposed to happen. It was bad enough keeping his entourage in line, without having to worry about his past-self going off-script.

'I'm not sure we can,' he said, a crack of actual fear in his voice.

'Looks like past-you is planning a Time Heist of his own,' said Hal, showing just a touch more excitement than the fear he should have been demonstrating. 'Luckily for you–'

'We know how to *own* that shit,' said Kara, pulling a pose akin to that of an action hero that would have been best served by an editor. One who could cut to the next scene where the action was actually happening.

But this was real life, and the reality was that

amidst Fearne's sigh, she was standing there watching this nonsense unfold waiting for someone to explain what the hell was going on.

'You *do* realise,' said Fearne, 'how ridiculous you two look when you set up some sort of *cliff-hanger*, and then just have to *stand* there, right? I mean, who are you even talking t–'

'Shh!' said Hal suddenly, staring behind her, causing her to turn around with fright. 'You *hear* that?' he whispered.

'Hear what?' said Fearne, wondering if their sanctuary was finally, after all this time, about to be invaded by a Dark Restarter after all.

'That's a scene break!' said Hal.

'Oh, sweet Lord,' replied Fearne, turning back to face him and being greeted by the sight of Hal pulling a thousand-yard stare up into the sky for dramatic effect. 'You are such a dic–'

CHAPTER FORTY-FOUR
The Rat-Catcher's Gambit

179th Restart – Friday, August 24th, 2018, 2:57pm

'More of a new chapter entirely, actually,' the Dark Restarter proclaimed, standing in the back of Kevin's truck, finishing one of what was now an innumerable quantity of self-aggrandising monologues that he was accustomed to indulging in, via the medium of shouting to his alive-self.

Having mere moments ago instructed himself to drive the vehicle just like he had acquired it; that is to say, as if he had stolen it, he continued onwards with his two-man show, painfully aware he was both performer and audience.

'Yes,' he repeated for no one's benefit but his own. 'Not a fresh start. Nor a fresh *restart*. But a chance to start a new life entirely.'

He was feeling elated.

Trying to manipulate the past had been challenging enough, but the arrival of the time-travelling counterparts he was trying so earnestly to eradicate had exacerbated matters far beyond his ability to predict. The introduction of these personified *wildcards* led to him reaching an unpredictable, and therefore potentially game-changing decision; by driving his physical self over the boundary line – and by extension, away from this cursed place – he would finally be free. After all, how could he *restart*, if he wasn't *here* in corporeal form to be restarted?

Malcolm grimaced, hating himself just a little bit for using the term of his enemies. But, secretly, he had to admit it was better than constantly having to sound intelligent by utilising so many synonyms. In the end he conceded it was better to stop wasting valuable thinking time on the matter.

*

Hal walked calmly onto the dusty road and squared up to the Restart Point, marvelling at how boring and unspectacular it looked, even from a mere several feet away. He found it odd how the road beyond it looked so…traversable.

For a brief moment, he allowed himself to imagine that his knowledge of the reality-bending properties that swirled malevolently within were nothing more than flights of fancy; a lie he had concocted, an urban-legend he had convinced himself to be true.

He made the sound of crackling lighting under his breath, as if that was the noise a gateway to a temporal nexus, and the self-contained trigger for a thirty-three-hour temporal anomaly such as this, should have been making.

Instead, it was more like a flawlessly-recreated, photo-realistic, animated snapshot of not only his own past, but an unattainable present and fluctuating future all in one. The road before him stretching out with all the hallmarks of terrain, with none of the follow through.

Sniffing belligerently, he forced a smile, followed by a half-hearted exhalation of amusement through his nostrils.

"It is what it is," he thought.

A statement everyone inevitably resorted to when the cause of something couldn't be defined or rationalised in a quantifiable way.

It was then that he heard the rumbling, and turned to face the real reason he was here.

*

The glint of the sun in front of The Dark Restarter was breached by the arrival of a strange sight; an outline of a man that wasn't *quite* a silhouette.

The sun didn't refract off the bodies of the restarted like it did with the living. One of the many curiosities he had uncovered on his journey.

Given that the now-lobotomised version of himself in the driving seat showed no signs of adjusting his speed or trajectory, Malcolm was certain this was exactly what it appeared to be; a last-ditch effort to thwart his departure.

'*Restarters*,' he growled, spitting the word out like the poison it was.

But he found himself smiling through his feral snarl, as the realisation of the futility surrounding the rat-catcher's gambit sunk in.

What did the fool expect he was going to achieve? They may not feel pain when subjected to blunt-force trauma from an inorganic object such as the out-of-phase vehicle he had commandeered, but they could still be run over.

'Speed up,' Malcolm muttered to his psychologically-compromised alive duplicate, grinning with delight. 'This is a *very* bad plan, Harold.'

*

Hal couldn't get over how much of a *great* plan this was.

He looked back over his shoulder as he walked, beyond the Restart Point now situated one-hundred-yards-or-so behind him, and stared up at the blistering sun that held no power over his vampiric skin, then looked back out to the road ahead.

Kevin's paint-chipped, midnight-blue truck was motoring towards him, and despite knowing what he knew, he licked his lips apprehensively, his imagination playing havoc with his sense of self-preservation.

He knew for a Stone-Cold Steve Austin fact that the car couldn't hurt him physically, no matter how fast it was going. It existed in the past, and he was occupying his own present…but it was still a truck. And he was just a man…

He shook away his counter-productive fears.

This was going to work.

He could run away from this, allowing the car to pass him by. But that would give the Dark Restarter exactly what he wanted, potentially leaving himself, Fearne, whatever was left of Peter, and – most importantly of all – Kara stranded in time.

That last thought grounded him.

Standing sideways-on in the direction of the vehicle that was increasing in size at an alarming rate, he raised his right hand theatrically, and with a flourish of over the top showmanship pressed play on the phone in his palm, which he had slyly charged during his recent extended contact with the others.

'Gotta have a soundtrack,' he muttered, smiling as the music blared from the speakers.

Hal was unable to resist the urge to bop, as the baseline of the Foo's "The Pretender" consumed every fibre of what was left of him.

Eyeing up the wagon of death that was speeding towards him, he casually unclipped the button on the holster that secured his gun, resting his hand on the grip like a true Brown Coat.

He knew the bullets couldn't harm anyone. But the man standing on the back of the truck? Staring down at him like some kind of vehicular themed horseman of a patent-pending apocalypse? *He* couldn't possibly know that.

As the Dark Restarter scowled at him like a top-tier extra from a Mad Max movie, Hal's mind unhelpfully reminded him of another fact that knocked his bravado somewhat; the car might not be able to hurt him, but the road warrior could.

In fact, he could actually *kill* him.

Hal spun the gun in his hand impractically, like a cowboy dispensing a gratuitous demonstration of showboating that served no other purpose than to look like a damn boss, and it slipped from his grip, clattering soundlessly to the ground.

'Shit,' he muttered, seriously hoping Kara hadn't seen that.

*

'What *is* he doing?' growled the surly spectator.

'Being Hal,' said Kara, who very much *had* just seen that.

But she didn't roll her eyes, she merely smiled.

*

Retrieving the chromed weapon from the ground, he looked down the sight, aiming it towards the oncoming vehicle, unable to wipe the smirk from his face as he discarded the doubt from his mind.

"You got this, Callaghan. This is going to be legen–'

*

"–dare he?" thought Malcolm unable to get his head around what was clearly a demonstration of pure, unbridled stupidity. He replayed the thought again. "How dare he?!" having just witnessed the Restarter clumsily dropping a gun onto the ground like a delusional moron of unquantifiable idiocy.

But as the fool had composed himself and picked up the weapon, Malcolm wondered if there was more to all of this tomfoolery than met the temporally-displaced eye. The thought lasted for just a fraction of a second, but the seed of doubt was there; did the cavalier cretin before him know something he didn't?

As Malcolm's physical-self changed gear, taking his foot off the gas for a brief moment, the faintest sound of music met his ears over the ferociously revving engine of the truck. It was then that he knew he was *truly* being mocked.

He thought back to the niggling feeling that something was amiss. Was it impossible?...

*

'This is possible,' Hal said to himself, taking a deep breath and releasing a pep talk. 'I mean, sure. On the one hand you're jousting with a truck that's moving eighty miles per-hour armed only with a pellet gun.'

He really hoped Kara was watching, as he arced the gun downwards in a quick motion, bringing his phone-wielding hand to the forefront.

Pointing it at the car, he turned his body and

adopted a stance that seemed to indicate he was bracing himself for impact.

Kevin's truck surged towards the Restarter, now less than twenty feet away, both Malcolm's staring at him, one peering over the top of the vehicle's cabin, the other inside it. Hal and the Dark Restarter shared a moment, staring into the whites of each other's eyes; Malcolm's face a savage sneer, and Hal's adorned with a defiant smile.

'Top left,' muttered Hal, waving his phone-wielding arm like a Jedi, into the direction of the trees to his right.

Malcolm would have laughed, were it not for the version of himself that was driving the car suddenly pulling the steering wheel into a sharp full lock to the left, sending the Dark Restarter careening out of the vehicle and landing face down into the dirt, rolling for a comically extended length of time.

The truck, meanwhile, ploughed purposefully into a trio of burly looking fir trees that had, up until that point, been minding their own business, their disturbed branches now waving like Team Hal cheerleaders, as the bonnet and engine of Kevin's truck crumpled like a soda can being struck by Mjolnir.

Hal brought the barrel of the gun to his lips, and blew away the non-existent pistol smoke, shooting a look instead of bullets to where Kara, Fearne, and Future Malcolm were hiding.

*

The Malcolm of their future held his outstretched arm in place, eyes closed in concentration, drawing on the Restarter energy of the others to bolster his equally innate ability to control his physical-self remotely.

Their plan was, first and foremost, to prevent his alive-self from stepping over the boundary line and into the world beyond.

But he'd never done it from this distance before, and didn't know how long he could keep his alive-self from overcoming the whiplash he had surely sustained…

*

'You okay their mate, you took quite a nasty tumble,' said Hal, walking towards the recently-jettisoned Dark Restarter. 'Can I get you anything? A cloth for the egg on your face, maybe?'

The darker Malcolm of the past pressed downwards towards the ground he was laying on, as if doing a very slow and deliberate press-up, all the while maintaining eye-contact with the person he was about to kill.

And then he faltered, as Kara and Fearne flew past him, each collecting one of his two large knives, and running off into the woods. Presumably to discard them.

'Ouch,' said Hal, tapping his foot to the beat of the music. 'Yeah, no knifey-spoony for you today. This really is a *bad news bears* kind of day for you, isn't it?'

The Dark Restarter didn't speak. He was beyond

such triviality. The *boy* before him had just carved the biggest bullseye into his own flesh. If Malcolm's hatred was bad before, it was now spilling over the sides of the thimble-sized container that ensconced his sanity.

Hal felt it too; a prickling sense of danger that made him realise he'd just pushed a literal serial killer over the edge.

The Dark Restarter took a step towards him, and Hal pulled back the hammer on the Colt Python he had firmly trained on the man, absolutely counting on the fact that Malcolm's past-self had no idea it was a fake.

'Don't move,' ordered Hal, his instruction as effective as the type of command he issued to his dog Shelby when she'd caught a whiff of a particularly delicious cat-poop she wanted to investigate. And consequently devour. That is to say, entirely fruitless. 'I mean it, I'll shoo–'

Malcolm didn't hesitate, he simply pulled the gun from Hal's hand and grabbed the Restarter by the wrist, killing the music emanating from the phone instantly.

Hal suddenly felt weak, his retained charge of energy rapidly revoked.

Malcolm, however, clearly wasn't suffering from the same problem, and was positively glowing. His eyes blazed with a terrifying red hue, which served as an unwanted invitation made solely to Hal. One inviting him to what was surely an imminent death.

Malcolm looked with disdain at the weapon he had stolen from the Restarter, back at Hal, then threw it with little effort, somehow managing to lob it all the way into the rear storage area of the vehicle his alive-self was currently still occupying.

'Sick throw, to be fair,' said Hal, genuinely impressed.

A compliment Malcolm rewarded by pulling Hal towards him and grabbing the Restarter by the throat, lifting him into the air.

'Gak!' gargled Hal, unable to produce any other response.

'No more jokes?' whispered Malcolm. 'Not even a little smile? Or are you now realising that your luck truly has run its course?' he added, throwing Hal to the ground away from both the Restart Point and the blue truck, which was now billowing smoke from its engine, as if trying to give everyone the heads up that it wasn't feeling all that great, and would quite like any spectators to take a step back in case it lost control of the situation and, well, exploded.

'Who needs luck,' croaked Hal, his face an unwell-looking red, thanks to his recent foray into recently administered strangulation. 'When you look as good as thi–'

Malcolm brought his boot down hard against Hal's face.

'Please,' said Malcolm, reaching down and grabbing Hal by his brown, leather jacket and dragging him several more metres across the dirt-covered concrete, 'stop,' he added, releasing his grip and squatting down next to him like a garish gargoyle, '*talking*,' he whispered, placing Hal's head in his enormous hands, and beginning to squeeze.

Hal clawed desperately at Malcolm's wrists, trying to somehow force him to release his grip, but was entirely unsuccessful. He was outmatched by the man's strength, and it took all he had just to remain conscious, as the taste of copper trickled lazily across his taste buds and down the back of his throat.

Small, swirling black wisps began to fill his vision, tantalisingly proposing that perhaps a quick rest and a sleep would solve all his problems.

'*Bad* wavy lines!' he croaked, swatting them away with exaggerated eye movements, as if that would cast them out.

He could have really used his *own* Malcolm right about now to even the odds of what was evidently becoming an increasingly-unlikely survival scenario, but that was never on the cards.

They couldn't risk tipping their hand so early on. Having a Malcolm from the future on their side, at least in theory, was the only ace they had. Though, admittedly, it wasn't exactly doing Hal any favours in the immediate sense.

But Hal knew *their* Malcolm had a far more important task to contend with.

Hal, as agreed, was just the bait.

*

Kara quickly stashed the knife in a suitably dense

patch of tall grass, glimpsing a flurry of Fearne's dress as she ran off to do the same.

As she made her way back to the wreckage of Kevin's truck, she watched as *their* Malcolm froze, overcome with an unexpected hesitancy.

'Malc', what's wrong?' asked Kara.

His eyes were glazed over, as if he were stuck in place by an unexpected bout of emotional memory.

"Is that *fear*?" thought Kara, before feeling the urge to get back on track and placing her hand gently on the man's shoulder.

'Malcolm?' she said softly.

Whether it was her words, or the jolt that flew through him thanks to the unexpected contact, he was back in the room, and reached in through the open passenger-side window. Ducking down low to make sure he remained unseen, he took advantage of his close proximity to his considerably more alive – yet utterly-stupefied – past-self, unlocking the door.

'How long will it take?' asked Kara, as he placed his hand through the body of his corporeal self and muttered a slew of words.

'I'm not changing the battery in a smoke alarm, Kara,' he replied, spitting the words in the irritated manner of someone much akin to that of a writer being asked a question whilst they were painstakingly trying to complete a particularly tricky sentence.

'Jeez, just give me a ball park timeframe,' she said with a frown, not wishing to draw this out any longer.

The Restart Point was closer to her than it was to

Hal. It would have been so easy for her to just end this madness then and there without risking–

'Oh shit!' exclaimed Kara, as the Dark Restarter across the road from her shifted his position, revealing Hal's bloodied and bruised face.

She watched helplessly, as Malcolm's past-self grabbed her friend by the throat, causing her own out-of-phase hands to grip the lip of the trailer of the truck. Whilst she deliberated on what to do next, a familiar glimmer of chrome caught her eye, and she smiled mischievously.

'Oh, hello you!'

*

'What *is* it with you people,' mused the Dark Restarter, as if he were engaging in a friendly catch-up over a cup of tea, rather than choking the life out of a young man.

'*You* people? That's–' Hal spluttered, blood filling his throat, '–kinda narrow-minded, Malc'. Is it,' he struggled to finish, 'because I'm *blue*?'

Malcolm pressed harder against his wind pipe.

'Why couldn't you have just *left* things alone? You *saved* yourselves. Why did you have to come back here and risk it all just for the golfer?!'

'He owed me…' croaked the Restarter. 'A tenner.'

'I suppose you think of yourselves as time travelling superheroes don't you. That the *universe* rewards *goodness*? Punishes the *bad*? But it's all *relative*, Harold. You *must* understand this? After all, *you* yourselves are killers, in your own dull way of–'

'Hey, Rambo!'

Malcolm turned his head towards the source of the other bane of his life. A female voice he recognised immediately. The second personified thorn in his side.

He couldn't help but chuckle.

There she was; the orange secretary, no longer wearing orange, true, but still very much as he remembered her, standing in the back of the pickup truck, aiming a gun at him no less.

This was going to be interesting.

*

Kara teased the trigger, knowing that as soon as she fired the gun, the jig would be up.

Malcolm would know it was as harmless as a mouse deciding it wanted to become President of The United States.

But she didn't need to pull the trigger, she just needed to stall him.

'You look *smaller* than I remember,' said Kara, goading him into focusing on her.

'And you lack less courage in your convictions than I recall,' retorted Malcolm's past-self.

'Blah, blah. Got it *all* figured out, don't you,' she said with a sneer. 'Big man that likes to kill people half his size, and then calls it art. Tell me,' she said, attempting to channel the spirit of her friend Robert and looking at him with as much sardonic pity as she could muster. 'Was it because your mother didn't *love* you enough?'

'Careful, girl,' said Malcolm, throwing Hal to the ground like yesterday's Cornetto.

'Ohhh,' Kara continued, her eyes lighting up like an epiphany had revealed itself to her. 'Or did she love you *too* much, maybe? If you *catch* my *drift*?'

He caught her drift. One handed. And crushed it to dust with a look of hatred so pure it would have killed her, if looks possessed the ability to kill. Luckily for Kara, that was little more than trite hyperbole.

'I,' said Malcolm, preparing to unleash a response so brutal, so *perfectly* crafted that it would have broken her in ways she would never have assumed possible.

But his intricately-designed wordplay was cut down before it had a chance to escape into the world, as Kara did something entirely unexpected; she turned around, jumped off the truck, and ran.

*

'You done yet,' snapped Kara.

'A little more,' replied Future Malcolm, hiding in the footwell with his hands firmly planted inside the brain of his living self.

'You boys will be the death of me,' said Kara under her breath, trying to locate Fearne with furtive glances, frustrated that she was nowhere to be seen, and continued onwards.

*

Fearne knew the plan. They had spent the last two hours piecing it together, erasing all trace of any unexpected loopholes. She knew she was meant to stow the blade she had swiped into the long grass, as far away from the dark Restarting monster that was Malcolm's past-self.

And yet...

The weapon seemed to hum with the promise of vengeance, whispering to her the things she wanted to hear.

She allowed it to wash over her, as she approached Future Malcolm from behind, noting how vulnerable and pathetic he looked, pressing his body down in the compacted footwell of the drivers-side of the truck.

She had been told it belonged to the man named Kevin.

Jerry's owner.

"Where *was* Jerry?"

Her thoughts were an erratic collage of swirling maybes, but one clear idea shone through, as she looked down at the business-end of the enormous blade in her hand, and she set her gaze back towards the man who had *killed* her boyfriend.

"Such a flimsy term," she thought. "Boyfriend."

It didn't do Peter justice. Once you reached the age she was, such terms felt...juvenile, almost.

He was her *lover*.

Potentially would have been her future husband. The father to the children they would now *never* have.

He had taken that away from her.

"From *them*."

That made her see red, quite literally, and her eyes filled with the red power Malcolm was now so well-known for.

"Yes," she reasoned.

He had indirectly *killed* her children. Past, present, future, it didn't matter. All this time travel bullshit was lost on her.

Would plunging the knife into the back of the man that was claiming to help them bring Peter back?

"Unlikely."

Would killing him erase the murderer's past-self that was unleashing sickly-sounding kicks and punches to Hal's Restarter self?

"Who knew," she thought. Or, more importantly, "Who cared?"

This would be her only moment. The *window* of opportunity she had been waiting for.

She stepped closer and raised the knife, her footsteps silent, until the pain inside her brought her more into phase with the timeline they were travelling through, solidifying her presence and causing a twig to snap beneath her foot.

Future Malcolm glanced over his shoulder at her, and grinned.

*

'Well, enough chat,' the Dark Restarter chirped, as he turned his attention back to Hal and placed his boot firmly into the small of the Restarter's back, who, he noticed, had been trying to crawl away. 'It appears that for all her brave words, even your orange friend has abandoned you. Running to the *barrier*, I expect. Off to trigger another one of your restarts.'

'I'mjustthedistraction, douchebag,' mumbled Hal, his words so faint Malcolm couldn't catch them.

'Speak up, Harold, you're *embarrassing* yourself.'

Hal mumbled the same words, even quieter than before.

The Dark Restarter groaned, removed the pressure his leg was applying to the young man's back and dragged him up by the collar, staring him square in the face.

'I can't hear you! Enunciate, or die quietly,' barked the Malcolm of their past. 'It matters not, even if your moronic friends trigger another loop, I'll simply try again, then again, until I make it out of this cursed place.'

Hal laughed.

A cringe-inducing, fake-sounding work-laugh that he usually reserved for Susan who worked in Legal, whenever she lamented that the weather was rather cold out.

During the peak of an English winter.

Or summer, for that matter.

Man, Susan sucked…

It was an ugly laugh too, more like a death-throw gargle thanks to the blood in Hal's mouth that continued to fill up like a self-replenishing goblet. Presumably due to the tooth Malcolm had dislodged that was bobbing against his cheeks, the nerve ending having only just given in and disconnecting from the enamel.

Malcolm was used to his art *crying* as the life ebbed

away from them. He always felt closest to his work at this point. But never laughter. The boy was clearly insane.

'Yeah,' said Hal, his voice wheezy but nonetheless defiant, as he spat out his rogue tooth. 'It's almost as if we *thought* of that.'

The Dark Restarter was taken aback.

'What did you say before, on the ground?'

'I said,' Hal cleared his throat and spat yet more of the red gooey contents from his mouth, though not at Malcolm. He wasn't *that* brave. 'I'm just the *distraction*,' he added, taking a pause before whispering the last word, his eyes like fire. '*Douchebag*.'

Malcolm looked over his shoulder to the car, seeing Fearne through the smashed driver's side window, then back to Kara who had just made it to the boundary line where the portal to a renewed past awaited her.

*

Future-Malcolm had done all he could, and grabbed Fearne by the wrist before she could introduce Malcolm's back with the pointy end of his own death-bringer.

The knife still managed to find its way into the top of his leg, but only by about an inch.

'I know you are hurting, and we *will* have this talk, but *right* now, you need to tell Kara we are ready.'

Fearne stared back him, nothing but red sparks spitting from her wrist thanks to their connection.

And zero blue.

'*Fearne,*' said Malcolm soothingly, trying to pull her back from wherever it was her head was at.

There was something incredibly disarming about the way he had said her name. If she didn't know any better, she would have almost believed he was speaking to her as an equal, rather than someone he would slaughter should the whimsical mood have struck him.

'Right,' she said, releasing her grip on the blade. 'Right,' she said a second time, as if doing so would erase the fact she had just been caught in the act of trying to kill him.

Having revealed her true intentions, Fearne almost felt embarrassed, as she backed out of the truck's cabin, then snorted in a sharp intake of air, before running to Kara.

*

Kara could see Fearne approaching, flapping her arms, and could just about make out her saying the deed was done as the truck exploded, a trickle of leaking petrol having seemingly kissed the smoke-cloaked flames from the engine.

None of them knew if *their* Malcolm had escaped, but they knew for a *fact* the living version of Malcolm hadn't, which meant they would need to restart this party soon, before their actions took hold and became cemented in time.

"Or should they?" thought Kara, in hesitation.

They didn't have enough information to know what killing their killer before he killed them would do to everything they had set in motion so far. There was no telling how that would affect the future.

She needed a moment, but saw Hal was in trouble, then smiled, as an idea *so* simple it was *genius* presented itself to here.

Kara thought of Hal's black wellington boot, and the last time he had thrown it through the restart portal. How it had reappeared on his foot. How Hal's brother Alex's phone had reformed in his pocket following the first explosion they had caused by time-travelling.

For a fleeting moment, she looked at the gun in her hand, at Hal, then at her feet where the invisible barrier resided.

The Colt Python suddenly represented caution, and the Restart Point became the wind, as she threw the weapon into it.

*

Malcolm's past-self was contentedly strangling the life out of Hal. 'You just *killed* me, you idiot! The *real* me!' he barked.

It was then he saw it; several wisps of blue light circling around Hal's hand, which was currently clawing once again at Malcolm's vice-like talons. Hal clearly saw it too, opening his hand and moving it away from them both.

They couldn't help but both watch with fascination, as the strips of light quickly multiplied into billions of blue fragments, until finally solidifying to form a rather inconvenient object.

'What *are* you people?!' said Malcolm, beguiled by the constant surprises they kept throwing at him.

'We're The Restarters,' said Hal, pulling back the hammer and shooting Malcolm in his mouth at point-blank range.

The pellet embedded itself into the back of Malcolm's throat, which promptly filled his mouth with blood.

The pain was tremendous, and shocking enough to cause the killer to release his hold on Hal, who fired another round into the man's cheek, then leg, causing the monster of a man to fall to one knee, comically looking like he was mid-proposal, his hands now wrapped around his own throat, still not knowing it wasn't a real bullet.

Hal raised the gun and aimed it at the forehead of the man kneeling before him, and stood there for a moment.

A thought occurred to him, and he glanced to his right, as if expecting to see a glimmer of someone watching the show; a former version of his Restarting-self staring back at him with awe over the man in a brown jacket holding a bad-ass gun.

But there was nothing there.

Coming to his senses, Hal took advantage of the precious seconds that had been afforded to him and hobbled away towards Kara, before turning around, smiling mischievously, and shooting the man in the arse for no other reason but shits and giggles.

Kara and Hal raced towards each other, with Kara

taking all of his weight before he keeled over, blue sparks erupting between them.

'You look like shit,' said Kara, her smile warm, yet anxious.

'Next time, *you're* the bait,' joked Hal, strangely feeling a lot better thanks to the energy flowing between them. 'Great shout on the gun, by the way. Total Bill and Ted moment.'

A menacing wave of white, static fog rolled through the trees, like a weary caretaker coming to investigate what the *hell* the two of them had instigated now, as if they were a couple of dogs fouling on the perfectly manicured lawn of linearity.

'Time to bounce,' said Hal.

'Nobody says that!' snorted Kara.

'*We* say that,' contested Hal.

'Can you even walk?'

'I actually feel pretty great, thanks for the boost.'

And they dragged themselves to the Restart Point, the sound of the Dark Restarter's gurgling profanity drowned out by the sound of rushing air, as they wiped the slate clean and converted their current reality into one of a more alternative variety…

One, for a change, operating by the rules *they* dictated.

CHAPTER FORTY-FIVE
Eternal Darkness of a Broken Mind
1,078th Restart – Friday, August 24th, 2018, 12:01pm

The Dark Restarter reappeared at the exact moment in time his own personal Restart-chain always began, stumbling outside of the small shack and falling to his knees. The residual memory of the burning in his throat, caused by the metal ball-bearing that had embedded itself into his soft flesh, caused him to gag reflexively. He tried to cough the bullet out, with zero success.

He absently acknowledged the sound of a dust-sheet being shaken out behind him, but had more on his plate at the moment, not particularly fancying the idea of having to deal with *that* wrinkle in his own timeline.

Malcolm calmed himself, reached into his mouth, and fished around with his perfectly clipped nails, hoping to gain purchase on the foreign object, before quickly realising that not only was it gone, the hole in his throat has also miraculously healed.

He cursed, reasoning that the "bullet" must have returned to the chamber of the rat-catcher's weapon, the damage to his body now merely a memory that acted as little more than a souvenir to their encounter.

The Dark Restarter breathed through flaring nostrils and clenched his eyes shut, expecting to feel pain, preparing to shut off that part of his brain, compartmentalising it and drawing upon the more analytical side of his mind to assess the entirety of his run-in with the self-proclaimed Restarters.

Calming the ocean of anger that ran through him, he smiled to himself.

All was not lost.

They had tipped their hand. There was no way they could recreate what they had just achieved a *second* time. All that was required of him was to try again, safe in the knowledge that, sooner or later, he would inevitably succeed.

There was a singular incongruity he needed to address, however, and that was how his corporeal-self had deviated so dramatically from the path he himself had set him on. Malcolm knew his physical body was a puppet to *him*, but how on earth Harold had literally taken the wheel remotely was a mystery.

He recalled the scene; Harold waving his arm at the last moment, Malcolm's physical-self seemingly acting on his instruction, and sending the truck careening into the fir trees lined up along either side of the road.

"Unless…" thought Malcolm, wincing.

Not through pain, but due to the arrival of the most logical answer presenting itself to him.

'No matter,' he gargled, still not quite right after being shot in the face, and proceeding gingerly back to the shack that served as his chronologically-decreed point of re-entry into the past. His "point of origin", as he had taken to calling it.

He outright refused to check himself over by applying pressure to his rear end, as if doing so would somehow give a sense of victory to the man who shot him in it. He would pay for that. They all would.

As Malcolm returned to his shack he surveyed his living, former-self with contempt. A shadow of the man he once was, his cerebral synapses severely frazzled and fractured, no longer able to formulate thoughts of his own.

In his arrogance, Malcolm automatically assumed he would be able to piece together his mind once they had successfully escaped, reasoning that in doing so all of his reprogramming would be undone and erased from history, taking the damage he was surely inflicting on his own psyche with it. With that in mind, he barked an order at the shadow of his former self.

'Get to the truck, we're going again.'

But the hulk of a man, whose shoulders now sagged despondently in a way that made him look almost frail, or at the very least mentally exhausted, merely stood there, swaying slightly.

'Malcolm,' he said to himself again, taking a curious step forward, knowing the increased proximity to each other would amplify his hold whilst reducing his alive-self's ability to resist him.

At least that's how it had worked.

For years, in fact.

And yet, the man remained firmly in place, defying his orders without so much as a troubled frown.

Malcolm felt a surge of anger, and plunged his hands into the brain of his physical self, the connection causing the eyes of the lobotomised doppelgänger to light up like a set of traffic lights urging oncoming traffic to stop.

'Get to the truck,' he ordered dispassionately.

But something was wrong. Different. *Altered*, somehow.

The Dark Restarter was flooded with garbled memories; the woman in the white dress, who he recognised as Fearne, walking towards the truck, a knife in her hand.

Was he seeing the memories of his alive-self watching Fearne? Or was it something else? Some*one* else?

He was repelled from delving deeper, pushed several steps back across the room by a force unlike anything he had encountered before. Whatever had happened whilst he had been distracted, the time-travelling thorns in his side had done something.

Malcolm had no idea *how* he knew, but he *did* know. A simple notion telling him that, from here on out, he would never again be able to manipulate his alive-self into getting into that damned truck.

The *red* flared within him, and he pulled the second knife that was concealed behind his apron, pressed between his jeans and shirt, kept in place by a sturdy belt. The second of two knives he had brought back in time with him, and threw it with all his might.

It flew right through his replicated out-of-phase head, and connected soundlessly with the wall of the shack, tumbling to the floor pathetically.

CHAPTER FORTY-SIX
The Trigger

180th Restart – Friday, August 24th, 2018, 12:01pm

Hal and Kara came with the wind, with Fearne hot on their heels a minute later.

But still no Peter, nor the radio that he had inadvertently brought with him into the past, which served as a callous reminder that their victory over The Dark Restarter was nothing if not bittersweet.

Hal spoke first, trying to begin their new restart on a positive note.

'Oh, I bet he's pissed off now,' said Hal gleefully. 'Throwing things around in a right hissy fit.'

Kara was more reserved, noting Fearne's stern

expression, as they took up residence on Hal and Kara's favourite bench, waiting for their Malcolm to catch up with them.

*

'Here he is,' said Hal, as Malcolm made his way over to them twenty-or-so minutes later, hands raised in peace so they knew it was their version of him. 'Looking pretty dope for a guy who just survived an explosion!'

'Hmm,' growled Malcolm.

'What happened back there?' asked Kara.

'Nothing,' he said curtly, keeping his words brief in an attempt at reaffirmation, intentionally avoiding eye-contact with Fearne, who he could feel staring at him as if wondering which way he was going to go.

Would he rat her out? Try and turn her friends against her? Or would he stick with what he did best, and lie his way through this...

As Malcolm uttered his next words, Fearne's third assumption was immediately validated, confirming to her that secrets were the only currency the killer traded in.

'It took longer than I expected,' said Malcolm, lying effortlessly. 'Luckily the blast was harmless to me in this state. Though I suspect my alive-self was not so fortunate. Thank you for triggering the restart when you did, Kara.'

Hal mulled his words over, taking the opportunity to fish around in his mouth with his finger whilst prodding his gums with his tongue, happy to confirm his formerly dislodged tooth had been returned to him.

'Damn,' said Hal. 'I guess what happens in Vegas stays in Vegas,' he mused, removing his finger from his mouth, relieved to see no trace of red residue between his fingers and thumb.

'Not that,' said Kara. 'You wanna talk about why you froze when you saw Kevin's car wrapped around a tree?'

'Not particularly,' said Malcolm, his tone ringing with unexpected honesty.

'Fine. But did it work, do you think?' said Kara, having just replayed their plan in her head and comparing it with the way in which they had all implemented it. 'Will it stick?'

'It will stick,' said Malcolm.

Their plan had been so simple in theory, which – for them at least – usually meant it could have gone wrong in so many ways that it was a miracle they were all still here and talking at all; Hal would act as bait, drawing Malcolm's murderous Dark Restarter-self into the open. Meanwhile, Kara and Fearne would boost Future Malcolm's energy levels, allowing him to theoretically reach across both time and space to issue a last-minute instruction to his alive-self who was driving the truck. Two simple words;

"Sharp. Left."

With the Malcolm of the past out of commission, and the Malcolm of the present having been thrown from the rear of the vehicle, this allowed the Malcolm of the future to backtrack through the forest, crossing the road back to the crash site. Once there, Future Malcolm proceeded to imbed what Hal was referring to as "an unbreakable vow" into the mind of his own alive self.

In essence, their goal was for Malcolm to implant a deep-rooted instruction, along the lines of "stay away from that damn truck, no matter what I say in future", thus preventing The Dark Restarter's tactic to leave the Pentney Lakes via vehicular means going forward.

It wasn't just a suggestion being imparted, more a long-lasting idea they were implanting.

Hal waving his arm was just the showboating icing on the cake, providing enough cover for Dark Malcolm to question Hal's true abilities, whilst allowing them to conceal Future Malcolm's existence entirely.

'What's he doing now,' asked Kara.

Malcolm folded his arms and closed his eyes, searching his own memories, as glimmers of faded recollections swam into focus.

'Licking his wounds,' said Malcolm, following his words with an uncharacteristic chuckle. 'He's very *angry* at you Harold. And especially you, Kara.'

'I think we'll live,' said Hal.

'Goading me by slandering my mother? What *were* you thinking?' the former killer added, trying to figure out what on earth had possessed her.

Kara shrugged. 'I mean, I took a gamble. There

must be *some* kind of reason you are the way you are.'

'Why *do* you do it?' said Fearne, the question filling their eardrums like a large glass vase of "don't go there" connecting with the concrete floor of "oh she's going to go there despite the aforementioned warning."

'Do what?' said Malcolm, knowing full well where this was going, but attempting to put an end to the line of questioning all the same.

But Fearne wasn't prepared to let this go. And if anyone had the right to ask him, it was her.

'You *know* what. Why do you kill innocent people?'

'Does it really *matter* why?' said Malcolm, genuinely curious. 'Why do *any* of you live the way you do?'

'Because we choose to,' said Kara.

'Precisely,' said Malcolm.

'But what makes someone wake up one morning and decide to be a serial killer?' said Hal.

'You keep using that term,' said Malcolm. 'It's rather reductive.'

'Well consider this a casting of the *Reducto* spell,' said Hal, waving an imaginary wand and adopting a pose befitting a wizard preparing for battle. 'A rose by any other name and all that.'

'What would *you* call yourself?' asked Kara curiously.

'If I were to label that which cannot be labelled, I have always thought of myself more of an *artist*. The people I encounter the canvas.'

'Yeah, that's…not normal, Malc'' said Hal, shivering slightly.

'You are viewing this from the perspective of someone who has been nurtured to conform to a societal structure,' he countered.

'No,' hummed Kara. 'We're viewing this from the perspective of basic human decency.'

'Oh c'mon Malc',' said Hal, utterly engrossed. 'It's not like any of us will remember anything you tell us when we bust our way out of here.'

'Hal's got a point. How often is it that you get to tell your side of the story to people like us? It's not every day you get to chit-chat with a serial…artist,' added Kara, changing her mind mid-sentence in the hope of perhaps appeasing his ego.

'Some would see that as a *good* thing,' countered Malcolm. 'I do not have to justify myself to you.'

'You may not owe it to *them*,' said Fearne, 'but you *do* owe me. Tell me why Peter had to die. What *art* was there in that? It was just pointless bloodlust.'

'Fearne, I…' he struggled, unable to find a suitable response.

He could tell his explanation wasn't good enough. That they needed more. Or at the very least, Fearne deserved more.

For the first time since *it* happened, he dropped the eloquent enunciation he was so fond of, and dialled back his inherently patronising tone.

'If you're asking what caused me to be this way, I

suppose there *was* an incident that one could argue served as a *trigger...*'

Kara's mind was taken back to the first time she saw all of the newspaper articles lining the walls of Kevin's basement.

'What *happened* to her?' said Kara, taking a leap and reasoning it must have been about a woman.

"His wife, maybe?"

Kara felt a splash of unexpected regret when it occurred to her that maybe she had been more on-point about it involving his mother, and suddenly felt very lucky to be alive. Or at least the Restarter equivalent.

And then Malcolm did something he very rarely indulged in. Something he usually only shared just before he ended the life of the person he was standing over.

He told them how he was reborn.

CHAPTER FORTY-SEVEN
Origins

Thursday, December 14th, 1995

Ophelia Moreaux was the kindest woman you could ever hope to meet. The sort of person who would bring you doughnuts as well as a coffee, even if you only asked for the latter latte, and would not expect money for either, despite it being your turn for the fourth day running.

She was simply built that way. Generous to a fault. And literally the only person Malcolm could stand. Ophelia understood him like no other.

She was also Malcolm's sister.

Five years his senior, the two of them shared the same mother, a woman of French descendancy named Lilith, who was stern in demeanour and incredibly tough. Malcolm and Ophelia would never have become family at all were it not for the untimely demise of Ophelia's father, which led to a rather quick remarriage to her second husband, boringly named Mark. That wasn't to say Mark was a boring person. If anything, he had spent his final moments on Earth doing what he loved; namely, *breathing*. It just wasn't the name you'd expect for a man who would inadvertently sire a serial killer.

Not that the name "Malcolm" screamed "*Zodiac*."

Despite being a mere twenty-two years of age, Malcolm had never been good at communicating with others. It wasn't that he *couldn't*, of course. He just had no desire to do so.

It was for this reason that meeting with his sister filled him with such ambivalence. She always demanded they met in public places, to test him he supposed, a means of dragging him out of his comfort zone.

Despite being five years older, she never lorded over him. They were equals.

Even though she *was* smarter than he was, both literally and emotionally.

She knew exactly what to say to someone to get what she wanted, and always made them feel like it had been their decision all along. It was through these innate people skills that she had successfully climbed the ranks within her career as a forensic scientist. She was paid less than the men she worked with, but nobody questioned that in the nineties. Additionally, Ophelia had an ace up her sleeve that she would utilise in various interviews, and that ace was that she was categorically adamant that she would never have children.

What difference that made to potential career advancement Malcolm had no idea, but apparently it meant something to those that employed her.

Back then he often wondered if times would ever change, and if such things would be trivial compared to the equality someone of Ophelia's intelligence and capabilities so rightly deserved.

He doubted it.

'Aren't all the lights beautiful?!' she said to him enthusiastically, her hair as thick and dark as his, but cascading to just below her shoulder blades and far better maintained.

She was wearing an expensive black cashmere three-quarter length coat, her gold stud earrings subtle and elegant, with black high-heels almost definitely matching the black power dress she always wore on a Thursday for her weekly team meeting.

Malcolm looked around, the smell of roasting chestnuts from the vendor several feet away traversing across the crisp London air that was still somehow humid, because, well, London was *always* humid. He fought the urge to throw up the admittedly empty contents of his stomach, much in the same way he fought the urge to stab the man who had just brushed past his shoulder with just a fraction-too-much vivacity.

'*Truly* a thing of *beauty*,' he said in a droll tone that was dripping with a truth only she could see.

'Have you even been *remotely* trying what we spoke about?' said Ophelia.

He absorbed the look of teacher-like disappointment on her face and shot her one of equal fervour that implied he would kill for less, but Ophelia merely laughed and hugged him.

Her hair smelt like coconut. Her preferred scent when choosing conditioner. It mingled with the thick chestnut smell that still lingered in his nostrils and he felt sick again.

'Come on, grumpus' said Ophelia. 'It's nearly eight, which means I know you haven't eaten. I've booked us a table at O'Reilly's.'

Malcolm groaned. 'Of course you have.'

*

The following evening, having caught the train from London to Chelmsford, Malcolm was naturally early, despite the universe conspiring against him.

It was Christmas time in England, which meant that trains were about as reliable as Malcolm taking up a career as a door to door knives salesman.

He waited patiently on the corner of Market Road for Ophelia to arrive, his mood unusually positive. The distant chatter and sounds of shutters closing from the nearby market square mingled with the infuriating relentlessness of archaic Christmas music.

Malcolm focused on the plumes of his breath

reacting to the cold air, a constant stream of exhalation that kept him centred enough not to snap under the mild anxiety being generated by being so exposed to the unpredictable idiocy of the human race.

Over dinner the night before, they had discussed an unexpected opportunity for Malcolm; a position had opened up for a trainee post within her team. One that, if he were successful in his application, would mean that they could work together.

The benefits her career had afforded him thus far were plentiful, but there was something intoxicating to him at the prospect of actually having a role in a specific field that would further facilitate his chosen…lifestyle.

Despite having not actually applied for the job, Ophelia had done so for him, rationalising that he would work better under pressure and with no notice to object.

She had been right of course. And for the past hour he had waited for her here, surprisingly eager to tell her how it had gone.

Ophelia had been pulled in as a consultant for a training day with the local police force of Chelmsford, to impart wisdom on a topic that was something of a speciality for her, given her published thesis on crime scene contamination. He found himself smirking at that, as a familiar voice caught his attention.

'Sorry to keep you Mal',' said Ophelia, looking notably frazzled. 'Why they run this thing on a Friday

I'll never know. No one can concentrate on a Friday. So…'

'So what?' said Malcolm, still staring at the reverse waterfall of his own breath.

'You *know* what!' said Ophelia, scowling at him. 'How'd it go?!' she added, jabbing him in the arm.

'It was…as expected.'

'Jesus Christ Malcolm, did you get it or not?'

'I did.'

'Squeeee!' she chirped, hugging him, causing the scent of coconut to fill his senses. 'Could I *be* any prouder of you right now?! You know what this means don't you? I have some really great cases that you'll–'

And she kept talking, as he urged her to walk whilst doing so, to wherever it was that she had parked.

*

Ophelia repeated the same statements over and over, as Malcolm pulled out of the multi-storey car park. Things such as "you had the qualifications needed for an entry level job." How she'd "pulled a lot of strings" to make this happen.

He hadn't so much as offered to drive, as he had been *forced* to, the keys thrust into his hand by his over-excitable sister. She had kicked off her heels, her bare feet up on the dash, seat-belt, as always, unfastened.

'Seat-belt,' said Malcolm sternly.

'Oh please, with *you* as the driver? You always

stick to the speed limits, and—'

'And feet off the dashboard,' he added, like a cantankerous driving instructor.

'It's *my* fucking car!' exclaimed Ophelia, sticking her tongue out at him but lowering her legs anyway.

Malcolm chuckled.

They had a system that worked.

From a young age, Malcolm had showed an increasing fascination with dark obsessions. It started small, such as wanting to know how machinery worked. But it soon became apparent that his desires leaned more towards the biological variety. At least that's what he had told her, that time she found him carving his way through a fox he had captured during a particularly depressing trip to the Norfolk Broads.

But rather than recoiling, or running away in fear, she reached out to him.

From then on, she kept him grounded. Whenever his urges got the better of him, Ophelia alone knew how to bring him back around to the realm of rational thinking. Which is how she knew he would be perfect for this job. She reasoned that being exposed to such crime scenes would soothe his already desensitised sensibilities. That he could, in theory, get the *hit* he needed without actually needing to, well, *hit* anything at all.

He often wondered what life would be like without his sister around to keep him in check. Would he finally act on his impulses? Would he graduate from fantasising about ending the lives of others and actually follow through on them?...

On numerous occasions, Malcolm found himself experiencing a surge of what he assumed must have been diluted guilt. Having no barometer to determine the authenticity of such emotions, he had merely labelled it as such, so as to expedite the process of getting on with the dark fantasy itself. The days when he added an extra layer to his dark secret;

Dreaming of a world where Ophelia was *not* around just so that he *could* act on them.

He took a sharp intake of breath, expelling the notion once more from his conscious mind, but it was still there, lurking...yearning to be released. Aching to be acknowledged and explored.

As they made their way through the city streets, the roads oddly dead, considering the time of year, his sister leant over and switched on the cassette player between them.

'What the hell is this?' barked Malcolm over the top of the odd music that filled the cabin of the vehicle.

'I...don't know,' said Ophelia, as the cassette continued to churn out a frenetic number she had never heard before in her life.

She wasn't sure if she liked it, but felt reluctant to turn it off until she knew for sure.

'Turn it off,' said Malcolm, eyes wavering from the road and glancing down at the cassette player.

Ophelia did nothing, until Malcolm reached out to eject the cassette, and she slapped his hand away.

'I'm listening!' she hollered.

Malcolm swatted her hand away, accidentally cranking the volume up further, the unusual music drowning out their squabbling.

'It's my car,' Ophelia reminded him through a playful laugh. 'Lighten up,' she added. 'Why does everything new scare yo–'

Her words were cut horrifyingly short, as Malcom's head hit the wheel, a vast whiteness filling his vision, the confusion causing him to accelerate violently, sending the car into the central reservation and snagging on a guard-rail, pushing the vehicle back out into the road, until eventually their progress was halted by a sickening crunch, followed by an incessant bellowing of the car's horn.

Malcolm's eyes shot open, a blackness filling his peripheral vision and stinging his eyes. A blackness he quickly realised was his own blood filling the canvas that was the air bag his face was currently pressed against.

He stared at Ophelia, her glassy eyes staring right back at him.

"No…*through* me."

The vacant eyes of the dead.

His mind didn't try to shield his feelings with something as trivial as hope, he simply wasn't wired that way. She was quite dead. And yet, he felt compelled to say her name.

'Ophelia…'

His voice still lost amidst the deafening,

intermingling decibels of the car horn and ear-splitting music, Malcolm tried to move. He felt a surging pain in his leg, and realised quickly that something sharp had sprung forth from the compressed front of the car that housed the engine.

Malcolm sensed movement ahead of him, and attempted to reposition himself again, as the cassette player gave up the ghost, though the horn continued on like a banshee.

Straining his aching neck, he was able to just see into the left corner of the windscreen, which had shattered but not fallen in, past Ophelia's empty shell of a body, and over the crumpled dashboard. It was then that he witnessed the distorted occupants of the car that had collided with them, their faces fractured thanks to the fragmented glass.

As the pitch of the horn shifted, the electrical current that powered it having trouble maintaining its connection to the relay, Malcolm could just about hear the fleeting words and broken sentences of those responsible, *bickering*, seemingly debating *whether* to help them. Or, most likely, flee the scene.

He managed to isolate two voices; that of a man with a growling voice, and a second voice so high-pitched he reasoned it must have either belonged to a woman, or a man indulging in a spot of helium inhalation.

'No, no, no!' said the helium-absorbing observer. 'How can this be happening?!'

'*You* did this!' growled the man, the three simple

words echoing in Malcolm's mind, creating an inexplicable feedback loop, ingraining themselves in his psyche as he committed them to memory. In that moment, he made a promise to Ophelia; if he lived through this, he *would* find them.

'Help me open the door,' Malcolm heard the man shout.

Still unable to turn his head fully, due to the air bag keeping his head predominately faced towards his dead sister, he realised the man was trying to force the driver's side door open.

'We can't,' replied a third voice. A second woman. Firmer. As if she were taking charge. 'You *know* we can't.'

'Need to leave,' said the high-pitched coward. The last words of his sentence faint, as if he were further away than before. Malcolm could only catch brief words now. 'Stay. Think. Mistake.'

'Then *go*,' barked the man. Not a request. Not even an order. He simply didn't seem to care whether his cohorts remained there with him or not, as long as it didn't act as an interruption to his goal.

Malcolm suddenly felt giddy, and he knew he was losing consciousness.

As his head grew heavy, and his eyelids fluttered, his remaining senses were overloaded with nonsensical gibberish.

A sound of thunder.

A rush of air.

Then darkness.

CHAPTER FORTY-EIGHT
The Relativity of Truth

180th Restart – Friday, August 24th, 2018, 12:47pm

'Is *any* of that true,' said Kara, feeling both moved and doubtful all at the same time.

Malcolm's detailed recounting of what apparently sent a man with violent thoughts over the edge into a life of violent acts was perfectly delivered. His tone adopting sadness when it mattered most, inflecting anger over what had been taken from him, and notable melancholy over his all-too-real discovery that death operated without discrimination. That, much like a Black Friday sale weekend, it was cold, heartless, and ultimately out of everyone's control.

But it also seemed almost *too* perfect. Too convenient. Too…*well* told. *Rehearsed*, even.

Though it did more than explain his reaction to the crash site on their previous restart, making it seem not only justified, but an indication that he was indeed human after all.

Malcolm smiled, his previously softened, almost *tender* features hardening once more, and forming an all-too-familiar trademark sneer, his eyes showing a flash of reciprocated cynicism.

'Does it matter to you if it isn't?' he replied darkly.

Kara didn't respond, instead merely searching his eyes for the faintest glint of anything remotely resembling a soul, before ultimately coming up empty.

All she wanted to know was what drove him to this life. But she couldn't help but wonder if she was looking for logic where there was none. Projecting her own moral code on that of a sociopath.

She was shaken from her ruminations with a start, as Malcolm responded with what appeared to be some kind of residual telepathy. For a moment she wondered if such abilities were that far-fetched in their current state, and instinctively clenched her jaw, as if doing so would bring up a cerebral shield around her thoughts.

'That's your problem, Kara,' said Malcolm, almost humming the words, upping the creep-factor considerably. Hal and Fearne seemed to feel it too, both shrugging off an unexpected shiver. 'You're looking for *logic* in my actions. Searching for the *best* in me. The problem you're facing is that you're looking for what you want to see, instead of what's really there. It's precisely why you are not ready to face the younger version of myself.'

'And what is that, exactly?' asked Kara. 'What's *really* there?'

Malcolm seemed perturbed by the question. Almost as if he hadn't predicted it. Though Kara wondered if she was misinterpreting anxiousness for ambivalence.

'Nothing, Kara. Nothing at all.'

Kara exhaled sharply, feeling like she'd just taken one step forward with the man and two steps back. 'I refuse to believe that.'

She rested her head in her hands, sensing an inbound migraine.

'Some things are true whether you believe them or not,' replied Malcolm bluntly. 'The three of you…always thinking in absolutes. That good and evil are quantifiable terms. But who *defines* those terms to begin with?'

'Well,' said Fearne, having heard all she could stomach on the matter. 'I personally think you're full of shit,' she said simply. 'I doubt there even *is* an Aurelia.'

'O*phelia*,' said Malcolm, enunciating the syllables before pursing his lips, as if containing a crackling rage.

'Whatever,' said Fearne. 'Maybe we should focus

less on *psychopath story-time* and more on getting on with this.'

'I'm just amazed Malcolm here has a *mum*. I just assumed he was forged in the caverns of Mordor or something,' said Hal, stirring from his own close examination of the exchange between Kara and Malcolm. 'But I agree with Fearne. If past-you is currently licking his wounds, sooner or later he's going to figure out he can't drive his way out of here.'

'We hope.'

'So what's his next move?' said Hal, ignoring Fearne's pessimism.

Malcolm sucked his teeth as he processed the variables.

His past-self going off-script like that had left him in a bit of a quandary. He knew what was going to happen, but it seemed his younger self was able to make decisions outside of the predetermined path he was attempting to re-enact.

Which wasn't good.

His memories, once perfectly catalogued, now felt alarmingly jumbled. At odds with each other even, and he was begrudgingly forced to admit he had no idea what was coming next.

'Well, we can't keep running,' said Hal. 'We need to find a way to end this before it gets even more out of control.'

'Running is the only thing keeping you all alive. He's demonstrated that none of you are a physical threat to him.'

'What if we capture past-you?' said Hal, going back to an old idea that the Malcolm of their future had already vetoed. 'Try to reason with him?'

'It won't work,' said Malcolm, rationalising that if he had no memory of such an encounter they must not have gone that route, much less succeeded. 'The only way forward is to take him down. Permanently.'

'Yeah, not going to happen.' said Kara, the quiet words of her former conversation with Malcolm echoing in her mind. 'Besides, with you out of the equation, you said it yourself; we're no match for him. I'm with Hal. We try this first. It's decided.'

'I don't...' said Malcolm, a recollection swirling into his mind.

The memory of being tied to something.

Being interrogated. Being–

'Damn it.'

The Restarters stared at him, waiting for him to spill whatever it was he had just seen. They knew that look; it was the face of a man obtaining a new memory.

Hal smiled.

'Did we just Timecop you?!' he said excitedly.

'I literally have no idea what that mean–'

'Ha! We placed an idea of a plan into the time-stream, and just by discussing it we're making it solid! Tell me you don't remember us catching you.'

Malcolm wanted to, but clearly hesitated for too long.

'Maaaalcolm,' sang Hal. 'Don't hold out on us.

When does it happen?'

'Tomorrow,' he said miserably.

Hal stood up and started playing air guitar, muttering something about wild stallions.

'We'd best prepare,' Malcolm said glumly.

*

Malcolm told them everything about the memories that had been crowbarred into his brain. Most notably, the small inconsistency that pulled into question the validity of Malcolm's claims that the events leading to the capture of his past-self were indeed going to take place in the next twenty-four hours.

'You saw that?' said Hal, his brow furrowed.

'Yes. You were wearing your costumes from your original restarts.'

'But we don't have those,' said Kara. 'Are you *sure* it was us?'

Malcolm knew she meant the versions of Hal and Kara from their current timeline, and not somehow an iteration of themselves from the past.

'I am sure.'

'So we need…disguises,' said Hal, clearly excited by the conundrum that presented.

It made sense.

If Malcolm's past-self was on the lookout for their current incarnation, switching their look to mimic a former appearance would certainly give them an edge. The problem was that none of them were in-phase with the costumes that were frustratingly waiting for them on their respective beds back at Fir Lodge.

With the exception of Fearne, who was currently wearing hers.

'Perhaps…there *is* a way,' said Malcolm, disappearing like the crack of a whip.

*

Malcolm returned a good hour-or-so later, holding Hal's Ghostbuster outfit and Kara's Velma Dinkley costume.

There was blood on his shirt, and more than a dash on the garments he was clutching.

Kara, Fearne and Hal shared a troubled look.

'Where did you get those?' said Fearne, her voice laced with a quiver that implied she'd probably rather not know.

'Is that *blood*?' said Kara incredulously.

'Do not worry,' said Malcolm. 'It is not my own.'

'That was not the thing that worried me,' said Kara, bewildered that he would assume that.

'Tell me you didn't just jump into a previous restart and kill a version of us for those?' asked Hal, already knowing the answer.

'Of course not!' said Malcolm defensively. 'Well, not exactly,' he added, neglecting to mention that obviously he had to jump slightly further into the future and reach the Restart Point to access The White Lodge first, before making his way back to them, using their vibrant, blue energy signature as an anchor to get back.

Hal sighed in relief.

'Then, where the hell *did* you get them from?' said Kara.

Malcolm explained how he had chosen a very specific, and ultimately inconsequential restart.

Their 56th restart to be precise. The day Hal and Kara had accidentally punched a hole through time itself, causing reality to rupture and releasing hundreds of versions of themselves into the world. Some from alternate timelines that never solidified past the point of hypothetical probability. He had come up with the idea following all their talk about Time Echoes.

'How do we not remember that?' Hal said to Kara.

'Once I located suitable…*candidates*,' Malcolm explained, 'far away from the prying eyes of those that may be watching, it was merely a matter of incapacitating them. Before finally–'

'Stealing our clothes?!' said Hal, shuddering at the thought. 'What if they were versions of us from the future you idiot!' he added angrily.

Malcolm shrugged.

'It seems unlikely,' said the universe-bending garment thief, almost sheepishly. 'For you to be wearing these costumes in the future, that is. Much more likely they were from an *alternate* timeline that refused to take.'

'Unlikely?' balked Kara. 'We're literally about to wear these costumes again in our current future!'

'Kara's right,' said Hal anxiously. 'Maybe now the only way for us to stay alive is not to put them on?'

'You guys are the worst time travellers in the history of ever,' said Fearne.

'Regrettably, I could not obtain Kara's glasses,' said Malcolm, ignoring their concerns and feeling confident it had been a well-calculated risk. Though he said it in a way that implied he had let them all down, and that the plan was surely now a complete wash-out that they should abandon immediately.

Kara chuckled.

'Unbelievable,' said Hal, shaking his head and smiling in disbelief.

'I know, it is indeed a shame...' said Malcolm with false sadness. 'But perhaps this will make you understand that this course is one that we simply cannot follow after all.'

'No, not that,' said Hal, raising a hand to silence him. 'Show 'em Kar'.'

Kara slowly retrieved the black-rimmed glasses and magnifying glass from her jacket pocket.

'How?' said Malcolm, seemingly offering up a genuine compliment amidst his awe at the unveiling of the impossible objects.

'I had them on me at the coffee shop,' said Kara, looking down at the spectacles with fondness. 'Before we phased out.'

'But that would imply that you retained some memory of your time here? In the present. The future. The future-present that is...'

Kara knew what Malcolm was getting at.

If any of them had any remaining doubts that this plan was meant to be, the fact that Kara had brought such a crucial piece of her disguise all the way from the future without even knowing she would need to, surely did the trick in terms of eradicating them.

Now they had the threads for what came next, it was time to set events in motion and attempt their boldest mission yet;

It would be one thing trying to catch themselves a Dark Restarter. Of that, they were certain.

But it would be another thing entirely negotiating a truce with one.

CHAPTER FORTY-NINE
To Catch a Killer

180th Restart – Saturday, August 25th, 2018, 12:47pm

The plan was, at best, ambitious. At worst, it was a sure-fire way to get one of them killed.

With Hal and Kara dressed as they were at the time of the barbecue on their first ever Saturday at Fir Lodge, they could pass for exact duplicates of their past-selves. The tricky part would be luring the Dark Restarter to the party. Then there would just be the small, easy-peasy matter of getting close enough to restrain him.

Malcolm's past-self was armed with two knives presumably forged by the God of War himself. On top of that Ares-endorsed nightmare, he also possessed enough rage to fuel a Red Lantern battery. They had made peace with those facts, but after forty minutes of Hal and Kara wandering around trying to look the part, mingling with the party-goers of the past, it became apparent that there was a huge flaw in their plan.

'What if he doesn't show?' said Kara, getting antsy.

'He'll show,' said Hal, not all that convincingly. 'He knows his only way out of the time loops is to change something here. He's tried everything else.

Kara frowned.

'He's *going* to show…' said Hal.

*

It was growing ever closer to 8:15pm and there had been no sign, or so much as even the faintest shimmer of red energy, let alone a fully manifested Dark Restarter. The four of them regrouped, as agreed, in the communal area in the moments before Jerry arrived to whisk whoever was destined for the chopping block this time around off on a merry adventure into death.

'Can't you just, I dunno, *use* your Spider-Sense to tell us where he is?' asked Hal.

'Can *you* remember where you were a decade ago?' asked Malcolm sharply, hilariously attempting to hide his massive frame behind a sofa bed. 'It doesn't *work* like that.'

Hal knew this. And what was more, even if it *did*

work like that, by changing the flow of Malcolm's past by deciding to capture him, they had released all manner of flutterby effects into the world around them.

The whole evening seemed to be playing out a second or two out of sync, throwing them all off their game. Malcolm felt the brunt of it more than the others, as his own memories swirled around in his mind like a Hal and Kara fuelled Escher painting.

*

At 8:44pm, just as they were all about to write the whole plan off as little more than a waste of restarted time, the universe seemed to give in.

And there he stood, at the bottom of the driveway of Fir Lodge, just in view from their new vantage point in the rear garden.

'Yes! Showtime,' said Hal, nodding to Kara.

They ran along the side of the building and headed Jerry off before he could make his way fully up the driveway.

'What are *you* doing here,' said Hal, walking past The Dark Restarter who had taken position on the far side of the parked cars. Hal kept up the act, pretending he couldn't see the murderous monster and, instead, approached Jerry. 'You're far away from home kid! Kara?!' he shouted, causing Kara to step out into the cool night air that wasn't cool to them at all.

'What?' she replied, cringing internally at what she felt was terrible acting.

'Look! It's Jerry. Someone needs to take you home, come on boy!'

Kara acted as if she was torn between remaining at the party and partaking in the proposed errand.

'Can I at least grab my drink first?' she added irritably, as if she possessed the corporeality to actually lift a glass in her Restarter state.

The Dark Restarter didn't seem as if he were sure they were the versions of themselves they were pretending to be, and he took a step towards Kara, raising his blade and reaching out a massive hand towards her shoulder. Kara pretended not to notice, shooting Hal a look.

If past-Malcolm made contact with her he would know they were in-phase with each other, and the gig would not be so much as up, but thrown off its axis entirely.

'Leave the drink,' said Hal as calmly as he could. 'Poor little guy is lost.'

Kara didn't waste time milking her chance to act her heart out, chucking the few lines of extra dialogue they had rehearsed to the curb, moving quickly away from past-Malcolm's hungry hand, the stones offering a slight crunch under her feet thanks to the retained charge she had built over the past twelve hours.

She looked down at her orange shoes, doing her best to ignore the droplet of blood on the tip of her toes and smiling at how much of a convincer that must have been from the perspective of the man bearing down on her.

And off they went, wondering exactly when this plan would go south and result in a potentially life-threatening failure.

*

What surprised them most, however, was that the plan didn't fail as quickly as they expected. As they made their way to Kevin's, with Jerry sniffing away at various piles of pine needles, they could tell they were being followed, though neither dared to look back. They had caught the killer's attention, and just prayed Fearne and *their* Malcolm would be ready.

'He's buying it,' Hal mumbled under his breath.

'Shut up!' snapped Kara, her voice muffled between equally zipped lips, before putting on the next part of the show. 'I think he lives this way,' she added, wincing slightly at how forced the words sounded.

This was a deal-breaker moment; she was proposing to take Jerry past his house entirely, deeper down the winding road. Something she had never done in any of their prior restarts. A deviation Malcolm would know to be a red flag.

The statement was designed to maintain the killer's curiosity. The *why* of such a change, getting the better of the *how*.

The Dark Restarter had stopped behind them, seemingly thrown by the deviation in what was, as far as he knew, a temporal constant. *Unbeknown* to him, however, was that the considerably *more-alive* Hal and Kara were all the way back at Fir Lodge. Nice, safe, and getting drunker.

There were only Restarters here now.

Time travellers with multiple agendas that neither could predict, all participating in a game so outlandish it didn't matter who believed what at this point.

'What are you talking about Kar', pretty sure this is his house?' said Hal, feigning confusion and gesturing towards Kevin's cabin. 'Number fifty-one, you said so yourself, it's on Jerry's collar?'

The curveball.

'Weird,' said Kara, playing along. 'I feel like…we've done this before…I don't think…we should go in there,' she added for extra kick. As if she were experiencing a bout of temporal dysplasia. Intense déjà vu brought on by a Restarter's meddling.

She threw in a simulated ice-pick headache for good measure.

It was Oscar worthy.

If said Oscars were being awarded by seven-year-olds.

Hal rolled his eyes. It felt a bit much in his opinion.

'What's wrong,' he said, his desire to laugh in her face at her wooden acting counteracted by the fact an actual serial killer was closing in on them. 'Headache again?'

'Yeah, I keep getting them.'

She turned her head and stared through the Malcolm of their past and present, perfectly nailing the look of someone who may have just left the oven on at home and needed to know for sure.

"And the award for best breakout duologue goes to,' thought Kara.

"This is worse than Revenge of the Sith,' thought Hal.

But he followed her gaze all the same, and saw up-close the cynicism on the killer's face, realising they needed to wrap up this improv, given that they were dangerously close to over cooking it.

'Uh huh, come on,' said Hal a little *too* quickly. 'Let's get this done already.'

He whistled for Jerry, and led the way up the driveway, using the moonlight for guidance just like always, and into Kevin's home, the door helpfully fully open, rather than being merely ajar.

That meant Fearne and Malcolm had got here first, and must have been inside.

*

Something was off.

He could *feel* it.

The rat-catcher and orange secretary were behaving strangely, making odd deviations from a timeline he had spent years memorising. He had initially suspected this was some kind of trick, but this was definitely them. Their clothes proved that. Malcolm knew the newest incarnations of the self-proclaimed Restarters would not have had access to clothes from a different timeline.

And yet, as he reached the door of Kevin's lodge, so much was wrong.

He had left his physical-self to play out his day just as always today, which meant both Harold and Kara should be gasping their last breaths right now inside the building before him.

Instead, there was nothing. Not so much as a barking dog.

If they were inside and alive, why had they stopped talking?

Kevin was tied up in the basement, but where was the alive version of his own body? Had all of his attempts at manipulating himself finally led to severe consequence? Was he even still on the grounds of the Pentney Lakes? Or merely wandering the woods aimlessly, unable to form thoughts for himself at all.

Malcolm closed his eyes and focused, searching his memories for this night. Looking for answers his alive-self already possessed. Recollections that would surely filter into his brain at any moment.

But there was nothing.

No new memories.

Just darkness.

His alive-self must have been somewhere nearby. Had he left the Pentney Lakes he wouldn't be having these thoughts to begin with.

But he had to know.

And so, against his better judgement, the Dark Restarter stepped inside the lodge where the answers he craved resided.

*

The room was empty, the radio off, and the basement

door wide open.

Malcolm's immediate assessment of the room merely generated more questions. He peered down the staircase, but his eyes wouldn't adjust, he could only hear what he assumed to be the rat-catcher's hushed voice emanating from the darkness below.

As he descended the staircase, he heard a ruffle of material below him and caught a glimpse of what appeared to be a black strap, which wrapped around both of his feet, an unseen force yanking it backwards sharply, causing him to lurch forwards.

He tried to reach out with his hands to support himself but was rewarded with nothing but the empty expanse of darkness, and little in the way of steadying support.

The Dark Restarter hit the stairs hard and tumbled all the way down them, his face suddenly smothered by a black sheet that smelled identical to his rubber apron, though he was still wearing his own.

He reached for one of his knives but realised they were both missing, and growled as he heard the tell-tale ripping of heavy-duty tape, which his assailant wrapped frantically around him, binding his hands and legs.

Peter's killer felt himself being hoisted up and thrown down onto a chair, heard more tape being utilised and felt it wrap around his body, before hearing the voice of a young woman.

'We've got this, wait for us upstairs.'

The instruction was followed by loud, slow

footsteps which ascended the stairs, a slamming of the basement door sending reverberations that he was unable to fully experience thanks to them passing through the forever-shifting atoms of his now-restricted body.

His abductors, clearly satisfied their quarry was secure, whipped off the apron, revealing the furious face of a very pissed off Dark Restarter.

Hal and Kara stared at him smugly.

'Funny meeting you here,' said Hal, all confidence and zero tact.

'You dare–' attempted Malcolm.

'Oh, we dare. We dare very much,' Kara shot back, her tone dense with the disrespect of someone who couldn't have known how much danger she was in.

No.

Worse.

Someone who didn't *care* how much danger she was in.

'How?' muttered the Malcolm of their past, the word dripping with malice, despite him having a pretty damn concise idea of exactly what had happened.

He stole a barely perceptible glance towards the floor at the disregarded apron and knew precisely what that meant.

Hal caught him doing so, and kicked it under a work table.

'This is how this is going to work,' said Hal. 'Our

good friend Fearne is on the way to the Restart Point so none of this sticks, which means we've got very little time to get shit sorted.'

Malcolm looked down at his taped ankles.

'You think *tape* alone can hold *me*? Keep me *contained*?!'

'I do,' said Hal. 'On the basis that it's literally doing that and *only* that right now.'

'Plus,' hummed Kara. 'It's not any old tape.'

'It's *Restarter* tape!' said Hal gleefully, so glad he had brought it back with them, having wondered if this particular back-pack treasure would ever have had its time to shine on their journey. 'Patent pending.'

Malcolm struggled, but was embarrassingly unsuccessful in his attempt to free himself. It seemed that adhesive lined tape from the future was every bit as stubborn as its past and present brethren.

'We need to talk,' said Kara.

'Untie me, and we can talk about all manner of things,' the man growled, a dark smile flashing beneath laser-focused eyes.

The Restarters ignored him.

'This thing we're doing?' said Kara, 'Chasing each other across time? It has to stop, Malcolm.'

'How are you even back here?!' asked Malcolm, seemingly ignoring her too.

'Because,' said Hal with a heavy sigh. 'You keep ballsing up time Malc'. You brought us back here by going all 12 Monkeys on us.'

'I did no such thing!' their prisoner snarled. 'It was *done*,' he added, utterly confused. 'The golfer took your place, all three of us were free!'

That surprised them for a moment. Up until now they were certain he had been responsible for their return to the past.

They shrugged it off, interpreting it as plausible deflection.

'You don't have to tell us how you brought us back,' said Kara tiredly. Honestly, it didn't really matter at this point. 'But we're proposing a way out for *all* of us. *Including* Peter,' she added.

'A bit late for him isn't it?' said Malcolm, laughing thickly.

'Fake laugh.'

'No it wasn't,' said Malcolm.

'*So* was.'

'Both of you, shut up,' said Kara, and to her surprise, they did.

She took a breath and exhaled slowly, pinching the bridge of her nose as if summoning the negotiating prowess of Olivia Pope.

She and Hal broke it down for the killer, alternating between universal truths that all led to the same conclusion; that in order for them all to be free, they would need to work together. How none of them could truly fathom what damage they were causing to the future of thousands by indulging in their perpetual game of cat and mouse and, lastly, that in the end a truce was the only thing that could truly salvage their shared past.

Hal reasoned that by breaking the chain and by working together they could simultaneously manipulate their past-selves into achieving anything.

Malcolm listened far more intently that they could have hoped, before wetting his lips and offering up his response to the request of parlay.

'You've both done exceedingly well,' he said, in a tone that possibly could have sounded like respect, were it not for Malcolm's innate ability to make every syllable that left his rotten lips sound condescending.

"More like a teacher speaking to school children who weren't doing very well at all," thought Kara.

'But for all your efforts,' he continued, 'you are working on the assumption that you know all the facts.'

'Of *course* we don't know all the facts!' scoffed Kara. '*None* of us do! Yourself included.'

'Oh, I know more than you think I know,' The Dark Restarter chuckled enigmatically, in a manner true to his unchosen namesake.

'Maybe it's all the time travel turning your brain into scrambled eggs,' said Hal, getting just a bit too close to their captive, ignoring Future Malcolm's very clear instructions to keep their distance at all times. 'Or maybe you've *always* been a special kind of stupid. Either way, we don't want to fight you! We can *all* get out of here if we just agree to stop this Spartan-kick-madness!'

Kara scrunched up her nose. 'That a video game

thing?'

'No not…it doesn't matter,' said Hal.

Malcolm glared at them, before inhaling the out-of-phase air his mind continuously tricked him into thinking he needed, for the summary he was about to provide.

'So, we stop this tit for tat one-upmanship?' posed Malcolm. 'I cease my own methods of obtaining freedom. And in exchange, you stop your attempts at interrupting the implementation of *my* plans? And we work together to uncover a mutually beneficial solution to our chronological quandary? Is t*hat* what you're proposing?'

'Yes!' blurted Kara. 'That! Exactly that. No one else needs to die.'

'Very well. *Untie* me.'

Hal and Kara shared an uncomfortable glance, and turned back to their prisoner, whose eyes looked fully black in the dim light that refused to reflect in them.

'And this is why,' said Malcolm, 'this will never work.'

'It *can* work,' said Hal, the words feeling hollow despite him wanting them to be solid. 'We just need…*time* to get our heads around the…*concept* of working together.

'You expect me to entertain this when you don't even believe it can work yourself? And of course, there's the small matter that Kara is wrong, wrong, wrong.'

'What are you talking about,' she said, slumping against the workbench and feeling foolish for ever thinking this would work.

Did she really think this version of Malcolm would be interested in an amicable solution? After all, the mere existence of Future Malcolm was testament to this being a fool's errand. If the Malcolm of the past had agreed to their plea-bargain, Future Malcolm would have simply ceased to *be*. Which in turn would have meant he couldn't have come back to aid them as he had done, which meant neither her or Hal would have ever even *made* it to this damn basement, let alone this very specific restart.

'About no one else needing to die,' their captive said, as if pointing out that the sky was blue. 'Surely even *you* are not naïve enough to believe any of us can escape without at least *one* casualty? A life for a life, Kara. That's how this works. It is the one rule we simply *cannot* bend. You know it to be true. After all, you both had to *kill* me to escape your own prison.'

'It doesn't have to be that way. We *can* beat this,' her words a faint whisper, laced with the harsh reality that she didn't really believe them herself. 'We just–'

'Don't feel bad. All is not lost,' their hostage said wickedly. 'You have at least highlighted an interesting point. Admittedly, in your own typically moronic way.'

Their ears were greeted with the sound of an approaching rush of air, a bank of fog rolling in from nowhere, consuming the staircase and the floor. A fog that appeared white to the Restarters, and black as wood-smoke to Malcolm.

'I think we're done here,' said Hal dismissively.

'What point?' said Kara, unable to help herself.

'You still don't see it?' The Dark Restarter cooed.

'Kara, we should leave.' The last thing Hal wanted was for the killer to have another chance to get in their heads, but it was too late for that. This was what he did. And he was dragging them down to his level, intent on beating them with experience.

'If it wasn't *I* that brought you here…who did?'

The question caused their stomachs to lurch.

'It seems we *are* done here,' said Malcolm happily, content that he had clearly succeeded in driving a maliciously delivered railroad spike into their lives. 'Regretfully, I must *decline* your offer. Though I will offer you one parting piece of fair warning; stay out of my way. And I'll do my best to spare you too much pain. Probably.'

Before Hal could splutter a witty response, his body, along with any misguided hopes of an alliance, disintegrated into nothingness, as the three of them were swallowed up by the universe, and spat back out into a brand-new day.

CHAPTER FIFTY
Time Crisis

187th Restart – Friday, August 24th, 2018, 2:47pm

His words, even seven restarts later, hung over them like a sickness.

They knew the secret to his ability to get under their skin was that he tended to lace his malice with just enough cyanide-coated sprinkles of truth, in order to make them linger long after he had spoken them.

If it wasn't I that brought you here...who did?

"That sonuva bitch," thought Kara, angry at herself for giving him power.

Of course it had been him. It had to be. The how didn't matter. He did it. He did do it.

Didn't he?

She shook off the memory, knowing it would return in force soon enough anyway.

Kara could tell this was going to be a nothingy kind of restart, and instead busied her mind unpacking what she assumed to be another undocumented truth; that when it came to time travel, it wasn't just the Flutterby Effects and trans-dimensional traversal that dragged you down, nor was it the emotional anguish that simmered quietly along the fringes of her consciousness. In fact, she tried not to dwell over how – in her current out-of-phase state – she was an ambassador of a future that no longer existed, or that she was a relic of a past that didn't want her.

Nope. It wasn't any of those things that bothered her the most. Despite all that temporal mumbo-jumbo, there was one thing she resented more than anything else;

The *waiting*.

It was during such a restart that she had decided to kill some time by shooting the reformed bottles of water and cans with Hal's hand-cannon, making sure to remove the gunpowder caps to maintain their current cloak and keeping them off the grid.

Their attempt at bringing past-Malcolm around to their way of thinking had proven to be a total bust, and each of them had expected all hell to break loose, waiting for whatever twisted retaliation he settled on to drop down on them like an atom bomb.

But over the next seven restarts their assumptions had been all but disproven. In fact, The Dark Restarter has seemingly fallen off the map entirely.

They had spent a lot of time brushing up on their fight training, but boredom was starting to take hold, and Kara found herself feeling guilty for wishing something would happen.

Heck, that *anything* would happen. Just something they could latch onto to refuel their sense of purpose.

She pulled back the hammer, closed her right eye, and looked down the sights at her unsuspecting targets, situated an impressive fifty yards-or-so away on what she bizarrely realised had become her favourite log.

Kara exhaled and *pressed* the trigger, rather than pulling it, letting the gun do all the work, and the bullet sailed through the air at a blink-and-you'd-miss-it speed, unimpeded by the soft breeze she knew was there, but was failing miserably at connecting with the temporally-misaligned metal pellet.

The bottle quivered as the bullet of the past connected with it, and flew backwards off the log. Kara, shot the next bottle, then the two cans of energy drink, each attempt hitting the mark until the log was barer than today's itinerary.

The Restarter lowered the weapon, deciding to check her handiwork, and walked towards her no-frills fairground attraction, dragging her feet with boredom.

Jumping over the log and taking a seat, she noted

how the contents of the bottles had spilled onto the dirt, dispersing like translucent blood, the liquid stubbornly refusing to seep into the ground. She tapped the water with her foot, and whilst it adhered to her boot, the action had also sent a ripple across the water, making it shift across the ground like mercury, until it eventually embraced the neighbouring liquid of the bullet-ridden energy drink.

The fluids found solace in their mutual alignment with the universe, swirling together like two desperate humans eager to make a connection.

Kara felt a pang of guilt as she thought of Greg. Where even *was* he right now? Was her boyfriend even alive? Did the future exist without her?

She shook away the thought, wincing at the notion.

Of course it did. To think otherwise was insanely narcissistic. She simply wasn't that important in the grander scheme of time.

The future was there. It was just a future without her in it.

'You're really good at that!' said Hal, catching her off guard, and for a moment she interpreted his words as meaning she was good at moping, as he hopped over the log and forced her to shift over to make some space for him to sit down.

'Where did you learn to shoot like that?'

Kara smiled, his presence lightening her mood in that typical *Hal* kind of way that he didn't even know he was capable of.

She stood up, restacked the targets, and marched back even further than she had been standing before, eager to increase her range.

'Oh sick, you're going again?' said Hal, trailing behind her and watching her excitedly as she lined up her shot.

Their Malcolm, a term that was firmly cemented into their shared lexicons as the norm at this point, skulked up behind them, causing Hal and Kara to roll their eyes in unison. They really weren't in the mood for another "I told you so" speech. But instead, he said something relatively unexpected.

Fun, almost. For a Malcolm.

'You need to adjust your wrist, you're aiming at an angle.'

'Since when are *you* a gun expert?' said Hal. 'Besides, I figured you more as a sort of "I *despise* weapons of this *ilk*?" kinda dude?' he said, totally nailing his Malcolm impression.

'That… is *not* how I sound,' said Malcolm.

'Actually, it was bang on,' said Fearne, who had returned from wherever it was she was hiding these days, having reverted to distancing herself from the group.

Hal had asked Kara to speak to Fearne about it, reasoning that going lone wolf throughout a restart chain was not the best way to stay sane. But Kara had decided to give her some space, assuming it was just another stage in her grieving process.

'Just because I find them *distasteful* does not mean

I'm incapable of using them,' a faint shimmer of competitiveness in his voice. 'Here, give it to me.'

'Sure,' said Kara, before firing off the remaining two rounds of the six-shooter, each one hitting the restarted objects she had carefully lined up.

'Woah,' said Fearne.

Kara raised the gun into the air, blowing the non-existent smoke from the barrel, the afternoon glare of the sun stubbornly refusing to reflect itself onto the out-of-phase chrome.

'Knock yourself out,' said Kara, passing Malcolm the gun, knowing it would be devoid of pellets until the next restart.

'That was the last bullet wasn't it,' said Malcolm grumpily.

'Oh, was it?' Bummer.'

Her top lip curled with more than a hint of smile.

'Seriously, where *did* you learn to do that?!' said Hal, more than an edge of jealously sprinkled amidst his equally-blatant admiration.

'My brother Justin and I used to play Time Crisis a lot, in the arcade at Southend,' said Kara, with a modest shrug.

They looked at each other for a moment, before bursting into laughter.

'Time....*Time* Crisis?' said Hal, struggling to get the words out due to his splitting sides.

Kara couldn't help but laugh along with him, the ironically absurd name of the game she played religiously in her teens suddenly becoming the funniest thing in the world. 'We...we...could never get pass the final boss,' she added, cracking up further.

'St-stop. Too much!' said Hal, his laughing fit sending tears streaming down his desynchronized cheeks.

'It seems unlikely,' said Malcolm, chiming in, 'that anyone could have predicted such a juvenile endeavour would end up proving to be a transferable skill for actual time travel.'

And for the first time ever, the three of them laughed together, Hal and Kara continuing their seemingly endless tirade of guffawing, with Malcom's own quiet chuckle sending an out-of-character shaking to surge across his shoulders, as Fearne stared back at them with a barely-there smile.

'Ohhh doctor,' said Hal, their laughter winding down to a simmer of giggles before petering away into nothingness. 'Amazing. Time crisis. Brilliant.'

'I needed that,' said Kara. 'So, what now? Malcolm's gone dark, so to speak.'

'Heh. *Nice*. What's his next move...guy who...was...the killer on the...Orient Express?' said Hal, grimacing at how tenuous and poorly formed his latest attempt at burning Malcolm with a killer reference from a movie had landed.

'Ugh, Hal, that sucked,' said Kara, embarrassed for him.

'It's been like twenty weekends now,' said Hal, not so much defensively, but more as an apology. 'I'm running out of bad guys.'

'You could try stopping altogether?' suggested Malcolm.

'Oh, you'd like *that*, wouldn't you Hans Gruber!'

'Annnd he's back. So, what *is* his next move?' said Kara, as if the man from the future was a Magic 8-Ball with all the answers on the Dark Restarter's whereabouts. Which, as it happened, he kind of was.

'I've told you, it doesn't work like that,' said Malcolm. 'He appears to be in-between decisions, which leaves us with…little in the way of pre-emptive opportunity.'

'Maybe he's reconsidered,' suggested Kara, taking a seat on the ground once more. 'About working with us?'

'That is…unlikely.'

'Whatever happens next, we need eyes on the future,' said Hal. 'This "life for a life" business can't be the only way.'

'You need to accept what I am telling you,' said Malcolm. 'The only way to reach the future you're so keen on glimpsing is to end my past-self. Only *then* can we rebuild and…'

Fearne listened, as a penny dropped in her mind, as if seeing the world clearly for the first time.

"Again with the talk of killing his past self," she thought.

Since the moment they got here, the Malcolm of their future had been saying the only plan worth following was to kill his younger-self.

"But how did he even know it was possible to kill

someone in Restarter form to begin with? Unless…" and then it dawned on her. She was starting to gain concrete evidence that *their* Malcolm had known what would happen to Peter all along...

Re-joining the conversation, Fearne's eyes fluttered as she banked the additional facts.

'The younger you said something about us not having all the facts,' said Hal, addressing Malcolm directly and deciding it was time to let that fact out into the world. 'What do you suppose he meant by that?'

'Did he now? Showing off, I expect,' replied Malcolm, with barely a nanosecond of hesitation.

'Hmm...' said Kara, sensing yet another lie.

'So *what* if he knows something we don't,' said Hal, using the opportunity to return to his idea of glimpsing the Sunday they were creating as they manipulated the past in real time. 'What if we could learn things he had no *way* of knowing?'

'We've tried everything,' said Malcolm, not so much frustrated as he was weary. 'Explored all of our theories.'

Hal thought about that.

There was so much at stake.

They had lost Peter, and it felt as if every road they took towards reaching a peaceful resolution with Malcolm's past-self led them further and further towards the darkness they were fighting so hard to avoid.

A thought flitted through Hal's mind, one so

obvious he would have urged his physical self to kick, well, *himself*, had he been close by. They had spent so much time running through their own history, towards a goal that Future Malcolm had assured them was unavoidable, that they hadn't truly taken time to breathe. But they had a wildcard up their Restarting sleeves that they had yet to take advantage of.

'Exactly,' agreed Hal, which threw Malcolm off for a moment. 'All of *our* theories…' he repeated.

Kara sat up, her interest piqued, excitement brewing deep inside of her. This was the Hal she remembered. What's more, it also felt a lot like the cure to the boredom she was so thirsty for.

'What if we got some other input,' said Hal. 'Perhaps from some *Restarters* past-you doesn't even know about.'

'What are you talking about,' said Malcolm, a slight snappiness in his words.

Hal smiled. There was something innately rewarding in frustrating a time traveller from the future. Like thinking of an idea before your boss does and everyone loving it.

'Is that even possible?' asked Kara, seeing where he was going.

'I don't see why not…'

Kara clambered to her feet, her eyes bright. Not blue with restarter energy, but infused with intrigue thanks to Hal's mischievous smirk.

'What *other* Restarters,' said Malcolm, all but losing his shit.

He had explored almost every one of their restarts in minute detail. But not once had he come across an instance where other Restarters had been added to the mix, with the exception of Robert of course.

Hal and Kara grinned, feeling elated that they had information that Malcolm didn't.

'Well, what are we waiting for,' said Kara, clapping her hands with a new lease of invigoration. 'Let's go get the band back together.'

And with that, she span around and walked off in the direction of the Restart Point.

'You're all insane. What is happening right now?' grumbled Malcolm, feeling like he had just lost complete control of the situation.

Hal thought about the best way to word it, recalling the intro from a TV show from the 80's, trying to remember how it went.

'Where *everyone* goes if they have a problem,' the Restarter hummed. 'When no one else can help, and *if* you can find them…maybe we need to hire ourselves some soldiers of fortune,' said Hal, resting his hand on the grip of his holstered gun and clucking his tongue, just to really wind Malcolm up and send him over the edge.

Hal noted the flicker of red in the two eyes latching onto him. Eyes which eventually fluttered and returned to their regular colour. He decided it may be prudent to put Malcolm out of his misery.

'You're taking us to The White Lodge, Jeeves,' said Hal. 'We need your help to find something.'

'And what could possibly be of use in that *curs*ed place?!' said Malcolm, adding extra emphasis to the last syllable of the word, in a way usually reserved for those reciting Shakespeare.

Hal grinned at him and set off after Kara, shouting two words back at Malcolm without so much as looking back over his shoulder.

'Smoke signals,' said Hal, with a hearty chuckle.

CHAPTER FIFTY-ONE
The A-Team

187th Restart – Friday, August 24th, 2018, 3:32pm

The four Restarters reached the boundary line of Pentney Lakes, which meant only one thing; it was time for Malcolm to stress his relentless objections for the eighth time in as many minutes.

'Absolutely not,' said Malcolm.

'You said that already,' said Kara.

'This is a complete waste of time that we simply do not have.'

'You've said *that* already too' said Hal. 'And like *I* said before, we've got nothing *but* time.'

'Relatively speaking, perhaps,' conceded Malcolm,

'but from a chronological standpoint this little excursion of yours is, at best, muddying a timeline already fraught with paradoxes.'

Hal had thought of everything. He knew precisely *when* he wanted to travel to, and knew Malcolm could get them there. Seeing Hal throw Malcolm's plans completely out the window seemed to breathe new life into Fearne, who was considerably more present and lucid. If nothing else, Hal's plan was already proving to be worth it, if only to bring Fearne back to them, even just a little.

'We're really going to see Alex and Rachel?!' said Fearne excitedly. 'And they'll be able to see us?!'

'Better than that,' said Kara, equally relieved to see their friend opening up to them once again. 'They'll be able to talk to us too!'

Truth be told, Hal's plan wasn't really much of a *plan* at all. Once they reached the desired moment in time, Hal was hoping for good ol' fashioned free-will to take the wheel. He knew Rachel and his brother Alex would see their situation with fresh eyes.

Not willing to kill them a second time – primarily because the last thing they needed was Malcolm's murderous past-self knowing that blowing up Fir Lodge was even remotely an option – they had decided to take a more low-key approach. All they had to do was return to The White Lodge, locate the Restarter versions of both Alex and Rachel, allow their previous conversation to play out. And then, when past-Restarter-Hal-and-Kara triggered the restart, the *current* Hal and Kara could continue their conversation right where they left off.

'If what you're saying is accurate,' said Malcolm brashly, 'you will have but a moment before the restart sends them hurtling back to the land of the living.'

'Oh, come on Malc', you're not even trying. You can slow down time like you did for Fearne and...' Hal hesitated, but Fearne gave him a nod that it was okay to say his name. '...Peter,' referring to the way Future Malcolm had done just that when they came back into phase with the Dark Restarter so the killer couldn't see them.

'It is...not an exact science,' said Malcolm cagily. 'And we have no way of knowing how long I can sustain it with a restart licking at our heels.'

'Fine,' said Kara, not ready to be dissuaded by what was clearly an excuse. 'Then we bring *them* to The White Lodge, say what needs to be said, then you pop them back.'

'They will not be easy to locate,' said Malcolm, clutching a straw that Hal was already prepared to cut into pieces. 'From what you've described, they exist in an alternate restart that—'

'I know,' said Hal, hoovering up the aforementioned metaphoric straw into the woodchipper of proactive time travelling. 'But we don't need to look for *them* exactly, we just need to look for the smoke signal they don't even know they're generating.'

Malcolm stared blankly, not even dignifying the obtuse words Hal was uttering with a verbal response.

'We just need to look for a lodge on fire,' added Hal helpfully, before fully explained how his brother and best friend had even made their way into a restart in the first place.

Malcolm grumbled, clearly unhappy, but finding himself unable to offer a counter-argument meaty enough to sway them.

The echoes of a burning lodge would indeed be easy to find. He had even caught glimpses of such a sight whilst the multiple timelines had cycled before him, now possessing the answer to a riddle he had not bothered to seek a resolution to.

'Fine,' said Malcolm, firing the word at them with more than just a sprinkle of unwarranted salt. 'If you are adamant on taking this route, I'd rather leave immediately.

'Sure,' said Hal. 'But first, I'm going to need a moment with the others.'

'Now is not the time to be harbouring secrets, Harold,' his stare piercing through the Restarter as if trying to read his mind.

Actually, his eyes looked more like they were trying to carve whatever Hal was contemplating hiding from his very soul.

'Just piss off over there for a minute, not everything is about you Malcolm,' said Hal, using the former-killer's full name in the hope it would facilitate a granting of his request.

'Hrrrm,' Malcolm mumbled unhappily, before putting some distance between him and the three Restarters.

Hal gestured for them to huddle round, speaking in a hushed voice to Kara and Fearne.

'Look, I know I'm selling this thing as a means for chuckles over there to get to Sunday, but I want us to be on the same page before we get to where we're going.'

'Oh God, is this a *Hal* plan?' said Fearne wearily.

'What do you mean,' said Kara, ignoring her friend's frostiness.

Hal shot her a smile, realising that he often took Kara's willingness to follow his ideas for granted.

'Dark Malcolm said he wasn't responsible for bringing us back here.'

'Here being back into the Restarter life?' asked Fearne.

'Exactly that,' beamed Hal. 'Which means Captain Future here may have been economic with the truth in terms of his part in that.'

'So you want to see if Alex and Rachel can come up with ideas on what he may have changed?' confirmed Kara.

'When in Rome, right?'

'If *we* can't figure that out,' said Fearne, clearly having bought shares in negatively reinforced de-motivational speaking, 'what makes you think Rach' and Alex will fare any better?'

'Because,' said Hal, 'they're smarter than us.'

'Speak for yourself,' said Fearne.

Malcolm, having had enough of the incessant whispers, made his way back over to them.

'Allons-y then,' said Hal happily, indicating that the conversation was, at least for now, over.

'Are we ready?' Malcolm's bitterness at being excluded more than evident.

'Let's do it,' said Kara.

They formed an orderly line, taking each other's hands, and traversed the extra few metres to the boundary line.

With the decision made, they stepped into the Restart Point, the space they were formerly occupying filling with a sharp snapping sound, reminiscent of someone shaking out a heavy tarpaulin, and vanished into the ether, The White Lodge embracing them with unusual enthusiasm.

*

Hal had instructed Malcolm on what they were looking for whilst within the realm of The White Lodge; a billowing smoke that filled the white sky, caused by the utter obliteration of Fir Lodge.

Once the correct cycle presented itself, Malcolm reached into a nearby shadow and pulled the four of them through the veil between timelines, into phase with the past version of themselves that were standing outside the destroyed building.

Under the cover of a dense patch of woodland, as the embers drifted down and fluttered amidst the Restarters, Kara and Hal both smiled, feeling a sense of relief as two of their closest friends walked towards them. Or rather, towards a past version of themselves from an alternate timeline.

Malcolm had in fact visited this restart before, but given the short duration of the restart, had assumed it was a mere anomaly, leaving it behind without much further thought. As he stared up at the inferno lighting up the sky, he couldn't help but ask.

'What did you use as an accelerant?'

But Hal offered little more in the way of explanation than a shrug.

'Now what,' said Fearne, watching as Alex and Rachel made their way from the burning structure towards a past version of Hal and Kara standing a fair distance away from them all.

'Now we get to the boundary line and wait,' said Kara.

*

'This is going to be so much fun,' said Hal excitedly, as they crouched down low and out of sight amidst the cover of a grassy knoll a few hundred yards from the Restart Point, waiting for their past-selves to bring David Bowie and an additional Ghostbuster closer to them. They'd gained a pretty decent head start, as the versions of themselves from an earlier restart tried to convince Rachel and Alex to follow them.

'There's something we need to discuss,' said Kara, glancing over her shoulder at Malcolm, who was sulking and muttering to himself with his arms crossed and leaning against a nearby lodge. Satisfied that she, Hal and Fearne could not be overheard, she added 'about Rachel.'

'Shoot.' Nothing could bring Hal down from the ninth cloud he was on, now that he was involved in a far more exciting stakeout than their last.

'We can't let on to Rachel that she's pregnant in the future,' said Kara, as if it was old news.

'What are you talking about?' said Hal, not even bothering to take his eyes off of the soon to be occupied road ahead. 'Rach' isn't having a kid.'

'Wait,' said Kara, kicking herself. 'You didn't know?'

Hal turned to face both Kara and Fearne, his eyes narrowing as if he was being pranked. 'Did my first "what" lack conviction?'

'Why are boys so dumb, Fearne?' she sighed, rolling onto her back and staring up at the amber, smoke-filled sky, realising she could have got away without even mentioning it. 'Why do you think she was drinking lemonade at the funeral?'

'Because not everyone drinks before noon like we do Kara,' said Hal, before falling silent, then eventually feeling like a crap friend for not noticing the signs. Rachel had really hidden it well. 'When did she tell you?' he conceded, not taking it personally that Rachel hadn't brought it up.

He knew there were a million reasons why people kept the early stages of pregnancy a secret, not least in case complications arose.

'She didn't. I just have a sense for these things. You must have known, Fearne?'

Fearne remained silent.

The truth was that Fearne didn't remember anything from this alternate future they kept mentioning. Least of all Peter's funeral.

'I know what you're like Hal, don't tell her,' said Kara, warning him. 'I know how terrible you are at keeping secrets.'

'Oh puh-lease,' he scoffed. 'I'm the *bomb* at keeping secrets.'

'No, what you *are* is someone who gets all sweaty and makes stupid jokes when you're anxious and only *think*s he's the bomb at keeping secrets.'

'Wow, don't hold back or anything.'

'I'm serious,' pleaded Kara. 'On the off chance she has even an *inkling* of what's to come, you could screw up her entire future.'

'Kara,' said Hal, leaning on his elbow and propping his head up with his hand, 'chill. I've *got* this.'

Though secretly, he simply knew Rachel wouldn't retain anything he said when she returned to the present anyway, so it didn't really matter what he said.

Before she could make him take a blood oath, their quarry arrived.

The Restarters stared in fascination, as the prospect of what they were witnessing sunk in. The three of them were more than accustomed to seeing echoes of themselves going about their business in the past, but this was so much more. They were witnessing time travelling versions of themselves recruiting additional support in the form of their friends Rachel and Alex, watching it unfold from an entirely new vantage point.

'This is so cool!' said Hal, craning his neck to get a better look but being pulled back down to the ground by Kara.

As the conversation played out just like it had before, Hal and Kara straightened up, as their past Restarter-selves approached the boundary line and said their goodbyes to Rachel and Alex.

'Okay,' said Kara, 'you guys ready? We're up.'

Fearne and Hal nodded, the latter shooting a short, sharp yet muted whistle to get Malcolm's attention. Hal pointed to his own eyes with two splayed fingers, directing Malcom's line of sight to the road over the mound of grass they were currently hiding behind.

Malcolm half-heartedly pushed himself away from the wall of the lodge and took a stroll towards them.

'And remember Hal,' said Kara sternly. '*No* baby talk.'

'I've got this Kara, will you just relax already? You're stressing me out.'

*

As Alex's phone pinged to life in his hand, and a familiar fruit-shaped logo popped onto the screen, Alex raised the handset in an attempt to get his brother's attention, but all he could muster was the start of a word, which for the first time Hal was in a position to hear in its entirety.

The current Restarters watched as their past-selves jumped into nothingness, and were pulled apart into shards of blue light.

'–uck,' said Alex, as he turned his back on the Restart Point, only to see his brother appearing from over the top of a small mound.

Alex wondered why Hal was waving his arms, as if he were being chased by a Tyrannosaurus Rex and was trying to give Alex the heads up so he could save himself.

Which wasn't far from the truth, if the T-Rex in this equation represented the fast-moving mass of fog that was hot on his brother's heels and obliterating everything it came into contact with.

Hal collided with his brother and grabbed him by the shoulders, as Kara did the same to Rachel, with Fearne and Malcolm creating a link between the six of them.

'Hal,' said Alex, his mind clearly overloaded. 'The phone! It charged! Look!'

'Way past that point bro', but it was a great idea!'

'Wait,' said Rachel. 'What's with your clothes?' suddenly feeling overdressed in her David Bowie getup.

'Oooooh,' said Alex excitedly, realising in that moment that this was not the version of his brother he had initially thought. It was a version of him from a different time.

'Did you just *Back to the Future Part Two* us?!' Alex swooned. 'That. Is. Awesome!'

'Harold,' warned Malcolm. 'It's now or never.'

'I know, I know! Nobody likes a backseat Restarter, Malcolm. You guys may want to…buckle up,' said Hal, providing no time at all for Rachel or Alex to find a buckle at all.

As the fog surrounded them, accompanied by a deafening sound of rushing air, Hal and Kara – with considerable assistance from Malcolm – yanked Rachel, Fearne and Alex through the Restart Point, and into the Fir Lodge Nexus beyond.

CHAPTER FIFTY-TWO
The Nexus that Connects Us
RI Timestamp error: Recalculating…

Rachel and Alex couldn't help but stare at the abrupt change in their surroundings. Everything was ice-white, as if it were the middle of winter, and a heavy snowfall had taken hold over the entire landscape. It was only when Alex took a closer look that he realised it wasn't snow on the ground, but rather it *was* the ground.

Rachel swiped her hand with awestruck curiosity through the motes of temporally-distorted snowflakes that swam around them, as they bounced along the outskirts of her invisible, polarised aura.

'I feel *knackered*,' said Rachel sluggishly.

'Yeah,' said Hal. 'The journey takes it out of you. Plus, the bus driver that brought us here loves to hog the blue,' he added, casting a thumb over his shoulder to Malcolm.

'I have to admit,' said Alex, 'I hadn't expected to see you both again so soon.'

'We're…from the future,' said Hal, just in case there was any doubt lingering over that fact.

'Well, obviously,' said Alex, feeling almost hurt that his brother had to clarify that.

'Nooo, you didn't make it out?!' asked Rachel, wondering if they had even managed to leave following their last conversation, trying to wrap her head around how that was barely a minute ago from her perspective.

'We did,' said Kara, 'then…we got brought back.'

'How?' said Alex, his brow suitably furrowed.

Hal moved closer, muttering to his brother so that Malcolm, who was keeping watch a fair distance away, couldn't hear him.

'That's the thing,' whispered Hal. 'We have no idea. I told the big guy we needed you for something different, which we'll get into. But honestly, we were hoping you could help us figure out exactly what he could have changed to bring us here. If nothing else so we can plan a Time Heist to fix it if things go south.'

'Or, south-*er*,' noted Fearne.

'Oh,' said Alex awkwardly, sensing the resentment

radiating from Fearne. 'And how did *you* get dragged into all this Fearne? And who's the big guy?' he said finally, gesturing towards the towering slab that was Malcolm.

Hal had forgotten that from Alex and Rachel's perspective, they were carrying on a conversation right where they left off. One of the reasons Hal had chosen this moment in time in particular.

'Okay,' said Hal. 'Take a seat. This is…going to take a while.'

Alex cracked his knuckles and clicked his neck, the sound of which causing a muted crack to reach their ears in reverse.

*

'That didn't take nearly as long as I expected,' said Kara a mere nine minutes later. 'You guys really have a strong grasp on Restarting.'

'We had good teachers I guess,' said Alex, rummaging in his pocket in an attempt to locate a cigarette. 'You wouldn't happen to have smokes in that fancy backpack of yours, would you?' he said, his voice full of hope.

Hal retrieved one and offered it to his brother, but returned the box, resisting the urge to have one himself. Alex noticed, but merely nodded in approval.

'I'm telling you, man,' said Alex, after sparking up and finally being brought up to speed on everything that had happened since they last met, which felt like an awful lot of happenings in such a short space of time from Alex and Rachel's perspective. 'It *has* to be then. That moment. No other change would matter. I'm certain of it.'

'He wouldn't be that stupid,' said Hal, refusing to accept it.

Whichever Malcolm, be it dark, future or otherwise, that had altered the past to bring Hal, Kara and Fearne back into the restart game, one thing was certain; neither would have been insane enough to change the moment when Kara and Hal had stopped Malcolm's heart.

'What makes you so sure?' asked Rachel.

'Hal's right,' said Kara. 'For Malcolm to change that moment in his own history, it would undo everything that came after. For one thing, the Dark Restarter would cease to exist entirely, and Future Malcolm–'

'–couldn't be here now,' finished Hal. 'We wouldn't even be talking without him being here to bring us to The White Lodge.'

Alex closed his eyes, clicking his fingers absently, as if trying to organise his thoughts, before finally speaking again.

'Occam's Razor then,' he said. 'Maybe they're *both* telling the truth.'

'But if it wasn't Dark Malcolm or Future Malcolm…' began Kara.

'There could be another possibility,' said Alex, frustration lining his features.

'Oh!' said Rachel, clearly collecting the morsels of broken sentences and reorganising them into a wonderful collage of a marginally more sensical brainstorm. 'What if you did something yourselves! Like, a future version of yourselves. It just hasn't happened yet!'

'That would explain why we can't remember our past being altered,' said Kara pensively.

'But not why I can't remember Peter's...funeral,' said Fearne bleakly.

'Peter's *what* now?!' blurted Rachel.

'Malcolm went all in. Plucked Peter and I out of time and...'

'Peter's here too? Where is he?' asked Rachel excitedly, realising instantly that the question was a mistake.

'Gone,' said Fearne coldly.

'What do you mean gone?' asked Alex.

Fearne told them how Peter had gone to retrieve past-Malcolm's knife, and was slaughtered before their very eyes in his Restarter form, and how he had disintegrated into nothing. Her words caused doubt to spread across Alex's face.

'But if that Malcolm is from the future, why didn't he warn you?'

'Exactly Alex. Exactly,' said Fearne, glad that someone understood.

'So, you're trying to find Peter?' asked Alex.

'They *say* they are,' said Fearne bluntly. 'But I've yet to see any evidence of that.'

Hal and Rachel shared a knowing glance and the latter instantly knew a change of subject was in order.

A form of body-language intuition that only years of friendship, or perhaps Restarting together, could provide.

'So, ah, what's the future *like*?' said Rachel, unable to help herself.

'No one's having kids or anything!' blurted Hal, causing Kara to do nothing but stare at the space ahead of her.

'That was…*oddly* specific,' said Rachel, frowning at the strangely-timed statement.

'It was only six weeks from now,' said Kara, in an attempt to rectify Hal's rampage against the timeline she was trying so desperately to salvage and get back to. Luckily, Rachel didn't seem to notice all that much.

'Come on then, hand it over,' said Alex, gesturing with his hand as if plucking at invisible harp strings, unknowingly saving his brother from ruining Rachel's future altogether.

Hal smiled, having noticed his brother had been eyeing up a certain six-shooter as soon as he showed up. Popping the clip of his holster, he handed over his gun without hesitation. The act surprised Kara, seeing as how Hal had been so averse to letting anyone mess about with his pride and joy. Clearly, it was a sign of how much he loved his brother.

Alex whistled in appreciation.

'Oh wow! A Python? Isn't that the gun–'

'Yup,' confirmed Hal. 'Rick Grimes!'

'Niiiice.'

Hal looked over at Malcolm, noting that whilst he was keeping his distance, he had been edging ever closer in incremental amounts, presumably to listen in on the Restarter conference taking place without him.

'There's actually something else we wanted to talk to you about' said Hal, before dropping the next agenda item into the laps of Alex and Rachel.

*

Having shared everything regarding their new lofty goal, Kara and Hal were waiting patiently for the combined lateral thinking of Rachel and Alex to offer up some ideas they hadn't thought of.

'Thoughts?' said Kara, eager to hear what they had to say.

'Well,' said Alex, spinning the gun in his hand, as if it eliminated procrastination and helped him to form a livewire loophole. 'You're looking at breaking out from the time bubble, sending Vigo the Carpathian over there–'

'I used that one once!' said Hal, his brother merely nodding that this was inevitable.

'–into Sunday, to see if you're on the right track in terms of fixing this thing?'

Hal and Kara nodded enthusiastically.

'But,' said Alex, taking a deep drag on his cigarette, exhaling his thoughts along with the smoke, 'you guys can't cross the boundary line without triggering a restart...'

'That's right,' said Hal.

'And when Malcolm steps into the Restart Point

he gets sent here, to Fir Lodge Winter Wonderland…' Alex took another deep intake of partially out-of-phase, nicotine-free tobacco. 'What if…' began Alex.

"Here it comes," thought Hal excitedly.

'What if you cross the boundary line *whilst* you're in the White Lodge Nexus?'

And there it was. Something so simple, and yet so utterly outside of the box only his brother could have thought of it.

'Wow,' said Rachel, flexing her fingers as if she were preparing to literally grab onto the prospect of what Alex was suggesting. 'Then you could explore the…*nexus* world beyond Pentney Lakes!'

'The nexus that connects us,' said Kara, smiling at the way it rolled off the tongue.

'Entirely unbound by the restart loop,' said Hal rubbing his eternally five-o'clock stubbled chin. 'That…could actually work. Oh, and Kara?'

'Yeah?'

'The nexus that connects us? Very nice,' said Hal approvingly.

'Thanks. One question though; nothing exists in this realm?' said Kara. 'I mean, sure, the *surroundings* do, but no one is here to watch or gain hints from, in terms of the future that is.'

Hal was about to say "almost no one," remembering the horrifying creatures that were drawn to their Restarter energy like moths to a bonfire, but thought better of it, as if mentioning them would jinx them all and lure the beasts to their current place in the nexus they were residing in. He knew on some level that the entire concept of tempting fate and jinxes was inherently ridiculous. If something was going to happen, it would happen regardless of someone speaking of the outcome out loud. But still…she had a point.

What good would surveying the Sunday of their future be if it was a lifeless facsimile of the real world, with nothing happening within it to draw updates from.

'Maybe,' said Rachel, her nose scrunched in thought as she ran her fingers through her thick red hair, 'you could do that thing? Grab onto an "anchor" or whatever, and *pull* yourselves into the present?'

The five Restarters turned to face the boundary line, each of them wondering what would happen if they crossed it now, in their current state, whilst occupying a realm that served as a nucleus for the entirety of time in all its forms.

'We could try it now,' said Alex excitedly, envisioning the countless adventures they would all have together by taking the plunge.

'No,' said Kara. 'We need to get you back to where we brought you from.' Kara's eyes unconsciously dipped to Rachel's stomach, the gesture washing over everyone but Hal.

'Kara's right,' said Hal. 'Besides, who knows how many *flutterbys* we'll release into the world if we don't take you back. We may have already totally borked up time in ways we can't even imagine.'

Malcolm strolled over, all but refraining from tapping the wrist-watch he wasn't wearing, signalling that they needed to wrap this up.

'Two secret Restarters,' said Malcolm, his words a mix of wonder and suspicion, slicing through the two of them like an ice-pick. 'I must confess, I'm amazed you slipped past me. I've heard you two are quite the problem-solvers.'

'We heard *you're* a serial killer,' said Rachel, biting back.

'Former,' chuckled Malcolm thickly. 'My, you look positively glowing Miss Bowie,' he added, addressing Rachel. 'What's your secret?'

It was in that moment that Kara knew that he knew. Had he been listening to them? Was it a lucky guess?

'Time to go, Creepy McCreepyson,' said Hal.

Alex and Rachel looked troubled,

'Bro,' said Alex, lowering his voice. 'We've seen enough movies to know how this guy's character arc ends. No matter what he says, you know you can't trust him right?'

The five Restarters formed a tighter circle.

Hal could feel Malcolm's eyes burrowing into the back of his head, knowing he was close enough to hear what Hal was about to say, and chose his next words wisely.

'He isn't the man he was,' said Hal. 'I really believe he's changed. Or is at least *trying* to.'

'I don't get the vibe from him that he's changed,'

noted Rachel, Fearne's expression showing clear signs of agreement.

'Hal, you need to listen to me,' began Alex, but Hal interjected before his brother could cause any more damage.

'You remember that time we played beer pong,' said Hal. 'Gavin and Jon utterly destroyed us?'

Alex nodded, not sure where Hal was going with this.

'And how I drank your drinks to spare you from drinking too much? Remember what I said just before it went south and I threw up all over the damn place.

'You threw up in my sink, Hal, it was disgusting!' said Rachel,

'You said you've got this,' said Alex.

'Exactly,' said Hal with a wink, and his brother knew in that moment what he was trying to say, despite not being able to say it, as he looked over his shoulder and saw the enormous killer bearing down on them.

'This is the same thing,' said Hal. 'Only this time, Kara, Fearne and I—'

'Tick-tock, time-travellers,' said Malcolm. 'We must depart.'

Without warning, Alex moved in and went to hug his brother, the sparks between them fizzling immediately as Hal pulled away as quickly as he could.

'Alex, no!' said Kara.

'What? Just wanted to say goodbye?' he said, not seeing the problem. He had done just that the last time he had seen them. Even hugged Kara.

It was then that they heard the squeals, echoing in reverse from beyond the tree line.

'You just rang the dinner bell,' said Hal, causing a look of horror to appear on Rachel and Alex's faces.

'What?!' said Rachel, eyes wide.

'Time Vampires,' said Hal as casually as he could.

'That's a thing?!' said Alex, his eyes just as wide in horror as Rachel's, but his smile betraying him and giving away how cool he thought that was.

'Bring it in guys, we've officially outstayed our welcome,' said Kara, pulling everyone together, as Malcolm strode towards them and grabbed Fearne and Hal's arms.

Alex had just enough time to glance over his shoulder, as a flock of what appeared to be humanoid creatures flooded across the horizon like an oil spill.

'They come at night,' said Hal. 'Mostly.'

'You wanna pick up the pace a little here Malc',' said Kara, the desperation to get the hell out of Dodge more than evident.

'I...can't,' said Malcolm.

'What do you mean you can't,' said Hal. 'Now is not the time to get performance anxiety! It's not that common, it doesn't happen to every guy–'

'–and it is a big deal,' said Kara, smiling at the reference to the only TV series she had seen a dozen times over.

They stood there like petrified statues, as if their visibility to the creatures that were becoming clearer by the second was based solely on movement, as the interlocked arms of the time travellers generated a notable burst of electricity, like a flare being fired into the skies of yesterday.

'I am joking,' said Malcolm, his attempt at humour falling flatter than a restarted carbonated drink.

And with a whip-like crack, they were gone, teleported back to Rachel and Alex's first ever restart, and Hal and Kara's 52nd respectively.

Back to the very second before Rachel and Alex were erased in their Restarter form.

CHAPTER FIFTY-THREE
Licence to Feel

52nd Restart – Saturday, August 25th, 2018, 3:37pm

The Restarters found themselves amidst a mind-bending scenario, as they arrived back in Hal and Kara's 52nd restart. They had arrived early, waiting out of sight and from a distance as they watched a past version of themselves jump through the restart portal, and gawped as yet another version of themselves ran across the road to great Alex and Rachel.

The six of them watched in awe, as they witnessed a duplicated Future Malcolm (who was now technically a Malcolm of their past) whisking them all to The White Lodge to embark on the conversation they had just had.

'Anyone else struggling with an identity crisis right now?' said Alex, looking a little green.

Hal, Kara and Rachel all raised their hands slightly in agreement.

'Well, weirdness aside, it's been fun! Take care guys,' said Rachel, as she and Alex took up the spot their past iterations had only moments before been occupying, waiting for the restart mechanism to claim them as it had done the first time.

With their friends in position, Hal and Kara gave Malcolm the go-ahead to take them back to the timeline where the Dark Restarter was waiting for them, as the world crumbled into nothingness around them.

'What do you think Hal meant,' said Alex, turning to Rachel and filling their last precious seconds as bona fide time-travellers with a delayed response to a seemingly innocuous outburst from his brother. 'When he said no one's having babies in the future?'

Rachel clenched her jaw, trying admirably to cloak the smile that was causing the corner of her mouth to quiver.

'Oh, I think I have an idea,' said Rachel, unable to contain her smirk.

'No waaay?' said Alex excitedly. 'Really? How long?'

She was about to tell him Jon and her had only found out a couple of days ago, but was distracted by the temporal wave that was making its way towards them both, disintegrating everything in its path.

'Boy or girl?'

'It's way too early Alex, but…I'm thinking a g–'

They felt the ground rumble beneath them, Alex's eyes drawn to a small blue spark erupting from his hand.

'Ouch,' said Alex. 'I feel weird. *You* feel weird?' he added, as an odd sensation of retained current coursed through him.

'Actually,' said Rachel. 'Ye–'

And they were gone.

*

"You know," thought Kara, glad to be back in-phase with the slightly more predictable environment of Restart 187. "The weirdest thing is, everything we just did must have been happening during *and* after we jumped through the portal on that restart," she noted, made giddy by the cyclical nature of travelling through time, and referring to their 52nd trip back through it, which Hal knew thanks to their current connection.

"I'm pretty much certain of it," thought Hal, transmitting his response to Kara. "Which means you, me and Fearne were already there when our past selves met with Alex and Rach' the first time around.'

"Isn't that crazy?" thought Kara. "The thought of us three being there, and past-us having no idea? Kinda makes you think, doesn't it?"

"It kind of gives me a headache, to be honest,'

thought Fearne, causing the collective of Restarters to chuckle in unison.

'What are you three doing?' said Malcolm suspiciously, like a teacher walking in on some naughty school children.

It was becoming an increasing occurrence for him, and he didn't enjoy it.

They broke the connection, their eyelids fluttering until eventually re-joining the relative present.

'Practising,' replied Fearne, being intentionally obtuse in the hope it would piss Malcolm off.

'Practising *what*?' asked Malcolm, in a tone that made her realise she had succeeded.

Having dropped Rachel and Alex back into Hal and Kara's 52nd restart, the three of them had decided to find a quiet place to practice sharing their thoughts through a sustained connection of their out-of-phase bodies. It had been slow going, but with Fearne's grief over Peter as an emotional anchor, and Kara's seemingly innate affinity with generating a mental link, they had both pulled Hal along for the ride and successfully set up a rudimentary three-way communication network.

'A three way,' said Hal, without thinking.

'Annnd you're banned from using words,' joked Kara.

'Could've worded that better,' agreed Hal.

They were preparing for their next attempt to send Malcolm into the future, to glean whatever he could in the hope it would provide them with valuable insight into the world that was being generated by their meddling.

A concept that seemed all the more possible now they were armed with Alex and Rachel's idea to use The White Lodge as a sort of *back door* out of the bubble they were trapped in. They didn't know if their plan would work, but if it did, they knew Malcolm would need as much information as possible to get to a point of personal interest to them all.

Hal explained his reasoning that it would take Malcolm hours to reach their Sunday-selves by car, let alone on foot, and with no way of knowing which way to go he'd just be wandering the Earth aimlessly like some kind of post-Winter-Soldier Steve Rogers.

'So if we can generate enough…Restarter energy feedback, if we focus everything we've got, I can literally *give* you the memories of how to get to my house!'

Malcolm recoiled, utterly surprised by Hal's willingness to impart such personal information. Of course, had Malcolm wanted to find Hal in the present, he would've been able to do so a number of ways. Stalking, mainly.

It was, after all, amazing how much his previous works of art were willing to share across a multitude of platforms. Details they freely spewed out across the internet. But still, the gesture was not lost on him.

'You…*trus*t me enough to impart such details?' said Malcolm, almost giving Hal a chance to back out, as if he were protecting him from himself.

'Don't go all teary-eyed on me Malc',' said Hal, rolling his eyes. 'I'm not going to be inviting you around for dinner when this is all done. But yes. I trust you. We need you. I'm putting all my cards on the table.'

'Are you sure this is a good idea, Hal,' said Fearne. 'I mean you're literally about to tell a serial killer where you live. Where *Jess* lives!' she added, reminding him of his unsuspecting fiancée.

"The convincer," thought Hal. "Trying to talk them all out of it." He had to hand it to her, it was perfectly delivered.

'Here,' said Hal retrieving his wallet from his trusty backpack of treasures. 'Take this.'

Hal passed Malcolm a small rectangular piece of salmon-coloured plastic.

'What am I supposed to do with this,' said Malcolm, staring at the driving licence.

'Well, you can *start* by reading it,' said Hal. 'So you can learn my address, dumb ass. In case the fog tries to mess with your head. And you'd better take *this* too,' he added, removing his gun from its holster and handing it to Malcolm.

Malcolm was about to ask what use he could possibly have for a pellet gun, when Kara answered the question for him.

'You're heading into Uncharted Time,' said Kara, just like they had rehearsed, smiling at how cool that sounded. It was *classic* Hal. 'You may even run into other Restarters out there. Stuck in other time-bubbles of their own. Better to have it as a deterrent and not need it…'

'…Than need it, and not have it,' said Hal, finishing her sentence. 'Okay, now that this Secret Santa is done with, I need to show you exactly how to get to my place.'

'Shouldn't we wait until we've made changes?' said Malcolm, almost suspiciously.

'Well, obviously,' said Fearne. 'But we might as well figure out how to do this in preparation for when we actually need you to do some actual recon.'

'Very well,' said Malcolm. 'Proceed.'

'Okay,' said Kara, 'just empty your mind. Fearne is going to give you a boost of emotion, Hal's going to project his thoughts into your mind and I'm…'

'Kara's the powerhouse,' said Hal simply, his words causing Kara to blush.

'This is just my thing,' said Kara.

Gripping each other's hands, the energy crackled between them angrily, as if it knew what they were attempting and was extremely agitated by it.

'Okay Fearne,' said Kara. 'Time to drop the needle. Show him how you feel.'

'Gladly,' said Fearne, finally getting to the part of the plan that had led to her agreeing in the first place, as the killer's unique ability to soak up restarter energy like a sponge suddenly became his undoing, her eyes lighting up and unleashing a landslide of raw, pure emotion directly into Malcolm's cerebral cortex.

CHAPTER FIFTY-FOUR
What's Mine is Yours

187th Restart – Friday, August 24th, 2018

Soul crushing agony hit him like a landslide, as he relived the moments when his boyfriend and future husband was toyed with by the maniac wearing his own face. The unbridled glee in the killer's eyes made Malcolm feel sick to his stomach as he was assaulted by a blast of sheer shame. The realisation that he was powerless to prevent any of it sunk deep into the ocean of his heart, colliding angrily with the seabed of his hopes and dreams.

They had such plans, Peter and he.

They were going to move in together in just a few short months.

Build a family.

Probably get a cat or something.

And now, here he was, faced with the inescapable fact that none of that would come to be.

That he would never again feel the sensation of Peter's fingers running through his hair, or the feel of his kiss as–

'Enough,' barked Malcolm, jerking violently as he attempted to pull away from the Restarters that had commandeered his mind.

But Fearne wasn't done with him yet, refusing to yield in the slightest, her grip tightening, throwing more and more of her own memories and feelings at him until a voice broke through the electrical crackle that filled all of their eardrums.

'Dial it back, Fearne,' said Hal. Not scolding her, but clearly equally overwhelmed by the power of her mind; unfiltered emotions that were bleeding into their own and tricking all of them into thinking they were experiencing their own thoughts and recollections instead of the true instigator.

Kara, Hal and Malcolm all gasped in unison as she released them from the psychological bombardment, as if a tap had been turned off, and they were all permitted once again to think independently, though still very much connected.

'That was…' began Kara

'…intense,' wheezed Hal.

There was no other word for it.

'Righty oh,' said Hal, shaking off the residual aftershocks of losing a lover that was not his own.

'Time to check your memory inbox for the thought email I'm about to wing your way.'

Hal focused his mind on his driveway, imagining that he was approaching the front porch as his car keys jangled by his side. The key slid into the lock as if it were magnetised, and then he was inside his home.

His dog Shelby greeted him, delighted that her dad had returned. Early, it seemed, given her over-excited reaction. Usually, Hal would have flipped on the kettle and prepared himself a coffee, but this was an exercise in data duplication, designed solely to give Malcolm the lay of the land, and Hal proceeded onwards down his short hallway to his modest living room, before scanning the area, allowing himself to drink in every last detail.

Malcolm looked at the slightly messy lounge area, feeling oddly at home, before leaning down to stroke Shelby, who he now knew wasn't over-excited because he had returned home early, but rather this was always how she reacted, regardless of time.

As Malcolm stared at the magnolia coloured walls of his home, his eyes rested on the mantlepiece of a wood burning fire, adorned with photographs of his fiancée…

"Jessica," he thought, smiling warmly.

He found it odd that he had to search for her name. And even stranger that he had referred to her by her full name, which felt wrong on the tongue. "Jess," he thought, correcting himself, and feeling pleased that it felt truer.

Suddenly, the room began to shrink, as if Malcolm were being lifted by a grappling hook, torn away from his home, pulled up through the roof, a sound of electricity pulling him away from what he now knew was a fabricated construct, and back into temporal purgatory.

'So,' said Hal, his throat unusually hoarse and somewhat despondent. 'That's my place. You get all that?'

Malcolm found himself needing to take a moment, having to shake off the feeling that he had been in his own home, not Hal's. An unexpected side-effect to sharing memories via the medium of crude telepathy, he wagered.

'I did,' said Malcolm. But a building alone did not a map make. 'But I still have no idea how to get there?'

'Dammit Hal,' said Kara, realising the reason Hal hadn't imparted the most pertinent of information was that he simply couldn't get anywhere at all without a bloody sat-nav. 'Everybody link arms.'

Hal literally had no idea how to get back to his house from Norfolk.

Kara imagined driving over the boundary line of the Pentney Lakes, towards the nearest motorway, and then quickly navigated herself back in her mind's eye on how to reach their home town.

To Malcolm, it was as if he were watching a memory in fast-forward, until the connection between them was once again severed.

'Okay,' said Malcolm. 'I am ready.'

'Be careful with that,' said Hal, still not sounding like himself, but looking down at the gun he had given Malcolm all the same. 'I want it back.'

Malcolm grinned, retrieved Hal's driving licence from his pocket, and read over the details once more for good measure.

'Well,' said Malcolm, 'let's attempt a *house call* shall we. Would you like me to say hello to Jess for you?' he added.

Hal, uncharacteristically, said nothing. And without so much as a razor-sharp quip or a wave of the broadsword of banter, he merely walked away.

'What's with him?' asked Fearne, worrying if perhaps she had been the cause, having somehow broken his spirit. Her target had been Malcolm, but in her eagerness to cause the killer pain, and perhaps in the hope of shedding some of her own by jettisoning the dead weight lodged firmly in her broken heart, she felt almost guilty.

Kara shrugged. 'I…don't know.'

'And need I remind you,' said Malcolm sourly, utterly oblivious to Harold's quietness, 'try not to cross the boundary line whilst we attempt this fool's errand. On the off chance it leads anywhere but *back* here, I have no desire to get trapped in a nexus realm *between* time.'

Admittedly, they hadn't even thought about that.

Kara was about to pretend they had, by offering

some words of comfort, but Malcolm disappeared before she could do so, like a crack of the whip, presumably well on his way to The White Lodge.

'Are we sure this was a good idea,' said Fearne.

Assuming Malcolm could even make it to Hal's home, they had just willingly given a serial killer enough personal information for Malcolm to set up a bank account in Hal's name.

Fearne noticed that Kara was smiling, and she suddenly felt incredibly irritated.

'Relax,' said Kara. 'We know what we're doing.'

Fearne bristled. 'Maybe you could let *me* in on it?' all but spitting the words. 'For once. Assuming it's okay to join your little secret time travel club?'

'It was never about sending him to Sunday,' said Hal, who had taken a seat on a nearby log.

'What?' said Fearne. 'But that's all you've been going on about since we got here. "Sunday is the key. Future events will tell us how to beat this thing," blah bloody blah.'

'That's not how I sound,' said Hal, not so much dismissively as he was exhausted by her seemingly unquenchable desire to pick a fight with him. 'You said it yourself,' he continued, looking decidedly shaken up. 'What *point* would that serve? We'll just restart anyway, and it'll all get wiped. There's nothing to gain from glimpsing a future that hasn't set yet.'

Honestly, Hal had no idea how far Future Malcolm would get on his impossible quest, but he doubted it would amount to much more than a long commute back to Restart-Ville. All that mattered was what the killer's absence would bring them; the solitude the three of them needed to speak in peace and run through–

'So why go to all this trouble?' said Fearne, interrupting his thoughts.

During their foray into telepathic espionage, they had imparted to Fearne that the plan was to connect with Malcolm, flooding him with enough Restarter energy to create a link between the four of them. A link that would facilitate providing Malcolm with enough personal information about Hal to make the killer believe their motive was solely about giving him what he needed in the event he managed to breach through into Sunday.

The key to this being Fearne's intense emotions towards the loss of Peter, and how that emotional boost would surely expedite the process of allowing the three of them and Malcolm to share their thoughts more succinctly.

What they *hadn't* told Fearne was that Kara could have triggered that without her help, and that what they actually needed was for Fearne to act as a buffer; a distraction brought on by her loss that was so consuming, that it would overwhelm Malcolm. Overload his mind just enough so that they could use his disorientation against him.

'The thing with mind-reading between Restarters,' said Hal, his voice containing more than a hint of an incoming mic-drop, 'is that it's always a two-way street.'

'And once we get out of this mess,' added Kara, 'he's not going to remember any of it anyway.'

'A two-way street?' said Fearne, starting to understand. 'Oh my god...you read *his* mind?!'

Hal shot her a wink.

'Why thy hell didn't you tell me?' asked Fearne, clearly hurt that they didn't trust her enough to let her in on it.'

'Well, with Malc' receiving Fearne FM,' said Kara, 'we figured what you didn't know couldn't be...used against you, I guess.'

'So, you saw how all of this really ends?' asked Fearne, the excitement building in her voice and overriding her damaged pride. 'That was...*really* smart!'

'Don't seem *too* surprised!' joked Hal, feigning hurt feelings, despite his heart clearly not being in it. 'Yes...and no. I didn't expect to get drawn in by the whammy you were throwing at the guy. It took me a while to refocus on what I was looking for. By that point I only had time to grab on to the glimmers of his memories.'

'So, what did you see?' said Fearne, her elatedness palpable, knowing for certain she was about to be vindicated. That Future Malcolm's true agenda was surely to destroy them all. Perhaps Hal had even discovered a way to rescue Peter…

'Is he telling the truth?' added Kara, wanting to know if Malcolm really was as reformed as he claimed to be, her heart sinking as Hal shook his head.

'It's…hard to describe,' said Hal, turning to face Kara. 'It wasn't as clear as when you and I have shared our thoughts. It was more like…a series of images playing at super-high speed.'

In truth, it was hard to garner any real opinions on Malcolm one way or the other. He had expected to see fully formed scenes of betrayal, or conversations they were yet to have playing out in their unabridged, unedited entirety.

The reality was far less fraught with game-changing drama than he had hoped for.

'He's lying, right?' said Fearne matter-of-factly, as if all of her concerns were one sentence away from being verified, date stamped, and bagged up for evidence.

'Honestly,' said Hal, 'I think he's on the level. I saw the moments we'd all shared together, only from Malcolm's point of view. And I felt…I think *he* feels…' Hal hesitated. He was about to go as far as saying Malcolm had feelings for them, but that made him feel like a bit of sick was going to rise up in his throat, so he settled on something easier to swallow, keep down and digest. '…I think he *likes* us?'

'What do you mean, *likes us*?' said Fearne, the scepticism in her voice borderline tangible, and not for the first time since this nightmare started, feeling like she was drifting further and further away from both Hal and Kara.

'His thoughts seem to dwell on training us. His

reasons for doing so…he feels *happy* when we improve. Like he wants us to be ready for when the time comes to confront his past-self.'

'Like he wants us to win?' asked Kara.

'Yeah,' he replied, his face twitching in equal surprise, confirming that the only sensations he experienced were positive and genuine.

Fearne, meanwhile, found herself finding it hard to breathe.

It had been one thing wishing they would finally see what Malcolm truly was, but another thing entirely seeing them get sucked in by yet another deception. She had gone from feeling like someone had walked over her grave, to feeling like her friends were digging a fresh one reserved just for her.

'Fearne,' said Kara, sensing the sudden change in her friend and starting to worry. 'What's wrong?'

'Nothing. Nothing at all,' she lied, knowing in that very moment that she was truly alone now.

That when it came to saving her friends, and saving herself in the process, it would be down to *her* and her alone to bring an end to the pantomime.

"Or, more precisely," she thought, "an end to the so-called *Future* Malcolm."

'So, what now?' said Kara, folding her arms and blowing a stray strand of her reddish fringe that was obstructing her line-of-sight.

'I think we just chill here for a bit,' said Hal, unintentionally mimicking her body language. 'There's no way in hell he's actually going to make it further than the boundary line,' he added, with the same level of certainty he displayed during his first viewing of "Deep Blue Sea", when he had declared Samuel L Jackson's character was totally protected by plot armour.

But ultimately wasn't.

Malcolm Unbound

R.I Timestamp Error: Recalculating…
System Error. Timestamp Failure.

For all of his newfound abilities, such as fast-forwarding through timelines, and accessing the nexus between what once *was* and what could one day *be*, there was a singular, inconvenient truth that reeked of limitation.

Malcolm could move among the echoes of the past with a freedom the other Restarters could only dream of. Indeed, they could only access The White Lodge – where he currently found himself – if he alone *chose* to take them there.

It was off limits to the more conventional brand of Restarters, and only accessible by him due to the mind-frazzling paradox caused, presumably, by him having taken his own life when he had switched off his own life support. At least, that's what he had told them…

Malcolm reasoned that his unrestricted access to such a place was clearly only granted to him thanks to the fact he could not affect or interact with the real world in any tangible way.

He had learned, thanks to their recent altercation, that he could whisper sweet nothings in his own ear just like his "Dark Restarter" self was penchant to, forcing his alive-self in the past to do his bidding. But Future Malcolm felt confident that was a trick he could only perform once. His younger, darker-self had far more of a hold on his living body that he now had.

As Malcolm approached the boundary line on the outskirts of the Fir Lodge Nexus that doubled as a Restart Point in Hal and Kara's current phase, his mind raced at what rules the same location abided by in this alternate universe, that both existed between the land of the living, and the land of the dead.

He stopped short in hesitation, deliberating over what the ramifications would be if he stepped over the threshold, into the netherworld beyond. Across the line in the sand that represented the adhesive bond which held the past, present and future together like a pliable but unbreakable glue.

Those living in the present, outside of the confines of this thirty-three-hour time bubble, could surely not be influenced by his presence in their world, though he feared time itself would not be so forgiving by the potential loophole he was attempting to exploit.

Future Malcolm felt a rush of fear, wondering if he would simply disintegrate.

What if his essence, his *spirit* – or whatever the scientific or metaphysical term for his now wraith-like existence was these days – was eviscerated if he attempted to leave? Or perhaps he would simply be returned to Hal, Kara and Fearne? Or would he single-handedly break the universe entirely, sending time into a spasm of irreparable chaos?

He sniffed stalling for, of all things, time…and smiled.

He knew Harold's true reason for sending him on this nonsensical voyage, of course.

His incessant claims that viewing the future would somehow yield vital information on how to escape their purgatorial prison?

Utter nonsense.

It was clear as the sky on a first restart to him that Hal's… "*Harold's*," he corrected, true motive was solely to use the opportunity to fish around the dark lakes inside the killer's head, looking for answers on Malcolm's true…*raison d'etre*.

He had prepared for this very eventuality,

obviously.

Ever since he first heard Peter mutter about how the transference of thought via the medium of telepathy, brought on by extended contact and the sharing of the energy that fuelled them all in this cursed place.

And he had prepared.

Admirably so.

Despite the onslaught of Fearne's emotions, which admittedly ran him through his paces, he had focused intently on showing whichever one of them it was that was trying to probe his thoughts – Harold, presumably. It was *classic* Harold – exactly what they *needed* to see in order to nudge them, ever-so-slightly, towards the endgame.

His endgame.

The key to his release. The end to *all* of this.

And the end, not that it mattered, to those that had placed their admittedly reluctant trust in him.

Knowing there was far more to come in the approaching restarts, he took comfort in possessing the memories of events that were yet to transpire, his resolve suddenly fortified by the fact that the future literally couldn't function without him, and walked without doubt across the duplicated boundary line of the nexus that contained him.

Maybe there was more to this idea than the laughable attempt at subterfuge Harold was trying to facilitate…

"One small step for a damned man," he thought,

as he stepped across the invisible line, waiting for the rushing air or the black liquid-like tentacles of death to wrap themselves around his un-beating heart and drag him into the chasm of eternity, intent on punishing him. To torture him for his unwillingness to follow the rules of his extended parole. A reprieve that time had selflessly afforded him, and that he was now abusing…

It was therefore, understandably anti-climactic when nothing happened at all.

He was simply…*there*.

Standing on the other side of the boundary line, a mere leaf in the cosmic winds of self-perpetuating time, unwatched, unseen and unmonitored.

At least that's how it appeared at first, as he looked back towards the bubble that contained countless iterations of both himself and his frien–

'Steady, Malcolm,' he said out loud, reprimanding his sub-conscious for having the audacity to even whisper that type of terminology when describing *The Restarters*.

He held up the gun that had been gifted to him by Harold and marvelled at the paradox; surely it should have dematerialised, catapulted back to its rightful owner as soon as he crossed the invisible barrier?

And yet, here it was, the chrome refusing to reflect the insidious whiteness that surrounded him. The nexus was nothing if not full of unexpected quirks when it came to the objects that were tangled in the web of reality on a quantum level.

As if in direct response to his slip in vocabulary, or perhaps brought on by the anomaly of the gun itself, the world he had been trapped in became increasingly opaque, like a car windscreen steaming up due to rivalling temperatures from either side of the glass that separated Malcolm from the present and past, until eventually his vision was entirely obscured.

The complete lack of visual stimulation sent a surge of panic through him, as he turned frantically on the spot to look out at the brave new world he may or may not have been granted access to, and heard his own sharp intake of breath as the unnaturally-pristine white hue began to fill with colour, like droplets of paint colliding with water and spreading outwards, unleashing a glorious technicolour into everything they came into contact with.

His concerns on wondering just how he would be able to pull himself out of the nexus in order to re-enter a notably more solidified timeline – what with there surely being no disembodied arcs of electricity for him to latch onto on this side of the boundary line, blue or otherwise – were quickly dispelled.

Time, it seemed, had taken care of that for him.

Future Malcolm had no need to find an anchor; he had *become* one.

Struggling to tear his eyes away from the overwhelmingly glorious sight of the *real* world, he snapped his head back towards the white screen of the Restart Point, which was now as innocuous and vibrant as what lay behind him.

He chuckled in disbelief, and then descended into full blown hysterics.

'I'm free?' he muttered. 'I'm...I'm free!' he shouted, screaming the words at the top of his out-of-phase lungs, before rather embarrassingly being clipped by an oncoming red car, which sent him spinning out of the way of the numerous additional convoy of cars that had burst forth from nowhere, the drivers of which equally unfazed or even remotely aware of his presence.

Malcolm caught a glimpse of the passengers in a white car, noting that the vehicle contained both Harold and Kara, who were just arriving for the first time, en route to their stay at Fir Lodge.

'Today is Friday?!' he said aloud, as if expecting an answer from Harold or Kara themselves as they shot past him.

He felt the faintest twinge of...what? Sadness? That felt odd to him, so he decided to actively ignore the fact that, for the briefest of heartbeats, he felt unhappy that he was unable to share this moment with someone...*anyone* else.

Shifting the large knife – which he had thus far kept secret from his unlikely allies by hiding it in the forest at the beginning of each new restart, or concealed behind his apron in the earlier days – he made room for Harold's arguably useless gun, which he shoved into the waistband of his black trousers.

Despite the Restarters failed attempt at

subterfuge, Malcolm suddenly felt even more obligated to continue with the plan. He couldn't rationalise why, but if he was truly free, he felt it was the very least he could do to see this thing through to the end, eager to embark on what was surely a journey fraught with impossibility.

*

The journey was long, but made shorter by hitching lifts on coaches that had stopped for refuelling at a nearby service station, and as he made his way into the more rural areas leading to his destination, he downgraded to a form of public transport that made him glad he wasn't in-phase with the occupants; that of the county bus service.

He loathed using them, and reasoned that even the less-murderously inclined would surely have been driven to such lengths after being subjected to several short trips on them.

Despite being considerably better at applying directions to navigate the world than Harold (though to be fair, that was a universal truth; *everyone* was better at geographical traversal than Harold) it had been Kara's transferred memories that had proven most useful in getting Malcolm where he needed to be.

Indeed, having initially relied on Harold's memories, Malcolm had ended up very much lost over the course of the next 24 hours, leading him to experience panic at the thought that Sunday may just have passed him by without him ever making it to Harold's house.

But, as he walked into the quiet cul-de-sac that felt oddly like home, thanks to the residual transference of emotion-memory he had obtained from the Restarter, he finally made it.

Retrieving the small rectangular piece of plastic from his pocket, Malcolm looked down at the driver's licence for the millionth time, going over the details;

'165 Kent Street,' he said out loud, looking around the peaceful suburban surroundings, drinking in the dull and ordinary backdrop with notable contempt.

He felt exposed in the bright afternoon sun.

A man to his left was focusing intently on cleaning his expensive-looking silver car, utterly oblivious to Malcolm's presence. The former killer waved at the man, who dutifully ignored him, adding to the reassurance that he was definitely invisible.

To Malcolm's right, a door opened, and a young woman marched out onto the front grass, encumbered by a black sack of household rubbish. Hot on her heels, a small black dog followed her out, embracing unexpected freedom and sniffing along the edges of the grass, drinking in the scents of the local cats that had traversed across it the night before.

The woman lifted up the lid of a grey wheelie bin, placed the bag inside it, then headed back inside the house, which was adorned with the number 165, printed in gold writing against a jet-black plate, affixed to the light-coloured brickwork.

"Harold's home," he thought, releasing a chuckle.

CHAPTER FIFTY-SIX
Netflix and Kill

Saturday, August 25ᵗʰ, 2018

Malcolm walked briskly, taking advantage of the inexplicable serendipity of not having to wait outside forever, slipping in through the front door, as the woman called out to the dog, who was munching on some blades of grass that Harold clearly hadn't bothered to strim.

'Shelby, in now, come on,' said the woman who Malcolm would soon learn was Hal's fiancée, Jess.

As Malcolm crossed the threshold, he felt a sense of temporal dissonance wash over him.

When *was* he exactly?

Shelby stopped at the door and looked up to him, continuing to chomp on a long blade of grass that had got caught in her back teeth, her eyes narrowing with suspicion as if trying to gauge the measure of the man who had walked into her home.

Inhaling the remainder of her snack, Shelby emitted a guttural growl, as if warning him to behave, then burped at him. She waddled past the time traveller, and shook from head to tail, his presence having generated a shiver deep within her, as Jess closed the door behind them.

Future Malcolm followed Jess into her kitchen and watched with fascination as she popped the kettle on, moved towards the stainless-steel sink and rinsed any residual bin juice from her hands.

He glanced to his right, where a calendar was pinned against the back of the kitchen door; a calendar with a picture of Shelby chasing bubbles stared back at him, but it was the image beneath that held true value.

All other days leading up to the 25th of August had a line through them, the words "Hal Fir Lodge" written in the unmarred square in a bubble-gum-pink permanent marker.

"Remarkable," he thought, smiling to himself at the irony that the calendar contradicted the use of the word.

He had not only travelled to a location that had been incepted into his brain by a time traveller, but – relatively speaking – had also travelled not into the future, but to the present of the current restart he and his temporally-displaced allies…"acquaintances?"

were occupying.

Any reservations he may have held that this was all just a coma-induced hallucination were finally debunked. He had no prior knowledge of this place, or this woman, or the creature that had just given him a burp-laced warning to follow the rules whilst on the dog's turf.

He thought on that for a moment, before the most fantastical observation of all manifested in his mind as a cold, hard fact; the mundane events playing out before him were surely occurring in tandem with what they were experiencing back at Pentney Lakes.

This meant that the world outside of their bubble of time was operating in parallel with their plight.

He mused over how this specific date was largely immune to their meddling. This day would play out exactly as destiny dictated. Indeed, it was tomorrow, Sunday the 26th of August, that was open to obliteration and alteration.

With little else to do, he made himself at home, Jess utterly oblivious to the fact that she was now house-sharing with a serial killer.

A murderer, no less, that had killed her actual fiancé more times than she had told Hal to get off his phone in the past week.

*

Malcolm and Jess streamed movies together, took the dog for a walk, spent some time on a video-call with her parents and generally doing a mish-mash of other ordinarily bland things.

Ordinary, that was, with the exception that Jess was none the wiser he was even there.

Shelby, on the other hand, was considerably less inviting.

When she wasn't growling or barking in his general vicinity, she was sitting in her bed staring at the man who smelt oddly like the colour red.

Shelby knew, deep down, that her dad would not be happy about him being here.

Her animal instincts flared under the certainty of that.

But there was nothing she could do about it, besides protect her mum the only way she knew how.

Whilst Malcolm maintained a notable level of respect when Jess showered and changed, Shelby held the line, making sure she kept between him and Jess at all times, acting like a sentinel charged with protecting a person of interest and not *once* taking her eyes off the killer. As she munched her dinner, not even the allure of food could pull her away from keeping one wary eye on the uninvited time-travelling house guest.

It was during a particularly mundane episode of MasterChef that Jess was bizarrely engrossed in – specifically the part of the show Malcolm was learning he despised the most; where each judge proceeded to eat the food, quietly emoting how great everything tasted, lips slapping together to the dulcet tones of cutlery clinking against ceramics. The act inadvertently making a pretty good argument in

Malcolm's favour for why his "work" may have actually merited advocation – that Malcolm decided to broach the subject with Shelby.

'Have I not proven myself to be honourable, Shelby?' said Malcolm, as Shelby panted, her ears tweaking in response to the utterance of her name. 'Your…*father* sent me here himself. You can relax.'

Shelby growled, then moved away from him, jumping from the sofa and onto her bed, before placing her head on her paws, desperate for sleep but knowing her work was not done, her heavy eyelids fluttering every few minutes as she tried desperately to fight the urge to close them.

*

It was during the fourth episode of Grey's Anatomy that Malcolm developed a notable sense of Stockholm syndrome, becoming as emotionally invested in Doctor Owen Hunt's past as he was in determining whether or not being here was actually more of a purgatory than the restarts he had left behind.

With the setting of the sun, Jess tried a second time to phone Harold to no avail, before heading into the garden to blow some bubbles for Shelby's amusement, filming their antics and sending the video to him.

Malcolm watched, feeling awkwardly in the way, as Jess tidied the house and prepared herself for bed, and resigned himself to the decision of sleeping on the couch. Not that he could have made it upstairs with Shelby blocking the doorway, hackles raised, refusing to answer Jess's call to come to bed.

Malcolm sighed.

'I promise I will stay down here, little dog. Go to bed.'

Shelby sniffed, shook off her stress, then panted for a second. She looked to her left towards the staircase, back at Malcolm, then reversed awkwardly from the room before heading upstairs, where she continued to stand guard on the edge of the bed until her heavy eyes grew too much for her.

Malcolm waited until the early hours of Sunday morning, noting the wall clock.

"3am."

Not needing to sleep in his current form, he stood up and stretched unnecessarily.

The red light on the motion detector of Jess's dog camera situated on the mantle-piece sprung to life and, for a moment, he wondered if the crude technology had just detected his presence.

*

Jess's phone pinged with an alert tone, which she recognised as a notification bouncing through the ether from their downstairs webcam they had installed to check in on Shelby whilst they attended their unavoidable adulting duties knows as "day jobs".

She opened the app, more out of boredom than to check if there was a burglar, though deep down she did feel uneasy.

The camera often detected false readings of movement, but as the image loaded, she was slightly unsettled by what she saw; a bright white mass of light that appeared to be standing in front of her sofa.

She knew the camera took still-frame shots, and suspected it was just picking up a moth.

Probably a moth.

Placing her phone back on her bedside table, Jess reached out for her glass of water, downing it with the grace of a sailor. She looked over to Shelby, who was clearly relishing the extra space afforded to her by Hal's absence and taking up the entirety of Hal's pillow, dead to the world.

Her phone spoke again, and she grabbed it to check the second image that had just been captured; notably humanoid in shape, the intensity of the light dominating the room, without actually illuminating it.

Shelby awoke with a start, and growled.

*

Early that Sunday afternoon, Malcolm was busying himself with checking the balance of his blade, which see-sawed gently as he teased it to topple off his fingers, reasserting his mastery over the weapon at the last moment and starting the process all over again, as Shelby perked up. Malcolm raised an eyebrow, noticing as an internal struggle took hold of Jess's protector.

Shelby stared at the killer, then at the front door, then back to Malcolm, sensing the impending arrival of Hal well before Jess and the time traveller in front of her, before emitting a whine of confliction.

Sure enough, a car pulled up on the driveway

shortly after, causing Malcolm to marvel at her phenomenal senses. He was beginning to understand why people invited these creatures into their lives, and felt a sudden pang of an emotion he couldn't quite get a handle on, but that he ultimately defined as wistful melancholy.

'It's okay. You've done admirably. Off you go.'

Shelby huffed at him, darting from the sofa to the door and whined for attention, not for the first time resenting the fact she couldn't open doors without human aid.

Malcolm hoisted himself up from the dining room chair, which refused to grumble under his weight, and made his way into the kitchen to gain a glimpse through the window of what he knew must surely have been Harold, returning from his stay at Fir Lodge.

A partially transparent tendril of black fog slithered across the floor of the kitchen, almost sentient in the way it seemed to hone in on him, attempting to wrap itself around his ankle, but Malcolm merely stepped over it.

'Not yet,' he muttered, watching Harold intently through the window, as the one named Jasmine killed the engine, and his own would-be killer leapt from the passenger seat, making his way to the boot of the car.

Heading into the hallway, Malcolm rolled his eyes as Harold uttered muffled thanks to the driver. Why people felt inclined to drag out social exchanges such as these was a mystery to him.

Jess flitted down the stairs, rushing through Malcolm and indulging in a shiver as she opened the door that Shelby was huffing at, allowing the Staffordshire bull terrier to make a bolt for the outside world.

Malcolm peered around the door frame, watching as she jumped at her dad incessantly.

'Ha-ha, I've missed you *too* girl, get orf me!' said Hal, but Shelby refused to listen, continuing to wag her tail regardless.

Realising Hal was going to be a while, Jess stepped onto the grass, giving him a hug, then chatted to Jasmine, whilst Shelby rolled onto her back, legs kicking into the air eager for attention.

Hal let out a sigh of contentment as he rubbed Shelby's belly.

'Feels like I've been gone a year!'

'You've only been gone since Friday, weirdo,' said Jess, shooting him a wink that held no meaning to Malcolm.

Love, perhaps?

Malcolm ducked out of the way, pressing himself against the wall of the hallway as Hal made his way into the house and switched on the kettle, Jess closing the door behind him.

'Coffee pleeeeease,' she shouted, as she shot off into the living room out of sight.

Hal glared upwards, grunting under his breath, but secretly smiling. For what reason, Malcolm had no idea. This entire dynamic was entirely alien to him.

Encumbered with a cup of coffee in each hand, Hal made his way to the living room, walking straight through Malcolm, who failed miserably to get out of the way in time.

Hal shivered, spilling some of his hot beverage, the liquid within his cup sloshing over the side and onto the carpet.

Malcolm raised an eyebrow, as the snake-like wisps of black fog lurking behind Hal retreated immediately, pulled back into the alternate dimension from whence they came. At the exact moment Hal passed through Malcolm's chest, a flash of red manifested briefly, topping up his out-of-phase body.

The killer flexed his fingers, feeling invigorated, albeit marginally, and wondered if it was possible Hal's alive-self had been altered somehow…that perhaps his numerous trips through time had imbued him with a residual reserve of Restarter energy all his own.

It begged the question; were any of them truly going to be the same on the other side if they managed to escape? Or would they be changed forever. In ways they could not yet fathom?

'Oops,' said Hal sheepishly, now behind Malcolm, rousing him from his daydream. He cursed at having lost focus, Hal now occupying the living room and in the process of passing Jess a cup of coffee.

Malcolm took up a spot in front of a large plant situated in the corner of the room, observing the two of them as they exchanged banal small talk about window cleaners, and Hal recounted his time at Fir Lodge. Or, at least, the time spent at Fir Lodge from the viewpoint of *this* version of himself.

Shelby placed herself between her parents and the unwanted spectator, unintentionally cutting their conversation short with a growl of warning.

Malcolm remained motionless, feeling oddly exposed as they turned to face him, looking him squarely in the eyes.

'What's up with Shelby?' asked Hal, taking another gulp of coffee.

'Eesh, ignore her, she's been growling at that plant all day.'

'We've had that thing for over a week now, you'd think she'd be used to it.'

'Tell me about it. Don't stop, carry on, what did I miss?!' said Jess eagerly.

As Hal continued to fill her in on everything that had happened during his stay at Fir Lodge, Malcolm stared at Shelby, who was blocking him from progressing any further towards her dad.

From the corner of the room, he looked up from her, and stared at Hal. His eyes dropped down to his left hand, and he once again inspected the pink plastic rectangle of information, reading it out loud.

'Harold Callaghan, 165 Kent Street, thirty-three years of age,' he said out loud, despite having already committed it to memory.

He looked up from Hal's driving licence, placing it back into his out-of-phase pocket, and reaffixed his gaze back to his would-be murderer. It had taken him an incomprehensible amount of time to reach this stage in his plan. Countless years spent planning his revenge, obsessing over every detail; what weapon to use, whether he would kill the orange detective first, or last.

"Better to make him watch," he had thought, all those years ago.

It suddenly dawned on him that his hand had drifted unconsciously to his waist, and was now gripping the hilt of the large blade that was tucked into his belt. Malcolm blinked to clear his mind, and then grinned, baring all of his teeth like the hungry shark of old.

Retrieving Hal's gun, he raised it towards Shelby, miming the act of pulling the trigger, and blowing the sound of a fake gunshot through his pursed lips, before smiling at her warmly.

She had proven to be something of an unexpected friend to him during his impossible journey through the Sunday that was soon to be erased.

Unable to help herself, Shelby responded by rolling onto her back, and playing dead, as if hoping to be rewarded with a treat. Malcolm having seen it was a customary reward for a trick well done in this household, Jess having done just that earlier that morning.

It felt…*odd* to Malcolm. A betrayal of his character, even. He was never one for indulging in play, least of all with dogs. Unless you counted toying with the victims of…

"*Canvasses*," he thought, correcting himself for the bizarre slip.

They had been canvasses. Nothing more.

Yet, with no one to bear witness, he found himself powerless to resist the dark urge within him, and redirected the weapon towards Jess, once again mimicking the action of firing off another pretend bullet into *her* forehead, then one at Hal, just for good measure.

Malcolm chuckled to himself.

"Much better to be up-close," he thought, as he remembered the blood that flowed from–

'*Focus* Malcolm,' he said to himself sternly, suddenly sensing that the black, liquid-like fog was reforming around him, sending his thoughts spiralling off tangentially along a path of irrelevance.

Lowering the gun back down to his side, he *felt* the darkness before it arrived.

It swirled around his body, sliding across his shoulders and coiling around his chest like an oil-drenched python, eager to claim him once more.

But he wasn't in the least bit concerned. He had achieved more than any of them had ever dreamed possible.

The all-too-familiar sound of rushing air filled his eardrums, as his surroundings were systematically obliterated from his vision, with Hal himself being the last to vanish.

Malcolm closed his eyes, realising he was about to be recaptured. Sent back to his friends. Or the closest thing he had ever had to such a thing. That he had expended the seemingly arbitrary allowance of time that had allotted for his exploration of a slice of reality he should never have been in to begin with.

'See you soon, Harold,' he whispered into the dark black fog, his words thick with iciness, and seasoned with resentment.

A resentment aimed partially at the ruthless fog that thickened all around him. An abominable anachronism acting as a proxy for time itself, wrapping around him proudly as if it had finally sought him out. And additionally, towards the sobering reality that those that trusted him would never forgive him for what came next.

Hand in pocket, the once and future Malcolm clenched the driver's licence, the sharp plastic digging into his palm, a sensation he used as a reminder that he was here, that he was real, at least in some form, as the darkness consumed him and erased him into nothingness. Sending him hurtling back into the past, with a single, simple agenda; to restart the past, and change the future.

CHAPTER FIFTY-SEVEN
The Voice in the Shadows

7,150th Restart – Saturday, August 25th, 2018

As Malcolm's body solidified and his consciousness returned, he knew immediately something was wrong. The room he had appeared in was empty, for one thing.

A first, for sure.

He flexed his fingers, the gun having vanished, and pressed against his trouser leg to feel for a driving licence that was no longer there.

The weary traveller made his way out of the abandoned cabin into what he was expecting to be dazzling sunlight, but was greeted instead by a domain thick with a static fog, mixed with the unsettling hue of twilight. Having not been returned to the beginning of his restart cycle threw him off his game, and for a brief moment he thought that perhaps he had returned to the nexus realm. But as his eyes adjusted, he realised there *was* colour in the world around him, on the fringes of his perception. It was just incredibly saturated.

'Where have *you* been,' said a familiar voice, cutting through the shadows behind him like a figure-skater turning sharply through fresh ice.

Not feeling the need to turn around, Malcolm was instantly alert all the same. In his experience, turning suddenly could lead to finding yourself intimately acquainted with the business end of blade. At least that's what his victims could attest to. Not only that, he knew the temporal dysplasia could be kept at bay as long as he didn't make eye contact whilst the impending questions rolled.

'I have been working,' he said with his face still turned away.

'How is it possible, exactly,' said the voice, smooth as silk despite the razor-blades that rested underneath, 'that you have not graced me with your presence in over three weeks?'

"Three weeks?" thought Malcolm. Surely that was impossible. He had assumed his journey into a *relative* present would have run parallel to the time loop taking place at the lakes. "Clearly," he thought as the voice continued, assuming his questioner could be trusted, "that was not the case."

'I've been watching them, in your absence.

Unbeknownst to them of course. They read your mind before you left.'

'Did you hurt them?' asked Malcolm, trying to keep his voice steady.

'That's an odd question.'

'I've been careful,' said Malcolm, changing tack.

'You've been *careless*,' said the visitor. 'I have been patient. Forced to live in your shadow under the proviso you would not…outlive your usefulness.' His interrogator released a murmur of curious disapproval.

'What's *that* supposed to mean,' said Malcolm irritably, the after-effects of his journey leaving him notably weaker than he would have liked.

'I have devised my own solution. You would do well to refrain from further intervention.'

'I need more time. Just a little longer, you need to–' began Malcolm, concerned by how methodical and concise the words being sent his way sounded. How *dangerous* they were.

'Say the word *patient* again, and not even your *age* will protect you. Your time, in every sense, is up. Now, run along. And do whatever it is you *do* here outside of delaying the inevitable.'

Malcolm turned on the spot, brandishing a glare of such intensity that he knew it would bring the insolent child to his knees for speaking to him in such a way, but the entity had vanished.

Presumably into the future. Or present. Or even a nearby hedge.

Malcolm sighed, knowing it made little difference, and set off to find those of a far more hospitable disposition.

*

Malcolm had checked everywhere, but was perturbed to discover there was no sign of the Restarters at all amidst the bleak surroundings.

Over the past few hours he had checked Fir Lodge, their makeshift campsite, and various other key locations they could have been holing up; including Kevin's, and as a last-ditch effort even neighbouring lodges, for the faintest trace of either Hal, Kara or Fearne.

I have devised my own solution.

The words echoed through his mind.

"So soon?" he thought. He had expected it to take longer to reach this point, before remembering it had been years already, and truly long enough.

The impatient child in the shadows would cool off.

He always did.

'Where *are* you?' he muttered to the wilderness, once again coming up empty.

He had at least managed to ascertain that it was currently Saturday. As he returned for a second time to the clearing that had become their base of operations, he was greeted by the sound of a sickly click, and the feel of metal against the back of his head, which felt soothingly cold thanks to being in-phase with him.

Malcolm turned, welcomed by the sight of a gun barrel millimetres away from his left eyeball, which was being held by a very pissed-off looking Kara.

Hal and Fearne had flanked him from either side, creating a wall behind him, and gradually moved towards him, closing into a tighter circle. All three of them had a look of power about them, and Malcolm realised they had obviously built a charge.

'Not quite the welcome home I was expecting,' he said in a tone as dry as yesterday's mashed potato.

'But more than the welcome you deserve,' said Kara. 'Just so you know, if it were up to me I'd have pulled the trigger as soon as you popped up, but Hal convinced me to wait, on the off chance it was really you and not your past-self.'

'Thank you, Harold,' said Malcolm. 'Your fiancée and animal are fine by the way.'

'We'll get to that in a minute,' Hal's eyes clearly showing a notable mix of *wonder* that a plan guaranteed by its very design to fail had actually worked, and *fear* over giving his home address to a serial killer.

Kara glanced over and noted Hal's expression was the same look of dread one might display after realising a psychotic ex-girlfriend had acquired the login details for all of your social media accounts.

'You can put the gun down now, Kara,' more than a hint of warning in Malcolm's tone. 'It's not as if it can do any real harm.'

'I don't know, I'd reason a gas-propelled metal

ball-bearing at point-blank range could do notable damage to an eyeball…'

Malcolm grinned, narrowing his eyes as if attempting to stare directly into her soul.

She reaffirmed her grip, ready for firing.

'It's been three weeks since you left,' began Hal, eager to diffuse the tension somewhat, knowing that testing Kara was not the smartest of moves on Malcolm's part. 'We didn't think you'd come back.'

'It seems you haven't quite been the beacon of honesty and transparency you were selling yourself as,' said Kara.

Malcolm sighed, assuming they were referring to the thoughts Hal had gleaned from him.

'Good show Harold, very clever. How much did you see?'

'What?' said Hal, having all but forgotten that, given how much time had passed. 'This isn't about the little mind-meld exercise. It's about past-you. Dark Restarter you. He's been stalking us since you left!'

'Yeah,' said Kara. 'He kept saying the end was coming.'

'Hardly news,' said Malcolm, dismissing it immediately.

'There's more,' said Fearne quietly. 'He knows you're here Malcolm. He said…he said we're going to die and you've already seen how it happens.'

Malcolm grumbled in acknowledgement of the inconvenience of that.

'The fog seems to have...intensified...' noted Malcolm.

'It took hold pretty quick a few restarts after you left,' said Kara.

'If there are things you haven't told us,' said Hal, pressing the issue, 'now's the time to talk Malc'.'

Malcolm cleared his throat.

It was hard to argue with how his past-self knowing his future-self was *here* changed things.

'Of *course* there are things I've kept from you! From *all* of you. I have just as much to lose if my past-self is left unabated. If we fail here, the future my past-self is so focused on creating *will* come to pass. I have spent a year reviewing where his actions will lead us all, looking for a loophole that we can expose to destroy that version of myself, so that I can become *this* version of myself.' Malcolm offered up a pregnant pause to allow them to absorb the ramifications of that. 'If we do not defeat him I will *cease* to be, and then you will be left alone in the dark to fight an iteration of *me* that does not possess patience, that would not entertain — let alone *allow* — a *childish girl* to hold a *gun* to his head. So perhaps we can truly begin to take this seriously instead of wasting time fighting each other? In the hope that we can prevent the end of *all* our days? Would that be *acceptable?* Are you capable of acting like *adults* for once in your damn lives to...'

Malcolm fell to his knees, three weeks' worth of altered memories boring their way into his skull like thousands of hungry beetles.

'What's wrong?' said Kara, aiming the barrel of the gun into the sky for a moment.

Malcolm experienced another bout of debilitating anachronistic nausea, and growled in what appeared to be barely suppressed agony, before slowly lowering the palms of his hands from his temples, releasing the firm pressure he had been applying.

'No…' said Malcolm forebodingly.

'What did you see?' asked Hal, knowing an inserted memory when he saw one.

Whatever it was, it must have been big.

'*When* are we?!' asked Malcolm urgently.

'By our count, roughly our 202nd restart,' said Kara, not understanding the question.

'Not what *restart*, what *time*!' he snapped, with the same level of panic Hal often displayed when realising he'd pressed the snooze button on his alarm so many times that he was roughly 44 hours late for work.

'Just how much coffee did you drink in the future?' said Hal. 'It's Saturday, half eight-ish.'

'You need to get to Fir Lodge,' barked Malcolm. 'Now!'

Hal and Kara stared at each other, a look of "why" on their faces.

'Fearne, you're with me,' added Malcolm feverishly.

'What?' exclaimed Fearne. 'No way!'

'I can't trigger a *restart* in this form, I need one of you with me at the boundary line! Harold, Kara, delay him for as long as you can.'

How could he have been so stupid? Leaving them all like this. Changing his own past merely by his absence.

'I…' added Malcolm. Struggling to find the words. 'I had no idea so much time would pass for you all by doing this. I am…'

'*Sorry*?' said Hal, offering up the only word that fit the bill. 'You *can* say that you know? You don't have to be such a little bitch about it.'

'*Responsible*,' corrected Malcolm, not ready to make that leap.

Fifteen restarts. It may as well have been fifteen years.

'What's he planning?' asked Kara. 'What are we walking into?'

'He's going to kill you all,' said Malcolm simply. 'Every last one of you and your friends.'

'We can stop him,' said Hal casually. 'We'll leave now and prepare before he gets there.'

'You don't understand,' said Malcolm. 'It has already begun!'

Both Hal and Kara looked as if they were going to ask more questions, but seeing Malcolm this way, like a man who for the first time in his life was losing control, the wheel of time having been pulled from his white-knuckled hands and pushing him out of the vehicle…

'Just go!' barked Malcolm, not wishing to engage in a poorly timed display of democracy.

CHAPTER FIFTY-EIGHT
The Fir Lodge Massacre

202nd Restart – Saturday, August 25th, 2018, 8:27pm

The Dark Restarter watched as his alive-self stepped onto the gravel driveway of Fir Lodge. A party was in full swing, and he could sense the reluctance brewing in his doppelgänger's posture.

He leaned in close to himself, whispering tenderly into his own ear.

'No turning back. Proceed,' he said, placing his hand through his own back, causing his past-self to shiver.

It seemed to have the desired effect as he shook off the self-doubt and made his way closer to the lodge.

Malcolm strode ahead of the past incarnation of himself, satisfied that no further convincing was needed, slipped in through the side entrance and made his way up the staircase to the upper level. He grinned as the light above the dining table reflected off the phone screen, strutting happily towards it as he passed through the young man standing in his way.

Gavin shivered, his eyes darting around suspiciously, fear brewing in his heart for a reason he couldn't quite fathom.

'Something...*country* I think,' the Dark Restarter chirped, as if addressing Gavin directly.

He concentrated, placing his finger onto the phone, a solitary red spark dancing from his fingertip, as he changed what was currently playing to something far more fitting, remembering fondly the day he had learned that he could manipulate electronic devices when so close to his physical form.

As the music began, he waited until he heard it, then smiled with joy as the first scream reached his ears.

*

The Restarters, minus Future Malcolm and Fearne – who were hopefully well on their way to the Restart Point – arrived at the lodge of their shared past in record time. Just in time, in fact, to witness another Malcolm walking towards the double entrance doors of the lodge.

'Which Malcolm is that?' said Kara, hoping Hal

could somehow clarify. This was all becoming far too confusing.

Her question was answered as whichever Malcolm it was they were spying on pulled down on the door handle and let himself inside.

'Okay, said Hal, 'so that's "Alive-Malcolm." Restarter-Malcolm wouldn't be able to open the door like that.'

'Unless he's holding a charge.'

'Dammit, good point,' said Hal, realising she was right. 'Come on, let's go,' he added, running towards the now open entrance door.

Kara rushed after him, as Hal quickly pulled his phone from his pocket, lobbing it at the Malcolm who was walking in front of them. The phone passed straight through the killer's shoulder, connecting with the wall of the lodge and landing on the floor with what should have been a clatter, but wasn't a clatter at all, thanks to the soundless nature of the phone's existence.

'Well, that clears that up,' said Hal, entirely unaware of how little things were going to be cleared up at all in approximately eight seconds time. 'This is Alive Malcolm. Malcolm 1.0.'

Kara noticed how Malcolm was mumbling to himself.

'He's receiving instructions.'

'Never a good sign.'

*

August 25th 2018

Peter was interrupted mid-knock, as he tapped on Hal's door looking for a charger, when he felt a sharp pain in his chest, akin to a trapped nerve becoming rambunctious.

He looked down and saw the horrifying sight of a steel blade protruding from the centre of his body, glistening with a sickly-looking claret which he just about realised was his own blood before his body hit the floor, vaguely aware that someone was screaming from the top of the staircase behind him, just as the sound of Dolly Parton's "9 to 5" reached his ears. Regrettably he was dead before the vocals kicked in.

Will recoiled in terror, clutching his pool cue as if he had walked in on something he really wished he hadn't.

Malcolm glared at him, unknowingly mimicking his Dark Restarter-self and baring his shark-like teeth as Will scrambled backwards, losing his footing and pressing himself against the rear wall of the lodge, frozen in fear.

Past-Hal came out of his bedroom to see what all the fuss was about as the very real Malcolm span on his heel, closing the gap like a hungry velociraptor. In a move notably un-raptor-like, he placed Hal in a headlock before slitting his throat with all of the compassion of someone cutting a loose thread on a T-shirt.

Hal clutched at his neck, trying to stop the life from escaping his body as Malcolm discarded him against the wall of the corridor. The last thing Hal could think of as he fell to his knees being how he hadn't heard this song in ages.

*

202nd Restart

The Restarters observed Malcolm's murder of both Peter and Hal's younger selves, unable to do anything but watch as he continued to unleash hell in the physical world. A billowing crack of thunder blasted through the sky above them, attacking Hal and Kara's eardrums with all the discretion of man attempting to jump over a chained gangway in a supermarket but misjudging the barrier's height by a few inches and colliding with the floor, with only the carton of eggs he had been clutching to break his fall.

"That was a really shit day," thought Hal, remembering that particular shopping trip all too well.

'What was that?!' said Kara, looking upwards to the ceiling.

'Maybe it's me?' said Hal.

'I doubt that, unless you've been moonlighting as Zeus in your downtime?'

'Funny. Not me *literally*. I mean, I'm not meant to die yet. If I die *now*, how can I be here now when—'

But his thought was cut short, as a static fog rolled over the hedges outside the lodge and crept into the building through the open door on the opposite side of the room, on the prowl for something.

"Or someone," thought Hal, taking a tentative step backwards.

'What does Malcolm think he's doing?!' shouted Kara above a second crack of thunder.

'Working theory? I guess he figures if he takes everyone off the board…'

'There won't *be* a board to worry about anymore…'

Kara was unable to deny it was smart, despite being literal overkill.

'Oh my crap,' muttered Hal, spotting a second Malcolm at the top of the staircase on the floor above him.

Hal dragged Kara by her arm, pulling her out of view to the side of the front entrance doors, their bodies pressed awkwardly against each other, as the energy from their contact crackled between them.

She looked into his eyes, searching for an explanation, noting the wildness within them as he glared intently over her right shoulder.

Thanks to their proximity to each other, coupled with the charge they now shared, she caught a brief waft of his aftershave.

Kara was about to pull away and ask what the hell he was doing, until she too craned her head around the corner of the door and saw exactly why he had grabbed her so abruptly.

*

The Dark Restarter jumped down the stairs, barking a laugh.

'That's the *spirit*, Malcolm!' he shouted to himself, a delirious edge to his voice. 'Behind you. Top left.'

His past-self subliminally acknowledged the instruction from his Restarter-self just as Jon brought down the pool cue hard, aiming for Malcolm's head.

Malcolm dodged the incoming attack, and it collided instead with his shoulder causing the killer to growl ferociously in agitation. He lashed out in response, his duel-wielded blades flashing at an alarming speed.

Jon moved to his right, grabbed the wrist of his assailant, then used Malcolm's own momentum against him, pulling him forward and sending him stumbling towards the staircase, which Malcolm grabbed to support himself.

'He's your biggest threat, Malcolm,' the Dark Restarter warned himself. 'Take him out quickly, and the rest will fall easily.'

Alive-Malcolm nodded, seemingly understanding the trans-dimensional instructions he was receiving, assuming it was his own inner-monologue that was behind the wheel, rather than that of his malevolent time-travelling counterpart.

Jon and Malcolm began circling each other, walking around the staircase, which Jon was using as a shield of sorts. A shield that simply couldn't last forever.

*
202nd Restart

Hal and Kara ran to the side of the lodge, the latter freezing on the spot, peering up to the balcony, an idea forming.

'Give me a boost,' said Kara.

Hal shrugged, and placed his hand on her shoulder, the displaced energy causing her to recoil.

It was far more powerful this close to the lodge, and she remembered her alive-self must have been mere metres away in the kitchen.

'Not *that* kind of boost, the other kind!' said Kara, jerking her head in the direction of the balcony.

'Oh, my bad.'

Hal squatted down and nodded his head at his clasped hands indicating he was ready for her to place her foot into them.

With the extra height afforded by Hal's assistance, she attempted to gain purchase on the floor above her, her fingers a few inches short from success.

'Higher,' she said,

'I'm trying, you're…heavier than I–'

'Oh no you don't. Don't you *dare* put this on me! It's not my fault you never work out.'

'Fair point.'

And with a concerted effort fuelled by not wanting to look as weak as he was, Kara was finally able to grab at the lip of the balcony with her fingertips, before awkwardly pulling herself up and over the wooden barrier.

'Now what,' said Hal, sending the words up to her in a whisper devoid of sense, what with it being louder than if he had just said the words normally.

'Head around the side. I'll keep an eye on the top floor.'

Hal saluted sarcastically, but Kara had already moved inside, and he huffed at the wasted effort.

Darting around the rear side of the lodge, he glanced through the rear side-entrance doors, the mirrored layout of the lodge mercifully offering a multitude of entry points, and ducked down low as he dashed across the doorway, now back-to-back with Will, both of them separated by the wall of the building.

Hal closed his eyes and concentrated.

'Come on Will, get involved mate!' his words only a whisper as they left his lips, but that of a scream in the form of his projected thoughts.

*

August 25th, 2018

Will shook his head, the fogginess clouding his thoughts expelled by an idea that had just been incepted into his brain.

The monster before him had his back to him, and Will realised now was the time to act.

'Come on Will, get involved mate,' he said to himself.

Clutching the pool cue tightly, he bellowed a

poorly conceived war cry that was completely out of character for him. Pool cue raised, he sought to bring it down ferociously on their unexpected guest, but Malcolm had been granted an advanced preview of Will's intentions, thanks to him announcing his arrival and diminishing even the faintest trace of elemental surprise.

Malcolm casually stepped to the left of his hapless attacker, dropping the knife in his left hand, and grabbed the pool cue from Will with a growl. Meanwhile, Jon took advantage of Will's distraction, ceasing their game of musical staircases, running towards his would-be killer at full speed.

Malcolm turned back to face Jon, swiping savagely at his forearm with his second blade, a sickly red spewing from the wound, before sending his knife-wielding fist into Jon's stomach, winding him so completely that it brought him to his knees.

*

202nd Restart

Finding it difficult to see, what with the ever-increasing fog clouding his vision, Hal seized the moment; with both the Dark Restarter barking orders and regular vanilla-flavoured Malcolm facing away from him – currently occupied with tackling Jon head on – the Restarter made a break for the communal staircase, taking advantage of the chaos.

Hal had never been more thankful for his soundless footsteps, affording him a level of stealth he never would have got away with in the real world. He winked at Kara as he met up with her at the top of the stairs.

Kara, having made her way past the large oak dining table, stopped at top of the communal staircase and allowed him to pass, staring down in horror, as she noticed the Dark Restarter turning over a black object in his hand.

'Shit,' said Kara.

The jig was up.

The Malcolm pulling the strings of the murderous puppet the occupants of Fir Lodge were currently facing knew both she and Hal were here, as his alive-self surged onwards under the instruction of systematically eliminating their friends in the past.

'We have to do something,' said Kara, 'This is…this is a massacre!'

The Dark Restarter looked up at Kara from the bottom of the stairs, then to Hal, smiling horrifically and extending his arms as if gesturing at everything that was unfolding, shrugging as if he had just been caught eating the last Rolo. The killer mouthed several words at them being sure to enunciate so they could lip read without hindrance. "You're too late."

'What can we do?! said Hal, swatting away a persistent swirl of irksome fog.

Kara frowned. 'What's with *you*?'

'Just the fog.'

'What fog?' asked Kara, her frown transforming into a look of worry.

Everything seemed crystal clear to her. Truth be told, the sheet of fog had retreated considerably since she'd been pressed against him at the side of the lodge, the remaining wisps eradicated entirely following the charge she had drawn from him giving her a leg up onto the balcony.

'Jon won't last long,' said Hal, totally missing the concern in her voice, far more preoccupied with stealing another glance downstairs, just as Alex entered the fray. 'Ahh fuck.'

*

August 25th, 2018

Alex sauntered past the pool table, blissfully unaware of what was going down, before freezing on the spot, drinking in the sight before him; Alex stared at Will, then Malcolm, then back to Jon, who was doubled over on the floor trying to catch his breath and losing a worrying amount of what Alex's brain struggled to reconcile as being blood.

Alex clenched his fists and was about to ask just what the hell was going on and who this man was, but was prevented from doing so thanks to Malcolm's lightning-quick reflexes.

Malcolm flipped the knife in his right hand, catching it by the blade end, then drew his arm back, launching the weapon towards Alex, the fluid traversal of the knife ending abruptly on account of it being obstructed by Alex's heart.

Will suddenly felt a pang of shame at the mixed

emotions he was experiencing; on the one hand, what he had witnessed showed a level of practise and expertise that generated authentic awe. On the other, his mate Alex now had a blade embedded firmly in his chest.

Alex collapsed into a heap on the floor, as Will, now unarmed, turned back to face their attacker, instinctively taking a step back in horror.

'Listen man, we can…we can *talk* about this?' Will's words more a plea bargain than a statement, and his tone that of a man who had accidentally swooped in to a parking space someone had clearly been waiting for, as evidenced by the flashing indicators that sung "back the hell off" to all that thought they would try their luck, leaving Will now floundering to prevent an all-too-British passive-aggressive confrontation from occurring.

'Pool cue, Malcolm. Pay attention,' whispered the Dark Restarter once again into the ear of his past-self.

The Malcolm of the past nodded, snapped the pool cue in half as if it were a mere Twiglet, and plunged the jagged, splintered wood into Will's neck, pulling it out and sending arterial spray arcing over his own head, making impromptu wall art on the wood structure around him.

Malcolm dropped the bloodied wood to the floor and it landed with a ringing hollow clatter.

With half a pool-stick in one hand, Malcolm leant down and picked up his second knife from the floor with the other, noting that Jon was crawling away to the entrance doors of Fir Lodge.

The killer smiled savagely.

'Where do you think *you're* going?' the Dark Restarter cooed, clearly amused, his words repeating through his past-self's mouth so Jon could hear them.

Jon's eyes widened with urgency as he looked with faltering, blurred vision back towards the man striding towards him. Not through fear for his own life, but for that of Rachel's, who had been hiding in the en-suite bathroom of her bedroom up until this point, and was now attempting to sneak up behind the killer with the discarded remnant of a splintered, blood-soaked pool cue shaking within her firm grip, as adrenaline took over her body.

Jon tried to keep his eyes locked on Malcolm, as the mother of his unborn child snuck across the room in an attempt to save him.

A decision that was already sending countless ripples across time. Innumerable flutterbys that would change their family dynamic forever, as well as altering the shared future of billions.

CHAPTER FIFTY-NINE

Memento Mori?

202nd Restart – Saturday, August 25th, 2018, 8:36pm

Kara span around and bolted to her doppelgänger, who was currently pressed against the kitchen sink, not knowing what to do or how to help her friends below.

"Still time," she thought, contemplating drawing a charge from her alive-self.

Maybe then they could influence the events that were unfolding.

Thrusting her hand into the duplicated copy of her own body she did just that, in a last-ditch effort to draw *something* from herself.

Anything.

She noted the familiar shrill sound that indicated she was now drawing a charge. Her mouth filling with the taste of the colour blue.

'Kara!' Hal shouted, causing her to look over her shoulder far too late, as Malcolm grabbed her physical-body by the shoulders.

Kara could do nothing but watch, taking in the surreal sight of seeing her own body being thrown down the stairs, her corporeal-self colliding with the wall at the bottom with a grim crunch.

The man pressed on, about to make his way towards Jasmine, before being summoned to return downstairs.

'Hal, come on, we need a charge!'

'There's no time, Kara,' he replied, wafting his hand across his face as if fighting off a wasp she couldn't see. 'You need to get to the Restart Point and end this now!'

'Why me?' asked Kara, less than eager to leave Hal behind. 'Fearne's on the case already.'

'Something must have happened…' He didn't want to think of what. 'You're the fastest out of both of us,' reasoned Hal, remembering how she could move almost as fast as light itself if she really set her mind to it.

'That was a long time ago,' mumbled Kara, realising that he was referring to her minor meltdown on that fateful restart, where she had tried to escape the confines of their time bubble.

Without warning, the air around them began to crackle, as a thousand tiny grains of electrified sand swam into a frenzy, forming a shape.

'What now?!' said Kara snappily.

Will appeared next to them with a short-but-punchy rush of temporally-displaced air, followed by yet another alarmingly-loud crack of thunder from above them.

Hal and Kara looked upwards in unison, wondering what the hell was forming above the lodge.

'Oh, hey guys!' said Will happily, though looking a bit confused over how he had ended up here with them. 'Fancy a game of pool, Hal?'

Hal and Kara shared a look, rolling their eyes in unison, both realising that their problems were exacerbating wildly.

'Are you kidding me?' said Hal, as yet another curveball landed onto their plate;

Their slaughtered friends were beginning to re-materialise. Reappearing in a terrifyingly familiar form…

'They're Restarting!" blurted Kara, gulping audibly.

'Wow, *this* can't be good,' said Hal helpfully.

'Ya think?'

'What do we do?' squeaked Hal in a moment of high-pitched delirium.

'Sooo, is that a no for pool?' said Will sadly.

'Really not a good time right now Will,' said Hal. 'This doesn't make any sense,' he added, turning back to Kara. 'Why aren't they reappearing thirty-three hours ago in the past?'

'You're forgetting the *first* time. The first time, we reformed moments after our death.'

Hal slapped his forehead.

'Kara! Hal!' said Alex, springing up next. 'What brings you guys here? Surely not another time travel board meeting and–'

'Time travel *what* now?' said Will, looking utterly dumbfounded.

Alex raised an eyebrow.

'Umm, is Will *meant* to be able to see us?'

'Who even *knows* anymore,' said Hal despondently, pressing down on the corners of his eyes with pinched fingertips, before dragging them across his immortal stubble, and turning his frown upside down with relief, thankful for the small mercy of his brother retaining all of his memories from his previous time spent as a Restarter.

'Boys,' said Kara. 'Enough chit-chat, in case you hadn't noticed everyone's dying and restarting and we've got a fuckton of Malcolm's to deal with.'

'Uh, guys?' said Rachel joining the fray, oddly holding a pool cue.

'Holy–' said Hal, jumping in fright. 'Everyone back up! We need time to think! It's hard enough with all this fog!'

'Hal, *what* fog?!' exclaimed Kara.

And just like that, Hal and Kara's usually quiet slice of time was quickly becoming far too crowded, busier and louder than it had ever been as everyone started to converge and converse, two distinct groups forming of their own volition; those that knew how bad this was, and those that had no idea of what a restart even was.

'Quiet!' shouted Kara, cutting through their chatter, ushering in a brief moment of silence.

'Wow, Restarter Code Red,' said Alex.

Kara had never considered what a Restarter Code Red would look like, but as she looked around at the group, each of them looking to her and Hal with expectant eyes, she realised it would surely look a lot like this.

She took a deep breath, noting that the Dark Restarter was staring up at them, seemingly deciding on his next course of action whilst whispering sweetly into his own ear to finish off Jon, now that his past-self had nipped back downstairs, granting Jasmine a few extra moments of allowance to inhale air.

'Right,' said Kara. 'Malcolm's killing us all, Fearne is attempting to trigger a restart, *Dolly Parton* is playing on *repeat* for some goddamn reason and if we don't put an end to this quickly, all of us are going to be very *dead*, *very* soon! Get it? Got it? Good. Any questions?'

Will licked his lips, torn by the obvious rhetorical nature of the question and his desire to know more.

Kara sighed. 'What *is* it Will?'

'Oh, just...who's *Malcolm*?'

*

202nd Restart – 1 Minute ago

The Dark restarter smiled, turning the restarted phone in his palm, discarding it with contempt.

For it to be there, the *rat-catcher* and *the orange secretary* had to be also.

Always meddling.

The killer turned and looked up the stairs finally catching sight of the Restarting double act, and mouthed the words "You're too late", slowly and cleanly.

Deciding to abandon his current plan, he whispered to his alive-self.

'Up the stairs, the orange one next.'

Malcolm's alive-self attempted to ignore the instruction, instead yanking the pool cue from his hip and applying pressure to the stab-wound in his side, somewhat overloaded by the incessant nagging of his inner-voice.

Having just dispatched with Rachel – her fingers having slipped from the cue she had thrust into his body as he choked the life out of her – he continued onwards towards the man crawling along the floor

"Malcolm," he found himself thinking, the voice far sterner and more authoritative this time. "Leave him."

The killer growled, frustrated by his contradicting thoughts, but knew better than to second-guess his own instincts, and turned away from Jon to make his way up the staircase.

The Dark Restarter waited patiently, as Kara's body flew down the stairs shortly after and into the wall, landing with a beautiful crunch.

He was about to make Jasmine his next target, but grew concerned by Jon, and how he appeared to be stemming the flow of blood from his arm with a makeshift tourniquet made from the shirt he had just removed.

'Back here,' shouted Malcolm, and his alive-self trundled back down the staircase.

He glared up at Harold and Kara once again, raising a curious eyebrow at the gaggle of friends now standing by their side, and grinned. The sound of Jon's gurgles music to his ears, as his alive-self set about strangling him.

"Time to finish this," he thought, gesturing for alive-Malcolm to ascend the staircase.

*

202nd Restart – 8:37pm

They watched as the Dark Restarter version of the man Will had just asked about looked up at them from the bottom of the stairs, and Hal did the honours of introducing them.

'Will, meet Malcolm. He's a time travelling serial killer that likes big knives, rubber aprons, and long walks in the park on his way to dropping body-bags into the nearest river.'

The Dark Restarter gestured for his physical-self to ascend, following him up, but was caught off guard by a pleasant popping sound as a replicated version of Peter sprung into existence directly behind the two Malcolms.

'Hey,' said Peter, patting down his body and resting his hands against his pockets, 'I'm back!' he added, chuckling in amazement.

'Peter, look out!' said Kara, just as Malcolm's Restarter-self drove a blade through his back, causing him to fall to the floor, signs of disintegration already showing.

'Holy shit!' said Alex.

'Man,' said Hal, 'Peter *really* can't catch a break, can he? Maybe best we don't mention this to Fearne,' he added glumly, with a side glance to Kara, trying to wave away the fog that was getting so dense he could barely see her at all.

A fog that, unbeknownst to him, only he could see.

'Agreed,' said Kara. 'So, recap! Knives are bad. Do not get stabbed by them.'

'Noted,' said Alex.

'Hal and I are going to–*FUDGE MONKEYS!*' screamed Kara, her orders cut short thanks to the unexpected arrival of Jon, who popped up next to her, having clearly just died of his own accord thanks to the savage slice Malcolm had cut into him during their tussle. That or the strangulation. Who knew.

'Oi, Oi! That's what she said!' said Jon, replying to

Kara's fragmented sentence. 'What's everyone doing up here anyw–'

'Annnnd Jon's here,' said Hal. 'Glad you asked. We're all being unceremoniously murdered by a serial killer, you're a time traveller now, and the "beginners guide to Restarting" induction seminar is being held in the living room.'

'What?' said Jon, blinking at Hal's nonsensical rambling.

'If you hurry, there still might be some cake left,' added Hal.

'Wait,' said Kara. 'Who's down there with Malcolm?'

*

202nd Restart – 8:37pm

'Hey,' said a surly voice that caused both Malcolms to turn around on the staircase.

'Leave him,' the Dark Restarter barked, having just disposed of the Restarted golfer and eager to claim the real prize; that of Harold and Kara in their Restarter forms.

'67 Pentney Lakes,' said the voice, his words delivered with boredom into what Malcolm realised was a phone. 'Please hurry,' the man added.

Robert stared at the two killers, totally unfazed, one leg crossed in front of the other as he leant against the doorframe, arm extended, swigging the dregs of his beer from a bottle with his free hand, wearing nothing but shorts and a Santa Claus hat.

The Dark Restarter scowled at Robert, realising he must have called the police.

Which meant he was alive.

It was, admittedly, getting hard to keep track.

Cursing under his breath, Malcolm grimaced over how his plans for a quick getaway would be somewhat hindered with the involvement of outsiders.

He looked all around him, at the carnage he had wrought; so much blood. So many bodies. So much of his own DNA sprinkled about the place, thanks to the lucky stab from the one named Rachel.

And he felt ashamed. It was sloppy work. At worst, with no time to sanitise, it would lead to a manhunt.

'Fine,' spat the Dark Restarter, 'Malcolm. End him.'

His alive-self turned on the stairs and plodded back down towards Robert, who simply stood there and feigned a yawn of indifference.

'Got it all figured out, don't you,' said Robert. 'I imagine the police showing up is really going to piss on your cornflakes though, amiright?'

Malcolm's corporeal-self strode towards him, the knife gripped so tightly that his knuckles had turned white.

The killer squared up to Robert, who didn't so much as move a muscle, but instead stared right back into the murderer's dead eyes, daring the killer to blink first.

'There's just one problem. I've got a *pregnant* wife upstairs, and I'm sure as shit not about to let a *bell-end* like you touch a single hair on her body. Knife or no knife,' he added, eyeing up the man before him, paying the darker, Restarting version of Malcolm no attention at all.

Robert went in for another swig of his beverage.

Malcolm brought the knife down with tremendous force, and it ripped all the way through Robert's neck, a sickening gurgling noise filling the room.

The blade travelled onwards through his midsection, and imbedded itself firmly into the door frame of Hal's room.

Robert ceased his gargling, swallowing his mouthful of beer, then shot a wink over to the Dark Restarter.

Malcolm blinked, his mind piecing together all the answers he had sub-consciously possessed all along.

Robert being completely dry; despite having come from the hot tub where he lived.

The phone; clearly the one he had discarded earlier. The battery as dead as a Restarter.

A Restarter…like Robert.

'It's okay to face-palm like Picard,' said Robert. 'I won't tell anybody.'

'Clever boy,' The Dark Restarter conceded. 'You're one of them, aren't you. A Restarter.' It wasn't really a question.

The blade passing through him like butter and not

leaving a mark had already proven that.

'It's not my first time,' said Robert. 'Third actually. Looks like your knives can't hurt me,' he added smugly.

'*That* knife, perhaps…' said Malcolm, with a wicked flicker in his eyes, his physical-self standing tall like a sentinel waiting to be unleashed. 'But *this* one?' he added, brandishing his own out-of-phase blade, Robert having no idea how wrong he was in making that assumption.

'I was wrong…' said Robert.

'…About what?' said Malcolm, well and truly distracted.

Robert finished off his beer, spinning the restarted beer bottle in his hand, tiny droplets of out-of-phase froth hitting the floor. Outstretching his arm through Malcolm's living body, he directed the bottle towards the Malcolm he was now in-phase with, tipping the end of the container in a gesture reminiscent of a Kung Fu master summoning an adversary to try their luck, before responding with a sentence that Hal would have loved.

'Restarters.…When I said that sounded like a terrible name for a movie? It's actually not that bad.'

*

202nd Restart – 8:39pm

'Oh man, it's Robert,' whispered Alex. 'Should we go help him?'

'We should stay up here,' instructed Kara, hoping

Fearne and Future Malcolm would trigger a much-needed restart any second now.

'There's cake?' said Jon.

'Just kidding. There's never any cake, Jon,' said Hal sadly. 'The cake is a lie.'

'Erm, bro…' said Alex, addressing Hal, or more specifically Hals' *arm*, which had just turned invisible.

Dropping the sarcasm for a moment, Hal stared at his own hand, twisting it in front of his face, watching as it phased in and out of existence. 'Umm, Kar'? I'm kind of Marty Mcfly'ing over here.'

For once, Kara almost wished that was a reference she didn't get, as all of their attention was pulled away from Robert to the issue of Hal falling to literal pieces.

'Kara…I don't feel so good…Somethings wron–' but Hal's sentence was cut off like the arm he was now missing.

His whole body seemed to shake in agony as he keeled over onto the floor.

'Hal!' shouted Kara, the final syllable being drowned out by an almighty crack of thunder that caused the whole lodge to shake, forgotten fragments of wood shavings and dust showering over them all from the load bearing supports of the structure, like sprinkles of pixie dust that passed right through their bodies.

Hal heard a scream so blood-curdling that he actually would have recoiled, were it not emanating from his own voice box. Well, that and not having control of his body, which was convulsing in an agony of such intensity that he found himself wondering if a wizard had just blasted him with the Crucio curse.

The wisps of fog wrapped around his frame, as Alex tried to pull him upright.

But the hungry serpents were ruthlessly efficient.

Consuming him. Claiming him.

"Eating me," he thought deliriously.

And then his scream became muffled, as the fog flew down his throat, eager to erase his internal organs, and he realised this must have been how it had felt to Peter when he was taken.

Kara stood there, feeling utterly useless, an inconsequential onlooker. From her perspective, all she could see was her friend disintegrating into a million tiny blue shards of energy, the savagery of the fog not meant for her or Alex or anyone else's eyes, until Alex was clutching little more than a memory of his brother.

'No, no, no!' shouted Kara, as it suddenly dawned on her that if she wasn't hideously out of her depth before, she sure as shit was now.

Hal was gone.

CHAPTER SIXTY
The Santa Clause

202nd Restart – Saturday, August 25th, 2018, 8:30pm

Fearne and Malcolm travelled silently, making their way to the boundary line as quickly as they could, as Malcolm once again fell to his knees.

Fearne looked up at the night sky, pleading to be blessed with a patience she in no way felt.

'Malcolm, we need to go! Now.'

'I'm sorry I….'

'You may have *them* fooled,' said Fearne. 'But I'm not buying any of this. So get *up*, and keep *moving*!'

Malcolm pressed his palms against his temples,

indicating more memories were flooding into a fifty-eight-year-old brain housed within a forty-five-year-old body.

'Malcolm. Get. Up.'

Malcolm stopped, pulling his hands away from his head and dropping the act.

'I'm no expert on time travel, not like *Hal*,' said Fearne, the inflection of her friend's name surprisingly bitter. 'Or rather, not like Hal *pretends* to be. But I know enough about how all this works to spot a huge plot-hole in your claim that your past-self is going off script.'

'*Pretends* to be?' said Malcolm, curiously.

'Oh, you know, Hal bases his entire knowledge of our situation on movies he's seen. Chucking in the word "Temporal" and "Phased" in front of everything as often as possible to hide the fact he's just as lost as we are.'

Malcolm stood up, not bothering to dust himself down. A habit he had long since forgone unless he was trying to fool others into forgetting he was far older than he appeared to be. At least mentally.

'How long have you known?' he said calmly.

'That you're a big fat faker? Round about the time Peter died,' she said icily.

'I see.'

'There's no way in hell you didn't know that was coming. Just like all these *new* memories you keep harping on about. You've had them all along. So, cut the shit and help me restart this nightmare so we can start formulating a real plan.'

'Are you intending on telling the others?'

'Of course I bloody am! As soon as we get back. Assuming there's anything to go back *to* if you refuse to hurry up.'

'Very well,' said Malcolm.

They sized each other up.

'And before you get any ideas, you can't *touch* me, remember? You need me to trigger this restart.'

'I have no *desire* to harm you, Fearne. I *need* you,' he said, in a statement truer than she could ever know. 'You're no good to me dead,' he added for good measure.

'Whatever. Now come–'

A thunderous bolt of lightning cut across the sky, causing the ground to tremor.

'What the hell was that?' said Fearne, her ears covered and eyes wincing.

'Okay, now we can go,' said Malcolm, the anger of the world around them acting as his clock.

*

Kara's world stopped.

Hal was gone.

The same way Peter had been taken from them.

His Restarter-self erased entirely due to Malcolm killing him in the past earlier than was destined.

But if that were true, why hadn't a freshly-Restarted Hal reappeared?

'Time travel is bullshit,' muttered Kara.

'Kara,' whispered Alex, 'Tell us what to do.'

'Right. Right!' she said, shaking off the loss of her best friend. Something told her she'd have all the time in the world to mourn. But right now, her other friends were depending on her.

With Hal gone, there simply was no one else to guide them through this.

'Everyone back up,' ordered Kara, pointing to the balcony behind them at the far side of the communal living room. 'We all have one job now. Stay alive. And protect Jasmine, Daisy, Michaela and Gavin.' She added, the last remaining survivors frantically trying to stay hidden whilst Jasmine called the police.

Kara took a deep breath, then looked back down the staircase.

'Actually, scratch that. Everybody link arms with me…'

*

For all of the Dark Restarter's planning, after all his countless years of observing, in his excitement to execute his plan and…well…*everybody* in Fir Lodge, he had overlooked one key factor;

That time itself was working tirelessly to counteract his meddling, and was reshaping the time-bubble they were all occupying to stop the monumental changes he was trying to cement into a permanent state.

In the 165th restart that they were all reliving, Hal had tripped the trip switch on the hot tub, causing Robert to get out.

What no one could have possibly known is that

when Malcolm erased Hal from time, he also upset the balance of their 165th restart entirely. With Hal not around to carry out that tiny act, or any others for that matter, The Dark Restarter had inadvertently created a vacuum in history that needed to be filled in order for it to stabilise.

As time worked frantically to rearrange itself, the universe's answer to that paradox was apparently to revert to a previous restart, one where Hal had accidentally killed Robert.

And so it was that Robert came to be, retaining all of his memories from his previous two restarts.

Robert knew Hal and Kara would be on top of the shitstorm that was unfolding.

They would have a plan.

But from the squabbling upstairs he also knew that him being here was no accident.

It held *purpose*.

And he reasoned that purpose was to keep every version of Malcolm – Restarter or otherwise – as *far* away from his wife as possible.

Right or wrong, that was *Robert's* goal.

Stalling for time seemed like a great place to start.

'So much like your friend Harold,' said Malcolm, his distaste in Robert's pose of apparent challenge falling notably flat. 'She will fall just as they all will,' The Dark Restarter muttered, waving his blade as if swirling a fine glass of wine to allow it to breathe.

Robert's eyes flared blue, and he felt a power similar to the time Hal and Kara had tried to pin him down in the rear garden the first time he had attempted to investigate a scream emanating from Fir Lodge. A scream he still remembered.

"Was that now?" thought Robert, fear filling his heart. "Was her scream due to this man running steel through her? Was he already too late?"

It wasn't of course. That scream from his wife had merely been in response to her discovering his floating corpse in the hot tub.

But he had no way knowing that, as the power within him amplified.

Malcolm raised an eyebrow, taking the minutest fraction of a step backwards, but Robert merely grinned, looking down at his hands as energy arced ferociously between them.

'You must be fucking up time pretty bad for a side-character to get pulled into all of this,' said Robert candidly.

'You people and your oddly chosen words,' said Malcolm, sighing deeply. 'Come on then, let's finish this up.'

As the time-travelling incarnation of Malcolm ran at him, Robert held the line, preparing to put all of his weight into bringing the killer to a halt.

It wasn't bravery exactly, more the fact Robert believed he was immortal, having not seen what a restarted knife to the heart would do to him if he didn't keep his distance.

They locked arms, and Robert bonked Malcolm repeatedly on the head with the beer bottle he had died with. Another gift from the world of the living.

'Stop that!' said Malcolm irritably.

'Man, glass acts weird here,' said Robert, equally mystified by why the bottle refused to crack despite him giving it his all.

With his back pressed against the long edge of the pool table, Robert got in a surprising amount of decent punches, bottle attacks, and even a cheeky knee to the killer's groin before his luck ran out, and he fell to Malcolm's superior might.

Ultimately, his downfall rested within the reserves of Restarter juice Robert was haphazardly tapping into, fuelled by his desire to protect the ones he loved.

With no practice under his belt on how to wield it, he found himself in a vicious transference, as all of his best laid plans were siphoned off into Malcolm, hoovered up like an insatiable smart-phone that had too many applications running all at once.

In a moment of eternal finality, Robert felt the blade run through him.

As Robert dissolved back into the timestream, Malcolm refocused his mind, span on his heel and re-established his connection to his alive-self, who responded by pulling his very real knife out of the doorframe.

'Upstairs,' he ordered, his foot brushing against the phone Robert had dropped. The Dark Restarter kicked it angrily, sneering at the belated revelation, and feeling incredibly idiotic for falling for the pantomime. Pretending to call the police on a phone that was deader than he was showed undeniable genius.

*

Kara stood there continuing to draw a charge from her friends, her face contorted in frustration as if she were desperately trying to refuel her car despite already being late for an important work meeting.

'Come on, come on,' she said to herself, clenching her eyes closed in case it helped. She suddenly felt the connection falter. She stole a look, greeted by a thick fog which began to spill across the upper level of the lodge, this time coming for her, she was sure of it.

She clenched her fists and strode towards the staircase, locking her sights onto the only thing that mattered; the alive Malcolm of the past. A towering behemoth, existing out-of-phase to her, occupying a slice of time which she knew she couldn't interact with physically.

But Kara was never one to be told what she could and could not do.

She drew back her hands, as a familiar blue energy sparkled in her eyes, allowing her body to embrace the unparalleled anger she was feeling, knowing that this monster was about to attack the last of her remaining friends that were still drawing breath, and that the Dark Restarter was surely hot on his heels, preparing to *truly* end the ones who had *already* fallen.

If she really was about to be erased, she would go out swinging.

Alive-Malcolm had reached the top of the stairs now.

'No,' she whispered, as she shoved her hands directly into the man's chest, dispelling the entirety of the small charge she had managed to draw through her palms and into her attacker, stopping him in his tracks, forcing him to take a step backwards, then another, backtracking and falling victim to his own momentum.

Malcolm's alive-self lost his footing, and tumbled backwards down the staircase, landing on the broken body of Kara's past-self.

If she wasn't dead before, she certainly was now.

*

The Dark Restarter grimaced at the pathetic sight of his past-self, who was trying to pull himself up from the floor in an attempt to regain his composure.

Leaning over the banister rail of the staircase, he peered upwards, catching a glimpse of a familiar blue light, as Kara stared back at him, a crack of thunder ringing out above Fir Lodge like gunfire.

'You're in over your head, little girl.'

His past-self echoed his words and he smiled, happy that they were finding their way into the ears of those that dared to stand against him, sounding more like an automated recording than a man thinking of his own volition.

Kara's rebellious smile waned, however, thanks to a tingle in her arm.

The Dark Restarter breathed a sigh of elation. 'It seems my work here is done,' he said happily.

She looked down, horrified to see her hand was out-of-phase with time, shifting in transparency.

'Super,' she said to herself, trying to run the numbers on what this chaos would mean for her and Hal.

The sheet of fog increased in density, wrapping around her legs, moving up to her knees, and claiming her chest. She looked upwards at the ceiling, as the now-solid whiteness made its way towards her mouth, her eyes wide in terror.

With her mouth now covered, the only air she could draw was through her nose, until that too was smothered.

Kara's suffocation took an even darker turn, as her sight was stripped from her.

Finding herself suddenly blinded thanks to her slowly disintegrating eyes, she tried to scream, but the insatiable fog refused her the indulgence, cutting through her vocal chords as it travelled down her throat.

Without reason, the static mist stopped, releasing its hold on her, freeing her nose, allowing her once more to draw the air she had forgotten she didn't actually need to stay alive in this place, and Kara felt a surge of relief.

A new wave of fog rolled into the lodge, wiping her surroundings from existence, clearing away the dead bodies of her friends that littered the lower level of the lodge, their Restarted duplicates, and both incarnations of Malcolm.

Finally, she was claimed as well, possessing just enough cognitive resilience to think about where she was being taken next, as her temporally-displaced body and sense of consciousness were torn to shreds.

CHAPTER SIXTY-ONE
Full Blue

203rd Restart – Friday, August 24th, 2018, 12:01pm

Kara reappeared outside Fir Lodge in a fresh restart to the dual sounds of rushing air and screaming. She covered her ears to determine the source, before experiencing a sense of relief so intense she could have cried.

'Hal?'

But her friend was far too busy rolling on the floor to hear her.

'Hal!' she shouted, more firmly this time.

'Oh,' said Hal, stopping mid-scream. 'Sup. Had a bit of a…*situation* there,' his embarrassment clear as the sky was blue, as he picked his restarted gun off the floor and holstered the weapon.

She hugged him tightly, fighting against the current.

'I thought I'd lost you!' she whispered.

'Looks like the universe had one last spare sheet of paper in the photocopier,' he replied, before lowering his volume to that of an equal whisper. 'But you'll never lose me, you know that.'

As Fearne began her own re-materialisation process, they pulled away from each other, the shared moment brought to an end.

'Where the hell were *you* guys?' said Hal, switching to a notably more accusatory fluster.

'I'm sorry,' said Fearne. 'We ran as fast as we–'

'What the hell happened?' said Kara, cutting Fearne off, showing no desire to hear her excuses. 'We were waiting on you! We nearly lost everything!'

'It was Malcolm! He kept stopping, saying he was having memory…*episodes*! There's something I need to tell you,' she added.

'Bench?' suggested Kara.

'Hell yes, bench,' said Hal, confirming that the motion had been carried to adjourn to their make shift war room.

'It's about Malcolm,' said Fearne, taking a seat next to them. '*Future* Malcolm.'

But having spoken of the devil, the devil himself appeared beside them.

'Since when can you get here so quickly?' asked

Kara, eyeing him suspiciously for making a journey that had always taken him longer than it took for them to reach their bench.

'I'm so glad you're safe,' replied Malcolm, his words sounding oddly authentic.

'You okay?'

'I will be, Harold.'

Fearne bristled.

'Are you *kidding* me right now? He's the reason it took us so long!'

'Fearne,' said Malcolm. 'Perhaps now isn't the time to go into–'

'Oh, it bloody well *is* the time!' she barked, standing up from the bench and stomping towards him, poking him directly in the chest, before spinning on her heels and facing her so-called friends. 'Malcolm's been lying to you. To *all* of us. Those *memories* of his aren't just appearing now, he's had them all along.'

'I figured,' said Hal.

'And another thing,' began Fearne, having clearly been rehearsing this speech. '…wait, what?'

'Well, time travel doesn't work like that. What's happening here had to have happened the first time around, for Malcolm at least. It would be a temporal impossibility for his past-self to go off track from his fixed timeline, regardless of Future Malcolm here being in-phase with him.'

'*Temporal*,' said Fearne pinching the bridge of her nose and clenching her eyes shut in frustration.

'*Phase*,' she hissed, repeating Hal's words.

'I'm sorry you lost Peter again,' said Malcolm, directing his words to Hal and Kara, who stared back at him slack-jawed.

'What?!' said Fearne, opening her eyes in outrage. 'What does he mean, *again*?!'

'I, erm…' began Hal.

'Peter came back,' said Kara. 'It was only for a second, but…'

'And you didn't think to *start* with that?' her eyes both hurt and angry in equal measure. 'Then let's go get him!'

'It…I don't think it's going to work like that,' said Hal.

'And why not?!'

She should have known there would be another excuse. Another patented Restarter reason for them not to search for Peter just because it didn't fit in with whatever Hal and Kara felt was important that day. 'Let me guess, is the *phase* not *temporal* enough?' she said viciously.

'That's…not even a sentence, Fearne.'

The rage circled her like an almost perceptible heat-vapour, Hal's response seemingly lacking in even the faintest sign of empathy, as if she had just been told publicly that she'd been caught using "your" instead of "you're" in a social media post.

Fearne turned away from the three of them, picking a direction at random and hoping to put as much distance between her and the lot of them as she could.

'Fearne,' said Kara, 'don't leave. Who knows where Evil Malcolm is right now, it's too dangero—'

Fearne stopped, not wanting to face them, instead talking to the forest in front of her.

'*Evil* Malcolm,' she said, her words only slightly louder than a whisper, 'is standing less than a metre away from you. You're just too *blind* to see it.'

'Fearne, we're sorry for not telling you about Peter,' said Hal. 'I just thought it would…there was nothing we could do.'

'It's funny how there's nothing you can do when it isn't about you or Kara.'

'Fearne, that's not fair,' said Kara.

'I just…I need some space,' said Fearne despondently, walking away from Fir Lodge.

Away from *them*.

'I should be going too,' said Malcolm.

'What are you talking about,' said Kara. 'You got a haircut appointment you didn't tell us about?'

'Clever,' said Malcolm. 'No, I thought perhaps it prudent to glimpse the present again? See what damage my past self has caused, if any.'

'You must be joking?' said Kara. 'And disappear for another three weeks? That's what caused this all in the first place!'

'I have a theory I may be able to simply transport myself to your home, cutting the journey from the equation.'

'How does that even *remotely* make sense?'

'Temporal phasing,' joked Malcolm.

'Seriously Malc, feel the room,' replied Hal.

'Whatever,' said Kara, honestly feeling like having some time to speak with Hal alone wouldn't necessarily be a bad thing.

'Try not to *die* whilst I am gone,' Malcolm chided.

Before either Restarter could respond, a sharp cracking noise filled the air, and he vanished.

'You think he's really going where he says he is?'

'Who cares,' said Kara. 'We need to talk anyways.'

'About what?' said Hal, realising he was standing following Fearne's outburst, and returning to his seat.

'Malcolm's past-self is out of control. I think we may need to prepare ourselves for the ugly truth here.'

He knew Kara was referring to the elephant in the room.

'More like a brachiosaurus,' mumbled Hal.

'What?'

'Nothing. You mean killing Malcolm's Dark Restarter self. Like he did to Peter.'

It wasn't a question.

'I think it's the only way,' a battle-weary look spreading across her face.

'We're not ready,' said Hal, thinking back to the massacre they had just witnessed at Fir Lodge. 'Even at *Full Blue*, Malcolm managed to take on Peter, Me, You, Rachel, Will, Alex…hell, even *Jon* without breaking a sweat.'

'*Full Blue*?' said Kara, remembering the utterance

of the term which had fallen from the lips of a very different Hal.

'You know, like fully charged Restarter? Full Blue.'

'Oh! I like that,' she smiled, finally in possession of a fragment to a larger puzzle that was far from solved. It was the little things.

'I'm sure you can convince everyone you came up with it,' he said, shooting her a kind-hearted smile.

Kara paused, a sudden obligation washing over her. She wanted to tell him all about the encounter by the lakes, but was hindered by her promise. It seemed important to the Hal from their future, and that should have been good enough for her. And yet…

'I really thought I'd lost you,' she said, more than a hint of a glisten in her eyes

'You said that already,' Hal replied playfully, his smile full of warmth and his tone equally heartfelt.

'There's something I need to tell you,' said Kara, leaning in close enough for him to feel her breath on his cheek.

'What,' Hal's voice uncharacteristically croaky enough to warrant him clearing his throat and taking another stab at it. 'What's up?'

Kara looked over Hal's shoulder, watching as his past-self moved closer, seconds away from claiming the bench they were sitting on.

'If you ever die on me again, I'll kill you, understand?' she whispered, before leaning away from him and punching him hard in the arm, causing a savage spark to erupt.

'Oww, dick! Did you intentionally drag that out just so my past-self was closer to me to make the feedback bigger?' said Hal, rubbing the affected area.

'Obviously! Now come on zombie boy, we need to find Fearne.'

CHAPTER SIXTY-TWO
Five Little Words

203rd Restart – Friday, August 24th, 2018, 12:17pm

'You're a long way from Fir Lodge,' said the Malcolm of Fearne's future, having materialised directly in front of her and blocking her path.

'You seem to be able to move around far easier than you let on,' she replied, highlighting yet another one of the innumerable inconsistencies to the half-truths he had fed them.

'Yes, I *have* rather undersold it, haven't I...'

'Whatever. Get out of my way,' said Fearne, changing direction and attempting to walk around him.

He phased immediately, now several meters closer to her and blocking her new course.

She faltered, unconsciously taking a step back.

'I came here to tell you something,' said Malcolm. 'Something I've never told anyone.'

'Let me guess, you're a huge fan of Grey's Anatomy?'

Malcolm recoiled, then chuckled, his hands clasped behind his back in a show of aloofness, bridging the gap between them with slow, incremental steps.

'Whilst that program does grow on you, no…that's not what I wished to tell you. You know, when I returned here, *after* the hospital that is, I genuinely had no idea how to get you all on board. I had the memories from the past, of course. But no *playbook* on how to actually implement them.'

Fearne rolled her eyes as if she couldn't be more bored, but nonetheless matched every step he took to ensure she maintained her distance.

'But through it all, I had one glimmer of hope. A single thought to work towards. I made that the focal point to everything we've been through together thus far.'

'And what was that?' she whispered, her senses flaring, seeing a look in Malcolm's posture that was dripping with historic familiarity. They were circling each other now.

Or rather, he was circling *her*. Like a vulture.

'*You*, of course!' as if it were the most obvious thing in the world. 'You're the *key* to everything!'

'Is that why you killed Peter? Was that part of…whatever *this* is?'

He sighed in frustration. 'How many times do I have to tell you? That wasn't *me*!'

'Semantics.'

'Facts,' said Malcolm.

'Bullshit,' she countered with finality.

'I realise now that it's time to tell you what no one else can know. A vision of the future that, until now, I haven't shared with anyone. Are you ready to know what that is?'

'Not really,' lied Fearne, forgetting to take a step backwards to counteract his movements.

'Fearne, how many times have we gone around in this *circle*? Flitting around through time, always hitting the same brick wall. I'm offering you what you've wanted. The key to bringing Peter back.'

'There *is* no bringing Peter back,' replied Fearne sourly, at least remembering to keep moving despite the crack in her voice betraying the hope which was quickly squashing the more logical compartments of her mind.

'But he *did* come back. You *heard* the others. I'm not asking you to trust me, I'm just asking you to listen in order to save the man you love! After that, you can make up your own mind.'

'I knew it, he's not dead is he! There's a way! To make things right?!' she said, ceasing the dance they were engaging in and coming to a full stop.

'There is a way to make *everything* right! To make up for the actions wrought by my monstrous past-self. But it comes with a price, to us all. Knowledge of the future always does.'

'Whatever it is, I'll pay it,' said Fearne.

'I know you will,' his smile far warmer than it had ever been, so powerful in its sincerity that Fearne experienced involuntary empathy. 'You did before. The last time I gave you this choice.'

'How do we save him?' said Fearne, allowing Malcolm to get closer, ignoring the oddness of his words.

Too close.

He took another step towards her, legs apart, allowing his shoulders to slump down. Due to his shift in posture it felt like she was truly seeing him for the first time; not *The Boogey Man*. Just…a *man*. Trying to get home, just like her.

Vulnerable, almost.

'We need to work together to attain victory. I know I've given you nothing but justifiable reasons to doubt me, but I haven't just *seen* the future Fearne…I *am* the future. There is no better weapon at your disposal than me.'

'Tell me what to do,' she said, her eyes filling with determination, desperate for the emptiness within her to be once again filled by the laughter of her soulmate.

'Nothing,' said Malcolm.

Her eyes widened as he leant closer to her and whispered into her left ear. The revelation he had kept from them all finally dawning on her. She understood now why he had kept these words to himself for so long. Hearing them answered everything.

She replayed the five little words over in her head. A single sentence from the future that held the key to their escape.

'You see now,' he said, 'why I couldn't tell the others? They wouldn't understand.'

'I…s-see,' she stammered, looking down at the dust covered ground, droplets of crimson dripping onto it and resting on top of the dirt, unable to blend with it, the fluid as out-of-phase as the rest of her body.

Malcolm smiled sadly, retracting the blade gently from her torso, lowering the hilt slightly so the serrated edge didn't catch unnecessarily on her flesh, catching her limp body to prevent it from hitting the ground.

Her vision became blurry. A symptom, she assumed, of being erased permanently from existence. Fearne took comfort in the fact that the pain was minimal; akin to a sharp sting that slowly waned in intensity.

She smiled, feeling grateful that perhaps Peter had felt the same lack of pain, as the words Malcolm had whispered to her echoed in her mind.

"You were right about me."

CHAPTER SIXTY-THREE
The Man in the Mirror

203rd Restart – Friday, August 24th, 2018, 12:48pm

The Dark Restarter felt the presence of his guest the same way he always did; an unnatural stillness overpowering the air, followed by an electromagnetic wave that besieged the hairs on his body, causing them to prickle and rise, as if magnetised towards the duplicated abomination.

Despite knowing his visitor was from the future (or rather, a potential variant from an as yet uncemented timeline) Malcolm considered himself to be the one *true* Malcolm.

This pretender was little more than a child born

of cause and effect, one that could be erased and usurped by him with little more than a small adjustment to future decisions.

And yet, as much as Malcolm hated to admit it, this futuristic facsimile did hold some power over him.

Power in the form of knowledge over what was yet to come.

The Dark Restarter fought admirably against the need to fall to his knees as the man drew closer to him, gripping onto the edge of the table with his back to the door of their new Kill Room. Or, as the younger Malcolm preferred to call it, "canvas table."

'As promised,' said Future Malcolm, carrying a near-lifeless Fearne in his arms, her blood having covered a large portion of his black apron.

Future Malcolm had grown to hate these visits. His younger self had become incredibly unhinged throughout his time here. To the point he almost didn't recognise himself. Though, if he was brutally honest, it would have been disingenuous to insinuate he himself had changed all *that* much.

The younger Malcolm turned to face his senior, regretting doing so immediately, experiencing an intense misalignment in the way reality was interpreted by his mind.

'You need a second?' said Future Malcolm, feeling the residual echo of his own words before he heard them.

'You need a second,' spluttered Malcolm's past-self, desperately trying to regain control of his body. 'I'm fine,' he snapped, hating his involuntary display of weakness, despite it being unavoidable.

Both Malcolm's had learnt that this was the price of conversing with other iterations of your own self when travelling through time.

Whereas a conversation between two separate minds always led to unique interactions that could not be predicted, when conversing with an identical mind, the variables became…corrupted.

A feedback loop, that was generated when a person had already experienced the response to a question they themselves had yet to ask for the first time, and would one day be forced to participate in again from a paradoxically impossible perspective.

It appeared to be a universal constant that Malcolm was powerless to alter the flow of quantum-entangled thoughts in any meaningful way. And so it was that The Dark Restarter found himself feeling the intense temporal dysplasia brought on by attempting to do just that; conversing with a version of himself from his own potential future.

Both men took a breath and exhaled slowly, the simultaneous act not helping matters.

'I must admit,' The Dark Restarter recalled, struggling to fight through the relentless nausea, 'when you appeared before me with the golfer and actress it was incredibly challenging to pretend as though I could not see the three of you.'

'You sold it well,' said Future Malcolm calmly.

'I was sceptical when you told me they would accept your invisibility bubble routine so willingly,' said Malcolm's past-self, and they shared a gruff chuckle together, which to the outside world would have sounded like gravel being churned in a cement mixer, only in surround-sound.

'They would do anything to defeat the great, *Dark Restarter*,' said Future Malcolm with false theatrics.

'*Dark Restarter*?' said past-Malcolm, hearing the term for the first time and trying to decide if the misnomer met his fancy.

'That's what they're calling us these days.'

'A little…*reductive* for my taste,' said the owner of the mantle.

'It'll grow on you,' said Malcolm with the flash of a smile, surprising even himself when it hit him that he actually meant it. 'They do enjoy their little labels. Almost as much as they love to embrace the fantastical attributes of this place. They would have believed anything I had told them at that point. So much so, that they often forget to question the more realistic limitations of the prison they're contained in.'

'You looked so serious,' The Dark Restarter chirped. 'Concentrating, as if you were slowing time. I was almost embarrassed for you.'

Future Malcolm had a bone to pick with his past self, and dropped the pretence of self-fulfilling allegiance.

Though initially wary to explore the issue, he found himself remembering that the words had been thrown at him already, many years ago, and eventually took comfort from the knowledge that it was inevitable.

'Trying to leave the lakes in Kevin's truck? That was not what we agreed. What the hell were you thinking?'

'I needed to exhaust all possibilities,' said Past Malcolm. 'That failure proved to me that your claims were true; the past cannot be changed. At least, not *your* past.'

It had been one of the few genuinely-implanted memories Future Malcolm had received; the instance where his past-self had gone off script in order to test Future Malcolm's claims that his path was predetermined. The instances of alleged memory insertion that followed were easy to fake thereafter.

'It was foolish and nearly cost us everything,' said Future Malcolm.

'You can place her over there,' said Past Malcolm, ignoring the pathetic sulking of his future-self and not wishing to release his grip on the table top, instead using his head to gesture to the cage behind him.

'All I ask,' said Future Malcolm, 'is that you keep her alive until I can bring the others to you. Do you think you can handle that?'

The question triggered another instance of severe chronological dissonance, though Past Malcolm appeared to feel it more, a nonsensical word being all he could muster.

'Gak.'

Future Malcolm realised it was probably better to phrase his words as statements rather than questions.

'No doubt a side effect from poking around in your own past too much. It will pass.'

'How is it that you seem less affected!' said Past Malcolm. 'Do you not feel it too?'

'No,' he lied, struggling to stay upright following the receipt of the question and wanting nothing more than to vomit violently.

He compartmentalized the notion and proceeded onwards.

'And that business at Fir Lodge? You see now why that approach will never work,' said Future Malcolm. 'Killing them in the past isn't the answer. You need to kill them in their time-travelling form. They simply can't bounce back from that. Only then can you proceed with our mission.'

'And what *is* our mission exactly?' he said sceptically.

Malcolm smiled wearily, recalling the words he had heard himself utter many moons ago, ensuring he got them right, despite knowing they would come naturally regardless. 'The same as it's always been brother, to bring an end to the rat-catcher and orange menace. To remove them from the board, once and for all.'

'And then we'll be free?' The Dark Restarter said longingly. *Desperately.*

'Not exactly. You will become *me*. And *I* will be free.'

'I keep forgetting that part,' his younger self grumbled. 'I'm not looking forward to that. You seem to have lost the joy in your work.'

'It will be our *greatest* masterpiece,' said Future Malcolm. 'To Ophelia,' he added.

'To Ophelia,' the Dark Restarter seconded, issuing a meaningful nod, in lieu of a glass he could raise.

'The second Restarter, as promised,' said Future Malcolm, placing Fearne's unconscious body down gently inside the cage. 'I know it killed you, being captured like that. I apologise.'

'I must admit, I was sceptical. I thought I'd gone soft in my old age,' Past Malcolm said dryly.

'Never. We're closer than we've ever been.'

'The rat-catcher first,' said Past Malcolm, mimicking his future-self's method of communication by communicating via statements rather than questions. 'On his own, that was the arrangement.'

'Of course,' said Future Malcolm. 'I will deliver him to you shortly.'

'And how do you plan on separating them?' asked Past Malcolm. 'They always travel together.'

'You leave Kara to me. I know what I'm doing. Just be ready. Once Hal is down, the secretary is yours to do with as you wish.'

'You mean *Harold*,' said Past Malcolm, his eyes narrowing at the slip.

'That is what I said.'

'No, you called him *Hal*.'

Future Malcolm was hoping his past-self had missed it, but knew that was optimistic. Instead, he tried a different approach to cover his mistake.

'Are you *sure* that's what you heard?' asked Future Malcolm, speaking quickly, barraging his past-self with a collection of follow-up questions, knowing that doing so would cut his mind to ribbons given their close proximity. 'Because if you aren't hearing me correctly, are you sure you can handle this? Perhaps you're losing your edge? Do I need to make alternative arrangements?'

Past Malcolm was shaking, the words creating an endless feedback loop in his brain.

'Stop,' he whispered, reaching his limit.

'Then we understand each other,' said Future Malcolm. 'I have but one request.'

'It's the least I can do, out with it,' the Dark Restarter spat, swaying slightly, the aftershocks still coursing through him.

Future Malcolm shifted uncomfortably, knowing the words he used next could be a deal breaker. He pulled himself together, also knowing he was simply repeating what he had heard himself say, albeit many moons ago. 'Make it…quick. There's no need to draw out their suffering.'

Malcolm's younger self pushed away from the table, sizing himself up.

'That…is an odd request. Don't tell me you've grown *attached* to them? After everything they've *done* to us? Everything they've *taken* from us?'

It was Future Malcolm's turn to fight back against the onslaught of questions, the tide threatening to drown him. 'Of course not,' he fired back. 'It's just imperative not to draw this out. We need it done and we need it done quickly. Their resilience is…unprecedented. Their bond allows for miraculous improvisation.'

'It would be quicker with your help,' said Past Malcolm, pressing an old issue he had posed at the very beginning.

And every restart thereafter, in fact.

Ever since Future Malcolm had realigned himself with the specific restart his past-self was occupying, he had re-materialised next to him.

Future Malcolm would then relay to his past-self what the order of business was for the next thirty-three hours. Everything had been by design;

The murder of Peter in his Restarter form.

The massacre at Fir Lodge.

The carefully orchestrated second murder of Peter when he reformed during said Massacre.

That had been crucial. It led to a divide in trust between Fearne, Hal and Kara. One which Future Malcolm had exploited in order to bait them to come here; the place where the Restarters would be laid to rest once and for all.

'We all have our parts to play,' said Future Malcolm finally. 'Mine is merely to facilitate their arrival. That's how it was then, and how it must be now. I've come too damn far to risk changing the outcome just to assuage your damaged pride.'

'You forget who you're talking to,' the Dark Restarter challenged.

'I know *exactly* who I'm talking to,' said Future Malcolm, his eyes flaring crimson, unable to hide a notable look of distaste in his features.

'Is this what I become?' said the Malcolm of the past. 'A voice in the *shadow*s, an echo of my former self, frolicking around the forest, fraternizing with the enemy?'

'That so-called fraternization has yielded more results in barely two months that you've made in the years you yourself have been here. Perhaps, instead of analysing the *man* in the *mirror*, you would do better to heed my advice. As opposed to questioning my apparent emotional attachment to our *murderers*.'

Malcolm's past-self stared, his expression switching from fury to a smile so quickly it was impossible to tell where it would lead, until, eventually, it evolved into a barking laugh.

"It *does* have a fakeness to it," thought Future Malcolm, realising that perhaps Hal had been right. "Something to work on."

'*There* he is,' said Past Malcolm, a flash of respect dancing across his face, finally at ease.

'You've removed all the devices that can generate music from the room?' asked Future Malcolm.

'As instructed. Oh, and you'll need *that*,' said Past Malcolm, pointing towards a thin, neatly folded garment situated behind his guest. 'You've got *red* on you.'

Future Malcolm looked down at his blood-soaked apron. He quickly removed it, crunched it into a ball and threw it to his past-self, carefully replacing it with the much cleaner variant from the past waiting for him on the work surface.

'Very good. And you've made the necessary arrangements for our corporeal-self to be nearby, so you can draw charge from him if needed?'

Malcolm's past-self smiled darkly, and snapped his fingers.

From the shadows, the incarnation of himself that was whole and in-phase with the physical world lurched forward, only he didn't look as whole as Malcolm remembered himself to be. Not in the slightest…

Future Malcolm surveyed the *alive* version of himself, now entirely under the thrall of his Restarting counterpart, and cringed internally.

Once a mind fully in control of his own destiny, now a weak and mindless lacky, forced to enact the commands of the time travelling version of his own consciousness. It made him feel ill, though not as unwell as his physical body clearly looked; still as muscular as he ever was, of course, but the eyes…the eyes were dead. The embers of whatever quantified as his soul truly extinguished, his face little more than an expressionless husk. A slab of granite, devoid of even the faintest glimmer of free will.

It was worse than seeing himself comatose.

'It begins then,' said Future Malcolm, ignoring how uncomfortable seeing himself this way made him. 'The epitaph has been carved. *Harold* and Kara die tonight. And this time,' he added, his smile savage, eyes full of nothing but long-overdue vengeance. 'There's no way for them to return. It will be irreversible.'

CHAPTER SIXTY-FOUR
Manifesting Destiny

203rd Restart – Saturday, August 25th, 2018, 2:04pm

The White lodge.

Covered by the eternal snowfall let loose by infinity.

A battle appeared to be playing out before him, but his thoughts were scattered. He both recognised the participants and yet…equally saw them as faceless strangers, their names on the tip of a tongue that didn't exist, let alone one that could be used to utter them.

Black figures joined the fray.

"Time Vampires", he had thought.

Eager to feast upon the dregs of energy from a body sputtering with blue sparks. A fallen combatant on their last legs, so desperately in need of being revived.

He extended a hand to help the fallen warrior.

Then darkness.

Then screaming.

His screaming.

'And then I was back,' said Hal casually, recounting what it had felt like to be erased temporarily during their run in with a Restarting Terminator.

'Weird dream,' noted Kara.

'Definitely the kind you get after eating too many Coco Pops before bed,' acknowledged Hal.

'You're thirty-three Hal, you really need to work on your diet.'

'You don't own me,' said Hal defiantly. 'I hope to God we don't end up in an alternate timeline where we're married.'

'Oh Lordy, that *would* suck.'

They shared a laugh, the momentary reprieve weighing heavily on them.

It had been over 24 hours since they had last seen Fearne, and it was starting to seem a lot less like a soul-searching time out, and lot *more* like she'd dropped off the small slice of Earth they currently called home.

They had made their way back to Fir Lodge once more, in the hope that maybe they had all missed each other somehow, and were currently taking a break in the rear garden, as Malcolm re-materialised behind them.

'Sonuva–' squealed Hal. 'We need to get you a bell or something.'

Hal and Kara had been reluctant to leave their friends unguarded following the events of the night before, but equally felt uncomfortable leaving Fearne to roam the lakes all on her lonesome now that a murderous Restarter had seemingly gone into self-destruct mode.

'Any change in the future?' asked Kara, not believing for a second that he had even gone to check.

'None,' said Malcolm. 'Thankfully the rampage of my former self has been *Restarted* without consequence.'

Future Malcolm had decided to remain hidden, feeling that returning back immediately would arouse suspicion, but judging by Kara's facial expressions, he needn't have bothered.

'Uh huh. Sure.'

Malcolm surveyed the rear garden, his eyes falling onto a version of Fearne from the past, already in her costume, making the time approximately early afternoon on the Saturday of their eternal stay.

'She's still not back,' said Kara, following his line of sight.

'Perhaps we should look for her?' said Malcolm, his voice containing just the right amount of concern.

'What do you think we've been doing for the past twenty-four hours?' said Hal with a justified scoff.

'We could just go the boundary line,' suggested Kara.

It was a solid plan. Triggering an early restart would bring everyone back together.

'You're right,' said Hal. 'Enough is enough. I'll go,' he added, pulling himself up from the grass and grabbing his backpack of restarted objects, collecting his replica gun from the ground, holstering it with a spin.

Kara stared at him.

'What?' he asked.

'Nothing, just you being all Wild West. It was funny.'

'I was going more for a *Mal Reynolds* kind of vibe.'

'I don't know what that means.'

'My mother used to call me Mal,' said Malcolm.

'Annnnd now you've ruined Firefly,' said Hal, rolling his eyes, causing Malcolm to shrug with indifference.

'I'll run to the perimeter. And–'

'Since when do you say perimeter?' laughed Kara.

'What, it's a word,' said Hal snootily. 'That people use.'

'Yeah, but, ya know. You're not running a police operation.'

'Time Police,' joked Hal, tapping an imaginary sheriff badge. 'We've only got about six hours until sundown, which means about seven hours until the next restart kicks in. I'd rather have her back before then.'

'Be careful.'

Hal shot her a mischievous look before taking his leave. 'I aim to misbehave, ma'am.'

Malcolm fell to his knees, causing both Kara and Hal to stare at him in amusement.

'Malc', we've been over this. Inserted memories are not a thing for you,' said Hal, turning away from the allegedly reformed killer's amateur dramatics.

'He *has* her,' said Malcolm shakily, his words catching serious attention.

The Restarters knew he meant Fearne.

'You knew this would happen,' said Kara, losing patience.

'I did. But it's too soon,' confessed Malcolm. A truth hidden within a lie that neither Restarter could contest. That was, after all, what compulsive liars did best; hiding in plain sight. 'She must've sought him...*me* out. She's changing the past!'

It didn't matter if they believed him or not. The only thing that mattered was saving Fearne before she was erased just like Peter.

'Okay,' said Kara, standing and getting her thoughts in order. '*Where* has he taken her?'

'He's on the move,' said Future Malcolm, closing his eyes and placing his fingers to his temple like he was running a school for gifted folks with power-affording mutations.

'Urgh, fine,' said Kara. 'Don't tell us. We'll do this

ourselves. Let's go,' she said, pulling Hal by the arm with the intention of reaching the Restart Point before any harm could come to their friend.

*

As they reached the boundary line Malcolm slowed down, as Hal ran straight into the invisible force field preventing any of them from triggering a restart.

He rubbed his noise, checking his hand to see if there was any blood.

'Oww.'

'Of bloody course,' said Kara, spinning to face Malcolm. 'Why can't we leave?'

'He must have journeyed into the future.'

'How far?!'

'You said it yourself,' said Malcolm. 'It would technically only require a single minute. That would be enough to prevent you from accessing the Restart Point.'

'Oh c'mon!' said Hal, turning in circles with impatience, trying to find a loophole he could exploit, but coming up empty. 'Okay, then we find her the old-fashioned way.'

'You mean, search the entirety of Pentney Lakes?' said Kara, letting the unrealistic success rate of that option wash over him.

'There's…something else you I need to tell you,' said Malcolm.

'Shocker,' said Hal. 'Spit it out.'

'My physical self, he's taken a captive.'

The Restarters stared at him with incredulity.

Future Malcolm had one job; to give them the heads-up to prevent these sorts of things from happening. It seemed incredibly unlikely that everything would come unstuck all at once by sheer chance.

And it was happening with increasing regularity.

'Wait? So *Dark Restarter* you has Fearne, and *Alive* you has…who?'

'Kevin, Harold. He has Kevin.'

'Are you kidding me?' said Kara. 'If he kills Kevin, we'll have another Restarter to contend with!'

'Or worse,' noted Hal, 'we could disappear entirely. We know we die either way, but having Kevin here could replace our 165th restart. How can past-us save him from the basement if he's dead before we get there?'

Kara was about to lay down the support beams of what was surely going to be a good plan, but was interrupted by an unexpected guest.

As if attempting to pull off one of Hal's mic-drop moments, none other than Jerry sauntered up to them like a canine superhero.

'Oh, hey Jerry,' said Kara. 'Haven't seen you in a while! You've missed a lot of drama!'

Jerry squeaked, then exhaled through his nose, clearly meaning business.

'You don't suppose Jerry has gone full on Lassie and happens to know which *well* Fearne is trapped down?' said Hal, half-joking.

'With us to the end, huh little guy?' said Kara.

Jerry panted enthusiastically, looking up to her

with adorably wide eyes.

'Okay,' she continued, realising time was too much of the essence to waste it deliberating over Malcolm's sincerity. As much as she hated to admit it, they were going to need the killer's help. 'Here's what we're going to do…'

CHAPTER SIXTY-FIVE
A Kiss through Time

203rd Restart – Saturday, August 25th, 2018, 4:12pm

At first glance, their goal seemed impossible, given that they needed to be in two places at the same time. Luckily, for Hal and Kara, that was something of a natural forte.

Or at the very least, an occupational hazard.

'We need to split up,' Kara had said. 'Hal, we need to focus on Fearne. Malcolm, who better than to talk your living-self out of murder than you. Assuming you *want* to help us?'

'Of course I do!' Malcolm had said, before muttering diatribes about how this 'wasn't supposed to be happening yet' "blah blah blah," thought Hal, replaying the scene in his mind.

They both had a part to play. But before Hal moved on to carry out *his* role in their plan, there was something he needed to do…

Taking advantage of their time away from the hustle and bustle of jumping through time, Hal stole a moment. He knew the hunt for Fearne would take everything they had, and how important that was, but this needed to be said.

In fact, there was *so* much Hal needed to say to his fellow Restarter.

Even now, he knew there was still so much that would forever remain *unsaid*. He felt both sadness and comfort in the fact that when all this was done, his words would be forgotten and discarded into the void of nothingness.

Such was the curse of time overwritten.

Hal looked lovingly into the eyes of his Restarting colleague, wetting his lips so that the words would flow true.

'We've been through so much together,' he said, releasing a sigh which was laced with equal parts regret and melancholy. 'But for this to work, I have to leave now and…' his fellow Restarter stared back at him, eyes wide as if asking him why.

How could he leave her? Why *now*?

Surely they could *make* time?

Eyes that were asking *how* he could leave her here, all alone? But the words failed to come, refusing to be given life, as if it would make everything that bit more real.

Hal chose to fill the silence, and continued onwards.

This was difficult enough without more guilt being piled onto him.

'It's okay, you don't have to say anything. Maybe I'll see you again, maybe I won't, but I want you to know that there's no one I'd rather have been on this journey with…'

His partner in time stared back.

'I'm going to kiss you now…' said Hal.

And with that, he leaned in tenderly, kissing the Restarter on her lips.

Or rather, *beak*, and placed the rubber-duck-sized flamingo that he'd retrieved from his backpack onto the wooden gate post so it could be seen from a distance.

This was the place. He knew that for a fact.

It wasn't some existential sixth-sense, or knowledge which had downloaded itself through his soul and into his cerebral cortex.

Nor was it because Jerry's alive-self had led him here.

It was more the fact Hal had literally just seen Malcolm's Dark Restarter-self sprinting across the grass and into the lodge before him through an open back door.

'That's not possible,' he muttered, looking up at the building before him.

Of all the places The Dark Restarter could have chosen out of the countless other options available to him, Hal had no idea what had led him to this one.

He experienced a wave of nausea at the realisation that maybe there was no such thing as *chance*. That maybe everything *was* predetermined after all. That perhaps there was no free will…

Hal shook away the unhelpfully distracting notion. But the sight of the familiar building still sent a shiver down his spine.

'I dunno man…you think she's in there, boy?' Hal said to Jerry, hoping that if ever there was a time Jerry would reveal he had a voice it would be now.

Jerry, did his best, emitting a tiny growl, before shaking from nose to tail, his ears and jowls flapping wildly, before laying on the ground and laying a sulky head on his paws.

'Yeah, it *would* be just our luck, wouldn't it…' Hal agreed pensively.

He couldn't help but smile. He had often wondered what Jerry got up to when he wasn't hanging out with him and Kara on their adventures. But the fact he was with Hal now, during an entire new restart cycle, made him wonder if Jerry was always with them, in some form or another.

Hal looked back towards the imposing structure.

Had the Dark Restarter known the significance of this lodge when he had chosen it as his new base of operations?

Hal remembered fondly the first time he had

brought Kara here.

He had picked it at random to prove to her they weren't living in a construct of their own minds. How the couple inside had argued about over-priced kale whilst their children had played outsi–

'Dammit,' he grumbled.

He'd forgotten about the kids.

That…complicated things.

Hal knew he was supposed to wait if he was successful in finding Fearne, but he was entirely wrapped up in the moment. Casing the place to see what they were up against was surely a wise move. Not to mention the fact that innocent children were almost definitely inside, at the very least being scarred for life emotionally by the invasion of a serial killer wind-milling into their lives.

Or what if it was worse than that? What if the kids were insurance?

Did Malcolm have a rule about not hurting children? He couldn't remember it ever coming up. Hal grimaced at the vulgarity of how questions like that were his life now. That he would need to start categorically asking the company he kept if they would harm young children if temporal-push came to time-travelling shove.

He once again adopted the mantra of the prophet Taylor Swift, and shook it off.

'Bloody kids,' he groaned, the stakes having just been raised, noting how children always seemed to find a way to become a liability at the most inopportune of times.

If Future Malcolm was on the level, the only man who could hurt this family was currently preoccupied with Kevin. Which meant it was only a Restarter he needed to worry about. Albeit one of the dark biscuit variety.

Hal weighed up his options, glancing back at the flamingo, positioned like a beacon of reassurance, and put faith in the theory Kara would see his breadcrumb when they caught up with him.

'Bye Felicia,' he said in his best American accent, shooting her a wink before moving towards the lodge, onwards in his pursuit of Malcolm, being sure to stay close to the ground in the hope he could get the drop on him.

*

Kara had reluctantly agreed to split up, allowing Hal to follow Jerry in the hope it would lead him to where Fearne was being held captive.

They had agreed it was best for her to stick with Malcolm in case he tried any funny business, or worse, didn't bother to help Kevin at all.

'After you,' said Malcolm, gesturing to the staircase that led to Kevin's basement.

Kara scowled.

'What is this? My first restart? After you. I *insist*,' she pressed, wondering if Malcolm had genuinely believed she would be that compliant. Or that stupid.

As she and Malcolm made their way down the steps, she made sure to keep her distance, gently pulling back the hammer on the gun Hal had given her under the cover of false pretence.

Malcolm looked over his shoulder as if she had hurt his feelings. A look that would have possibly carried more weight if he had the emotional range of anything beyond that of a cactus.

'What?' said Kara with a level of defensiveness that numerically equated to precisely zero.

Malcolm grinned, his aggrieved expression replaced with something much worse than his murder face; a look of respect.

Kara exorcised a cringe in the form of a full body shudder.

The plan was simple; Malcolm would latch on to his physical-self, preventing him from acting upon the instruction to kill Kevin, whilst Kara sought out a way to free the man from his restraints.

But, like all previous entries in their back-catalogue of "simple" plans, she quickly realised that this one in particular was about to go south even faster than usual.

'Malcolm…' said Kara, her voice a hushed whisper, her body shaking at the sight before her which told her everything she needed to know. How much *danger* she was now in. 'What have you done?' she had just enough time to add, as she felt two large arms wrap around her, attempting to drain her of every last ounce of retained charge they had managed to muster prior to her and Hal going their separate ways.

*

Hal snuck around the back of the lodge, feeling an intensely powerful twinge in his chest, reminiscent of the ones he used to get before he realised Malcolm had snuffed out his life with less regret than the network that had cancelled Firefly.

He pulled himself together, pressing firmly against his chest to alleviate the momentary agony, now pressed against the wall of the black lodge.

Not just *any* black lodge, either. The *Third* Lodge.

"It couldn't be a coincidence. Could it?"

Something was wrong. He could feel it.

Hal instinctively reached for his phone, then realised he had given it to Kara in case they needed an anchor. Or a distraction…

He cursed, remembering that it wasn't as if he could have called her anyway, making a mental note to add walkie-talkies to the list of things every Restarter needed to carry with them at all times.

"Or was that stupid?" he thought. Did radio-waves work the same way as they did outside of a time bubble? "If they were in-phase with each other," he reasoned, "Surely?"

He heard a soft whimper from inside the lodge and refocused, noticing a thin veil of static fog was lining the floor.

"Great."

The one thing he needed right now was a loss of cognitive coherence brought on by the surly sheriff of time that was Restart Fog.

No wonder he was day dreaming about bloody walkie-talkies.

The whimper evolved into an ear-splitting scream, sending a surge of ice to course through him as he realised exactly who it was coming from.

"Fearne."

'Pick up the pace, Kara,' whispered Hal, sighing deeply and psyching himself up, knowing it was down to him to slow down whatever this shit was, before slipping in through the double patio doors.

*

'Will you settle down,' said Future Malcolm brashly, 'Everything is fine! I have a plan!'

As the electricity surged from Kara's body, before being hoovered up into Malcolm's own, lighting up Kevin's basement with pulsating flashes as they tussled, she fought against the light-headedness she was experiencing, wanting so badly to demand answers…but wrestling instead with the fact it was taking all she had just to stay conscious.

Malcolm released her and she fell to the floor.

'Sonuva…' muttered Kara, shaking off the nausea. 'You have a *plan*? *You* have a plan?!' she repeated, her eyes suddenly filling with a new lease of blue energy, as she dragged herself up off the ground.

'How are you…' Malcolm tried to ask, wondering how she had regained a charge so quickly.

'That's funny. No, actually I'd go as far as to say freakin' hilarious! Because what it *looks* like you have is a chronic case of the *bullshits*!' she snarled, whipping a hand in the direction of a lone empty chair in the centre of Kevin's basement.

A chair that was notably devoid of a Kevin.

Malcolm went to speak, but fell silent as Kara raised a solitary finger like a lightsaber powered by a shut-the-hell-up crystal.

'We came *all* this way,' her words concise, oddly calm now, and notably brisk, 'to *save* a man you *told* us was in danger. Splitting up at the *worst* possible time to stage a two-pronged intervention on two versions of *you* from the past and–'

'I…'

'I swear to God Malcolm, if you say *one* more word, I'm going to rip your heart from your chest,' said Kara, surprising herself with how unhinged she sounded. How…*Malcolmy* her choice of words were... 'And here *I* am, Kevin's *nowhere* in sight, and then you try to, what?' she struggled to find a way to describe his actions. '*Bear-hug* me to death?!'

'It is not what you think.'

'What *I* think? What I *think*, Malcolm, is that you've been *playing* us from the start. What I *think*, is that you just sentenced *Hal* to a showdown he can't *win*, and you're keeping *me* busy so we can't take on the Dark Restarter together! That sound about right? My thoughts *loud* enough for you? Are you picking up what I'm putting down?'

'We told Hal to wait for us,' said Future Malcolm.

She scoffed, hissing loudly and looking up at the basement ceiling begging for a patience that refused to present itself.

'This is *Hal* we're talking about! He's probably in there *already*, trying to *bore* past-*you* with abstract movie references long enough for us to get to him and save him. Which we can't *do* when we're miles away from…where even *is* he?!' she said with a start.

Panic began to sink in, realising she didn't even know how to reach him.

'A third lodge.'

'*What* third…' and then it hit her like a truck. A truck full of baby– 'No, no, no Malcolm!' She knew of only one other lodge that held any significance to her. 'There are *kids* there! What have you done?!'

Kara went to push past him, but Malcolm grabbed her forearm.

The Restarter's eyes lit up, and Malcolm suddenly found himself feeling two distinct sensations;

Charge.

And pain, as the energy tried fervently to repel him away from her.

He looked down at his hand and saw the skin starting to crackle, burning under the intensity of the blue energy she was generating.

'I suggest you take your damn hand off me before I send it into the next restart,' she said coolly, barely managing to hide her sense of wonder at the pain Malcolm was clearly failing to hide between his clenched teeth.

'*Release* me, woman,' said Malcolm, his words making her realise that he wasn't trying to maintain his grip on her anymore…he was *trying* to let go.

She closed her eyes for a split second, calming herself, and the Restarter energy died down to a gentle thrum.

Malcolm peeled his hand from her arm, leaving fragments of singed skin behind in his wake.

'Ah balls, I really liked this jacket,' she said, grimacing at the sickly handprint he had left behind.

'You *must* listen to me Kara. I fully intend to save Hal, but you *must* listen.

'Oh, for fff…ine. Talk,' she relented, knowing deep down she didn't have any other options, before warningly adding 'Quickly.'

*

As Hal moved through the living room of the swanky lodge, dodging his way through a jungle of wallet-bustingly expensive furniture, he heard a second cry, this time calling his name.

He followed the sound and came across a door that was trying to be helpful by being ajar, but was ultimately letting the side down by not being open *quite* enough.

'Ahh…*door*,' he grumbled, as if addressing an arch-nemesis from his past with a tone which implied that perhaps it had been this *very* door all along that had been responsible for everything that was happening to him.

Realising he was a long way away from Fir Lodge – and therefore his past-self – *and* with Kara currently in the wind, he had nothing to draw a charge from.

There *was* Fearne, of course, but *she* was currently messing with his would-be zen on account of being on the other side of the dastardly, hindrance-spewing door itself.

If he had her, he wouldn't need to be having this conversation with himself.

He slumped against the wall and peered through the gap into the darkness beyond, seeing the hint of what appeared to be steps that led downwards.

'*Basement*,' he sighed, pulling off a pretty solid Harrison Ford Impression. '*Why'd* it have to be *basements*?'

A childlike sniffle made its way up from what lay below, met with the whispering reassurances of a woman's voice trying to ease the girl's shattered nerves, culminating with what Hal assumed to be a cheek being kissed.

"A kiss through time," Hal thought poignantly.

A dispassionate rumble of a voice – whom Hal recognised instantly as belonging to a nemesis far more accomplished than Mr Door – uttered a smattering of chilling words, addressing his captives directly.

'Quiet child. Listen to your mother.'

Hal's eyes flared with anger, his body tapping into a source of power hitherto out of reach, as he pulled the door open savagely, the wood yielding under his exertion without so much as a hint of resistance.

He stood there in the doorway for a moment, staring down the classically foreboding, text-bookishly cliché staircase that The Dark Restarter had seemingly rented out following its overuse in…well, every horror movie in the history of ever.

'No backup, creepy basement, imminent death? Check, check, and check,' Hal grumbled, making a mental list of the itinerary of his current situation, before smiling darkly.

His mind filled with imaginary Time Demons with skin as slick as oil and serial killers alike, all wanting a piece of him, their gnashing maws and dancing blades all flickering in the shadows, *daring* him to enter.

'*Classic* Saturday,' he said with a shrug, as he stepped willingly into the lion's den.

CHAPTER SIXTY-SIX
Outatime

203rd Restart – Saturday, August 25th, 2018, 4:21pm

Kara sprinted in the direction Hal had headed towards before they had split up, covering ground at such an almighty pace that Future Malcolm struggled to keep up with her.

It was as if she was flitting in and out of phase, *gliding* more than running. In the end, he had to resort to teleporting ahead of her. It was all he could do so as not to lose her.

Kara cursed. She was usually so good with directions, but she'd only been to the black lodge once and, at the time, had no reason to commit the route to memory.

In fact, Hal had chosen the building for the exact reason that they had never been there before.

'Which way?' she asked, more to herself than to Malcolm.

'You'll figure it out,' he said unhelpfully.

Kara glared down at her shoulder, not dignifying his words with eye contact as she continued onwards.

As she blitzed her way across the Pentney Lakes she found herself reaching a dip in the road, and stared down at what was apparently a recently developed collection of lodges, most of them black.

'Are you kidding me with this?' she squawked indignantly, shielding her eyes from the afternoon sun that was beating ineffectually down on her.

'There is more I must tell you,' said Malcolm, catching up with her.

'I'm not interested in anything you have to say.'

He'd made his position quite clear. He wanted this to happen. All of this was by his own design.

'Put your childish hurt feelings to one side and listen to me, woman! Hal's life literally depends on it!'

There was something about his tone that elicited an involuntary reason to listen. That and the way he had referred to her friend as "Hal", instead of "Harold".

Kara turned to face him, unsure as to why she was even entertaining the prospect of being a receptacle for what was surely going to be yet another lie, but quickly deciding Hal's life meant more to her than sticking to her guns on going it alone.

'I know how this looks,' said Malcolm, relieved she was prepared to hear him out and running a singed hand through his thick black hair. 'You think I've betrayed you, but I'm stalling you for a reason. Only *you* can save him, but everything *has* to happen in a *very* specific order for you to achieve that goal.'

'You killed Peter, Malcolm.'

'Not in the way you think.'

'Our friend is *dead,*' said Kara, letting the word hang in the air between them for a second. 'Because of you. And your twisted games. We *believed* in you. I can't decide if you actually believe the shit you're spouting, or if you think I'm stupid enough to believe anything you say from here on out. And then there's…wait…what do you mean "Not in the way you think"?'

'Both Peter and Fearne are special, Kara. They are the key to everything. To our salvation.'

'I feel like this is something you need to elaborate on.'

She sensed a greater subtext to his already overcooked delivery of that sentence.

'I will. You have my word. But now is not the time,' he said dismissively, once again skirting the subject.

It wasn't time yet. It was never time.

Malcolm sighed. They were so close now…

'You can't *reason* with him, you *must* remember that,' said Malcolm sternly. Almost desperately. 'He is besotted, utterly *infatuated* with enacting vengeance on the two of you. All *this*,' he said gesturing around him and up to the sky. 'It's all to get you as far away from your physical forms so you have no charge to draw upon. To make you powerless.'

'We're *never* powerless,' whispered Kara with a look of defiance that could have set light to water.

Malcolm let out a chuckle as thick as syrup, and raised his burnt hand in-between them.

'You are preaching to a choir that I myself assembled,' he said, clearly in agreement.

'I'll talk him round,' said Kara simply. 'No one else has to die.'

'Kara,' said Malcolm disapprovingly. 'That isn't even remotely true. I think, at this point, we both know that you know that.'

'Not everyone sees the world like you do, Malcolm!'

'Clearly. But I assure you, *one* person does. The only person that matters; *I* see the world like I do.'

'Oh, very clever,' she said sarcastically. 'You stay up all night writing that one?'

'Cemeteries are full of heroes, Kara. I'd rather quite like for you to realise that before you decide to join them.'

'I'll turn this thing around,' she said, their eye-contact cutting the space between them like a blade forged by the legendary *Hattori Hanzō* himself. 'Now, if you're done squawking, I could really use your help finding this damn lodge!'

*

Timestamp Error. Recalculating…

Hal took each step slowly, not wishing to generate a creak despite his weight unloading ineffectually on the wooden staircase.

Old habits.

As he reached the bottom he was greeted by the sight of a dimly lit room; an open space which housed a large metal cage to his left. Each of its two sides stretching from floor to ceiling and connecting to the back and side wall, creating a complete cube of containment.

He evaluated the enclosure quickly, his eyes glancing over mountain bikes, fishing equipment, deflated lilos and what appeared to be an inflatable dingy of some kind. Amidst it all was a sickly sight that changed the tone of the container from a practical storage solution to that of a jail cell, as his eyes fell upon the only thing in the room that could turn the tide enough to keep him alive. At least, alive long enough for the cavalry to arrive.

'Fearne,' he whispered.

He moved closer to the open section of the cage and took stock.

There was a puddle of blood pooling beneath her, refusing to coagulate as she pressed her hands to her lower torso, her white dress now predominately crimson. She appeared to be drifting in and out of consciousness, her head bobbing forwards, then snapping backwards as she rested her back to the rear brick wall, shifting awkwardly in her sitting position.

A dull clap erupted behind him, and he looked to his left, looking back beyond the staircase.

Hal realised the room was larger than he had first deduced, as he scowled in an attempt to mask his fear, but came up more than a little short, failing miserably.

'He said you would come,' The Dark Restarter hissed, like a snake attempting to lure its dinner into a false sense of security. 'Alone, no less. I must confess, I was sceptical.'

Hal saw the outline of what was surely Malcolm's alive-self, skulking in the shadows behind his time travelling master.

Keeping watch, presumably, over the father and mother of the two children who were trying their best not to let the side down by whimpering, lest it garner the attention of the man who had brought them here.

The family appeared utterly oblivious to Hal and Malcolm's more…*Restartery* existence, let alone the exchange of words they were about to share.

The next of which, Hal chose very carefully.

'Well, I'm here now. What say we let these kale-loving hipsters go, yeah? It's a lovely day, and you're really pissing on their holiday.'

'How does it feel,' The Dark Restarter purred, seemingly desperate to revel in ambiguous rhetoric.

'Being this pretty? I do okay.'

'To *know*...' The Dark Restarter continued, ignoring the rat-catcher's attempt at humour. After all, he'd rehearsed this speech. He hadn't factored in improvised interruptions. '...that you were *betrayed* by my future-self. To *know* that you're going to *die* here. That your friend, *Kara,* will *die* here?'

There was something about the way he lingered on her name that made Hal's blood run cold, as he remembered she was with the Malcolm of their future right now, presumably in imminent danger.

Hal rolled his eyes as the truth hit him like a brick to the face.

'Kevin's not in danger is he. I mean, he can't be, if *Lurch* over there is here with us.'

The Malcolm of the past smiled, baring those pearly great whites.

'Let them go, Malcolm,' said Hal, his voice strong but quiet, not daring to use anything but the killer's full name. He figured it would show respect, whilst also throwing the man off, thanks to the overfamiliarity it insinuated. '*Us* I can understand. This is a *done* thing. But bringing this family into all this just risks messing up time even further. You're an intelligent man. You know I'm right.'

"Flattery," thought Hal. It was worth a punt.

Hal considered the children, who had surely just accrued enough emotional baggage to keep them in and out of therapy for a lifetime.

Malcolm clicked his fingers, his alive-self moving out fully from the shadows.

'Take them away, secure the house. Especially the basement door,' The Dark Restarter ordered of his own body.

His living-self obliged the instruction, ordering the parents to take their children and run.

An instruction, Hal was relieved to see, that they didn't hesitate to follow.

The killer stalked them slowly up the stairs like a weary groundskeeper, until he too was out of sight.

Hal heard the sliding of patio doors, the locking of a door, and the creaking of wood as the shadow of what was formerly Malcolm returned.

The Dark Restarter moved his head from left to right, stretching out his neck until it clicked, content that they were finally alone.

Just him, his alive duplicate, the dying Fearne, and the soon to be *dead* young man that had humiliated him on countless occasions.

So many instances…

'You gonna stand there for the whole restart, Bronson?' asked Hal, ruining yet another moment for the killer. 'Or you wanna dive right in?'

Always talking.

Always goading.

Always *insolent*.

Malcolm glowered with the sullen intensity of a man who had just dropped his car keys down a drain, before diving from the springboard of manifested destiny into the ocean of long overdue vengeance.

"Shame," thought Hal, having secretly hoped that

the *standing still* option had the legs required to buy him the one thing he was used to having in abundance. But now, like a spinning licence plate of a recently departed DeLorean, he was completely and utterly out of.

CHAPTER SIXTY-SEVEN
Battle of The Restarters

Recalculation complete. R.I Timestamp Verified: 203rd Restart – Saturday, August 25th, 2018, 4:47pm

Kara stared down at Jerry – who had drawn the Restarter to him with a bout of frustrated barking – then up at the pink flamingo placed on the fence post which acted as a beacon, left by Hal solely for her to find, and smiled.

'This is the place,' she said with certainty.

Any doubt she may have had eradicated instantly as a man and his family exited the rear garden and hobbled towards them, his face bruised and his partner and children in tears.

At least they didn't have to worry about the family now.

'Good work Jerry. Now, go find your daddy, we've got this.'

Jerry snorted, reluctant to leave her side, as if there was surely more work for him to do.

Kara leaned down and simulated the action of scratching behind his ear, causing his tongue to lop out between his canines.

'It's okay,' she whispered, thinking it more than saying it.

Jerry understood, trotting off to his next adventure.

Kara made her way to the rear of the lodge.

'Can you open this?'

Future Malcolm nodded, moving closer to the patio doors and sliding them open, his proximity to his alive-self proving invaluable, as Kara slipped inside, hearing a large bang beneath her.

She began to panic, looking for some kind of access point to the room beneath her, her eyes snapping towards the only door that mattered.

She reached for the handle, turning it frantically, her newfound and inexplicably-self-perpetuating charge being no match for a door which was clearly–

'Locked,' she muttered. 'Do something!' she pleaded to her Malcolm.

'I may be close to my -alive self, but I'm not a Swiss army knife,' he said sourly.

'Actually…maybe you are. Can't you…I dunno, take control of *real* you and get him to throw us a bone here?'

Malcolm closed his eyes in concentration for a moment, before allowing them to flutter open. 'He's too close,' he said, referring to his younger, Dark Restarter self.

He wasn't sure how he knew, but he could tell his tether to his physical body and mind was no match for the depth in which his younger self had embedded his hooks.

Kara sighed. She didn't have time to bother with asking if that were true or not.

'If we can't open it, we'll go through it.'

'Even if you were close enough to *your* past-self, that would take a tremendous amount of energy,' said Malcolm, all frowns that seemed reluctant to be turned upside down.

They heard a sickening crunch, followed by a yelp of despair from who they knew to be Hal, clearly getting the beat down of his presumably-limited life.

Kara's eyes flared with blue, as she focused with grim determination, and realised if ever there was a time to punch the rules of Restarting in their smarmy little face, it was very much now.

She couldn't lose him too…

She *wouldn't*.

Kara slammed her fist into the door, which remained as uninterested as the acoustics of the building, the dull thud generated by her efforts not so much mocking her, as it was denying for even a second that her existence meant anything at all.

He's going to die.

Again she punched, and again the wooden barrier refused to yield.

Alone.

Again, she lashed out.

And you'll fade without him.

She wasn't sure if these were her own thoughts, or if Future Malcolm was talking to her. All that mattered was the door.

'Just open already!' she growled, punching again, refusing to surrender.

She saw it then. Faint, but there. Just like her.

A splinter sized indentation; not just etched into the wood, but etched into the present.

It was then she knew the rules were buckling.

She pulled a black mirror from her pocket, and continued her assault on the gateway that may as well have been a solid wall of concrete. Damned as she was, and tortured by a thirst for results, the dam of time reluctantly burst, the rivers of quantum-fuelled energy filling every fibre of her being. Spilling outwards not only into the device she was clutching, but over the Malcolm of her future as well. Washing over them both like a tidal wave, giving Malcolm more of a charge than he had ever experienced before.

He knew the significance of her actions, and offered some unwarranted advice.

'He's going to need–'

'A soundtrack,' said Kara, her body surging with cosmological foresight.

'If I could offer a suggestion?' said Future Malcolm, taking the device from her, now functional and ready for action.

'Go nuts,' said Kara, returning her focus to the door.

*

'Any last words?' The Dark Restarter said cruelly, having grown tired of toying with the Restarter for what felt like an eternity to Hal, but in reality was merely just shy of thirty-or-so minutes.

'I still can't think of anything,' mumbled Hal, attempting to chuckle but choking on his own blood, notably ruining the effect he was striving for.

'Always joking, always laughing. I suppose that's meant to be time-travel humour?'

'Flashback humour ac–' Hal coughed, his voice as hoarse as Kara's after a night on the tequilas, words fractured as he cleared his throat, '–tually.' His ability to speak diminishing rapidly.

Malcolm grabbed Hal by his shirt, lifting his crumpled frame from the ground, as the electricity arced between his enclosed fist and the Restarter's chest.

Hal's mind refused to cooperate, a fog only he could see clouding his thoughts, preventing him from focusing.

Raising his arm, Malcolm brought up the hilt of

the trusty serrated blade he was clutching.

'The time of *The Restarters* is over, I am all that's left,' The Dark Restarter said with an obscenely large dollop of grandeur. 'I have travelled across *countless* timelines, erasing your future. And now? I will finally kill you in the present. All that remains is–'

Malcolm's perfectly rehearsed monologue was abruptly interrupted by the arrival of a small rectangular object, that travelled down the staircase innocently. Its lack of clatter made up for with the angry music spewing from it like a cavalry of cacophony, filling Hal's heart with joy, and his attacker's chest with shock and anger.

The phone bounced off of the cage and landed nonchalantly between Hal and Malcolm, causing them to temporarily cease their deadly embrace.

An illuminated rectangle of glass filled Hal's vision, and he became vaguely aware that it was more like a screen. In a clock-tick between moments, they both stared at the device. Then at each other. Then back at the phone, utterly bewildered by its inexplicable intrusion as it filled the room with the sound of music, a tune continuing to splurge from the speakers, bouncing off of the eardrums of the duo, unable to do the same to the surrounding walls.

Malcom's eyes widened, knowing that the arrival of the unwanted stimulant would have a potentially disastrous impact on his plans, and he quickly pulled back the blade, aiming for Hal's heart once more, eager to finish this before further complications had the opportunity to bleed into his present, but it was too late.

The killer froze, the music meaning far more to him that it did to Hal.

'It can't be,' The Dark Restarter muttered, and for a moment Hal thought the killer was referring just to the phone.

But it was more than that; Malcolm wasn't just displaying frustration…he was visibly *haunted*. As if his mind had been transported back to somewhere else entirely.

Hal took advantage of the brief respite, as a band Hal knew to be called "Freak" filled the dead space between them like an air horn, the song "No Money" levelling the playing field.

Malcolm remained in a state of seemingly perpetual hesitation, his eyes now fully-glazed by a painful memory.

'But that would mean,' The Dark Restarter whispered, his words utterly lost under the chaotic onslaught to both their senses. All this time, he thought it had been a stranger. But now he knew the truth. 'It was…*you*?'

Hal didn't know what that meant.

Actually, he simply didn't care at all, as he closed his eyes and inhaled deeply.

As The Dark Restarter pulled himself together and applied pressure to the blade once more, Hal grabbed Malcolm's wrist in one swift, effortless movement, preventing the tempered steel from entering his body and ending his life.

As each note connected with the next, the fog clouding Hal's mind lifted, his memories returning in full force as the floodgates of time itself were ripped open, his focus no longer revoked, but returned to him with a boundless tenacity.

'I remember…' whispered Hal. 'I remember *everything.*'

"It's never too late," Hal thought, recalling the advice of a stranger from his past. 'To restart from scratch,' he muttered, releasing the end of his thoughts into an existence beyond that of his own mind.

A sense of disbelief washed over him, as the faint echo of a forgotten memory drifted onto the shore of his conscious mind; a message in a bottle, that had traversed the infinite ocean of time with a singular purpose; to make him remember something important. A memory from his childhood that, thanks to the music, was so vivid, he knew without a shadow of a doubt that he could win this.

He chuckled at his own ingenuity, feeling as if he were cheating on a test by receiving answers he had no right possessing. Hal thanked his future-self for the gift…not yet realising the implications that having such a recollection would mean for him in the long run.

Using his legs to slowly lift himself up from the ground, Hal found his footing and pushed back against the force Malcolm was exerting onto him.

Malcolm snarled as a mixture of blue and red energy ignited between them, violent arcs of electricity spitting viciously and landing on the floor in a pile of temporally-charged embers, lining the ground like the epicentre of a blacksmith's forge.

Malcolm stared in disbelief, as his strength was inexplicably matched by Hal – who was somehow keeping the knife at bay – and concentrated fully on attempting to drain his opponent.

But something was different.

It wasn't…*working* like he knew it should.

With his eyes still closed, Hal's mind was filled with thoughts that were fuelled by positive reinforcement; he found what he was looking for quickly, as he relived the day he rescued Shelby from the shelter.

"More than enough," thought Hal.

His eyes sprang open, glowing an ethereal blue, the connection between his hand and Malcolm's wrist spewing another wave of freshly-baked sparks, generating an enormous feedback of power that sent Malcolm flying across the room.

Malcolm collided savagely with the wall alongside the metal cage that imprisoned Fearne, as Hal dusted himself down for no other reason than to show his attacker he was rallying.

For the first time in a long while, The Dark Restarter was utterly lost for words, but collected himself all the same, pulling himself up from the floor, managing to utter a curse as his eyes darted around the room demanding answers on where the phone had originated from.

Hal spat out a mouthful of blood, wiping a stray trickle from his chin, before releasing a humble laugh into the room at the killer's expense.

'You see, that's the difference between you and me Malc', I have *one* thing that you'll *never* have…' said Hal goadingly, his mind once again firing on all of its restarted cylinders.

Malcolm bristled at his adversary's insolence.

'Do tell,' his eyes filling with the fire of red energy that only a true Dark Restarter could generate.

The refuelled time-traveller shrugged, and walked slowly towards Malcolm, stopping a few metres in front of him as he looked down at his hands, stretching out his fingers in relief as blue energy danced between his fingertips.

Hal smiled darkly, his blindingly-blue eye sockets casting a fluctuating glow on his cheeks. And then, he uttered two simple words; a truth that, for all his intelligence, Malcolm couldn't possibly fathom.

'A *team*.'

Malcolm used his shoulder-blades to push off from the brickwork, and they began circling each other, both men waiting for the other to react first.

No longer an underdog and an undefeatable giant.

But as something worlds apart; as equals.

Shaking away the nonsensical doubt, Malcolm struck first, running towards Hal, the blade in his hand singing through the air as he did so. But Hal didn't step away.

Officially done with running, the Restarter instead strode *towards* his attacker.

Malcolm dropped his arm downwards, the blade slicing the air, on a collision course with Hal's shoulder, who merely leaned back on his heels, effortlessly dodging the incoming attack, sending Malcolm off balance as the momentum of his actions carried him onwards.

Hal knew in that moment that all was not lost.

After all the training Future Malcom had insisted on…Hal knew something the younger Malcolm before him couldn't; he hadn't been preparing Hal for *multiple* outcomes, he had been training him entirely for this *exact* fight.

For every blow that the killer threw at him, for every *attempt* Malcolm made to connect with Hal, a response was now ingrained so deep within his muscle memory that Hal knew what was coming next before Malcolm had even made the decision on what move to make.

'I know Kung Fu,' muttered Hal gleefully, his eyes lighting up with joy as the true majesty of that dawned on him.

Regaining his balance, Malcolm swung again, as Hal ducked heavily to his right.

Ever the chameleon, Malcolm changed his approach, bringing the knife back around in a horizontal motion towards Hal's head, but Hal did what no one ever did when such a threat to life occurred; he moved closer to his attacker, bringing up his left forearm, blocking the blow, the electricity sparking between them physically repelling Malcolm's knife-wielding arm like a steel bar connecting with adamantium, the force of the connection sending an earth-shattering reverberation through their bodies, causing Malcolm to lose purchase on the weapon.

The blade flew from his hand and slid across the floor behind him, Malcolm not bothering to follow its path, instead reaching out to grab Hal by the throat.

Hal ducked underneath him like a professional boxer, landing a lightning-fuelled uppercut to Malcolm's jaw, causing him to stagger back.

The music hilariously hit the end of a chorus at that precise moment, as if lamenting the impossibility of what had just happened.

Harold Callaghan.

A complete novice in combat, who would sooner take a punch to the face than embrace even the mildest form of confrontation, had just caused a legitimate serial killer…one proficient in multiple fighting styles and a behemoth by comparison in terms of strength…to stop.

To hesitate.

It was a thing of such rare beauty that Hal genuinely felt saddened by the fact Kara hadn't been there to witness it, or that even *he* would be unable to remember it, assuming he made it out of this whole mess and back to a future that was perfectly content to go on without him.

'That's…impossible…' mumbled Malcolm, spitting an irksome mouthful of blood that had filled his mouth, legitimately dazed. 'Who taught you to fight?'

As Hal picked up the phone from the ground, he marvelled as the power levels of the phone shot from nineteen-percent back up to one-hundred.

'Oliver Queen,' replied Hal, putting on his best rasp before muttering 'and Malcolm…you have *failed* this city…'

Malcolm growled, and sped towards him, collecting the blade now resting by his foot and thrusting it outwards towards Hal's throat.

Hal lowered his body in an almost-kneel, crossing his wrists to form an "X" with his arms, and pushing upwards, guiding the un-glinting metal to the left of his own head, where it narrowly missed cutting off his ear lobe.

Moving his wrist and taking the notable heft of Malcolm's right arm, his knees buckling slightly under the load, Hal fluidly turned his whole body, using Malcolm's own weight against him and causing the monster to stagger forwards, before unleashing several jabs to his assailant's torso in quick succession.

Malcolm regained his balance and brought up a hand, savagely lashing out at Hal's head, which Hal deftly ducked under, allowing him a free moment to casually punch Malcolm square in the face.

The Dark Restarter recoiled in pain, dropping his advantage, the knife landing once more with a muted clatter that only a Restarter could hear.

They both stood there for a moment, breathing heavily, the severity of what Hal had just done truly dawning on both of them.

Malcolm lifted his hand up to his nose, pulled it back into view and saw the staining of blood on his fingertips.

Hal kicked the knife away from them both and into the corner of the room, remembering Future Malcolm's advice that if there was a weapon in play, it was best to keep it as far away from an opponent as possible.

"*You'll be tempted to use it*," Future Malcolm had said. "*You will think it will change the tide. But all you will be doing is bringing him a weapon he can use against you.*"

For a brief second, Hal felt like he had taken this too far, and had pushed his luck to the point where if Malcolm *were* to show any mercy at all, that option had just officially been taken off the table. Hal was also privy to the fact that there wasn't much of his tutor's training left to run through. A few moves at the most.

The Restarter suddenly found himself resisting the potent desire to apologise, as if doing so would result in Malcolm laughing it off. That perhaps he would decide to go easy on him. Maybe even grab a cup of tea and a biscuit. Allowing them to discuss how silly this all was.

Hal could almost hear the belly laughter they were both indulging in over this entirely imaginary coffee shop meet-up, over the clinking of dishwasher-safe crockery and the whirr of milk-frothing apparatus. Perhaps they even split the bill before going their separate ways.

He was pulled back to reality, thanks to Malcolm's eyes which seemed to suggest such a fantasy was a no go.

'Malcolm,' said Hal, regaining control over his shortness of breath, the exertion having really done a number on him thanks to his charged state of self. 'It doesn't have to be this way. We can work together, find a way to—'

But Hal's plea was evidently falling on deaf ears. He had damaged more than Malcolm's temporally-displaced body…he had damaged his *pride*.

There was no coming back from that.

As if to cement that truth, the door above them blew apart, shards of wood exploding inwards and trickling down the staircase, causing both Hal and Malcolm to instinctively divert their attention to it.

Two hovering orbs of blue light stared out at them down into the darkness, a familiar silhouette filling the doorway.

Hal chuckled, but the relief in his voice betrayed the levity.

'Cutting it a little *fine*, aren't we?' he said to the powerful being, which to Malcolm seemed to glide down the stairs, rather than walk.

'It's not *my* fault your plans are terrible.'

'You found Felicia then?'

'If you're referring to that poxy plastic flamingo,' said Kara, in a playfully irritated tone, the relief that her friend was still alive lining her words. 'Yeah.'

They shared a smile.

'Wanna tag in? I'm sort of doing all the heavy lifting here,' said Hal.

Kara was about to mention how she'd just disintegrated a door when Malcolm growled, running towards them and causing the Restarters to end their ill-timed banter.

As the music continued, they began exchanging blows with the man from two fronts instead of just the one.

This felt odd to them both. They had practiced the moves that followed, sure, but never in tandem. Never as one.

Hal knew it wouldn't be long before he himself came unstuck and evolved into a liability, having always lost interest at this point in his tutelage. Kara clearly didn't have that problem, as she weaved around Malcolm, jabbing him in the spot above his kidneys, continuing to dodge him expertly.

Merely getting by, Hal's luck eventually ran out as Malcolm's fists collided with his face, throwing him hard into the open cage door where Fearne – a few pints of blood shy of truly living – continued to swim in and out of whatever dregs of consciousness she was somehow clutching onto.

'Close it,' The Dark Restarter shouted to his alive-self, who traversed the room, passing through both

Kara and Malcolm himself, shutting the gate, and sealing Hal inside with a simple click of a padlock.

'Hal!'

It was just her and Malcolm now.

'Ready to die again, little *girl*?'

'Ready to have your arse handed to you by a *woman*?' she retorted, pleased that her voice didn't contain a single iota of the self-doubt she was feeling, or the shakiness being brought on by her surging adrenaline.

Malcolm found himself momentarily distracted, noticing a large frame in the doorway above them, which nodded slowly, all deliberation nullified.

The Dark Restarter smiled, nodding back, as the silhouette retreated. To *where*, he would only know when he *became* him.

Kara seized the opportunity to land the first blow of the next wave, forcing the palm of her hand upwards into Malcolm's nose.

Hal's eyes fluttered open, and he began to pull himself up from the ground, knowing that Kara would need his help. However, the display before him seemed to indicate anything but.

Kara and Malcolm's parries were being exchanged at such speed, that they seemed to be juddering in and out of time itself, becoming little more than a flurry of red and blue sparks, as their respective blows and counters connected.

Kara, fuelled by what Hal knew to be hope and the sheer will of needing to succeed…and Malcolm, channelling the entirety of his hatred and resentment, until finally, Kara's luck ran out too.

She staggered backwards, no longer a blur, her body realigning with the present moment, her slender frame coming back into focus, her hands pressed against her nose, blood pouring from between the gaps in her fingers.

'It's over,' The Dark Restarter barked, trying to catch his breath far more than he should have been.

But Kara merely closed her eyes, and concentrated.

Her short auburn hair began to rise, defying gravity, held in place by a static charge of some kind. She lowered her fists to her side and clenched them.

Eyelids flashing open, blue energy coursed through her eye sockets, arcing down her arms and all the way to her hands, causing her entire face to glow blue, her features no longer visible.

Hal and Malcolm covered their eyes, shielding themselves from the intensity Kara was emitting until, eventually, the light retreated.

Malcolm took a step backwards. The tiniest of steps. But definitely definable as a step all the same.

Hal had pulled himself upright and ran to the grill of the cage, peering out to witness Kara being lit up like Christmas and tearing his gaze away from her towards her attacker.

Was that fear Hal could see in his eyes?

Hal attempted to force the cage door open, eager to rejoin the battle, with zero success.

Kara shot Hal a look of surprise, as she looked down at her own hands in fascination.

Her broken nose had been fully-healed as the rest of her injuries diligently repaired themselves, leaving her with a feeling of aching invigoration.

'How?' said Malcolm, looking to the doorway behind her and clearly debating with himself as to whether he should just make a run for it.

None of this was going to plan.

Malcolm faltered, then shook away the notion of running. Regaining his resolve, he flexed his muscles and clicked his neck menacingly.

"That seems to be his thing," thought Hal, as he scrambled to the other side of the cage, and reached out beneath the gap, trying to gain purchase on the blade that resided on the other side.

He flexed his fingers, but it was *just* out of reach.

Remembering he couldn't be harmed by objects in the real world, he forced his wrist through the gap, the metal unable to break his skin or cut him like it would have done had he been in-phase with it. "Come on, come on," he thought, as his fingertips kissed the hilt of the time-travellers knife.

'No matter,' said Malcolm, an uncharacteristic inflection of self-doubt in his voice.

'Malcolm, *enough*,' said Kara like a teacher telling off a child under her charge. 'I have an *offer* for you.'

'Unless it's these *walls* painted with your *blood*, I suggest you cease stalling me so that we can end this.'

'That's *exactly* what I'm offering.'

'What?' her words not computing, as if the telephone line was bad and clarification was required.

'Let them go,' she said, pointing to the Restarter Zoo that housed Hal and Fearne. 'Spare my friends at Fir Lodge. And I'll give you what you've been after since this nightmare began. No resistance, no retaliation. You can have *me*.'

The offer genuinely seemed to strike a chord with Malcolm, as if he were legitimately weighing her attempt at haggling against his darkest, most innate desires. And for a brief second, he almost forgot why they were fighting at all. The fog did that. Even to him. But that was the problem; *almost* just wasn't quite *enough*.

'The rat-catcher…' began Malcolm.

'Off the table. Non-negotiable. The deal is me, in exchange for everyone else.'

'Kara, what are you doing?' said Hal, still trying to reach the blade.

'Do we have a deal?' she pressed, ignoring her friend entirely.

Malcolm looked up at the ceiling, his eyes darting left then right as if he were trying to locate missing tiles. He slowly weaved and bobbed on the spot, before chuckling darkly.

'No, no, no, no, Kara, you know that won't *cut* it,' he said, remembering and retrieving his second restarted blade from under his apron. Truthfully, he had refused to resort to using it, as if doing so…as if *needing* it would have forced him to accept that he was indeed outmatched. He began brandishing it at her as if he were a wizard casting a spell. 'It has, to-be, the *both,* of you,' he sang rhythmically, 'that's the *only* way I can acquire *true* freedom from this place.'

As tantalising as the thought may have been to him, eliminating half the cause behind his temporal incarceration would simply leave him with the same problem.

It had to be the both of them.

'Noooo deeeeal, Kara,' he sang, his eyes indicating that so much time spent alone had clearly sent him so far past the edge of reason that the edge itself was little more than a dot on the horizon to him now. 'I think I'll just take all three of you and be done with it.'

'Please don't do this,' Kara pleaded, her voice strong, but loaded with sincerity. 'It's not too late, we can work *together*, we can *all* get home.'

'The only way I'm getting home is by ending your life Kara. And then, when I'm done, I'll kill the ratcatcher. And *then*, just to remove *every* last feasible way in which you can meddle in my affairs, I will kill *each* and *every* one of your friends.'

'Okay, I get it,' she said, tears of anger forming.

'*Do* you, though? Do you *really* "get it"? I don't think you do,' The Dark Restarter drawled, popping out of existence and reappearing inside the cage with Hal and Fearne.

Hal cursed, clambering into the opposite corner of the cage and trying to claw at a nearby bike pump to defend himself, which remained unmoving despite his best efforts.

Malcolm reached down and hoisted Fearne from the ground, disappearing with another pop and reappearing on the outside of the cage, holding his knife to her already severe wound.

'You see, whilst there is even the faintest *memory* of you, I run the risk of repercussion. For me to be free, *truly* free, I must destroy even the most tenuous of connections to your existence. Your *family* first of course, then Harold's. A boyfriend perhaps? We can't have that. I will *not* stop, Kara. I will destroy *everything* you have *ever* loved, and not only will I take pleasure in it, I will *savour* it. As every last drop of blood *drips* into the *dirt*, I will devour everything you hold dear. Case in point,' he added, plunging the blade into Fearne's spine viciously.

Repeatedly.

'Fearne!' Kara screamed in horror.

As Fearne began to disintegrate, Kara's recently restored form simmered once more with energy, crackles of blue suddenly darkening in hue…into a shade that didn't suit her.

A shade of red.

Her light hair turning black, red electricity coursed through her veins and spewed wildly from her clenched fists.

She ran at The Dark Restarter, intent now on killing him.

There was simply no other way.

Kara had exhausted all other options.

But as she grabbed his shoulders Malcolm tried to phase away from her, using his unique ability to pull himself further along in both time and space on their current restart.

'Let go,' barked Malcolm, realising something was wrong, but Kara held on tight and pushed him against the wall of the basement, their combined red energy causing them both to phase, like an image glitching in and out of focus.

The air between them rippled savagely, as if desperately trying to repel them apart until, in an instant, they vanished.

Knowing the coast to be clear, Future Malcolm trotted down the stairs and inspected the wall where his past self was once standing. Placing his palm down flat upon it, his alive-self slumped to the floor, as if The Dark Restarter had been his power source.

Or, perhaps, simply with exhaustion.

'No, no, no! Where did they go?!' said Hal, his mind blown.

'Remarkable,' said Future Malcolm, still holding his palm to the wall. 'Seeing it from this perspective. An outsider of my own past, looking in through the window of eternal–'

'Stop monologuing! Where did they go, Malcolm?! We need to find them!'

'Where they're going, we simply cannot follow.'

Hal scowled, utterly done with riddles that weren't so much riddles, as they were withheld facts.

Somehow, despite his apathy, Malcolm managed to feel the room, deciding that ending Hal's torment would not be detrimental to the outcome. After all, what harm could Hal really do from here anyway?

'The nexus,' said Malcolm. 'They are between us both, now.'

'The White Lodge? But how? You didn't acquire that level-up until after you pulled the plug on your life support?!'

Malcolm growled under his breath, wading deep between the rivers of faded daydreams.

'I didn't *acquire* that ability at all. It was Kara that passed it on to me. Just now, in fact. At least, that's the only explanation I can think of that makes any sense.'

'Whatever,' said Hal. 'So, we go to the Restart Point and go after her!' he reasoned feverishly, as if it were obvious.

'Even if I wanted to, which I do not,' Malcolm clarified, 'The boundary line is closed for business, remember?'

'But with past-*you* gone, it might…'

'It *won't* work,' said Malcolm, leaving Hal on the cusp of asking how he knew, before diving straight in and providing the simple explanation as to how he knew that to be true. 'Because you and I weren't there for what comes next.'

'Well, you wanna at least let me out of this cage?' said Hal, trying a different approach, unable to process "no" as an answer, but reasoning there was little he could accomplish from inside his metal prison.

'Not really,' said Malcolm.

'Dick.'

*

Kara and The Dark Restarter landed hard on what looked like snow but felt a lot more like face-breaking concrete.

After an ungraceful time-traveller landing to say the least, Kara pulled herself up from the ground and realised she was on the upper level of Fir Lodge. Or rather, an intensely vibrant, almost *glowing*, white equivalent.

She swatted away some rogue snow-like particles, which barely had time to become displaced themselves following her arrival, but which continued to circle her with curiosity regardless.

'Oh no,' said Kara. 'Not good. *Not* good!'

'What *is* this place,' said Malcolm, taking a break from the fight to take in their new surroundings. 'Where have you brought us?!'

'I didn't…this is…we call it The White Lodge.'

'Imaginative,' said Malcolm drolly, momentarily dazed as he tried to swat away what appeared to be flakes of perpetually dancing ash, marvelling at how they seemed determined not to settle onto either the ground or his body. Collecting his weapon from the floor he strode towards her. 'Anyway, where were we?'

'Malcolm, stop, you don't understand, we *can't* do

this here, it'll draw—'

But her words were cut short, literally and figuratively, as he slashed at her arm, drawing a sickly slice that she prayed was a graze, but quickly opened like a mouth, a red lacquer smiling back at her.

'You are *such* a bastard!' she screeched, trying to stem the flow of blood, and focusing her anger in the hope of repairing herself like she had done just moments ago down in the basement. Unfortunately, the energy refused to cooperate.

Malcolm stared blankly, then chuckled. 'It looks like you're running on empty,' he said happily.

'Dammit,' she muttered. He was right.

Whatever it was that had brought them here had taken a tremendous amount of Restarter energy out of her, resulting in her being little more than regular old, puncturable Kara.

He came at her again with the knife, but she backed away just in time, and made her way to the communal staircase, losing her balance and hitting the wall hard at the base of the stairs.

Malcolm slowly dragged the tip of his blade against the spokes of the bannister as he followed her down, generating a scratching noise between clacks that somehow met her ears in reverse.

She froze in fear, powerless, alone, and trapped in the nexus that connected not only her multiple incarnations of existence, but *all* of time, knowing that it would be just a matter of the latter before the vampiric creatures that dwelled here…

"The creatures," she thought. "It just might work."

Pulling herself away from the wall, Kara made her way to Robert's bedroom, opening the door as she passed it and leaving the room behind as she made it into the rear garden of Fir Lodge.

She ran across the garden, but came to an abrupt stop as an open expanse of blackness greeted her. The edge of the garden was now a cliff-face, separated from the rest of the Pentney Lakes and extending into a void of nothingness.

Kara turned her back to the edge of the universe, noticing that the entirety of Fir Lodge was surrounded by the same blackness; a white gemstone cut off from the rest of time. She watched ineffectually as Malcolm strode towards her, the killer smiling at the development in their surroundings that had left her with nowhere to go.

She thought quickly, and spoke faster.

'If you kill me, you'll be trapped here,' she said trying to recount some fancy-sounding terminology to hook him in with, only then realising how easily Hal made it look.

There was definitely an art to it.

'I'll take my chances,' Malcolm shouted across the garden.

'We're...we're quantumly-entangled to our past-selves, if you sever yourself from the restarts you'll be stuck here forever in...temporal purgatory.'

A valiant effort. At least she *thought* it was, but she

needed to dig deeper. Malcolm didn't seem to be buying what she was selling and seemed reluctant to barter with the extra time she so desperately needed.

'There's only one way out, and that's with *me*,' said Kara. 'You can only absorb energy, but I can…I can *create* it.'

A truth contained with a presumption, but surely an appealing one.

Malcolm stopped a mere several feet in front of her.

'Then I'll just take what I need,' said Malcolm, grabbing her by the wrist of her bleeding arm and siphoning off the dregs of the retained charge she held.

But it was enough. It *had* to be.

She knew it before she saw them. A single spark was like a drop of blood in the ocean, and the megalodons were hungry.

Always hungry.

She saw their slick oily outlines filing out from Robert's room and blocking the hallway, quickly reasserting her gaze back to Malcolm in case he caught-on that they were about to have guests.

'How utterly heart-breaking,' Malcolm's voice devoid of the compassion his words implied. 'Such *promise*. When you came at me like you did, I almost experienced a hint of *worry*. That, perhaps, inexplicably, I had my work *cut* out for me.'

'Last chance,' said Kara. 'Work *with* me, and you can still live. We can get out of here…together.'

'How many times, Kara? You will *never* beat me. And I don't *need* you! Look at you; a desperate mess of pathetic second chances. All that *power*, and this is how your story ends.'

'That's always been your problem, Malcolm. You're always so focused on *us* that you never fail to miss the bigger picture.' She smiled. 'I'm not *trying* to beat you. I just needed to keep you busy long enough.'

'Busy for what?' he said, a raised eyebrow coexisting with a smirk brought on by the fact he had this in the bag.

'For *them* to find us.'

She jutted her head towards something behind him, and for the first time in his miserable life, the Dark Restarter felt what his victims felt when they laid eyes on him.

'All that energy you've been siphoning? It's a beacon. Like moths to a flame...' said Kara, feeling weak, but her contempt filling her cold body like a fire.

Malcolm dropped her, lashing out with his knife at the reflective, midnight-black skin of the nearest creature, slicing into its arm, causing it to shriek.

The act achieving little but sending the others into a frenzy, as more of them piled out of the trans-dimensional recreation of Fir Lodge and on top of him.

Kara could do nothing else but watch, feeling utterly drained and rolling onto her back. If this was how she was going to go, it was a good death.

Taking that bastard with her…

She smiled up at the white, featureless sky, feeling oddly at peace now that the battle was over. That she had won, in her own little way, on her own terms.

Two of the creatures appeared above her, stepping into her view and blotting out the relentlessly-white, perpetually-restarting sun, their slick skin contrasting against it and making her wonder if that was really a sun above her at all.

As their hands reached out to her, presumably to shred her flesh and bleed her dry, she drifted into unconsciousness, wondering on that for a moment.

Every time they restarted, were they creating a separate universe? Were they *duplicating* an entire galaxy? Or was it localised to just their little corner of time, confined to their time bubble?

The talons of the Time Vampires dug deep into her, feeding on the meagre scraps that were left, and she was relieved that the pain didn't last long.

As the creatures of the nexus fed on her, she slipped into a peaceful, almost meditative state, swirling white fireflies dancing in the sky above her, giving her space, and reluctant to land on her cheeks, as the sounds of Malcolm's screams took on the role of a reassuring lullaby that sent her into the oddly welcoming arms of death.

Hello?

She called out into the void, as if checking she was truly alone, her disembodied voice floating away like an autumnal leaf into the heart of oblivion.

Death was not as terrifying as she thought it would be.

An existence without pain.

Warm.

Inviting, even.

Her mind, or what was left of it, drifted listlessly, as she tried to absorb this new world, staring without emotion at a pitch-black horizon separating an ocean of oil and a sky made from a swirling black fog.

A place both devoid of light but, paradoxically, shielded from darkness also.

"Peace," she realised. This was the truest definition of the term.

A voice reached out to her from the darkness.

"You shouldn't be here…" each word dragging across her soul like forgotten nails along a metaphysical chalk board.

"Where am I?" she thought, both asking herself and the disembodied voice.

She was greeted by silence, until a new presence revealed itself via the faintest whispering of a single word.

"Kara."

A word from another time.

Its utterance filling her surroundings with a faint blue hue, as if by magic casting an outline around a previously unseen structure.

A *Black* Lodge?

Odd.

"Kara," her drifting consciousness echoed back at her.

She knew that word once. As well as the owner of the voice that had used it. It belonged to someone she knew, long ago. Someone close to her. Someone named—

"Hal?"

She sensed a flicker of electricity.

Followed by a surge of power.

Too *much* power!

And there was that pain again, arriving like an unwanted sales call...

If she had eyes, they would have rolled in their sockets.

What did it want?

Surely, this was one accident nobody would be willing to insure her for...

Stir of Echoes

R.I Timestamp Error: Recalculating…

System Error

As the claws gripped her arms, the Restarter felt a warmth flow through her body. A heat that stripped away the fog addling her mind until she regained the strength to open her eyes, only to be greeted by two very unexpected faces.

Kara gasped, her body eager to suck in some oxygen, as she was pulled from the black abyss of a partially de-molecularised mind, electricity coursing through her veins and refusing to plateau, increasing steadily as if searching for an unattainable amplitude. She gripped the wrist of her formerly damaged limb with her free hand, the gash on her arm having fully repaired itself and allowing her to flex her fingers. Kara expected her arm to burn with at least a flicker of residual pain, but all she could feel was the pulse from her wrist, which throbbed against her clenched hand as each finger waved back at her without protest.

'araK,' a female voice repeated kindly.

'Rachel? How?' she was clearly hallucinating. She looked down at her arms which were glowing blue, presumably thanks to the contact between herself and her fellow Restarter. That at least explained where the sharp jerking sensation of being electrocuted was coming from.

Hal popped into her field of view, turning the duo into a trio, and making her feel suddenly both exposed and embarrassed by the crowd.

She noted Hal's clothes; his brown leather jacket and blue jeans throwing her sense of when and where she was off entirely.

'How are you here?'

'thgir wonk I!' said Hal, rather unhelpfully.

His voice rose in pitch at the final syllable, and she suddenly realised he was talking in reverse. Or at least that's how it seemed from her perspective.

'Where *am* I?' said Kara, pulling herself upright and looking over to the mound of figures keeping Malcolm at bay.

Hal pulled a face, seemingly trying to concentrate, but instead looking somewhat constipated, before speaking again.

'Vampires. Time. The. *We're*,' he said, smiling and nodding as if he was impressed with the result.

Kara laughed, realising he was trying to speak in his version of reverse solely for her benefit, in the hope it would translate into something she could understand. To be fair, she discovered it was a solid effort, as she tried to mutter a single word backwards, immediately appreciating how hard it was.

'iH!' she said.

'Hi,' he said back, smiling with joy and laughing, the act coming across quite creepy as the sound played out backwards. 'og ot toG!' he added, before pulling a face of frustration and huffing at how much he sucked at this.

'Got to go?'

Hal nodded at his friend enthusiastically, as if they were playing a God Tier level of charades.

Kara nodded, then shrugged over-dramatically as if trying to order something in a foreign land having no prior knowledge of the dialect or customs, spreading her arms as if to say "How?"

Hal flapped his arm, rocking a come-hither sort of vibe and pointed beyond his duplicated brethren.

Kara watched the creatures with fresh eyes, as more of them appeared, no longer the faceless monsters of her nightmares, but something far more recognisable. They continued to tussle with Malcolm, draining him of his darker brand of Restarter energy as they did so, the shadows of what Kara now realised were the discarded echoes of their former selves taking on a much more familiar appearance, their features phasing into view as the realisation hit her like a freight train of obviousness; an army of Ghostbusters, Velmas, Golfers, Marilyn Monroes, and David Bowies all working towards a singular goal; to buy her some much needed time.

Hal and Rachel shared a dark look of understanding, and with a barely perceptible nod from Hal, the latter ran off to join the fray.

'They're...us...' said Kara.

All this time they had assumed that the featureless creatures were some kind of malevolent beasts feeding on the energy between timelines.

Time Vampires, they had called them. But now she knew the conclusions they had vaulted towards were way off.

They weren't the enemy after all.

Three Hell Hounds slinked in from several of the multiple entry points to the garden, each growling as they held position; ink-coloured sentries keeping guard over the monster that was threatening what they each remembered to be Kara.

They released a single unified bark, that hit Kara's ears in all kinds of wrong, the sound reverberating in reverse.

"Not Hell Hounds," she realised with renewed excitement. "Nexus Jer–"

'What *are* these things?' The Dark Restarter growled, throwing the humanoids off of him with ferocity, apparently unable to see them for what or who they really were.

'They're us. All the versions of us you killed,' Kara shouted back to him. 'And they're really fucking pissed with you!'

That was her working theory, but there seemed like too many for that. And then a darker truth dawned on her. It was *more* than that. They were–

Her thoughts were fractured by Malcolm's fearful shouts.

'We need to get out of here,' she murmured, more to herself than for Malcolm's benefit.

Kara turned to face the echo of Hal, who nodded and ran off towards the lodge, rolling his eyes back at her when he realised she hadn't taken the hint, once again gesturing for her to follow.

In an instant, she was beside…whatever version of Hal this currently was.

Kara didn't recall following him, but now found herself in Robert's room, where she was met with the sight of an empty bedroom, with Hal pointing excitedly towards the bed.

'Thanks Hal, but I was thinking of *leaving*, not sleeping. Wait,' she said, her eyes narrowing playfully. 'What are you asking me to *do* here?'

Hal looked confused, his eyes growing wide and waving his arms as if to cross out the relevance of the bed, seemingly mortified at what she was insinuating, and not at all what he was suggesting.

'Head of out gutter,' he exclaimed, his smile betraying the appalled glare in his eyes.

'Hey, you're the one who kept pointing at the bed,' she laughed, not even bothering to try and say that in reverse.

'drawkwA,' he muttered, before placing a hand on her shoulder.

She felt another surge of energy run through her, and suddenly saw that he wasn't actually suggesting a controversial method of spiking their energy, but was instead pointing at what appeared to be a *fracture* in the wall that was suddenly perceptible to her.

Thanks to Hal's touch, she assumed.

"No," she corrected in her mind. She was thinking too small again. "A fracture through *time*." She stared at the beautiful veil of shimmering, emerald-green energy. A rip in reality that shared more than a passing resemblance to that of a doorway.

"Not beautiful," she thought. "Dangerous."

'Is this what the Time Vampires,' she corrected herself, 'sorry, Time Echoes were feeding off?'

Hal and Kara had assumed it was the paradox caused by Peter the creatures had been staring at during their first trip into the nexus; that by changing his own timeline and him being pinned to the bedroom wall he had given the occupants of the nexus some scraps to latch onto…but as it turned out, it was merely an unseen gateway into the past they were being drawn to.

At least, *unseen* by Hal, Future Malcolm, and her the first time they had come here…

A considerably more murderous Malcolm arrived in the doorway, looking positively exhausted.

'*You*,' he growled, rushing at Kara, who allowed him to collide with her, dragging him with her through the split in space-time, as their bodies dematerialised and re-entered a much more predictable dimension.

Left behind like a rejected prom date, the echo of Hal walked slowly to the temporal schism and reached out towards it, but it shrunk with every step he made, shying away from him, until he placed his hand directly onto the space it once was, closing the breach completely.

He smiled, as the colour of his features bled away, replaced instead by a sickly-black oily complexion, his clothes tightening and morphing into nothingness, until he was once again nothing more than a mindless creature.

Other humanoid shapes made their way back from the garden, taking up the spaces next to him, until the room was completely full of them once more, the last of them closing the door behind themselves.

And they waited.

For *what*, they did not know.

An opportunity?

Freedom?

It was then that the door of the bedroom opened behind them, and they all turned around in unison, a shared jerking movement of surprise, and stared with eyeless faces at the intruder.

A man in a brown leather jacket, who reeked of power.

Power they craved.

Needed.

The man before them slowly extended an arm out towards the handle of the door, eager to close it to lock them back inside, but stopped himself, his hand halting just before it reached the door handle. The now-androgynous being that had formerly assisted Kara moments before mimicked his action. The others follow suit, their arms now extending towards him and drawing a wisp of electricity from the man's cheek.

'Ouch', the uninvited guest muttered.

'hcuO,' replied the Time Echoes all at once, a feedback loop befuddling their confused minds.

But to anyone experiencing time chronologically, such as the interloping time-traveller standing before them, the way the syllables bounced around in reverse sounded a lot more like "Chew."

CHAPTER SIXTY-NINE
All Good Things…

203rd Restart – Saturday, August 25th, 2018, 5:07pm

'Soooo, got any plans for the future? Should all this work out and we manage to escape, I mean?' said Hal, in a dismal attempt at making small-talk.

Kara, and the considerably more *killerish* version of Malcolm, had been gone for what had felt like hours, though in reality it had only been a fistful of minutes.

'I was thinking, perhaps, of taking up…fishing?' said Future Malcolm, as if asking Hal advice on if that was something normal people might do. Those of a more stable disposition who didn't indulge in murder, for example.

'Cool,' said Hal. 'Cool, cool, cool, no doubt.'

The Dark Restarter and Kara were thrust back into the land of the almost-living, caught in a deadly tussle, neither of them releasing their grip on each other.

'Oh, thank God,' said Hal, partially glad to see Kara alive and well, but mainly more because he didn't have to engage in laborious, banal chit-chat with his Malcolm any longer.

Future Malcolm kicked the blade Hal was still trying to reach gently with his foot, so Hal could pick it up from underneath the metal grill of the cage, then popped out of existence before his past-self had time to see him.

'Kara!' Hal shouted, sliding the blade across the floor to her.

She ducked down to avoid a vicious swing from Malcolm, catching it by the hilt and spinning it in her hand. Kara brought the knife downwards in a sharp, fluid motion as The Dark Restarter closed the gap between them.

He grabbed her wrist effortlessly, blue and red sparks spewing between them.

'You have nerve, girl, I'll give you that,' said the Malcolm of the past, smiling at her trembling arm that was no match for his strength. 'How did you bring us back here?'

'I...have a lot of friends across time these days,'

she said, straining against his might.

'What *are* you?' The Dark Restarter questioned, more out of genuine interest than as a stalling tactic, marvelling at how she was able to hold him at bay at all.

'Endahyou,' Kara mumbled, and Malcolm leaned in closer to her, their faces mere millimetres apart. The energy that was fuelling Kara had all but depleted, that much was clear. Instead of the wildly powerful glowing eyes, it was just her regular green-tinged orbs that stared back at him, her stimulated pupils dilating. A frightened woman, seriously out of her depth.

'Say again?' he said, revelling in the moment before her death. Drinking it in like a fine wine.

Kara pursed her lips, the blade held in place above Malcolm. 'I said…the *end* of you.'

The Dark Restarter's eyes widened in bemusement, as Kara released her grip on the blade from one hand, allowing it to fall freely between them, landing perfectly into the open palm of her other, her fingers wrapping cleanly around the handle.

She relaxed her left arm entirely, surrendering to Malcolm's superior strength, causing him to fall towards her, and into the knife, which slid through his chest with a sickening crunch.

They stood there, pressed against each other, Kara with a look of combined horror at what she had done, and Malcolm with a look of…was that a congratulatory look in his eyes?

She couldn't tell.

She wanted to throw-up, feeling almost cheated that she couldn't.

As blood began to trickle down from his body and down her arm, there was the briefest crackle of red energy emanating from Kara's hand.

They both saw it.

The Dark Restarter brought his lips to her left ear.

'Interesting, isn't–' he spluttered, as blood rose up to fill his mouth, and he puckered his mouth as if trying to swallow, but instead allowed the black liquid to dribble down his chin so he could continue speaking, before trying again. '*Isn't* it?'

'What?' she whispered, choosing to focus entirely on the wall in front of her as Malcolm's body began to increase in weight.

'All this time, you were–' he growled defiantly, the act of talking clearly becoming a struggle. 'You were chasing me, chasing the *darkness*…what was it you called me? The *Dark* Restarter?…' his body convulsed, but he kept it together. Just a little longer. 'When, in truth, you were only chasing yourself…'

'Shut up,' she said defensively.

She knew what he was trying to do. Future Malcolm had warned her he would do this.

But she was powerless to resist hearing the words splurging from the mouth of the snake, his forked tongue so calm and laced with conviction. Wrapping around her thoughts like a parasite.

'Chasing your destiny,' said the mortally wounded Malcolm. 'But we both saw it…' she knew he was referring to the flash of red energy. 'You'll make a *fine* Dark Restarter, Kara…'

The words hung in the air like a stagnant truth, blue and red sparks showering between them onto the ground. Intermingling in such a way that it made it impossible to truly tell which of them was channelling which.

Past Malcolm began to chuckle. A guttural noise that would have made even Lucifer grab his coat and make his excuses to leave.

And on that dire note, she savagely twisted the blade counter clockwise, then clockwise, just as Malcolm's future-self had instructed her to, and pushed the lumbering giant off of her, where he landed with a soundless thud, his words still ringing in her ears.

Her second murder now under her belt.

Only this one was far more brutal. Up close. Personal.

Was she any different from Malcolm?

All he was trying to achieve was to change the past so that he could be free of this place. Travelling through time, killing all those that stood in his way to reaching that singular goal…

As she looked down at her blood-soaked hands, thankful that she had no sense of smell in her current state, and looked down at the body beneath her, the blade sticking upright from his chest, unable to shake a bitter question from her mind;

The notion that perhaps, after all this time, her

and Hal were the true Dark Restarters all along.

The Restarter fell to her knees, tears forming.

Not because of having defeated Malcolm, but because he had forced her hand.

She stared at the blade, which was now resting on the ground, thanks to the body it had perforated now little more than cosmic dust, returning to the winds of time. The blade itself began to fade away, its work well and truly done here.

She felt a sudden burst of anger, and reached out for the weapon.

The object seemed confused, as if unsure if it should be ceasing to exist or if Kara had become its rightful owner by default.

As a compromise, it solidified in her hand, not wanting any trouble until the rules could be ironed out.

Pushing it between the flimsy latch and the metal gate that held the metal grills in place thanks to the pesky padlock, Kara used the blade as leverage in an attempt to break it.

'That won't work, Kar', we're not in phase with–' began Hal, his argument immediately invalidated as it snapped effortlessly. 'How did you–'

'Where is he,' said Kara, her eyes filled with a shine that seemed to peer straight through him.

'It's over, Kara,' said Hal, reaching for the blade as if hoping to take the burden from her.

'Not quite.'

She made her way to the staircase, in search of the

final loose end to their nightmare that only she could tie up.

*

Kara didn't waste a second, marching through the double patio doors and into the rear garden where Future Malcolm was waiting for her.

She grabbed Malcolm by the scruff of his shirt and drew back the blade, slicing it through the air and stopping its traversal just before his Adam's apple.

A shower of red electricity surging between them.

'Kara, what are you doing?' asked Future Malcolm, utterly perplexed by her actions.

'Say their names,' she spat savagely.

'I don't know what you want me to—'

'Say. Their. Names!'

'Peter. Fearne,' he muttered, not entirely sure what was happening.

'Is there even an Ophelia at all? *Did* you just make her up to manipulate us?'

'...'

'Answer me!' she screamed, causing a wave of vicious red energy to erupt from her eyes, generating a mini shockwave that blew the dirt from underneath them in an outwards circle.

She pushed the blade further, causing blood to flow from the small cut she was carving into his neck.

She felt a hand on her shoulder and turned around to face her assailant, realising it was Hal. She attempted to shrug away from his grip, but Hal held on tight, his teeth chattering under the duress the connection was causing, the last dregs of his own power siphoning away into her.

'K-Kara, put down the knife.'

She attempted to shrug Hal off her shoulder with a minimal exertion that somehow sent him reeling backwards and into the patio doors, the force sending an impossible crack to spread across the glass.

Something was wrong. Deep inside her. She felt…broken. She could feel it. The physical world around her was bending to her dark desires in a way that shouldn't have been possible.

Returning her focus back to Malcolm, she applied more pressure to the restarted blade, his grip on her wrists doing little to slow her progress. She lashed out, pushing him hard in the chest and sending him into a nearby tree trunk, leaving him winded, gasping for the air that did little to quench his body's thirst.

Kara suddenly felt like she was being ganged up on, that the person she trusted more than anyone else in this godforsaken circle of hell had been fooled, tricked, and was now siding against her. The red energy crackled as she gripped the hilt of the knife even harder.

She wanted to tell Hal everything. That Malcolm's Dark Restarter form had literally just told her what his plan was. That the only way Malcolm could feel truly free was to kill everything they loved and cared about. That he would not rest until he achieved that goal. That, even now, he was playing them. It had been *he*, the soothsaying Future Malcolm, who had knowingly sent Peter to the slaughter, that had kept them in line this whole time, not allowing them to diverge from his meticulously devised and orchestrated plan.

Were they really expected to believe that a bunch of restarts in a hospital after the events that transpired here would seriously reform a psychopathic murderer?

Were they *really* stupid enough, in their innate nature to see the best in people, to be blinded by the fact that all they were really doing was assisting the very person that had killed them in the first place?

And what? Now they would restart his *heart*? Freeing him from the bubble that protected the innocent lives outside the Pentney Lakes?

He had to be stopped. Permanently.

'Kara,' whispered Hal, returning to her side, his eyes equal parts kindness and worry.

"But mostly kindness…" she thought.

She could always rely on him for that.

The one constant.

Her compass in the dark.

But he was wrong *this* time. He was wrong to see the *good*. There was only *death* here. Only one way to protect her friend. *Friends* plural. Her *family*. Oh God, her family.

A life for a life. Those were the rules.

'Kara', Hal repeated, reaching out and wrapping his fingers around her knife-wielding hand.

She tried to pull away, red energy arcing out across the blade and upwards like a lightning rod; a conduit for the strength she would need for this final act, swirling in amongst the blue of Hal's own dwindling Restarter energy.

The contrasting colours of temporally-charged power swirled with such tenacity that the random patterns began to form what appeared to be a double helix.

'He's going to *kill* us, Hal,' she whispered, her cheeks feeling wet from what must have been tears. 'I…have to *save* us…I…'

'You've done enough saving for one day,' he said softly, his words full of comforting reassurance and more than a sprinkling of sadness. 'I'm sorry you had to go through that alone. But you can *stop* now. Just *stop*. Let go of the knife. I've got you.'

The red began to die down in intensity until, after what could have been minutes, maybe hours, the dark energy she was channelling brightened, returning to a far more manageable blue.

Begrudgingly, she let go of the knife, severing their connection as Hal took it from her.

The blade dissolved instantly in Hal's hand. Less than dust.

Malcolm sat there on the ground, eyes wide with wonder.

Kara's legs buckled beneath her, suddenly feeling like sun bleached ink on withering parchment.

'He *made* me kill him, Hal! There was no other choice. I tried to…' her sobs becoming more uncontrollable, the words harder to understand.

'I said he could take me but he wanted you and the others our families and Greg and he wouldn't stop he meant it I could see it I...I...' she gasped for air.

Hal kneeled down next to her.

'I know. There was no other choice. I saw and heard it all.'

Malcolm pulled himself onto all fours and slowly crawled towards the Restarters, then reached out hesitantly, his hand hanging in mid-air, as if waiting for Hal's consent.

Hal nodded, and Malcolm placed his hand on her shoulder in a comforting manner.

Kara swished her hair out of her eyes and balled her hand into a fist, as if attempting to summon the time traveller's knife back into phase, fully expecting to see the red energy radiating between Future Malcolm's hand and her shoulder.

Only the red electricity had changed. Mutated. Shifting into something she would never have believed had she not seen it with her own eyes.

The Restarter energy Malcolm was siphoning from the past, from *them*, from the *universe* itself...whatever it was that was powering them wasn't important. What *was* important, more than anything, was one simple fact;

There wasn't a trace of red between the three of them.

Only blue.

CHAPTER SEVENTY
The Immortal Instruments

203rd Restart – Saturday, August 25th, 2018, 5:19pm

Hal had expected something transformative to occur after defeating Malcolm's considerably darker past-self.

Like a gong being sounded, as if to signify they had completed their challenge and had levelled up. As if the heavens would split, showering them in congratulatory sparkles of shimmering blue Restarter shards that maybe they could cash in at the Starbucks gift shop before they left. It seemed plausible to Hal that the coffee chain would have found a way to facilitate breaking into the trans-dimensional market.

But the reality was far more anticlimactic. They simply…continued to exist.

'So…what happens now?' said Kara, vocalising their shared thoughts.

Hal was equally stuck on how they should proceed.

'I know, right? Do we just…ride this restart out?' opening the question to the floor but steering it slightly more towards the man from their future.

'Why are you looking at me?'

'Well, ya know,' remarked Hal. 'This was essentially the end game of the plan you've spent the best part of *three hundred-or-so* restarts putting together. I figured you'd have a contingency once we took out Bowser. You better not be telling us our princess is in another castle…'

'I honestly have no idea why you insist on using words in such a ridiculous order,' said Malcolm, feigning fatigue to mask the fact he was stalling whilst he got his thoughts into something resembling order.

'Malcolm….' said Kara, singing his name with a questioning tone.

'Yes, Kara?'

'Oh, for fu–' she replied, before revealing what was suddenly all-too-apparent. 'He has *no* idea. Look at him! He has no *idea* what to do next!'

'Well, this is just perfect,' said Hal, in a way that truly displayed the utter lack of perfection in the absence of any notable paradigm shift to their situation. He sighed irritably. 'Well, I guess we could just head back to Fir Lodge and see what's going on.'

Hal and Kara stared at Malcolm expecting an objection, but he simply broke eye-contact and stared at a dried-out patch of grass.

'Great,' said Kara. 'Just great.'

*

'So,' said Hal, having made their way back to the more comforting territory of their home turf at the rear of Fir Lodge, plonking himself down on an unused deck chair as he addressed Kara, instead of the essentially useless time traveller Malcolm, who insisted on standing. Presumably just for stylistic purposes. 'With The Dark Restarter out of action, where does that leave us?'

'Well, I guess it works the same as Peter,' mused Kara. 'Since Malcolm teamed up with himself and stole Pete's life from him, he hasn't returned. I think it's safe to say the same will apply to Malcolm's past-self and…' she struggled to finish her sentence. But they all knew she was going to say "Fearne."

'I feel like now would be a good time to discuss that,' said Malcolm.

'Discuss what? You murdering another one of our friends?' said Kara sharply.

'I told you, they are not dead in the way that you think.'

In truth, she had forgotten about that little morsel of information he had dropped. She reasoned that stabbing a temporally-displaced serial killer through the chest and erasing them from time itself would probably tend to do that to a person.

'You keep saying that as if you didn't kill them,' she said. 'As if it wasn't *your* hand that took them from us. But it *was*, Malcolm.'

"A younger hand maybe," she thought, but one that belonged to him all the same.

'Wait' said Hal, his voice suddenly filled with unexpected hope. 'You mean we can bring them back?'

'No,' said Malcolm flatly. 'They were Echoes,' he added quickly and simply to ease Hal's torment. 'Not the *true* versions of your friends. I discovered them purely by luck during one of my earlier expeditions to The White Lodge.'

Hal and Kara stared blankly.

'And they didn't *betray* you. At least, not until I intervened,' clarified Malcolm. 'They failed.'

'What do you mean, *failed*?' asked Kara.

'They were stuck,' Future Malcolm continued. 'Barely sentient shadows. I found them in Fir Lodge, on what would soon transpire to be their last ever "Repeat". After I manipulated them into exchanging their lives for yours, they should have faded away…'

The Restarters knew what he was getting at.

By Peter and Fearne changing their own past, they would have dematerialised. Sent hurtling back to the present, none the wiser of their dark deeds. Leaving Hal and Kara to pick up the pieces. A truth they knew all too well from first-hand experience.

'But,' Future Malcolm added, his use of the word

seemingly brimming with revelation. 'A unique opportunity presented itself.'

'Of course it did,' groaned Kara.

'Before they were fully reclaimed by the fog, I latched onto them. After all, if their present-selves were alive and well, what harm could it do? Using the last of their retained charge I placed them into a new timeline.' *One of his own design*, he neglected to add. 'One where they could…serve an even greater purpose.'

Before reality had a chance to shift.

Before Kara and Hal's first ever restart could take hold.

'Imagine my amazement once we arrived, when the fog stopped chasing their…*echoes*. Echoes that possessed all of their prior memories, no less,' lamented Malcolm. 'Entirely self-sufficient.'

In truth, Malcolm hadn't known for sure just how convincing these facsimiles would be. Nor how they retained their sense of self to the point of making new decisions of their very own, acting entirely independently, their minds a perfect replica of their predecessors.

Fearne especially.

She, in particular, had been right about him all along. How he was using them like puppets to facilitate his own dark deeds and opportunistic agenda.

Indeed, that had raised a philosophical quandary in his own mind; how real were *any* of them, if their consciousnesses could be replicated so easily? Like a severed limb, somehow evolving into an entirely new body, one with its own hopes and dreams, whilst the phantom limb of the future continued onwards through time.

'I needed you to experience true loss,' continued Malcolm. 'So that when the time came for you to act, you would no longer require the proximity of your past-selves. Though I must admit, I assumed you'd need at least another Restarter to generate a charge. You're very special Kara.'

Kara's skin crawled as if she were in the middle of a work appraisal chaired by Satan, and she brought her guard back up.

'More importantly,' continued Malcolm, 'I needed my *younger self* to believe the stakes. I needed him to trust my intentions were to serve mutual benefit. And what better way to do that than…'

If what Malcolm was suggesting were true, Peter and Fearne were never in real danger at all.

'Offering up Peter and Fearne to him,' said Hal. 'That explains why Fearne couldn't remember Peter's funeral. She simply hadn't lived through it yet.'

'And why Peter didn't return to the future without us,' said Kara. 'When we stopped Past Malcolm I mean. And barged through that door when we first got here?'

'I know not of Peter's funeral,' said Malcolm, 'but yes. I was concerned that would have given the game away in terms of Peter's…chronological affiliation.'

Hal and Kara shifted uncomfortably, feeling like rookies for missing such a glaring inconsistency. Luckily, Malcolm was in a talky mood, and permitted them to gloss over it.

Malcolm continued, highlighting how not only *delivering* two Restarters to himself, but also permitting him to *kill* them by his own hand was a powerful means to gain his own trust.

'I'm sorry for not telling you,' said Malcolm, an odd truthfulness lining the words. 'But the reaction you and Kara displayed upon witnessing their respective deaths had to be genuine. I would have known if it wasn't.'

Suddenly, Malcolm's claim didn't seem that far-fetched.

If he had indeed retrieved a version of Peter and Fearne from a timeline that was scheduled to collapse, then brought them into phase with the version of Hal and Kara that had arrived from the *actua*l future, it would have meant that Peter and Fearne were alive and well in the present.

"Little more than immortal instruments," thought Hal. Instruments strung with strings that could never truly be snapped.

'Oh my god,' said Hal in sheer awe of Malcolm's gamble. 'They're *alive*, Kara.'

'That is my understanding,' said Malcolm. 'What happened to their echoes should not hold any duress on their present selves.'

'You can't *possibly* know that,' said Kara angrily.

She had always worked on the assumption that their Restarter-selves were transported back into their living bodies once they had fixed whatever broken timeline they were living within. But she found herself wondering just how certain she could really be. After all, she had seen a frightening display of evidence to the contrary whilst fighting Dark Malcolm at The White Lodge.

She really needed to tell Hal what she saw. How there were countless versions of both her and Hal, speaking oddly in reverse. How–

'Everything I have done I have done to free us *all*,' said Malcolm, breaking Kara's train of thought.

'Oh, that's rich,' said Kara. 'Don't dress this up. Everything you've done you've done for yourself.'

'Kara,' said Hal quietly.

'What?' she snapped. 'There's no *way* he could have known killing the Restarter versions of Pete and Fearne would have guaranteed their safety in the present Hal! He's just not that smar–'

'We have to restart his heart.'

Hal's words cut the air between them and landed like an anvil.

'Why?! If we don't, he'll cease to be and we can...we can *fix* time. We won't be interrupted now. We've done it before, we can do it again.'

'That's just it,' said Hal. 'If we don't, he'll never make it to the hospital. Never come back and bring us into phase with Pete and Fearne's echoes. The Dark Restarter version of himself will never be destroyed, and all this...' he added, raising his arms to encompass everything around them. '...All this will just keep going around. An endless cycle. An infinity loop that we'll never, *ever* escape from. It's the only way–'

'To break the chain,' said Kara angrily, finishing his sentence and hating him a little for how right he was.

'Exactly,' said Hal glumly.

'We can't *do* this Hal. If he ever wakes up from that coma...'

'I'm not saying there won't be consequences, I'm saying we don't have any *choice*. Besides, you said it yourself, the potential brain damage alone...if we're lucky he'll be a vegetable for the rest of his life.'

'You know I'm standing *right* here, don't you? I can hear every word you're say–'

'Honestly, Sauron, it's like you're actively *trying* to sabotage yourself. The heroes are talking.'

Malcolm scowled, but remained quiet, as the silence between the three of them grew louder, until Kara finally exploded.

'Fuck!' she shouted. 'Fucking fuck! Fine. Let's go do this so we can get out of here.'

'So,' said Hal, rubbing his hands together in preparation for a good old-fashioned Time Heist. 'All we have to do is run over to Kev's Saturday evening, give ol' *Frankenstein* here a jump-start and–'

'Technically, you will both be playing the role of Victor Frankenstein. It is a common misconception that the *monster* was named Frankenstein, when in actuality–'

'Really?' said Hal in disbelief. '*Now's* the time you decide to chip in to correct a reference?'

'If you're going to reference a literary classic, you might as well reference it correctly. Besides, I'm afraid it's not going to be quite as simple as "Jump starting" Frankenstein's monster,' said Malcolm.

'Malcolm, I swear to God,' said Kara, reaching breaking point.

Malcolm raised his hands apologetically in an attempt to show it had not been his intention to antagonise her.

'What I mean is, we must first ensure your 165th restart plays out exactly as it did before. *Everything* must be identical.'

'We'll figure it out as we go,' said Hal. 'You in?' he added, shooting Kara a look that implied if she wasn't, he'd back her all the way.

'You mean, am I ready to resurrect our killer?'

She held Hal's gaze, before throwing up her hands in defeat.

'Why the hell not. It's not like we have anything even remotely plan-like to fall back on. I'm in.'

'Well then,' said Hal, pulling himself up from the chair and dusting himself down. 'Let's get this party Restarted.'

His words causing Malcolm to groan, and Kara to protest that they were all better than catchphrases like that.

CHAPTER SEVENTY-ONE
Restart my Heart

204th Restart – Friday, August 24th, 2018, 12:01pm

'You know,' said Hal, having just passed through the Restart Point and unclenching his stomach, utterly nailing a flawless time-traveller landing, 'I don't think we're going to have to actually *do* all that much.'

'How so?' said Kara, looking for Fearne and accepting she wasn't going to restart along with the rest of them.

Not this time.

'Well, I know for us this is like our billionth restart, but technically we're just reliving our 165th, right?'

'Oh,' said Kara, seeing where he was going. 'So, you think there's a past version of us already putting our plan in action?'

'Exactly,' said Hal, shivering for a moment and taking a step backwards, as if he was somehow treading on the toes of an out-of-phase version of his past-self.

'So, all we need to do,' surprised that she wasn't on the verge of getting a headache from all the time travel theory, 'is make sure nothing gets in the way of our past-selves carrying out their Time Heist?'

They stood there for several minutes, mentally twiddling their thumbs and wondering what they should do next, as a shrill popping noise signalled the arrival of Future Malcolm.

'Man,' said Hal. 'Wouldn't it be awesome if we could just generate a montage and skip to the end when all this grafting is done?'

'That *would* be pretty great, yeah.'

Malcolm smiled at them, a look of mischievousness in his eyes.

'Urgh, please don't smile. There's nothing creepier than when you're in a good mood,' added Kara.

'I was just contemplating your idea on skipping to the end,' said Malcolm.

'Oh, don't you *dare* leave all this for us to deal with you–' began Kara.

'See you tomorrow evening. You know when to find me,' said Malcolm, dematerialising into their respective future.

'Such a twat,' remarked Hal with prolific incredulity.

'Let him go,' said Kara with a flimsy wave of her hand. 'We work better without him anyway.'

Hal nodded in agreement. 'Okay, so where do we start?'

Hal checked his non-existent watch, trying to remember exactly where they were at this point in what their past-selves had assumed would be their final restart.

'Friday. Twelvish. I guess we just stay out of each other's way,' said Hal pulling out his phone from his pocket. 'Can I steal a charge?'

'Only if I can choose the music?'

Kara smiled at the impending payment for his services as Hal shrugged at her terms, and they held hands causing the phone to spring to life.

'Woah, it doesn't usually charge that quick,' noted Kara, taking the phone from him and turning her back on him. 'What's your passcode?'

'No,' said Hal, a look of concern on his face that went entirely unnoticed by Kara. 'No, it doesn't…'

'Hal. If you want me to drop the needle, I'm going to need your passcode,' she repeated.

'Huh?' he responded, pulled away from his worry over Kara's increasingly innate ability to bend the rules he was still very much shackled by. 'Oh. Sorry. One, six, five, zero. Please don't pick anything rubbish for the soundtrack to our last restart.'

'No pressure then,' said Kara, shooting him a wink. 'You know, you're an identity thief's dream,' remembering he had used that code for his gun's lockbox as well, and that he probably used that code for everything. Temporal lucidity, it seemed, was nothing if not repetitive.

She spun around having settled on a song, aiming the phone at him like a Starfleet-issue ray-gun before pressing play, as Good Charlotte's "The Chronicles of Life and Death" began blaring from the speakers.

'Emo much?'

'Hey, it's *your* music library,' she countered.

'Touché.'

*

The afternoon breezed by, as they relived a very familiar Friday, until 3:33pm, when Hal started to get antsy. They were standing at the end of the rear garden, watching the events unfold.

'Where did you go?' said Hal, plonking himself down on the grass. 'When you and Evil Malcolm went all *Hayden Christensen* and teleported, I mean.'

'The White Lodge,' she said simply.

'Yeah, that's what Malcolm suspected. But that shouldn't be possible should it? Going there without Future Malcolm?'

'Maybe it's because I *was* attached to Malcolm? *Dark Restarter* Malcolm I mean?' she offered.

Hal wasn't convinced. 'He said he didn't score that gift until after his stay at the hospital, though.'

'What do you mean?'

'I mean he wasn't able to access The White Lodge until after his battle with you…'

They watched idly as their alive-selves blasted a weathered shuttlecock between them, the sounds of laughter meeting their ears amidst the energetic thwacks of the rackets.

'How did you get out?' asked Hal eventually, assuming the answer may have rested somewhere within the question.

'You saved me. And Rachel. I was done.'

She recounted how Malcolm's past-self had her on the ropes, had cut her badly. How the edges of the nexus had been burnt away to nothingness. And how they had been swarmed by the Time Vampires that stalked the eerie dimension of folded space-time. How Hal himself had led her to a *breach* of sorts; a gateway back to *her* Hal and Future Malcolm.

'At first I thought it was really you. But…we were wrong about the creatures Hal. They weren't what we thought they were.'

'How do you mean?' said Hal, brow furrowed.

'I think…I think they were *us*.'

Hal stared in disbelief. That was a huge claim to process.

Kara attempted to elaborate, trying to piece together the limited facts she had at her disposal

'I think…every time we restart, a version of ourselves gets transported to that White Lodge Nexus place.'

Hal shivered.

Up until now they had simply assumed that once a restart was done, they were transported to the next one. But if Kara was right, it meant they were not only disintegrated at a molecular level, but *duplicated*, just as Future Malcolm had claimed.

The implications of that made him sick to his stomach.

If he and Kara, right here and right now, were copies of their original selves, were they even the real Hal and Kara at all?

'That could explain the static fog,' said Hal, referring to the seemingly sentient mist that swirled around them and hindered their minds during prolonged exposure to multiple restart cycles. 'As the fog gets thicker, what if that's as close to Restarter death as you can get.'

'You mean if you were to stay here too long? In a restart loop?'

'Yeah. Stay too long and eventually you end up there?' Hal theorised, referring to The White Lodge.

'I think that's why they wanted to draw power from us,' said Kara sadly. 'So they could be whole again. If just for a little while. So they could communicate.'

'Wait, you said you saw Rachel there?'

'I did. Though I don't know how she could have been there. Not unless–'

'*Everyone* who has Restarted has been duplicated…' said Hal, finishing her sentence. 'Were there lots of Malcolms there too?'

'Nope. Just a bunch of "*us's*". Well, and a handful of Peters and Fearnes, with some Rachels and Alexs for good measure as far as I could tell. It was weird.' She couldn't be certain, but she was sure she even saw a couple of Santas.

'I'll bet.

'No, I mean, they tried to *speak* to me. But their words were garbled. They were speaking in reverse.'

'Sounds creepy,' said Hal thoughtfully, and Kara nodded in agreement as she recollected the experience.

'Kinda makes you think, right?" said Hal, sitting upright.

'About what?'

'Well, if there are hundreds of "us's" running around in that nexus...'

'Oh...'

'Yeah. Where were the Restarted Malcolms?'

Kara mused over that bombshell for a moment. Where *were* the Restarter Malcolms?

'Heads up,' said Hal. 'We've got company.'

She put the disturbing question aside as Jerry appeared to her left, peeking out through the hedge like a ninja, before sprinting towards the badminton quartet. Hal chuckled as they heard Kara's past-self crying out about a dog attack.

'Oh, bloody hell, the hell hounds at The White Lodge! They must've been–'

'Restarted Jerrys!' said Hal, slapping his forehead. It was so obvious to him now. All those Restarts Jerry had spent with Peter and Fearne, each time recreating an echo of the four-legged honorary Restarter.

Hal was about to dive into the ramifications of that, when the hairs on his arms rose.

'Something's wrong. I feel like we've forgotten something…'

'How so?' replied Kara.

'It's gotta be *exact*, right?'

'Yeah, what are you thinking?'

'Well, right now, Jerry should be running to check out that flowerpot, shouldn't he?'

'Oh yeah, Jerry came over to see us.' It was the first time they realised Jerry could seem them in their Restarter form.

'No, Jerry came over to see us on our first *ever* restart,' corrected Hal. 'There's no reason for him to leave the group right now. Because there's nothing to attract him. But he definitely ran off somewhere when we were alive, remember?'

'Oh,' said Kara. 'Oh! Shit!'

He watched, as *his* Kara set off at a sprint towards the flowerpot, charging after her upon realising she got what he was getting at.

'Here boy!' Jerry seeming to sense her Restarter-self rushing past him, his ears twitching as they caught a sound only he could hear.

He moved away from the badminton game he had interrupted, shaking from head to tail, and shot off after the Restarter to see what all the fuss was about, sniffing at her ankles as she stood by the potted plant.

After a reasonable amount of time, and the timeline seemingly back on track, Kara started to panic. Jerry hadn't stayed in this spot for this long, had he? He had run off around the side.

She heard someone calling Jerry's name and was relieved to see it was her Hal, who had taken the long way around the lodge, trying to get the dog's attention, though Hal needn't have bothered.

In fact, neither of them had needed to intervene at all.

Jerry was already sauntering over to another patch of grass, and began rolling on his back, interacting with what Kara knew to be a version of herself invisible to her own eyes; one occupying one of her latter repeats of their 165th Restart.

And so it was that Jerry's timeline for Friday had come full circle, with Kara and Hal marvelling over how Jerry could sense them from across multiple phases of existence, countless restarts apart.

'Because time travel,' said Kara, releasing a short puff of air and aiming her sarcasm at the plant pot which remained entirely inanimate and forever unhelpful.

*

At 11:04am the following morning, Kara and Hal watched in silence as the box of screws slid across the floor towards a worktop, smiling as a screwdriver fell into the box from the counter, then made its way once more of its own volition and into the storage room that would later become Kevin's prison.

'Man, that would be super creepy if you walked in on that, right?' noted Hal. 'Like, coming down here and seeing a box moving on its own like that?

'Time Heist? Check!' said Kara. 'What's next? Pretty much just the balloons, champagne glasses and cork–'

'Oh my,'

'–left to go, right?' said Kara, ignoring his Wizard of Oz joke.

'Oh my crap,' said Hal, suddenly worried. 'Will Peter and Fearne still be glitching tonight if their Restarter-selves aren't there to, ya know,' Hal shook his hands and made a noise that was meant to sound like lightning.

'I guess we'll just have to be ready if that plays out differently.'

'But there are only two of us, and they're at opposite ends of the lodge,' said Hal, showing signs of stress. 'It'll take both of us to keep one of them occupied, let alone both.'

'Will you calm down,' said Kara. 'You're starting to make *me* panic, Hal.'

But he had a point.

*

Luck was for once on their side, as the past crimes of their Restarted counterparts played out as normal, with Peter being held in place in the physical world by his past-self and the assistance of what was confusingly a *past* incarnation of a *future* Malcolm.

Both Kara and Hal refused to dwell on that too much, deciding to circumvent paradoxical insanity by taking comfort in the realisation Peter and Fearne's actions across time had cemented themselves as a temporal constant.

Fearne's alive-self spun around, knocking into some champagne flutes, but instead of letting them fall, Hal instinctively reacted and reached out to prevent them from toppling, his out-of-phase molecules reverberating with solidity given how close he was to his alive-self.

'What the hell did you do that for?' said Kara.

'I'm sorry, I just reacted!'

'Well, I guess now we know when the champagne flutes stopped falling,' said Kara sourly.

'Yeah, my bad. Who knew? Righty oh,' said Hal. 'Next stop, Kevin's. I'll run ahead and make sure that's playing out as it should be.'

'I guess I'll stay here and watch the shop, then.'

Hal saluted, and Kara reciprocated, finding herself in the utterly bizarre reality of knowing there was the echo of herself moving pool balls around, none the wiser that, less than three feet away, a version of herself from the future was chaperoning her actions to make sure she didn't bodge it all up on the last stretch.

Kara watched as her alive-self departed with a still-living version of Hal, then recoiled in horror as they closed the door behind them. She glanced back to the pool table, then at the double entrance doors.

They needed to be open. She remembered them being open.

She was about to panic, until an unprecedented truth dawned on her.

Kara walked towards the entrance doors, her alive-self having just departed and therefore close enough for her to draw a modest charge. Not that she needed it any more. Unlike Hal, she seemed to be able to draw a charge whenever she pleased.

She reached out for the handle, feeling a sense of relief as it yielded under her touch. She let go of it and pressed her palm gently against the glass, pushing outwards.

Kara thought back, to when her time-travelling-self had been leaning on that pool table; how she had forgotten her own name, entirely freaking out over her lack of memories as they had drained away from her.

She looked back over her shoulder, her past-Restarter-self still presumably leaning against the exact same pool table, albeit out of phase, noting the black 8-Ball was still in play. This meant her Restarter-self was yet to pot it accidentally by brushing against it.

"I wonder," thought Kara, wandering closer and reaching out into the space above the table, twisting her hand in the empty air, a brief spark erupting from her hand and disappearing into nothingness. Or, perhaps, giving her past Restarting-self the nudge she needed to snap out of it.

Kara looked down, the 8-Ball moving of its own accord and falling into the centre pocket.

She smiled, realising that she had been supporting herself all along, and she hadn't even known it.

'Run Kara…' she murmured. 'Run.'

*

'Something's wrong,' said Hal, who had been greeted at Kevin's by Future Malcolm. 'That plate isn't budging'

They peered at it together, as if searching for a divine intervention that had apparently got held up, perhaps nursing a nasty hangover.

'Maybe I should knock it off?' said Hal. 'Our Restarter selves are doing their thing, but everything needs to be like it was before…'

'Do not touch it. It will fall when it is meant to fall.'

'It's not going to fall, Malc,' said Hal impatiently.

'If you knock it now and it's too early, it could ruin everything!'

Hal moved closer to the circular anomaly, causing Malcolm to push him away, until eventually they were both heatedly slapping at each other, both of them looking utterly ridiculous and neither displaying the finely-honed skills of combat Malcolm not only possessed, but had also imparted onto Hal.

Eventually, Hal won the scuffle, reaching around Malcolm and flicking the plate with his finger, causing a muted ding to fill the room, which in turn made Malcolm's alive past-self stop in his tracks, until finally the plate tipped over the edge of the drainer and collided with the floor, the ceramic shattering violently.

Alive-Malcolm groaned, and turned his back on the basement, proceeding to clear it up.

'Was that it?' said Hal, feeling let down that the ripple they were sending back through time served no other purpose than to temporarily delay Malcolm from his inevitable path. 'Lame.'

Future Malcolm sighed, wondering what he had done to deserve being trapped here with such people.

'I don't know, maybe killing all those *other* people?' said Hal.

Malcolm's expression was one of a man having been caught in the socially awkward act of belittling someone in their presence. He was about to ask how Hal knew what he had been thinking when he realised he was still holding Hal's arm.

He released his grip on the Restarter and snapped his arm away from him.

'Stay out of my head, Harold.'

'Don't look at *me*. It's not my fault our abilities have gone *Super Saiyan*. Maybe you're drawing on your alive-self more than you realise. And past-*me* is only up the road.'

'Hmmmmmm….'

Kara burst through the open front door of Kevin's lodge causing Hal to squeal in shock. An act he tried to cover up by clearing his throat.

'I thought you were–'

'—The *othe*r Kara. Yeah, yeah,' she said rolling her eyes. 'I'm not even wearing the right clothes! You scare *way* too easily.'

'Sorry. It's just…we're so close now.'

'We should make our way to the basement,' said Malcolm.

'And at number one,' said Hal jokingly, 'on the list of the ten things you don't want to have said to you by Malcolm is…'

Malcolm growled faintly once again, before leading the way to a place of particular significance to not only the Restarters, but him especially.

It was, after all, the room where each of them had died.

*

They watched as Malcolm's alive-self was held in place by the unseen Restarters of the past, a wild energy filling the room which offered Hal and Kara a unique perspective on how they managed to defeat a man they would never have been able to defeat in the physical world.

At least, not *then*, anyway…

The three time-travellers were all but patting themselves on the backs for a job well done. Everything was happening as it always did; they had covered all of their bases, accounted for every eventuality, and it was just a matter of allowing this final piece of cemented history to play out as it always did. In fact, it was at precisely this moment that everything went to shit.

'Uh, Malcolm,' said Kara, her eyes widening with confusion. 'You should be dead by now, shouldn't you?'

It was true; at this point Malcolm's alive-self should have hit the dirt, lying lifelessly on the floor. Instead, he was still raising a knife to an invisible assailant.

As the energy coursing through his veins weakened, a darkness began to materialise in the centre of the blue storm Hal and Kara's presently invisible past-Restarter-selves were generating, creating a rift that seemed to be *assisting* the killer of their past rather than incapacitating him.

They heard their familiar voices above them, their own alive-selves now in the house and tending to Jerry's hydrational requirements.

'No,' said Future Malcolm. 'It can't be…'

'Oh, it very much be, Malc,' said Hal, panic surging through him.

'It's…' began Malcolm.

'You!' said Kara, as a flutterby took hold of the room around them.

Sure enough, a form had manifested inside the rift, sharing more than a passing resemblance to none other than Malcolm himself.

Suddenly, the missing piece of the puzzle engulfed them.

Until this point, they had assumed that it had been a certain Dark Restarter who had changed something big to bring Hal and Kara back into their restart cycle, and back into the past.

'Malcolm,' said Hal softly. 'Tell me it wasn't you that went back and changed this moment to bring us here?'

Malcolm was frozen in place. Honestly, he had assumed he'd gotten away with it. After all, they were all still here, and Hal and Kara had no memory of this moment. He was confident it had slipped through the net, unnoticed by whatever it was that acted as the guardian of cemented time.

'This is bad, isn't it,' said Kara.

'This is *worse* than bad,' said Hal, spinning to face Future Malcolm. 'How could you be so stupid? Changing *this* moment?! The one event in all of this that has to remain unchanged!'

It was true. All of it.

To bring them here, Future Malcolm had revisited his own past, saving his alive-self from the onslaught of the Restarters. The ripple effect of that was that no matter how many Dark Restarters they took out, this was a version of Malcolm they couldn't stop. Unless…

'Tell me you haven't done this yet,' said Hal, thinking quickly. 'If you haven't done it yet, this is a future we can change. This is–'

'I did this…' said Malcolm, slower than he had ever spoken before, each word a nail in a coffin. *Their* coffin. '…*before* you arrived. To bring you here.'

And in that moment, Hal realised Malcolm had broken everything. They couldn't stop what was unfolding now even if they wanted to.

If they did, Hal and Kara would cease to be, everything they had achieved thus far would come undone. And *their* Malcolm, the Malcolm from the future, would be caught in an infinity loop for all eternity.

'But how?' said Kara, their time running out as the being in the rift became clearer, forcing its way into phase with them.

'You must *know* how I did it,' said Malcolm, your memories should have realigned themselves by now?'

Hal and Kara thought back to that night, probing their memories, as a dull ache wormed its way across the top layers of their recollections of an already-altered past, their thoughts shifting as they attempted to absorb an equally altered truth.

How they had combined their energy to keep Malcolm in place between them, how they had ended his miserable life there and then…but suddenly they weren't so sure. There were black spots in the order of events that led to that moment. A black shadow appearing between the three of them, reaching through Malcolm and forcing their hands apart, disrupting the flow of their combined energy and preventing them from keeping him in place. They were forced apart somehow.

No.

By some*one*.

And their killer had continued on his merry way, up that staircase in Kevin's lodge, and–

Hal and Kara clutched their heads in fleeting agony, as the memory was stripped from them.

'What the hell was that?' said Kara, rubbing her temples to alleviate the residual discomfort.

'An implanted memory, maybe?' said Hal, 'He's creating a *new* restart! A *sixth* timeline! One that–'

Hal turned to face the Malcolm of their slowly unravelling future, realising that everything from here on out was entirely out of their control.

'You get to decide, Malcolm,' Hal said earnestly. 'What happens next…only *you* can change it.'

'I don't know how,' said Malcolm, in what appeared to be genuine sadness. 'I'm sorry. For all of this. I…I needed you here.'

The void within the sea of blue parted, generating a roaring wind, a humanoid shape taking an even denser form as it held the two invisible attackers at bay, not looking too dissimilar from the creatures that resided within the nexus of The White Lodge. Suddenly, time froze around them, creating a vacuum in space as well as time; as if the universe itself had no idea what should come next.

'You think this is why there were no Malcolms at the White Lodge?' said Kara, shouting over the hurricane of air that was attacking their senses.

It made sense. How could the back catalogue of Malcolms be *there* if–

'He's trapping himself inside a paradox!' shouted Hal, his words almost lost amidst the uproar. 'And us along with it!'

Future Malcolm stood there, utterly stupefied.

He had to act quickly. It was the only way.

And with that, he lunged recklessly towards the entity.

Hal latched onto his arm and tried to hold him back, shooting a glance towards Kara that screamed "A little help would be nice."

She caught on quick, grabbing Malcolm's other arm, their restarter energy crackling wildly, both noting how Future Malcolm was no longer generating a pleasant blue, and instead reverting to a tried and tested red variant.

'Malcolm, no!' shouted Hal.

Hal didn't know how bad it could possibly get if someone from their own future connected with an alive-version of themselves from the past, whilst a duplicated *time travelling* echo of themselves was simultaneously phasing through multiple timelines to alter the amalgamated history of everyone in the entire room, but he felt safe in his assumption that the answer was somewhere along the lines of "pretty fucking bad."

Standing in front of Future Malcolm, Hal released his grip for just a moment. Staring him straight in the eyes, he mimed the action of breaking a twig, then splayed his fingers as if the movie he was tasked with relaying during this hopeless game of charades was "Armageddon."

Malcolm stared back, eyes momentarily delirious, but once again present, as he mulled over his limited choice of options; he could jump into his own Echo, and hope that making contact would sever the connection to his alive-self, allowing the Hal and Kara of Restart 165 to succeed in defeating him.

But that would erase the Hal and Kara he was currently in-phase with from existence.

Or, he could do nothing; allowing his alive-self to regain control and ultimately kill the alive Hal and Kara who were upstairs.

Starting this entire cycle over again from the very beginning.

Suddenly, it wasn't about him. Not since Ophelia had he felt so certain of that. The words replayed in his mind like the endless loop he was surely condemning himself to.

It wasn't. About. Him.

He had made a promise to this Hal and Kara. One that he intended to keep.

He broke free from Kara's grip and continued onwards towards the entity occupying the space within his physical-self, slamming into him, his own eyes red with anger.

To his surprise, he managed to grab hold of what he assumed would be an intangible ghost, pulling him from the rift and into phase with all of them.

Blue energy filled the gap instantly, time continued onwards, and Malcolm's physical-self finally fell to the ground, very much dead.

Malcolm pinned the Echo of his former-self to the ground, little more than a disembodied central nervous system of red electricity, writhing in confusion, as Future Malcolm wrapped his hands around his own neck and squeezed.

Then kept squeezing, drawing on the energy his Echo was made of.

Memories flooded into his mind as he recalled being strangled, his life ebbing away, the darkness claiming him. An impossible contradiction of opposing realities converging, as alternate timelines wrestled with temporal constants and culminated in the bright red man of energy disintegrating into a billion blood red, restarter blue, and emerald green shards.

A shade of green lost on all except Kara, who recognised it as the same brilliant shade of emerald as the breach between dimensions she had used to escape The White Lodge during her last stand with The Dark Restarter.

Future Malcolm remained kneeling over the body that no longer was, over his own *past* that no longer was, panting like the animal of old.

The Restarters stood there in silence, waiting for Future Malcolm to vanish.

Perhaps keel over in agony?

Explode, maybe? That would have been kind of cool.

But he did neither.

Eventually he looked up at them and laughed. An anxious laugh, laced with disbelief and confusion.

'That was…' began Hal.

'Intense,' agreed Kara.

There was no other word for it.

'We're all still here?' said Hal in utter fascination, patting himself over. 'We should all be…gone.'

'You…kind of saved us!'

'It was my mess to clean up, Kara,' said Malcolm, playing down the moment.

'How are we here?' said Hal, like a broken record.

'Quickly,' said Malcolm, moving towards his dead body. 'My past-self is about to restart for the very first time, he should have made his way up the stairs by now.'

Malcolm recalled the moments after he had been brought into phase with Hal and Kara…into the world of Restarting. He had been disorientated. Unaware that he was no longer in the world of the living.

'He'll come back down, find me, then vanish,' said Malcolm, projecting his memories of that moment with them. '*That's* our window!'

'We can't *be* here,' mumbled Hal, certain they would cease to exist at any moment.

They waited, as Malcolm continued kneeling, re-enacting his movements in his mind before the darkness had claimed him the very first time. Reliving every moment. Seeing Hal extend his middle finger next to the ghost he would later realise was Kara. All the way up to and including when the thick black fog had whisked him away, until his eyes eventually surged open.

'It's time,' he said feverishly.

'But if we revive you, what happens when Kevin busts out of the room behind us?' said Hal.

'We will wait and protect him if necessary. If it comes to that.'

'We won't BE here Malcolm!' said Hal, in a flash of frustration. 'If we restart your heart, all of us will vanish!'

'I think we've established that the three of us aren't going anywhere,' said Malcolm, clearly clutching at straws.

'Kara,' said Hal. 'You need to listen to me. This doesn't make *any* sense. H G Wells over here just strangled the version of himself that brought us back here. Which means–'

'Hal,' said Kara. 'You don't have to keep saying it. I *get* it. We *all* do. Let's just…get this over with.'

Kara had a point. At this juncture, time was so screwed he was finding it hard to imagine what difference anything they did would make going forward.

Hal growled in resignation, joining them and kneeling down next to Malcolm's body

'I want this on record that I have a bad feeling about this.'

'Noted. So how does this work?' asked Kara, rubbing her hands together and preparing to apply the imaginary paddles from what could only be described as some form of internalised defibrillator.

'Link arms,' said Malcolm, 'and just place your hands into my chest. Then release some of the power you both share.'

Hal looked at Kara, who shrugged, and they did just that, their touch sizzling, ready to discharge some bolts that surely wouldn't lead to anything resembling resuscitation.

'Let's sling some blue,' said Hal. 'On three?'

Kara nodded.

'Okay…three,'

'Wait! Are we counting *down* from three?'

'As evidenced by my opening with the number three, Kar'. Yes.'

'Can we count up from *one* instead?'

'You're seriously overthinking this,' said Hal with a frown.

But he obliged, counted upwards to three, and they plunged their hands into the heart of their killer.

CHAPTER SEVENTY-TWO
The Impossible Girl

204th Restart – Saturday, August 25th, 2018, 9:04pm

The crackle of energy fluctuating between them was met with a crescendo of thunder above them, as the un-beating heart within the deceased man beneath them restarted, a faint pulse surging throughout his lifeless body, causing him to convulse, until he eventually stopped shaking and drew a single, raggedy breath.

The Restarters exchanged a brief glance of amazement that it had actually worked, as the cabin above them shook with such intensity that Hal felt certain a re-evaluation of the Richter scale may be in order, and for a New York Minute Hal and Kara wondered if they'd finally taken things too far.

Neither of them had any point of reference for what a thousand suns colliding simultaneously would sound like, but felt safe in assuming it would hold more than a passing similarity to the soul-shattering rumble they had just experienced; an apparent by-product of having just been responsible for creating a crack in time so gargantuan that it was felt across the present, past and future of every timeline in existence, including those that had yet to even form.

Unbeknownst to the time travellers a momentary occurrence of global déjà vu rippled outwards from where they were kneeling, one that was well on its way to engulfing the entire Earth.

They had broken the cycle, but at what cost? Once again, they had jammed the fork of defiance into the electrical socket that represented time itself, affecting not only the lives of everyone they would ever come into contact with, but everyone in-between, sending potentially thousands of futures belonging to strangers they hadn't even met into disarray.

A notable cracking sound filled their eardrums.

'You think that cracking noise was a good thing?' asked Kara.

'It's probably fine,' lied Hal sarcastically.

Thunder bellowed once again in the sky above them, an angry roar that seemed to call Hal out on his bullshit, as swirls of fog rippled in and out of phase around them, cracks of blue and red light opening like hungry mouths, before vanishing just as quickly, then springing back into existence moments later; Angry sneers of trans-dimensional energy bleeding from the innumerable nexuses that seemed to cackle with glee at their unexpected release into a realm of corporeality.

Kara shuddered, perceiving the curved cuts in reality as frowns, but they could just have easily been disembodied smiles, awkwardly flipped on their axis.

'This was a mistake,' muttered Kara.

'I'm sensing that,' Hal agreed emphatically, as another bout of thunder boomed in apparent agreement. 'And it sounds like Odin agrees with you.'

Future Malcolm crawled towards them, his body rippling with a red energy that seemed eager to tear him apart, but instead fluctuated wildly, allowing him to remain very much whole, like a teleportation experiment gone horribly awry.

A thunderous rush of air flooded the basement, a heady mix of both an audible and physical variety assaulting the three of them.

'You've got red on you,' yelled Hal, pointing towards him.

'It's done,' bellowed Malcolm. 'We're finally fre–'

Malcolm's glaringly presumptuous claim that everything was still on track, as opposed to clearly being so far off the rails that the metaphoric train of best laid plans was going to need one hell of a parachute if it had any hope of landing on terra firma any time soon, was ultimately cut short, as he saw the same rippling energy that was afflicting him surging around the two Restarters.

Energy, albeit of the *bluer* variety, that pulsated savagely, as if trying to dismantle their bodies. Desperate to dematerialise the trio, so that they could be reinserted into whatever new timeline they had so carelessly created.

It was the first instance Malcolm had seen the Restart process up close, yet somehow caught mid-phase, snagged on a paradox that seemed reluctant to release the three of them back into the wild until it had run the numbers on exactly where to send them.

Seeing the look of wonder on Malcolm's face, Kara looked down at her hand, and twisted her fingers. It was surely a matter of time before the pain of what was happening to their bodies would kick in, and yet…they remained. Unchanged, unclaimed, and still somehow in phase with the past.

'Why haven't we Restarted?' hollered Kara with an understandable frown.

'To be fair, looks like the universe is *trying*,' shouted Hal, marvelling as his body phased between a blue tinged opacity and an electrically charged transparency, then back again.

'Seems like an odd time for *time* to get performance anxiety, don't ya think?'

'What?!' screamed Hal, the wind drowning out the back end of Kara's sentence.

The incessant gusts made way for a belligerent

thwomping sound, like that of a projectile leaving the tube of a grenade launcher, minus – so far at least – the ensuing explosion.

Instead, the rushing air was sucked from the room and replaced with an eerie silence, and the three of them felt a tingling sensation across their skin, as an intense static charge washed over them.

'Oh man, you feel that?' said Kara, her ears now ringing thanks to the unexpected quietness.

'I've got chills,' said Hal, pulling up the sleeve of his jacket and seeing the hairs on his arm standing to attention, before quickly shooting a look at Kara as if to warn her not to go there.

'They're electrif–'

'Come on man,' his tone one of reprimand. 'You're better than that. Mind you, your *hair* is losing control!'

Kara raised a hand to her usually neck-length hair, gingerly tapping the rogue strands that were all standing to attention, as if an invisible prankster had rubbed a balloon against her head, dangling it above her.

The three of them turned as one to face the staircase, as footsteps filled the quietude, the dimness of the hour working in tandem with the thin streak of moonlight cascading from the small window of the basement to reveal an outline of what appeared to be a young woman.

The impossible girl stopped in her tracks, having reached the halfway point of the rickety staircase, before speaking to the empty room.

Her voice rang out, feeling remarkably amplified, thanks to both the acoustics and the apprehension they were all feeling due to the unexpected guest, the latter of which having forced them into forgetting to breath since catching sight of her.

'Pssst, you three dead? I'm sorry, that was insensitive. I meant, like...*Restarted*...or whatever? Hang on...' the visitor raised a hand just below her right temple, causing two bright blue discs to appear at her own eye level, partially lighting her cheeks to reveal a purplish-hued leather jacket, long hair draping over the top of the lapels. 'That's better!'

The girl continued her decent of the staircase, jumping the final few steps, and twirled around the three of them, making her way to the counter where Malcom's bag of murder paraphernalia rested, and reached towards the pouch that housed the syringes of what both Hal and Kara referred to as Malcolm's "Death Juice."

She held one up to the light, the green liquid within glistening thanks to the blue light radiating from her glasses, as she flicked the glass tubing with her free hand.

'They always do that, don't they?' said the girl with a devilish smile. 'Flick the vial, then depress the plunger to release a droplet of whatever they're about to inject?'

The time travellers stared at her, not sure if she was talking to them or, more likely, just utterly insane.

'I always wondered why they do that in the old movies, but now I know,' said the young woman, pressing the plunger and reducing the quantity of green liquid until only half remained. 'It's when they need to reduce the amount inside. How dope is that? The more you know.'

'Rachel?' said Hal, the poor lighting and the glasses being sported by the stranger making it hard to be certain, but the similarity was uncanny.

'I get that a lot,' said the girl with a chuckle.

Future Malcolm and the Restarters stared in utter bewilderment as she walked towards the barely-alive version of Malcolm on the floor they had just revived, spinning the syringe in her hand so the needle was pointing downwards, before jabbing it into Malcolm's leg.

It pierced through the fabric of his trousers as well as his flesh rather effortlessly, as she emptied the contents into his bloodstream with a happy hum.

'Bosh,' said the woman, disregarding the now empty relic over her shoulder, where it collided with the wall, the small tinkle of broken glass raising a satisfied smile beneath her blue-hued cheeks. 'That should keep him out of our hair for a while. Oh man...I can see you need some time to process. I'm totally spooking you. Dammit,' the young woman added, as if chastising herself for ruining their first impressions of her. 'Come on up when you're ready!'

And without further explanation, she balled her fists, stuffing them into her jacket pockets and twirled her way back to the stairs.

Pulling her hand from her left pocket, she yanked at the rickety old bannister rail, using it to boost her ascent, leaving the three of them unequivocally slack-jawed.

Unseen by all of them, a small piece of paper fluttered back down the staircase under cover of darkness, landing lazily on the dusty floor.

Hal was the first to broach the question on the tip of all their temporally-displaced tongues.

'Who the hell was that?'

'Was she talking to us?' said Malcolm.

'Well, Kevin's unconscious in the room behind you, your time echo is dust and your alive self can barely breathe,' said Kara.

'Probably brain-dead too,' said Hal helpfully.

Malcolm scowled.

'What? I said *probably*?' joked Hal, trying to resist a chuckle.

Malcolm stole a glance at his unconscious body, as if mulling over whether a lifetime of coma-induced survival was really something he could live with, before nodding solemnly.

Kara was up on her feet, making her way to the staircase.

'Kara, wait! None of this makes any sense. We have no way of knowing who she is or what she wants!'

'Or how she can see us,' added Malcolm.

'Only one way to find out.'

Seeing no other course of action and eager to get out of the tomb that was starting to feel a little bit too much like a home away from home, Kara headed up after the strange visitor, leaving Hal with no other option than to follow.

*

As the three of them reached the front door of Kevin's home, they were greeted by the intense glare of several xenon-bulb spotlights.

'We have company,' said Hal, apparently determined to state the obvious.

'Thanks detective,' said Kara, shooting a classic glance of dismay upwards into the infinite void of superfluity.

Malcolm stood behind them in the doorway, his instincts telling him he should slip out the back door, before realising how pointless that would be. Not least of which because there was nowhere for him to run to.

Hal and Kara both went to exit the cabin at the same time, getting caught in the doorway.

'Oh, sorry, you go first.'

'I'm trying, move backwards I can't get past.'

'My bad,' said Hal, pulling himself out of the doorway causing Kara to stumble out.

She glared at Hal for embarrassing her in front of the two silhouettes that were standing in front of the spotlights.

'Two of 'em now,' said Hal.

'Will you stop narrating what we can all see?' chirped Kara snippily out of the corner of her mouth.

Hal took up position by Kara's side on the path, with Malcolm gingerly bringing up the rear, maintaining a metre or so distance behind them.

'This. Is. *Insane*!' said the young woman, all her attempts of restraint bubbling over like a cauldron as she bridged the gap between them with barely contained excitement. As she came into focus, Hal realised the jacket she was wearing was actually bright red, as opposed to the purple he thought he had seen. 'I can't believe I'm finally *here*, meeting you guys. *For cereal*. Gosh. The *OG* Restarters.'

'*Oh Gee*?' said Kara, realising that the similarity she shared with Rachel really was quite striking.

'Original Generation!' said Ava, squealing a little bit too much.

'Stop fan-girling Ava, you're embarrassing yourself,' said the man to her right, absently staring at a tablet and tapping on the screen in-between scrutinising whatever it was he was reading.

'Don't you *dare* ruin this for me, Ross,' hissed the young woman they now knew to be called Ava, ditching her chirpy enthusiasm and replacing it with unbridled resentment towards her colleague.

Ross yawned, flapping his free hand dismissively as if signalling her to get on with it.

'Sorry,' said Ava, composing herself and unnecessarily straightening the bottom of her red biker jacket. 'Ignore him. This is a *huge* day for me. It's kind of my *first* day in the *field* and I've studied *everything* about you and now I'm *finally* here and *you're* here and–'

'Who are you people?' said Kara, fearing that if she didn't interject, ten restarts might roll by before she could get a word in edgeways.

Hal couldn't keep it in any longer, his foggy memories from a future that had all but been obliterated coming back to the forefront of his mind. 'I know you! You were at the coffee shop. In the future. Your hair was purple though…'

'Hmm,' said Ava thoughtfully, seemingly trying to recollect exactly when he was referring to. 'Yes! Sorry, that was like…six months ago. When I placed the goober under the table at the coffee shop! Gotta have a stakeout disguise, amiright?'

'Goober?' said Hal, only now recalling the device that had clattered to the floor after the table was atomised. It felt like forever ago.

'You think it was an accident you were able to bring all that sick swag with you in that backpack of yours?' replied Ava, notably amused. 'And those fancy duds you're both wearing?'

'I really like her,' Hal whispered.

'Figures,' Kara muttered back.

'I switched it up,' Ava's focus returning to that of her hair colour and running her hand roughly through it as if scratching an itch. 'Ross said it looked lame.'

Ross continued to ignore them, tapping away on his tablet.

'Are you kidding? It looked great,' said Hal.

'Really?' Kara crossed her arms, her eyes narrowing.

'What?' said Hal defensively. 'It did.'

'You're doing this *now*? Hitting on a complete stranger?'

'I'm not *hitting* on anyone! I just said her hair looked nice!'

'Ha! Mum would love this right now,' said Ava. 'Right. Of course, introductions!' as Kara sized her up; she appeared to be in her early twenties, her hair long and black as the night. She wore it just like Rachel did, only a little more wildly. As if styling was an afterthought. 'I think it best the head poncho–'

'You mean honcho?' said Hal. 'It's head honcho, not poncho.'

'I know! That was a reference! Ya know, to uncle Robert? How he always gets his metaphors in a tizz? Classic Rob.' Ava wobbled her head slightly, her eyes scattily looking up to the sky as if they were all sharing the same in-joke.

'You know Rob – wait, did you say *uncle*?' Kara was beginning to feel both irritated that she herself was derailing the path to the answers that mattered, her confusion on how this Rachel lookalike could know Robert throwing her off.

'Of course!' said Ava. 'When he tricked Dark-Restarter-Malcolm with the old "I'm actually a Restarter too" routine? Gah. That was *so* badass. I was all like–'

'Ava,' said Kara in restrained frustration. 'You said there's a boss or something?'

'Right,' said Ava, wincing. 'We knew this would be a lot to take in. Which is why we thought it best to bring the big guns.' She raised a hand to her ear and spoke quietly. 'It's time, boss.'

A third silhouette of a man appeared from the woodland behind Ross and Ava, two electric-blue discs lighting up around the space where his eyes should have been as he switched on his glasses.

'Sort of milking the entrances, don't you think?' Hal whispered to Kara, who was already nodding.

As the man walked into the light, Hal noticed he was in his late fifties, dressed in a suit and a dark-yet-vibrant blue three-quarter-length coat. He reached up to his white shirt and adjusted his blue tie as he made his way towards them, clearing his throat in that way people tended to when it was their turn to take the microphone for the next round of karaoke; nervous and not nearly drunk enough for what was coming, feeling one extra rehearsal *short* of ready for what would follow.

'Yes,' said the smartly dressed man. 'It *is* about time.'

'No...' said Hal, recognising the man immediately. A man who looked considerably more weathered since the last time Hal had seen him.

But no amount of ageing – nor a pair of futuristic specs – could hide that all-too-familiar hint of a rebellious smile.

And that voice…He *knew* that voice.
'Remarkable,' said Malcolm.
'How?' spluttered Kara.
'Dad?' said Hal.

CHAPTER SEVENTY-THREE
"R" is for Restarter

204th Restart – Saturday, August 25th, 2018, 9:16pm

Kara scrunched up her nose for a moment, then frowned in confusion at Hal.

'I've met your dad, Hal. That's not him. Actually, he looks way more like...'

'Oh,' chuckled Hal. 'I know, it just felt like a cliff-hanger ending kinda moment, ya know?

'For who?! What are you even talking about?' said Kara, utterly confused.

Hal shrugged.

The man Ava had referred to as Ross looked up from his tablet, clearly disinterested by their banter, and reaffirmed his focus on reading the complex data that was streaming across the screen.

The older man before them exhaled sharply, before addressing them.

'I forgot how irritating I used to be,' he said. 'As Kara has so acutely deducted, I am not your father. I am *you*.'

Before the words even left the man in the blue coat's mouth, Kara, Hal and even Malcolm knew it to be true. There was no subterfuge, no subtext, no games being played. Merely a universal truth that held no other purpose than to be heard and accepted.

'Damn,' said Hal, feeling like it was his responsibility to break the silence given that it had technically been a future version of himself that had caused it to begin with. 'How are you resisting dropping the mic right now? It must be killing you? Me. Us.'

Hal's future-self stepped closer to them with the gait of a man that was more than accustomed to holding a room's attention. 'I'm sure you have a lot of questions. Not least of which, how you're even still *here* at all – talking to me – instead of being vaporized back in that basement.'

'I feel weird,' said Kara, unable to bear the uncomfortable sensation that was wracking her body any longer 'Like my whole body is vibrating.'

'That'll be the TDA's we've set up around the cabin,' said Ross, his words laced with a very acute level of boredom, one that could only stem from countless years working in tech support. He might as well have asked them to try turning it off and on again for all the explanation it gave, the personality he had inflected in his tone of equal fervour to that of a fork.

'Yeah,' said Hal. 'I'm still sort of getting my head around how I'm speaking with a version of myself from the future, let alone trying to backwards engineer acronyms. What's a TDA?'

Ross began to answer, before being rudely cut off by an over-excited Ava.

'Time Dilation Amplifiers!' she blurted, at a tempo just short of light speed.

Her colleague scowled at her, then sighed deeply, as if he were more than used to his thunder being stolen, before taking back the reins of the conversation.

'We're currently generating a stasis bubble around us to stop you from returning to whatever botched future you've just created here. That tingling you're feeling? That's your bodies trying to restart.'

'Which, by my count,' said Future Hal, 'should have happened no less than twice; once when Malcolm here killed a past incarnation of himself, ultimately breaking the continuity of his own timeline…'

'And then again when you restarted his heart,' said Ava helpfully. 'Heh…*restarted*. That's funny.'

'Yes. That,' said Future Hal. 'In truth, time is actively trying to reintegrate you both back into the present. All we're doing is…slowing down the process.'

'Surrrre…' said Kara, not really understanding how any of this equated to making any sense. She had so many questions, but decided to start small. 'How are you all even here? Are you Restarting right now?'

'God no!' said Ava, visibly abashed by the implications of such a theory. 'We're committed to the cause, but not to the point where we'd kill ourselves just to speak to you.'

'Plus,' said Malcolm, 'we saw her pick up an object in the physical world,' referring to the syringe, the contents of which they had seen Ava inject into Malcolm's physical body, which Hal and Kara presumed was now dead in Kevin's basement thanks to the administering of what was surely a Death Juice overdose.

'Yeah,' said Hal. 'What was *that* all about?'

Future Hal fielded the question, his hands interlocking in front of him.

Hal clocked the silver ring his future-self was sporting as it caught the moonlight. It was hard to make out, but at barely a metre away he was able to tilt his head, trying to decipher the significance of the logo which looked like an upside-down tree next to a building.

'It is imperative, for the sanctity of history, that when solidified time takes hold, certain…*constants* are kept intact.' Future Hal stared directly at Malcolm as he delivered what was clearly a well-rehearsed sentence.

Malcolm caught every ounce of subtext, knowing exactly what the time traveller was implying.

'Yeah,' said Ava, chiming in. 'When ol' Kev' escapes from that room down there, he's going to check Malcolm's pulse. If he feels one, he'll *for cereal* drive a screwdriver into his throat.' Ava mimed the action, making the noise of someone who had just been stabbed.

Future Hal winced, as if it were in bad taste. Which, of course, it was.

Hal and Kara were both sensing Ava and her boss clashed often in terms of their work dynamic.

Malcolm nodded knowingly. 'So, you injected me with my own serum. One that creates the illusion of death. Very clever. Though I fear you were a little…over-zealous with the dosage.'

'Should it worry me that I'm so used to hanging out with Malcolm now that I wasn't even remotely creeped out by that?' Kara offered up to the time travellers that were slowly but surely beginning to outnumber the regular visitors of the lakes.

Hal shrugged, clearly feeling the same way.

'Quite,' said Future Hal. 'One of the benefits of Tetrodotoxin – besides inducing paralysis – is that it inhibits the central nervous system from carrying messages through the body, preventing muscles from flexing in response to stimulation.'

'Did you know that?' said Hal, whispering to Malcolm.

'Of *course* I knew tha–'

Future Hal continued. 'Whilst Malcolm's unique concoction doesn't completely cloak the pulse of an individual–'

'It'll slow it down just long enough,' said Ross, not bothering to look up at them, 'for Kevin to miss it when he checks for one. Forty-one seconds between each beat to be precise. If Ava got the dosage right.'

Ava mimed Ross's words, refusing to look at him, the dig at her capabilities flicking off her like water off a duck's back.

The once and future Hal's lip trembled, fighting against the smile which was desperate to escape. He had every faith in Ava. Despite her incorrigible attitude, she was bloody good when it counted. 'And as Kevin will only check for forty of those seconds, he will not, as Ava so eloquently put it, *drive a screwdriver into Malcolm's throat.*'

'It seems you've thought of everything,' said Malcolm, nodding thoughtfully, with a look of intensity directed squarely at Future Hal. A penetrating glare of understanding which the time traveller interpreted exactly as Malcolm intended him to, the two older men now privy to an unspoken truth; that Malcolm knew it wasn't time, or restarts, or even a delayed resuscitation that had caused his coma. It had been this new version of Hal that had seen to that.

Future Hal returned a barely perceptible nod, the

exchange allowing both men to know it wasn't personal. Merely insurance to ensure a temporal constant was kept on course.

After all, everything had to happen once, for it to happen again.

Whilst there was a chance Ava had known what she was doing when she carried out Future Hal's orders, Malcolm sincerely doubted it, given the breezy demeanour she was emanating. Which meant in the years that were to follow, Hal was clearly now taking a page out of Malcolm's approach to manipulating those around him…

'Wow, you guys really run a tight ship,' said Kara. 'How do you even *know* all of this stuff?'

'We've had a lot of time to perfect the details,' said Future Hal, breaking eye contact with Malcolm, seemingly flattered by the acknowledgement of how much precision his team was displaying.

'So, where's Future *Me*?!' said Kara, suddenly excited.

Tension filled the air, as if the question had generated a rehearsed response from their visitors. From the barely perceptible action of Ross ceasing his data entry on his tablet, before returning to his responsibilities to sustain their time bubble within a time bubble, to the slightly more obvious sight of Ava's smile freezing in place unnaturally. Future Hal continued onwards, hiding his unwillingness to answer the question by filling their heads with more pressing matters.

'Truth be told, we've been following your exploits for quite some time. Years in fact. It wasn't always straight forward. Every time you restarted the past, we had to attempt to lock on to you all over again. There were times when we lost you entirely. A last-minute decision here, a small change there…'

'Yeah,' agreed Ava. 'You guys are like a magnet for Timestamp errors!'

'Urgh, you seriously are,' agreed Ross, recalling the countless hours of overtime he had accumulated, waiting for their unique signatures to pop back up so he could re-establish a lock.

'For *frosted* cereal,' said Ava, her impossibly good mood surprisingly infectious.

'Timestamp error?'

Future Hal waved his hand dismissively at Kara, as if explaining the minutia of such admin was not something she needed to trouble herself with.

'How is it that you are communicating with us right now?' asked Malcolm. 'And how can you even see us in our current…condition.'

Kara found herself thinking back to her brief exchange with a version of Hal from the future. Not the older man in front of her, but a version far more reminiscent to the Hal she knew and lov–

'I'm guessing,' said Kara, 'it has something to do with those earpieces and glasses they're all wearing.'

Future Hal and Ava stared at her, somewhat perplexed. Even Ross looked up from his tablet, for a solid second this time. Each and every one of them wondering how she could possibly have known that.

'That is…correct,' said Future Hal suspiciously.

'Oh, come on,' said Kara, sensing the vibe and attempting to play it down. 'You've got a bright blue light in your ears and shades with luminous blue lenses. It's not *that* much of a leap.'

'The earpieces act as a receiver, picking up even the faintest residual electronic voice phenomenon,' said Ross, like a proud father.

'You mean like…an EVP receiver?' chuckled Hal.

'What's so funny,' Ross suddenly becoming quite protective of his baby.

'Let me guess, you've met my brother Alex?'

'Well, he *was* involved in the feasibility study…'

'The glasses on the other hand,' said Ava with just a little bit too much enthusiasm. 'They were actually my mum's idea! They cycle through multiple phases of temporal reality like–'

'Ava,' said Future Hal, cutting her off with notable warning. 'Perhaps another time?'

'Right, sorry boss.'

'And please stop calling me boss.'

The request seemed to cause her to glitch, and she stood there with her mouth open, unable to respond, before turning back to face Hal and Kara.

'You guys should know; the RI doesn't just show up in person for anyone.'

Kara sniffed deeply, feeling irked by how much the future was clearly all about annoying shorthand labels. But it was Malcolm who saved her from sounding like she was only there to fish questions out of the stream of time.

'RI?'

Future Hal sighed, looking at Malcolm with eyes that seemed to indicate there was more history between the two men than just the current batch of restarts alone. Or perhaps he was just taking a moment to get over Ava jumping the gun. 'The RI is an organisation that specialises in closing breaches in space time,' he said with a hint of his younger self's swagger.

Though there was an air of fatigue in the delivery of those words, as if he had been forced into uttering them in that exact order countless times, to innumerable ears.

"If only they knew," he thought, spotting that his audience had noticed his tiredness, recalling the nightmarish quantity of mandatory meetings he had not just attended, but chaired. Conferences that had gone on longer than all of his historic restarts combined.

He pressed onwards. 'Primarily, breaches caused by the three of *you*, actually.'

'Oh my goose, Kara,' said Hal, his body tensing up as if he were about to explode. 'You know what this means don't you?'

'The Time Police *are* a thing,' said Kara calmly, though admittedly she too felt a small surge of adrenaline at the prospect.

'The Time Police are a *thing*!' said Hal, jumping on

the spot. 'And not just that, we *are* the freakin' Time Police!'

'More an *initiative*,' said Future Hal.

'What kind of initiative?' said Malcolm, taking on board far more than anyone was giving him credit for, as he skulked in the background of a conversation that would have sent most men mad.

'Wait...RI,' said Hal, the cogs turning. 'Oh, that is dope. It became a *thing*? It's–'

'Your legacy,' said Future Hal. 'Or should I say, *our* legacy.'

'TDA's are winding down,' said Ross. We need to wrap this up.'

The Hal of the future nodded.

'Indeed. We've been here too long already. Open up a bridge to The Shire, we're nearly done here.'

'Shut the front door! Did he...I mean did *I* just say the *Shire*?' said Hal, turning to face Kara, realising she was a lost cause and having to resort to getting the response he needed from Malcolm, and ultimately hating both of them for not being remotely fazed by that.

'Once we shut down the stasis field, you will be returned to the present, but before that happens, I need to ask you something.'

'What is it?' said Kara, having trouble reading Future Hal's expression. It was as if he was holding back, somehow.

'He *totally* just said The Shire! You guys *heard* that, right?'

Everyone continued to ignore regular Hal, as his future-self continued.

'We have travelled a long way to bring an end to the singularity at Fir Lodge. We thought that ending this cycle would repair the damage that is rippling through time and damaging the future, but...'

'Seriously? Is nobody picking up he said Shire?' said Hal, wondering if perhaps he was now in a different phase altogether to all those around him.

'...we were working on the assumption that the events which transpired here were the cause of this damage. After countless probability simulations, we discovered a disturbing truth.'

'What truth?' said Kara, not liking where this was going.

'That we were *wrong*. The facture in time did *not* originate here. It merely *culminated* here. What's worse, the RI can't fix this by ourselves.'

'Why?' said Hal. 'I mean you clearly have some kind of time machine deal going on here. How old are you? Like, seventy years old?'

'I'm only *fifty-seven*!' exclaimed Future Hal, before catching himself, straightening the lapels of his jacket and clearing his throat, realising he had stupidly imparted more information than his past-self should ever have known. "Dammit," he thought. "Been here less than twenty minutes and you've already let slip your point of origin. Stupid Harold. Stupid."

'Wow, okay,' said Hal, noting that clearly his future-self was way more sensitive about the age thing than he could have predicted. 'Moving on…So, you're me. From the future. You've jumped back in physical form somehow to 2018. What do you need *us* for?'

'Hal has a point. I don't really see what we can offer you here.'

'Do not sell yourselves short, Kara. The three of you are more important to the future than you could possibly know.'

'Ah maaaan,' said Hal. 'The three of us? You mean Biff Tannen here has to come too?'

'I'm standing right here, Harold,' said Malcolm coldly.

'Sssh,' said Hal, 'the adults are talking. Spill then, what do you need us to do?'

Future Hal looked over at Ross, who nodded to indicate the bridge was ready to rock, then back to Ava, before nodding and smiling at her, making good on his promise that she could have her mic-drop moment. He was too old for them these days anyway. He lacked the required…energy.

Ava smiled back, a small squeak of joy escaping her lips, as she walked closer to the three Restarters.

'Oh, you know. No big deal,' shrugging as if it were just that, before adopting what Hal assumed was an attempt at mimicking Batman. 'We just need you to save the world.'

'Was that your Batman impression?' said Hal, staring back at her.

'Maybe,' replied Ava, maintaining the intense

stare, a rebellious smile cracking beneath the blue glow of her glasses, which danced across her jacket like a drunk Kryptonian using X-Ray vision to find their house keys.

'Pretty solid,' conceded Hal.

'Thank you!' Ava replied gruffly.

'Okay, you can stop now,' said Kara.

'I don't know how,' continued Ava, now in full-on Dark Knight Mode and apparently stuck there for the foreseeable.

'So how does this work?' said Hal. 'When we get back to the present, we won't remember any of this. And surely you'll all cease to exist now the Fir Lodge problem is done and dusted?'

'It's…complicated,' said Future Hal, responding to his younger self.

'Isn't it always?' replied Kara.

'I want to bring you in. I can find you. But I wanted to give you the choice I never had.'

'Are we joining a Time Travel police force?' asked Hal, raising an eyebrow and refusing to accept his future-self had chosen those words specifically without knowing their significance. 'Or becoming vampires?

Future Hal smiled knowingly, as if the act caused him pain of some kind. 'So, are you in or out? We can leave you to your present and you can take the long way around, just like I did, or you can get a head start on your own destinies.'

'Will we get cool time travel gadgets?' asked Hal,

as if that would be the deal breaker.

'Urgh,' grumbled Kara. 'Don't say it like that!'

'Why not?'

'Because it sounds ridiculous!'

'Time travel gadgets?' Future Hal cut in, ending their bickering. 'They're all packed up and waiting for you,' he added, reaching up to the frame of his Restarter-blue lensed glasses, pulling them fractionally down the bridge of his nose and dispensing an awkward wink, that oddly didn't suit him quite the same way it suited his younger incarnation.

Ross and Ava shared an uneasy glance. One that was entirely missed by the Hal of the present as he turned back to face Kara.

'What do you think, Kar'? Couldn't hurt to take a look, right?'

Kara could see how actively her friend was trying to play it down, as well as how much it would crush him if she decided she wasn't on board. She made him wait for two seconds longer than necessary, sensing the imminent explosion that was building beneath his nonchalant exterior.

'Why the hell not,' she said finally, defusing the Hal-Bomb by clipping the blue wire of his anticipation and putting him out of his misery. 'If anything, it'll be worth it just to meet my future self!'

'Excellent,' said Future Hal, utilising selective hearing to ignore her reasoning. 'Ross, shut it down.'

Ross nodded, showing what appeared to be relief that he had carried out his duties without any unexpected hiccups.

'A moment, if you will,' said Malcolm, causing all eyes to land on him. 'If I may, I'd like to confer with my...with Hal and Kara?'

'Oh my god, were you about to say friends?!' said Kara, half joking, but half wondering if that was indeed what they were now. They'd been through so much together, and yet it was a hard dynamic to quantify.

'I hardly think that misnomer applies to us,' said Malcolm, lowering his voice so that only the two of them could hear him. 'Nevertheless, I want to thank you both. For everything you've sacrificed. For your help in ending this hell.'

'So, what's your plan now,' said Hal, trying to figure out what would happen to this incarnation of Malcolm now that his chain of restarts had been truly severed. With his Dark Restarter-self defeated, it seemed to Hal there was nowhere for this version of him to go.

'There's nowhere left for me to go,' said Malcolm, as if reading his mind, his words causing Hal to steal a glance downwards to make sure they weren't inadvertently connected. 'At best, I will awaken in the hospital. At worst...'

The three of them knew he was referring to the far more likely reality that he would remain comatose. Though for how long was anyone's guess.

'Wait!' said Hal. 'I almost forgot! Yo, Future Me? Pump the breaks, we need a bit longer.'

His future-self looked up from the huddled discussion he, Ava and Ross were engaging in, nodding curtly before returning to whatever it was time travellers from the future discussed in their down time.

"Phase 10 of the MCU probably," thought Hal, certain he'd cracked it.

He slid off his backpack and dropped it to the floor, squatting down as he unzipped it, rummaging around with urgency. 'Come on, come on you bastard, where are ya?' he muttered.

'Hal, what are you–'

'False alarm! Found it!' he said, revealing a mini-bar sized bottle of alcohol and standing back up to attention.

'You didn't?' said Kara, laughing at her ridiculous friend.

'Oh, I did,' said Hal, dispensing his classic wink that suited him just fine.

He removed the tiny cap and discarded it onto the shingle, where it landed soundlessly.

'A toast,' Hal declared, raising the bottle. 'To life and death…' he took a swig and passed the tiny tequila to Kara.

'To tequila!' she added, taking a gulp, and to Malcolm's surprise leaving enough behind for him to join them.

She held out her arm, offering him the bottle.

'I…don't drink,' said Malcolm, utterly taken aback by their willingness to include him.

'Don't ruin the moment, Malc',' said Hal, a playful scowl dancing across his face.

Malcolm took the bottle, smiled at it, then at them.

'To time travel,' he quipped, downing the remaining mouthful and hiding his disgust at the aftertaste like the veteran chameleon he was.

'I'd apologise for doubting you,' said Kara, 'but you don't make it fucking easy, man.'

Malcolm chuckled. 'It has been said.' Ophelia had always criticised him for that. 'Despite what you may think of me, it's important to me that you know this; I am…not the man I once was. A by-product of our time together, I expect. Something about you both has a nasty way of…rubbing off on people.'

'Does that mean you're going to stop…well…*killing* people?' asked Hal.

'Baby steps, Harold. Baby steps,' said Malcolm with a wink that looked more like he was having some form of brain malfunction.

'Not very committal,' Hal mumbled.

Malcolm stared at them, as if wanting to say more. And in truth he did want to, but couldn't bring himself to let the words out. How he had grown fond of them. Protective of them. Even *proud* of them, in his own contorted *Malcolmy* sort of way.

'Farewell, *Restarters*,' he said, stepping away from them and notifying Hal's future-self he was ready via the medium of a deliberate nod. Malcolm began making his way back to the front door of Kevin's cabin, eager to check what condition his past-self's condition was in, his back to them as he did so. 'And should we meet again…' he added.

'You'll spare us and never try to kill us again, right?' Hal said hopefully.

Malcolm stopped at the threshold, dipping his head to the left, but not looking back.

'Malcolm?' pressed Kara. 'You'll leave us alone, right? Our families? Friends?'

Malcolm looked back into the darkness of the cabin in front of him.

'I was *going* to say; stay out of *my* way, and I'll do my best to stay out of *yours*.'

And on that menacing note, he vanished into the shadows.

'*Classic* Malcolm,' said Hal. 'All righty then. How do we do this thing? Click our heels? Swallow a red pill? Shout *Shazam*?'

Future Hal gave the go ahead to Ross, who faffed about on his tablet in a dramatic manner, causing Kara to wonder if he was just milking it to look the part.

'Do you think he's just dragging that out to look the part?' Hal whispered to Kara.

'Definitely.'

'I can *hear* you,' said Ross curtly.

'Would you like some cornflakes to go with all that milk?' said Kara, Ava's eyes lighting up and laughing an inch away from Ross's face.

'She got you, man,' said the red-jacketed livewire.

'Catch you on the flip side,' said Hal turning to face Kara, moving in close so there was barely any space between them. 'You wanna hold hands for this or...?'

He was expecting her to tell him to man up, and was surprised when she took his hands in hers. They both noted the lack of electrical feedback between them. Presumably a side effect of the TDA's.

'Sure,' she said with a smile. 'So, *Time Cops* huh? Who'd have thunk it?'

With a pop of air, the triangulating generators cut out, ending both Hal and Kara's conversation as well as the sweet spot of dilated time.

The de-molecularisation process of their bodies now unimpeded, Time arrived promptly, angrily efficient in its eagerness to reclaim them

And, amidst little more than a flash of blue light, they vanished.

CHAPTER SEVENTY-FOUR
The Consequence

Saturday, August 25th, 2018,
9:28pm

F uture Hal, who could once again be referred to as just "Hal", pulled back the cuff of his shirt and jacket, stealing a glance at his watch; simplistic in design, but secretly being the only thing that kept him from exploding into a billion blue shards.

'Great work everyone. First Contact went as well as we could have hoped.'

In truth, he had assumed it would have taken much longer than it did. Mere minutes, instead of hours. Hours they didn't have.

'Are you sure this is a good idea,' said Ross for

the billionth time. 'Bringing them into this…it's…'

'Risky. Yes. You've said that before. I know what I'm doing. You need to trust me, Ross.'

'It's just,' said Ava, licking her lips quickly as if her next words were forbidden. 'You were kiiinda told not to, is all.'

'Ava…'

'And by *kinda*, I mean you were explicitly instructed by UNTAC to do the complete *opposite* of that.'

She was right of course. He had only been allowed to come back here, to this time, under the double-edged proviso that he left Brexit the hell alone, and that under no circumstances whatsoever was he to engage with his past self.

And especially not Kara.

And definitely not Malcolm.

Research and report, whilst the singularities were in their infancy and burning bright enough that their point of origin could be catalogued and timestamped. Only then would a decision be made.

The political implications were forever hindered not so much by red tape, as they were by cast-iron gates with angry barbed wire, every contemplated action analysed from every conceivable angle so that the ultimate consequences could be categorised into three distinct grades; Blue, Red, and Green.

"Ad infinitum," thought Hal irritably.

'It was numero uno on the "things not to do" list that we signed to even get here is all I'm sayi–'

'Ava! The *theorists* at UNTAC have no idea what's truly at stake here. I told them what they needed to *hear* to get us when we needed to *be*. By the time we get back they won't even be aware of what they made us sign.'

Ava nodded, noting the resentment in the way he said "theorists", then smiled. Hal returned the gesture with shared contempt before she asked the question he knew was coming.

'Are you going to tell her?'

There it was. Hal played dumb. 'Tell who what?'

'You know who and what,' said Ava with a look of worry.

'She can't know. Not yet, at least.'

'She's going to find out one way or another,' said Ava warningly. 'Especially now you've decided to bring them in on this. It just feels kind of…out of order not telling her, you know?'

'Ava may have a point,' said Ross, stealing a look away from his trusty tablet. 'Maybe it *would* be better coming from you?'

'Enough,' said Hal. 'Everybody dies, Ava. Even us. We're all immortal until proven otherwise. Knowing the when and where…it's no way to live.'

'But not *everybody* is in a position to prevent it,' she contested. 'I know what she meant to you.'

Hal tensed, deflecting her words by shutting down his feelings, just like always. 'And that's the problem. If we tell her, she'll undoubtedly tell the younger version of myself. And he'll do *everything* in his power to change the future to save her. I have mourned her passing. Just like my younger self will when it happens.'

'That's kinda cold boss. And you don't know that past-you will go against what you say. He has no reason not to trust you. Unless you make one…'

'It is what it is; History. And I know that's what he'd do because it's exactly what *I* would have done back then. He'd sooner destroy time itself than let one of his friends take a bullet. *Especially* Kara.'

'Then why bring them in at all,' argued Ross. 'If none of this happened in your own past, why are you forcing it?'

'You *know* why,' he said simply, feeling that they had spent far too long discussing this out in the open already. It was neither the time, nor the place. 'And on our *next* first contact, please don't call me *boss* in front of potential candidates, Ava. It sets a derogatory precedent.'

'Bridge is ready, boss,' said Ross.

'Excellent. Take us home.'

'Why is it okay for *him* to say it? said Ava, full of sulk.

'Can we *please* just return to the Shire?'

'It's because of mum isn't it.'

'No,' Hal replied. Even though it was.

The darkened doorway of Kevin's lodge was replaced with a bright green shimmering portal of light, the shadows beyond now filled with what the three of them knew to be work stations.

Hal's future-self took the lead, walking directly through the gateway that led to their base of operations, his blue jacket appearing green from the other side of the threshold, as he made his way to his office on the top level.

Rolling her eyes at her uncle's inability to open up to her, she stood on the edge of their current side of the bridge to what they now referred to as home, glancing over her shoulder at Ross.

'Don't forget to kill the turds,' she said, her crude nickname for the TDA's that she knew her colleague hated.

'Such a backseat Restarter,' Ross muttered under his breath, but ensuring it was loud enough for Ava to hear.

She hopped around to face him like an overexcited rabbit, her back to the portal they had created, before flicking him the double bird, and jumping backwards hundreds of miles and landing on the other side in a blink of an eye.

Ross breathed a sigh, a rustle in the trees drawing his attention away from the gateway separating the mind-boggling distance between Pentney Lakes and the Shire, that was now pressed together by a mere few inches of folded space.

He'd been doing this for long enough to know when something felt off.

It was something of a gift.

The time traveller cycled through the filters built into his glasses, slow deliberate clicks throwing the empty road that connected the countless lodges into varying hues of translucence.

Clicking from blue, to red, to green, to white, and black, before switching the perception-altering specs off entirely, the real world reverting to its moonlit default.

The surroundings remained undisturbed.

Nothing.

He huffed, berating himself for getting so spooked for no reason. A side-effect of always being the last one to leave the scene. They had prepared for everything, and today's encounter went far smoother than even he had dared to hope.

There was nothing here but the living, and the Malcolm beneath his feet in a state of simulated death.

Ross shuddered at the thought as he gathered his things. Positioning himself on the cusp of the doorway, he entered the Kill command on his laptop before walking through the portal back to The Shire.

The bridge in space-time closed behind him, air rushing in to fill the void it left behind. In his wake, the Time Dilation Amplifiers ignited, their power-cores set to self-destruct, causing them to disintegrate, removing any trace they were ever there at all as the green embers dissolved into the night sky.

*

As pliable time stabilised into a concrete constant, the surroundings remained entirely unaffected, until the stillness of the evening was interrupted with a crackle, heralding the arrival of a small tear in the fabric of reality.

A hand reached through the breach, black as oil and just as slick, causing the splinter between universes to widen, allowing for more of the creature's body to make its way through; an arm, a torso, a leg, until eventually it had dragged its way to full freedom.

The creature looked up at the moon, its eyeless face seemingly drinking in its surroundings, taking sharp breaths in through what should have been its nostrils, but were instead quivering ripples of stretched flesh, before looking down at its hands.

With fervent curiosity, the figure twisted the object it had brought back with it; an equally slick, black blade that was an identical replica to what Malcolm had been so fond of.

Shoulders jerking, the Echo attempted a laugh, but it landed more like a shrill squeal. Growing bolder, it tried its hand at speaking. A gargled mess of syllables putting to rest the question of if a tree falling in the woods could be heard at all if no one was around to hear it.

'aaaaarrrraaaaaK.'

The creature jerked its neck unnaturally, focusing on the bright light pulsing from the rupture in time behind him, feeling intense elation that he was now free of the nexus beyond, its maw opening to reveal shark like teeth which formed a horrifying smile, as another hand clutching a blade forced its way through.

Followed by another.

And another.

*

The army of Echoes juddered their way through the night towards the boundary line of Pentney Lakes, a blend of nightmarish horror wearing a scarf of ridiculousness. They had no power to draw on, so were forced to take each step at a time, like a Butlins holiday-retreat tribute act on their first practice run of Michael Jackson's "Thriller".

Indeed, it was fortunate Hal wasn't around to witness it, given that he would have chosen that as the soundtrack to what was unfolding.

The Thriller rejects continued onwards until reaching the Restart Point, the first of them to make it through to the realm of the living taking point as the others stopped for a moment, willingly allowing their self-appointed leader to claim the title on the basis he would shortly cease to exist anyway.

It raised its blade, jabbing it into the point of no return – or more accurately, the point of *infinite* returns – slicing the black knife across the barrier.

Cocking its head in wonder, it continued onwards through the barrier, which rippled against the being's presence, but allowed safe passage all the same.

Breaking through the temporal mesh of former incarceration, a red energy flowed along the surface of its hideous body as it marched onwards.

And its brothers followed.

A squadron of serial killers unleashed.

An army of Dark Restarters unbound.

With even time itself unwilling, or perhaps unable, to stop them.

CHAPTER SEVENTY-FIVE
Time Cop

Sunday, August 26th, 2018, 10:06am.

Stephanie Hawthorne was assessing the circus playing out in front of her through the faint haze of steam that curled out from the slit of the lid in her coffee cup.

She'd asked for it to go.

Always to go.

Occupational necessity.

The morning sun lashed against her fair skin, but she still held the cup with both hands, revelling in the unspoken glory that came from the rarity of having access to caffeine that wasn't at best lukewarm and at worst tepid.

She leant against the police van she'd hitched a

ride in, watching as armed police officers raided the too-quaint-to-be-threatening log cabin, and continued to do so as a young constable jogged back, requesting a gurney be brought in for a body they needed to relocate.

A body, if the rumours were to be true, that belonged to the serial killer she had been hunting for the past 6 years after the case had been passed to her by her father.

"There's no way this guy is the one."

It never was.

And yet, as he was wheeled unceremoniously into view looking like he'd caught a bad case of the deads, her mind was once again drawn to the cow-leather bound journal.

The dates stacked up. That much was true.

And that meant that the second diary would be delivered to her later today.

So it was written.

Foretold in the etchings of an imaginative individual, years ahead of his time.

But not once, until now, did she assume it would be literally.

"Ahead of his time," she repeated to herself, and scoffed.

Even though she knew in her heart the scoff was for the benefit of the dead who would no longer care either way if she *bought* what was being *sold* to her or not.

'Lodge is clear, detective Hawthorne,' said an

overly keen Special Constable.

'Hmm,' she said idly, feeling an intense wave of Déjà vu. 'It's Steph, Tom. Call me Steph.'

'Yes…Detective,' said Tom, doing his level best to break a habit of a lifetime.

She winced, and passed her cup to him.

'Hold this, would you,' she said, kicking herself away from the support of the van and making her way to the threshold allegedly belonging to the man who had called them here.

"Kevin Barker," she thought.

It may have seemed like a fast response on her part. That her team got here so swiftly. That the licences had been approved for so many firearms, and the whole squad had made it to the arse-end of Norfolk in less time than it took to reach the control room when dialling 101.

My god they had response time issues. Everyone knew it. And no amount of tax rises seemed to change it.

"Pot-holes over plods," she thought, reaching the doorway.

And yet there were still *so* many potholes…

But then, she'd had all of that sorted *well* in advance. She'd staked her reputation on selling this to her superiors.

Sargeant Holtzmann wasn't one for hunches. She'd had to dress it up as an anonymous tip.

She cringed at the thought of the paperwork she'd have to embellish.

Steph heard a screech from down the road, and ducked her head back out from the doorframe, her brow furrowed. She thought she could see Kevin Barker, clearly still in shock, speaking to someone in a car. She imagined the occupants were rubber-necking like there was no tomorrow.

Armed coppers, big ol' vans. Perhaps even a rumour of a murderer.

She couldn't blame them.

This was Netflix level stuff.

She made her way back inside and immediately took stock.

It was very twee. Not really her style of décor. Or building. Or…okay she hated it. But she wasn't here to judge.

Her eyes fell upon the basement door, and off she popped.

*

Each step creaked under her weight, and she descended carefully.

The lights were on below, but the glow was dim, and she retrieved her pen-sized torch from her trouser pocket, clicking the switch on the end, allowing the light to dance in front of her like a searchlight looking for escapees from Alcatraz.

Her feet finally reached terra firma, and she couldn't help but whistle at the paper cuttings, nor the knife that had been marked with a small yellow cone with a number 3 on it, signalling it was evidence, as two lads in blue plastic onesies took their photos.

She called the Scene of Crime Officers "Onesies" to their faces too. They didn't seem to mind.

'Well, shit,' said Steph to the closest of the two SOCO's. 'We've even got some syringes over there! Leather satchel and everything. Are we *sure* they weren't just shooting a movie?'

'We should be able to tell what's in them by end of working day Monday,' replied the onesie wearer.

'Tox reports be what they be,' said Steph.

'You *really* think it's him?' said the younger of the two men in literal blue, voice muffled thanks to his fetching mask.

'It's *never* him,' she said, smiling weakly.

And then she saw it, hidden by shadow, the white corner catching thanks to her relaxed torch-wielding arm resting by her side.

She squatted down, popping her pen-torch between her lips, and reached down for it.

'You find something?' asked the keener-eyed of the two Onesies. 'Don't touch it or we can't use it as evid–'

She picked it up anyway, shooing them away to focus on their photography.

'That's not possible,' she whispered to herself, her gut instinct flaring wildly.

A simple receipt.

Not in itself all that miraculous.

Coffee shop.

Not local.

But it wasn't any of that which sent a chill down

her spine.

It was the date that was printed on it.

An impossible date that read "October 6th, 2018, 10:29am."

And in that moment, she knew it was true.

All of it.

If this really *was* the killer she had been looking for, it was all just the beginning.

Now she had to find herself the real cause behind all this mess.

A man destined to become the killer of everyone on board Flight MAL651. Followed by thousands more, if not *millions*.

A man who would go down in history as being the cause of an eternal darkness. One that would *restart*, over and over, until everything unravelled.

She had to find him before the girl died. Or rather, the *young woman* that went by the name of "Kara".

That's how it started. If she could prevent that from happening, if the journal was as accurate as it had been today…

But all she had to go on was a name. That and a receipt, which might have meant nothing at all. Tills needed date recalibration all the time. It was hardly concrete.

But that didn't stop her believing what she knew in her heart to be true.

She shivered, wondering if he was here with her right now, out-of-phase…kneeling next to her...staring into her face with the manic eyes of the murderer he was destined to become.

A killer armed with the ability to travel through time.

A master of the afterlife who currently went by the name of "Hal", but would forever be remembered by his countless victims as something else entirely.

"*The Dark Restarter*," thought Steph, her blood turning to ice as she reached to the hidden chain around her neck that rested beneath her shirt. Her fingers pressing idly against the bullet it supported, which vibrated softly thanks to the swirling blue energy contained within.

A bullet with Hal's adopted name metaphorically etched onto it.

Entirely unaware that the consequences of her actions were about to change everything.

The Restarters will return.

I'm here, Hal.

Acknowledgments

Howdy, Restarters! Thank you so much for investing your time on the second instalment of the Restarter series!

This acknowledgement section is for everyone who has helped me to achieve one of the hardest challenges I've ever faced; that of writing a sequel. For cereal. In many ways it was so much more challenging that writing Fir Lodge.

Firstly, thank you once again to my wonderful returning editors; Amanda Gliddon, and Christopher McMahon.

In order to give you all what I hope is the best possible final version of this story, I upped the ante even further by head-hunting a further two editors; Rebecca Greenwood and Katie Hagaman. And, oh boy…am I glad I did. Thank you all for your honesty, advice, and invaluable input. Not to mention being the quickest readers I know. I owe all four of you more than I can ever repay. <Thwip Thwip>

Onwards to the readership! Or as I like to call you, the *real* Restarters. When I started this journey, I had no idea Fir Lodge would resonate with so many of you. Your support and kindness has changed my life in more ways than you know. To everyone who has left a review, taken part in a competition, and reached out to me just to say "hey", thank you. It truly keeps a writer going.

Thank you once again to my photographer, Russell Whitcombe, who exceeded my wildest dreams in terms of getting the shots we needed. Without his commitment, perseverance, and sheer skill, we never would have got those shots for the cover and trailer.

Which brings us to Roy Clark…you are all closer to him right now than you may realise. A man who, despite the sweltering heat on the hottest day of the year – not to mention a particularly rambunctious wasp nest – picked up a blade, donned a rubber apron, and took on the role of Malcolm with such enthusiasm that…honestly…he frightened me a little bit. You can see him in the trailer, as well as on the cover of The Dark Restarter.

Speaking of covers, special shout out once again to Sam Moore, who worked tirelessly with me to create the cover for TDR. Your ability to translate the words I'm dispensing and transform them into the images from my mind is nothing short of remarkable.

To my writing group, whom I speak with daily (if not hourly) Katie, Sarah, Corry, Gil, Paul, Kenny and Jordan. Your support has been phenomenal.

Thank you to Christina Alvarado and to Pearl Khatri for featuring Fir Lodge on their respective YouTube channels. Seeing Fir Lodge in that context was…mind blowing. So many feels.

Special thanks to Mike Chapman, a man who not only agreed to interview me, but has now interviewed me twice.

Thank you, good sir. Your kindness and support to both myself and the indie community in general is a privilege to be a part of.

And Marnye Young…the Audio Sorceress. Who, with the support of Silverton Audio, brought me onto her podcast for one of the most fun and rewarding experiences becoming a writer has afforded me thus far. Thank you.

Thank you to Sam Jenkins and Rebecca Braybrook for allowing me to gatecrash Hospital Radio Chelmsford, and for making me feel like a superstar.

High five to Zev Good, a fantastic author and friend who took me to school on the differences between Bar Mitzvah's, Bar Mitsvoth, and B'nai Mitzvah. Who knew plurals could be such tricky dragons to tame?!

To the forever awesome Danny Wyatt, owner of Fir Lodge – who I'm now lucky enough to call a friend. A man that, despite me blowing up the joint in Book One, was still on board for the sequel. None of this would exist without you.

Not forgetting the Reverends of Saint Mary's Church in Bocking, Essex. Namely; Reverend Rod Reid and Reverend Mark Payne who allowed this plucky nobody to not only film footage and feature it in the trailer, but also gave me their blessing, so to speak, for me to feature the location in my work. If anyone is wondering what it's like to be left alone in a church? Well, it's an eerily beautiful experience.

Lastly, thank you to Steve Gore, Kerri Muldowney, and Rebecca Greenwood for their Restarter-themed artwork, which has taken pride of place above the work station in my War Room.

So…what next? I hope I've delivered on my promise to you all and you've enjoyed the second part of this story. And that perhaps you'll join me for what's next, all the way to the last restart. We're in this together now, you and I. All the way to the end. Until we reach the beginning…

There's just one more thing I need to tell you. It's imperative that you follow these instructions to the letter. The secret to everything rests not in the future, but the past. The only way to–

Wait…can anyone else hear the sound or rushing air?...

Onwards to Book Three.

Your friend in Time,

Sean

Become a Restarter!

For news, giveaways, exclusive content, or even just to reach out to me, you can find me by visiting the Restarter's Lodge

at:

www.restarterlodge.com

Thanks to the internet, you can also follow the Restarters by punching the above website into your communicative weapon of choice, and clicking on the Twitter, Instagram, and Facebook icons.

Thanks, internet!

About the Author

Sean McMahon has only managed to save the world once this year.

Having single-handedly defeated the Sinister Six, Sean lives in Essex with his family, and was totally going to copy and paste this section from his last book, but decided against it, reasoning that if a reader got this far, they deserved one last Easter egg.

Wait!
What's that *behind* you?!
Just kidding. You're okay.
Probably.

Sean still claims to be an avid gamer – despite having no time to…ya know, *game* – and loves walking his rambunctious dog, Mindy.

Because she's a good girl. Aren't you girl?

Mindy will wag her tail happily every time someone reads the above sentence out loud.

Sean also once took a leak standing next to Simon Pegg at a press event. Since the release of Fir Lodge, several people now care.